THE MAYA CODEX

Adrian d'Hagé was educated at North Sydney Boys High School and the Royal Military College Duntroon (Applied Science). He served as a platoon commander in Vietnam where he was awarded the Military Cross. His military service included command of an infantry battalion, Director of Joint Operations and Head of Defence Public Relations. In 1994 Adrian was made a Member of the Order of Australia. As a brigadier, he headed defence planning for counter-terrorism security for the Sydney Olympics, including security against chemical, biological and nuclear threats.

Adrian also holds an honours degree in theology, entering as a committed Christian but graduating 'with no fixed religion'. In 2009 he completed a Bachelor of Applied Science (Dean's Award) in oenology or wine chemistry at Charles Sturt University, and he has successfully sat the Austrian Government exams for ski instructor, 'Schilehrer Anwärter'. Adrian is presently a research scholar and tutor at the Centre for Arab and Islamic Studies (Middle East and Central Asia) at ANU. His doctorate is entitled 'The Influence of Religion on US Foreign Policy in the Middle East'.

ALSO BY ADRIAN D'HAGÉ

The Omega Scroll
The Beijing Conspiracy

ADRIAN d'HAGÉ

THE MAYA CODEX

MICHAEL JOSEPH

an imprint of

PENGUIN BOOKS

MICHAEL JOSEPH

Published by the Penguin Group
Penguin Group (Australia)
250 Camberwell Road, Camberwell, Victoria 3124, Australia
(a division of Pearson Australia Group Pty Ltd)
Penguin Group (USA) Inc.
375 Hudson Street, New York, New York 10014, USA
Penguin Group (Canada)
90 Eglinton Avenue East, Suite 700, Toronto, Canada ON M4P 2Y3
(a division of Pearson Penguin Canada Inc.)
Penguin Books Ltd
80 Strand, London WC2R 0RL, England
Penguin Ireland
25 St Stephen's Green, Dublin 2, Ireland
(a division of Penguin Books Ltd)
Penguin Books India Pvt Ltd
11 Community Centre, Panchsheel Park, New Delhi – 110 017, India
Penguin Group (NZ)
67 Apollo Drive, Rosedale, North Shore 0632, New Zealand
(a division of Pearson New Zealand Ltd)
Penguin Books (South Africa) (Pty) Ltd
24 Sturdee Avenue, Rosebank, Johannesburg 2196, South Africa

Penguin Books Ltd, Registered Offices: 80 Strand, London WC2R 0RL, England

First published by Penguin Group (Australia), 2010

1 3 5 7 9 10 8 6 4 2

Cover design by Dave Altheim © Penguin Group (Australia)
Text design by Elissa Webb © Penguin Group (Australia)
Cover photographs by istock
Typeset in 12.5/18.5pt Granjon by Post Pre-Press Group, Brisbane, Queensland
Printed and bound in Australia by McPherson's Printing Group, Maryborough, Victoria

National Library of Australia
Cataloguing-in-Publication data:

D'Hagé, Adrian
The Maya codex / Adrian D'Hagé
1st ed
9781921518195 (pbk.)
Manuscripts, Maya – Fiction

A823.4

penguin.com.au

FSC
Mixed Sources
Product group from well-managed
forests and other controlled sources

Cert no. SGS-COC-004121
www.fsc.org
© 1996 Forest Stewardship Council

To Tammy and Catherine

PROLOGUE

Aleta Weizman stared at the falling snow from the window of her apartment, contemplating the future with a deep sense of foreboding. Winter had come early this year and a biting wind from across the Danube whipped the snow into flurries above the old cobblestones in the Stephansdom Quarter; but it was more than the chill winds worrying the brilliant Guatemalan archaeologist. Her studies of the ancient civilisation of the Maya had led her to believe they'd left behind a terrifying warning, one her grandfather had devoted much of his life trying to unearth. Now she had discovered another piece of the puzzle. In Vienna for an international conference on the Maya, Aleta had been browsing her grandfather's books when she'd come across a signed copy of Erwin Schrödinger's *Science and the Human Temperament*. Curious about her dear grandfather's old friend, she'd flicked through the book and a page of yellowed notes and a small photograph of a pectoral cross had fallen out.

The notes, written in Levi Weizman's meticulous handwriting, captivated her.

- The Fibonacci sequence is prominent in the construction of all Mayan pyramids and temples.
- Greek letter Φ – if you are to find the Maya Codex, look for Φ and the centre of the golden mean – Pacal.

Look for Φ, and the centre of the golden mean – Pacal. Who was Pacal? It was unlike her grandfather to write in code, so presumably he had not solved the puzzle but simply written it down word for word as he'd received it. And why were the notes hidden in a book? Had he suddenly been disturbed? What information was needed? Aleta turned over the photograph of the pectoral cross but there was no inscription on the back. Her father had mentioned the cross to her once, when they'd been fishing together on Lake Atitlán, telling her how the priceless family heirloom had been taken by the Nazis when he was a boy. She sighed, her dark-brown eyes troubled. The loss of her father still haunted her.

Curtis O'Connor adjusted his binoculars and focused on the woman standing near the window of the upper-floor apartment. Whatever else she might be, O'Connor thought, Dr Weizman was tall, young and very attractive. Her long black hair tumbled onto her shoulders, partly covering the fine features and tanned olive skin of her oval face. She seemed deep in thought as her dark eyes probed the night.

O'Connor remained hidden and kept his target under surveillance. At six feet tall, the CIA agent was fit and solidly built. Originally from

Ireland, he had trained as a microbiologist. His face was tanned and his blue eyes were mischievous, but deceptive. His thick dark hair fell roughly into place. Very much his own man, O'Connor had one of the sharpest minds in the CIA, and his mission to assassinate Dr Weizman had troubled him from the outset. Why, he wondered, did his superiors on the seventh floor of headquarters back in Langley, Virginia, want this beautiful woman eliminated?

Aleta stared across *Judengasse* towards Saint Ruprecht's, Vienna's oldest church, failing to see the man in the shadows of the ivy-covered stone belltower. What must it have been like to live here under the brutality of the Nazis? Aleta knew that the narrow lanes of the old city once housed Vienna's Jewish community; now they were home to designer-clothing shops and an eclectic collection of bars and discos, dubbed the 'Bermuda Triangle' by backpackers from around the world. Bar patrons had been known to disappear from *Judengasse*, or 'Jew's Lane', in the small hours of the morning. Usually they reappeared a day or two later, a little the worse for wear but otherwise unharmed. In the more sinister Bermuda Triangle of the Atlantic, a small area to the north-east of the ancient Mayan lands of Guatemala and the Yucatán Peninsula, whole ships and aircraft sometimes disappeared without trace. Had Aleta known that her every move was being observed, she would have realised that, for her, Vienna's Bermuda Triangle was every bit as dangerous as its Atlantic counterpart.

She gazed past the old square tower of Saint Ruprecht's, past the trams running on *Franz-Josefs-Kai*, towards the *Donaukanal*, one of the many canals the resourceful Viennese had built in the late 1800s to control the persistent flooding of the Danube. Aleta maintained an open mind towards the ancient Maya's warning of impending disaster, but she found it hard to dismiss the concrete scientific evidence that seemed to support it. Many of the events the Maya had declared as precursors to the coming disaster had already occurred. She reflected on the ancient stela, the stone monument inscribed with Mayan hieroglyphics she'd discovered in the *Museo Nacional de Arqueologia y Etnologia* in Guatemala City. The Museum of Archaeology had many stelae on permanent display, but it was the small stela in one of the storage rooms that had excited Aleta's interest. It was the only stela she had ever seen inscribed with Φ. And now she'd found the same reference in her grandfather's notes.

Aleta closed the heavy velvet drapes. She thought about exploring the streets of the elegant Austrian capital but decided against it, though not out of any concerns for her safety at night. The city where Mozart had spent his most successful and creative years was one of the safest in Europe. It was more that she wanted to be fresh for the opening day of the conference, which included several presentations by academics working to decipher Mayan hieroglyphics. The eminent Mayanist Monsignor Matthias Jennings would also be speaking tomorrow on 'The Myth of the Maya'. She strongly disagreed with the pompous Jesuit priest's views of the Maya as bloodthirsty, warmongering savages, but he was always controversial, which inevitably attracted the media and she relished the opportunity to publicly challenge his theories.

Aleta retrieved her glass of wine from the marble mantel above the fireplace, turned and felt a floorboard move under her weight. The natural curiosity of an archaeologist might normally have prompted her to investigate, but she was weary from the long flight from Guatemala City and retreated to her bedroom. The tin box that her grandfather had hidden there in 1938 remained undisturbed, just as it had when Hitler's Brownshirts stormed the apartment over seventy years before.

O'Connor left the shadows of the Saint Ruprecht's steeple, descended the short flight of icy steps to the *Morzinplatz* and jumped aboard an old number 1 tram at the nearby *Schwedenplatz Strassenbahn-haltestelle*. He settled onto one of the wooden seats and, as the tram rattled along the famous *Ringstrasse*, the roofs of the *Neues Rathaus*, the Parliament and the Opera House covered in snow, he reflected that he never tired of the dignified Austrian capital. He alighted at the *Kärntner Ring* and walked the short distance to the Imperial Hotel, the former palace of Prince Philipp of Württemberg. Nikita Khrushchev, Indira Gandhi, Liz Taylor and Richard Burton had all stayed there, as had Bruce Springsteen, Mick Jagger and Hillary Clinton. O'Connor had heard that in the 1960s a young Rudolf Nureyev had asked for a room, but was refused – back then jeans were unacceptable in formal settings – until Lord Snowdon walked in and recognised the up-and-coming dancer. Snowdon had escorted him to the bar and Nureyev got his room.

O'Connor headed for the very same softly lit bar, and one of the hotel's blonde pagegirls, dressed in an elegant olive-green suit trimmed in gold, flashed him a charming smile. O'Connor nodded, but wary of any entanglement he climbed onto a soft leather bar stool.

'Champagne, thank you, Klaus.' There were two people O'Connor always got to know in a hotel. One, the head concierge; the other, the head barman.

'The Dom Perignon or the Moët, Mr O'Connor?'

'The Moët will be fine, thanks.' O'Connor glanced around the smoke-filled room. In the far corner a group of distinguished-looking Austrian men and their attractive wives were in quiet conversation around a coffee table near a window that was curtained in gold and crimson.

'Gold seems to feature prominently in this hotel,' he remarked, glancing at the stylish gold epaulettes on the pagegirl's uniform.

The barman smiled, allowing the fine bubbles to disperse as he filled O'Connor's crystal flute. 'During the war, when my father worked in this bar, the clientele were mainly Nazis. The bunkers where they stored their gold are still in use.'

'They stored gold *here*?'

'Hitler used to stay in this hotel whenever he came to Vienna, and his foreign minister, Joachim von Ribbentrop, set up an annex here for the Third Reich.'

After the Führer's triumphant entry into Vienna following the Anschlüss, the hotel's balcony had been decorated with huge red-and-black banners displaying the swastika and the *Reichsadler* – the German eagle. When O'Connor reached the jungles of Guatemala, he would have cause to reflect on the irony of his choice of accommodation.

'Not many people remember, Mr O'Connor, but the Nazis used reinforced concrete to construct bunkers beneath this bar. The tunnels they built led through the walls of the hotel cellars into a concealed entrance underneath *Dumbastrasse*,' Klaus added. O'Connor knew that *Dumbastrasse*, the street on the western side of the Impe-rial, connected with the *Kärntner Ring* at the front of the hotel.

'Bombproof,' he observed.

Klaus smiled. 'The Imperial was very lucky. The State Opera House and the *Burgtheater* were destroyed, and the Ambassador Hotel and the Old Bristol were bombed as well, but even if we had been hit, the tunnels beneath where you're sitting are a metre thick. The doors are solid steel and the filtering systems were made by Dräger, the same construction company that made the filters for Hitler's bunker in Berlin. I can remember my father saying that when the SS Captain Otto Skorzeny rescued Mussolini in 1943, he brought him into the hotel through the secret *Dumbastrasse* entrance.'

'And the gold?'

Klaus shrugged. 'The only gold left now is on the hotel plates and cutlery that is stored there. Still, there are rumours . . . My father told me that before Himmler fell out with Ribbentrop, he used to stay here frequently. My father showed me a photograph of Himmler and one of his protégés, an SS officer by the name of Karl von Heißen. Von Heißen finished up as the commandant of the concentration camp at Mauthausen. A terrible place. He was also involved in the disappearance of a large quantity of ingots just before the fall of the Reich. The ingots were rumoured to have been stored here, then shipped to Central America through the Vatican Bank, I think. Per-haps they are still to be found, Mr O'Connor?'

O'Connor left a twenty Euro note with the bill, and left the bar. He climbed the narrow red carpet secured with gold strips to the centre of the long marble staircase, the same staircase that Hitler, Himmler and countless other characters from the dark pages of history had used. At the top of the stairs a huge oil painting of Emperor Franz Josef in the dress uniform of an Austrian field marshal dominated the landing. O'Connor passed a tastefully lit statue of a naked goddess and his thoughts turned to Dr Aleta Weizman.

He locked the door of his suite behind him and checked the single hair he'd left at the bottom left-hand corner of the wardrobe safe. Satisfied nothing had been disturbed, he dialled the combination and extracted the disc containing the Weizman data. He'd already committed it to memory, but he wanted to be sure there was nothing he'd missed, and he inserted the disc into his laptop.

The file was classified 'SECRET – NOFORN', meaning that in addition to the watertight security accorded CIA secret files, the information was not for release to foreign nationals. It didn't make sense to O'Connor. The information on the combined FBI/CIA Weizman disc was sparse, and most of it could have been obtained from government departmental records in Guatemala City anyway.

WEIZMAN, ALETA REBEKKAH
Born: 15 November 1972, San Marcos, Lake Atitlán, Guatemala. Grandfather, Professor Levi Weizman, distinguished archaeologist. Parents and siblings deceased.

O'Connor grimaced. The word 'deceased' concealed a raft of information.

Physical characteristics: Height, five-foot eight; hair, black; complexion, olive; eyes, dark-brown; scar just above the right buttock.

Marital status/Social pursuits: Does not appear to be in a relationship. Married an American in 1999, but the marriage lasted only eighteen months and ended in divorce. No children. Holds a PADI qualification, including high-altitude diving certification, but does not appear to dive on a regular basis.

Religion: Describes herself of 'no fixed religion'. Catholic upbringing; Jewish ancestry.

Education: BSc, BArchaeol (Hons), PhD (Harvard).

Political outlook: No evidence that Weizman is a member of any political party or organisation, but she can be outspoken on human rights, especially on behalf of present-day descendants of the Maya.

Publications: Mainly confines herself to writing academic papers on ancient Mayan civilisations, but has also authored a paper on the science behind changes in the earth's magnetic field and its connection to an ancient Mayan warning (see attached list at Annex A). Took a major in mathematics in her BSc.

O'Connor paused for thought, reflecting on what he'd learned during his last posting to one of the United States' top-secret research stations at Gakona, in the icy wastes of Alaska. Was Weizman getting close to some uncomfortable truth about the earth's magnetic field and a possible pole shift? As catastrophic as such an event might be, she wasn't the only one probing for answers; and even if she had linked the chilling scientific facts to an ancient Mayan warning, it didn't remotely justify an assassination mission. O'Connor scrolled down the page.

> More recently Weizman has authored articles critical of US policy in Central America (full texts are at Annex B).

> **Surveillance priority**: Low.

O'Connor scanned the remaining pages, which included the full texts of Dr Weizman's journal articles, her academic papers, including one on a missing 'Maya Codex', and a few transcripts of interviews in the Guatemalan national papers *El Periódico*, *Nuestro Diario*, and *La Hora*. Still puzzled, O'Connor took out the disc and returned his laptop to the safe. The Weizman dossier raised many more questions than it answered.

O'Connor stripped off and adjusted the pulse on the shower, one of the great pleasures of staying at the Imperial, he thought as he soaped his lean, hard body. But his mind quickly returned to Dr Weizman. An obscure archaeologist working in the jungles of Guatemala shouldn't be registering on Washington's radar. Based on what was available on her file, she didn't even come close to the 'clear and present danger' test that might give the President justification to order the current mission. There had to be more to it, O'Connor thought. Much more. He resolved to break in to her apartment. Perhaps there he might discover something that would explain the mystery.

BOOK I

I

VIENNA, 1937

Professor Levi Weizman removed the priceless jade figurine from the large wall-safe in his study and placed it on his desk. The intriguing milky-green sculpture had been carved in the shape of a ceiba tree, a tree revered by the ancient Maya as the *Yaxche*, 'tree of life'. The powerful figure of a male jaguar was etched amongst the tree's buttress roots, and through the roots there was a hole in the shape of Φ, the Greek letter phi. At the apex the Mayan artisans had faithfully reproduced the ceiba tree's distinctive flat crown. Long, intricately carved branches radiated horizontally in the four directions of the compass. Levi had encountered the tree many times on his field trips. In the highlands of Guatemala the ceiba soared above the jungle canopy, providing a roost for the harpy, the largest of the eagles, but for the figurine the Maya had replaced the eagle's nest with a black-and-gold obsidian cup in which rested a large shimmering crystal.

The Weizmans' third-floor apartment overlooked *Sterngasse* and *Judengasse* in the old Jewish sector of Vienna's fashionable Stephansdom Quarter. It was early evening and light snow was falling, the flakes drifting onto the cobblestones below. Deep in thought, Levi thrust his hands into his pockets. The Mayanist scholar was well into his fifties, but he maintained the fitness of a much younger man. His grey hair was brushed straight back from an oval face, and his white moustache and beard were neatly trimmed. Levi adjusted his square rimless glasses and stared at the figurine. The markings on it were, he knew, consistent with it being made around 850 AD, a time when the Maya had occupied the great city-state of Tikal, deep in the jungles of what was now Guatemala.

In the summer of 1936 Levi had discovered the figurine in a secret chamber in Pyramid I, one of Tikal's many tombs. The trip had been a sabbatical from the University of Vienna, and Levi knew that eventually he would have to make his find public; but he was convinced the figurine held an ancient secret which he was determined to unlock before he made any announcement.

'*Es ist fast Abendessen*. It's almost dinnertime, sweetheart. The children are getting restless.' Fifteen years younger than her husband, Ramona Weizman had maintained her own career as one of Vienna's leading fashion designers and milliners. Her label was sold exclusively from her street-level boutique beneath their apartment and her 'Greta Garbo-style' Fedora slouch hats were the toast of Vienna, rivalling those of the Parisian milliner Schiaparelli. Tall and slim, with dark curly hair and deep-brown eyes, Ramona was a woman of warmth and charm.

'You've been in here all day, Levi,' she remonstrated gently, rolling her eyes as she spied the myriad mathematical calculations lying beside the figurine on her husband's desk.

'I've been looking at the figurine and trying to work out what it means,' Levi said. 'Do you remember that stela I found in Pyramid I at Tikal?'

Ramona looked sheepish. 'Vaguely,' she said, perching on the only corner of the desk not covered by papers and crossing her elegant legs. 'You showed me photographs. The stone monument with all those squiggles and dots and dashes?'

'Hieroglyphics and Mayan numbers,' Levi responded with a smile. 'I'm pretty sure the Mayan hieroglyphics were referring to the winter solstice, and it's occurred to me that the solstice and this figurine might somehow be connected.'

Levi took the figurine over to the large table on which he'd constructed a model of Tikal's major pyramid temples and placed it on top of Pyramid I.

'You know, even without telescopes, the Maya were accomplished astronomers, and their buildings reflect that. At the winter solstice the pyramids in Tikal and the sun are aligned with Victoria Peak in the Mayan Mountains,' he said, pointing to the wooden models. 'Each pyramid is part of a matrix, see? If you stand on top of Pyramid IV before dawn on the solstice of 21 December, for example, the sun will rise directly over the top of Pyramid III and vice versa for the sunset.'

'So what does that have to do with the figurine?'

'I'm still not sure, but I suspect part of the answer lies in this crystal at the top.'

'You'll have to forgive me, Levi,' she said, sensitive to her husband's fascination with all things Mayan, 'but it's a very ugly reproduction. I thought the ceiba tree was tall and stately. That one's squat and stubby.'

'Exactly 33.98 centimetres high and 21 centimetres wide,' Levi agreed, 'but I think these dimensions are no accident. If you divide 33.98 by 21, you get 1.618.'

Ramona smiled as she raised her eyebrows.

'Which is the value of Φ, the Greek letter phi, or the "golden mean". It comes from the Fibonacci sequence, which is at the core of the natural world —'

Ramona held up her hand, just as Levi was getting into stride. 'And I'm sure good old Fibonacci won't mind if you take a break to eat.'

Levi gave his wife a hug. 'You do ground me.'

'Someone has to. Come on. The children are famished and so am I.'

Levi reluctantly turned out the light and followed his wife out of the study.

'*Ow!* Stop it!' Rebekkah said, pushing her brother away. 'Mama, Ariel's hitting me with a cushion!'

'That's enough you two. Go and wash your hands; dinner's nearly ready.'

The two silver candles represented God's commandments, and Ramona positioned them both on the simple white tablecloth. She placed a covered loaf of braided challah bread alongside a silver six-pointed Star of David. Once they were all seated, Levi intoned the blessing in Hebrew:

Barukh atah Adonai Elohaynu melekh ha-olam
Blessed are You, Lord, our God, King of the Universe

Ha-motzi lechem min ha-aretz. Amein
Who brings forth bread from the earth. Amen.

Levi poured one of Ramona's favourite Austrian white wines, a grüner veltliner, and raised his glass. '*Prost, meine Liebling.* Good health.'

'*Prost*,' Ramona replied, giving her husband a loving look. 'Here's to cracking the code of your figurine. What do you think it means?'

'I suspect the Maya were trying to leave us a message. At the time that figurine was made, over a thousand years ago, the Mayan civilisation was thriving. Its pyramids and temples stretched from the Yucatán Peninsula in what is now Mexico to the jungles of Guatemala, El Salvador and Honduras. But less than fifty years later, the entire civilisation just disappeared, leaving its city-states and pyramids to the ravages of the jungle.'

'Do we know why?'

'There are theories, ranging from a catastrophic viral haemorrhagic fever to a meteorite, but none of the evidence stacks up. A lot of us suspect that the warring between city-states, coupled with deforestation, did so much damage to the environment that the Maya were no longer able to grow the crops they needed to survive. Whatever the cause, it remains one of the great mysteries of the ancient world. Do you remember that Mayan elder I got to know the last time I was in Guatemala?'

'The one from Lake Atitlán? Roberto?'

'Roberto Arana. He told me it's a great honour to have found the figurine, although he urged me to keep it quiet. The figurine's existence is a closely guarded secret, known only to the elders. But he also told me there are two more, each with a crystal embedded in the crown. The one I have is *ah-ton,* or male, but neutral and female ones are still to be found.'

'Any idea where they might be?'

Levi smiled ruefully. 'If only . . . I asked Roberto, of course, but he was very cryptic. He said, "The remaining two will not be found until they're meant to be found." A divine timing, if you like.' Levi glanced at the children and decided against revealing all the details of his conversation with the Mayan shaman. 'He also said the figurines will lead the way towards a very important secret codex – the Maya Codex – but whoever searches for the codex will need all three of the figurines to find it.'

'What's a codex, Papa?' eight-year-old Rebekkah asked, her soft blonde curls shining in the candlelight.

'A codex is a very old book, sweetheart, made out of bark, and it folds out like a concertina.'

'Funny stuff to make a book out of,' Ariel declared. Tall for his ten years, and already a brilliant student, Ariel had inherited his mother's dark curly hair, olive skin and warm smile. This evening, though, that ready smile was not much in evidence.

'Not really, Ariel,' Levi said gently. 'Paper was invented centuries ago in China, but the printing press wasn't invented until 1448. You see, a German by the name of Johannes Gütenberg —'

'Suffice to say,' Ramona cut in with a smile, 'the Maya had to use what was available.'

'So, how was school today, Rebekkah?' Levi asked.

'It was all right,' Rebekkah murmured, her eyes suddenly downcast. Levi exchanged glances with Ramona. Their daughter was normally an effervescent ball of energy, but tonight, like her brother, she was strangely subdued.

'Just all right? And you, Ariel?' Levi asked.

Ariel played with his food.

'Was your day all right as well, young man?'

'Sort of. We've got a new teacher,' Ariel said finally.

'And he's horrible and mean!' Rebekkah made a face.

'Really? What happened to Herr Löwenstein?' her mother said, surprised there had been no warning to parents. Ariel shrugged. 'The new teacher is Herr Schweizer, and he says Herr Hitler's Third Reich will last for a thousand years.'

Levi and Ramona exchanged glances again, but any further conversation was interrupted by the phone ringing in the study.

'Professor Weizman.'

'*Ein Moment, bitte, Herr Professor. Berlin ruft an.*' The line crackled while the operator made the connection.

'*Guten Abend, Herr Professor. Mein Name ist Standartenführer Wolff. Stabschef auf Reichsführer Himmler.*'

Levi listened intently as the German SS Colonel outlined Heinrich Himmler's proposal for an archaeological expedition to Guatemala.

'*Gute Nacht*, Papa!' Rebekkah and Ariel each gave Levi a hug.

'Who was on the phone?' Ramona asked after the children had tripped off to bed.

'Standartenführer Wolff, Himmler's chief of staff in Berlin. Reichsführer Himmler wants to see me next week at his SS headquarters in Wewelsburg.'

Ramona was instantly alert. 'What on earth for?'

'Apparently he's thinking about mounting an expedition to Guatemala to search the Mayan tombs and pyramids for archaeological evidence of Hitler's master race. Hitler has yet to approve it, but if he does, the expedition will be led by a young SS officer, Haupsturmführer von Heißen, and Himmler wants me to assist him.'

'You're not going to, are you?' Ramona asked, suddenly alarmed. 'I wouldn't trust them, Levi. Hitler, Himmler, Goebbels – they're all just beer-hall thugs.'

'I know. But if they're prepared to fund a full expedition back to Tikal, it will give me an opportunity to search for the other two figurines.'

'Are you sure you're not walking into a trap, Levi? Why would they be asking *you* to help them? Hitler and Himmler both think Jewish intellectualism is dead; they've said so publicly. All our friends . . . Einstein, Schrödinger . . . all of them have left. If it gets any worse, we might have to go as well.'

'Well, let's just see what Herr Himmler has to say,' Levi responded gently. 'I think I should do everything in my power to discover the other two figurines – and prevent them from falling into the hands of the Nazis.'

Ramona put her arms around her husband. 'I don't know, Levi. I was listening to the radio yesterday: Chancellor von Schuschnigg was warning us not to trust the Nazis. I have a very bad feeling about this.'

'It'll be all right. I promise, *Liebchen.*'

'Are you coming to bed?' Ramona asked, her eyes moist.

'Soon,' Levi promised. 'I just want to test the crystal on the figurine.'

Once Ramona had left, Levi set up a slide projector to simulate sunrise at the winter solstice. He checked the figurine's position on top of the model of Pyramid I and switched on the light beam.

Levi's pulse quickened. The crystal on top of the figurine became strangely energised. A laser-like beam of deep-green light deflected at a precise angle, irradiating the top of Pyramid IV.

2

OBERSALZBERG

Reichsführer Himmler's driver eased the big black Mercedes through the Bavarian town of Berchtesgaden. The tyres buzzed on the cobbled roads as they passed the twin-spired *Stiftskirche* near *Marktplatz Strasse*. It was midmorning and the narrow streets were crowded with shoppers: the men in their traditional leather jackets and feathered alpine caps, and the women in colourful *dirndls*.

They travelled down the *Bahnhofstrasse* before turning east onto the bridge that crossed the swiftly flowing River Ache. The river banks were still covered in deep snow. Here and there, the water tumbled over the natural sculptures of ice that had formed on the rocks. The road meandered towards the foothills of the Obersalzberg, a soaring mountain overlooking the town. Occasionally the sun struggled from behind heavy clouds scudding across the sky, illuminating the snow-covered countryside that changed from open fields and cherry orchards to thick pine forests.

Oblivious to the scenery, Reichsführer Himmler sat in the plush red-leather seat in the back, resplendent in the sinister black uniform of the Schutzstaffel-SS, Hitler's Praetorian Guard. In civilian clothes Heinrich Himmler might easily have been mistaken for a bank clerk or an accountant: his round gold-rimmed glasses supported by a sharp nose, his head seemingly too big for his slight body, his fine black hair trimmed ferociously and shaved well above his ears.

Himmler continued to make meticulous notes on a file marked *Geheim – Nur Durch Offizierhände* as he read the cable he'd received from the German ambassador in Guatemala City:

PERSONAL FOR REICHSFÜHRER HIMMLER:

Report on possible links between Aryan race and Maya in diplomatic bag soonest. Austrian Professor Levi Weizman last here November, when he visited Lake Atitlán, as well as Tikal. Weizman Jewish but undoubtedly best hope to decipher Mayan hieroglyphics. Catholic priest in Tikal, Father Wolfgang Ehrlichmann, believes we will find Aryan skulls amongst ruins. Uncorroborated reports of an ancient Mayan codex rumoured to contain warning of "coming Armageddon". Codex may also provide link between Aryans and ancient Maya.

Himmler underlined the words 'Maya codex' and 'coming Armageddon', and thought back to the 1933 Conference of the Nordic Society, where he'd encountered a crusty old colonel from the Austrian Imperial Army, Karl-Maria Wiligut. Wiligut had produced a yellowed leather-bound manuscript containing a fragment of a warning.

When all the trees are destroyed, a day will come when the temperatures will soar; when fires will increasingly ravage the land; when earthquakes will bring pestilence and flood and the land will wither; when mankind will become lovers of pleasure; religion will fight religion and the Catholic Church will be destroyed. A prince, with links to the Aryans and an ancient civilisation, will arise from obscurity. He will wear an iron cross on his chest and it is he who will deliver his people.

According to Wiligut, the complete warning was contained in an ancient Mayan codex that had never been found, one that would explain the links to the past and the destruction of the Maya, and the steps that must be taken in order to avoid a similar catastrophe in the future. Himmler stroked his chin. *A prince with an iron cross on his chest, who will arise from obscurity.* The Führer had been awarded the Iron Cross during the Great War . . . He went back to the cable.

```
Whereabouts of codex unknown. Papal nuncio
requests Ehrlichmann to assist the expedi-
tion in an official capacity. Vatican interest
not clear but most likely related to codex.
Request advice before approving. Logistics
support for expedition being evaluated. Will
```

require construction of an airfield at Tikal.
Will advise soonest.
    Friedrich Waltheim, Ambassador.

Himmler's Mercedes reached the first of the heavily guarded check-points on the outskirts of the Obersalzberg. The boomgate and the right arms of the guards went up in unison. Himmler was expected. With the Nazis' rise to power, the traditional residents had been unceremoniously evicted from the beautiful Bavarian mountains, and the Obersalzberg was now a Nazi stronghold. Hitler's beloved country chalet, the Berghof, was here, and other senior Nazis, including Hermann Göring and Nazi Party Chief Martin Bormann, had acquired extensive estates. More soldiers saluted as the Mercedes swept past another heavily guarded entrance adorned with the Eagle of the Third Reich. The greystone buildings belonging to the Gestapo, Himmler's hated secret police, appeared cold and forbidding. Beneath them, kilometres of tunnels and bunkers had been dug deep into the mountainside.

Himmler returned the salute and opened the Gestapo file on Levi Weizman. Was the Austrian professor hiding something on the ancient Maya? While Austria remained outside the greater Deutschland it would be difficult to openly search the Professor's apartment in Vienna. He studied the photographs of Professor Weizman's wife and two children. A devoted husband and father. Good. That might be useful.

The road twisted through the pine forests as they climbed 6000 feet towards the *Kehlsteinhaus*, or Eagle's Nest. In an engineering feat that exemplified those of the Third Reich, the mountaintop resort had been a birthday present to Hitler, and Martin Bormann had personally supervised its construction. Himmler's driver changed gear again for the last five kilometres of Germany's highest road, carved from the side of the cliff, but the big Mercedes' engine handled the climb with ease. Fifteen minutes later, Himmler alighted outside the entrance to a long tunnel. It was lined with Untersberg marble and lit by big square gothic lamps suspended at intervals from the rock. Two SS guards snapped to attention and their commander, a young tall blond Untersturmführer, saluted.

'*Heil Hitler, Herr Reichsführer!*'

'*Heil Hitler,*' Himmler responded with a perfunctory salute. The Untersturmführer accompanied him into the tunnel that led to the heart of the mountain, their boots echoing on the polished stone. Two more guards snapped to attention at the end of the tunnel, where a circular room contained the base of an elevator shaft. Hitler's elevator was lined with brass and dark-green leather. It had been decorated with Venetian mirrors, a telephone and a large brass clock from a U-boat. The Untersturmführer pressed the 'up' button and the elevator hummed quietly as they rose 500 feet inside the mountain towards the *Kehlsteinhaus* above.

Hitler was on the sun terrace, hands spread on the stone balustrade, staring across the border into Austria. The snow-capped granite peaks of the Hoher Göll, Watzmann and Hochkalter mountains soared into the clouds. Thousands of feet below, Himmler could make out the Königssee. Surrounded by mountains on three sides, the surface of the King's Lake shimmered in the cold morning sun.

Himmler hesitated, gathering himself before interrupting his leader. Adolf Hitler was the only man Himmler genuinely admired; the one man who could raise the Fatherland to its rightful place in the world. At the same time, he was wary of the Führer's notorious moodswings.

'*Guten Tag, mein Führer.*' Himmler clicked his heels.

'Ah, Himmler.' Hitler turned back towards the Alps, brushing at the black thatch of hair hanging over his left eyebrow. 'You see that?' he asked, sweeping his hand towards his native Austria. 'Soon that will all be part of the greater Reich!'

Himmler nodded as he surveyed the vista of the Austrian Alps. It was a cold, clear day and, far below, the Berchtesgaden Valley reached towards Austria. It was as if they were on the roof of the world. Up here, the power of the Reich seemed limitless.

'I have a proposal for you, *mein Führer*,' Himmler began, emboldened by Hitler's ebullience. 'We believe we may be able to discover new archaeological evidence that will prove the Aryan master race to be the driving force behind some of history's great civilisations.'

'Excellent!' Hitler responded, slapping his thigh. 'We'll discuss it over lunch. I have some ideas for you as well, on this Jewish question and the Catholic Church.'

Lunch included one of Hitler's favourite dishes: baked potatoes and curd cheese with unrefined linseed oil. The two men sat in the pine-panelled Scharitzkehl room, where an expensive Gobelin tapestry hung on the inner wall. The large window afforded both men views over the snow-dusted pine trees to the Austrian border.

'I met with the Pope's financial advisor, il Signor Felici, this morning,' Hitler said. 'He tells me that Pius XI's health is causing increasing concern in the Vatican.'

'Terminal?' Himmler asked.

'It would appear so. Heart disease and some complications from diabetes.'

'A new pope will need careful watching, *mein Führer*, and we can't trust Felici. He's very close to that pompous Cardinal Secretary of State, Pacelli, whom, I'm informed, is taking a close interest in our archaeological expeditions.' Himmler was wary of the Vatican. It was not the first time Rome had intervened in the affairs of the Maya. In 1562, during the Spanish Conquistador's conquest of the Yucatán Peninsula, the Catholic Church ordered that the priceless Mayan libraries be burned. The literary history of an entire civilisation was destroyed and only four codices had survived. Himmler suspected Friedrich Waltheim was right: the Vatican's interest in the jungles of Guatemala was probably related to the Maya Codex.

Hitler nodded. 'You are right. The Vatican is not to be trusted, but there are twenty-three million Catholics in this country, and once we return Austria and the Sudetenland to their rightful places in the Reich, there will be over half that number again. The German and Austrian bishops must be kept on a tight leash, and we stand a much better chance if Secretary of State Pacelli takes over as Pope.'

'Do you know where Pacelli will stand if he's elected?'

'I've asked von Bergen to find out.' Diego von Bergen had been Germany's ambassador to the Vatican since 1920. 'But if Pacelli wants me to sign a concordat so he can retain control over the German curricula in his precious Catholic schools, then he'd better support us. And I've told von Bergen to pass on to Pacelli that if the German

Catholic Centre Party continues to oppose us in the Reichstag, there will be *no* concordat.'

Himmler looked thoughtful. 'Do you think Pacelli . . . *if* he gets up . . . do you think he might side with the Jews?'

'I think Pacelli takes the view that the Jews have brought retribution on themselves, so it will be useful for us if he succeeds Pius XI. But it's one thing to exterminate the Jews here,' Hitler added, looking towards the Austrian Alps. 'There are a lot more of them across the border.'

'*Jawohl, mein Führer*. As best as we can estimate, about 185 000.'

'Which is 185 000 too many. The question is, what do we do with them?' Hitler mused matter-of-factly. 'Dachau is already full of them, not to mention all the homosexuals, squinters, gypsies and other subhuman species.'

'We'll need many more camps,' Himmler agreed, 'and I've already drawn up plans for the Austrian takeover. I've been informed that several camps can be built around Gusen, and we have a proposal for another large one at Mauthausen. There's an old quarry there that can be brought back into use – the Jewish scum can quarry the stone.'

'Preferably with their bare hands.'

'You've only to give me the word, *mein Führer*, and by the time Gusen and Mauthausen are finished, you'll be able to walk around any quarter of Vienna and not encounter a single Jew.'

Hitler nodded thoughtfully. 'Good. However, the Austrian Chancellor is somewhat obstinate. I've arranged a show of force on the border to compel him to comply. I'm also having an agreement drawn up for the Austrians to sign. Kanzler von Schuschnigg's ban on the Austrian Nazi Party is to be lifted and our people in his jails are to be released!' Hitler banged his fist on the table. 'It shouldn't be long before you start construction, Himmler.'

A cold smile spread across Himmler's sallow face.

'Now, what's this archaeological evidence you were talking about?'

'I've received a cable from our ambassador in Guatemala City. There's a possibility the Aryans were instrumental in the rise of the great Mayan civilisation.'

'That wouldn't surprise me in the least. I've been reading *Der Mythus des Zwanzigsten Jahrhunderts* – it's excellent, *excellent*,' Hitler emphasised, slapping his thigh again. 'Alfred Rosenberg has it absolutely right. The lower race of Jews has corrupted the Aryan culture, and we must pursue the purification of the master race with every fibre of our being. We are building the foundations for a Reich that will last a thousand years!' Hitler's eyes blazed as he warmed to his theme. He got up from the table and placed his hands on the window casing.

'With that in mind, *mein Führer*,' Himmler said, quickly seizing his moment, 'I'm planning to set up a research establishment to promote the purity of our ancestral heritage. The bulk of the funding will come from big industrial conglomerates like Bayerische Motoren Werke, which will also fund archaeological expeditions to the Middle East, Tibet and Guatemala. For Guatemala we're planning to use an Austrian, Professor Levi Weizman.'

'Weizman? That sounds Jewish?'

'We're looking into that, *mein Führer*,' Himmler replied evasively. 'The Mayan hieroglyphics are notoriously difficult to decipher, however, and Weizman is one of the most eminent scholars in the field.'

'I wouldn't trust him,' Hitler warned, 'any more than I'd trust Felici or Pacelli.'

'Weizman will not be difficult to control. We already have a great deal of information on him, including the fact he has a young wife and family. After our mission is complete, we can dispense with all of them.'

Hitler grunted.

'The expedition will be led by Hauptsturmführer von Heißen, a promising young SS officer,' Himmler continued.

'Ah, yes, I met him at the Reichstag. A fine young man. If we're to undo the damage the Jews and the Christians have inflicted on the Fatherland, Himmler, we're going to need many more like him.'

3

STEINHÖRING, NEAR MUNICH

Tall and blond, with piercing blue eyes, Hauptsturmführer von Heißen embodied Himmler's vision of the powerful male of the master race. Von Heißen stood at the bar of Heim Hochland, the first of the Aryan-breeding homes Himmler had set up in the countryside to assist German girls to give birth to racially pure children. In a memo to the SS, Himmler had stressed the need for German births of good blood and urged his SS officers to spread their Aryan seed. Heim Hochland provided von Heißen with the opportunity to sleep with a young woman of the right breeding, one who was free of the syphilis he'd encountered more than once in the brothels of Berlin.

Doctor Rainer Drechsler, a small, thin man with a nervous twitch in his right eye, watched without interest as one of the women under his care put on a gramophone record. Couples began to circle the dance floor to the sounds of a Decca recording of 'Darling, My Heart Says Hello To You'. Von Heißen had never mastered the art of dancing. Time to plant some seed, he thought, and he poured himself another Glenfiddich, spilling the malt whisky onto the white damask bar runner. He wandered over to Doctor Drechsler, glass in hand.

'The sultry one in the red dress over there in the corner. She's mine. Introduce me,' he demanded thickly. Drechsler shrugged and moved towards the tall blonde sitting on her own at a table.

Von Heißen followed unsteadily, stumbling against a table and knocking it over, sending the wine glasses to shatter on the wooden floor.

'May I present Miss Katrina Baumgartner,' the doctor intoned impassively.

Katrina looked up. Her eyes were pale blue and her skin milky white.

'Von Heißen. Hauptsturmführer Karl von Heißen,' the SS captain slurred, clicking his heels. 'What are you drinking, Fräulein?'

'I don't drink, Hauptsturmführer,' Katrina Baumgartner replied coolly, eyeing von Heißen with disdain.

'Nonsense.' Von Heißen snapped his fingers at one of the dining-room staff. '*Rotwein für das Fräulein*. Where are you from?' he asked, pulling out a chair.

'Berlin,' Katrina replied, her eyes glazed with boredom.

'And what brings you here?' Von Heißen leered.

'I've been assigned to the Lebensborn program, so I didn't have much choice. But surely you know that, Hauptsturmführer.'

'Quite an honour,' von Heißen observed, 'for a woman to be able to serve the greater Reich. I myself am about to deploy to the jungles of Guatemala, although that is top secret. Tomorrow I will meet with Reichsführer Himmler, who has personally selected me for the mission. We are going to search for archaeological evidence that the Aryans were at the heart of the great Mayan civilisation.'

Katrina raised a sceptical eyebrow.

'We will also be looking for a secret codex that's been missing for centuries. It could be of great value to the Reich!'

'If it's top secret, then perhaps you shouldn't be talking about it?'

'You, I can trust,' von Heißen slurred. 'You're on the program, and you're of good German stock. If you were a Jew or a gypsy, it would be quite a different matter.'

'And if I told you I have a number of Jewish friends who are good, decent citizens?'

'Then I would advise you to be careful, Fräulein. Very careful. Have you read *The Protocols of the Elders of Zion*?'

'Should I have?'

'Most certainly. I will arrange for a copy to be sent to you. The Führer himself has endorsed it . . .' Von Heißen reached for his glass, almost toppling out of his chair. 'Anyway, for the moment, I'm going to have to put up with a Jewish professor on my expedition, although he will have a use-by date.' Von Heißen's laugh was deep and guttural. 'But it's very noisy in here,' he added, standing and reaching unsteadily for Katrina's hand. 'Let's go to your room.'

She looked at him, contemptuous of his highly polished knee-high boots and the immaculately tailored Hugo Boss uniform, all black save for the red-and-black Nazi swastika armband. She reluctantly rose from the table.

Von Heißen sat on the side of the bed and wrestled with his boots. 'I'd get into something very comfortable if I were you,' he said lustfully.

Katrina Baumgartner let her red dress fall to the carpet of her large, comfortably furnished room. Her black lace bra and knickers contrasted with her smooth white skin.

Von Heißen ogled her long legs and struggled out of the rest of his uniform. He stood up and lurched towards her. Katrina sidestepped his advance and von Heißen stumbled back against the bed.

'Not very ready, are we, Hauptsturmführer?'

'What do you mean?'

'Well, look at it,' she said, laughing as she slipped into bed. 'Any smaller and I wouldn't be able to find it.' It was a dangerous, albeit calculated ploy. Katrina knew well that the more pressure a man was under to get it up, the higher the failure rate, especially amongst the arrogant Officer Corps. She couldn't have known, of course, that von Heißen's first girlfriend had also had a fit of the giggles, or that von Heißen had been forced to find solace in the brothels of Berlin ever since.

'*Fick dich!*' Von Heißen swung his fist at Katrina, but she deftly swayed to one side. He bellowed in pain as he connected with the bedhead, falling back onto the pillows.

'I wouldn't try that again, if I were you, Hauptsturmführer,' she warned, picking up the buzzer from the bedside table. 'I might have been forced on to this program, but this alarm is connected to the Security Office, and unless you behave, I will call them. Now,' she said, raising one eyebrow, 'are you going to get that thing up? Perhaps you'd like another whisky before you try?'

Von Heißen sat back against the pillows and nursed his hand, his bloodshot eyes blazing with anger. Katrina got out of bed and walked over to the sideboard. 'Down this,' she said, returning with a large tumbler of Chivas, 'it'll put you in the mood.'

Von Heißen glared at her, drained the tumbler in one gulp and handed it back. Katrina refilled it and wandered over to the gramophone player. She took her time sorting through the records, finally choosing some soft music. She turned to find von Heißen lolling against the pillows, his eyes half closed.

The next morning, Katrina eased herself out of bed, dressed quietly and went for a long walk. Depressed and trapped, she followed the narrow path up into hills shrouded in mist.

It was getting on towards midmorning when von Heißen's driver reached Kassel, where the Brothers Grimm had lived and written their fairytales. They turned east towards the Alme Valley, but von Heißen didn't notice. He was still seething over the night before, the details of which he recorded meticulously in his diary. Less than an hour later, the big Mercedes came to a halt in the stone courtyard of Wewelsburg Castle. Von Heißen alighted and stretched. From the hillside above the village of Wewelsburg, the castle had views over the Westphalian forests and the rolling farmland dotted with small stone cottages. Von Heißen stared up at the castle's massive stone walls. It had been built on a rare, triangular footprint and three towers commanded each apex.

'*Heil Hitler, Herr Hauptsturmführer!*' The young SS lieutenant snapped to attention and gave the Nazi salute. 'I am Untersturm-führer Bosch. Welcome to Wewelsburg.' Leutnant Bosch was a centimetre taller than von Heißen, and his light-brown hair was thick and wavy, brushed straight back off his broad forehead. His deep-blue eyes held an intensity of purpose.

'I've been assigned to look after you while you're here, Herr Hauptsturmführer,' Bosch said. 'Professor Weizman is already in his room and will join you and the Reichsführer for lunch. Please follow me and I'll take you down to the hall where Reichsführer Himmler is addressing the officers.'

Bosch led the way across a cobblestone bridge. The stone arch spanned the castle's protective moat. Von Heißen followed him through the huge arched wooden doors and down a flight of heavy stone steps. Wrought-iron lamps threw an eerie glow against the solid rock walls.

'This is the Grail room,' Bosch explained, as they passed a chamber containing a huge, illuminated rock crystal representing the Holy Grail. 'And in here,' he said, lowering his voice, 'is the Obergruppen-führer Hall.' Bosch eased the heavy wooden door open and led the way to the rear of a hall that was decorated with ancient runes. The inner walls and arches were supported by stone columns and a large black iron wheel hung from the ceiling. It supported seven lamps, and a mirror image of the wheel had been reproduced on the marble floor. About fifty SS officers, all dressed in their black uniforms, were listening intently to their Reichsführer.

'Breeding will be the basis of our success, gentlemen. In animal breeding one has known it for a long time. If anyone wants to buy a horse, he will sensibly take advice from someone who is a horse expert.' Himmler had a high-pitched voice, but, like Hitler, his oratory was charged with a hypnotic power. 'The best bloodlines will always produce champions, but centuries of Christian education have caused us to lose sight of this,' he said, looking over his gold-rimmed glasses. 'The Christians regard a shapely human body in a bathing suit as somehow sinful!' Raucous laughter echoed off the stone walls.

'It is your duty to breed from sound, shapely Nordic stock. We will have fought in vain if political victory is not followed by births of good blood. The question of multiplicity of children is not the private affair of the individual, but his duty towards his ancestors and our people. The existence of a sound marriage is futile if it does not result in the creation of numerous descendants. The minimum number of children for a good marriage is four. That doesn't mean I want you or your officers to marry the first girl who might appear to meet our requirements. Without being tactless, you should get the girl to tell you a little about her family. If she discloses that her father shot himself, or an aunt or a cousin is in a lunatic asylum, you must do the decent thing. At all times the SS officer must behave with decorum. He should say openly, "I'm sorry, but I can't marry you; there are too many diseases in your family." '

Von Heißen nodded approvingly.

'Now, before we break for lunch, we have time to take one or two questions.'

A tall flaxen-haired major rose to attention. 'What do you think is the greatest problem facing Germany today, Herr Reichsführer?'

'Identify yourself.'

'Sturmbannführer Austerlitz, Herr Reichsführer.'

'That is an excellent question,' Himmler said, coming out from behind the lectern. The SS major sat down, beaming at the compliment.

'Quite apart from the need for Lebensraum – more land for the Third Reich to reach its potential,' Himmler responded, 'we must recapture the lost world of the Nordic race. We must restore *das Herrenvolk*, the master race, to its position of pre-eminence, and to provide a foundation for that, we have to reconstruct the lost history of the Aryans. With that in mind, we are shortly launching several archaeological expeditions to prove the origins and influence of the master race, including one to the highland jungles of Guatemala. Hauptsturmführer von Heißen, who has now joined us, will be leading this expedition. Perhaps you might like to comment on your mission, von Heißen.'

'Certainly, Herr Reichsführer. The source of the pure Aryan race is crucially important, gentlemen,' von Heißen explained, unfazed by the more senior ranks in the room. 'Why? Because ancient Germanic tribes demonstrated far greater intellect and creativity than any other civilisation of their time. If our research can recover this knowledge, it will help the Third Reich to once again excel in science, medicine, agriculture and every other field of human endeavour. The German Nordic race is at the apex of humankind, while races like the Jews, the African Bushmen and the Australian Aborigines are at the very bottom.'

Himmler beamed at his young protégé. 'For the moment, the Africans and the Australians don't concern us, but the Jews, together with gypsies and homosexuals, are quite another matter. The Führer will very shortly introduce the Law for the Prevention of Hereditarily Diseased Offspring. This will enable us to sterilise the mentally retarded, the blind, the deaf, the schizophrenic – anyone who is likely to impede our glorious progress. The Jews will require special attention, of course.' Reichsführer Himmler nodded to Obersturmbannführer Manfred von Knobelsdorff, the commandant of the new SS Nordic Academy, indicating to the colonel that it was time for lunch.

Levi Weizman perused *Der Angriff*. The paper was, he knew, sponsored by the Nazis' Minister for Enlightenment and Propaganda, Joseph Goebbels, but it was the only one in his room. To his surprise Levi found a story on Catholics, but his surprise at it appearing in a Nazi paper turned to excitement:

Archbishop of Paris
Crowns Our Lady of Hope

THE CATHOLIC ARCHBISHOP of Paris, Cardinal Jean Verdier, has crowned a statue of the Virgin Mary at Pontmain in the north of France. The Virgin Mary appeared to two children in Pontmain on 17 January 1871, during the Franco–Prussian war. The war ended in a crushing victory for the German and Prussian forces, which saw the unification of the German Empire under King Wilhelm I, and the total destruction of the French Empire.

Levi now understood why the article had been approved for publication. The detestable little Goebbels never missed a chance to trumpet a German victory.

> In a message to the children at Pontmain, the Blessed Mother asked them to pray, giving the war-torn community hope, and the Armistice was signed a few days later in Versailles. The Cardinal Secretary of State, Eugenio Pacelli, in a decree issued from St Peter's Basilica in Rome, has affirmed the veneration of 'Our Lady of Hope' of Pontmain, as the appearance has become known, and declared that her statue be honoured with a crown of gold.
>
> Cardinal Verdier crowned the statue of the Blessed Mother in the presence of other bishops and priests. There have been several verified appearances of the Virgin Mary, the most famous of which was at Fátima, Portugal in 1917. Watched by a crowd of several thousand, many of whom confirmed the sightings, the Blessed Mother appeared at Fátima a total of six times, on the thirteenth day of each month, from May until October.

Levi took a deep breath, recalling the stela he'd discovered in Pyramid V in Tikal. Although the Maya had not specified an exact year, the ancient hieroglyphics had indicated that such a series of events would occur on the thirteenth day of each month from May until October – events that would be of great consequence to humankind. Was there a connection between the warnings the Virgin had delivered at Fátima and the Maya Codex, Levi wondered. Could that explain the Vatican's interest in the ancient civilisation and the presence of a Catholic priest in Tikal? How could the ancient Maya have known these appearances would occur? And what might it have to do with 2012? Levi shook his head. So many questions, but, as yet, so few answers. Levi was convinced there was a great deal more to the ancient Maya than even he had previously thought.

Levi had been taken aback by his host's genial charm. It hadn't been long, though, before the façade of bonhomie had completely vanished. The study room in the Wewelsburg Castle north tower was sombrely decorated with swastikas and runes, matching Himmler's change in mood. It was already clear to Levi that his participation in the Tikal expedition would not be voluntary.

'Are you familiar with craniometry and the cephalic index, Professor?'

Levi nodded without commenting. He had long believed the Nazis' philosophy of using 'head shape' and 'nose shape' as measures of racial categorisation to be a dark stain on the social science of anthropology.

'Then you will not need reminding of the importance I attach to the collection of Mayan skulls. They are to be brought back to Wewelsburg for examination and classification. It will be in your own interest to give us your full cooperation,' Himmler added, before turning to his young protégé. 'Hauptsturmführer von Heißen will be in charge of the expedition, although you will, of course, direct the archaeological exploration, so we will need your lists of supplies as soon as possible. Von Heißen will ensure that the necessary officers are on hand to assist you.'

Levi nodded, Ramona's warnings ringing in his ears. Himmler

THE MAYA CODEX 45

got up from the table and walked over to a small stone aperture overlooking the village.

'In time this castle will represent the zenith of racial science,' he said, leaning on the stone ledge. 'The village of Wewelsburg will be an SS city, and this castle will be the Vatican of the world. I wish you a pleasant stay, Professor,' Himmler said, dismissing Levi with a curt nod.

'I want you to depart as soon as possible,' Himmler ordered von Heißen.

'*Jawohl, Herr Reichsführer.* We've already started assembling the stores, and I've made contact with our embassy in Guatemala City. They're doing everything possible to clear the diplomatic hurdles.'

'Excellent! Generaloberst Göring has assured me that an aircraft and crew will be made available for the duration of your time in Guatemala. In the meantime watch Weizman carefully, von Heißen. The Jew is as cunning as a sewer rat and is never to be trusted.'

'There was no one else, Herr Reichsführer?'

'No one with the necessary skills in reading the Mayan hieroglyphics, no. But we can dispense with him once the expedition is successful. More importantly, I've also met with the papal envoy, Signor Alberto Felici, who plans to visit the expedition. Felici's arranged substantial sponsorship from Vatican finances, so he's to be treated well. In return, he's asked for a Father Ehrlichmann to join the expedition in an official capacity. Amongst other things,

Ehrlichmann is an expert on craniometry, so he'll undoubtedly be useful, but he's to be trusted no more than Weizman or Felici.'

'There is another agenda, Herr Reichsführer?'

'Perhaps. The Vatican only shows an interest in archaeological digs when they fear what might be found. You've seen the cable from our ambassador in Guatemala raising the possibility of a missing codex purported to contain a catastrophic warning for the human race. As to the precise nature of that warning, Weizman and the Vatican will both have their theories . . . We shall see. But if the codex does exist, the Jew can lead us to it.'

4

TIKAL, GUATEMALA 1938

Levi Weizman glanced into the cockpit of the Luftwaffe Junkers Ju 52. The pilot had started his descent and the co-pilot was leaning forward. His leather helmet obscured the instrument panel, but he appeared to be tapping on one of the fuel gauges.

Levi turned in his seat and looked out of the big square window of the Junkers. Nearly 5000 feet below, wispy grey clouds drifted amongst the thick jungle of the Guatemalan highlands. The Junkers was slow, cruising at only 160 miles per hour, and it was cramped: there were just twelve seats, six either side of the centre aisle. The flight had taken a bum-numbing ten days from Berlin. Having finally crossed the Gulf of Mexico and landed at Mérida, the bustling, wealthy capital of Mexico's Yucatán Peninsula, it would be ironic, Levi thought, if they were to have a fuel problem now. He glanced at von Heißen sitting opposite, but the arrogant German, whom Himmler had promoted to major, seemed unperturbed.

'Tikal seems a remote place to establish a city, Herr Professor.' von Heißen said.

'It might seem that way today, but the Maya chose their sites very carefully. Tikal was built on top of a continental divide, astride one of their most important trading routes, one that linked the Gulf of Mexico and the Usumacinta River in the west with the rivers that flow into the Caribbean in the east. So the inhabitants of Tikal, under kings like Great Jaguar Claw, had control over international trade.'

'Reminiscent of the way the Aryans would do things?'

'As an archaeologist, I'm always careful to ensure there is concrete evidence before reaching any firm conclusions, Sturmbannführer.'

Von Heißen scrutinised Levi's map of the ancient city. 'There seems to be a great many ruins,' he observed.

'Construction took place over many centuries. By the middle of the sixth century, we know that Tikal covered some thirty square kilometres and was inhabited by over 100 000 Maya. It was a huge city.'

'And the pyramids?'

'The stepped pyramids were constructed in the form of the Witz, the sacred mountain of the Maya,' Levi replied. 'Other structures served as palaces for the royal families, and as tombs.' He chose his words carefully, not wishing to reveal his theories on the Maya architects' employment of Φ, the golden mean, or their use of the Fibonacci sequence. Levi was now convinced the construction and alignment of the pyramids were linked to the missing figurines and the Maya Codex itself.

Further conversation was cut short by an abrupt spluttering from the port engine. A trail of smoke poured from the cowling.

'Everything will be okay. We have two other good engines,' von Heißen observed with a throaty laugh, but the starboard engine, and then the nose engine coughed, and Levi felt a pang of fear in the depths of his gut. The pilots were working frantically to restart the engines, and the radio operator was furiously tapping out an SOS in morse. Levi knew that in this part of the world, radio communications were tenuous at best.

'*Befestigen Sie Ihre Sicherheitsgurte!* Fasten your seatbelts!' the engineer yelled as the aircraft began a steep descent towards the jungle below.

Levi fastened his belt and silently began the Shema Yisrael, the prayer from Deuteronomy that all God-fearing Jews recited in the morning and at night:

Sh'ma Yis'ra'eil Adonai Eloheinu Adonai echad . . .
Hear, Israel, the Lord is our God, the Lord is One . . .
Barukh sheim k'vod malkhuto l'olam va'ed . . .
Blessed be the Name of His glorious kingdom for ever and ever . . .

The wind tore at the stationary propellers and whistled over the corrugated wings and fuselage. The aircraft shook violently. In the cockpit, the two pilots worked feverishly at the controls, but all three engines were dead.

'All three gauges are showing empty now!' Leutnant Müller, the young Luftwaffe co-pilot, yelled.

The pilot, Colonel Hans Krueger, motioned to the younger man to remain calm. Oberst Krueger had seen service flying Fokker biplanes with Göring in the Great War, and had been shot down three times.

He'd been awarded the Iron Cross First Class, and Generaloberst Göring had personally selected his old friend for 'Operation Maya'.

'I can't see the airfield, so we'll have to land on top of the trees,' Krueger observed matter-of-factly, peering out of the windscreen. 'Airspeed?'

Müller, white-faced, glanced at the airspeed indicator. 'One hundred and five miles an hour.'

'Flaps, ten degrees,' Krueger ordered.

'That exceeds the limit, Herr Oberst,' Müller replied nervously.

Krueger smiled and turned to his young co-pilot. 'It would be most helpful, Leutnant Müller, if you could forget about what they taught you in flying school and give me ten degrees of flap. I don't fancy hitting the trees any faster than is necessary.'

Müller nodded and reached for the flap lever. The aircraft slowed, although Krueger knew their airspeed was still way too fast.

'What was the forecast wind direction this morning?' Krueger already knew the answer, but he also knew this was the young man's first forced landing, and he was subtly teaching him what every good pilot needed in a crisis: an ice-cool calm and a methodical, ordered approach.

'Fifteen miles an hour, from the north-east.'

Krueger pulled back on the big control column and gently turned the wooden flight wheel, his foot lightly on the rudder pedal.

'Flaps, twenty-five degrees.'

Müller moved the flap lever instantly and the aircraft slowed further, the wind whistling eerily past the cockpit.

Levi Weizman stared out the window at the jungle rushing towards them, still silently mouthing the Shema.

'Two o'clock! Two miles! The airstrip!' Leutnant Müller shouted and pointed through the windscreen.

'I see it,' Krueger replied calmly, altering the falling aircraft's course slightly towards the break in the jungle. 'Airspeed?'

'Ninety miles an hour.'

Krueger grunted. It would be touch and go. On the one hand, he'd need around forty degrees of flap to land, but applying that much flap at anything above seventy-five miles an hour might tear the wings from the airframe. On the other hand, he needed to maintain speed to make the clearing, and if he allowed the Junkers' speed to fall below sixty miles an hour with flaps down, they would stall and head nose first into the trees.

'More flap, Herr Oberst?' Müller queried anxiously, his hand on the flap lever.

'Wait.' Oberst Krueger mentally fixed the glide path and adjusted the aircraft's heading. 'Wait,' he commanded again, sensing the young co-pilot's nervousness. 'Now!'

Müller immediately adjusted the lever and the aircraft shook violently as the big flaps bit hard.

'*Scheisse!*' Krueger swore as the aircraft's nose came up too fast. He pushed the control column forward to maintain airspeed and aimed at a point just beyond the trees at the start of the clearing. At the last moment he pulled back on the column and flared the aircraft. It shuddered as the tailplane clipped the top of a big ceiba tree. Krueger braced himself as the aircraft slammed onto the makeshift airstrip and bounced. He calmly kept the control column forward and they bounced twice more before he could bring the Junkers to a halt near the end of the dirt strip.

'Everyone okay?' Krueger asked, turning in his seat to look into the cabin.

Von Heißen turned and made a quick check of the cabin. '*Alles gut, Herr Oberst!*' he replied.

Levi said a silent prayer of thanks and followed von Heißen down the steps propped against the ribbed fuselage. A Catholic priest was waiting to meet them.

'Welcome to Tikal, Sturmbannführer von Heißen.'

'Father Ehrlichmann, how good to see you again. And this is Professor Weizman. Father Ehrlichmann is an expert on craniometry and the cephalic index,' von Heißen explained to Levi. 'He'll be in charge of the preliminary classification of any skulls before they're shipped back to Wewelsburg.'

'*Guten Tag, Herr Professor.*'

'*Guten Tag, Father Ehrlichmann.*' Levi shook hands, immediately wary.

The next morning Levi woke just before dawn. He dressed in a light safari suit and quietly pulled back the dirty brown canvas tent flap. The expedition tent lines had been pitched along the eastern side of the airstrip, and Levi's tent was just two down from von Heißen's.

The stars were fading as Levi made his way towards the thick jungle at the north-west corner of the airstrip. He knew from his previous visits that the narrow jungle-track led to the Central Acropolis, the sacred heart of the great Mayan city. The air was cool, and already the jungle was coming alive in the soft pre-dawn light. Suddenly, a series of enraged roars pierced the foliage. Levi looked up to see a group of howler monkeys, the biggest nearly a metre tall, their squat black faces staring down at him from the tops of massive, buttressed strangler figs. The killer trees started life as a tiny seed. Eventually, the seed's tendrils wrapped around a host tree, strangling it, as the crown of the fig tree soared above the canopy. Figs were a favourite of the howler monkey. The troop moved on, noisily alerting the rest of the jungle to Levi's presence. Further into the rainforest, Levi spotted two keel-billed toucans, croaking and barking in the half-light, their bright-yellow hooked beaks contrasting with their jet-black feathers, but it was the large paw marks and droppings nearby that made him proceed more cautiously. Levi recognised them instantly; a jaguar was on the prowl. He moved silently on the forest floor of decaying leaves, peering through the low-lying ferns, orchids and mosses that grew in abundance alongside the balsa, chicle and myriad other trees and vines growing thickly around the ancient city.

Twenty minutes later Levi emerged into a clearing, surrounded by moss-covered limestone pyramids. The jungle was noisier now. The howler monkeys competed with the chirps and trills of the hummingbirds, the *hoot-oot* of the blue-crowned motmot, the insistent *kyowh-kyowh* of the orange-breasted falcon and the *squark-squark* of the brilliantly coloured macaws and parrots.

Levi moved through the East Plaza, skirting the sacred court where the Maya had played humanity's oldest and most brutal ball game. He reached the Great Plaza and the base of Pyramid I, built by Jasaw Chan K'awiil, the twenty-fifth ruler of the ancient city. Levi looked up. The limestone steps of the huge pyramid connected nine separate levels, culminating in the roof comb, nearly forty-six metres above the plaza.

Breathing hard, Levi at last reached the summit and turned to survey the jungle below. A heavy white mist drifted through the tops of the thirty-metre-high ceiba trees, sacred to those who had once occupied the ancient city. Huge mahogany, cedar, chicle and ramon trees towered over the smaller copal trees and escobo palms, forming a thick green carpet as far as Levi could see. To the west stood the imposing Pyramid II, and to the south-west of the Great Plaza he could see Pyramid III. Further west the roof comb of Pyramid IV thrust defiantly through the mists, while to the south, the top of Pyramid V was also visible, as was the Pyramid of the Lost World. Levi walked to the east side of Pyramid I. The mists on the horizon were tinged with a brilliant orange-red glow. A fiery sun rose slowly and majestically, bathing the ancient city in its light.

Levi felt a sense of awe as he reflected on the ancient Maya. To the east of the Great Plaza the jungle had taken over the magnificent paved causeways that once controlled the entry of traders into a bustling marketplace. The pyramid temples of a mighty city that had glimmered in a brilliant shade of salmon pink had now eroded to reveal a dirty limestone, covered here and there in a dank, dark moss. Levi shivered. The sudden fall of the Maya was an eerie reflection of humankind's vulnerability and mortality. He turned towards Pyramid IV, pulled a compass from his pocket and took a bearing, then a second bearing on the Pyramid of the Lost World.

Far below, von Heißen adjusted his binoculars. He stood in the shadows of the ball court and watched as Professor Weizman put the compass to his eye.

Roberto Arana, the shaman from the shores of Lake Atitlán, was also watching. He was short and stocky and his sun-weathered face looked older than his years. His jet-black hair was tied in a ponytail and he wore a bright-red bandana. More at home in the jungle than either von Heißen or Levi Weizman, Roberto kept both men in view from his position in the rainforest beside Pyramid II.

Levi waited while the mother-of-pearl disc steadied. His pulse quickened as it stabilised. His experiment back in Vienna with the light beam had predicted that the prism on top of the first figurine would deflect the sunrise, aligning the sun's rays on precisely the same bearing, directly towards the top of Pyramid IV. Was the second figurine somewhere in the depths of the partially explored Pyramid IV? And where was the third?

Levi replaced the battered compass in the pouch on his belt and began to descend the steep blackened limestone steps on the eastern face of Pyramid I. His thoughts turned to Ramona, Ariel and Rebekkah. In Vienna, he knew, things had gone from bad to worse. Hitler was more threatening than ever, and the Austrian Nazi Party's Brownshirts were firmly in control of the streets.

Von Heißen put down his binoculars and waited.

5

VIENNA

Ariel Weizman started up the steps towards *Judengasse*, fighting back tears. Rebekkah was already crying and Ariel took her hand, determined to protect her. The humiliation at the hands of their new teacher had been crushing.

'You! Weizman and your sister! *Jude Kinder!*' Herr Schweizer had yelled at Ariel and Rebekkah as soon as the bell rang to signify the start of classes. Schweizer was thin and balding with a wispy moustache.

'Filthy, stinking *Jude Kinder*! You're lucky to even be allowed in this class. From now on you will both sit at the back of the room. The world would be better off without your type, and the rest of us don't want to be contaminated!'

Laughter echoed off the old *Hauptschule* walls, and Ariel looked around. Even his friends were laughing at him. He made his way to the back of the class with Rebekkah and sat down. Numb. What had they done to deserve this?

Herr Schweizer, a senior vice president for his region in the banned Austrian Nazi Party, addressed his new charges.

'There are going to be some changes around here, for the good of Austria and the greater *Deutschland*. We will deal this morning with the Treaty of Versailles. Can anyone tell me what that was and why Germany should never have been a party to it?'

Rebekkah clung to her brother's hand as she dragged her satchel up the *Donaukanal-Judengasse* steps, her blonde curls bedraggled; the cracks between the steps fuzzy through her tears.

It wasn't until they'd almost reached the top that Ariel noticed the crowd. Suddenly a stranger grabbed him by the ear. His assailant was a large, rotund man in breeches. The man wore a felt hat with a large feather. His coat looked several sizes too small and he was wearing a swastika armband on his sleeve.

'What are you doing here?' the man demanded, his face florid.

'Let go of me! We live here!' Ariel replied, trying to shield his little sister.

'So! *Jude Kinder!* Gutter-dwelling *Jude Kinder!*' the stranger bellowed, addressing his remarks to the jeering crowd. Though it was the second time Ariel had heard the words that day, the sting was no less vicious. He caught sight of Herr Lieberman and his wife, who owned the carpet store a few doors down from his mother's boutique. They were scrubbing the steps with toothbrushes. Herr Lieberman looked sad yet somehow dignified as he shook his head at Ariel and Rebekkah, indicating they shouldn't resist.

The stranger thrust a paint can and brush into Ariel's hand.

'*Schreiben Sie hier Jude verrecke!*' He grabbed Ariel by the neck and forced him roughly to the ground. The crowd began to chant menacingly. In a futile gesture, Rebekkah flailed at the stranger who held her by the hair.

'*Sieg Heil! Jude verrecke! Sieg Heil! Jude verrecke!*'

Through uncomprehending tears, Ariel began to paint the words in large black letters on the steps. *Jude verrecke!* Death to the Jews!

When Ariel finished, the crowd reacted with a roar and the stranger kicked him behind his knees. Ariel's legs buckled and he fell backwards down the steps. The man kicked the paint can after him and thick black paint splashed over Ariel's face and school uniform. The crowd cheered wildly.

Ariel wiped his nose and mouth and looked up to find three older boys in brown shirts crowding over him. He yelped in pain as one of them kicked him in the ribs.

'I wouldn't walk to school tomorrow, Jew boy, and that goes for your bitch of a sister too. We'll be waiting.'

Ariel missed his father more than ever, and once again he fought back the tears. He put his arm around Rebekkah to shelter her and together they made their escape.

Himmler strode past the high-backed red-and-gold armchairs and tables interspersed at regular intervals down the Hall of Marble, a long impressive room at the front of the new Reich Chancellery. His boots rang on the marble floor, echoing off walls decorated with priceless tapestries. The magnificent red marble had been specially quarried from Untersberg. Designed by Hitler's architect, Albert Speer, the Chancellery took up several city blocks on *Wilhelmstrasse* and *Vosstrasse*.

Two SS guards stood beneath the marble archway that led to the double doors of Hitler's vast office.

'*Reichsführer Himmler, mein Führer.*' Hitler's adjutant Oberst Friedrich Hossbach clicked his heels.

Anyone admitted to Hitler's office in the Reich Chancellery could not fail to be impressed. Hitler's huge desk at the far end of the room was exquisitely finished with inlaid wood and upholstered with the finest red leather, and was matched with a high-backed red-leather chair. A map table was positioned near the French doors overlooking the courtyard. Some of Hitler's favourite oils hung from the walls, and indoor plants in large Egyptian-styled vases on the floor added to the ambience. A large golden eagle was suspended over the double doors.

'Our expedition has arrived in Tikal, and they've begun their search,' Himmler advised his leader after they were seated on the comfortable powder-blue lounges in front of a vast marble fireplace at one end of the office.

'Excellent,' Hitler affirmed with a satisfied look.

'I've received a cable from our ambassador in Guatemala City,' Himmler continued. 'It appears that during his last visit to Lake Atitlán, Professor Weizman met with a Mayan shaman and discussed the existence of a priceless codex. We've not been able to confirm it, but Weizman may have also discovered an ancient figurine that may hold a clue to the whereabouts of the codex.'

'How does the ambassador know that?'

'Our ambassador and the papal nuncio in Guatemala City keep in close contact, *mein Führer*. Father Ehrlichmann, the Catholic priest to San Pedro and Tikal, is a useful source of intelligence.'

'Von Heißen has been warned?'

Himmler nodded. 'Weizman's belongings have been searched and von Heißen has him under constant surveillance.'

'You can never trust a Jew, Himmler, never! But the search for the origins and secrets of the Aryan race must go on. Keep Weizman alive, but only for as long as he's useful.'

'*Jawohl*, *mein Führer*. When you take over Vienna, we will turn his apartment upside down.'

At the mention of the city in which he'd known desperate poverty, Hitler became agitated. He got to his feet and began to pace the length of his huge study.

'There are those amongst us who think invading Austria is a mistake.' Hitler glared into the courtyard through the French doors, arms akimbo. 'But I'm meeting with the chiefs of staff and that lily-livered foreign minister, von Neurath, this afternoon to inform them that not only are they to be ready to invade Austria, but Czechoslovakia as well.'

Himmler nodded approvingly. 'We must have more land, *mein Führer*.'

'*Lebensraum!* It's a question of space for the master race, gentlemen.'

The Führer's energy crackled through the silence around the vast cabinet table. Just six men were seated in the burgundy chairs, each embroidered with a black eagle atop the swastika: Reichsmarshal von Blomberg, Commander in Chief of the armed forces and Minister for War; Baron Konstantin von Neurath, Foreign Minister; Admiral Doktor Erich Raeder, Commander in Chief of the navy; Generaloberst Baron Freiherr von Fritsch, Commander in Chief of the army; Generaloberst Hermann Göring, Commander in Chief of the air force; and Colonel Friedrich Hossbach, Adjutant to the Führer. The long polished mahogany table was covered with a burgundy tapestry runner embroidered with gold swastikas. Gold tassels overhung the table at either end. Lighting was provided from small candelabra lamps spaced at intervals down the centre. Crimson files embossed with the golden eagle and the swastika and marked *Streng Geheim* – most secret – lay unopened on the cabinet table. Each man knew the contents well, and each was now contemplating the enormity of the Führer's plans.

'We're now rebuilding our armed forces, and as I predicted, Britain and France have done nothing,' Hitler stormed. 'Nothing! Already we have thirty-six divisions in the army. Germany has a right!' Hitler's eyes blazed with the fires of his own destiny. No one spoke.

'The German *people* have a right to see the Fatherland restored to its place as a great power – *the* great power of the world. And we can only do that by force.' Hitler's voice rose and fell as he made his points. 'We have retaken the Rhineland without a shot being fired. Now we must turn our attention to Austria and Czechoslovakia.'

Baron von Fritsch, Commander in Chief of the army, made the mistake of raising an eyebrow.

'You look worried, Generaloberst?' Hitler glared.

'*Mein Führer*, no one doubts the progress we've made since you became Reich Chancellor,' von Fritsch responded evenly, 'but I would be remiss in my duty to you and the German people if I did not remind you of the risks involved in what you're suggesting. If the British and the French oppose your plans to invade Czechoslovakia and Austria, a major war would risk disaster for the Third Reich. From the army's point of view, we've made good progress in raising the thirty-six divisions you require, but it takes time to train over half a million men. More importantly, we do not yet have the logistics to sustain such a force in the field. I would urge you, *mein Führer*, not to move too quickly.'

'There are always risks!' the Führer shouted, thumping the tapestry on the heavy table. His face was flushed and his eyes bulged. As his commanders in chief were beginning to learn, the Reich Chancellor could become enraged very quickly. Hitler pushed his chair back, got to his feet and strode over to a large globe of the world supported in an ornate wooden frame. He gave it a spin and it turned soundlessly on its bearings.

'You obviously don't know much about history, Herr Generaloberst,' Hitler sneered. 'The leaders of all great empires – the Greek, the Roman, even the stupid British – have always been prepared to take risks.' Hitler paused, then approached the head of the table and leaned on it.

'The aim of German policy, gentlemen,' he said more quietly, 'is to preserve our racial superiority and enlarge it. Germans are the greater people, and, as such, we have a right to a greater living space than others.'

Suddenly it were as if he had withdrawn into a trance. His eyes bulged again and he pounded the cabinet table. 'The most precious possession on earth lies in our own people! And *for* these people, and *with* these people, we will struggle and we will fight! And never slacken! Never tire! Never falter! Never doubt! Long live our movement! Long live our people!'

Hitler stormed out of the Cabinet Room and strode across the corridor towards his study, furious with weak generals like von Fritsch who failed to recognise the genius of his plan. They were irrelevant, he fumed. The swastika would soon fly from the elegant buildings of Vienna, and the streets of that great city would be free of the accursed Jew.

6

TIKAL, GUATEMALA

'So, what have you discovered, Professor? And so early in the morning, too.'

Levi jumped back, startled by von Heißen's sudden appearance from the overgrown jungle of the ball court.

'Do you normally creep about like this, Sturmbannführer?' he demanded.

'That depends, Professor, on whether those around me have something to hide, something that might further the greatness of the Reich. I see you were taking bearings. There is presumably a reason for that?'

'It's quite common archaeological practice to take bearings before we grid an area.'

'Yet you don't find the need to take any notes? Fascinating. I will watch your progress with interest. Now,' von Heißen continued, 'Father Ehrlichmann is keen to make a start. I plan a meeting for after breakfast. If Ehrlichmann is right, we'll find skulls not far from here.'

'The ancient Maya were a very proud race, Sturmbannführer, and their victory ceremonies included the sacrifice of enemies. Centuries ago, teeming ranks of painted warriors thundered onto this very ball court, stamping to the rhythm of pounding drums and the scent of burning temple fires. They led their prisoners up those steps over there.' Levi pointed towards a large stone at the top. 'They ripped their hearts out while they were still beating. Then they decapitated them. The last time I was here I found several skulls in the jungle behind the ball court.' Levi was more than happy to distract von Heißen with Himmler's obsession with craniometry.

'And you didn't take any back to Austria?' von Heißen probed.

'Museums might be interested, but I don't collect skulls, Sturmbannführer, nor do I disturb sacred ground.' Roberto Arana, the shaman, had reminded Levi of the curse the ancient Egyptians placed on the tomb of Tutankhamen: *Death shall come on swift wing to him who disturbs the peace of the King.*

Levi knew that those who had opened Tutankhamen's tomb had succumbed to mysterious deaths. Roberto had warned that the Maya protected their pyramids and sacred ground with equal ferocity. 'The secondary jungle has taken over,' Levi observed, looking past the ball court, 'and it's very thick now, but the skull racks where the Maya displayed the heads of their victims should still be there.'

'Excellent,' von Heißen exclaimed. 'I wouldn't be at all surprised if the measurements of any skulls there are well within the cephalic index for the Nordic Aryans.'

'Ah, yes. The mathematical formula for the shape of a head, on which you base your judgements on intelligence and race. If I remember rightly, it's the ratio of head breadth to head length multiplied by a hundred. A fairly simplistic way of looking at things, I would think. Although your Reichsführer seems to place great faith in it.'

'As do I,' von Heißen replied icily. 'Perhaps you should stick to your compass bearings, Professor, and leave the intricacies of craniometry to those who understand it.'

Levi said nothing. Clearly von Heißen was unaware of Mayan beliefs about the shape of the human skull. An elongated head was considered to be a sign of nobility, and Levi had discovered that the ancient Maya had bound babies' heads, compressing them between boards for days to change the shape of their skulls.

It was midafternoon by the time the team of indentured labourers from the local village, beads of sweat glistening on their brown skin, hacked their way far enough into the dense secondary undergrowth surrounding the ball court.

'Maestro!'

Levi moved forward but von Heißen and Father Ehrlichmann both shouldered him out of the way.

'There! Look at the shapes,' von Heißen enthused.

The local villagers, the modern descendants of the Maya, had uncovered the first of several grisly rows of skulls. Macabre, eyeless sockets stared at the intruders. Levi shivered. The heads remained impaled on the moss-covered rack, just as the original inhabitants of the city had left them more than a thousand years before. To disturb them now seemed to invite the retribution Roberto had warned of, Levi thought. Not far away, a large masacuata stirred at the sounds of its territory being invaded. The boa constrictor was the largest snake in Central America, and this one measured well over five metres.

Von Heißen ran his hands over the first of the skulls. Centuries ago, the racks had been drenched in drying blood, the stench of death heavy in the air, but now every skull was creamy smooth and yellowed with age. 'Look at the size of them! Aryan!'

Father Ehrlichmann reached into his canvas satchel for a pair of sliding callipers. 'An index of around seventy-five,' he announced after he'd finished measuring the first skull. 'Unusually broad, but I think Reichsführer Himmler will be pleased.'

Again, Levi said nothing. Ehrlichmann might be an acknowledged authority on the dubious science of craniometry, he thought, but like von Heißen, Ehrlichmann seemed unaware of ancient Mayan customs.

A week later, the Junkers returned on the first of its weekly resupply runs. Levi leaned back in the canvas chair outside his tent and looked towards the skies, his spirits lifting. Perhaps there would be a letter from Ramona. The aircraft circled the clearing in the jungle and then disappeared before lining up for its final approach.

Inside the plane, il Signor Alberto Felici tugged nervously at his large black moustache. Beads of sweat ran down his pale, pudgy face. He detested flying, and the DC-2 flight from Rome to Guatemala City, followed by the flight from Guatemala City in the Junkers, had done nothing to lessen his apprehension. Felici maintained a fierce grip on the armrest, but he needn't have worried. Under the patient tutelage of Oberst Krueger, Leutnant Müller eased the Junkers onto the rough strip, turned at the far end and taxied back. He cut the power and the propellers phutted to a stop in quick succession.

Levi watched as a bald-headed, portly little man dressed in a fawn safari suit and carrying a large leather briefcase descended from the Junkers. Von Heißen and Father Ehrlichmann were waiting to welcome him. They disappeared into von Heißen's tent and Levi wondered who would take the trouble to travel to such a remote part of the world, but he was not left wondering for long. The visitor, accompanied by Father Ehrlichmann, emerged almost immediately and they both headed in Levi's direction.

'Il Signor Felici is an advisor to Pope Pius XI,' Father Ehrlichmann enthused after he'd made the introductions, 'and he's here on a fact-finding mission at the personal direction of Cardinal Pacelli, the Cardinal Secretary of State.'

'Why would the Vatican be interested in the Maya?' Levi asked politely after Ehrlichmann had left.

'May I call you Levi?' Felici asked smoothly. Levi smiled and nodded. 'And I'd be grateful if we could keep our conversations confidential: the Nazi machine is not always to be trusted.'

Levi nodded again. Perhaps, at last, he had a friend in court.

'The possible existence of a Maya codex has not gone unnoticed in the Vatican. Bishop de Landa's burning of the Mayan libraries was a terrible loss to civilisation, and although the Vatican will never publicly admit to any involvement, privately, the support for this expedition is in recognition of a grave injustice.'

'It will take a lot more than that to make amends, Signor Felici. Imagine the outcry if the Maya had invaded Rome and burned all the public libraries and art museums!'

'It's been a painful lesson,' Felici agreed, 'and one that should not be forgotten, but in the meantime I'd very much appreciate a briefing on your progress.'

'What do you expect this codex to contain?' Felici asked after Levi had dismissed the Nazi's craniometry theories and brought the papal envoy up to speed on the expedition's findings.

'The Nazis think it will provide proof of a link between the Aryans and the Maya, but I think they're wrong. The Maya were amongst the greatest astronomers of the ancient world, and from my study of their hieroglyphics, I'm convinced they're trying to warn us of a rare planetary alignment that will occur in 2012. It won't affect you or I, of course, but anyone who's alive in 2012 will need to prepare against the full force of the cosmos. And there may be a link between the warning in the codex and the warnings of the Virgin at Fátima, which makes me wonder why the three secrets the Virgin entrusted to the children at Fátima have been suppressed. Are they just a threat to the papacy, or do they speak of the annihilation of our civilisation?'

'I wasn't aware they had been suppressed,' Felici replied, feigning surprise.

'The Maya predicted the Marian appearance at Fátima, a thousand years before the secrets were transcribed,' Levi continued, searching Felici's face for any reaction.

'How?'

Levi smiled enigmatically. 'They left a warning on a stela which was found not far from here. We still have a lot to learn about the Maya, Signor Felici. We're only scratching the surface. Astronomers have now confirmed their predictions for 2012, down to the last second. If humankind is to have any chance of responding, it's vital this codex be found.'

Von Heißen poured another generous shot of whisky into his tumbler.

'Whisky, Signor?' von Heißen offered Felici, who had returned to von Heißen's tent.

'Thank you, Herr Sturmbannführer. You're well set up out here.'

'I like to think so, and, please, it's Karl,' von Heißen replied, conscious of Himmler's dictum to treat the papal envoy well. 'So, what did the Professor have to say?'

'He's convinced the lost Maya Codex exists, although I wouldn't trust him, Karl. He is, after all, a Jew,' Felici intoned, raising his glass. '*Prost.*'

'Yes, but don't worry, we're watching him very closely. *Prost!* Did he give you any idea what the codex might contain?'

Felici shook his head. 'Other than being convinced it's here somewhere, he was very vague, Karl. But if he does find it, I'd be very grateful if we could discuss it before any release to the wider world.'

'Of course. We're on the same side here. And how are things at the Vatican? I gather the Pontiff is not well.'

'Deteriorating rapidly, I'm afraid,' Felici agreed.

'Any word on his likely replacement?'

'Are you a betting man, Karl?'

Von Heißen smiled. 'I've been known to have the odd wager, Signor.'

'Then I'd put your money on the Cardinal Secretary of State, Eugenio Pacelli. If Pacelli's elected, it'll be a great boost for German–Vatican relations . . . The Cardinal Secretary of State is quite well disposed towards your Führer.' Felici was stretching the truth a little. Pacelli, he knew, had serious reservations, but the concordat between Hitler and the Vatican had greatly strengthened the power of the Holy Church in Germany, and Pacelli saw the Nazis as offering the best hope against the advancing tide of Communism.

'We should stay in touch,' von Heißen opined, as he farewelled Felici from his tent. 'Your proposal for a new Vatican Bank sounds very interesting. I've received word from Reichsführer Himmler himself that once this expedition is concluded, I will most likely be posted to Mauthausen in Austria. If you're ever in Vienna, I know some excellent restaurants.'

Felici nodded, slightly unsteady on his feet. 'I'm in Vienna two or three times a year on business, so I'll look forward to that. *Gute Nacht und danke schön.*' Felici weaved his way towards his own tent, reflecting on the powerful forces gathering to Italy's north, and von Heißen's impeccable connections to the highest levels of the Reich.

Von Heißen reached for his diary and began to record the day's events in characteristic detail.

Levi felt frustrated. In the nearly three months they'd been at Tikal, despite having sent several messages via the local villagers, Roberto

Arana had not made contact. Levi leaned back in his canvas chair and looked out through the tent flap across the red-dirt airstrip. The day before, he'd received word to join the elders in the local village for a meal, and he wondered if Arana might at last appear tonight. In the time they'd been here, 129 skulls had been collected from around the ball court. Father Ehrlichmann had meticulously measured each one and made copious notes. And in that time Levi had also received several letters from Ramona, letters he was convinced had been opened. Levi was more homesick than ever for her touch, her laughter, and he worried about her safety and the safety of the children. He re-read the last paragraph of the letter he'd received earlier in the week.

I hope you won't be away too much longer, darling. There are more Brownshirts on the streets than ever now, and Hitler is making more threats. I've sent you copies of Wiener Zeitung *this week, and as you can see from the headlines, our own chancellor is stoically resisting the Nazis, but we are all wondering for how long. I miss you terribly, my sweet. I long for your touch.*

Your Ramona. Always. xx

Levi knew he was running out of time. He'd thoroughly investigated Pyramids I, II, III, and IV, but without success. In Pyramid IV, he'd discovered a secret niche, much like the one where he'd discovered the male figurine in Pyramid I all those years ago, but the niche was empty. Had one of the figurines already been discovered by someone else? In the past week, he'd attempted to examine the small room beneath the decorative comb on top of Pyramid V, but each time he'd been disturbed by either von Heißen or Father Ehrlichmann. It was as if his every move was being watched. Somehow he would have to find a way to examine Pyramid V late at night, after von Heißen and Ehrlichmann had retired.

Levi looked at his watch: 5 p.m. Dusk was only an hour away. He would pay a courtesy visit to von Heißen's tent on his way to meet the village elders.

'Well, Herr Professor. To what do I owe this unexpected pleasure?' von Heißen sneered. The level in the bottle of Glenfiddich, one of several dozen von Heißen had insisted be included in the cargo, was well down.

'Just to let you know I'm sharing a meal with the villagers tonight. I'm not sure what time I'll be back.'

'Why do you want to eat with the hired help?' Von Heißen refilled his metal tumbler.

'If you are to understand Mayan hieroglyphics, Sturmbannführer, you must first understand the culture, and in any case I consider it an honour to share a meal with these people. They have much to teach us.'

'Well, that's your view, Weizman. If you want to go and eat beans and bananas, I'm not going to stop you. But you might remind the head honcho down there that I've yet to see the young woman I pointed out to him. Her name was Itzy something or other . . .' Von Heißen was already slurring his words. 'We Germans are the descendants of the master race, Weizman, remind him of that, too.'

Levi turned on his heel, his anger rising. In von Heißen and Himmler's twisted world, ancient skulls could somehow provide proof of the master race, while the modern Maya descendants some-how fell outside of their bizarre mathematical calculations. Levi strode across the dirt airstrip and when he reached the jungle track that led to the village, he stopped and took several deep breaths. It was pointless enough arguing with von Heißen when he was sober, he reminded himself, let alone when he was full of piss and wind.

The village was nearly three kilometres from the ruins, but Levi had only gone about half a kilometre when he sensed he was being followed. He turned to look back, peering past the heavy leaves and foliage hanging over the jungle track, but apart from a troop of howler monkeys above and the throaty squawks and screams of a pair of red macaws ahead, the track seemed deserted. Half an hour later he reached the river. The water ran swiftly, and the roar of the falls grew louder as Levi approached the rickety rope bridge that spanned the crossing point. It was hard to see in the eerie half-light, but again, Levi sensed movement a hundred metres or so along the track behind him. He moved off the track and waited.

7

VIENNA, MARCH 1938

It was still dark when Chancellor von Schuschnigg's phone dragged him from the depths of an exhausted sleep. The Austrian Chancellor groped for the bedside-lamp switch and looked at his watch: 5.30 a.m.

'Schuschnigg.'

'Es tut mir leid Sie zu wecken, Herr Bundeskanzler,' the Austrian Chief of Police apologised, 'but the Germans have closed the border at Salzburg. All rail traffic has been halted and I have reports German troops are massing on the other side.'

Von Schuschnigg thanked him and hung up. Wearily he swung his feet out of bed and headed for the bathroom. An hour later his black Mercedes turned into the *Ballhausplatz*. A light dusting of snow glistened in the headlights.

Herr Seyss-Inquart, a young pro-Nazi lawyer, was waiting for him in the otherwise eerily quiet Chancellery.

'It was a grave mistake to take a plebiscite to the people, Herr Bundeskanzler.'

'The people were asked whether or not they wanted a free, independent Austria, *Ja oder Nein*,' von Schuschnigg responded angrily.

'Hitler is furious. He sees it as an act of betrayal, a broken promise.'

'You seem to have a direct line to Berlin,' von Schuschnigg observed icily.

'These are difficult times. I'm merely trying to achieve what is best for the Austrian people.'

'We're all trying to achieve that. And as far as promises go, I seem to remember we had an agreement with Herr Hitler that he would respect Austrian independence.'

'He will still hold to that, Herr Bundeskanzler, but on one condition.'

'Which is?'

'You are to resign and I am to take your place,' Seyss-Inquart replied bluntly, his face inscrutable.

'Anything else?' von Schuschnigg growled.

'I can assure you such a move will save a lot of bloodshed. It is for the good of the Austrian people and for them alone.'

'That is your view. I will give you my answer directly.'

The young women in the basement of the main telephone exchange in Vienna were keenly aware that something was afoot. For three hours, in a flurry of activity, they'd connected the President and the Bundeskanzler to some of the most important people in Austria and

Europe. By early afternoon, von Schuschnigg and President Miklas had both given way to the inevitable.

Von Schuschnigg stared pensively out his office window at the snowy courtyard. Perhaps the agreement to restore some prominent Nazi officers to their posts in the police force had been a mistake, he thought grimly. The Chief of Police had warned him the government could no longer rely on its own police force. The army would fight, but von Schuschnigg knew they would eventually be overwhelmed. The cost in young Austrian lives would be horrific. It would be better,' he'd assured the President, to accede to the German Führer's wishes.

Her boutique devoid of customers, and she herself fearful for the safety of both Levi and her children, Ramona listened to the radio with growing disbelief.

'The roads are lined with huge crowds anticipating the arrival of the Führer,' the announcer crowed. 'In every town the swastika of the Third Reich flies regally from the *Rathaus* and other community buildings.'

Hitler's massive six-wheel Mercedes crossed the Inn River at Braunau at 3.50 p.m. on the twelfth of March, flanked by a large motorcycle escort and a motorised armed guard. The convoy sped beneath the towering snow-capped Alps, slowing at the towns.

'People are cheering and waving to the German Chancellor as he heads towards Linz, and then on to Vienna,' the radio announcer continued, 'where over a half a million people are expected to gather in the *Heldenplatz*, the Heroes' Square.'

How could the Austrian people be so stupid, Ramona wondered incredulously.

Hitler's driver eased the Mercedes into the *Heldenplatz* behind a German infantry band playing 'In Treu Feste'. Hitler stood in the open back and raised his hand. The crowd went wild.

'*Sieg Heil! Sieg Heil! Sieg Heil!*'

The beat was primeval, echoing ominously off the historic walls of the Hapsburg Palace. Huge red-and-black swastika banners flew from the palace, the *Rathaus*, the balcony of the Imperial Hotel and the *Burgtheater*. The crowd was still chanting as Hitler walked onto the palace balcony, placed both hands on the edge and looked down onto the sea of people below. Hitler was home. He moved in front of the microphone and held up his hand. The vast crowd fell silent.

'Years ago I went forth from this country, and I bore within me precisely the same profession of faith which today fills my heart! Judge the depth of my emotion when after so many years I have been able to bring that profession of faith to its fulfilment.' His stirring words echoed around the *Heldenplatz*. Young women wept as they chanted and a rising hysteria gripped the crowd.

'*Sieg Heil! Sieg Heil! Sieg Heil!*'

The beat never lessened and Hitler stood motionless, triumphant over the city where, a quarter of a century before, he'd wandered the streets unshaven, his hair matted, a filthy black overcoat his only protection against the biting snows of winter, selling his postcard paintings on the street for a few paltry pfennigs, begging at the soup kitchen on the banks of the Danube while the patrons of the *Burg-theater* sipped champagne and delighted in the works of Mozart and Haydn and the waltzes of Johann Strauss. Vienna. It was the jewel in the crown of Austria. It was here Hitler had studied the Jews, and the more he'd studied, the more he'd come to detest the vile race. They were like maggots in a rotting body. There wasn't any form of filth, prostitution or white-slave traffic they weren't involved in. Innocent Christian girls were seduced by repulsive, crooked-legged Jew bastards. The Jews were the evil spirits leading his people astray. They must be destroyed, he mused. And they would be. Soon Adolf Eichmann would arrive in Vienna to implement his instructions.

Trembling, Ramona Weizman wiped away a tear and turned off the radio. She closed her boutique and went upstairs to the apartment to retrieve her prayer shawl.

8

TIKAL, GUATEMALA

Levi Weizman moved back onto the track, away from the balsa tree he'd used for cover. He froze immediately. A two-metre fer-de-lance, one of the largest and deadliest snakes of Central America, slithered towards him, the black diamonds on its dark chocolate-and-grey back clearly visible in the moonlight. Levi backed slowly into the jungle. The pit-viper could detect a change in temperature to one thousandth of a degree, enabling it to strike its prey with lethal accuracy. The dose of venom fatal to humans was just fifty milligrams, and Levi knew that a fer-de-lance could deliver up to 300 milligrams in a single strike. The huge snake slithered past and headed towards the river in search of frogs and rats. Levi could hear the troop of howler monkeys further up the river, but the track behind him was clear. Perhaps he'd been imagining things, he thought, and he turned towards the rickety rope bridge that spanned the swirling river separating the Mayan village from the ruins of Tikal.

'It's been a long time, Professor Weizman.' The jungle to the right of the bridge parted and Roberto Arana appeared, wearing his customary red bandana atop his weathered face. Roberto was smiling and he stretched out his hand.

'I was beginning to wonder if you'd received my messages,' Levi said as he followed the shaman across the bridge, holding on to the swaying ropes and carefully choosing his footholds across the gaps between the worn wooden planks. 'Was that you following me?'

Roberto shook his head. 'A jaguar.' The jungle suddenly reverberated with a spine-tingling roar, confirming the jaguar's presence. 'But don't worry, warriors from the village will escort you back. As to your messages . . . that which you seek has remained hidden for centuries, Professor. The codex and the remaining figurines will be revealed when the timing is right, but already, the elders sense that timing is near. They have some information for you.'

Levi's pulse quickened. 'On the figurines, or the codex?'

'If you decipher that which they disclose, you will find what the ancients want you to find,' the shaman answered enigmatically.

The jungle track on the far bank of the river was narrow and Levi followed in Roberto's footsteps. A short while later they reached a big clearing by the river bank, around which ten thatched huts were grouped. Smoke from the cooking fires drifted towards the fast-flowing river. The women of the village had soaked maize kernels in lime the night before, to soften them, and during the day they had ground them into traditional *masa* dough. Blackened pots hung over the fires, and next to them the *comales*, or griddles, were warming, ready for the tortillas. A savoury aroma wafted into the jungle: chicken simmering in jalapeno chillies, diced peppers, oregano and limes. Some of the younger women were still working their looms by the firelight, sitting on mats with one end of their looms strapped behind their backs, the other tied to trees along the river bank. Colourful *huipils*, traditional Mayan ponchos, were taking shape as the village women deftly moved the loom warps back and forth, the cedar worn smooth by countless hours of use. Every village and town in Guatemala could be identified by its unique *traje* or traditional dress, and here, bright reds and yellows were wonderfully interwoven with diamond patterns of blues and turquoises. The women and older girls all wore the *corte*, a long wraparound skirt with a wide woven belt.

The elders were waiting, dressed in their traditional *kamixa*, colourful cotton shirts and straw hats. Levi smiled politely as solemn introductions were made and he was offered a seat on one of several cedar logs grouped around the central campfire.

'*Hach ki'imak in wo'ol in kaholtikech*. We are very happy to meet you,' said Pacal, the village chief. There were gaps in his warm and welcoming smile.

'*Ki'imak in wo'ol in wilikech*. And I am very happy to be here.'

The elders nodded, smiling broadly as Levi responded in their own tongue. Long hours spent studying the Mayan language had paid off handsomely.

'*Bix a k'aaba?*' Levi asked the young woman who'd been designated to look after him.

'My name is Itzel,' she replied. Her white teeth sparkled in the soft light of the fire.

'*Dios bo'otik*. Thank you,' Levi said as Itzel handed him a wooden platter of hot tortillas and salsa, together with a small pottery cup filled with *pulque*, a heady Meso-American beverage made from the agave plant.

The elders raised their cups, first inclining their heads towards Roberto and then Levi. Even though Roberto's home village was on the shores of Lake Atitlán, it was clear that he was revered here just as much as he was in San Marcos.

Venus had risen well into the night sky by the time the conversation turned to two vital issues.

'Your German colleague could cause problems for you here,' Pacal observed. The village chief's wizened brown face was etched with lines of wisdom.

Levi nodded. 'I must apologise if his behaviour has caused any offence.'

'It is your safety we're more concerned for,' Roberto observed. 'The Catholic priest should be watched as well.'

'Father Ehrlichmann has attempted to prevent us conducting our cultural ceremonies. He calls us pagans,' Pacal explained, 'and as a result, he and his church have remained ignorant of the ancient warnings. But you're a spiritual man with an open mind, Professor. It may fall to you to unravel the mystery.'

'I've been looking for the two remaining figurines, but without success.'

'One of those you seek is still here,' Pacal intoned. 'The other has been removed for safekeeping,' he added mysteriously. He reached into the woven satchel he wore over his shoulder and withdrew two maps inscribed on fragments of bark paper, the first of which he passed to Levi. A strange yellow shape had been painted on the bark. Three lines, each annotated with a bearing and all starting at different points outside the shape, met at a single point on the edge.

'The Germans have been here before,' Pacal said, 'and they vandalised Pyramid IV. The pyramid's sacred figurine was removed for its protection, and it's now some distance away, but if you are meant to find it, you will. This map gives the clue to its whereabouts. As to the final figurine,' Pacal said, handing Levi the second map, 'it's still here. Together, the three figurines will indicate the location of the codex.'

Levi examined the second map. Three points were marked on the map, forming a triangle.

'The ancients constructed calendars according to the movements of the planets,' Pacal continued. 'You would also be aware, Professor, that the Mayan calendars are cyclical, unlike the western calendars, which measure time in a straight line. As a result, the Mayan calendars are far more accurate, and our predecessors were able to predict the future based on recurring past events. The next great event will occur on 21 December 2012.'

'A planetary alignment,' Levi observed.

Pacal nodded. 'For the first time in 26 000 years, our solar system will be aligned with the stargate at the centre of the Milky Way galaxy. Are you familiar with the Fibonacci sequence?'

'Yes . . . but I thought that was a western discovery,' Levi replied.

Pacal and the village elders just smiled. 'The Maya, the Inca, the Egyptians knew about it: all three civilisations were much further advanced than your history has so far revealed,' Pacal said. 'And if you're familiar with the Fibonacci sequence, you will also be familiar with phi, the golden mean?'

Levi nodded. 'One point six one eight.' He'd long been fascinated with the ratio designated by Φ. The Fibonacci sequence, he knew, was a sequence with each term obtained by adding the previous two terms:

$$1, 1, 2, 3, 5, 8, 13, 21, 34, 55, 89, 144, 233 \ldots$$

The extraordinary ratio of 1.618 was obtained by dividing one number in the sequence by its previous number, and Levi also knew that the golden mean was part of life itself. It determined the ratios of the spirals on things as small as nautilus seashells, right up to the ratios of the massive spirals of the galaxies themselves. Even the distance between leaves on plants yielded a Fibonacci number.

'The ratio is at the very foundation of the universe,' the village chief observed, 'and the Maya, Inca and Egyptians all used it in the construction of their pyramids. If you're to find what you are looking for, look for the centre of the golden mean,' Pacal intoned.

'*Dios bo'otik*. Thank you,' Levi said. 'I will keep looking.'

'But be careful,' Roberto Arana warned. 'The German officer and the priest are both watching you.'

Four young village men, descendants of the warrior class of Tikal, escorted Levi back to the airstrip. As they crossed the bridge, another spine-tingling roar rent the night air, but the blazing torches they all carried kept the magnificent jaguar at a distance.

The camp was in darkness. Levi hid the precious maps in a cavity he'd dug near a corner of his tent, grabbed his weathered leather bag containing his archaeological tools, and set off for Pyramid V. He held a flaming torch in front of him, picking his way through the jungle towards the tomb of a Mayan king. Carefully, he climbed the jumble of blackened limestone steps that led to the small room at the top of the second-tallest pyramid in Tikal. At least there was a full moon, he thought.

In the jungle below, von Heißen positioned himself behind a huge cedar tree and watched.

9

THE VATICAN, ROME

The Cardinal Secretary of State, Eugenio Pacelli, his soutane immaculate and edged in crimson, was deep in thought. He stood at the window of his office on the third floor of the Apostolic Palace and stared unseeingly towards the Tiber and the ancient City of Rome. The second-most powerful man in the Catholic Church was tall and spindly. His long oval face was lean, his cheeks hollow, his nose hooked and aristocratic. Among the myriad challenges confronting the Vatican's principal foreign diplomat, some took priority. Above him, on the top floor of the palace, the papal physician was attending Pius XI; Pacelli was now the favoured candidate to take the Keys of Peter. The rise to power of Adolf Hitler and the Nazis was equally grave.

The Cardinal lowered his gaze towards *Piazza San Pietro*. The dark cobblestones shone in the soft glow of the Vatican lights. They seemed to hold a message of dark foreboding. Pacelli moved away from the window and returned to his desk, turning his mind towards the other grave matters of concern: the Vatican's finances and a Nazi archaeological expedition being carried out in the distant jungles of Guatemala. On the wall behind him a two-metre-high black-and-silver crucifix hung in silent observation. Had the solid silver Christ been able to speak, He too might have uttered a warning. Pacelli's thoughts were interrupted by his private secretary knocking on the double doors.

'*Avanti*.'

'Il Signor Felici is here, Eminence.'

'Show him in.'

Signor Alberto Felici, Gentleman of His Holiness and Papal Knight Commander of the Order of Sylvester, bowed deferentially as he entered.

'*Benvenuto, Alberto*.' Pacelli kissed the ambitious diplomat on both cheeks. 'Have a seat,' he said, indicating one of three comfortable lounge chairs. '*Desideri acqua minerale, caffè, tè?*'

'No, *grazie*, Eminence, I've not long eaten.' Alberto patted an ample stomach that was testament to his fondness for food and fine wine.

'Thank you for coming at such a late hour,' Pacelli began, after his secretary had closed the doors, 'Before we get on to your reports, I hear that congratulations are in order.'

'*Grazie*, Eminence, you are most kind.' Alberto had finally married in his late forties and now his wife had given birth to their first child.

'Have you settled on a name yet?'

'Salvatore Giovanni Felici, Eminence, and if your busy schedule

THE MAYA CODEX 89

allows, Maria and I would be honoured by your presence at Salvatore's baptism.'

'We can do it here in *San Pietro* if you wish. Who knows, the young Salvatore Felici may grow up to become one of us. The priesthood is always looking for good candidates, *non è vero?*' Pacelli smiled.

'Maria would be very pleased, on both counts, Eminence.'

'Good. Now, what have you discovered about our friend Nogara?' Pacelli had become increasingly suspicious of Signor Bernardino Nogara, the financial advisor to Pius XI. In 1929 the Italian Prime Minister Benito Mussolini had signed the Lateran Treaty, finally recognising the sovereignty of the Holy See as a separate state. As reparation for lost papal territories, the Italian government had paid an enormous sum to the Vatican, but now rumours of failed businesses, Nogara's links to an ultra-secret Masonic Lodge and his luxurious lifestyle had been swirling around the Vatican's corridors.

'When I worked alongside Signor Nogara during the negotiations on the Lateran Treaty, he kept very much to himself, so I was prepared for anything, Eminence. Even so, I've been surprised by what I've found, and I can assure you the investigation has been very, very thorough.'

Pacelli braced himself for the worst.

'Signor Nogara lives very simply, Eminence. In the time he's been involved with the Vatican's finances, he's drawn a modest salary and his bank account contains less than US$200. As far as I can determine, he gives generously to charities, all of them Catholic. He attends Mass every day and his entertainment appears to be limited to a weekly visit to the movies.'

Pacelli looked puzzled. 'And women?'

'There are no women in his life, Eminence, and there is no evidence of . . . how shall I put this . . . soliciting sex. He has no connections with the Masons, or any anti-Catholic organisations, and he confines his reading to the financial journals.'

'The accounts?'

'The Special Administration of the Holy See is in excellent order, Eminence, and Signor Nogara is well on his way to turning a hundred million dollars into the Vatican's first billion.'

Pacelli's eyes widened.

'Signor Nogara is very much a man after your own heart, Eminence. He is devoted to the Holy Church.'

'I have done him an injustice,' the Cardinal Secretary of State observed quietly.

'In matters of finance, Eminence, it's always better to be sure. I suspect the rumours originated from those who are jealous of Nogara's access to you and the Holy Father, and, of course, your concordat with Reichskanzler Hitler has realised far greater revenue than we anticipated.'

Pacelli nodded. The agreement he had signed with Hitler had been a masterstroke. Not only were German Catholics now subject to Canon Law, but criticism of Catholic doctrine was prohibited by German law. In return for the Vatican's support of his regime Hitler had agreed to a *Kirchensteuer* or 'church tax'. This meant that in addition to 'Peter's Pence', which flowed into the Vatican from dioceses all over the world, practising Catholics in Germany now had their pay cheques docked at a rate of nine per cent of income tax.

'It will be important to ensure the agreement on the *Kirchensteuer* stays in place, but I understand the Holy Father is preparing to issue an encyclical.' Felici's Vatican connections were impeccable, and he'd already heard that the dying Pius XI was about to release his long-awaited treatise *Humani Generis Unitas* – On the Unity of the Human Race. 'If such an encyclical were to criticise Hitler's treatment of the Jews, Eminence, it might endanger the concordat itself,' Felici warned. 'Ambassador von Bergen is quite worried.'

Pacelli nodded, only too well aware that all his hard work might be unravelled by a single stroke of the ailing Pontiff's pen. 'I've assured the German ambassador of the Vatican's continuing support, especially in the fight against the Bolshevik Communists. In my view they're a far greater threat than Hitler and the Third Reich. As for the Jews . . . they're not our concern.'

'That's good news, Eminence, because Nogara will shortly suggest a change in the Vatican's financial arrangements.'

'Why, if we're doing so well?'

'The Special Administration has served its purpose admirably, Eminence, but with so much money flowing in, the Vatican will shortly need its own bank. A separate entity that can operate as a normal bank on the international financial stage.' Felici knew well that the Vatican Bank would be anything but normal. Immune from any scrutiny by Italian or international authorities, and even from the Curial Cardinals, the Vatican Bank, or the *Istituto per le Opere di Religione*, would be exempt from any Italian government tax. In time the bank would provide a mechanism for the Mafia and prominent Italian businessmen to launder billions of lire into secret Swiss bank accounts. In the nearer future, the Vatican Bank would become a conduit for Nazi gold and treasures confiscated from millions of murdered Jews.

'A bank might contradict the Church's teaching on usury,' Pacelli observed thoughtfully, reflecting on one of the most grievous sins in Catholic dogma. St Ambrose and the councils of Nicaea, Carthage and Clichy had all condemned the practice of earning interest from loans, as had Pope Benedict IX.

'There are ways around these things, Eminence – especially when it is for the good of the Holy Church.'

Pacelli nodded. 'Would you be prepared to serve as a *delegato* on the board, Alberto?'

'Of course, Eminence. Of course.' Felici maintained a neutral expression, but he felt a surge of satisfaction that his plans were falling neatly into place.

'Good. Then I will give Nogara's proposal careful consideration.' Pacelli closed the file on Nogara and reached for the one marked *Maya*.

10

TIKAL, GUATEMALA

Levi Weizman struggled over the last of the broken steps that led to the small stone room at the top of Pyramid V. Breathing hard, he turned to survey the jungle below. A wind had sprung up, stirring the jungle canopy, and the moonlight danced eerily on the thick foliage. Levi reached into his satchel and took out a measuring tape. It took only a few moments to take the measurements of the small opening at the top of the pyramid, and Levi quickly worked out the ratio of height to width in his head.

One to 1.618. Levi whistled softly. The small room on top of Pyramid V had been constructed with the sacred ratio of the golden mean. Levi took out his compass. The tops of Pyramids I and IV were silhouetted, like shards of obsidian reaching for the centre of the Milky Way. *Look for the centre*, Levi thought. The middle of Pyramid I produced a bearing of 15°30′, while the middle of Pyramid IV revealed a bearing of 352°, or 8° west of north. Would the crystals in the figurines reproduce those bearings at the winter solstice? Levi turned. As best he could judge, both bearings would intersect on the far wall of the room behind the opening. Levi took his measuring tape and calculated half the ratio distances on the wall. He played his torch over the masonry and his heart began to race.

It had faded over the centuries, but he could just make out the faint outline of the letter phi on a large brick in the centre. Levi took a small pick from his satchel and began to scrape at the sascab, the mortar the ingenious Maya made from crushed and burnt limestone. At first the mortar came away fairly easily, but as Levi reached areas that had not been subjected to the dampness of the air, the resistance increased. He took a finer pick, and a few minutes later it penetrated what appeared to be a cavity behind the stone. *Look for the centre.* He'd found a similar cavity in Pyramid IV, but that one had been empty. Now he knew why. It had contained another figurine until the shaman and the elders removed it for safekeeping. The brick began to wobble and Levi carefully inserted another pick and pried it loose.

The stubby rectangular figurine had lain there for centuries, just as the ancients had planned. A milky-green ceiba tree carved from exquisite jade, it was almost identical to the one Levi had brought back to Vienna, except there were both male and female jaguars etched among the buttress roots at the base. The presence of both male and female cats balanced the figurine, Levi reflected, so this was surely the neutral one. Now, if he could only find the female figurine that represented the lost feminine . . . the final balance for a world that was now dominated by males.

Even though 2012 was still more than seventy years away, perhaps the world needed the time to prepare, or to attempt to reverse whatever catastrophe the Maya were predicting in the codex. The Meso-American jade glinted softly and Levi held it up to catch the moonlight in the crystal. He could see the ancient artisans had again carved a hole through the ceiba tree roots in the shape of Φ.

'So, what have you discovered so late at night, Herr Professor?' Von Heißen appeared in the narrow doorway, his Luger pistol cocked and pointing straight at Levi. 'Ah, the figurine. How very interesting. May I take it?'

Levi reluctantly handed over the priceless artefact.

Von Heißen pointed the pistol at Levi's head. Levi could smell the whisky on the Nazi's breath and he could feel his own heart pounding against his chest, but he forced himself to remain calm.

'If you were not to return from this mission, Professor Weizman, it would be just another unfortunate accident.'

'Perhaps. On the other hand, a pistol shot will not go unnoticed in the jungle, and, more importantly, Reichsführer Himmler will be less than pleased if you return with the figurine without knowing its significance for the master race.'

'So what does it mean?' von Heißen demanded.

'I would suggest you put that thing away. I will report back to you once I've analysed the figurine tomorrow.'

The SS guard outside the tent lit a cigarette, but Levi was oblivious to his presence. He'd been studying the figurine all day, but still couldn't believe it. Levi focused his magnifying glass on the hieroglyph beneath the sculpture of the jaguars. The date was unmistakeable: 21 December 2012. The two hieroglyphs next to it were equally clear, designations for 'winter solstice' and 'annihilation', but it was the next hieroglyph that took his breath away. Levi knew that the series of sawtooth markings were the Mayan designation for immeasurably powerful electromagnetic energy, and the markings pointed towards another hieroglyph that represented the stargate at the centre of the galaxy. Running on adrenalin, he put down his magnifying glass and gently moved the figurine back into the centre of his small collapsible table. Pacal had confirmed that the third, female figurine would be critical to locating the missing codex, the one item that Levi was increasingly convinced would hold the key to surviving 2012. But even if he was successful in finding the other figurine, the Nazis now had control.

The barking of the howler monkeys and the chirrup of the crickets, the sounds of the Tikal jungle at dusk, were already being drowned out by the singing coming from the mess tent at the end of the airfield. Someone had put on a recording of a brass band playing German drinking songs. Levi sighed. He was feeling tired and dejected, and he knew that after dinner he would have to brief von Heißen on his findings. He deeply missed Ramona's calm and gentle counsel, and he missed her touch even more. As important as the hidden Maya Codex might be for humankind, Levi wanted nothing more than to be back in Vienna. The way he felt right now, he could happily leave the discovery of the codex to another archaeologist.

'So, Herr Professor. What are we to learn from this discovery, hmm?'
Von Heißen blew some imaginary smoke from the barrel of his
Luger and put it back on the table alongside a half-empty bottle of
Glenfiddich.

Levi struggled to hide his contempt. The Nazi was even more
drunk than usual.

'As you can see, the figurine is in the shape of a ceiba tree, which to
the ancient Maya was revered as the sacred tree of life. If you want an
analogy, the Aryans who swept down from the north of Afghanistan
about 3500 years ago to occupy the Indus Valley considered the birch
tree in a similar vein. There is a parallel here.'

'Reichsführer Himmler will be delighted,' von Heißen slurred.
'Perhaps you have your uses after all, Herr Professor.'

Levi said nothing, knowing his analogy was absolutely baseless.

'I'm curious, though, as to how you knew exactly where to look.'

'I've been looking for artefacts for a long time, Sturmbannführer.
Very occasionally, you get lucky and find a loose stone, and, even
more rarely, you discover a set of steps that will reveal a hidden
tomb.'

Von Heißen refilled his metal tumbler. 'Then you'd be well
advised to make your occasional discoveries in the daylight, Herr
Professor, when we can all share them.' He glanced over Levi's shoulder. Levi turned to find the beautiful young Itzel standing nervously
in the opening of the tent flap.

'*Brunnen! Was haben wir hier?*' von Heißen leered.

Itzel turned away shyly and looked at the red-dirt floor. She was
dressed demurely in her native *traje*: a colourful *kamixa* shirt, and
an ankle-length wraparound skirt secured by a wide woven belt.

Levi knew the shaman and the village elders would have sent her, but why?

'I'm not used to being kept waiting, Fräulein. I expected you three days ago.'

Itzel looked at the floor again before reaching into her woollen shoulder satchel. She withdrew a pottery jug and a single mug fashioned in the shape of a monkey. Itzel placed the mug on the table and poured from the jug. The elders had mixed the *pulque* with mango and pineapple.

'*Hatsh mal-ob*,' Itzel said nervously, but von Heißen was already focused on the top of her blouse. Itzel's flawless brown skin gleamed in the flickering light of the oil lamp.

'She doesn't speak German or English, Sturmbannführer, but she is offering you a small gift of friendship.'

Von Heißen picked up the mug, and tasted the *pulque*. '*Fruchtsaft!* Fruit juice!' He drained the mug and poured some Glenfiddich into it. 'Have a real drink, Fräulein,' he said, guiding her to a chair and letting his hand pass over her thigh.

Levi knew it was futile but he had to try. 'I would caution you against doing anything that might make things difficult between your expedition and the villagers.'

'*Verpiss Dich!* Piss off, Herr Professor! I'll deal with you in the morning.' Von Heißen got to his feet unsteadily. He reached for the figurine and locked it in his trunk, pocketing the keys.

Furious, and very worried about Itzel, Levi returned to his tent and turned up the oil lamp. Roberto Arana was sitting in one of his canvas chairs in the shadows.

'Don't worry about Itzel, Professor. Mayan princesses were often called on to make sacrifices and Itzel knows it is for the greater good of her people.'

'She is a princess?'

Roberto smiled. 'You must pack your things quickly,' he said. 'Just the bare essentials. It's no longer safe for you here and we are leaving tonight.'

'But the figurine ...'

'Do you know if the German drank the *pulque*?'

'Just one mug,' Levi replied, the meaning of Itzel's gift dawning on him.

'One mug is enough. The pulque was carefully prepared.'

'So, Fräulein, come and sit on the bed, where we can get better acquainted.' Von Heißen steadied himself with the help of the tent pole as he closed the flap. He turned, trying to focus, but the inside of the tent started to spin. He lurched towards Itzel but instead fell face-first into the red dirt, and Itzel did as she'd been instructed. She took the keys from his pocket, unlocked his trunk and placed the figurine in her satchel. She returned the keys to von Heißen's pocket and made her way across the airstrip to where the shaman and Levi, together with a protection party of six young warriors from the village, were waiting. Levi had only had time to pack a satchel containing some toiletries and underwear, his tools, the two maps and Ramona's precious letters.

'Put this in your bag,' Roberto said, handing Levi the jade figurine. 'There is still one more to be found, but the maps will guide you.

Safeguard the two figurines you have with your life, because together with the third, they will lead you to the Maya Codex.'

'But how —'

'It will happen when the cosmos is ready,' Roberto replied as the lead warrior re-lit his torch.

'What about the Germans?' Levi asked as they moved off down the jungle track.

'Leave them to us. The women and children of the village are already on the move to a safe hideout in the jungle. The warriors will take you by canoe downriver and on to Puerto Barrios and the Gulf of Honduras. One of our people will meet you there. We've arranged passage to Naples on a cargo ship, and from there you can make your way back to Vienna. It will take time, and it won't be very comfortable, but going through Italy will be safer. Von Heißen will probably report you missing and they'll be watching the airports.'

'I don't know how to thank you . . .'

'Safeguarding the figurines will be more than enough,' Roberto replied. He turned and smiled at Levi, his teeth flashing white in the torchlight. The sounds of the German marching band and the singing in the mess tent receded, supplanted by the crickets and a roar from one of the great cats.

THE VATICAN, ROME

'I've done as you requested, Eminence, and interviewed anyone who might have information on the lost Maya Codex, including Father Ehrlichmann and the papal nuncio in Guatemala City,' Alberto Felici said. 'I'm now convinced it probably lies hidden in or around Tikal.'

'So Himmler is on to something concrete?' Pacelli observed.

Felici smiled enigmatically. 'I'd be very careful of Reichsführer Himmler, Eminence, he keeps some very strange company. On the advice of a Karl-Maria Wiligut, a former colonel in the Austrian Imperial Army, Himmler has taken over a medieval castle in Wewelsburg and turned it into a Nordic academy for the SS. But I've discovered that Wiligut is a deranged, violent alcoholic who was only released from a mental asylum in 1927.'

'Why would Himmler take notice of a deranged alcoholic?'

'For one thing, Wiligut is a fierce opponent of the Jews, and he publishes an anti-Semitic paper called *The Iron Broom*. But there's a lot more to Heinrich Himmler than anti-Semitism, Eminence. He's feared throughout the Reich as a cold, hard, ruthlessly efficient administrator who doesn't miss the slightest detail, but behind the scenes, the Reichsführer is heavily into the occult. Wiligut has been presented as a mystic who has access to lost cities and civilisations via ancient channels . . . He's managed to convince Himmler that the final great battle for civilisation will occur around Wewelsburg in the valleys of Westphalia.'

'Then we're dealing with a crank?'

Felici shook his head. 'Never underestimate Himmler, Eminence. He's turning the SS into a new Aryan aristocracy, a noble order of warriors sworn to the Führer, modelled on the Knights Templar and the Jesuits. Himmler intends to develop Wewelsburg as an SS city, a pagan Vatican at the centre of the new world.'

Pacelli's eyes widened.

'Himmler is now relocating the villagers of Wewelsburg and remodelling the castle. He's established a concentration camp in the Niederhagen Forests, where Jews are being imprisoned and drafted into forced labour. We're dealing with the Devil here, Eminence. Outwardly Himmler's prim and proper, but his mind is medieval. He's cold, calculating and lethal; and as far as his treatment of the Jews is concerned, you may have to make some public remarks. International condemnation is growing.'

'I'm aware of that, Alberto,' Pacelli said, irritation in his voice, 'but there are bigger issues to consider than the plight of the Jews.'

'Are you also aware then, Eminence, that your papal nuncio in Istanbul is organising an escape route for Jewish children? Weizman confided in me that if things get any worse in Vienna, he may have to get his family out through Turkey.' Felici watched carefully for any reaction that might reveal enmity between the powerful Cardinal Secretary of State and his subordinate in Turkey, Angelo Roncalli.

Pacelli made a mental note to speak with the archbishop in the Vatican's foreign ministry. 'Did Professor Weizman give you any idea of what might be in this codex?'

'He thinks the Maya have encoded a warning of a coming anni-hilation; but he also thinks there could be a connection between the Mayan warning and the warnings of the Virgin at Fátima.'

Pacelli went pale. His own connection to Our Lady was strong. Pope Benedict XV had elevated him to archbishop on 13 May 1917, the very day the blessed Virgin Mary had first appeared to the three peasant children at Fátima in Portugal. The connection had never been lost on Pacelli, nor had the blessed Virgin's three warnings.

'Is the Vatican going to make these warnings public, Eminence?'

Pacelli didn't answer. A heavy silence descended on the Secretary of State's apartment. 'It's possible,' Pacelli said finally, 'that we may release the first two warnings. At present, all three are in the hands of the Bishop of Leiria in Portugal. The third – and this must remain strictly between you and me – the third contains a threat to the Holy Church itself, and it must remain hidden.'

'Perhaps all three should be moved to the secret archives, Emi-nence, where they will be better protected? The existence of the documents and the miracle of the sun are quite widely known.'

Pacelli's thoughts went back to the last apparition, on 13 October 1917, when on a wet and windy morning 70 000 people had gathered in the fields at Cova da Iria to witness the miracle the blessed Virgin had promised the three children at Fátima. As the clouds cleared, little Lúcia had called to the crowds and pointed towards the sun. Suddenly, the sun began to rotate like a catherine-wheel, shooting light in different colours, as the great crowds would attest. Several journalists from Portugal's most influential newspapers, including *O Século*, a pro-government and anti-religious paper, reported the sun 'zigzagging' and reversing direction across the sky. The Lisbon daily, *O Dia*, recorded the sun as having a deep-blue light emanating from its centre, illuminating thousands of people prostrate and weeping on the ground.

'The warnings are secure for now, Alberto,' Pacelli said, 'but, as you say, they should be moved to the secret archives. In the meantime I want you to keep a close eye on developments in Tikal. If the Maya Codex *is* linked to the warnings of the blessed Virgin, then it too must be secured in the secret archives.'

'I agree, Eminence. We will need to watch Weizman very carefully.'

Felici acknowledged the salute of the Swiss Guard as he left the Vatican through huge bronze doors. He descended the marble steps and headed into the night across the cobblestones of a deserted *Piazza San Pietro*. His conversation with Pacelli had been illuminating. A seat on the board of the Vatican Bank would give him power. But as he walked towards the Tiber, he reflected on the meeting he'd held with von Heißen before he'd left Tikal. Von Heißen's links to Himmler might put him in an even more powerful position. Felici was a master at the arcane art of the double agent.

12

VIENNA, 1938

The train slowed as it approached the Brenner Pass check-point on the Italian–Austrian border. The snow-capped granite of the Zillertal and Stubai Alps towered over the pass. When the train hissed to a stop, Levi watched in trepidation as the Nazi guards boarded. The closer Levi got to Vienna, the more insecure he felt.

'*Papieren!*'

Levi handed over his Austrian passport to the officious young border guards.

'*Zweck der Ihr Besuch?* Purpose of your visit?'

'I'm returning to Vienna,' Levi replied, as calmly as he could, feeling like a stranger in his own country.

'*Beruf?* Occupation?'

'Professor at Universität Wien.'

One of the border guards looked at the photograph in Levi's

passport, scrutinised Levi's face, looked back at the photograph and handed it back without a word.

Levi heaved an inward sigh of relief. Roberto had been right. Neither the Italians nor the Germans were yet completely organised. Benito Mussolini was busy supporting his ally, General Franco, in the Spanish Civil War, and the bustling port of Naples had been relatively free of scrutiny. Here, on the border, the arrogant but inexperienced young guard had asked his questions by rote. Four rows behind, and unseen by Levi, a large man in a grey trench coat flashed his SS identification to the border guards and they quickly moved on. The SS agent went back to his copy of *Corriere della Sera*.

Levi pulled his fedora down over his forehead as he alighted from the old tram on *Franz-Josefs-Kai* near the *Donaukanal*, not far from the steps that led up to *Judengasse*. Vienna was crowded with Nazi soldiers and Brownshirts: on the trains, the trams, the buses, the street corners and in the bars and cafés. He scanned the steps, instinctively clutching at the satchel hidden beneath the overcoat he'd purchased in Naples. He reached the top of the stairs and crossed into the shadows of the Saint Ruprecht steeple. At the far end of *Judengasse*, a group of Nazi soldiers were leaving a bar and their drunken singing echoed down the cobbled streets. The light was on in his apartment. Levi's heartbeat raced at the prospect of seeing Ramona and the children again. The Nazis disappeared towards the Hofburg Quarter, and Levi walked quietly to the back stairs which led up to his apartment.

'*Wer ist es?*' Ramona called from the other side when Levi knocked. Her voice was strong, but Levi sensed her fear.

'*Levi, meine Liebling* . . . I'm back.'

Ramona wrenched open the door but it banged against the

security chain. 'Levi! Levi! How . . . ?' Ramona tore at the security chain, opened the door and threw her arms around Levi's neck. 'Why didn't you tell me you were coming home? I've been so frightened, Levi!' Tears of relief flowed down Ramona's cheeks as she clung to her husband.

'Papa! Papa!' Rebekkah and Ariel came running down the hall. Rebekkah launched herself at Levi and fastened her little arms around his neck in a vice-like grip. Levi kissed his daughter and put his free arm around Ariel. 'We've missed you, Papa!' Rebekkah said, hanging on to her father for dear life.

'I wasn't sure if the Nazis were tapping our phone line, so I couldn't ring,' Levi said, after kissing the children goodnight. He took a seat at their kitchen table. 'I hardly recognised Vienna for the soldiers,' Levi added, after he'd explained his escape from Tikal.

'It's been terrible, Levi.' Ramona sipped her tea. 'Rebekkah and Ariel are too afraid to go out, and so am I. We can't even walk in the park. There are signs everywhere: *Juden Verboten*.' The Brownshirts have been here twice already this week, demanding that I close my boutique. Not that I have any customers any more,' she said, wiping a tear from her cheek.

Levi reached across the kitchen table and held Ramona's hand. 'We still have each other and the children, *Liebling*, and that's all that matters.'

'I'm frightened, Levi. Won't Himmler and this von Heißen be looking for you?'

Levi cursed himself for leaving his family unprotected. 'I should never have gone; not that I had much choice,' he added ruefully. 'Although I don't think von Heißen will have admitted to Himmler that he had the figurine in his possession, much less the reason it disappeared. But you're right, we'll have to leave, and quickly. I've made contact with Ze'ev Jabotinsky down at the Jewish Agency. They're setting up escape routes through Istanbul. If we can get to the United States or England, Albert Einstein or Erwin Schrödinger might be able to put in a good word for me at Princeton or Oxford. I can carry on my Mayan research,' he said, 'and you can start another boutique.'

'And what about the apartment? Even if we could sell, in this market we won't get anything.'

'My brother has German citizenship. He can look after it until things improve.'

'He's a Nazi sympathiser, Levi!'

'Yes, but that can work to our advantage. At least the apartment will stay in the family until all this is over.'

Ramona's sobs diminished, calmed by her own inner strength and conviction, which was in turn underpinned by an unshakeable faith. Suddenly shouting and the sounds of shattering glass carried through the cold night air. Levi got up and went to the front window. Further down *Judengasse* he could see torches.

'Turn off all the lights, quickly!'

The sounds of shouting and the smashing of glass intensified. A menacing group of young thugs – members of the Austrian Hitler Youth and Brownshirts – had entered *Judengasse*.

'Judenfrei! Judenfrei!' The yelling echoed off *Judengasse*'s buildings. 'Jew-free! Jew-free!' Just as Nebuchadnezzar and Titus had

destroyed the First and Second temples in Jerusalem, Hitler and Himmler were determined to destroy the Jews of Vienna. Bricks were being hurled through the plate-glass windows of every shop daubed with the Star of David.

'Get the children and lock them in the bathroom,' Levi whispered. In the shadows, he could feel Ramona's fear. Levi quickly picked up the precious Mayan figurine that had remained in Vienna, wrapped it in red velvet, lifted the carpet in front of the fireplace and hid the figurine alongside the other one in the long tin trunk he'd placed under the floorboard. He'd thought about putting them in the big safe in his study, but he knew that would be the first place the Nazis would look. Satisfied the figurines were as secure as he could make them at short notice, Levi hid his notes on the Fibonacci sequence and the pyramids in Tikal inside one of his friend Erwin Schrödinger's books, *Science and the Human Temperament*. He slid the book back on the shelf and turned to secure the apartment. He and Ramona moved a heavy dresser over the big trapdoor that concealed the stairs leading to Ramona's boutique below.

'Go and join the children now,' Levi said, and he moved towards the front window. The mob was getting closer; the sound of glass smashing was sickening. Levi drew back as a group of about twenty young thugs stopped outside Ramona's boutique.

'*Juden verrecke!* Death to the Jews!' one of them yelled, hurling brick after brick through the window. The mob, armed with iron bars, stormed in and began systematically smashing glass shelving, counters, cases, anything that would break. They splashed yellow paint over the designer dresses and hats. One thug climbed the stairs and began to batter the door with the butt of his rifle, but the rest of the mob was moving on, and he gave up. 'We'll be back, Jew bastards!' he yelled as he ran down the stairs to catch up.

'How long do you think we've got?' Ramona asked, her arms around Rebekkah and Ariel. Rebekkah sobbed and Ariel fought back the tears, both of them terrified. The sounds of smashing glass receded, replaced by sirens as flames began to pour from the Synagogue, just a block away from *Judengasse*.

'We'll have to pack tonight,' Levi replied, his eyes moist.

13

ISTANBUL

The sun bade farewell in a fiery salute, streaking the sky to the west of Istanbul with fierce red and orange. In stark contrast to Cardinal Pacelli, who when papal nuncio in Munich had travelled in a black limousine adorned with the Vatican coat of arms, the papal delegate to Turkey and Greece and future Pope John XXIII, Archbishop Angelo Roncalli, elected to leave his old battered Fiat in the garage. Dressed in comfortable civilian attire, Roncalli hailed a ramshackle taxi in the narrow road outside the Papal Embassy in *Ölçek Sokak*. In years to come, long after he had died, a grateful Turkish people would rename *Ölçek Sokak* 'Pope Roncalli Street'.

'Hotel Pera Palas, please.'

'*Evet*, Pera Palas!' The old driver engaged the gears with a frightening crunch and pulled out into the chaos that was Istanbul's traffic, waving his hand placatingly at those yelling abuse that was nothing more than ritual amidst the cacophony of screeching brakes and blaring horns.

'*Senin bir ailen var?* You have a family?' Roncalli asked the wizened driver.

'*Evet*.' The taxi driver's dark face creased with a smile at Roncalli's use of his native tongue, his smile punctuated by three missing teeth. 'Two boys and a girl,' he answered proudly. 'And you?'

Roncalli smiled and shook his head. '*Hayir*. Just me.'

The roadside was thick with traders, and the driver threaded his way past them with a practised ease. Tarpaulins were spread edge to edge with eclectic offerings of fish and chickens, leather and brass, shoes and shirts, and occasionally *uds* and *cümbüs*, Turkish lutes and mandolins. They reached *Refik Saydam Caddesi* and began the descent towards the Bosphorus, the long narrow stretch of water that connects the Black Sea to the Marmara. On the other side of the road, an old brown horse, ribs showing through his pitifully thin coat, nostrils flared and breath clouding in the cold, laboured to pull an impossible load up the steeply sloping hill. The rubber tyres on the rickety wooden cart had worn through to the canvas, and the hessian sacks of rice, spice and coffee, piled three metres high, defied gravity. Old men struggled past under the weight of big wicker baskets full of oranges, bananas and bread. Legless beggars sitting on small wheeled boards pushed their way between smaller carts, some supporting brass urns full of strong Turkish coffee, others containing braziers on which chestnuts and kebabs were roasting. Myriad smells of spices and meats wafted through the open window of the taxi.

'Thank you, my friend,' Roncalli said as they reached the Hotel

Pera Palas. 'A little extra for the children,' he added, pressing more lire into the taxi driver's hand.

Roncalli paused and took in the view of the Golden Horn. Across the harbour, the minarets of the great mosques of Istanbul rose like stone fingers towards the evening sky. Roncalli turned and headed towards the Pera Palas, an opulent rococo-style building on *Mesrutiyet Caddesi*. A young bellboy with dark curly hair, dressed in black trousers and a deep-purple military jacket topped with gold epaulettes, smiled broadly and sprang to open the brass-plated double doors.

Behind the dark polished wooden counter of reception, pigeon holes held the heavy brass room-keys. On one side of the desk stood a telephone with a black bell-shaped mouthpiece and a heavy Bakelite earpiece. To the right of reception, a wide, sweeping marble staircase carpeted in red wound its way around the steel pillars and wire mesh enclosing the lift well, where another young bellboy stood ready to open the heavy wooden doors.

Archbishop Roncalli made his way into the big chandeliered vestibule, the magnificent handmade Persian carpet soft beneath his shoes. At intervals down the centre of the room, tall pots were filled with flowers. Heavy carved wooden sideboards, gilt-framed mirrors and elegant Egyptian-styled vases lined the walls, but the Pera Palas was not all it seemed. Istanbul was on the Silk Road straddling Europe and Asia, and the city was ideally positioned midway between Eastern Europe and Palestine. As the world teetered on the precipice of war, the Turkish government was determined to remain neutral. But they had allowed the Jewish Agency, an organisation set up after the Great War to support the international Jewish community, to open an office in the hotel.

Mordecai Herschel was already waiting for Roncalli at one of the antique tables in the vestibule.

'Angelo, thank you for coming.' Herschel rose from his chair and extended his hand. Now in his fifties, but still lean and fit, he had been a major in the Haganah, the military wing of David Ben-Gurion's Jewish Agency in Palestine, where he'd been wounded in a clash with the British. His face still bore the scar on his right cheek. Herschel had been selected to set up an agency in Istanbul as part of the Zionists' desperate attempts to save their countrymen from the Nazis. In physical contrast to Herschel, Roncalli was a big bear of a man, not naturally inclined to exercise. He had thinning hair and a long oval face that was dominated by a large roman nose. They made an interesting pair, the fit-looking former freedom fighter and the rotund archbishop. Both were deep thinkers, bonded by a common devotion to justice and humanity.

'Any news from the Vatican?' Herschel asked.

'They're sending a papal envoy, although that could be a delaying tactic. I'm afraid Rome can be somewhat removed from the problems of the real world.' Cardinal Pacelli's silence in response to Roncalli's pleas for help for the Jews had been deafening.

Herschel nodded. 'I understand. Closer to home, one of our biggest problems is communications, Angelo. Finding native speakers with all the qualities we need has not been easy, but I've now got an agent in Romania and one in Hungary, and another two will leave next week for Yugoslavia and Bulgaria. I've also managed to infiltrate the Austrian concentration camp at Mauthausen.'

'If you need secure transmission of messages, I have some people I can trust in our embassies and we can use the black bag.'

'Won't the Vatican object?'

'Only if they find out.' Roncalli smiled broadly, immensely pleased with himself. 'God won't object, and he holds a lot of the votes.'

'Thank you, Angelo. I'm very grateful. The Turkish Post Office has been helpful, and we'll continue to use them for contact with ordinary citizens, but it's good to know there's a more secure line.'

Roncalli leaned closer. 'And,' he said quietly, 'I was thinking, too, of the children. If we were to produce Certificates of Conversion to Catholicism with the appropriate stamps of approval, would that help?' It was not the first time the elegant Pera Palas hotel had been host to a conspiratorial plot. The Mata Hari had drunk in the Orient Express Bar, as had Alfred Hitchcock and Ernest Hemingway; and after Agatha Christie's crashed car had been found abandoned, amidst false rumours she had drowned, Christie wrote *Murder on the Orient Express* in room 411.

'That would be an enormous help, Angelo. We're going to try to funnel as many of our countrymen as we can through here and on to Palestine, although the double-dealing British are preventing us from landing the refugee boats, so we're having to do it on the beaches at night.' Herschel raised his eyebrows ruefully.

'Will other countries take them?'

'We're looking at Central and South America.'

'At least that gives us more options.'

'Although for some, time is running out. Have you ever heard of Professor Levi Weizman?'

'The distinguished archaeologist?'

Herschel nodded. 'We've received some intelligence from one of our agents inside the SS: Weizman and his family are in grave danger.'

14

VIENNA

Adolf Eichmann stood at the podium of the ballroom of the recently commandeered Rothschild palace on the *Plosslgasse*, bringing to a close an address to SS officers, Gauleiter and Kreisleiter, the district and county political leaders who had bubbled to the top of the Nazi party in Austria like scum to the top of a drain. Obersturmbannführer von Heißen, now promoted to lieutenant colonel and newly appointed commandant of the Mauthausen concentration camp, was sitting in the front row.

Eichmann gripped the sides of the lectern, his SS cap at a rakish angle. 'The Jew, gentlemen, is a rank parasite. Apart from making money, his only other aim in life centres on the destruction of the German people and the Reich. But we Germans are a compassionate people and this filth will be encouraged to leave of their own accord.'

'And if they don't want to leave?' The buttonholes on the brown uniform of the Kreisleiter of Vienna's Third District were scalloped, straining against their fastenings. Kreisleiter Schweitzer was as ruthless as he was obese.

Eichmann smiled thinly. 'As of now, all Jewish businesses are to be boycotted. Any Viennese who patronises a Jewish store will be guilty of a crime against the State. Their names and addresses will be published on the streets of Vienna. In fact, no Austrian is to speak with a Jew unless it is absolutely essential.' Eichmann paused for thought and then decided against any further disclosure. His program to recruit young female clerks to work in Jewish stores and compile lists of the names of their customers would remain on a need-to-know basis.

'It will not be long,' Eichmann continued, 'before their wretched blood-sucking money-making ventures are on the market at rock-bottom prices, so that decent Austrians can buy into those businesses and run them fairly and honestly. In addition, by order of the Führer, all civil servants who are not of Aryan descent are to be sacked. That includes university staff. Universities are to be closed to anyone of Jewish blood. This is to apply to schools as well. Jewish lawyers and doctors are to be struck off. In the case of physicians, they are to be reclassified as "Jewish Healers", and they are to restrict their foul practices to their own kind.'

'Herr Obersturmführer, how can we be sure to identify every one of them?' Kreisleiter Schweitzer asked.

'With the help of their leaders, you are to compile a list of Jews for each district, and they will all be required to wear the yellow star,' Eichmann replied. 'The Law of Jewish Assets has now been passed, and Jews are to surrender all gold, platinum and silver objects as well as any precious stones, pearls and jewellery.' Von Heißen nodded in approval. 'Political prisoners, as well as those deemed to have information valuable to the Reich, are to be interned in a camp we have constructed at Mauthausen.' Eichmann nodded towards von Heißen in acknowledgement of his position as commandant.

Back in his office, once one of the Rothschild living rooms, Adolf Eichmann stood at the window overlooking the *Plosslgasse* with his hands clasped behind his back. He knew the measures he'd announced this evening would not be enough. A final solution would be necessary, and with that would come the opportunity to carry out some much needed medical research to improve the quality of life for members of the Reich. His thoughts were interrupted by a knock on the door.

'Kommen Sie!'

Eichmann's deputy entered and clicked his heels to attention. 'This cable's just arrived, Herr Obersturmführer. It's marked most urgent.'

Eichmann read it impassively.

```
      FOR: OBERSTURMFÜHRER EICHMANN
     ──────────────────────────────────

   By direction of Reichsführer Himmler, Jew-
   ish Professor Levi Weizman (55 yrs), Ramona
   Weizman (40 yrs), Ariel Weizman (10 yrs)
   and Rebekkah Weizman (8 yrs) all of 4/12
   Judengasse, Stephansdom Quarter, Vienna, to
```

```
be arrested immediately. Mauthausen Comman-
dant, Obersturmbannführer von Heißen, will
be coordinating search of Weizman's apart-
ment and surrounds and is to be given every
assistance.
     Brigadeführer Heinrich Müller
     Kommandant
     Geheime Staatspolizei
```

Eichmann initialled the cable and signed an authorisation for von Heißen to assume temporary command of a special detachment of SS Sonderkommandos.

'Give this to Obersturmbannführer von Heißen,' Eichmann ordered, handing over the authority. 'You'll find him downstairs in the ballroom.'

'Jawohl, Obersturmführer!'

15

VIENNA

The banging on the front door was unrelenting.

'*Öfnen Sie, Jude!*'

Ramona sat up with a start. 'Levi! Have they come?'

Levi put a finger to his lips. '*Shhh*. I'll deal with them.' He threw on his dressing gown, suddenly remembering the two bark maps he'd left beside the model of the Mayan pyramids in his study. He rescued them and went back to the bedroom. Rebekkah and Ariel, both wide-eyed and fearful, had run in to their mother. On an impulse that the Nazis might not suspect a child, Levi gave the maps to Ariel. 'Look after these for Papa,' he said. 'It will be all right, I promise,' he added reassuringly.

'Open up, Jew, or we'll break the door down!'

When Levi opened the door, the Sonderkommandos, supported by a group of young Brownshirts, knocked him to the carpet and stormed into the apartment. Levi struggled to his feet to find von

Heißen standing in the doorway, tapping his knee-high boots with a leather cane.

Von Heißen shoved the point of his cane under Levi's chin. 'Going somewhere, are we, Jew?' he asked, seeing the Weizmans' suitcases in the corridor.

Levi knocked the cane away. 'How dare you come barging in here like this!'

Von Heißen whipped his cane across Levi's face. 'Where is the figurine?'

The pain was excruciating.

'I have no idea . . . Somewhere in the jungles of Guatemala, I should imagine.'

Von Heißen slashed Levi across the face again. 'Where is it?'

Levi's eyes watered and he gritted his teeth, but said nothing.

Von Heißen fought to control his fury at the Jew's defiance. '*Scharführer!* Sergeant! Arrest them, and then search this place. We're looking for a jade figurine about thirty centimetres high.'

'*Jawohl, Obersturmbannführer*. There's a safe in the study, but it's locked.'

'Is there now?' A look of satisfaction spread across von Heißen's face. 'The Jew will open it,' he said, again raising Levi's chin with his cane.

Levi steadied his hand and inserted the key into the safe. He opened it and stepped back, silently praying for Ramona and the children.

Von Heißen surveyed the contents of the large strongbox in which Levi and Ramona stored their most precious possessions. The strong-box contained over 4000 schillings, proceeds from Ramona's boutique she had yet to convert to the new Reichsmark. 'No figurine,' von Heißen observed angrily. The disappointment in his voice was palpable. He rifled through the rest of the contents: Ramona's jewellery and three gold menorahs, the seven arms a symbol of the burning bush encountered by Moses on Mount Horeb. Von Heißen picked up a solid gold cross. At its centre was an exquisite ruby surrounded by twelve large diamonds. Von Heißen turned the cross over in his hand.

Levi struggled to remain calm. The pectoral cross had been discovered by his great-grandfather at an archaeological dig on the Mount of Olives, just outside of Jerusalem, and it had been in Levi's family for four generations. Its lineage could be traced back to the Third Crusade, Richard the Lionheart and Saladin, the Sultan of Egypt.

'Get this scum onto the trucks,' von Heißen ordered, closing the strongbox and pocketing the keys.

Levi wrenched his arm away from a Sonderkommando. 'I need to get dressed!'

Von Heißen's laugh was evil. 'Put him on the truck. He won't need any clothes where he's going.'

Von Heißen moved to the front window and watched the young Brownshirts shove Levi over the tailboard of the truck parked below. It had snowed heavily during the night, and the icy cobblestones glinted in the winter dawn. Further down *Judengasse*, more Jews were being rounded up for transportation to Mauthausen, but von Heißen still felt cheated. Behind him, the Sonderkommandos and Brownshirts were systematically ripping Levi's apartment to pieces, but there was no sign of the missing jade. Perhaps, von Heißen thought angrily, the figurine was in Guatemala after all. The Jew would still pay, he vowed. Von Heißen turned on his heel and headed back into the apartment, passing within one metre of the two figurines lying hidden beneath the floorboard.

Levi put one arm around Ramona, and his other around Rebekkah and Ariel. Rebekkah was sobbing as she buried her blonde curls into her father's chest. Ramona had managed to convince a sympathetic corporal to allow her and the children to dress, but Levi was still in his pyjamas, shivering in the cold.

'Where are these men taking us, Papa?' Rebekkah sobbed.

Levi kissed her curls and held his daughter more tightly. 'We'll see . . . it'll be all right, *Liebchen*,' Levi whispered, comforting his little girl as best he could.

They crossed the Danube at Emmersdorf, and Levi could tell they were now moving along the north bank, the trees heavy with snow. He rubbed his hands to get his circulation going, Rebekkah and Ariel asleep at his left shoulder. Ramona rested her head on his right. Nearly two hours later they slowed through the little town of Mauthausen, and a few kilometres further on the lorry wound its way up a small hill before coming to a halt at the massive wooden doors of the concentration camp. The guards checked the driver's papers and made a cursory check of the human cargo in the back before opening the gates. The truck ground into the lower courtyard and lurched to stop.

An SS captain and a dozen SS guards were waiting in the compound.

'Get them out of the truck and line them up against the wall,' the Hauptsturmführer barked.

Levi hugged his children and his wife. 'God will protect us,' he whispered.

Levi, Ramona and the children were in the middle of the line-up, and Levi looked around cautiously, shivering in his slippers and pyjamas. The camp was enclosed by high stone walls topped with barbed wire. At regular intervals along their length the walls were interrupted by massive granite watchtowers covered with slate roofs. Like some macabre university of death, the lower compound into which they'd been delivered was ringed by meticulously constructed stone cloisters. In the sentry box at the far end of the cloisters, Levi could see two guards silently sweeping the barrels of their machine guns across the group of prisoners. Levi detected a sudden apprehension amongst the guards as the big doors through which they'd just entered were opened again.

'*Achtung!*' A dozen guards doubled out from the main guardhouse and formed up, rifles at the ready.

'*Heil Hitler!*' The guard commander snapped to attention, his right arm thrust forward in salute, as von Heißen's black Mercedes swept into the courtyard. Von Heißen alighted, acknowledged the salute from his adjutant and strolled over to the group of prisoners, habitually tapping his leather cane against his knee-high boots. He slowly wandered down the line, and then stopped in front of Ariel, who had one hand in his pocket.

'What have you got in your pocket, boy?'

Ariel stared at the ground, not answering, his bottom lip quivering. Von Heißen levered Ariel's chin up with his cane. 'Give it to me!'

Levi moved to protect his son, but von Heißen lashed out with his cane and a guard slammed Levi back into the wall.

'I said, give it to me, boy!'

Ariel, tears welling in his eyes, handed over one of the maps he'd concealed in his pocket, the one with the bearings superimposed over Lake Atitlán. 'So, what do we have here?' von Heißen demanded, turning his attention to Levi.

'A child's drawing,' Levi responded quietly.

'Liar!' Von Heißen slashed Levi's face again and Ramona began to sob.

'You dare defy the Third Reich? *Sturmscharführer!*'

'*Obersturmbannführer!*' The short, dumpy senior NCO clicked his heels together. His uniform was stretched against his barrel-like form, his collar straining to contain thick purple jowls. Sturmscharführer Schmidt had been specially selected for the appointment as Mauthausen Camp Sergeant Major, not least for his vicious hatred of the Jews. In over twenty-five years in the Wehrmacht, and now in the SS prison guard 'Death's Head' division, Schmidt had never seen a shot fired in anger. Incapable of original thought, the sadistic and subservient Schmidt was determined to keep it that way. He was hated by prisoners and guards alike, but he had qualities von Heißen found useful.

'Take this scum to the guard barracks and have them clean the latrines.'

'*Jawohl, Obersturmbannführer!*'

Von Heißen pushed his cane under Levi's chin again. 'And you will clean the latrines until they sparkle. It will give you time to think about being a little more cooperative.' Von Heißen turned on the heel of his immaculately polished boot and strode away.

Schmidt marched the ragged column up the steps at the end of the cloisters and on towards the main entrance of the prisoner compound, where two massive stone towers stood sentinel on either side of the gate. Levi looked to the left. Men and women were chipping rocks from the face of a granite cliff and carrying them to large wooden hoppers. Several women were straining to push a full hopper, their screams carrying across the quarry when a guard bashed them with a heavy wooden club. Beyond the women, men were carrying large rocks on their shoulders, forced at gunpoint to run up a steep granite staircase that led to a cliff.

The guards shoved Levi and the rest of the group into the barrack-room toilet. A vile stink permeated the air.

'Most appropriate, don't you think?' Schmidt sneered. Ariel coughed and held his nose. 'Jewish *Scheisse* cleaning SS *Scheissen-häuser*!' Schmidt's laugh was harsh and he manhandled Levi towards one of the open cubicles. The stench was overpowering. Schmidt grabbed Levi by the neck and shoved his head into the bowl. He yanked the chain and reeking faeces cascaded through Levi's hair and up his nose.

Levi fell back and vomited.

'My tallit, Levi. They made me clean the toilet with my prayer shawl,' Ramona sobbed quietly as they were marched back towards an empty barrack block.

'*Lichte löchen*. Lights out,' *Scharführer* Schaub growled, and he flicked the switch. Levi had assessed the young German corporal as being one of the few decent guards he'd encountered during their arrest, so he was surprised when Schaub approached his bunk.

'You! Outside!'

Emotionally and physically exhausted, Levi offered no resistance when Schaub shoved him towards the door, closing it behind them once they were outside the barrack block.

'We don't have much time, so listen carefully,' Schaub said quietly, dragging Levi out of the circle of light thrown by a naked bulb hanging above the barrack-room door. 'I'm sorry for what you're going through. We'll try to get you out as soon as we can; but it's too dangerous at the moment, although we're working on a plan for the children. If Ariel and Rebekkah are transferred to laundry duties, don't try to keep them with you, and tell them to do exactly as they're told.'

'How do you know their names . . . Who are you?' Levi asked, struggling to comprehend the message from the SS guard.

'That doesn't matter. The Jewish Agency in Istanbul is all you need to know.'

The door to the barracks on the opposite side of the compound suddenly opened.

Levi winced as Schaub struck him across the face. 'You Jewish scum! What are you doing outside after lights out? Get back inside!'

16

The day had dawned overcast and cold, and von Heißen's boots crunched on the fresh spring snow as he returned from his inspection of the camp. Von Heißen was determined that Reichsführer Himmler's visit and the celebrations for Hitler's birthday would go off without a hitch. Reaching his headquarters, he descended the stone steps that led to a large cellar beneath the building. Only two people were allowed into what was effectively a strong room: himself and his batman, the latter charged with melting down Jewish jewellery and the piles of gold fillings that were extracted each time the bodies were cleared from 'the showers' beneath the hospital. Von Heißen felt the side of the small furnace he'd had installed alongside one of the stone walls. It was still warm from the night before. Satisfied, he dialled the combination to the huge safe at the rear of the cellar.

Excellent, he mused, picking up the ten-kilogram ingot his

batman had added to the six already stored in the vault. The bars were stamped with the eagle and swastika, giving the impression they were being produced to bolster the coffers of the Reich, but von Heißen had a very different plan. He'd already invited il Signor Felici to visit. The powerful envoy's contacts within the Vatican, a nation state outside the jurisdiction of either Hitler's Reich or Mussolini's Italy, would, he thought, be very useful. The SS colonel opened one of the vault drawers and extracted the pectoral cross he'd discovered in the Weizman safe, one of a number of items his batman had been instructed to store separately. Other than its possible monetary value, the cross held no particular attraction for von Heißen, but he'd already determined that it might mean quite a lot to someone like Felici. He returned the cross to its drawer, closed the vault door and headed back to his office.

Sitting behind his large mahogany desk, von Heißen turned his attention again to the strange piece of paper he'd recovered from the Jewish boy. A child's drawing? The yellow painted shape might be, but why would a boy of ten draw a series of lines and then assign what looked like bearings to them? Was it worth keeping his miserable father alive to find out? Under normal circumstances it might be, at least to give the usual methods of persuasion time to work, but von Heißen was very aware of the threat the Jewish archaeologist posed. The longer Weizman was alive, the greater the danger of word leaking out about the discovery of the figurine. There was only one man von Heißen genuinely feared: if Himmler ever found out, he'd be finished.

Deep in thought, von Heißen got up from behind his desk and stood at the window, absent-mindedly looking towards the quarry where the Jewish scum were already at work. He was convinced that if Weizman still had the figurine, he would have almost certainly hidden it in his strongbox. It was safe to assume the jade statue was still in the jungles of Guatemala, and therefore — His thoughts were interrupted by a knock on the door.

At five-foot nine, his adjutant, Hauptsturmführer Hans Brandt, only just cleared the SS height restrictions, but Brandt was well-connected and what the fair-haired, oval-faced, olive-skinned Aryan captain lacked in height, he made up for in ambition and naked ruthlessness.

'*Kommen Sie!*'

'The Jew is outside, Herr Kommandant, and I've been advised that Reichsführer Himmler's car is approaching Mauthausen. He will arrive in just under half an hour.'

'The guard is ready?'

'*Jawohl, Herr Kommandant.* I've inspected them personally. I've also been advised that Doktor Richtoff is accompanying the Reichsführer.'

'Everything is ready for the doctor?'

Brandt nodded. 'The technicians have finished installing the equipment, including the high-altitude pressure chamber, and Barrack Block 6 has been refurnished in accordance with Doktor Richtoff's instructions.'

Von Heißen grunted. 'Good. Bring the Jew in.'

'*Jawohl. Heil Hitler!*'

'Herr Professor, I'm told that your apartment has been thoroughly searched and there is no sign of the figurine. So where is it?' Von Heißen put his question very slowly, his voice ominously calm.

'I've already told you —'

'Liar!' Von Heißen lashed Levi with his cane. Levi gasped and stifled a cry.

'Filthy Jewish liar!' Von Heißen whipped Levi's face again, smashing his glasses. 'Where is it?' Von Heißen was shouting now, lashing at him uncontrollably. Levi's eyes watered, and he fought against the searing pain.

Von Heißen wondered again if the Jewish archaeologist might be telling the truth, but the moment was fleeting. 'And what does this map mean?' von Heißen asked, picking up the *huun* bark from his desk.

'It's nothing more than a small boy's drawing,' Levi answered defiantly, his knees starting to wobble.

'You're lying!' Von Heißen turned towards his adjutant. 'Have the guards take him away and when the Reichsführer has left, Sturmscharführer Schmidt can take him to the parachute jump.' As powerful as von Heißen had become, he knew he would have to seek approval from Himmler himself before he disposed of the Jewish professor.

'Achtung!' The guard of honour came to attention and saluted as an armoured car, followed by a new black BMW staff car, with a silver eagle and swastika pennant fluttering above the bonnet, swept through Mauthausen's gates. The staff car bore the registration plates: SS1. Von Heißen snapped to attention, right arm outstretched as the SS Commander alighted.

'Heil Hitler, Herr Reichsführer. Wilkommen zum Mauthausen.'

A hundred metres away, in the middle of the quarry, Ramona, Ariel and Rebekkah struggled to lift a large rock into one of the hoppers. Levi moved to help them and he winced in pain as an SS guard hit him with his rifle butt.

'Try to pick smaller ones, *meine Lieblings*,' Levi whispered. He turned and felt a cold shiver run down his spine as Reichsführer Himmler, accompanied by Obersturmbannführer von Heißen, appeared at the railing of the nearest watchtower. Suddenly a squad of SS guards doubled towards the quarry, rifles at the carry. At the far end of the quarry a line of marching prisoners, all in black-and-grey striped garb, were suddenly halted and ordered to turn to face the cliff.

A rifle shot echoed around the quarry, and the prisoner on the far left of the line crumpled to the ground, her face blown away by a bullet to the back of the head. Ramona fainted and Ariel and Rebekkah started to cry, cowering behind the hopper. For the next hour and a half the quarry reverberated to the crackle of rifle fire as every two minutes a Jew was shot in the back of the head in honour of the Führer's birthday.

Von Heißen watched Himmler's car disappear through Mauthausen's main gate before turning to walk back towards the quarry. It had been a very successful day. The Führer's birthday celebrations had gone very well, and Himmler had personally congratulated von Heißen on the efficiency of the camp. It was, Himmler said, the main reason Mauthausen had been chosen for Doctor Richtoff's top-secret medical experiments. The Reichsführer had even inti-mated that all going well, another promotion was in the offing. Standartenführer! Von Heißen could almost see the oak leaves on his collar. He felt a surge of pride and whacked his boots with his cane as he walked along the path leading to the top of the quarry cliff. He looked back towards the gates of the prisoner compound where, as per his instructions, the Weizman woman and her off-spring had been chained to one of the stone towers. Good, he mused, feeling a rising sense of satisfaction. From there they, too, would be able to see the quarry.

Schmidt shoved Levi over the rough ground towards the steps. 'There are 186 steps, Jew, and you're going to climb every one of them.'

Levi glanced back to where Ramona and the children were chained to the stone tower. Ramona's eyes were full of fear.

'Pick up that rock!' Schmidt shouted when they reached the nar-row stone staircase leading up to a high granite outcrop overlooking the quarry. 'On your shoulders, Jew man!' Schmidt's jowls were crimson now and a strong stench of garlic assailed Levi. He heaved the heavy rock onto his right shoulder.

'*Jetzt lauf!* Now run!'

Ramona, her hands chained to an iron ring in the wall behind her head, watched in horror as Levi struggled to climb the staircase, a massive rock teetering on his shoulder.

Schmidt turned to two young guards. 'You know what to do. Follow him!'

The taller of the two guards bounded up the stairs and yelled in Levi's ear. 'Come on, Jew, you're not even halfway yet!'

Levi's knees buckled under the weight of the granite boulder. He staggered and fell to the ground, and the other guard smashed a rifle against his ribcage.

'Get up, Jewish pig! I don't want to be here all fucking night!' Levi levered himself to his feet and hoisted the boulder back onto his shoulders, closing his mind to the searing pain in his ribs.

'What are they doing to Papa, Mama?' Rebekkah sobbed, her hands chained high above her head.

Levi rasped for breath and glanced ahead of him, not daring to stop. Ten steps to go. Nearing exhaustion, he staggered over the very last step and let the boulder fall at his feet.

'Who gave you permission to drop the rock?' The taller guard swung his rifle butt into the small of Levi's back. Levi fell face-first onto the rocks, breaking his nose and two of his teeth. 'Get up!'

Levi got to one knee, coughing blood and fragments of teeth.

One of the guards looked at his watch. 'We're losing fucking drinking time up here, Günther!'

'*Ja*. Get up, you Jewish shit!' Günther snarled, kicking Levi in the stomach. Levi stumbled forward onto a large flat rock that over-looked the quarry. A hundred metres below a jagged outcrop of granite extended from the cliff base to where the prisoners, their ribcages clearly visible, were quarrying stone with picks and shovels. Levi looked up to the left and a chill ran through him. The unmistake-able figure of von Heißen was silhouetted against the fading light.

Levi shuffled back, but he was shoved violently from behind.

Ramona watched in horror as Levi tumbled over the cliff, his arms flailing wildly. His scream pierced her very soul as he bounced off a rock halfway down, before smashing into the jagged granite at the base of the cliff.

'That's what happens when you criticise the Reich!' Schmidt shouted at the prisoners in the quarry. 'Now get back to work or you'll be next!'

Von Heißen's batman and the chief steward, the latter holding a large crystal glass of Glenfiddich on a silver tray, were standing at the ready, just inside the heavy cedar doors of the officers' mess. Flags of the Third Reich and the SS were mounted on one of the stone walls, and the bar had been decorated with a large gold eagle.

'*Meine Herren. Der Kommandant!*' Hauptsturmführer Brandt sprang out of his chair to announce von Heißen's arrival, and the other officers followed suit. Von Heißen handed his cane and cap to his batman and relieved the steward of the crystal tumbler.

'Hans, come and join us,' von Heißen commanded his adjutant, waving his hand towards an empty leather lounge chair beside Doctor Richtoff's. '*Ein Bier?*'

'*Danke schön, Herr Kommandant.*'

Von Heißen looked towards the bar and snapped his fingers.

'So, Eduard, everything is in order?' von Heißen asked, turning towards Richtoff.

Richtoff nodded. The SS doctor's skin was milky white. His spiky grey hair was cut short above his high, square forehead, and pale-green eyes peered from beneath bushy black brows. 'It appears to be, Karl. The equipment is being tested as we speak. We should be able to start our experiments tomorrow.'

'What is it that you're testing for, Herr Doktor?' Hans asked.

'The SS is to set the standards for the new Reich, Hauptsturmführer. The Mauthausen experiments are aimed at producing a new German elite – a human embryo that combines leader, scholar, warrior and administrator all in one. You will forgive me, gentlemen, but you are not perfect.'

'But a good start, Doktor,' von Heißen responded, signalling the steward to refill his glass.

'The experiments are also designed to provide data that may help with the conditioning of our troops for possible service on the Eastern Front.'

'How will you achieve that?' Brandt asked, keen to know how the German race might be perfected.

'Your *Kommandant* has kindly undertaken to provide me with fit specimens, both male and female. In the first experiment we'll strip them naked and put them in ice vats to discover how long it takes them to die. Of course, during the winter it will be easier,' Richtoff added, coughing, 'because we can just leave them naked in an outdoor cage to see how long they last. In the second experiment we'll lower the temperature to a point where most of them die, and from the remainder, we'll see which ones can be resuscitated. We've already done some testing in Auschwitz, where we forced iced water into their intestines . . . but all of them died. Unfortunately that method doesn't seem to have much promise.' Richtoff reached for his beer.

'And the pressure tank? What's that for?' Brandt asked.

'Low-pressure simulation of an oxygen-thin environment,' Richtoff replied. 'Your *Kommandant*, being a qualified high-altitude diver, knows quite a bit about this.'

'It's been a while now,' von Heißen replied.

'We've also tested this at Auschwitz,' Richtoff continued, 'but in Mauthausen we're planning to use women as well as men. The human body functions best at sea level, where the bloodstream is saturated with oxygen, but at altitudes above 15 000 feet, the oxygen levels are halved and the body needs to acclimatise. At Auschwitz we found that most subjects died once the altitude simulation reached 23 000 feet. At that height it's difficult to sleep and the digestion system breaks down. But one lasted past 25 000 feet and we've kept his organs for further analysis.'

'How many specimens do you need, Herr Doktor?' Brandt asked.

'Forty will do to start with. Twenty men and twenty women, but they must be fit.'

'Include the Weizman woman in the first batch, Hans – and make sure those brats of hers are forced to watch. Perhaps next time the boy will not be so keen to hide things from the Reich. In the meantime, in honour of your arrival, Eduard, I've ordered some very nice wine for dinner.'

Night descended on the quarry, and a team of soldiers finished removing gold fillings from the bodies at the base of the cliff. A large bulldozer, smoke pouring from the exhaust flap, manoeuvred into position and began shovelling the corpses towards a refuse pit. Back behind the forbidding stone walls of the prisoner compound, the inmates were standing in the cold between the barrack blocks, waiting for roll call. Ramona did her best to comfort Ariel and Rebekkah, her spirit unbroken but her heart torn apart, aching for the man she'd loved with every fibre of her being.

'Tomorrow, you'll both be transferred to work in the laundry, *Lieblings*,' Ramona whispered. 'If someone offers to help you, you're to do exactly as they tell you, all right?'

'But what about you, Mama?' Ariel asked. His face was white, his whole world shattered. Rebekkah looked up at her mother, struggling to understand what had happened.

'Mama will be fine . . . you look after your little sister,' Ramona said to Ariel, adjusting Rebekkah's blonde locks. 'Promise me.'

'I promise,' Ariel whispered, gripping his mother's hand more tightly.

17

MAUTHAUSEN

Ariel went to Rebekkah's aid. The laundry bag was nearly as big as she was, and Rebekkah was battling to load it into the back of a battered blue van that made the daily run, carrying the SS officers' laundry into the little town of Mauthausen. Ariel and Rebekkah turned to go back for the last of the bags, but the driver, a young woman with pale-blue eyes, beckoned to them from the side of the van that was hidden from the watchtowers.

'Listen carefully,' she whispered. 'My name is Katrina and you must do exactly as I say. There's a space in the back of the van near the cabin, and when the truck is full you must climb over the bags and pull them on top of you. I will lock the doors behind you.' Katrina glanced calmly to the left and right to make sure they were not being observed. 'Quickly now, get the last two bags.'

'But what about Mama?' Rebekkah pleaded with Ariel.

'Mama said we have to do exactly what the lady says,' Ariel said reassuringly, displaying a maturity beyond his years.

'*Was ist los?*' The Nazi guard's piggy eyes narrowed as he walked out of the laundry shed.

'*Beeilen Sie sich!* Hurry up, you lazy scum! I haven't got all day.' Katrina shoved Ariel and Rebekkah past the guard towards the doors of the loading dock. 'They're so lazy, those two,' she said, shaking her head at the guard and getting into the driver's seat.

'What do you expect? They're Jews!' The guard turned to follow Ariel and Rebekkah.

Katrina switched on the ignition. The engine turned rapidly, but didn't fire. Katrina tried again and then a third time, but the engine still refused to start. The guard, Katrina noted, was coming back.

'*Scheisse!*' Katrina swore. She lifted the van's stubby bonnet and retrieved from her pocket a rotor coated in green powder.

'It's the rotor,' Katrina said, looking at it in disgust. 'Do you have any sandpaper in your workshop?' she asked, slipping the guard a packet of Sleipner cigarettes.

'*Jawohl!*' the guard replied, smiling snidely at Katrina. 'Come with me.'

Katrina let the guard walk in front of her and turned back to Ariel and Rebekkah, giving a quick jerk of her head towards the back of the van.

Ariel grabbed a corner of his sister's bag and dragged it along with his own. He helped Rebekkah onto the tailgate, climbed in after her and closed the van doors quietly.

'Quickly,' he whispered, glancing through the van window. He could see Katrina walking alongside the guard, scrubbing something with a piece of paper. 'They're coming back!' They climbed over the piles of laundry bags, sat against the back of the cabin, and covered themselves with the bags in front. Rebekkah was breathing hard and Ariel reached for her hand and squeezed it.

'There's always something,' Katrina complained, snapping the plastic cover back onto the distributor and slamming the bonnet. '*Vielen Dank*.'

'*Bitte*. Any time. Perhaps you would like a drink after work?'

'We'll see.' Katrina let out the clutch and eased the van towards the heavy wooden doors and granite towers that marked Mauthausen's entrance. The fat guard gave a wave and headed off towards the toilet block for a smoke. Katrina drove slowly, expecting the guards to open the gates, but the thin, spindly man on duty climbed down from the watchtower and signalled for her to stop.

'*Was ist in der Lastwagen?*' he demanded.

'*Nur schmützige Wäsche*. Just some dirty laundry,' Katrina replied. '*Öffnen Sie!*'

Katrina shrugged, got out and opened the back doors of the van.

Ariel and Rebekkah instinctively pressed themselves against the metal back of the cabin. One by one the guard pulled the big blue bags out of the truck until there were only two rows remaining. Suddenly, the guard fixed his bayonet to his rifle and thrust it between two of the bags. Ariel and Rebekkah winced as the blade flashed between them and punctured the flimsy metal of the cabin.

'*Entschuldigung?*' Katrina inquired nonchalantly.

'*Was!*'

'I just thought I'd mention that Obersturmbannführer von Heißen's uniforms are in those bags. Perhaps the kommandant will not be too pleased if he finds a bayonet tear in his tunics?'

The SS guard grunted and got out of the truck. 'Load them back in and get on your way!' he ordered, turning on his heel and climbing back into the watchtower.

Ariel squeezed Rebekkah's hand again. With his other hand he checked to ensure the map he'd managed to keep from the Nazis was still in his pocket.

Half an hour later, Katrina slowed the van to a stop on a side road in a forest. She opened the back doors and passed in a small bag.

'There are some clothes in there. We'll be in Vienna in another couple of hours, but I want you to get changed while we're moving, because when you get out, you'll be going straight on board a ship.'

'Thank you,' Ariel replied numbly. 'Would you have a piece of paper and a pencil?'

'Yes; just a moment.'

'What do you want paper for?' Rebekkah asked as the van regained the highway.

'I tried to memorise those figures on the map the German took. Papa said they were important.' A tear dropped onto the paper as Ariel reproduced the map as best he could, but he could only remember one of the three bearings. When he'd finished, he carefully put both maps into the bag Katrina had given them.

A further two hours down the road Ariel looked through the window and recognised some of the buildings. 'I think we're near the docks,' he whispered. Suddenly, they stopped and the van doors were opened. A late-afternoon mist had descended on Vienna, and a small group of soldiers were lounging on some wool bales, smoking and telling jokes. No one was paying any attention to the small, rusted coal freighter rubbing against the tyres on the pylons. A wisp of smoke curled from the *Wilhelm Kohler*'s single grimy funnel, mingling with the mist. The Danube, brown but powerful, eddied past the steamer's rusted plates, while further out in midstream, a blackened barge loaded with timber chugged determinedly towards an unknown destination upstream.

'These are the last two,' Katrina said to the deckhand from the Jewish Agency in Vienna. She turned to Ariel and Rebekkah. 'Good luck, and may God go with you.' With that, Katrina was gone.

The deckhand ushered Ariel and Rebekkah up the narrow gangplank and below decks.

The children's escape from Mauthausen might have gone unnoticed until the evening roll call, but von Heißen was still furious over the missing figurine. Having ensured their father would never reveal the figurine's whereabouts, von Heißen was determined both Ariel and Rebekkah would witness their mother's demise, before they too were added to Doctor Richtoff's list of specimens.

The siren wailed ominously, warning the locals of a prison break.

'We've searched the entire camp, Herr Kommandant. They were last seen loading the laundry van, but they've disappeared.' Brandt was nervous.

'The laundry company?' von Heißen demanded.

'Their normal driver was off sick, and both his replacement and the van have disappeared, but the guard on the tower insists that he searched the van, and that's been corroborated by the other guards.'

'The Jews are behind this,' von Heißen seethed. 'Bring the laundry manager in for questioning.'

'Should I inform Vienna?'

'No! I will handle that myself,' von Heißen declared, determined there would be no blemish on his record. He would use his contacts in the Gestapo to seal off any escape route through Vienna or Istanbul.

'Do you want to cancel the experiment with the Weizman Jewess?' Brandt asked. 'Doktor Richtoff is ready to start.'

'Tell Doktor Richtoff to go ahead. I will be there shortly. We'll make other arrangements for the two brats . . . very special arrangements.'

'*Jawohl, Herr Kommandant!*'

In less than two minutes, von Heißen was through to Adolf Eichmann in Vienna, providing him with the registration number of the van.

'*Kein Problem, mein Freund*. The borders are sealed and if they're attempting to get them out through the docks, we'll intercept them.'

'*Danke, Adolf*. Much appreciated.' Von Heißen hung up the phone, satisfied the Weizman children would soon be back behind Mauthausen's walls.

Ramona lay naked on a stainless-steel gurney outside the pressure chamber. She shivered violently in the cold, unable to move. Black metal cuffs bit into her ankles and wrists, and behind her a series of leads attached to her body were connected to a machine. Fear for her children tore at her very being.

'As soon as you've recorded its temperature and blood pressure, have it placed in the chamber,' Doctor Richtoff ordered his assistant, a lanky pale-faced medical student in his early twenties.

'Jawohl, Herr Doktor.'

Von Heißen, together with Hauptsturmführer Brandt, stood at one of the observation windows. Two orderlies wheeled the gurney into the chamber and Brandt ran his eyes over Ramona's naked form. For a woman in her forties, she was in good condition, he thought. The doctor joined them in the observation booth. 'How long do you think she'll last, Doktor?' he asked.

Richtoff shrugged his shoulders. 'Hard to tell. This one looks pretty fit, but unfortunately we don't have much data on females, so we'll have to wait and see.' Richtoff picked up a small microphone at the side of the observation window.

'Ready?'

'Ja, Herr Doktor,' his assistant answered, his reply strangely muffled by the intercom. 'Temperature 99.9. Blood pressure 160 over 115 and heart rate 110.'

'So,' Richtoff observed, 'the specimen is running a fever and the blood pressure and heart rate are up. This may not take long, but we'll see.' He pressed a red button and a purple light started to flash above the steel door of the pressure chamber. The two orderlies and Richtoff's assistant evacuated the chamber, and one of them spun a silver-spoked wheel, sealing the chamber bulkhead.

'Achtung! Achtung! Wir beginnen!'

The Turkish captain of the coal carrier *Wilhelm Kohler*, Mustafa Gökoğlan, reached for a frayed cord just above his head. Three mournful blasts reverberated through the mist surrounding the docks. Gökoğlan looked out of his wheelhouse and waved the gangplank and mooring ropes away. He'd been reluctant to take on the human cargo, but he understood the language of money. Now that the twenty-one Jewish children were crammed into four cabins below decks, he was impatient to get away. The rest of his cargo manifest wouldn't stand too much scrutiny by the authorities either, and he was wary of the German soldiers on the docks. He leaned out of the wheelhouse. 'Let go for'ard!' The dockworker loosened the heavy hawser from its bollard. Gökoğlan took a sip from a battered mug of steaming coffee, grasped the smooth, brass handle of the telegraph and rang for 'slow ahead'. 'Let go aft!'

Three decks below, the *Wilhelm Kohler*'s wiry little engineer, a Kurd by the name of Hozan Barzani, wiped his dark brow with some oily cotton waste and reached for the old silver throttle wheel. He opened it gently and steam hissed into the Penn and Company triple-expansion steam engine. Barzani opened it a little further and more high-pressure steam shot into the first and smallest of the old cylinders, expanding into a second and then a third, each piston larger than the first to adjust for the progressive loss of pressure. The old engine towered over Hozan, and the worn big-end bearings on the one-metre-long connecting rods protested as the great pistons slowly gathered momentum.

'Son of a bitch!' Barzani swore in Kurdish. He'd been arguing with his obstinate captain for months, but to no avail. Not only were the con-rod bearings worn, but the bearings that held the drive shaft in place were dangerously overdue for maintenance and the lubricating oil was leaking badly, causing the bearings to overheat. Sailing the great river was not without its dangers, especially at night, but Barzani had been told that once they left the Romanian delta, they would cross the Black Sea and enter the Bosphorus Strait: fourteen nautical miles of twisting, turning waterway where thick fog could reduce visibility to a few hundred metres; where ships coming in the opposite direction were obscured by sharp turns. In places the straits were only a few hundred metres wide. When they reached Istanbul, ferries and other small craft would add to the hazards. From there Barzani had been told they were sailing for Palestine.

'Your father's a dog!' he swore, shaking his fist at the rusted deck above his head. It was madness.

Clouds of black smoke belched from the *Wilhelm Kohler*'s funnel, and the old tramp steamer moved away from the dockside and out into the Danube. Gökoğlan sipped his coffee, oblivious both to the insults being hurled at him from below decks and the sirens gathering in the distance.

The dark, dank cabin to the aft of the steamer smelled of rotting canvas and fuel oil. As the deck vibrated beneath her feet, Rebekkah felt as if she might be sick, and she reached for her brother's hand.

'I'm scared, Ariel.'

'We'll be all right, Rebekkah . . . I promise.'

Hauptsturmführer Brandt peered through the observation window at the pressure chamber. The specimen appeared to be crying, but other than that, it was all fairly boring. 'Not much happening, Doktor?' the young SS captain remarked, a note of disappointment in his voice.

Richtoff grunted. 'There won't be for a while. First we have to reduce the temperature to zero degrees centigrade and pressure to one atmosphere – what we call standard temperature and pressure, which replicates sea level. Under those conditions, our specimen would still take quite a while to die from the cold, but the pressure is dropping now, simulating altitude.' A large red needle on the pressure gauge started to quiver and slowly wound back over the black gradations that marked the millimetres of mercury.

Von Heißen watched the needle on the temperature gauge plunge past zero. He was still seething over the children's escape, but his connections with Himmler were well known in the Reich and he was confident the Gestapo would soon recapture the escapees. The borders were sealed and the docks in Vienna would be thoroughly checked, as would the shipping schedules and arrivals in Istanbul.

Ramona stared uncomprehendingly through her tears at the frost forming on the large pipes above her head, and she shivered violently on the bare steel gurney. Her head ached and every so often a razored needle seemed to pierce her wrists. Death would be a merciful escape, but she knew she had to hold on. The children were without their father now and they would need her; but it was becoming more difficult to breathe and she could feel her pulse quickening. Another bolt of pain burst through her brain and she gritted her teeth.

'Twenty thousand feet,' Richtoff observed. 'This one is tougher than I thought.'

Hauptsturmführer Brandt nodded, his eyes riveted on the

barometric pressure gauge. The experiment had been running for nearly twenty minutes and the red needle was falling more steadily now. The height equivalents were clearly marked in feet: 20 000 . . . 21 000 . . . 22 000 . . .

'It's twitching,' Brandt observed as the falling pressure simulated 23 000 feet.

'*Much* tougher than I thought,' Richtoff observed. 'Pulse is now 180. It's amazing how hard the heart can work before it collapses. See how its head wiggles. Even at this temperature it's perspiring.'

Ramona fought desperately for breath as violent cramps racked her body. 'My children. My children,' she gasped.

'I think it's finally unconscious,' Richtoff remarked casually. 'The breathing is slowing dramatically.'

'And there's frothing at the mouth,' Hauptsturmführer Brandt observed excitedly.

Richtoff turned to his assistant. 'Make a note of severe cyanosis.' The circulation of de-oxygenated blood had turned Ramona's face a deep blue.

'And now the breathing has stopped,' Richtoff observed. Five minutes later he turned to von Heißen. 'It's dead, but quite an amazing specimen. Nearly 25 000 feet . . . I can't recall one lasting for so long at that altitude, let alone a female. The autopsy will hopefully provide us with some more data.'

'Good. Let Hans here know if there's anything else you need.' Von Heißen headed back to his office where two immediate cables were waiting for him. The first was from Alberto Felici, indicating that he would shortly be travelling to Istanbul on Vatican business. The second was from Adolf Eichmann, indicating the Weizman children were believed to be on a tramp steamer bound for the Bosphorus, and giving him authority to liaise directly with the German Defence Attaché in Istanbul.

Von Heißen buzzed for his adjutant. This time there must be no mistake, he mused, vowing to see to it personally.

'*Herr Kommandant?*'

'Make arrangements for me to leave for Istanbul on the first flight out of Vienna tomorrow, and get this cable off to the Vatican,' he commanded, handing Brandt his reply to Felici, suggesting they meet at the Pera Palas Hotel in Istanbul.

18

THE *WILHELM KOHLER*

Hungry, cold and traumatised, Ariel and Rebekkah huddled underneath the *Wilhelm Kohler*'s wheelhouse. Further aft, some of the other children had sought shelter in the lee of the starboard wing. The rusty deck beneath their feet vibrated to the steady *thump-thump-thump* of the coal-steamer's engine. The rain sheeted in from the south across the Black Sea, but the cold air was far preferable to the fumes of the cabin. From the pocket where he kept his father's maps, Ariel carefully extracted a dry biscuit he'd saved from breakfast and broke it in two. As he passed half to Rebekkah, shouting broke out on the bridge above them.

'For three months I've been telling you the main bearings are too hot! Always you want full speed, but if you keep it up, they will seize!' Barzani's black eyes blazed with anger. It was a battle that was as old as the steam engine itself. For Barzani, the overheated bearings spelled disaster. For the stubborn old Turk on the bridge, any slackening in the ship's speed meant a bad-tempered owner and no bonus.

'I'm the captain of this ship, mister, and you'll follow orders. Maintain full revolutions!'

Barzani stormed off the bridge, his dirty overalls unbuttoned to his waist, sweat running down his dark, hairy chest.

'Son of a bitch,' he muttered as he clambered down the engine-room companionway. The thumping pistons, hissing steam and roar of the furnace were deafening, but amongst the cacophony, he sensed another noise. Like a great orchestral conductor detecting that an oboe was flat by a fraction of a tone, in amongst the thunderous cranking of the *Wilhelm Kohler*'s machinery, the engineer had picked up a slight knocking. Aft of the great engine, a single gleaming drive shaft ran the length of the keel, encased by semicircular bearing caps the size of a small car. Barzani checked the blackened steam gauges above the furnace and reached for his battered oilcan. He headed aft, stooping to fit through the cramped bulkheads that enclosed the pulsing drive shaft. He reached the first of the massive bearing caps and felt it. It was hot – far too hot. Barzani injected just the right amount of oil into the filler cup on top of the thumping case. He stopped to shake his fist at the deck above him. '*Pic!* Bastard!' he swore, and he headed along the shaft towards the next bearing.

The *Wilhelm Kohler* reached the entrance to the Bosphorus late in the afternoon. The Strait of Istanbul, Mustafa Gökoğlan knew, was one of the most dangerous waterways in the world. Sixteen headlands had to be negotiated along the seventeen nautical miles, and a surface current ran south from the Black Sea to the Marmara; but because of the different salt concentrations between the two seas, a second, deeper current ran in the opposite direction. Gökoğlan alternately puffed on his pipe and sipped from coffee laced with raki, the powerful white spirit the Turks called *aslant sütü*, lion's milk.

'See, Ariel: a fishing village,' Rebekkah said, pointing to their first sight of land since they'd left the Danube. The *Wilhelm Kohler* was less than 300 metres from the shoreline. Small, brightly coloured wooden fishing boats rocked in front of the fish market at Rumeli Kavagi. The rain had eased, and on the ridgeline behind the market, they could see houses beneath the plane trees. Further along, the ridgeline was dominated by a huge castle. The fishing villages on the European side gradually gave way to turreted wooden mansions; while on the Asian shore opposite, one of the former Sultans' many summer palaces commanded the top of a steep hill.

A thick fog began to roll in from the south. Gökoğlan yanked defiantly on the dirty length of rope hanging from the rusted roof of the bridge. Three short bursts of steam issued from the *Wilhelm Kohler*'s funnel as the foghorn sounded an eerie warning, one that was immediately absorbed by the mists. In defiance of the speed restrictions, Gökoğlan maintained course towards the Kandilli Turn, the notorious Bosphorus promontory that required a forty-five-degree change of course. Any ships heading south were blind to traffic going in the opposite direction. He peered into the gathering darkness, searching for the promontory he'd already passed, and the *Wilhelm Kohler* crossed into the northbound shipping lane.

Five deep blasts from a ship's horn, the international distress signal for an imminent collision, reverberated through the fog. A large Russian freighter loomed out of the mists.

Gökoğlan swore and wrenched the telegraph to emergency full astern.

In the engine room below Barzani leapt to the reciprocating lever and immediately brought the great engine to a stop in a cloud of hissing steam and protesting pistons. Just as quickly, he applied full throttle in the opposite direction. Whatever the engineer's views of his stubborn and irascible captain, Barzani was responding to a fundamental law of the sea. Above the thunderous noise in the engine room, the frenzied dinging on the telegraph meant the ship was in danger. Barzani watched the con rods slowly gather speed. On the bridge above Gökoğlan frantically spun the *Wilhelm Kohler*'s wheel to starboard, but as the huge Penn and Company engine reached maximum revolutions, the overheated bearing caps finally reached their limits. The number one bearing-case seized and shattered in an explosion of sparks. Freed of one of its supports, the glistening silver main shaft began to flex violently. Barzani rushed towards the reciprocating lever but he was too late. The shaft snapped just for'ard of the shattered bearing casing. Clear of the load of the propeller, the old engine reached revolutions for which it had never been designed. The little end-bearing in the number one cylinder was the next to fail, driving the con rod through the crown of the massive piston. The number two and three pistons shattered in sympathy and the engine disintegrated in an explosion of metal shrapnel. A lump of red-hot metal decapitated Barzani in a bloodied mist of escaping steam.

The Russian freighter hit the *Wilhelm Kohler* midway between the bridge and the stern on the starboard side. She sliced into the rusted plates in a grinding, sickening crunch. Rebekkah was knocked unconscious as her head slammed into one of the steel bulkheads. Ariel held his sister's limp body with one hand and clung desperately to a stanchion with the other.

The Russian captain immediately ordered full astern and ever so slowly, steel grating and screeching against steel, the Russian freighter freed herself from the *Wilhelm Kohler*'s grasp. Tons of icy water flooded the aft coal bunkers and the *Wilhelm Kohler* listed alarmingly to starboard, the sea foaming through the connecting bulkhead doors that had been left open.

'Launch the lifeboat!' Gökoğlan bellowed. One of the deckhands struggled with the ropes on the starboard lifeboat, but to no avail. Mustafa Gökoğlan hadn't conducted a lifeboat drill in years, and the pulleys in the davits were rusted solid. Gökoğlan fled the bridge to the fiercely listing deck below.

'Launch it!' he roared, swinging on the ropes, but the small wooden boat hung drunkenly from the davits. The *Wilhelm Kohler* shuddered and rolled past forty-five degrees, throwing Ariel and Rebekkah, along with those children not trapped below decks, into the icy sea.

Ariel spluttered and coughed up sea water as he surfaced a short distance from the stricken coal steamer. 'Rebekkah! Rebekkah!' he yelled, frantically searching for his sister in the dark, oily waters.

19

ISTANBUL

Alberto Felici leaned forward in the worn but comfortable armchair in Archbishop Roncalli's book-lined study in the Vatican Embassy on *Ölçek Sokak*.

'The Cardinal Secretary of State is sympathetic to the plight of *any* people who are oppressed, Excellency; but you must realise there are greater issues at play here than the fate of the Jews,' he insisted.

'I'd be interested to know what you might consider a greater issue than the lives of children,' Roncalli replied stonily. 'Hitler and the Third Reich represent a grave threat to world peace.'

'That's not a view shared by Cardinal Pacelli, Excellency. He believes Communism poses a far greater threat to the Holy Church than Hitler. And,' Felici added pointedly, 'with the Holy Father now gravely ill, Cardinal Pacelli may well be next to fill the Shoes of the Fisherman.'

'That will be a matter for the next conclave. It is poor taste, don't you think, Signor, to be discussing the next Pope before the current one is dead?' Roncalli's dislike for the Italian banker-turned-papal envoy grew by the minute. 'In the meantime Istanbul will remain one of the main escape routes for the Jews. The Nazis have stripped them of everything they have, and I need more funds to help them. But more importantly Rome must understand that the Nazis are committing *mass murder*. Instead of sending Hitler congratulatory birthday telegrams, Cardinal Pacelli should be urging the Holy Father to condemn this massacre in the strongest possible terms. If the Vatican won't condemn genocide, what hope do we have?'

'You don't seem to understand, Excellency —' Felici's protestations were cut off by the strident ringing of the phone on Roncalli's desk.

'Angelo Roncalli.' The archbishop leaned forward into the Bakelite mouthpiece.

'Angelo, it's Mordecai Herschel. There's been a terrible accident in the Bosphorus. The *Wilhelm Kohler* has been sunk in a collision with a Russian freighter.'

'Oh, no . . . the children?'

'We don't know yet. I'm on my way to the Kandilli Turn. We may not be able to get the children to Palestine now, but there's another steamer leaving for Central America tomorrow night. I'll keep you posted.'

'I will pray for them,' Roncalli whispered, and he replaced the receiver. He turned to Felici. 'I'm afraid I have to go, Signor. The *Wilhelm Kohler*, a ship bringing Jewish children out of Austria, has sunk in the Bosphorus.'

Obersturmbannführer von Heißen signalled the waiter. 'Another bottle of Château Latour.'

The Pera Palas dining room was one of Istanbul's finest. A magnificent crystal chandelier, heavy velvet drapes, crisp linen tablecloths and silver cutlery were complemented by a cellar containing some of the world's finest wines.

'Do you think the Vatican Bank proposal will go ahead, Alberto?'

Felici nodded. 'I suspect Pacelli will be the next Pope, and he's very keen to establish it. It's confidential, of course, but he's already asked me to be a delegate to the board.'

'Excellent news, Alberto.' Von Heißen raised his glass. 'I should imagine such a bank will be very well capitalised.'

'I expect that for the right clients, we'll be able to offer services more than comparable to those of any of our competitors in Zürich,' Felici replied smoothly.

Von Heißen smiled, momentarily thinking of the contents of the strong room beneath the SS headquarters in Mauthausen.

'On another issue,' Felici continued, 'I was with Archbishop Roncalli earlier this evening. There's apparently been a collision on the Bosphorus. It seems one of the ships was carrying Jewish children from Vienna.'

'Is that so? Well, it is a dangerous stretch of water,' von Heißen replied, choosing his words carefully. 'Any word on survivors?'

'Not yet, but Roncalli is taking a very keen interest in them.'

'How many were saved?' Roncalli asked the Mother Superior as he arrived at the Sisters of Sion Monastery in the old Pangalti Quarter of the city.

'Just three, Excellency. A boy and two older girls,' Sister Marta replied, leading the way down a narrow stone-walled corridor to a makeshift ward.

Roncalli took a deep breath and crossed himself. Eighteen young souls taken . . . At times like this he questioned God's presence in the world.

'The little boy in the last bed,' Sister Marta said quietly, 'his name is Ariel. His father was murdered by the Nazis; his mother is in a German concentration camp, and he lost his sister in the collision.' Her eyes filled with tears.

Roncalli held Ariel's hand in his. What could he say to this young boy who had already suffered so much in his short life? 'I'm so very, very sorry,' he said finally. 'I just want you to know you're not alone.'

Ariel nodded numbly, wiping away a tear.

Roncalli turned to find another of the sisters at his side. 'There's a German officer at the front door, Excellency,' she whispered.

Roncalli nodded. 'Tell him I'm coming.'

Ariel watched Roncalli walk from the room, sensing this was a man he could trust. He checked again under his pillow, and sighed in relief. The maps were still there.

A tall, immaculately uniformed SS officer was waiting for Roncalli at the front door. Everything in Roncalli recoiled at the sight of him, but he moved forward.

'Can I help you, officer?' he inquired mildly.

'I am Obersturmbannführer Karl von Heißen, Excellency. I have come to offer the condolences of the German government and my personal best wishes to the survivors. A shocking tragedy.'

'That's very kind of you, Obersturmbannführer. I'm sure you'll understand, however, that the children are still in shock. It may be some days before they're allowed visitors. Do you think you could come back the day after tomorrow . . . say just after lunch?'

Von Heißen fought to control his irritation. 'But of course, Excellency – the day after tomorrow.'

It was well after midnight by the time Roncalli and Mordecai Herschel had arranged for Ariel and the other children to be transferred to the greater security of the Vatican Embassy.

A candle flickered feebly on Roncalli's desk as he and Herschel worked on into the small hours of the morning. Never had certificates of Conversion to Catholicism been prepared with such loving care.

'The SS *Belize Star* sails tomorrow night for British Honduras and Guatemala,' Herschel said, rubbing his eyes. 'I've organised three berths, and we've an agent in Guatemala City who will meet the children. I'll take these papers down to the Immigration Department tomorrow morning and arrange Turkish passports.'

Roncalli smiled. 'Where I come from, that would take weeks . . . *domani, domani*, always *domani*.'

'Fortunately we're not in Italy, Angelo, and I have a contact who is sympathetic. I just hope the children will be fit to travel.'

'Children can be remarkably resilient, Mordecai, although I'm worried about Ariel Weizman,' Roncalli said. 'He's been through more than any adult should endure in a lifetime.'

Archbishop Roncalli drove his battered Fiat slowly along the darkened dockside on the southern shore of the Golden Horn. The concrete was still wet from an earlier shower, and the rail lines glinted in the feeble yellow light thrown from the portholes of steamers tied up at the dock.

'That's her,' Herschel said quietly, 'at the end of the pier.' Smoke was issuing from the *Belize Star*'s single stack, her crew preparing to sail. Roncalli brought the old car to a stop near the rickety gangplank, but as he pulled on the handbrake, the darkness was pierced by two powerful headlight beams from a Mercedes parked in the shadows. A tall, blond SS officer stepped out from the passenger side. Roncalli recognised him immediately.

'So, what brings you down to the docks so late at night, Excellency?' Von Heißen tapped his leather cane once, twice against his palm.

'I might ask you the same question, Obersturmbannführer,' Roncalli replied evenly, getting out of his car.

'I do hope you weren't planning to spirit these children out of the country,' von Heißen said politely, looking past Roncalli's shoulder to the three children in the back seat of the Fiat. 'I'm afraid my government has serious questions about the validity of these children's papers and how they themselves came to be in Istanbul.'

Fear gripped Ariel in the depths of his stomach. He looked his father's killer in the eye, not knowing that his mother, too, was dead. Ariel loathed the German with every fibre of his young being.

'I would have thought the Reich had better things to do than worry about the immigration of children, Obersturmbannführer.'

'What's going on? We're about to sail!' the short, stocky captain of the *Belize Star* demanded in a heavy Spanish accent as he descended the gangplank.

'These Jewish children are wards of the German government, Captain,' von Heißen said. 'If you take them on board, you will be guilty of kidnapping. I doubt your employers would be too pleased if their ship were impounded at your next port.'

Roncalli stepped forward. 'The Obersturmbannführer is mistaken, Captain. All these children are Catholic and in the care of the Sisters of Sion Monastery here in Istanbul.' He took the children's papers and passports from his briefcase.

The captain of the *Belize Star* glanced at the papers and shrugged at Roncalli. 'If there's doubt, that's not my problem, signor,' he said, turning back to his ship.

A slow smile spread across von Heißen's face.

Mordecai Herschel took three strides and intercepted the captain at the bottom of the gangplank. 'Their papers are perfectly in order, Captain, and the German government has no jurisdiction on a Turkish dock.' He fished a large wad of Turkish lire from his pocket. The captain's eyes glinted, his gaze shifting from the money to the children and back to the money. 'Get them on board,' he said finally, 'we sail in ten minutes.'

Ariel reached the rusted deck of the tramp steamer, one hand in his pocket, checking for the hundredth time on the maps his father had said were so important.

20

ROME, 1944

'*Gloria in excelsis Deo. Et in terra, pax hominibus bonae voluntatis . . .*' Eugenio Pacelli, now Pope Pius XII, read from the
Missale Romanum held by one of his secretaries.

'Major General William Joseph Donovan: for feats of arms,
writing, and deeds that have spread the Faith and safeguarded
and championed the Holy Church,' another of the Pope's secretaries intoned. He proffered the Holy Father a red velvet cushion,
in the middle of which nestled the eight-pointed gold-and-white
enamelled Grand Cross of the Order of Sylvester. One of the
most prestigious of the papal knighthoods, fewer than a hundred
men had received the honour since its inception in 1841 by Pope
Gregory XVI.

Franklin D. Roosevelt's intelligence chief and head of the Office
of Strategic Services stepped forward. In time the fledgling American intelligence service would be known as the CIA. The crusty

old general bowed his head, allowing Pius XII to place the medal's golden chain around his neck.

'A great honour, Holiness. Thank you,' he said, kissing the papal ring.

'The pleasure is all ours. It's very well deserved.'

Alberto Felici joined in the polite applause. The Papal Knighthood cemented what would become a lasting marriage between the Vatican and the CIA. Felici smiled to himself. Things were starting to fall into place. The new Pope had agreed to the recommendations on Vatican finances, the newly established Vatican Bank had an advantage no other bank could match – it was immune from external audit. Felici's own position as a delegate to the board provided him with unprecedented personal power. His appointment as the Vatican's liaison officer to Donovan's intelligence staff was not without power either. It was power Felici fully intended to wield at the meeting Donovan had scheduled in his Rome office later in the day.

'Communism is the greatest threat facing the United States since Hitler came to power!' General Donovan rasped. 'Wild Bill', as he was widely known, was in no mood for compromise. Felici nodded his head. The war against the Japanese in the Pacific was yet to reach its horrific conclusion in Hiroshima and Nagasaki, but the war with Germany was drawing to a close, and a new threat was emerging. An iron curtain was about to descend, one which would divide Europe in two. If the US and the Vatican's fight against Communism was to succeed, key Nazi intelligence officials and scientists would have to be smuggled out of Germany. General Donovan's staff had drawn up a top-secret list.

'The list you've got in front of you is provisional,' General Donovan advised the three intelligence officers detailed to oversee the escape routes. 'We're going to need every German officer with knowledge of Soviet operations, including Soviet logistics and industrial capabilities. Add to that every German scientist who can assist us with the war in the Pacific.'

'But not including those who have been members of the Nazi party, surely?'

Donovan glared at the bespectacled State Department liaison officer. 'Listen, sonny, every goddamned scientist in Germany is a member of the Nazi party. And that includes Wernher von Braun, arguably the best rocket scientist on the planet. So before you guys in Foggy Bottom start getting your knickers in a twist, ask yourselves whether you want these guys working for Stalin or Uncle Sam!' The general was convinced America should do whatever it took to curtail the growing threat of the Soviet Union. 'Their dossiers can be sanitised . . . the hard part will be getting them out.'

'I think we can help there, General,' Felici offered. 'The Brenner Pass on the Austrian–Italian border is still the main line of escape, but anyone as well known as von Braun might have difficulty getting through – unless he's disguised.'

'As what?' the man from the State Department asked.

'No one is likely to question a priest, particularly one carrying a Vatican passport. I've added a further name to this list, General,' Felici continued, passing the paper back across the table. 'Standartenführer von Heißen is one of Reichsführer Himmler's closest confidants. I think US intelligence might find him very useful.'

'The "fees" are fifty per cent, Standartenführer. Take it or leave it,' Felici told von Heißen. 'My intelligence links are impeccable, and the US 11th Armored Division has already crossed the Danube – they will be here within days.'

'That gold in the strong room is worth over three million Reichsmarks, Signor. Fifty per cent is exorbitant!'

Felici shrugged. 'A hundred kilograms of gold won't be easy to shift. Even if you can get it past the American patrols, your chances of getting it across the border into Italy, let alone to Central America without diplomatic protection are next to nothing, I would say.'

Von Heißen was like a cornered rat. 'It would appear I don't have many options,' he snarled. The radio in his office, tuned to track the advancing allied forces, beeped at the top of the news hour.

'This is the BBC World Service. Heading this special bulletin, the war in Europe is expected to be over within days. Following the German Chancellor Adolf Hitler's suicide on the thirtieth of May, General Alfred Jodl, Chief of the Operations Staff in the German High Command, is expected to surrender German forces unconditionally to General Eisenhower at his headquarters in Reims. The British Prime Minister, Winston Churchill —'

There was a knock at the door.

'*Herein!*'

Obersturmbannführer Brandt, now von Heißen's deputy

commandant, looked pale and shaken. 'We're getting reports of an American armoured car unit, the 41st Cavalry Reconnaissance Squadron, on the outskirts of Mauthausen, Herr Kommandant. They could be here within twenty-four hours.'

Von Heißen nodded angrily. 'The Wehrmacht have let the Fatherland down, Hans. Dismiss the guards and tell them to meld back into the community. The Jews can look after themselves. And tell my driver and batman to stand by.'

'Just how do you plan to get me out of here, Signor?' von Heißen demanded after Brandt had left.

Felici handed von Heißen a small package. 'The roads will be chaotic and I intend to take advantage of that. The soutane in this package has been tailored to your measurements. If anyone asks, you're on the German desk in the Secretariat of State in the Vatican. These papers confirm your new identity as Father Bartolo Hernandez. We'll need a small lorry for the gold, which is to be crated and closed with the seals of the Holy See. From here we will travel to Vienna, where the gold will be temporarily stored in the vaults of the Imperial Hotel, before being shipped to the Vatican Bank in Rome. If we're challenged, you're to leave the talking to me, understood? Now, if you don't mind, I'd like to inspect the vault.'

Von Heißen dialled the combination of the vault door at the back of the stone cellar and swung it open, revealing row upon row of gold ingots, each one stamped with the eagle and swastika of the Third Reich. He reached into the drawer that held Levi's pectoral cross. 'This was acquired from a Jewish prisoner,' he said. The large diamonds surrounding the huge ruby in the centre of the cross sparkled in the soft light of the vault. 'You may have it, but only after I am safely out of Germany.'

Felici struggled to contain his excitement. The cross was like no other he'd seen, and undoubtedly worth a small fortune.

The tall, lanky American soldier took his M1 carbine from his shoulder and waved the black Mercedes and small lorry to a stop at a roadblock just outside Mauthausen. Burnt-out German tanks and trucks littered the roadside, a road crowded with armoured cars and tanks from the US 11th Armored Division. A mustang fighter screamed low overhead as von Heißen's driver, dressed in slacks and a polo-neck sweater, brought the car to a halt.

'Your papers, please,' the corporal asked. 'You're a long way from home, Father,' he added, spotting von Heißen's Roman collar.

'*Ja* . . . but God's business doesn't stop, *nein?*' von Heißen replied with an urbane smile.

'Where you're headed, gentlemen, the road's a fucking – sorry, Father. It's bedlam between here and Vienna.'

'We'll have to take our chances, Corporal,' Felici replied. 'We're on Vatican business, and we need to be in Vienna tonight. As Father Hernandez says, God's work is never done.'

'Well, good luck,' the corporal said, handing back the passports.

'God bless you, my son,' Felici intoned.

Von Heißen returned his passport to the secure compartment in his briefcase, the same compartment that held Levi Weizman's tattered map. Despite the devastation of the Fatherland, von Heißen was determined to continue the search for the Maya Codex.

BOOK II

21

THE WHITE HOUSE, 2008

'The Iranians have successfully enriched over 1800 kilograms of weapons-grade uranium, Mr President, which is more than enough to construct a nuclear bomb capable of destroying the Old City of Jerusalem or Tel Aviv.'

Vice President Walter Montgomery, bald and overweight, glared around the polished mahogany table in the White House's newly renovated Situation Room, daring anyone to challenge him. The National Security Council was made up of some of the most powerful men and women in the United States: the Secretary of Defense, the Secretary of State, the Secretary of the Treasury, the National Security Advisor, the Chairman of the Joint Chiefs of Staff and the Director of National Intelligence. Their senior advisors were seated in the row of chairs beneath the new flatscreen televisions that lined the walls.

'I've asked the CIA to brief us on the Iranian situation,' the Vice

President concluded irritably, nodding towards the man waiting at the briefing lectern.

Curtis O'Connor had recently returned from a covert intelligence operation deep inside the Islamic Republic of Iran. He knew the risks involved if the United States were to open up a third front in the Middle East. The Taliban were already gaining the upper hand in Afghanistan, and further to the west over 4000 young Americans had been killed in combat in Iraq. Tens of thousands more soldiers were disabled for life.

'Operation Sassanid was launched two years ago, following President Mahmoud Ahmadinejad's refusal to halt the enrichment of uranium,' O'Connor began. 'Sassanid includes electronic intercepts of phone conversations, emails and fax transmissions, as well as satellite surveillance of areas where we suspect the Iranians are constructing nuclear facilities.' The National Reconnaissance Office's KeyHole spy satellites were the size of school buses, and travelled at over six kilometres a second. Orbiting as high as 36000 kilometres above the Islamic Republic, they provided imagery so precise that vehicle registration plates and street numbers on buildings were clearly visible. The sophisticated cameras also operated in the near infra-red and thermal infra-red spectra, and could peer through darkness and clouds. But as good as the coverage was, O'Connor knew there were still gaps.

'Despite our 24/7 coverage, we don't have reliable detection of Iranian bunker systems or tunnels, and we suspect they may be constructing more nuclear plants deep underground,' O'Connor continued. 'Nor can satellite imagery provide precise information on what might be going on inside a particular building. Up until now, Iran has only admitted to two nuclear facilities. The first is located in

Isfahan in central Iran.' O'Connor used a laser pointer to indicate the facility's location on the map behind him. 'Isfahan's main function is to convert yellowcake into uranium hexafluoride. The second facility is in Natanz.' He pointed to an area south of Tehran.

'Despite relying more heavily on technology, we have still managed to maintain *some* agents on the ground,' O'Connor said, glancing at the Secretary of Defense, 'and we now have both facilities under constant ground surveillance. One of our agents has confirmed that the Natanz facility contains high-speed centrifuges, perhaps as many as 50 000, which are used to convert the Isfahan hexafluoride into highly enriched weapons-grade uranium. Of greater concern is a new facility under construction deep inside a mountain complex at Fordo, near the ancient city of Qom.' O'Connor indicated a range of hills to the south-west of Tehran. 'This facility is located on an Islamic Revolutionary Guard base, and it's managed by the Atomic Energy Organisation of Iran – or AEOI – although few know of its construction, even amongst those who work for the AEOI.'

'But it's for military use?' President Denver Harrison looked tired and confused. Now well into his second term, he'd aged considerably. Curtis O'Connor had long thought this president out of his depth. The real power in the administration rested in the hands of the irascible Vice President Montgomery.

'Our agent in Qom thinks so, Mr President. He's counted just 3000 centrifuges. That's too few to enrich enough uranium for a nuclear power station —'

'But enough to create several nuclear bombs,' Montgomery cut in. 'Time is running out, Mr President. We need to take out all three facilities, and we need to do it now.'

'The Israelis are already considering that option,' the Secretary of State added. 'Ahmadinejad's threats to wipe Israel off the map have tried Israeli patience to the limit, and we fear they will launch a pre-emptive strike.' The Secretary of State went no further. Everyone in the room knew that Israel was an undeclared nuclear power, and there was already a precedent. In 1956, Egypt's charismatic president Gamal Nasser seized the Suez Canal and sank dozens of ships laden with concrete to deny its use to the West, and the Israelis acted without the imprimatur of their great and powerful friend. Without informing President Eisenhower, Prime Minister David Ben-Gurion ordered Israeli tanks into the Egyptian-held Gaza and General Ariel Sharon's paratroopers attacked deep into the Sinai Desert, surprising the Egyptians on the passes a few miles from the canal. Might Israel act unilaterally again? The question hung in the tense atmosphere around the table.

'Are the Iranians capable of striking Israel?' the President asked, looking at O'Connor.

'Not yet, but they're very close to testing a new version of their Sejil-2 missile.' O'Connor flashed up a photograph of the latest Iranian surface-to-surface missile on a screen. The gleaming black twenty-metre-high Sejil-2 stood on its launch pad amongst the foothills of a mountain range to the south-west of Tehran. 'The Sejil-2 will be capable of delivering a nuclear warhead and will be powered by solid-fuel rocket motors similar to those that powered our Minuteman 1 missiles. Although that's reasonably old technology by our standards, it represents a significant step forward for the Iranians, and will give their missile a range of over 2000 kilometres.' O'Connor pressed a remote and a map of the Middle

East and Eastern Europe came up on a second screen. 'The Iranians could then not only wipe out Tel Aviv and Jerusalem, but reach all of our bases in the Middle East, even from eastern Iran; and from western Iran, cities like Athens and Istanbul will also be in range.'

'All the more reason we should act before they do,' the Vice President urged.

O'Connor shook his head. 'All of our analysis indicates that a strike against Iran would be a disaster, Mr President. For one thing, it would almost certainly result in the Iranians closing the Straits of Hormuz. Eighty per cent of the world's oil supply flows through those straits.'

Montgomery was apoplectic, but O'Connor pressed on. 'Mr President, our intelligence indicates that the Fordo facility is buried so deep within the surrounding mountains, even our most powerful bunker-busting bombs wouldn't touch it. It's a widely held view amongst many of our analysts that rather than attacking Iran, the better strategy would be to establish a dialogue with Iran's ruling elite, and with Syria. The real power in Iran does not rest with Ahmadinejad, but with the Supreme Leader, Ayatollah Khomenei. If the United States were to adopt a more balanced foreign policy towards the Occupied Territories, and increase pressure on Israel to cease building settlements and to reach a solution on the Palestinian question, in our view, the Iranians may come to the table.'

'That's enough, O'Connor,' the Vice President rasped. 'You're operating well above your pay grade, and you're obviously not aware of the experiments being conducted out of Alaska.' The President looked puzzled. 'Seismic tomography, Mr President,' Montgomery explained. 'Extremely low-frequency radio waves that can be targeted to discover the precise locations of facilities underground. There are promising indications that if the power is increased to sufficient levels, the tunnels and the facilities within them can be destroyed.'

'Get me DDO Wiley on the phone, now!' Montgomery barked at his secretary as he stormed back into his office. The CIA's Deputy Director of Operations was responsible for all United States covert spy operations around the world, and Howard J. Wiley was now the second-most powerful man in the CIA. He often knew more than the director, an appointment held in the past by influential men like George Bush Snr and William J. Casey.

'Who the fuck does this O'Connor think he is?' Vice President Montgomery demanded after DDO Wiley came on the secure line.

'I've just heard, Mr Vice President. I can assure you, he'll be disciplined.'

'Disciplined? He needs to be fucking well sacked! If the O'Connors of this world get their way, we'll be inviting Ahmadine-jad and his mad mullahs to a fucking barbecue on the lawns of the White House! Get him out of Washington. He's far too cosy with those jerk-offs in the State Department. Send him off to keep an eye on Mugabe and his gangsters. Or better still, fuck him off to Alaska. The last time I was there it was forty below. Perhaps living with the goddamned huskies and bears will give him a better perspective.'

'Consider it done, Mr Vice President,' DDO Wiley responded, but he was wasting his breath. The line had already gone dead.

22

GAKONA, ALASKA

The blizzard was the worst in living memory. Icy winds tore up the Copper River Valley at over a hundred kilometres an hour. O'Connor glanced at the security-camera screen and shivered involuntarily. The mercury had dropped to minus fifty degrees. Alaska was a hell of a place to spend a forty-second birthday, he thought grimly, as another sub-zero blast shook the HAARP control centre.

HAARP stood for High-frequency Active Auroral Research Program, an ostensibly harmless scientific project , run out of a base in the Alaskan wilderness near Gakona, 320 kilometres north-east of Anchorage, but O'Connor was already wondering about the schedule of experiments. Outside the snow was piling up around the 180 high-powered antennae that were spread over nearly fifteen hectares. Each over twenty metres high and not dissimilar in shape to the backyard Hills Hoist, the combined antennae were capable of producing a staggering 3.6 billion watts of radio frequency power.

'That storm's packing one heck of a punch out there.' Dr Tyler Jackson, the CIA's senior scientist at HAARP, ducked through the outer door and ambled inside the control centre, brushing the snow from his long angular face and sandy beard. Ducking was a habit the gangly scientist had developed at an early age, but Jackson was now in his sixty-fourth year, and close to retirement. He had been with the Firm for over forty years, but, like O'Connor, he didn't always agree with the party line coming out of the CIA's headquarters in Langley, Virginia.

'Not the only storm brewing,' O'Connor replied. 'The Iranians have just test-fired another Sejil-2 missile.' In the two weeks since O'Connor had arrived at Gakona, a camaraderie had developed between the two men. Both had strong scientific backgrounds, both were cleared to the highest levels of security, and both were serving their country amidst the privations of the harsh conditions of Alaska.

'Have a look at this.' O'Connor rebooted the satellite images showing a powerful twenty-six-tonne missile rising majestically into the Iranian night sky from its launch pad at the missile test site at Semnan, outside of Tehran.

'They've come a long way in a very short time,' Jackson agreed. 'Their next step will be a three-stage motor . . . which will put cities like Rome and London in reach.'

O'Connor nodded. 'It may not be that far off, when you consider their first space launch – you could see bits and pieces falling off the rocket as it left the launch pad – yet barely a year later they've got a satellite into a stable orbit.'

'You think they're getting help? I've been a bit out of the loop up here.'

'I *know* they're getting help. I've seen the reports from one of our agents inside Iran. For starters, they needed maraging steel for the missile casing. That's a low-carbon, ultra-high-strength steel that's critical for low-weight missile skins. It's a controlled item under international agreements, but the Iranians have managed to buy it; so someone's selling. The tungsten copper alloy bars they needed for their solid-propellant control vanes are also a prohibited item, but somehow they've managed to get hold of them as well . . . probably out of China.'

'Why the tungsten alloy?'

'Solid propellant exhaust contains aluminium oxide, which is extremely abrasive,' O'Connor explained, 'but the Iranians have designed jet vanes that can withstand the entire sixty-second burn of the first stage of the rocket. If they can overcome the problems of an external heat shield *and* they develop a nuclear warhead, the balance of power in the world is going to change dramatically.'

'You think they're getting close?'

O'Connor nodded. 'The reports we're getting out of Iran indicate they're constructing a new uranium enrichment plant near the old city of Qom, but it's buried so deep into solid rock it will be almost impossible to attack, at least with ordinary bombs. The Pentagon is developing what it's dubbed a "massive ordnance penetrator" that contains thousands of kilograms of explosives. It'll be delivered by the stealth bomber, but even that may not be enough to deal with blast doors that are deep underground.'

'Which probably explains the pressure we're now under to fast-track our experiments here,' Jackson said grimly, 'which is madness.'

'Dangerous?'

'The science is untested, which is reason enough to be cautious.'

'Try telling that to the Vice President.'

'Exactly. Or some of the gung-ho brass in the Pentagon. Have you seen the proposals for Operation Aether?'

'Not the detail.'

'It's in three phases. The first involves a burst of three billion watts to heat and raise the ionosphere, to see if we can deflect a missile off course, and the last phase aims to develop ways of controlling the weather, which the military have been trying to do since Vietnam. But as dangerous as those experiments might be, it's the second phase that worries me most.' Jackson loaded a thumb drive into the computer on O'Connor's desk and fired up a PowerPoint presentation. It was headed 'Top Secret'.

'The second phase involves the generation of extremely low frequency, or ELF, waves directed at the earth's core, rather like the way the mining industry uses seismic tomography to search for deposits of oil and natural gas.'

'But the mining industry only uses power of about thirty to forty watts?'

'Precisely. At higher power levels we know we can X-ray the ground, and that can be useful in providing imagery on tunnels and bunkers, but the Pentagon wants to know if we can generate power levels at the extreme end of the range that can actually destroy underground installations – Iran's nuclear facilities being high on their list.'

O'Connor let out a low whistle. 'Are we seriously thinking of bombarding the earth's core with three billion watts?'

'There are powerful forces in Washington who are determined to see if it will work, and I'm afraid the director is just a puppet who'll do as he's told. Are you familiar with the Chandler wobble?'

O'Connor nodded. In 1891 an American astronomer, Seth Carlo Chandler, discovered that the earth wobbled on its axis by up to fifteen metres.

'Well,' Jackson continued, 'a highly respected Indian seismologist has pointed to data from the International Earth Rotation Service. In the three months leading up to the devastating earthquakes and tsunamis of 2004, the Chandler wobble increased significantly. Normally we might get one earthquake a year above seven on the Richter scale – what we call a "great earthquake" – but in 2004 there was a massive earthquake in the Macquarie Trench off New Zealand on 23 December, and that one measured 8.1. Just three days later, we had an even bigger earthquake . . . around nine if I remember correctly . . . triggering the tsunamis that killed hundreds of thousands on the coasts of Asia. The frequency of those great earthquakes is increasing, and the Chandler wobble is maintained by mass distribution within the molten outer core, as well as the crust and oceans.'

'So if we start bombarding the core with billions of watts of electromagnetic energy . . . '

'We might generate an even greater wobble. It's madness, but the admirals and the generals aren't listening.'

'Neither are the politicians. Is there any other data to connect the wobble with the frequency of earthquakes?'

'In 1967 two Canadian scientists came up with the Mansinha-Smylie theory connecting the earth's wobble with the big earthquakes, but mainstream science has largely ignored it. And it gets worse.'

Jackson turned to one of the centre's computers, keyed in a series of commands and pulled up an extraordinary photograph taken from the Hubble telescope. The space shuttle *Discovery* had carried the eleven-tonne Hubble into orbit in 1990. Bigger than a truck, the telescope orbited the earth every ninety-seven minutes. 'At a height of 360 kilometres, Hubble is free of any of the distortions of the earth's atmosphere, which enables us to take very clear photographs of some of the most distant objects in the universe. That's the galaxy NGC 1300, which in the scheme of things is actually quite close. It's about sixty-nine million light years away from earth, and 88 000 light years in diameter.'

O'Connor stared at the stunning image of the barred spiral galaxy, a massive swirling red-and-blue catherine-wheel in the Eridanus constellation. 'Huh. Eighty-eight thousand light years wide ... *big* doesn't seem to do it justice.'

Jackson grinned. 'No, and that's especially so when you think about the size of the universe. There are somewhere between 200 and 400 billion stars in our Milky Way galaxy alone. Multiply that by another 200 billion galaxies in the cosmos, and size is difficult to picture. With trillions of planets out there, it's absurd to think that earth is the only one with life on it, but I've chosen a photograph of the NGC 1300 galaxy because it's similar to our own and its centre is clearly visible.' Jackson pointed to the swirling image on the screen. 'The centre is a black hole of unimaginable gravitational and electromagnetic energy.'

'It looks flat – almost like a disc.'

'Precisely. As you and I both know, black holes are so power-ful they flatten everything around them. Nothing, not even light, can escape, hence the term 'black', and it's that power that keeps a galaxy's stars and solar systems in orbit. However, once every 26 000 years, our solar system travels through the same plane as the black hole in the middle of the Milky Way. In effect, if you imagine that black hole being in the middle of a dinner plate, our solar system rises to be level with the edge of the plate.' Jackson paused, weighing the impact of what he was about to say. 'That 26 000-year marker comes up again in 2012,' he said finally, 'at which time we'll be exactly opposite the black hole.'

'And that may explain some of the wild weather patterns?'

'Yes. And we're messing with the balance of the earth when its orbit is at its most unstable. On top of which, the earth's magnetic field is now at its lowest level in recorded history. The poles are skipping across the wastes of the Arctic and Antarctic at over thirty kilometres a year. If you couple that with the latest NASA data on sunspots, which are at an unprecedented power level, the planet faces an uncertain future, to put it mildly.'

'I've seen the magnetometer printouts,' O'Connor agreed, his mind racing at the size of the abyss the experiments out of Gakona might generate.

'And the sunspot power is still rising dramatically,' Jackson added, pulling up an image of massive explosions on the surface of the sun. 'NASA estimates sunspot power will also peak in 2012, at levels we've never seen before. Could be the Hopi Indians and the Maya were on to something.'

'You think there's something in all that mystic mumbo jumbo?'

'Perhaps. As a civilisation we *think* we're fairly advanced, but back in 850 AD, the Maya predicted that at 11.11 a.m. on Friday 21

December 2012 our planet would line up precisely with the Milky Way's black hole. Astronomers have now confirmed the Maya were right, down to the last second. If the Maya could make a prediction that accurate, 800 years before Galileo picked up the first telescope, maybe we should be sitting up and taking a lot more notice of their warning.'

23

WASHINGTON

Vice President Walter Montgomery was due to host some senior CIA officers at an evening function on the lawns of his official home, a stately white nineteenth-century mansion overlooking Massachusetts Avenue. He'd asked DDO Wiley to come early for a meeting in the first-floor library.

The vice presidential library was finished in white timber with light-beige wallpaper and matching lounge chairs. It had a certain New England charm about it, in the midst of which both men seemed distinctly out of place.

'I trust that asshole O'Connor's enjoying the delights of Gakona,' the Vice President said, indicating Wiley should take a seat.

'It's about as close to Siberia as I could send him, Mr Vice President. He'll stay there until I work out something more permanent.'

'Good. Now, have you seen the latest claims by that Weizman bitch?' Vice President Montgomery flung a copy of the latest edition of *The Mayan Archaeologist* onto the elegant white coffee table. The cover was dominated by a striking photograph of Dr Aleta Weizman, standing beside the Pyramid of the Lost World in the jungles of Tikal, Guatemala. The headline read:

Weizman Claims CIA Involvement in Guatemalan Genocide
Allegations made against the School of the Americas

Wiley knew the reality behind that headline lay deep in the Guatemalan jungle, and his reasons for ensuring that the truth didn't surface were far more pressing than those of the Vice President. Should he brief Montgomery on the diaries the CIA's man in San Pedro, the ex-Nazi commandant of Mauthausen, had kept? Diaries that were now missing —

'I need hardly remind you, Howard, that we go to the polls shortly,' Montgomery thundered on, 'and right now we're up to our bootstraps in hog shit in Iraq and Afghanistan. The last thing the President or I need is the media spotlight back on Intelligence or secret prisons and water-boarding. Or the fucking Guatemalans, for that matter. Or the Mexicans, Venezuelans or anyone else from that garbage dump down south. Nixon got it right about Central America. Nobody gives a fuck about the place.'

'I agree, Mr Vice President. It's a shit box.'

'I don't care how you do it, but put some heat on this Weizman woman. Find out who controls archaeologists' licences and send them a donation from a grateful nation with the proviso she gets blacklisted. Anyone who thinks that someone other than Columbus discovered America doesn't deserve to have a licence. And put her under surveillance. If she even looks like exposing our operations in Guatemala, Paraguay or anywhere else, get rid of her. Meantime, keep the CIA out of the fucking media.'

'Leave it to me, Mr Vice President. By the time I've finished with Weizman, and O'Connor for that matter, the AP numbers will look even better.' Wiley and Montgomery had both been greatly encouraged by an Associated Press poll that had claimed twelve per cent of Americans had either never heard of the CIA or couldn't rate it.

As the DDO left the vice presidential residence later in the evening, a move was already taking shape on Wiley's sinister chessboard. It was a move that would require the recall of O'Connor from Gakona, but it would eliminate Weizman permanently.

24

CIA HEADQUARTERS, LANGLEY, VIRGINIA

Unlike his predecessor, Howard Wiley always kept his office door closed. O'Connor, ignoring the protestations of Wiley's secretary, knocked firmly and walked in. The first thing O'Connor noticed was the modern furniture. His previous assignment had involved a Muslim terrorist threat against the Beijing Olympics. Back then the DDO, Tom McNamara, had been an understanding ally, pressing for negotiation with the Iranians and the Syrians, rather than committing the United States to another bloody war they couldn't win in the Middle East. The cracked and torn brown leather couches McNamara insisted on keeping had been almost welcoming; but they had gone, along with his old boss's familiar greeting of 'Come in, buddy. Have a seat.'

'You took your time getting here, O'Connor. Sit down,' Wiley ordered without looking up, gesturing to a small straight-backed chair as he continued to read from a crimson dossier that lay open on his polished desk.

O'Connor smiled to himself. Offering someone a small chair and then ignoring their presence was the classic authoritarian bully tactic, designed to make people nervous, and was often employed by individuals who were highly insecure themselves. O'Connor glanced around the refurnished room. The office was lit by a number of tasteful table lamps, and the panelled walls were decorated with oils of the Civil War. Myriad photographs of Wiley with various visiting dignitaries were scattered around the office. Amongst the most prominent was that of Wiley shaking hands with George W. Bush, and one with the Vice President at the School of the Americas, but it was the framed photographs on a side table that caught O'Connor's eye. The first was a photograph of Wiley and Pope John Paul II, together with an archbishop he couldn't identify. In time he would come to know Salvatore Felici very well.

Unlike the archbishop, the man with Wiley in the second photograph was instantly recognisable. A very young Wiley was standing outside Washington's Mayflower Hotel with a smiling J. Edgar Hoover, Director of the FBI. The DDO continued to ignore him, and O'Connor wondered about Wiley's early relationship with Hoover. Howard Wiley, O'Connor knew, had never married. He'd started his career in the FBI, and his stellar rise had attracted widespread comment in an old-fashioned media not renowned for their criticism of a public hero like Hoover. Within six months, a young, wet-behind-the-ears Wiley, with virtually no field experience, had been appointed to Hoover's personal staff at FBI headquarters.

'I've got a new assignment for you, O'Connor,' Wiley said finally.

'And I was just getting used to Alaska.'

The DDO glared at O'Connor. Howard Wiley was known

throughout the intelligence community as 'the Weasel'. He had a square face, a long thin nose and a high forehead. His reddish, spiky hair was brushed back without a part. Barely five-foot four, Wiley was vertically challenged, and O'Connor wondered whether Wiley's ruthless arrogance was a product of Napoleon Syndrome, an early close association with J. Edgar Hoover, or just a case of having the DNA of an asshole. Probably a combination of all three, O'Connor thought wryly. 'Our file on Dr Aleta Weizman,' Wiley said, pushing the slim file across the desk. 'She's an archaeologist working for that tin-pot Guatemalan government we silenced a decade ago. Archaeologists should stick to digging up old bones. This one's got a very big mouth.'

'I would have thought that with bin Laden and his Jihadists, not to mention the Taliban, we've got more important things on our plate than obscure archaeologists, Howard.'

Wiley's face turned the colour of his hair. 'I'll decide what's fucking important around here, O'Connor,' he exploded, clenching his fist and slamming it on the desk. 'Just find out everything there is to know about this Weizman bitch, then silence her!'

'That seems excessive. She might be on the front cover, but *The Mayan Archaeologist*'s probably got a print run in single figures. Hardly mainstream news.'

The DDO glared at O'Connor again, the veins near his temple clearly visible. 'You're skating on fucking thin ice, O'Connor. The Vice President's pretty pissed over your suggestions about negotiating with terrorists, so I suggest you leave the analysis to me, and do as you're fucking told!'

Wiley's words confirmed O'Connor's suspicions. This was coming right from the top, and the weasel was keeping to the letter of the CIA's manual of assassination. *Never write anything down.*

'Weizman is attending some archaeological circle wank in Vienna next month,' Wiley continued, his eyes still blazing. 'And you're going as someone who has an interest in Mayan archaeology, so I suggest you get busy on the jargon.' Wiley drew himself up to what he could muster in height, indicating the meeting was at an end. O'Connor suppressed a grin. Wiley looked shorter standing up than he did sitting down.

O'Connor left Wiley's office deep in thought. A sixth sense, honed by countless hours on assignment in the field, told him there was more to the Weizman case. Wiley was hiding something, but what? O'Connor knew the involvement of the CIA and the White House in Guatemala had been long and bloody. Had Dr Weizman somehow stumbled onto the CIA's operations in Central America? He headed for the CIA's archives.

Howard Wiley stared out the window of his office for several minutes, his anger still at boiling point. The Vice President was right: O'Connor had a bad attitude – he could not be trusted. As he opened his usual full inbox of emails, Wiley knew he would need a back-up plan to ensure his orders were carried out. He clicked open an email from Salvatore Felici, now a senior cardinal at the Vatican.

Greetings, my friend, and congratulations on your new appointment - very well deserved!

The Holy Father asked me to pass on his thanks for last

week's briefing on the Middle East. Most informative, and rest assured the Cardinal Secretary of State will do everything he can to support your president's efforts in this troubled region.

In the meantime, we are increasingly concerned over Central America and the threats this region poses to the Holy Church, and we are dismayed by the groundswell of support for liberation theology. Pope John Paul II was unequivocally opposed to this movement and the policy has not changed under the new pontiff. If anything, our opposition has strengthened.

I have also attached an article by a Guatemalan archaeologist, Dr Weizman. You will recall we had to deal with her father when we were in Guatemala City. The daughter presents an even bigger danger. She is not only critical of both the CIA and the Vatican, but I understand from my own sources that she is now investigating deaths in her family. This is a grassfire for the moment, but must be dealt with before it gets out of control and embarrasses both our interests.

Wiley sucked his teeth in annoyance. Emails between Felici's office and Wiley's were encrypted for transmission, but they remained unencrypted at the source and Felici had broken a very explicit rule. The operation they were contemplating should *never* be written down, he thought, scanning the rest of the correspondence.

It would be most useful to discuss these issues of mutual concern in person. How soon can you come to Rome? The regular briefing from your station staff here could focus on

the Central American region, and if time allows, we will organise a private audience with the Holy Father.

I have just received some cases of outstanding wine from
friends in Bordeaux, so we can discuss the finer points of
these matters over one or two excellent bottles of red.

Yours in Christ,

Salvatore Felici

Howard Wiley swivelled in his chair and stared unseeingly across
the grassland towards the trees and the Potomac River beyond. He
drummed his fingers on his desk. The mission he had given O'Connor
was totally deniable, and if O'Connor were to meet with an unfortunate accident, no one would question it. He needed to tap Felici for
contacts in some of the darker back alleys of Rome. Pope Pius XII's
decoration of General 'Wild Bill' Donovan with the Grand Cross of
the Order of Sylvester had paid dividends, and since World War Two,
the bond between the Vatican and the CIA had strengthened even
further. In 1978 President Carter's wife, Rosalynn, had a private audience with Pope John Paul II, during which she delivered a letter from
Washington that formalised what had been going on since Donovan's
time. The Carter letter approved regular CIA briefings for the pontiff
and his senior cardinals. Now, if they needed to, both the director of the
CIA and Wiley could reach His Holiness on his private line, Vatican
extension 3101, but Wiley routinely dealt with Cardinal Felici.

Cardinal Felici's email was timely. The CIA's station in Rome was
only a short distance from the Vatican, and it would be no trouble
to organise a special briefing on the growing threat to the Catholic
Church in Central America.

25

VIENNA

The Mayan conference was not due to start until 8.30 a.m., but O'Connor was in position by seven, choosing a nearby coffee shop from which he could observe the entrance to Aleta's apartment in the Stephansdom Quarter.

Three-quarters of an hour later, Dr Weizman emerged from her apartment wearing a tailored black pants-suit and spike-heeled ankle boots. O'Connor followed at a discreet distance, watching her descend the path that led towards the *Schwarzenplatz* U-Bahn station. Satisfied, he retraced his steps. The entrance to her apartment block was in Sterngasse, not far from Shakespeare and Company, one of Vienna's best-known British bookshops. The big double wooden doors that opened onto the lower courtyard were heavy, but for a man of O'Connor's expertise, they were not an obstacle. He checked the narrow street, but there were only three pedestrians and they were all heading away from him. The cast-iron latch flipped back easily under his knife blade. Closing the door behind him, he found himself in a deserted stone courtyard with several entrances, all protected by steel security doors.

Apartment number four was listed under the intercom on the nearest entrance and identified by just the name 'Weizman'. Like most security doors, O'Connor reflected, they provided more psychological peace of mind than actual protection, and he slipped a small tension wrench into the simple five-pin and tumbler barrel lock and applied pressure on the plug. Using a small diamond-shaped pick, he quickly raked the pins, before again working his way from the rear of the barrel to force up two that were not yet flush with the shear line.

The cam turned easily and O'Connor quietly swung the steel door open. Climbing to the second floor, he was again confronted with a pin-and-tumbler lock. At his first attempt, the lock didn't open. O'Connor delved into his soft leather briefcase and selected a pick with a finer head. Top student of more than one of the CIA's training courses, O'Connor fleetingly thought of the old master safecracker who'd been recruited from the dark side to teach CIA officers the art of break and enter. To the south-east of Richmond, Virginia, on Rochambeau Drive, was a place listed as the Camp Peary Naval Reservation. In fact, it was one of several top-secret CIA training bases where O'Connor had spent many hours honing the shadowy crafts of his profession. As he applied just enough pressure to hold the rear pins over the shear line, he carefully felt for the final pin and eased it up over the ledge he'd created with the torsion wrench.

O'Connor closed the solid cedar door quietly behind him. A short hallway led into the lounge room, which overlooked *Sterngasse* and *Judengasse*. To the left another corridor led past the spacious kitchen to the bedrooms and the bathroom at the far end. He looked around the lounge room. Soft white wool carpets and gold-and-black velvet drapes complemented the rococo Louis XV furniture. The walls were lined with mahogany bookcases, and O'Connor quickly ran his eye over the contents. Given Weizman's background, it was not surprising to find whole shelves devoted to archaeology, and in particular to the Maya. There were works by the legendary Alfred Maudslay, who in the late nineteenth century opened up the ancient Mayan civilisation to more modern research; as well as publications by J E S Thompson on *Maya Arithmetic* and *The Solar Year of the Mayas*. Other shelves were devoted to works by Newton, Einstein, Erwin Schrödinger and Max Planck, the latter three inscribed by the famous authors to Professor Levi Weizman. O'Connor whistled softly as he recalled his earlier years at Trinity College in Dublin, where he'd wrestled with Schrödinger's equations that described fiendishly difficult issues in quantum mechanics, like the movement of an electron around an atom. Levi Weizman had obviously rubbed shoulders with some of the finest scientists the world had seen.

The spacious apartment had three bedrooms, one of which was again lined from floor to ceiling with books. O'Connor tried the large wall safe, but it was locked. It would take time to crack it, so he left it for the moment and turned his attention to the main bedroom. He carefully went through it, but found nothing to explain Washington's interest. He picked up a folder entitled *Bad Arolsen Records* from the bedside table and flicked through it. In 2006 the German government had finally agreed to release the Nazi records on seventeen million people who had been imprisoned, tortured or murdered at the hands of the Third Reich. Two books were also on the bedside table, *The Popol Vuh*, the sacred book of the ancient Quiché Maya, one of the most powerful Mayan tribes of the Guatemalan highlands, and *The Hidden Maya Code* by Monsignor Matthias Jennings. O'Connor surmised that Weizman might be attending Jennings' lecture. He replaced the book exactly where he'd found it and headed for the bathroom.

O'Connor opened the bathroom cabinet. Amongst Aleta's personal toiletries there was a single bottle of medication labelled 'Sarafem', half-full of purple-pink capsules. He examined the capsules and compared them to the wide range of pills in different colours, shapes and sizes in his briefcase. He wondered why Aleta might have been prescribed fluoxetine, otherwise known as Prozac, and then as Sarafem for women. Might Aleta be taking it for a severe form of premenstrual syndrome? Or could she be clinically depressed? The latter might be more likely, he thought, although with the administration at 1600 Pennsylvania Avenue wanting her head on a plate, Weizman's medical issues were perhaps the least of her problems.

O'Connor selected a sachet from his briefcase and chose an identical pill to those in Dr Weizman's bottle, a pill the boys back in Science and Technology at Langley had dubbed 'aspirin roulette'. The purple capsule contained a massive dose of morphine, equivalent to 200 milligrams of heroin, more than twice the dose required to kill even severe addicts with high resistance. The Polizei would find morphine in her bloodstream and the media would speculate, but with a lack of motive and the absence of any other poisoned pills in the bottle, the Polizei would suspect she was on drugs, the media would lose interest and the coroner would be forced to reach an open finding.

O'Connor paused as he recalled his conversation with Wiley back at Langley: 'Find out everything there is to know about this Weizman bitch, and then silence her!' Again the question demanded an answer . . . why? 'You're skating on fucking thin ice, O'Connor.'

For the first time in a long career, Curtis O'Connor disobeyed an order that had been put to him as a 'clear and present danger', an order that only the President could approve. O'Connor doubted the President had any idea of what the Vice President, Wiley or the hotheads in the Pentagon were up to. He put the aspirin roulette pill back into the sachet in his briefcase. The CIA was not the same agency he'd joined nearly twenty years before; and not until he worked out why Washington wanted this woman dead would he comply.

26

THE VATICAN, ROME

The Prefect of the Congregation for the Doctrine of the Faith, Cardinal Salvatore Felici, was working at his huge desk in his opulent office in the *Palazzo della Sacra Inquisizione*. A forbidding grey-and-ochre palace, it still went by the name of the Sacred Inquisition. Felici's father, Alberto, had been a trusted advisor to Pope Pius XII and the cardinal was carrying on in his family's tradition of service to the Holy Church.

Tall and powerfully built, Cardinal Felici was proud of his good head of fine black hair, flecked with grey and combed straight back under his scarlet zucchetto, the distinctive skull cap of the College of Cardinals. He had a long rectangular face, and a large aquiline nose. His piercing grey eyes were hooded, underscored by dark circles, but, like a peregrine falcon, Salvatore Felici missed nothing. His anger rose as he again scrutinised an article by the Guatemalan archaeologist, Dr Weizman, dutifully forwarded to his office by the papal nuncio in Guatemala City. Felici's red pen was poised to strike as he absorbed her assertions on the existence of a lost codex, and tried to decipher the intermeshing glyphs on Aleta's diagram of the Mayan calendars:

Unlike our own linear calendars, the Mayan calendars, as the diagram shows, measured time in short and long cycles which enabled them to accurately predict major recurring events. The Mayan short- and long-count calendars intermeshed like gears in a gearbox. The larger wheel, the *Haab*, was based on cycles of the earth, using eighteen months with twenty days in a month giving 360 days. A short nineteenth month consisted of the extra five days, totalling 365. The smaller gear, the sacred *Tzolk'in*, was based on the cycles of the Pleiades star cluster in the constellation Taurus, so prominent in the night skies of planet earth. The twenty-first of December 2012 heralds a rare once-in-26 000 years meshing of calendar gears that can predict four days, 4000 or 40 000 days in advance.

We are living in the Mayan end times, an end time that is dictated precisely by the movement of the planets. The great 26 000-year cycle, or 25 625 years to be precise, consists of five smaller cycles, each 5125 years in length, and the Maya discovered that our sun, which they called *Kinich-Ahau*, synchronises with the centre of our galaxy once in each of the smaller cycles.

There is an abundance of evidence that proves the accuracy of Mayan predictions. Over a thousand years before it occurred, the Maya predicted the solar eclipse on 11 August 1999 down to the last second – 11:03:07 universal coordinated time – an eclipse that

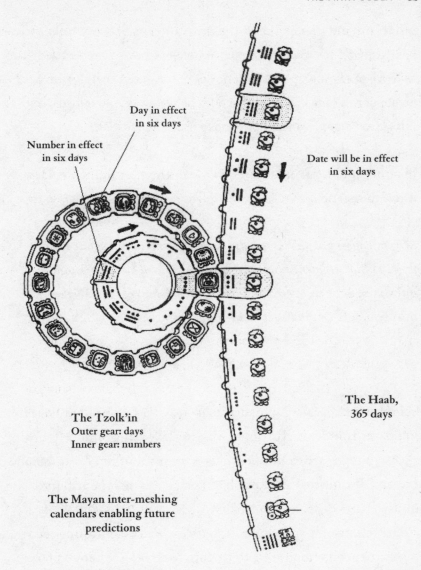

Number in effect
in six days

Day in effect
in six days

Date will be in effect
in six days

The Tzolk'in
Outer gear: days
Inner gear: numbers

The Haab,
365 days

The Mayan inter-meshing
calendars enabling future
predictions

was the most watched in history and the first visible in the United

Kingdom since 1927.

We are now in the fifth cycle of the sun. Mayan stelae recovered

from Guatemala record that four previous civilisations have been

totally destroyed by horrendous apocalypses driven by the alignment of the sun with the centre of the galaxy. Intense energy from the centre generates solar flares of unimaginable power, coupled with a reversal of the sun's own magnetic field. So, is there anything we can do about this? An ancient Maya codex holds the keys to our survival, but Mayan elders remain tight-lipped about its location.

In his fine, spidery hand, Felici wrote in the margin of *The Mayan Archaeologist* article:

Mayan pagan practices have always been a threat to the one true faith. Libraries burned for good reason. If Maya Codex exists, imperative it be recovered and stored in secret archives – Weizman is searching for it, and needs watching.

Felici returned the magazine to his in-tray and glanced at the photograph of Tomás de Torquemada displayed prominently on his bookcase, a man he constantly drew on for inspiration. Torquemada, the Grand Inquisitor of Spain, had been a staunch guardian of the Faith.

Felici rose from his desk, his Italian leather shoes sinking into the crimson carpet as he moved to the opposite wall where *St Jerome*, Leonardo da Vinci's priceless oil on wood, on loan from the Vatican's Pinacoteca, dominated the room. Saint Jerome was Salvatore Felici's favourite saint. In 393 AD Jerome had denounced sexual intercourse as corrupt, and Felici, too, believed that apart from the purposes of procreation, married couples should abstain from sexual activity altogether. He swung the painting aside, dialled the combination of his wall safe, extracted a crimson file embossed in gold with his personal coat of arms, replaced the painting and returned to his desk. The file held copies of the CIA documents on Dr Weizman that Howard Wiley had forwarded the previous week in the diplomatic bag. The file also held the regular reports from the papal nuncio in Guatemala City, many of them charting the rise of those left-wing governments in the Americas that were opposed to the Church in Rome.

Felici sank back into his plush red-leather chair. Deep in thought, he looked out the palazzo windows towards the 300-year-old columns of Bernini's Colonnade across the *Piazza San Pietro*. The *Palazzo della Sacra Inquisizione*, adjacent to the *Porta Cavalleggeri*, one of the ancient gates in the walls of the Vatican, had been built in 1571 by Pope Pius V to house what was then known as the Supreme Sacred Congregation of the Roman and Universal Inquisition. In the sixteenth century the Holy Church condoned the Inquisition's widespread use of torture. For those who refused to reconcile with the Catholic faith, that torture included burning at the stake, a policy that turned the Vatican's Inquisition into one of the most feared offices in Europe. The Holy Church's successor to the Inquisition had been given a softer title – the Congregation for the Doctrine of the Faith – but it was still housed in the same palace and still charged with investigating heresy. As Aleta had pointed out elsewhere in her article, Cardinal Joseph Ratzinger had towered over the modern-day Inquisition for nearly twenty-four years, earning the nickname of 'God's rottweiler', before being elected Pope Benedict XVI in 2005. It was a career path Cardinal Salvatore Felici had every intention of following. At sixty-two, in terms of being *papabile*, a future contender for the papacy and the Keys of Peter, Felici was still young; but he alone knew that if his past ever surfaced, his career would be finished.

Agitated, he fiddled with the solid gold pectoral cross that was suspended over his crimson silk sash on a heavy gold chain. The chain was attached to one of the thirty-three silk buttons of his soutane, each button symbolising one year in the life of Christ. The unusual cross, encrusted with a large ruby surrounded by twelve large diamonds, had been acquired by his father during the war. Felici turned his attention to the growing threats posed to the Holy Church in Latin America. The threat came not only from newly elected governments, but from outspoken academics, and of the latter Dr Aleta Weizman was at the top of his list. He opened her CIA file but was interrupted by a soft knock on the heavy office doors. Felici's private secretary, Father Cordona, closed the door behind him.

'The CIA delegation is on its way, Eminence. His Holiness's chamberlain has collected them and they will arrive at the Arch of the Bells in twenty minutes, from where they will be escorted to His Holiness's private library.'

Felici knew the procedure by heart, but it was his nature to want to be briefed on every detail of every visit.

'And the briefing aids?'

'His Holiness's private secretary has personally checked them, Eminence.'

'Who else is attending?'

'The Cardinal Secretary of State, and His Holiness has asked that the prefects for the Congregation for Bishops, the Congregation for the Clergy and the Congregation for Catholic Education be there as well.'

Felici clicked his tongue in annoyance. He networked and dined his fellow cardinals assiduously, but he had a low regard for all of them, and he guarded his own intelligence, especially from the powerful and ambitious Cardinal Secretary of State.

'His Holiness felt that since all of the prefects are asked to report on the appointments for our bishops in the Americas, they should be there, Eminence,' Father Cordona added, reading his cardinal's mind.

'You have scheduled dinner this evening?'

'Il Signor Wiley will join you for dinner at eight in your private dining room. The menu and the wine list are in your tray. Will there be anything else, Eminence?'

'No,' Cardinal Felici replied. Well accustomed to his cardinal's irascibility, Father Cordona withdrew.

Felici prepared to make the short walk across the *Piazza San Pietro* to the Papal Palace, his mind absolutely focused. The papal nuncio in Guatemala City had already provided evidence that Dr Weizman was not only searching for the Maya Codex, but that she was investigating the links between the CIA and the death squads in Central America. Worse still, Felici now knew she was also looking into the links between the CIA and the Vatican. Dr Weizman was far more dangerous than she appeared.

27

MUSEUM OF NATURAL HISTORY, VIENNA

.

The *Naturhistorisches Museum Wien* held one of the largest natural history collections in the world. Aleta Weizman had spent the break after the morning presentations wandering amongst enormous mammoths, dinosaurs, pterodactyls and other rare fossils of a bygone era. On her way back to the conference room, she crossed the main foyer, which was dominated by a huge stuffed elk. A massive lion, fangs bared, challenged the elk from the other side of the foyer. Aleta climbed a short flight of steps to the mezzanine floor and as she took one of the seats close to the front, she saw that Matthias Jennings was already on the dais. She wasn't surprised by the sizeable media contingent assembled at the back of the room; the controversial Jesuit priest created headlines wherever he went. Behind her, Curtis O'Connor slipped into the room and took a seat near the side wall at the back, a position from which he could observe the entire room.

'Ladies and gentlemen, it is my great pleasure to introduce

Monsignor Matthias Jennings, although to many in this audience he needs no introduction at all!' The President of the European Mayanist Society chuckled at his worn-out joke and Monsignor Jennings inclined his head.

Pompous prick, O'Connor thought, glancing at Aleta to gauge her reaction, but her expression told him nothing. He scanned the rest of the audience and noted that the swarthy, fit-looking young man who'd arrived late and sneaked into the back row didn't seem to belong. O'Connor felt in his pocket for the latest high-resolution miniature camera the agency's techs had provided and, choosing his moment, he quietly recorded the man's face.

'Thank you, Mr President,' Jennings replied, moving to the lectern. 'As a Fellow of this society, it is an honour to be able to update everyone on my latest research.' His garish yellow bow tie clashed alarmingly with his dark-red shirt. Monsignor Jennings not only had bizarre dress sense, O'Connor thought, he had a body to match. A large, portly man with a ruddy face, Jennings parted his thinning red hair down near his left ear, sweeping it up in heavily greased strands over a bald, pink pate. He wore thick black glasses on the end of a bulbous nose. His watery blue eyes were restless and his heavy, unkempt bushy red eyebrows seemed to defy gravity.

'There has been a great deal of alarmist speculation in the media about a coming cataclysm, including, apparently, a collapse of the earth's magnetic field and an increase in sunspot activity accompanying a pole shift in 2012. All this has been supposedly predicted by the ancient Maya,' he began, pointedly looking over the top of his glasses towards the media contingent.

'I've always been of the view that those who espouse this nonsense know nothing of the true nature of the ancient Maya. Far from being an educated, spiritual people who were in touch with nature, they were amongst the most ignorant and bloodthirsty people in the entire history of mankind. The Maya make Attila the Hun look a very suitable candidate for the boys choir in this very city. I've spent a lifetime researching this primitive civilisation, and in the past year I've had access to some exciting new hieroglyphs recovered from a recently discovered tomb in Tikal.' Jennings flicked on a PowerPoint presentation and a series of images appeared on a screen suspended from the ceiling. 'These stelae – for those at the back of the room, stone monuments on which the Maya engraved their complex messages in glyphs – clearly show the daily life in a Mayan city in all its gruesome detail. Stela One, shown here, depicts the mass rape of young boys and girls. Quite commonplace.' Jennings sniffed haughtily. 'Stela Two, which was discovered in thick jungle north-east of Tikal, clearly shows the absolute disregard for human life so typical of the Maya, who thought nothing of ripping still-beating hearts out of their captives' chests, in grisly and macabre sacrifices to their pagan gods.'

As the lecture ground on, O'Connor noticed that Aleta was studying the Jesuit priest with intense interest. At times she quietly shook her head, her full lips pursed in a thin angry line. Was it the savagery of the Maya, or the Monsignor's interpretation that had angered her? O'Connor breathed a sigh of relief when Jennings brought his dissertation to a close and the society's president invited questions from the floor.

'I note with interest your description of the Maya as ignorant and bloodthirsty, Monsignor.' The voice held a distinct authority.

'No one would deny that sacrifice was part of Mayan ritual, but I would suggest that it took place very much in the late post-Classical period and was linked to the warlike Aztecs and Toltecs to the north. Sacrifice was most often associated with war, and if we compare the Mayan propensity for fighting with our own readiness to wage war, I would put it to you that they were somewhat less bloodthirsty than we are.'

O'Connor grinned. There was a delightful Spanish lilt to Aleta's accent and her English was perfect. The eminent Jesuit priest looked furious.

'Not only that, the Maya were often known to settle their differences with their ancient ball-court game, rather than resorting to war, as we so often do. As to their gods, it seems to me that most of humankind's wars have at their base, disagreements in religious outlook: Islamic fundamentalists and terrorism, the Catholics and the Protestants in Northern Ireland, the President's claim that God told him to invade Afghanistan, Iraq, right back to the Crusades . . . I would suggest that far from being the ignorant race you have described, the Maya were responsible for some of the greatest achievements in astronomy and architecture, as well as being possessed of a deep spirituality; a belief that a spiritual force is clearly present in every aspect of the natural world.'

O'Connor could sense the anticipation of the media pack. Several journalists and cameramen were grinning broadly. The pompous Jesuit priest had at last been challenged by someone other than their own.

'Who's she?' one journalist whispered.

'Dr Aleta Weizman,' a journalist from *The Times* replied.

'A Guatemalan, but her grandfather lived and worked in Vienna. She's well on her way to being just as famous as he was.'

'I must say, I'm surprised, Dr Weizman, that your assessment doesn't demonstrate a more scholarly approach. Then again, you're a woman, and you haven't enjoyed the untrammelled access to ancient artefacts that is afforded to scholars of my standing.' Jennings sniffed again.

O'Connor watched the exchange with interest. To the outside world Aleta Weizman might be an obscure archaeologist, but she was obviously known to the Monsignor, and to some of the journalists.

'Why so surprised, Monsignor?' the *Times* journalist challenged in support of Aleta. 'Are you denying the ancient Maya's ability to chart the movement of the planets? And are you suggesting we should ignore the alignment of those planets in 2012?'

'That mystical nonsense is entirely overblown. I predict without a shadow of a doubt that 21 December 2012 will have as much effect on our planet as Y2K – another date you media people played for all it was worth.'

'You yourself have admitted that the Maya also warned that a geographical or magnetic pole shift would be associated with increased sunspot activity,' a journalist from Montreal's *Gazette* said. 'Some scientists, including those at NASA, have confirmed the Mayan predictions of a massive peak in sunspot activity in 2012, and there's evidence we're already experiencing increasingly violent solar storm activity. Two years ago solar storms brought down the entire electrical grid in Quebec. Long-range radio communications and GPS navigation satellites were crippled and aeroplanes had to be rerouted to avoid the worst of it. Don't you think if an ancient civilisation had advanced knowledge of what might happen in 2012, we should at least explore what that might mean?'

'Increased sunspot activity is nothing new,' Jennings responded irritably.

'There've been persistent rumours over the years of a missing Maya Codex, Monsignor.' The young journalist from *Women's World* seized her opportunity to turn the conference in a direction her readers might find more interesting. 'A codex that might give us advance warning of a catastrophe . . . one that might enable some of us to survive. Do you place any credence in these reports?'

'This so-called Maya Codex is nothing more than a figment of the media's imagination,' Jennings snorted and waddled over to a large whiteboard. 'Unfortunately most of the records of the ancient Maya were burned during the Spanish invasion. The few codices that survived, the Dresden Codex, the Madrid Codex and the Paris Codex – named after the cities in which they now reside – as well as the Grolier fragment, were produced on *huun*, the Mayan paper produced from the bark of the *Ficus continifolia* or *Ficus padifolia*, the largest of the strangler figs.' The journalist from *Women's World* turned to her photographer and crossed her eyes.

Jennings continued, '*Huun* being far more durable than the papyrus from ancient Egypt, I have had the rare distinction, the very rare distinction, of being able to study all the originals at first hand. Of the four, the Dresden Codex is the one that sheds most light on these bloodthirsty savages who would think nothing of sacrificing their own children, throwing them into the *cenotes*, the sink holes on the Yucatán Peninsula that connect with underground rivers. And while these codices have undoubtedly helped in deciphering the savagery of the Maya, there are no references to any forthcoming catastrophe – none whatsoever,' Jennings concluded decisively.

Aleta shook her head. Modern science had confirmed the rare planetary alignment the Maya had warned of, and Aleta knew Jennings had to be aware of the evidence for the missing codex, yet he dismissed it as a figment of the media's imagination. Who or what was he protecting? The Vatican? Could there be something in the codex that threatened the Vatican itself?

After the lecture, Aleta spotted Dr José Arana standing quietly at the end of the front row of chairs, and she made her way towards him.

'Aleta Weizman, Dr Arana,' she said, proffering her hand. 'We met once or twice when I was a child in San Marcos. I've been wanting to speak with you.'

'So . . . at last you have come,' he replied softly, taking Aleta by the arm. 'You are in grave danger.'

28

THE VATICAN, ROME

Earlier in the day Santissimo Padre, Pope Benedict XVI, had emerged from his high-ceilinged corner bedroom on the fourth floor of the Apostolic Palace on the northern side of the *Piazza San Pietro*. His two private secretaries were waiting for him in the corridor, and, together, the three men walked briskly towards the bronze door of the Pope's private chapel. Unlike his predecessor, Pope John Paul II, who frequently invited guests to the early morning mass, Benedict XVI preferred a private ceremony with his aides. Discarding the newer form of the mass that came into use following Vatican II, Benedict started his day with the 1962 Roman Missal in Latin.

'*In nomine Patris, et Filii, et Spiritus Sancti* . . . In the name of the Father, and of the Son, and of the Holy Spirit . . .'

The chapel was cold. The marble floor and walls offered little in the way of warmth, but the Holy Father didn't seem to notice as he concentrated on his communion. A soft light diffused through the Luigi Filocamo leadlight ceiling depicting Christ resurrected, mingling with the light from three candles flickering beneath the large bronze crucifix.

'*Gloria in excelsis Deo. Et in terra pax hominibus bonae voluntatis* . . . Glory in the highest to God. And on earth, peace to men of good will . . . '

Not far away, Sister Ingrid and the other nuns of the papal household were ensuring that everything was in readiness for the Pontiff's breakfast of coffee and fruit, laid out on the serving table in the dining room next to the Pope's bedroom. The carved walnut dining table could seat ten, but this morning just three places were set for Benedict and his two private secretaries, and Sister Ingrid had already checked to see that the major national papers were laid out on one of the two sideboards.

Salvatore Felici ignored the salute of the Swiss Guard as he passed through the bronze doors to the Apostolic Palace, his mind focused on the meeting ahead. He powered towards the lift that would take him to the Pope's private library on the fourth floor.

The library was dominated by Perugino's oil, *The Resurrection of Christ*, hanging in the centre of the wall opposite the door. The electronic projector for the CIA presentation seemed out of place alongside the two walls of heavy sixteenth-century bookcases containing an impressive set of all the Papal Encyclicals, as well as the complete collections of the Church Fathers. An old bible was open on a small sixteenth-century table, and Romano's *Madonna* panel highlighted the wall behind the Pope's desk. Three windows looked over the *Piazza San Pietro*. The Cardinal Secretary of State, and the Cardinal Prefects for the Congregations for Bishops, the Clergy and Catholic Education were already present, soutanes edged in red, gold pectoral crosses on solid gold chains over red watered-silk sashes, and each wearing a red zucchetto. Felici nodded politely to the assembled group before turning to Howard Wiley.

'Howard, how good to see you again,' he said. 'I trust the flight was not too arduous?'

'Even with a CIA jet, we all have to put up with airports, Salvatore,' Wiley replied. His smile was mechanical, and his grey eyes restless. 'You know my chief of station, Richard Snider?'

'Of course. Richard.' Felici offered a fine, bony hand as one of the Pope's private secretaries slipped into the library, quietly announcing that His Holiness was approaching. Moments later, he arrived, with a second secretary in tow.

'Santissimo Padre, may I present Signor Howard Wiley, Deputy Director of Operations for the CIA. And of course you know his chief of station, Signor Richard Snider.'

'Welcome to the Vatican,' the Pope replied with a charming smile, extending his ring for Howard Wiley to kiss. He spoke English with a thick Bavarian accent. 'I'm grateful for this briefing, Signor Wiley. Central America is perhaps not as stable as we would wish?' His Holiness observed, taking a chair.

'Indeed it is not, which is a cause for some concern,' Wiley replied, taking charge of the briefing and flashing up a map of Central and South America on the screen. 'Recent elections in Nicaragua, Brazil, Ecuador and Venezuela have seen Central and

South America moving well to the left, Holiness, and the United States is keeping a careful watch on these developments. As you're aware, a former Catholic bishop, Bishop Fernando Lugo has been elected President of Paraguay. The first bishop ever to be elected to the presidency of a country, Lugo has been much impressed by liberation theology. He's the first president of Paraguay since 1946 who has not come from the conservative Colorado Party, which up until this election had been the longest continuously serving party government in the world.'

Felici scrutinised the Pope for his reaction. Since Lugo's election, speculation had been rife that, having refused his resignation, the Pope would now defrock the man who was known throughout Paraguay as 'the priest of the poor'. The pontiff remained inscrutable.

'Lugo does not intend to move to the Presidential Palace,' Wiley continued, 'and he recently stated that Paraguay will no longer accept intervention from any country, no matter how big. That sort of rhetoric causes us some concern as it puts in doubt the viability of our Paraguayan military base, which we established in 2005 at Mariscal Estigarribia, 200 kilometres from the Bolivian border.'

'Do you have a presence there?' the Pontiff asked.

Wiley nodded. 'After Paraguay granted us immunity from prosecution by any Paraguayan court or the International Criminal Court, we deployed equipment and some 500 troops. That base is capable of housing up to 16 000 troops. It will be important, Holiness, with the enormous gas reserves in countries like Bolivia, for the US to maintain influence in the Andes. We do have a forward base in Manta on the coast of Ecuador, but since the election of the left's Rafael Correa in that country, the viability of that base is also in doubt.'

'Perhaps, Holiness, it's time to take a harder line with Bishop Lugo, and consider excommunication?' Felici suggested.

'Excommunication would be a very grave step, Holiness,' the Cardinal Secretary of State interjected. 'A bishop's sacrament is for life, and it is many centuries since the Church has taken such drastic action. Even if he has been influenced by liberation theology, if we take on Bishop Lugo, with his reputation as a priest for the peasants and the poor, it may weaken our position.'

'Appeasement didn't work with Hitler, Holiness, and it won't work with Lugo and Central America,' Felici retaliated, glaring at the Secretary of State.

The Cardinal Secretary of State raised a quizzical eyebrow. Given the Vatican's sordid involvement with the Nazis during World War Two, the irony of Felici's argument was heavy, but the veteran diplomat remained silent.

'They are arguments we will have to take into account,' the Pontiff replied, the use of the authoritative 'we' an indication that he wasn't going to be rushed. 'Do you have the same concerns over other Latin American countries, Mr Wiley?'

'Unfortunately yes, and if I may, Holiness, there are dangers for the Church there as well,' Wiley added, coming to Felici's aid. 'Hugo Chávez of Venezuela, for example, is not only a vehement opponent of the United States and our efforts to bring democracy to this region, but he's also fiercely critical of the Catholic Church.'

'Whilst proclaiming himself to be a Christian and calling Christ the greatest socialist in history!' Felici added.

Wiley nodded. 'In recent years Chávez's supporters, known collectively as the Chavistas, invaded the chancery of the Archdiocese of

Caracas, expelling Bishop Jesús González de Zárate into the street. It was perhaps fortunate that Cardinal Velasco was not there at the time.'

The pontiff nodded. 'Yes. They were claiming, quite erroneously, that we supported the 2002 coup attempt against President Chávez.' Felici and Wiley exchanged glances.

'Added to that, Holiness,' Wiley continued, 'almost every government in the region is leaning towards the left. Evo Morales in Bolivia, Michelle Bachelet in Chile, Tabaré Vázquez in Uruguay, Lula da Silva in Brazil, and the Sandinista, Daniel Ortega, in Nicaragua. Legislators in many of these countries are now preparing to liberalise abortion, as well as the morning-after pill, and they may well follow the lead of the Spanish president and legalise gay marriage. In the first year of that legislation 4500 gay and lesbian couples married in Spain and are now free to bring up children in the same way as their heterosexual counterparts. This may well spread, as we've seen in California,' Wiley added.

'A sad day for the Church in Spain and in the United States,' the Pontiff observed.

Felici looked on with approval as Howard Wiley's laser pointer roamed over the map, and Wiley expanded on the threat each country posed to oil supplies and to the influence of the United States and the Catholic Church. But with the Cardinal Secretary of State in the room, Felici reserved any further comment for his private dinner with Wiley.

29

MUSEUM OF NATURAL HISTORY, VIENNA

Nervous and on edge, Aleta sipped her long black coffee in the museum's Café Nautilus.

'I knew you would come eventually,' Dr José Arana said. Arana's voice was soft, but authoritative. Like many Guatemalans, he was short and stocky. His fine black hair was flecked with grey and tied back in a ponytail. Around his neck he wore a beautiful jade tablet, inscribed with his Mayan birth sign of the jaguar. His craggy brown face was etched with the wisdom of a shaman, and his dark eyes held a look of quiet peace and understanding.

'How . . . how could you know that, Dr Arana?' Aleta asked, still in a state of shock.

Arana smiled enigmatically. 'Call me José, please. My father, Roberto, who was the village shaman in San Marcos before me, passed on the wisdom of the elders. He gave me your name and told me that one day you would seek my help.'

'I don't understand —'

'Patience, my dear. Eventually all will be revealed. For now it is enough for you to know that you have a very important purpose in life. As you know, the ancient Maya left the present generation a warning.'

Aleta nodded. 'I've found some references to it in my grandfather's papers, and there's been talk of a codex in the media, but I wasn't sure if that was just speculation . . . if the codex really exists.'

'It exists,' Arana replied quietly, 'but we are running out of time. The winter solstice will soon be upon us.'

Aleta's pulse started to race. A quiet but unquestionable integrity emanated from the softly spoken Guatemalan elder. 'Do you know where it is?'

Arana nodded. 'Your grandfather came close to finding it before his tragic death.'

'I don't understand, José. If you know where it is, why don't you just retrieve it and announce its contents to the world?'

'If only it were that simple. Unfortunately most people dismiss the spiritual wisdom of the ancient Maya as mumbo-jumbo. In a time when happiness is sought from the material world, we ignore at our peril the wisdom of a civilisation that could accurately chart and predict planetary movements down to the last second, without the aid of a telescope. The signs of our own destruction are already with us.'

Aleta saw a great sadness in his eyes.

'In the last year,' Arana continued, 'chunks of ice twice the size of London have disappeared from the Arctic and Antarctic. The planet is providing continual warnings – an increasing number of powerful earthquakes, volcanic eruptions, fires, tsunamis and cyclones, hurricanes and floods. Yet many leaders dismiss global warming as rubbish. Some countries are also conducting experiments that are being kept secret from the public, but will ultimately put the entire planet at risk.'

'And you still don't think people would believe you?'

'People are driven by the herd instinct, Aleta. If the politicians and the media are sceptical, the public, too, becomes sceptical. If I were to make an announcement, the media would treat the codex as a curiosity and many would dismiss it as a fraud.'

'I still don't understand where I fit in to all of this.'

'Like me, you were born under the ancient sun sign of *Balam-Ix*, the jaguar, a spirit that is infused with a deep love of Mother Earth. The jaguar's energy, the ruling spirit of the jungles, is feminine, Aleta. The ancients were well aware of that spirit, and they have hidden the codex in such a way that it can only be discovered by someone who will understand how far the world is out of balance, and the real consequence of the alignment of the planets in December 2012. It is no accident that you have followed in your grandfather's footsteps. An *archaeologist* will have far more credibility than any Mayan elder and the warning that the codex contains will be considered more carefully by the media and the wider public,' Arana emphasised. 'But as my father warned your grandfather, the Maya Codex is fiercely protected. More than one fortune seeker has paid the ultimate price, as the ancients intended it to be found only by someone who possesses the inner spiritual balance to understand it correctly.' Arana gave Aleta a long, searching look.

'You can't mean me?' she gasped.

'You have been prompted to meet with me for a reason, Aleta, but the challenge is yours to accept or decline.'

'If I accept such a challenge,' Aleta asked slowly, as his words sank in, 'will you help me, José?'

'I can be your mentor, Aleta, but again, that is up to you. If I am to be your guide, you will have to undergo a cleansing and rebuilding of your inner spirit.'

'I'm not sure I understand.'

'You're not sleeping well, Aleta.' It was a statement rather than a question. Again Aleta sensed the power around this gentle man.

'No,' she admitted. 'Not for some time now.'

'I can see the unhappiness in your eyes.'

'Is it that obvious?'

'Not to the casual observer. Outwardly you are functioning at a very high level, but your eyes tell a different story, Aleta. You have intense brown rings around your irises, which is an indication of stress and acute depression.'

From his position near a display case in one of the museum's exhibition corridors leading to Café Nautilus, Curtis O'Connor observed the quiet conversation between Aleta Weizman and the man with the greying ponytail. O'Connor was not surprised to find that the swarthy young thug who had taken a back seat in Monsignor Jennings' lecture was also having coffee in the museum's restaurant, pretending to read a copy of the *Österreich Journal*. O'Connor reached again for his high-resolution camera.

'The brown rings . . . do they have something to do with the iris's connection to the brain?'

'Exactly,' Dr Arana answered. 'When you are first conceived, your eyes start as part of the brain, but after separation the nerves of the iris remain connected to a part of the brain known as the hypothalamus. The eyes actually reflect the condition of all organs, and we can detect a problem, such as cancer, long before the symptoms appear in the body itself. We can also detect depression, and if you are to be successful in finding and decoding the Maya Codex, that part of your spirit will need healing.'

'You said I'm in grave danger?'

'Because you have embarked on a quest to find out who murdered your family, especially your father and grandfather. Your grandfather was very close to recovering the missing Maya Codex when he was murdered by the Nazis.'

Aleta swallowed, her grief rekindled. 'What does "close" mean?'

'My father spoke with him many times when your grandfather visited Lake Atitlán and Tikal. Your grandfather eventually found two of the three figurines that are needed to recover the codex. He had begun to decipher the hieroglyphics that would lead him to the last figurine and the Maya Codex itself, but he was murdered before he could complete his task.'

Aleta sank in her chair, the past weighing heavily on her. 'My grandfather made some notes,' she confided, 'and he mentioned that three figurines would be needed to unearth the codex . . . but I've never seen any figurines.'

'I'm sure your grandfather took steps to ensure their safekeeping. There is a divine timing in these things, Aleta. Just as we can see the powerful warning signs that are now gathering in the natural world, the two figurines your grandfather found, the remaining one and the codex itself will all remain hidden until they are meant to be discovered – and that time is now close. Because of your quest to find those who have destroyed your family, you have come to the attention of both the CIA and the Vatican. There are two very powerful men who are determined you won't succeed. Both organisations are also determined, for different reasons, to recover the codex and keep it from the public.' Arana paused to allow Aleta time to reflect.

'There are two more men, one of whom will deal with the other,' he went on. 'You will come to trust one of these men with your life. If you decide to go on, you must come back to the shores of Lake Atitlán to prepare for your sacred mission.'

30

THE IMPERIAL HOTEL, VIENNA

O'Connor returned to the Imperial Hotel for dinner and then retired to his room. He recovered his laptop from the wardrobe safe, dialled in a series of codes to connect with the vast database held in the CIA's Cray supercomputers at Langley and waited while his request for access went through a series of encryptions and decryptions.

With access approved, O'Connor fed in the photographs he'd taken earlier in the day. Within seconds, a profile page for Antonio Sodano appeared, together with surveillance photographs provided by the *Guardia di Finanza*, the Italian financial and customs police:

Antonio Sodano - executive summary. Born Corleone, Sicily, 14 August 1987. Rising member of the Cosa Nostra and suspected hit-man, although young and inexperienced. Arrested in 2006 for the murder of a member of a prominent mafia family in Palermo in a dispute over protection money for quarries. Trial aborted for lack of evidence with a strong omerta surrounding the case.

Moved to Rome 2007. Has connections with a black Masonic Lodge, Propaganda Tre, an offshoot of the infamous Propaganda Due or P2 Lodge, suspected of involvement in the Red Brigades' assassination of Italian prime minister Aldo Moro. Sodano has links to the Vatican Bank (see attached photo). Now under investigation and surveillance by the Italian *Guardia di Finanza* for suspected drug-trafficking.

O'Connor scanned the rest of the report, but stopped when he came to the surveillance photographs. Sodano had been snapped at a dock-side in Naples, at Rome's international airport, and at La Pergola, one of Rome's finest restaurants, where he had been photographed at dinner with another man. The photo was grainy and O'Connor couldn't quite place him, but he looked vaguely familiar. O'Connor knew the restaurant well. Located on Via Cadlolo 101 in the Cavalieri Hilton, with panoramic views of the city from Rome's highest hill, La Pergola's cellar held 48 000 bottles. O'Connor had dined there with Kate Braithwaite.

O'Connor felt the old anger and hurt return, and he fought to control his deepest emotions. *Kate*. He pictured her in her level four spacesuit, calmly working with some of the deadliest pathogens known to humankind. She had been a brilliant microbiologist. They had worked together on an assignment in Beijing involving the biggest biological threat the world had ever faced. Their love-life had been a sensation between the sheets; but just when O'Connor was accepting there was someone very special in his life, Kate had been brutally taken from him – a needle stick in a lethal hot-zone laboratory at the Centers for Disease Control and Prevention in Atlanta. From the moment the Ebola virus had entered Kate's bloodstream, her fate had been sealed. Her agonising death was seared into his memory.

The coroner returned a finding of 'accidental fatality', but O'Connor hadn't believed a word of it. He and Kate had made some powerful enemies in Washington and at Langley, and the needle had punctured the *back* of her arm. He had considered resigning, but decided against it, knowing he would have a better chance from within the Agency of discovering how Kate had met her fate. He still harboured a hope that the CIA might change course – back to the old agency that had once been run by honourable professionals.

O'Connor took a deep breath and made a conscious effort to put Kate at the back of his mind, concentrating on the image on his laptop. Suddenly he remembered where he'd seen the other man in the photo. The suit had distracted him, for the man dining with Sodano was none other than the man who'd been photographed with Wiley and Pope John Paul II: Archbishop Salvatore Felici.

Never put anything on paper you can't afford to have someone read, and *never* be photographed, period, O'Connor thought. With a sense of rising anticipation he Googled the Vatican's official website. He'd never known Wiley to cultivate people who were not either powerful or in a position to provide information. The photograph on Wiley's desk had been taken nearly twenty years ago; there was every chance Salvatore Felici was now a cardinal.

Paydirt. O'Connor found his man on the biographical page of cardinals the Vatican thoughtfully provided for the faithful and the curious. According to his biography, Salvatore Felici had been the Pope's ambassador to Guatemala in the early '90s. Not only was Felici now a cardinal, but he was listed in the section for cardinal bishops, the highest of the Vatican's three cardinal rankings. O'Connor matched the unsmiling official portrait with the photo from the *Guardia di Finanza*'s surveillance. What would a nice boy like the Cardinal Prefect of the Congregation for the Doctrine of the Faith be doing dining with a young thug like Sodano? What was the relationship now between Wiley and Felici?

O'Connor flicked back into his encrypted log-in and dialled up Wiley's access code. While he and Kate Braithwaite had been working on the Beijing assignment, O'Connor had befriended and learnt from a brilliant young hacker whom the CIA had wisely put on the payroll at Langley. In his short life, Corey Barrino had worked under the pseudonym of 'Byte Blaster', hacking into the Pentagon's and NASA's classified networks. Byte Blaster had once hacked into the very bowels of Langley itself and left a little message for the Agency's director. The dent in the wall from the director's paperweight was still there.

Wiley must have changed his access codes, O'Connor thought, momentarily frustrated as *Access Denied* flashed on the screen. He knew that Wiley would have added a 'salt' to the DES, the Data Encryption Standard Algorithm. Corey's tutelage on Hacking 101 had taught O'Connor that two characters added to either end of a password – characters that could be chosen from upper- and lower-case letters of the alphabet, or the numbers zero to nine or a full stop or a forward slash – gave a choice of sixty-four different characters at either end of a password. That, in turn, provided a possible 4096 different salts. Even though Barrino had provided O'Connor with access to Langley's supercomputers, it might still take some time to crack Wiley's sophisticated encryption. The way this assignment was shaping up, time might not be on Aleta Weizman's side, O'Connor thought grimly.

Acting on a hunch, but one born of countless operations in the field, O'Connor dialled up one of Barrino's simpler but nevertheless devastatingly effective programs. The hacker had based it on a program which phishers used to acquire hundreds of thousands of email addresses. Criminal gangs used a similar system to dupe people into releasing bank account numbers by posing as Technical Services from Bank of America, Citibank or any of a hundred other financial institutions in order that 'a problem with the records might be fixed'. Unwary Americans lost more than $3 billion a year to email scams, and for someone like Corey Barrino, it would have been child's play to secure the cardinal's personal email address. Using standard Vatican email addresses, O'Connor typed in five possible email combinations for Felici and set the program to 'run'.

Corey's program would have seized most networks, but the Cray supercomputers in the basements at Langley were capable of 400 000 million calculations a second. It took less than ten seconds to confirm the email address and Felici's password. Felici@vatican.va; password: 'pectoralcrossmauthausen'. The password was unusual, O'Connor thought, as *Welcome Eminence* appeared on the screen. He scanned Felici's inbox without finding any emails from the CIA. Quickly he flicked to the sent box. The Cardinal had obviously not given much thought to anyone getting into his system. O'Connor opened an email to Wiley's personal address that revealed a whole thread of previous emails, including one that Felici had sent to Wiley a month earlier.

O'Connor read through the correspondence, quietly cursing

himself that he had even contemplated carrying out the DDO's orders. But the CIA instilled and demanded loyalty, and that loyalty had but one direction: upwards. O'Connor read Cardinal Felici's initial email with a rising sense of anger. Clearly Wiley and the then Archbishop Felici had both been involved in the disappearance of Weizman's family, but it was the last part of Wiley's response that rocked O'Connor to the core.

I plan to be in Rome on the 24th, and I'd be delighted to brief you personally on the situation in Central America, and perhaps we can discuss this missing Maya Codex that Weizman has raised in her article. For reasons I will explain, the codex poses a threat. If Weizman is searching for it, it will be important to get to it before she does. The Weizman issue is in hand, but I need a back-up plan. I understand that Sodano is back in Rome. If you can get me his contact details it might help me with an internal problem as well as the Weizman case.

O'Connor took another deep breath. Suddenly his mission had become personal. He had no doubt who the 'internal problem' was, and any lingering loyalty evaporated, replaced by a gut-wrenching realisation that he no longer had a future in the Firm. Worse still, as long as Wiley held the appointment of DDO, the mostly decent men and women who every day put their lives on the line for the CIA and the country were now at risk. Abraham Lincoln had abolished slavery. Thomas Jefferson had authored the Declaration of Independence and championed a separation of church and state. Theodore Roosevelt had been the first to recognise the need to conserve natural resources. But now, the debacle in Iraq had damaged the reputation of the US around the world and the country was losing its way. With the Vice President protecting him, Wiley was a loose cannon. O'Connor knew it was time to act, even if that meant being on the run until he could find a way to bring Wiley to justice.

O'Connor quickly made a copy of the correspondence and locked his laptop away in the safe. He took the lift to the lobby and then walked purposefully but calmly towards the nearest U-Bahn. The hacking operation had taken longer than he'd planned and there was no time for a leisurely tram ride tonight. Wiley had broken his own rules and those of the Agency, O'Connor thought, as he leapt aboard the train for *Schwedenplatz*.

Out of habit, O'Connor scanned the half-full carriage then returned to his thoughts, recalling the DDO's explosive burst of anger when he'd advised him against going ahead with the Weizman assassination. Wiley's email had been sent not long after that interview, which might explain his lapse in revealing Sodano's name. It was now very clear that Wiley had given Sodano the same mission as O'Connor, breaking another of the cardinal rules. Aleta Weizman had stumbled onto something far bigger than the ruthless murder of her family. What had Wiley and Cardinal Felici been up to in Guatemala that was so damaging, Wiley was prepared to have an archaeologist murdered? And what was in this mysterious Maya Codex that had caught the attention of both the Vatican and the CIA? Would it perhaps enable O'Connor to expose Wiley and Felici? He resolved to find out. Weizman undoubtedly held the key to discovering it, and if he was to get to the codex before Wiley or Felici . . . suddenly it became very important Aleta be kept alive. O'Connor looked at his watch. Ten p.m.

He had a sinking feeling he might already be too late.

31

THE VATICAN, ROME

Cardinal Salvatore Felici was known to keep one of the finest cellars in Rome. Invitations to his private dining room in the *Palazzo della Sacra Inquisizione* were much sought after, but rarely issued – unless the visitor possessed information or was in a position to influence a particular course of events to Felici's satisfaction. Howard Wiley was in a position to do both, and the two men took their seats at the oak dining table. Felici nodded to the attractive young nun who was hovering near the heavy Louis XIV sideboard. Sister Bridgette's appointment to Felici's personal staff had raised more than one eyebrow in the Vatican.

'Château Latour 1961, Howard,' Felici remarked as he poured from the crystal decanter. Felici's command of the English language was impressive, a hint of Oxford contrasting with Wiley's southern drawl. 'I've heard it said that the 1961 Bordeaux vintage in Pauillac was comparable to the great wines of 1928 and '29.' Cardinal Felici held the fine Waterford crystal glass aloft towards the chandelier, allowing a ray of light to stream through the deep pomegranate hue of the *grand vin* claret.

'Yes, although it's surprising that Pauillac has so few *châteaux* at the Premiers Crus end of the spectrum,' Wiley replied. 'From memory, the only other two are Château Lafite-Rothschild and Château-Mouton Rothschild.' Wiley sniffed the Latour's bouquet. 'Spicy. A hint of liquorice and leather.' Howard Wiley appreciated the finer things in life, and like his mentor, J. Edgar Hoover, the DDO was adept at using the public purse to attain them. Wiley's cellar, although not quite up to Felici's standards, was extensive.

'I read the file on the Weizman woman, Howard. She's becoming more than a nuisance. If she keeps digging into the demise of her family . . . ' Felici's voice trailed off while he waited for Sister Bridgette to serve the first course of scallops and garlic sauce, lightly grilled in their shells. 'It could get awkward for both of us,' he concluded, after she had withdrawn.

'I agree, Salvatore. I have the matter in hand. Perhaps people like Weizman shouldn't be surprised when unfortunate accidents befall them. That said, it doesn't hurt to have a back-up plan. The contact you gave me has already been briefed.' Wiley always operated on the need-to-know principle that was the cornerstone of intelligence agencies around the world, and he had briefed Sodano personally. Neither his chief of station in Vienna nor Felici were aware that Sodano had also been tasked with eliminating the troublesome O'Connor. O'Connor's demise in Vienna would be passed off as an unfortunate accident.

'Glad to be of help, Howard.' Felici replenished both wine glasses. 'Weizman has been very foolish, but there must be no mistakes.' Felici also worked on a need-to-know basis. He kept his real fears over what Weizman might be investigating to himself. Links between the Vatican and the CIA and the Guatemalan death squads could always be denied, but if Weizman dug too deeply into what had happened at Mauthausen, Felici's family connections to the Nazis would be exposed. He was determined that would never be allowed to happen.

'What's your take on Weizman's assertions on this Maya Codex?' Wiley asked.

'Why would the CIA be interested in an ancient codex, Howard?' Felici probed, his thin lips parting in a humourless smile. They were like two Olympic fencers, each *en garde*, each ready to parry, each ready with a riposte.

'A couple of reasons. Firstly, if such a codex were to be discovered by someone like Weizman, her profile would immediately rival that of Howard Carter when he discovered of the tomb of Tutankhamen, which would serve neither of our interests, Salvatore. It would be far better if it were found by one of our own.'

'All the more reason there must be no mistakes in dealing with her.'

'That's understood,' Wiley said, controlling his irritation. 'But if what is rumoured to be in the codex turns out to be true, it might be difficult to control public panic. Scientific data showing movement in the poles and a change in the earth's magnetic field are already available, but fortunately the media isn't taking much notice. The view in Washington is that the codex is just mystical nonsense, but if someone like Weizman were to find it and line up the scientific data with ancient Mayan predictions of a catastrophic pole shift, uncontrolled media headlines could blow this way out of proportion. Any suggestion that the financial centres of the world might finish up a thousand metres under water would cause investors to panic and seek safety in gold. There'd be a run on the banks and another stockmarket crash – one far worse than the 2008 panic. Worse even than the crash of 1929.'

Felici nodded, deep in thought, his mind more focused on the dangers the codex posed for the Holy Church.

'The President thinks any alignment with the current scientific data and what might be in this codex is sheer coincidence, but he agrees the public should be shielded from it.'

'I think your president is right. The Maya were uneducated savages who worshipped any number of pagan gods, and it's a pity that all of their codices were not destroyed, but I agree: fear breeds fear. When it comes to the financial markets, investor panic is an uncontrollable phenomenon that defies logic.'

'If this codex thing is not handled sensibly, Salvatore – and by that I mean if it gets into the wrong hands – it could threaten the entire financial system.'

'If this Maya Codex exists, it will need to be kept from public view, at least until after 2012 . . . and perhaps beyond,' Felici said, still more mindful of the threat the codex might pose to Catholic doctrine than the stockmarket. Cardinal Felici paused, reflecting on a more recent warning that had been delivered to the faithful by the blessed Virgin Mary when she had appeared at Fátima. Was her warning coming to fruition? Could the third warning and the Maya Codex be connected? Pope John Paul II had released a 'translation' of the third warning in June 2000, but Felici knew that the real warning was still buried in the Vatican's archives. 'We should maintain close cooperation on this, Howard,' he concluded.

'There is one other issue,' Wiley said carefully. 'When you and I were in Guatemala, one of our assets was based in San Pedro.'

'Ah, yes. Father Hernandez.'

'He kept detailed diaries . . .'

Felici felt a chill run down his spine, but in a habit born of long years of practice, he gave nothing away. 'Really? I thought Hernandez retired years ago. He must be in his late eighties by now?'

'Early nineties actually, but still very sprightly for his age, or he was the last time he was seen around Lake Atitlán. He and his diaries disappeared three years ago, we think possibly to Peru. He apparently received a tip-off that certain enemies were on to him.'

'Do we know what the diaries cover?'

'Not exactly. But I'm led to believe he recorded a considerable amount of information on this missing codex.'

'So if we find the diaries, they may lead us to the codex?'

'They may. But more importantly the diaries may also contain details of our operations in Guatemala, and Hernandez' escape from Nazi Germany. The CIA is not the only one looking for Hernandez – Mossad is more than a little interested as well.'

The blood drained from Felici's face. 'It would be extremely unfortunate if these diaries were to fall into the hands of the Israelis or anyone else, Howard. I will ask our papal nuncio in Guatemala City to keep his ear to the ground. Our papal nuncio in Lima can also be trusted, so I will make some enquiries on the possible Peruvian connection.'

Like two grand masters of the epee and the foil, Wiley and Felici watched each other's every move, revealing neither their fears nor their plans for the diaries and the missing codex.

32

VIENNA

Aleta lit the fire and poured herself a glass of wine. She was now determined to find the missing figurines and the Maya Codex, whatever it took; but first she would make the nine-hour train journey to Bad Arolsen, a spa town in central Germany. From there she would head to Mauthausen on the Danube, not far from Linz, where her beloved grandfather had last been seen alive. The Mauthausen concentration camp might not yield any clues, but she had to see it for herself.

Aleta retrieved her folder on the Bad Arolsen records from the bedside table. The six barrack buildings used by Himmler's elite Waffen SS, who were stationed in Bad Arolsen during the war, now contained shelves of documents stretching for twenty-six kilometres. The card index system alone occupied three whole rooms, providing critical links to medical records, transport lists, registration books and myriad scraps of paper. The records were not yet fully digitised, and in any case, having come this far, Aleta was determined to check them personally.

Schindler's list was there, with the records of more than a thousand Jewish prisoners whose lives Oskar Schindler had saved, convincing the Nazis he needed them to work on the production of enamel and munitions. So too were the records for 'Frank, Annelise M.' But even more important to Aleta than Anne Frank was her discovery that the Mauthausen concentration camp's *Totenbuchen*, or Death Books, were also at Bad Arolsen. She shuddered involuntarily at the thought of finding her grandfather's name. The Mauthausen *Totenbuchen* had been meticulously handwritten, and amongst the entries was one that was particularly chilling. Every two minutes, for ninety minutes, by order of the commandant, Obersturmbannführer von Heißen, a prisoner had been shot in the back of the head as a birthday present for Hitler. Had her grandfather met his fate on Hitler's birthday?

Aleta rose and wandered over to one of the old heavy bookcases that held a framed photograph of her grandparents. Levi and his tall attractive wife, Ramona, together with Aleta's father, Ariel, as a boy of ten, and his younger sister Rebekkah. It had been taken in 1937, when the Nazi juggernaut was already massing, but back then they were a smiling and happy family, standing on the deck of a riverboat cruising through a steeply rising gorge on the Danube. Behind them, the vineyards of the famous Wachau wine-growing region rose in rocky slate terraces above the church steeple of the village of Joching. Her father's smile was mischievous, just as she remembered it.

Aleta wiped away a tear as the memories came flooding back: sitting on his shoulders as he jogged down to the shores of Lake Atitlán. Together they would paddle the family canoe over to a secret fishing

spot. She knew now that it wasn't secret, and she suspected some of
the fish she'd pulled in on her line had been put there by her father
when she wasn't looking, but he had always been able to infuse her
life with a sense of mystery and magic. Now, like her grandfather,
he was gone. Weary and flat, she headed for the bathroom and shook
a purple-pink capsule from the jar labelled Sarafem. The pills and
a good night's sleep would allow her to function, but she knew they
would do nothing to help her lack of energy and the pervasive sense
of hopelessness that was her constant companion.

Three floors below, Antonio Sodano quietly entered the courtyard
to Aleta's apartment block. Using a lock pick remarkably similar to
O'Connor's, he dealt with the steel security door at the bottom of the
stairs. Sodano pulled a balaclava over his pockmarked, rugged face
and soundlessly ascended to the landing outside Aleta's door.

33

THE VATICAN, ROME

Cardinal Felici examined the latest file on Monsignor Jennings, forwarded from the papal nuncio in Guatemala City. A series of photos showed him emerging from a seedy bar in La Línea, a crime-infested, prostitute-ridden, gang-controlled ghetto on the outskirts of the city. The two boys either side of him looked to be no more than twelve. Another photo showed Jennings with the boys, booking into an even seedier 'motel', the rooms of which were made out of metal scrounged from shipping containers. Felici closed the file and pondered. So far, the Vatican Bank funding that financed Jennings' archaeological expeditions to Central America had ensured Jennings' loyalty, but it might not be enough. He also knew that an appeal to the Jesuit's faith would be problematic. Felici had known of Jennings' sexual proclivities for a long time, but this was the first concrete evidence he'd obtained. The papal nuncio had done well.

The Cardinal's private secretary knocked on the double doors of the office.

'Monsignor Jennings is here, Eminence.'

'Show him in.' Felici glanced at his rolled gold Rolex. 'And order my car for 11 p.m.'

'Certainly, Eminence.' Father Cordona stood aside for Monsignor Jennings and then closed the door. If he questioned why the Cardinal regularly ordered his car late at night, or why Cardinal Felici maintained an apartment in the fashionable but eclectic *Via del Governo Vecchio* on the north side of the Tiber, he never allowed it to show.

'*Benvenuto a Roma.*' The Cardinal extended his fine, bony hand.

'*Grazie*, Eminence.'

'I trust it was a pleasant flight?'

'As much as flying can be after 9/11.'

'Of course. Well. I won't keep you long, but something has come up. Have you come across a Dr Aleta Weizman?' the Cardinal asked, adjusting his soutane as he sat on one of the deep-blue velvet couches in his office.

'Unfortunately, yes. She was making a nuisance of herself during my address to the conference in Vienna.'

'Did she mention a missing codex?'

'She didn't, but a journalist did,' Jennings replied, glancing pointedly towards the cardinal's cocktail cabinet. 'A young bimbo from a women's magazine. I'm not sure why she was there. Like the rest of her colleagues, she showed no interest in my latest research.'

'Do you think Weizman suspects it exists?' Felici asked, ignoring the Jesuit's glances towards the whisky.

'While I was in Guatemala City, Eminence, I discovered Weizman had recently visited the *Museo Nacional de Arqueologia y Etnologia*. There's nothing unusual in that per se; she is, after all, an archaeologist. But my contact tells me she seemed particularly excited after spending some time in one of the storage areas.'

'And do we know what might have caused her excitement?'

Monsignor Jennings shook his head. 'The next time I'm in there, I'll make some enquiries.'

Agitated, Felici fingered his pectoral cross. 'The closer we get to 2012, the greater focus there will be on the ancient Maya and Guatemala . . . and the greater focus there will be on the Maya Codex.'

'There's not a lot we can do about that. I continue to play down 2012, as per your instructions.'

'Your funding from the Vatican Bank depends on you doing just that,' Felici reminded him.

Jennings shrugged. 'The media love a mystery.'

'Which means we must redouble our efforts to recover the codex before somebody else does.'

'That's easier said than done. The number of remaining Maya who might know the whereabouts of this codex could be counted on one hand, and all of them would be elders.'

'Which is a closed shop.'

'Precisely.'

'Money talks in Guatemala, you say? How much will it take?'

'There are still some people in this world who can't be bought, Eminence.'

Felici masked his irritation. 'Do you have any idea who these elders might be?'

Jennings shook his head. 'Not really. Although the most revered elder in the highlands region is a shaman, a Dr José Arana, who incidentally was also at the Mayan conference.'

Felici got up and walked over to the windows affording a view towards Bernini's columns surrounding the *Piazza San Pietro*. He stared out across the now-deserted piazza, hands clasped behind his soutane. The traffic past Vatican City on the *Via di Porta Cavalleggeri* was still heavy. The sounds of the Italians' love affair with the horn and motor scooters filled the evening air.

'For the good of the Holy Church,' Felici said finally, 'we must recover the Maya Codex for storage in the secret archives.'

'But what if we find it and it does contain a dire warning? The scientific evidence is mounting that the ancient Maya might be right. Should we not alert the world? People might have to move to higher ground.'

'My concern, as yours should be,' Felici responded icily, 'is that it may contain material that threatens the one true faith. Our responsibility, Monsignor, is to protect the Holy Church.'

Jennings shrugged. The Holy Church was the last of his concerns. Nor was he particularly concerned over the warning. Unbeknown to the wider public, scientists had already done some calculations, and Jennings had studied the maps that predicted the catastrophic consequences of a geographic pole shift. Based on that information, he'd purchased a property in one of the very few areas of the world that would provide safety in December 2012. But the possibility of discovering the codex itself had fired Jennings' interest, and for some time he had been far more focused on doing so than even Felici realised.

'The discovery of the Maya Codex would be an archaeological sensation, Eminence,' Jennings said. 'On a par with the discovery of the Dead Sea Scrolls, the Rosetta Stone, the Terracotta Army and the tomb of King Tutankhamen. Whoever discovers this prophecy will be immortalised in the annals of history.'

'And . . . ?' Felici challenged.

'If the codex is found, only to be hidden away in the secret archives, not only will a great discovery be lost to archaeology, but we will have abrogated our duty to broadcast the Maya's warning to the world.' Jennings sniffed smugly.

'I would remind you, Monsignor, that the funding for your archaeological expeditions is not inconsiderable. That funding depends entirely on your cooperation.'

'The Vatican Bank is not the only source of funding available for archaeological expeditions, Eminence.' Jennings had already sounded out alternative wealthy financial backers. It would have been more prudent to remain silent, but prudence had never been Jennings' strong suit.

'I had hoped it would not come to this,' Felici said, rising from his seat to retrieve Jennings' file, 'but you leave me no alternative.' He handed Jennings the folio of photographs and watched his reaction with a sense of satisfaction.

Jennings was speechless with shock, his face ashen.

'Fortunately for you, Monsignor, it is paramount that the image of the Holy Church be protected, and you are more valuable inside the Church than out,' the Cardinal said, relieving the hapless priest of his file. 'Now, having resolved the issue of what is to be done with the Maya Codex, there is one other matter which is of the utmost confidentiality.'

Jennings nodded.

'At the end of World War Two, in order to ensure the defeat of Communism, the government of the United States and the Vatican cooperated to release a number of German scientists and others who had valuable knowledge which could be used to defeat that threat. Amongst them was an officer of Himmler's SS, Karl von Heißen. In return for his cooperation, he was given a new identity as a Catholic priest in the parish of San Pedro.'

'Adolf Eichmann was another,' Jennings replied, still reeling over the photographs.

'Eichmann is dead, but von Heißen is still alive, or at least we think he is. You would have known him as Father Hernandez.'

'Yes, I remember him now. He had a thick Spanish accent – but you're saying he was German?'

'The Spanish schools in Antigua are very good, Monsignor, and von Heißen was given extensive training, but even the schools in Antigua can't erase cultural backgrounds. That said, in his role as Father Hernandez, von Heißen was very useful in the fight against Communism, and up until now his real identity has remained intact. Unfortunately, like you, he was careless, and we've recently discovered he kept detailed diaries.'

'Diaries that could be embarrassing to the Vatican and the US government?' Jennings sensed an opportunity to recover some ground.

'The diaries may also contain information on the whereabouts of the Maya Codex,' Felici replied stonily. 'Either way, we want them back.'

'Do we have any idea where von Heißen might be?'

'He retired in San Pedro, but he was apparently tipped off that Mossad were finally on to him and he had to leave in a hurry – perhaps to Peru.'

'So the trail has already gone cold.'

'Perhaps. Nevertheless, you are to make some discreet – very discreet – enquiries. As a cover, you are being assigned to the same parish of San Pedro on Lake Atitlán, which has been without a permanent priest for some time. Your primary aim remains the discovery of the Maya Codex, and you're to leave for Guatemala tomorrow. Father Cordona has your travel documents. Should you need to make contact, the papal nuncio in Guatemala City has secure communications, but even he does not know the real purpose of your return. In the meantime, these photographs will remain in my safe, Monsignor.' Felici waved the file at Jennings. 'I do hope you won't give me an opportunity to use them.'

34

VIENNA

Antonio Sodano quietly raked the pins of the lock to Aleta's apartment. Encountering the same problem O'Connor had experienced, he changed to a finer pick and raked them again. He held the tension with his torsion wrench and lifted the final pin over the shear line and turned the cam. Sodano eased open the cedar door and listened. A light was coming from the left, and he could hear the sound of running water. He silently moved forward and peered around the corner of the hallway. In the bathroom at the end of the corridor a woman was cleaning her teeth. She matched the photograph he'd been given. She was tall and shapely, standing now, examining her teeth in the mirror, an outline of her breasts straining against her nightshirt. He felt for the gag in his pocket and withdrew back into the front hallway.

Aleta turned off the light and headed towards her bedroom.

Sodano flattened himself against the wall and waited. The woman passed without looking into the hallway. He took two steps, clamped his right hand over her mouth and wrenched her hair back with his left.

Aleta let out a muffled scream and Sodano winced as she bit hard into his hand.

'*Schlampe!* Bitch!' He bundled Aleta into her bedroom and pinned her to the wall. Aleta's eyes widened in fear as she felt the knife against her throat.

O'Connor found both the heavy double wooden doors to the court-yard and the steel security door at the bottom of the steps to Aleta's apartment ajar. Fearing the worst, he drew his Glock 21 and silently bounded up the staircase, two stairs at time. The front door was unlocked. O'Connor paused at the sound of voices from inside.

'Not so feisty now, are we?' Sodano sneered as he ran his free hand up Aleta's inner thigh.

Aleta spat in his face.

'You're going to regret that, bitch.' Sodano moved the knife back against Aleta's neck and fondled her breasts.

O'Connor eased his way up the hall and cautiously looked around the door jamb, only to make immediate eye contact with Aleta. Her sharp intake of breath was enough. Sodano reacted in an instant, whipping Aleta around in front of him and pressing the knife harder on her neck. 'Drop the gun, O'Connor, or she gets it. Now!'

O'Connor reluctantly threw the Glock onto the floor in front of him. Sodano's use of his name was instant confirmation that Aleta was not the hitman's only target.

'Now step back.' Sodano shoved Aleta to one side. She stumbled on the rug beside the bed and for a moment, as he tried to hold her, Sodano was distracted. O'Connor swung his right leg in a round-house kick to Sodano's ribcage, pushing powerfully with his left leg. Sodano grunted in pain, releasing Aleta. The knife arced harm-lessly through the air, clattering against the wardrobe. O'Connor head-butted Sodano and then fought for balance as the tough little Sicilian hooked his leg behind O'Connor's right knee. They tumbled out into the lounge room, each searching for grip. Sodano drove his knee into O'Connor's thigh and they crashed against the fire-place. O'Connor slammed his elbow against Sodano's throat and rolled onto his back, wrapping his right arm around the Sicilian's neck. In the classic special forces choke, O'Connor secured his upper left arm on the struggling Sodano's shoulder and applied his left forearm and hand to Sodano's neck, forcing it forward. O'Connor squeezed his arms towards one another and Sodano's eyes bulged with fear. O'Connor held the mafia hitman's throat until the lifeblood drained from Sodano's face and his head fell limp in his hands. When O'Connor was certain his assailant was dead, he rolled Sodano onto the floor, and gasped for breath. Aleta stood above him, Sodano's knife in one hand.

'I'm on your side. So you can put that down,' O'Connor rasped between deep breaths.

'Not until you tell me who you are and what the hell you're doing in my apartment!' Her hands were shaking.

'My name is Curtis O'Connor. And strange as it may seem, I came to protect you.'

The shaman's words came flooding back . . . *There are two more men, one of whom will deal with the other. You will come to trust one of these with your life.*

'Who *are* you?' Aleta demanded again.

'That's a long story . . . '

'Give me the short version!'

'I'm with the CIA, and right now they want you out of the road. You've pissed off some seriously powerful people.'

'If you're with the CIA and they want me dead, how come you're here to protect me? And who's he?' Aleta pointed the knife at the corpse on her living room floor.

'Antonio Sodano, a hired hitman, or he was. But why don't you put the knife down and perhaps I can give you the longer version over coffee?'

'I'm calling the police!'

'That's the last thing you should do.'

'Why not? A mafia hitman just attempted to murder me!'

'Think about it,' O'Connor said quietly. 'If you call the police, you'll have every journalist in Vienna on your front doorstep. You won't be able to move without a camera crew following you, and because there's mystery surrounding who wants you dead, the journalists are going to keep probing.'

'Which might give me a degree of protection from assholes like you!'

'That's perhaps a little ungrateful?' O'Connor suggested with a lopsided grin.

Aleta said nothing. She felt like bursting into tears.

'And far from giving you protection,' O'Connor continued, 'if this gets publicity, the people who want you out of the way will redouble their efforts to silence you. These guys play for keeps and money isn't an obstacle, Aleta. You're going to have to trust me on this. The first priority is to get rid of the body.'

Again the shaman's words came back: *trust him with your life.* 'So we get rid of the body,' she said, her heart rate subsiding a little, 'but when it's found, the police are going to come looking for me. What then?'

'Only if it's linked to this apartment. When's the garbage collected?'

'Tomorrow morning.'

'I'll be back shortly, but if you don't mind, I'll use your bathroom first.'

O'Connor looked in the mirror. 'Not a pretty sight,' he muttered, as he gingerly dabbed at his battered face. Several minutes later he left the apartment. Sterngasse was deserted. With a bit of luck it would stay that way, he thought, as he walked quickly down the narrow cobbled street towards several wheelie bins that were already on the street just past the bookshop. O'Connor chose a full one and headed back towards Aleta's apartment, the load muffling the sound of the wheels on the cobblestones. When he reached the courtyard, he checked for any sign of activity in the rest of the block. Satisfied, he emptied the contents into Aleta's bin and carried the bookshop's empty bin up the stairs and into the living room. Aleta was sitting at the kitchen table.

'Are you okay?'

'I'll be fine.'

'Fine: one of the most dangerous words in the female lexicon.'

Aleta glared at him. 'So we just put the body out with the garbage, do we?'

'Look, I know you've been through a hell of a lot, but, like I said, you're going to have to trust me, because this isn't over — not by a long shot. Sometimes, the simplest methods are the best. If we're lucky, this bin will be picked up by a mechanical lever and emptied through the top of the truck. Unless someone actually sees the contents being tipped in, the body will be compacted with the rest of the garbage and may never be found. At worst, if the body's discovered, the police will identify Sodano, conclude it's drug-related and cross another young thug off their wanted list. They're not going to come swarming around here, at least not initially, and if they do, we're going to be well out of here.'

'We?'

'We. Because right now, whether you like it or not, you and I are in this together. If you put the coffee pot on, I'll explain when I get back.'

O'Connor searched Sodano's body. He left the wallet and Italian passport in Sodano's jacket but removed the cell phone.

'Why are you keeping his phone?'

'SIM cards can be tracked. But if I drop it into a passing barge on the *Donaukanal*, who knows where it might finish up?' O'Connor said with a grin. He picked up Sodano's body in a fireman's lift and dumped it headfirst into the wheelie bin. Sodano was stocky but he was short, and O'Connor managed to bend Sodano's knees and push his legs into the bin. He closed the lid and pulled the bin but one wheel had fallen into a hole in the carpet and O'Connor had to yank the bin free.

'I'm afraid there's a bit of damage to the floor,' he said, peeling back the carpet in front of the fireplace. The old floorboard had been dislodged and O'Connor pulled it clear. There, in the cavity between the floor joists, was a battered old tin trunk. It was nearly a metre long and about thirty centimetres wide.

Aleta, her animosity momentarily forgotten, helped O'Connor extract the trunk from its hiding place. Together they lifted it onto the carpet.

'If this belonged to your grandfather, he wanted it well hidden,' O'Connor observed, stepping back.

'I think I know why,' Aleta said, her fingers trembling as she pried open the latch. The lid creaked as she raised it to reveal an old yellowed notebook and two separate packages, each protected by red velvet cloth. Aleta unwrapped the first package to reveal an intricately carved jade sculpture, and she felt her heart skip a beat. 'My God. The figurines!' she gasped.

O'Connor watched her unwrap the second exquisite carving.

'You've been looking for these?'

Aleta didn't answer, turning the second figurine in her hands and examining it closely. She put the artefact down and looked O'Connor in the eye, her mind racing. Should she trust this man, as the shaman had suggested? He seemed to know who was out to kill her, and he *had* saved her life, but still she was wary. Very wary. 'Give me one reason I should trust you,' she challenged.

'You shouldn't trust anyone. At least, not until you get to know them, and maybe not even then.'

'You say there are people out to silence me. How do you know that?'

'Because I was sent here to kill you.'

'What?' Aleta recoiled in shock. 'So why didn't you?'

'That's a long story as well, but I'll give you the short version.'

Aleta listened in stony silence as O'Connor gave her a potted history of the events that had led to his interception of Sodano, and the involvement of Wiley and Felici. 'Look,' he said finally. 'We can spend the rest of the night arguing, or we can call a truce. I'm not asking you to like me, but you'll have to trust me . . . at least until I get you out of here.'

Aleta stared at him frostily.

O'Connor reached underneath his jacket, withdrew the Glock he'd recovered from the bedroom and proffered it to her. 'Take it.'

'What for?'

'Take it,' O'Connor insisted. 'I could have killed you at any time,' he explained, handing Aleta the weapon. 'I came to protect you,' he emphasised, pushing the barrel to one side. 'It's loaded.'

Aleta looked at him quizzically.

'And now you can kill me, or call the police, or both. Or we can call a truce and get the hell out of here.'

'Tonight?' She handed the weapon back to O'Connor.

He shook his head. 'Tomorrow. First I've got to deal with Pretty Boy Floyd over there and we both need some sleep. Have you got a spare bedroom here? I'd ask you back to my hotel, but it's only our first date.'

'Don't push your luck, *Mister* O'Connor.'

'Have you ever heard of the Maya Codex?' Aleta asked, plunging the coffee at the kitchen table.

'I was at Monsignor Jennings' lecture,' O'Connor admitted.

'Why am I not surprised?' Aleta shook her head, her feelings of being watched and stalked returning. 'Trying to pass yourself off as an archaeologist, no doubt.'

'I did a couple of nights' study, although it was a public lecture,' he added sheepishly.

Aleta nodded. 'Then you would have heard the question about the codex.'

'And Jennings dismissing it as a figment of the media's imagination. Is it?'

'It exists.'

'How can you be so sure?'

'Now it's your turn to trust me.'

'So you think these figurines will lead you to it?' O'Connor asked after Aleta had given him a thumbnail sketch of her grandfather's work, and Dr Arana's warnings.

'Well, I can't be sure of that. In any case, I still need to find the third one. The ancient Maya went to great lengths to ensure the codex would remain hidden until the time was right for it to be recovered.'

'And José Arana thinks that time may have arrived?'

Aleta nodded. 'The discovery of these two figurines may not be an accident, and if you look at them closely, you'll see that each one is in the shape of a tree, the Mayan tree of life. It's a very powerful symbol that represents creation, which right now is under extraordinary threat. The male figurine has a male jaguar at the base, while the neutral one is in balance with both male and female cats. The third figurine will undoubtedly have a female jaguar – the lost feminine.'

'The jaguar . . . one of the great cats of the Guatemalan jungle, and if I recall correctly, sacred to the ancient Maya.'

For the first time since O'Connor had burst into her apartment, Aleta allowed herself a smile. 'So those two nights spent studying had some benefit?'

'Not enough, unfortunately.'

'Don't feel too bad about it. My grandfather spent a lifetime studying the Maya, and he only scratched the surface. We think we are the most advanced civilisation in history, but we've yet to uncover the real history of the ancients. When we do, we will find that the Maya, like the Inca and the Egyptians, were all much more advanced than pompous historians like Jennings allow.'

'You're probably right,' O'Connor agreed. 'There is something in this codex that has both the Vatican and my government very worried. Both sides will do anything to get their hands on it, so that truce between you and I is going to have to last, at least until I help you find it.'

'Why do you think the Vatican or the US government is after it? And why would you want to help me find it?'

'I'm not sure, but I know they're both determined to get to this codex before you do, and if they do, I suspect they will bury it from public view.'

'What about the warnings?'

'They'll take a chance on them. Besides, it wouldn't be the first time the public has been kept in the dark.'

Aleta looked thoughtful. 'I'm not sure what's driving your government, but I think I know why the Vatican would be after it,' she said finally. 'The Vatican kept the Dead Sea Scrolls from public view for over thirty years because the contents threatened the uniqueness of Jesus' message. The Maya Codex might be a much bigger threat than the Dead Sea Scrolls.'

'Meaning?'

'My grandfather left some notes. He thought the codex would be found in the jungles of Guatemala, and that it would not only contain a warning of what might be about to happen to us, but it might be linked to the warnings the Virgin Mary issued at Fátima.' Aleta allowed herself a smile. 'The Vatican has always felt threatened by Mayan spirituality, Mr O'Connor.'

O'Connor smiled wanly. 'Do you think we might drop the "Mr O'Connor"?'

Aleta took a deep breath. 'Look, I *do* appreciate what you've done tonight . . . It's just that I don't have people bursting into my apartment with guns and knives every day of the week, and it's going to take me a little time before I can trust you – if I ever do. Although if what you tell me is true, and you've defied your boss to protect me, they're going to be after you as well.'

'That's probably an understatement, and all the more reason why we need to get out of Vienna and head for Guatemala.'

Aleta shook her head. 'Not before I find out what happened to my grandfather. Tomorrow, I'm catching a train to Bad Arolsen. The town houses millions of documents containing details on Holocaust victims, and they're finally available to the public.'

'Yes. I remember reading something about that. And you think your grandparents will be amongst them?' O'Connor asked gently.

Aleta nodded sadly. 'Along with my father and his sister, although they both escaped.'

'Well . . .' Now O'Connor's mind was racing. 'Bear in mind that as soon as Wiley discovers what's happened here, there'll be a manhunt on that will make the search for bin Laden look like a walk in the park. How long do you need at Bad Arolsen?'

'A day – two at the most. I've already booked my time through the International Tracing Service. The Mauthausen records will be grouped together.'

'And another day at Mauthausen itself. So allowing for travel, we need another five days in Austria. We might get away with it, but it'll be touch and go. In the meantime, you and I had better get some rest.'

O'Connor scanned the *Ringstrasse* behind and then ushered Aleta through the old brass-handled wooden doors of the Café Schwarzenberg.

They found a vacant booth in a quiet corner of the eighteenth-century café on the *Ringstrasse* opposite the Imperial Hotel, and O'Connor passed Aleta the breakfast menu. The café was only half full, and again O'Connor scanned the clientele, but there was no one out of the ordinary. They were mainly business people, heads buried in newspapers, with a croissant and a *mokka* or a *schwarzer* for company. It was too early for the tourists.

'*Kaffee, Kipferl, Marmelade und ein weichgekochtes Ei, bitte*,' O'Connor ordered. The old waiter's black suit and bow tie matched the ambience of the café's chandeliers, tapestries, wood-panelled pillars and old leather-padded wooden chairs.

'*Und eine Zeitung, Herr?*'

'*Die* New York Times, *bitte.*'

'*Und Ihnen, Frau?*'

'*Ich werde* Die Welt, *und die Wiener Frühstück als Gut, danke,*' Aleta replied in flawless German, ordering the German daily and the same Viennese breakfast as O'Connor.

'*Danke schön.*' O'Connor thanked the waiter for the newspapers and handed Aleta the wooden rod that had *Die Welt* attached. 'You're making me feel inadequate.'

'You seem to get by. How many languages do you speak?'

'I'm fluent in German, French and Italian, and I get by, as you put it, in Spanish, Russian and Chinese.'

'Very impressive. I dare say Russian was a product of the Cold War, but why Chinese?' Aleta thought she saw a momentary shadow in his eyes.

'That's another long story. I worked on security for the Beijing Olympics.'

'You're a man of few words, aren't you?'

O'Connor smiled. 'Comes with the territory, I guess. *Danke schön.*' He thanked the waiter again as the coffees arrived, grateful for the interruption.

'So what's the plan? You need to check out of your hotel?'

'Train leaves at 10.40 and my hotel's just across the *Ringstrasse,*' O'Connor said, indicating the Imperial through the high, curtained windows.

'The Imperial? You do travel in style.'

O'Connor shrugged modestly. 'It's a tough life, but someone has to do it.' His eyes met those of a tall, thin man in a black overcoat and beret, standing by a newsstand on the opposite side of the *Ringstrasse*. The man immediately went back to reading his newspaper.

'Don't look now, but there's a tall guy in a beret across the road who's got us on his radar. After I've left, wait until he follows me, then get a taxi to Westbahnhof. I'll give him the slip and meet you there.'

Aleta watched the man who had saved her life jog effortlessly across the *Kärntner Ring* towards the Imperial. As soon as O'Connor left, the thin man in the black overcoat and beret followed him down the *Ringstrasse*.

35

CIA HEADQUARTERS, LANGLEY, VIRGINIA

Howard Wiley flicked on the last briefing overhead for the new president's first visit to the CIA headquarters. From Wiley's point of view, the election had been a disaster: the new president eschewed the use of force in favour of negotiation. It was a language Wiley had never understood.

'In summary, Mr President, America faces many challenges around the world. Terrorist networks are widely dispersed and growing in number. Nuclear proliferation continues to be a cause for grave concern. We know North Korea has had access to reprocessed fuel rods and enriched uranium from their reactor at Yongbyon, and increasingly sophisticated ballistic missiles are now available from international arms dealers. Caution is also required in any negotiations with Iran,' Wiley warned. 'Tehran will not give up on enriching uranium, and unless we act against them, in a few short years Ahmadinejad's threat to wipe Israel off the map could be a reality.'

Wiley paused to judge the President's reaction, but the new leader of the free world gave nothing away. 'Despite the economic downturn, China continues to modernise her military forces, and this also poses a threat, not only to the balance of power in the Taiwanese Straits, but to our own forces in the region. Finally, while Prime Minister Putin is nominally subordinate to President Dmitry Medvedev, Putin remains in charge of the Kremlin and will likely run again for president once Medvedev's term expires. There is no doubt Putin aims to reclaim Russia's former position as the dominant power in Europe. We can expect the Russians to maintain a tough stance against Chechnya, the Ukraine and in Georgia, where Putin will seek to exert even greater control over the region's oil and energy supplies.'

'I received a briefing from your counterpart in DNI on our operations with HAARP in Alaska,' the President said.

Wiley controlled his anger. The Directorate of National Intelligence had been set up as a result of the failure of the FBI to detect the 9/11 terrorists' pilot training in Florida, Arizona and California. In Wiley's view, because of the FBI's incompetence, the CIA had lost its position as the country's pre-eminent intelligence agency to a bunch of shiny-assed rank amateurs at DNI in Washington, who big-noted themselves to politicians on every top-secret project they had access to. Wiley had been very careful to ensure that even his own director wasn't privy to those operations Wiley considered he alone was competent to run. Politicians who wanted to negotiate with the enemy, especially those like the newly elected president, were to be kept at arm's length. As far as Wiley was concerned, HAARP was far too sensitive to allow wide access or briefing, and he wondered how much the President had been told.

'What credence do you place on the Russians being able to control the weather?' the President asked.

'We have incontrovertible evidence that the Russians are conducting research on controlling the direction of hurricanes, Mr President, as well as increasing their intensity. They're also conducting experiments on the triggering of earthquakes.'

'And our own research?'

'Our research on this goes back to the Vietnam War. Project Popeye was aimed at changing the weather over North Vietnam by seeding clouds with silver iodide and dry ice. We had mixed success back then, sometimes churning the Ho Chi Minh trail into mud, but the Russians have been at this even longer. In 1962 we discovered they were beaming electromagnetic radiation signals at our embassy in Moscow, and, more specifically, directly at the office of our ambassador. In the '70s we discovered an extension of this experiment: the Russian Woodpecker. It was a series of electromagnetic signals in the three to thirty megahertz bands.'

'Woodpecker?'

'The Russians pulsed the signal at a rate of ten or twelve to the second – ham radio operators around the world christened it the Russian Woodpecker – but the signal is so powerful it is capable of disrupting communications here in the United States. We have reason to believe, Mr President, that Woodpecker was the forerunner to the Russians' version of HAARP.'

'And HAARP can change the weather? I thought there was a UN treaty banning those experiments?'

'Resolution 3172, passed by the United Nations in December 1976.' Wiley smiled condescendingly. He had anticipated the question. 'It bans experiments aimed at manipulating the weather as a form of warfare; but, of course, that doesn't prevent us from carrying out experiments for peaceful purposes, Mr President.'

Wiley returned to his office, satisfied that the President of the United States was none the wiser for his questions on weather wars, and that he was unaware of Operation Aether. Presidents came and presidents went, but the real power was here in the Agency, and Wiley was determined it would stay that way. His satisfaction was more short-lived than usual, though. A message had come in from the Vienna chief of station, marked for his immediate attention:

O'Connor observed having breakfast with target in Café Schwarzenberg. Unsure whether this is part of plan to elimi-nate her. O'Connor departed to Imperial Hotel but has not re-emerged, although cell phone is being tracked and is inex-plicably moving slowly away from the Imperial. Endeavouring to get another asset to Café Schwarzenberg and will attempt to regain surveillance on Weizman. Sodano's cell phone last tracked in vicinity of Bratislava, following the Danube towards Budapest. Request further instructions.

'Fuck!' Wiley slammed his fist on his desk. What the hell was Sodano doing in Bratislava and why was he headed for Budapest? Wiley had been in no position to haggle over the €100 000 Sodano had demanded up front, but if the little shit had done a runner, it would be his last. For now, there were too many unanswered questions. Wiley angrily punched in a response:

> For chief of station Vienna: 'Endeavouring' not good enough. Surveillance to be re-established at all costs, including airport, train stations and border crossing. O'Connor and Weizman assigned code names Tutankhamen and Nefertiti, respectively. Berlin station on full alert and able to assist. Advise re-establishment of contact SOONEST.

Wiley had chosen the codenames deliberately. Tutankhamen and Nefertiti had both met early deaths, and neither death had ever been explained. Wiley had every intention that history would repeat itself. He buzzed Larry Davis, his chief of staff.

'We have a situation. I want the ops room brought up to speed,' he ordered, 'and include the background to this Maya Codex. I'll be down there in three minutes.'

36

WESTBAHNHOF, VIENNA

Curtis O'Connor scanned the lower floor of Vienna's cavernous international railway terminal. The station was busy and the announcements in German and English echoed off the marble walls. Seeing nothing untoward, he and Aleta joined the queue in front of one of the ticket windows.

'*Zwei Karten zu Bad Arolsen, Business-Class, bitte.*'

'*Single oder zurück?*'

'*Single, bitte.*'

'*Das wird €480 bitte.*'

'*Danke schön.*'

'There's a coffee shop upstairs,' O'Connor said after he'd paid cash for the tickets.

'The train goes in twenty minutes. Is there time?'

O'Connor smiled. 'Always assume you're being tailed. The train leaves from Platform 6, but we'll get on at the last minute. That way it's harder for someone to organise a ticket – although the Austrians are so efficient you can buy them on board these days,' he added, his smile fading. 'And stick this in your bag,' he said, handing Aleta a new cell phone. 'From now on, I want you to assume everything you say on your cell phone is being monitored, and that includes texts.'

'Won't they be tracking yours?'

'They will. But as we speak, it's bound in bubble wrap and making its way out of the Imperial's toilets into Vienna's main sewer. Hopefully it will confuse them and buy us a little more time.'

They rode the escalator to the departure floor. Below them, the tall, thin man in the black overcoat entered the lower floor of the station.

The train sped quietly and smoothly westwards towards Linz, the capital of Oberösterreich, the city where Hitler attended high school with the great philosopher Ludwig Wittgenstein; a city from which the Mauthausen concentration camp was less than twenty-five kilometres away. The fields and distant forests were blanketed in a fresh covering of snow and the sun struggled to penetrate the low clouds scudding across the border from Italy.

'You don't slum it, do you?' Aleta sank back into one of just four leather seats in their business-class compartment. They had the compartment to themselves.

'Not if the CIA's paying. In about three hours we'll cross the German border near Passau. From there it's another three hours to Würzburg, where we'll change trains for Kassel-Wilhelmshöhe. Once there, we'll change again for Bad Arolsen.'

Aleta shivered at the thought of what she might find.

'How well do you know Monsignor Jennings?' O'Connor asked, picking up on her distress and changing the subject.

'Well enough, unfortunately, although I've never worked with him. It's always been a mystery to me why he's held in such high esteem in archaeological circles.'

'Overrated?'

'A self-opinionated, arrogant twit. He's very close to the Vatican, and they seem to have an unhealthy influence on him.'

O'Connor grinned. 'He speaks very highly of you, too.'

Aleta made a face. 'He's also rumoured to be fond of little boys.'

O'Connor's grin evaporated.

'That's the problem with the Vatican – most of them are hypocrites,' Aleta continued. 'Pius XII didn't lift a finger to help my grandfather or any of the millions of other Jews slaughtered at the hands of the Nazis, and nothing's changed. Now Benedict's given his blessing to a bishop who's denied the gas chambers even existed! What was his name —'

'Williamson,' O'Connor said simply.

'Richard Williamson! How could I forget? And Benedict, who in his time as Cardinal Inquisitor amassed detailed dossiers on everyone from Hans Küng to Teilhard de Chardin, now claims it was all a simple misunderstanding? That he should have consulted the internet? Give me a break!' Still angry at the injustice of being targeted by powerful institutions and finding herself on the run, Aleta was not about to cut O'Connor any slack. 'As for you Americans, you're the most powerful country in the world, and you throw your weight around so everyone knows it. You say you stand for freedom, yet when it suits your purpose, you think nothing of shipping people off to secret torture prisons around the world – prisons that you bastards in the CIA run – and most of these people just disappear. And as for that last idiot you elected to the White House, I doubt he's ever even read the Geneva Conventions. He picks a White House legal counsel who thinks water-boarding and leaving people out in the open to freeze in temperatures below zero are just fine. What did he say? "Terrorism renders obsolete the Geneva Conventions' strict limitations on the questioning of prisoners" . . . That's the sort of thing the Nazis did to my grandfather, and you bastards are no better. You *trained* the death squads who killed my father!'

'In other words, torture is okay,' O'Connor interpolated quietly. 'You're absolutely right: the Vatican and Washington have both lost the plot, and I'm not going to defend the indefensible. I can understand your anger at American foreign policy, too. Half the world hates us at the moment.'

'You flatter yourself if you think only *half* the world hates you. Where I come from it would be hard to find someone with a good word for an American, and don't kid yourself it's much better over here. I don't think you've got any idea how much damage your government's policies have done, Mr O'Connor.' Aleta reverted to formality. 'Or should that be Agent O'Connor?'

'That's the Hollywood version. It's actually "Officer", although when you're ready, Curtis will do just fine.'

'What I can't understand, given your views,' Aleta said, speaking more softly now, 'is why you're still working for the CIA?'

'Well, once they tumble to what happened back in your apartment, I'll be off the payroll. But despite what you think, with a few notable exceptions, the CIA is made up of basically decent human beings trying to serve their country.' O'Connor paused, trying to order his own emotions. 'I joined the CIA because I thought I could make a difference. Unfortunately it hasn't turned out that way. Although who knows? If we can recover the codex, that might redress the balance a little. Do your grandfather's notes throw any light on things?'

'I haven't had a chance to go through them in detail, although when Levi was in Tikal in the 1930s, he unearthed a stone carving.' Aleta opened the notebook at the page on which Levi Weizman had attached a photograph of a stela he had named 'Stela D'. 'The alligator represents the Milky Way,' she said, pointing to her grandfather's notations on his drawing of the intricate carving, 'and in Mayan hieroglyphics, the alligator's mouth is the Milky Way's dark rift or *Xibalba be*. The hieroglyphics surrounding the alligator all depict the December solstice sun of 2012.'

'Yet Jennings plays it down. Would he be aware of this?'

'He should be, because that stela is still in Tikal. It's similar to the Izapa stelae, which were excavated near the Guatemalan–Mexican border in the 1960s by archaeologists from Brigham State University and decoded by the noted Mayanist scholar, John Major Jenkins.' Aleta turned the page in Levi Weizman's notebook, now yellowed with age. 'I am convinced,' she said, reading from her grandfather's notes, 'that the hieroglyphics on Stela Delta indicate that this rare alignment of our planet and solar system with the centre of the Milky Way galaxy will be accompanied by a dramatic decrease in the earth's magnetic field and an equally dramatic increase in sunspot activity.'

The train slowed as the plough on the forward engine sliced

through an unusually heavy autumn build-up of snow on the tracks. Both O'Connor and Aleta were totally absorbed in Levi Weizman's notes, and neither noticed the tall, thin man make his way along the corridor outside. He glanced into their compartment as he passed.

Aleta continued to read from the old notebook: 'I have discussed this with Albert, and he is of the view we should take this seriously.'

'I gather your grandfather was a friend of Einstein's.'

Aleta nodded. 'Both of them detested the Nazis with a passion. You're probably aware that by the time my grandfather had unearthed Stela D at Tikal, Einstein had already published his paper on the theory of relativity.'

'The mathematics was a little complex, as I recall. Nonlinear partial differential equations.'

'Exactly, and from those you can predict the existence of black holes. My grandfather was not only an archaeologist, he was a passionate physicist, and even back then, these men were thinking about this.'

O'Connor looked out the window. The train had picked up speed. The lines ran beside the Danube now, and the trees on the banks were heavy with snow. 'It may be coincidence, but the earth's magnetic field is at its weakest in recorded history,' he said finally. 'I spent some time on one of our research bases in Alaska recently. The field is down to less than 0.5 gauss, and the poles are shifting very rapidly – more than thirty kilometres a year. The magnetic North Pole is no longer centred in Canadian territory, where it's been for the last 400 years. It's now located north of Canada's Queen Elizabeth Islands and moving rapidly across the Arctic Ocean towards Siberia. Since its discovery in 1831, it's moved 1100 kilometres, and as the magnetic field weakens, that movement is speeding up.'

'It's not the first time this has happened,' Aleta agreed solemnly. 'And if the magnetic field drops to zero gauss, we're all in big trouble . . . '

O'Connor nodded. 'Yes, not only do we lose all near-earth orbiting satellites, which would throw communications and ship and aircraft navigation into chaos, but if we lose the earth's protective magnetic envelope, there's no shield against deadly cosmic rays.'

'And there'd be altitude sickness at sea level. The only safety would be in underground bunkers,' Aleta added. 'I've seen some recent research published by respected paleomagnetists who've been drilling through ancient volcanoes, and their core samples prove the magnetic poles haven't always been in the Arctic and Antarctic.'

O'Connor and Aleta both knew that molten lava was rich in minerals, especially iron; minerals that oriented and then cooled along the prevailing magnetic field of the earth, providing an indelible record of the ancient positions of the magnetic poles. They also knew that as scientists mapped the ocean floor, they'd discovered that magnetite, the magnetic mineral in volcanic basalt, had left a similar footprint beneath the sea.

'The northern lights may not be the only thing Canada loses,' Aleta concluded. 'It's another indicator this planet may be in a lot more trouble than we think.'

'It's more your field than mine, but didn't scientists find tropical coral outbreaks when they drilled in Newfoundland?'

'The evidence is a lot more extensive than that. Scientists drilling through the ice in Antarctica have found fossilised tropical forests and ferns at depths that coincide with Mayan records of history. In the northern hemisphere they've found evidence of swamp cypress near the North Pole, as well as fig trees under northern Greenland, which means there's not only been magnetic pole shifts in the past but *geographic* pole shifts, devastating life on the planet.'

'The rise in sunspot activity is further proof that we're headed into very rough waters,' O'Connor agreed, 'but Monsignor Jennings wasn't buying the suggestion that the Maya knew about the sun's magnetic field?'

'Again, quite strange for someone in his position.' Aleta turned to another page in her grandfather's notebook. 'Levi says here "Stela F provides incontrovertible evidence that the Maya were well versed in the twenty-two-year cycle of the sun's magnetic field and the accompanying rise and fall in sunspot activity." '

'Does your grandfather give any clues as to how the ancients were able to investigate sunspots without even a basic telescope?'

Aleta shook her head. 'He just notes that he can't be sure if the Maya knew anything about the equator of the sun moving more quickly than its poles, or whether that's the reason the sun's plasma gets into such a tangle. And he also doubts they were aware of the intense electromagnetic radiation and solar winds. But he does say he suspects the Maya were aware of the effects of sunspots on the planet, and there's no doubt they were able to predict the cycles.'

'And the current cycle will reach its peak in 2012. A geographic shift, with the North Pole ending up in New York or the South Pole in Sydney . . .' O'Connor left the deadly prospect hanging. If the Maya Codex was predicting a geographic shift, both Aleta and O'Connor knew the human race would need to take extraordinary precautions, and even then much of life as we know it would not survive.

37

CIA HEADQUARTERS, LANGLEY, VIRGINIA

'Everyone here, Davis?' Wiley demanded of his chief of staff as he strode into the CIA operations room. A high-resolution computer screen showed a real-time satellite image of a train located some distance from the border between Austria and Germany and heading north-west. Another showed a map of the Danube with a blinking blue crosshair encoded with Sodano's cell phone number. The crosshair was moving south through Budapest. Yet another provided a map of the streets of Vienna with another crosshair annotated with O'Connor's cell phone. The track was leading away from *Währinger Strasse* and *Maria-Theresian Strasse* towards the *Donaukanal*.

'Ready to go, Sir. The chiefs of station in Vienna and Berlin are on secure video link,' Larry Davis confirmed. Davis was only slightly taller than Wiley. Overweight, bald and out of condition, Davis wiped the sweat from his brow.

'We have a situation,' Wiley barked at the six officers Davis had briefed into the top-secret compartment of Operation Maya. 'This is priority one. What've you got, Vienna?'

The encrypted video screen switched to the chief of station in a small operations room hidden in the bowels of the white four-storey US Embassy building in *Boltzmanngasse*, a quiet leafy street in Vienna.

'We have an asset on board the Vienna–Würzburg intercity express. He has confirmed Tutankhamen is with Nefertiti in Car 3. They've crossed the Austrian–German border and they're now ten kilometres north-west of Nuremberg. The train is scheduled to arrive at Würzburg Hauptbahnhof in fifty-two minutes.'

'Then who has Tutankhamen's cell phone?'

'Not known, but it's currently moving slowly east towards the Donaukanal.' Wiley glanced at the screen tracking O'Connor's cell phone, showing a location at the intersection of Schottenring and Rossauer Lande.

'Whoever's got it, I want them tracked down – now!'

'We've got the area under surveillance.' The Vienna chief of station, a grey-haired veteran CIA boss in his late fifties, was unperturbed by the DDO's fiery temper.

'And Sodano?'

'He appears to be still on a barge that has crossed the border into Hungary and that's now tracking south through Budapest.'

'*Appears?* I want to *know*!' Wiley glowered at the screen locked onto Sodano's cell phone. The blue crosshairs were hovering above the western channel of the Danube, abeam Margitsziget Island, just to the south of the Árpád Bridge. 'Get Budapest to put an asset on that barge,' Wiley barked at his chief of staff. 'I want Sodano brought in, and fast!'

Davis nodded towards his deputy, a slim, attractive brunette in her late thirties. Ellen Rodriguez had spent the last three years as Deputy Chief of Station in Lima, and before that she had worked at the White House. In the short time she'd been back, she had already clashed with Howard Wiley twice, and she was beginning to regret accepting the position on Langley's Latin American desk. Rodriguez logged into a spare computer in the ops room, but her attention was dragged back to the video screen almost immediately. Vienna's chief of station had been alerted to a live *Die Welt* online video update.

'Wait, we've got some breaking news here. The Austrian Bundespolizei and the Bundeskriminalamt are investigating the discovery of the body of a Sicilian national in a garbage truck.' The Langley technicians switched the camera feed to a live media conference with Gruppeninspektor Hans Boehm. The square-jawed police inspector was standing outside Vienna's state of the art waste-disposal unit near the *Donaukanal*. Its distinguishing landmark, a tall space-age silver tower, soared in the background. A large group of journalists were jostling for position.

'*Die Stelle zu sein scheint, von Antonio Sodano, Sizilianer, der nun Wohnsitz —*'

'Translation!' Wiley demanded.

'The body appears to be that of Antonio Sodano, a Sicilian who is now resident in Rome.' Ellen Rodriguez had not only served three years in Lima before working in the White House, she'd spent three years in Vienna and Berlin.

'*Haben Sie eine Idee von der Ursache der Tod, Inspektor?*'

'Do you have any idea of the cause of death, Inspector?' Rodriguez translated.

'It would appear that the deceased has been strangled, but we will not be able to confirm that until after an autopsy.'

'Where did this take place, Inspector?' another journalist asked.

'That's not clear either, although the truck in which the body was found had just completed its run through the Stephansdom Quarter in the city.'

'O'Connor!' Wiley muttered angrily.

'Is there a motive, Inspector?'

Gruppeninspektor Boehm smiled patiently. 'We do know that Mr Sodano was wanted in Rome by the Italian *Guardia di Finanza* for suspected drug-trafficking, so we haven't ruled out that it might be drug-related.'

'Fuck!' Wiley turned to the six officers who made up Operation Maya. 'Nefertiti represents a clear and present danger to the United States. So far, we have failed spectacularly to carry out what should be a simple elimination operation. It's also clear that Tutankhamen has gone over to the dark side.' Wiley turned back to the video feed. 'Vienna, your asset on board the train has a green light. Deal with them!'

'Both of them?' the Vienna chief of station asked, taken aback. He had worked with O'Connor in the field.

'Both of them!' Wiley barked. 'Sodano wasn't some two-bit punk. He could handle himself. This has got O'Connor's mark all over it.'

'Why would someone like O'Connor go over to the dark side?' Ellen Rodriguez asked. 'We don't have any evidence of that yet.'

Wiley turned, his eyes blazing. 'I make the decisions around here,

Rodriguez.' The other officers looked uncomfortable, but no one else spoke up in O'Connor's defence.

'Berlin. I want assets to move at a moment's notice,' Wiley ordered, turning back to the video connection, 'and get some observation on the Würzburg Hauptbahnhof. I want timetables of every connecting train and bus. If we don't get them on the train, I want to know where they're headed.' Wiley turned to Davis. 'Get hold of Nefertiti's movements in the last month. I want her cell phone connections, Blackberry, bank statements, credit cards, home-phone bills – anything that might give us a lead on why she's in Germany. And,' he said, lowering his voice, 'tell that bitch Rodriguez if she ever challenges me again, she'll be serving coffee in the canteen.'

'Watch your step, Rodriguez. The boss is pretty pissed,' Davis warned, mopping his brow after Wiley had left.

'*He's* pretty pissed? Jesus Christ, Larry. Have you thought about what we're doing here? I've worked with O'Connor. He's not the sort of guy to jump ship. And have you read the Weizman dossier? "Clear and present danger" got way overused in Iraq. Weizman's an archaeologist, for Christ's sake! Can someone please explain to me what threat she poses to Capitol Hill?' Rodriguez glared at Davis, her green eyes flashing angrily. One or two of the younger male officers smirked. Larry Davis was only marginally more popular than Wiley.

'Just get on with tasking Budapest to recover Sodano's cell phone,' Davis said. 'The rest of you, get cracking on Nefertiti and Tutankhamen's movements and phone calls. Let's go!'

'Asshole,' Rodriguez muttered as she went back to her desk.

38

NUREMBERG–WÜRZBURG, GERMANY

Three hours into the journey, the train rocked smoothly on a superbly engineered hydraulic suspension. A vista of fields and farmhouses flashed past the windows.

'My father escaped with just the clothes on his back and two maps,' Aleta said, taking the first of the maps her father had managed to secrete out of Austria. 'He always thought this one related to Tikal, but he wasn't sure.'

O'Connor scanned the *huun* bark diagram. 'A triangle in Tikal . . . That could mean anything.'

Aleta nodded. 'And this one isn't the original,' she said, handing O'Connor the second map. 'The original was given to my grandfather by some Maya elders and was also drawn on *huun* bark paper.'

'Where's the original now?'

'When the family was arrested, it was confiscated, but my father made a copy from memory. Unfortunately he couldn't remember all the figures and it's very rough. He always thought the shape was similar to Lake Atitlán.'

O'Connor took the map and examined it carefully, a puzzled look on his face.

'You don't think so?' Aleta asked.

'It may well be Lake Atitlán, although I've never been there. The problem is that only one of the three lines on the map has what looks like a compass bearing on it,' he said, pointing to the lines drawn across the yellow patch, 'and if it *is* a bearing, it doesn't match up with the north point on the map. Unless . . . unless . . . of course!' O'Connor exclaimed. 'It's a backbearing!'

'Backbearing?'

'It's an old military technique. We used it before GPS satellites took all the fun out of getting lost in the jungle. If you weren't sure of your position, you found a high point and took bearings to three points, like the top of a mountain or the mouth of a river, which were marked on the map, and therefore accurately known. By reversing the bearings, you can produce a small triangle where they intersect, and you should be inside the triangle. The smaller the triangle the more accurate the resection. Are there any prominent landmarks around Lake Atitlán?'

'The volcanoes! There are three of them, the largest of which is Volcán Atitlán.' Aleta pointed to the southernmost point on the map. 'Just to the north of Atitlán is Volcán Tolimán, and to the east is Volcán San Pedro, which has a small village at its base. They're all over 9000 feet, so you can see them from anywhere on the lake. Two of them are close together, and so are the lines on this map. They fit perfectly.'

'Although it's still not much help. There's only one accurate back-bearing, and the triangle of intersection is pretty big.'

'That's as best as my father could remember, and there's not much around where the lines intersect,' Aleta said. 'The nearest village aside from San Pedro is San Marcos, where I was brought up, further to the east around this inlet. It's mainly coffee and corn plantations. The people grow their own vegetables, chilli verde, tomatoes, onions, avocadoes, cucumbers, strawberries, pitahaya fruit . . . Life was simple until the death squads came.'

O'Connor nodded sympathetically. 'So what would be here?' he asked, pointing again to the triangle.

'A big rocky volcanic outcrop that drops into the lake. The whole area is volcanic. Without the other two bearings, it would be needle in a haystack stuff.'

'Are the volcanoes still active?'

'Volcán Atitlán is; it last erupted in 1853. Tolimán might be, although not recently. The lake itself was formed from a volcanic eruption. It used to have lots of fish species, until the Americans came in. Pan American Airlines thought it would be a really good idea to introduce non-native bass for American tourists to catch, but the bass ended up destroying all the native fish as well as causing the extinction of the giant grebe bird.' Aleta raised her eyebrows at O'Connor.

O'Connor winced. 'Are there many villages around the lake?' he asked, staying away from America's foreign policy record.

'Not many. Panajachel is the largest town on the north shore . . . about 14 000 people. Then you have the little villages like San Pedro, San Lucas, San Marcos and San Juan. You can see the Spanish Catholic influence, but Mayan spirituality is still very strong.'

'Even allowing for there being only one bearing, all three lines are drawn across the lake. Perhaps we're looking for something underneath the water?'

'Lake Atitlán's very deep, well over 400 metres, and there are caves.' Aleta fell silent as they both pondered the possibility. 'There's a diving school at Santa Cruz, but I don't think they dive this far south.'

'Diving at high altitude has its own risks.' O'Connor wondered whether Aleta would disclose her qualifications. 'Anything more than 400 metres above sea level and you need special training.' Both knew that diving at high altitude meant increased risks of decompression sickness.

'Lake Atitlán's well above that, around 1500 metres above sea level. Is diving amongst your skills?'

O'Connor nodded. 'I trained with the US Navy SEALS . . . ' His voice trailed off as he glanced through the compartment window. He was instantly on guard as a man in a beret and dark overcoat walked past their compartment.

'What's the matter?' Aleta asked.

'We've got company. The guy in the beret; he just walked past.'

'So maybe he's going to Würzburg or some place beyond?' Aleta suggested, more out of hope than conviction.

'I don't think so. Put the map and the notebook in your briefcase and pretend to be asleep. If he comes back, don't move. Breathe slowly and leave things to me.'

Aleta leaned back and closed her eyes, trust in her mysterious companion growing.

O'Connor pulled his Glock 21 from his leather jacket and screwed on the specially fitted silencer. He left his jacket covering the pistol, leaned back in his seat, half closed his eyes and waited.

Ten minutes out from Würzburg, the man with the beret returned. After observing O'Connor and Aleta sleeping, he quietly opened the compartment door. He took the seat next to Aleta and in one practised movement withdrew a razor-sharp KA-BAR Hawk-bill Tanto knife from his coat pocket.

O'Connor fired twice and the .45 calibre bullets slammed into the assailant's heart, hurling him back into the leather seat. The *phut phut* of the silencer seemed very loud and Aleta jumped as the knife clattered to the compartment floor.

'*Mierda!*' Aleta swore.

O'Connor motioned her to be quiet. He put on his leather gloves and returned the knife to his assailant's pocket. He searched the other pockets, keeping the hitman's cell phone. His mind racing, O'Connor checked the corridor outside and the toilet a few steps away at the end of the carriage. Empty. If the bathroom wasn't cleaned until the train terminated in Frankfurt, it might be possible to at least confuse the Bundespolizei for a while. A bright-red bloodstain was spreading over the man's white shirt. O'Connor buttoned up the black overcoat, hooked one of the dead man's arms around his neck, and dragged him down the still-empty corridor to the toilet, then sat him on it. He closed the door and locked it from the outside with the screwdriver blade on his pocketknife.

Aleta was white and shaken.

'You okay?'

She nodded. 'Does this happen often?' she asked, a tremor in her voice.

'Comes with the territory. Lord Acton got it right with his "power corrupts and absolute power corrupts absolutely". Wiley and Cardinal Felici fit the description, and unfortunately we're at the top of their hit list.'

The train began to slow on its approach into Würzburg.

'They may have the station under observation,' O'Connor said, lifting Aleta's bag from the rack above her seat, but they'll be looking for a couple, so we walk off separately. Look down, so the CCTV cameras don't get a clear picture of your face. The connecting train leaves from Platform 5 in fifteen minutes. I'll be watching your back.'

'Do I board?'

O'Connor nodded as he checked the corridor outside. 'They won't know our final destination – yet – and in a big station like Würzburg, they can't watch every platform. See you there.' He flashed Aleta what he hoped was a reassuring smile and headed for the carriage behind.

We're in luck, he thought as he followed Aleta at a discreet distance. Four trains had arrived within minutes of each other and the railroad hub for the Bavarian agricultural and industrial city was even busier than usual. O'Connor detoured onto another platform, boarded a train scheduled for Göttingen and dropped the assailant's cell phone into a bin in a carriage toilet. He was pushing his luck with another cell phone decoy, but Wiley would be tracking it, and he wouldn't be able to ignore the location feedback. O'Connor retraced his steps to Platform 5. When he reached their business-class compartment, Aleta was already sitting by the window; he took the other window seat. The two remaining seats were occupied by an elderly couple, and O'Connor breathed a little easier. Even if the boys in Berlin had tracked them and managed to get one of their assets on the train, Wiley would be wary of attempting anything in front of witnesses, and even more wary of disposing of an elderly couple in broad daylight, but only because of the heat that would follow the publicity.

The train pulled out, on time to the second, and O'Connor smiled to himself as he reflected on the energy Wiley would have expended tracking his small cell phone as it wended its way through the sewers of Vienna. For now, they were probably safe, but not for long. Incandescent with rage, Wiley would probably now be mobilising the CIA's considerable forces: command and control centres in US embassies around the world; trained killers of questionable background fluent in German, accommodated in boarding houses and motel rooms and kept on the payroll for just this type of emergency; international intelligence agencies; as well as foreign police forces and security agencies.

O'Connor resolved to get off at Kassel-Wilhelmshöhe and hire a car.

O'Connor scanned the surrounding fields with his binoculars. He had found a quiet farmstay on the outskirts of Bad Arolsen. There was only light traffic on Route 252, which connected Bad Arolsen with Mengeringhausen to the south, and the dirt tracks around the farm were deserted. The trip into town took them no more than ten minutes and O'Connor found a car park on the leafy Grand Avenue. The World War Two Waffen-SS barracks housing the twenty-six kilometres of Holocaust files had been renovated and a new headquarters constructed. The more friendly livery of the International Red Cross and the International Tracing Service fluttered in the garden outside the reception area.

'Frau Weizman, welcome to Bad Arolsen. We've been expecting you. The documents you've requested have been extracted from the archives. If you will just sign the register and follow me please.' The efficiency of the reception staff matched that with which the Nazis had recorded every detail of their savagery, although the purpose of the International Tracing Service could not have been more different.

Aleta's face was almost as pale as the gloves that had been provided for them to handle the files containing the pink Gestapo arrest warrants, the records of incarceration, *die Kontrolle Karten* recording in obsessive detail everything down to the number and size of any head lice on the prisoners, and the sinister *Totenbuchen* – the Death Books.

'Are you sure you're going to be okay with this?' O'Connor asked.

'*I have* to know what happened to them,' Aleta said. She opened the first file and began the awful task of scanning the names. They worked side by side in silence for nearly an hour, until O'Connor suddenly paused.

'There's an arrest warrant here confirming your grandparents and your father and his sister were taken to Mauthausen. The date is April 1938.'

Aleta scanned the four warrants: Levi Ehud Weizman. Ramona Miriam Weizman. Ariel Levi Weizman. Rebekkah Miriam Weizman. The place of arrest was *Judengasse*, Vienna.

'The commandant of Mauthausen was a young SS officer, Karl

von Heißen. One of Himmler's favourites. Levi worked with him in Guatemala,' Aleta said.

'Your grandfather worked with the Nazis?'

'He didn't have a choice. It was before the war. Himmler was convinced the Aryan master race had established some of the great civilisations of the world, including the Maya, and my grandfather was one of the few people who had been to Tikal and worked on the Mayan hieroglyphics. Himmler ordered him to join a Nazi expedition to the jungle highlands as the consulting archaeologist, and von Heißen was personally selected by Himmler to lead the expedition. My grandfather was very careful about committing anything to paper, though there are cryptic clues in the back of the notebook I showed you. But something happened between my grandfather and von Heißen on that expedition, and I have a hunch von Heißen had my grandfather marked out for special treatment when he arrived at Mauthausen.'

'Being on the Nazi payroll didn't count for much,' O'Connor observed. 'Von Heißen would have been quite young to be a concentration camp commandant.'

'Young, sadistic and brutal – just some of the qualities that no doubt impressed Himmler. I suspect Levi would have been less than cooperative on the expedition, and if he found anything of value, I think he would have made every effort to conceal it from the Nazis, as he did with the figurines. I know my grandfather tried to get the family out of Vienna when he returned from Guatemala, but by then it was too late.'

'Did your father talk about it much?' O'Connor asked gently, conscious of Aleta's enormous loss, a loss that was compounded immeasurably by the murder of her father at the hands of the Guatemalan government and the CIA.

'Only once. We were fishing on Lake Atitlán in the little native canoe we had. My father didn't say too much. It's hard to imagine what they went through . . . and even harder to work out why.' Aleta shook her head and wiped away a tear. 'It's still one of the great unanswered questions, isn't it? The Nazis finished up with enormous power, but how was it that so many ordinary Germans got into the sewers with them and behaved like animals? My father always suffered from terrible nightmares, but he was one of the few to escape from a concentration camp. He was one of those children saved by Archbishop Roncalli when he was papal nuncio in Istanbul.'

Aha, O'Connor thought. 'Forged Catholic baptism certificates?'

Aleta nodded. 'The Vatican has had its fair share of corrupt and power-hungry cardinals, but every so often they elect someone like Roncalli to the papacy.'

'Pope John XXIII,' O'Connor agreed. 'One of the truly great Popes. Was that the reason your father converted to Catholicism?'

'He never forgot Monsignor Roncalli's kindness when he reached Istanbul, and it was his way of repaying him.'

They turned their attention back to the Death Books. The books had been prepared with one name to every line, the columns recording prisoner numbers, names, the precise time and date and place of the murders and the method of killing. Aleta opened a book that was inscribed meticulously in black copperplate *Totenbuch – Mauthausen 1.1.37 – 31.12.38.*

'Bastards,' Aleta swore, as half an hour later, she came across a long and significant list of names.

O'Connor came around to her side of the table. 'Each of them murdered on the same day . . . but two minutes apart,' he said, noticing the regularity of the executions.

'There was a reason for that.' Aleta struggled to control her bitterness. 'It was Hitler's birthday, and as a present to the Führer, von Heißen gave orders that for an hour and a half, a Jew would be shot every two minutes.'

The Nazis obviously didn't believe in cakes, O'Connor thought darkly.

Aleta turned the page and gasped, her hand trembling over her mouth. O'Connor stood behind her. At the top of the page, were two names inscribed in copperplate:

LEVI EHUD WEIZMAN   20.4.38 1402hrs   Executed
RAMONA MIRIAM WEIZMAN 21.4.38 1131hrs   Died – medical experiment

'I'm deeply sorry, Aleta,' O'Connor said, resting his hand on her shoulder.

'Thank you. At least I know. It's closure, in a way.'

O'Connor's mind went back to the CIA archives and Father Hernandez, the CIA's asset in San Pedro. 'Was von Heißen ever brought to trial, do you know?' he asked finally.

Aleta shook her head. 'Not as far as I'm aware.'

'At the end of the war, the Vatican and the CIA worked together to arrange the escape of Nazi war criminals who were in a position to assist the fight against the rise of Communism. Some of them were disguised as priests and many were smuggled down the "Vatican Ratlines", including Adolf Eichmann and Klaus Barbie.'

'Yes. I wonder what Christ would have said about *that*?' Aleta pondered again the hypocrisy of some of the church's leaders.

O'Connor nodded, reflecting on his own bitter experiences at the hands of the Church. 'I think if Christ had been around, he would've done a lot more than just upturn the money tables in the Vatican Bank. The thing is, von Heißen was very close to Himmler. The CIA and the Vatican might have considered him a valuable asset.'

'You think he might have been one of those who escaped?'

'It's possible. And a lot of them were smuggled out to Central and South America, including Guatemala. It's only a hunch, but before I came to Vienna, I spent some time going through the CIA archives. The CIA smuggling operation was known as Operation Paperclip. The CIA had an asset on the shores of Lake Atitlán . . . a Father Hernandez.'

'I remember him! He was a nasty piece of work. And now that you mention it, his Spanish was very good, but he had a thick European accent, which could easily have been German. You think . . . ?'

O'Connor shrugged. 'I don't know. I've seen no concrete evidence that von Heißen and Hernandez are one and the same person. But from what you've told me, von Heißen spent quite a bit of time in Guatemala before the war. If he was given a choice of countries in Central or South America, it would make sense to go back to a place he was familiar with.'

'And if he did escape to Central America, he may have taken the original *huun* bark map with him. Which would have the precise bearings to the location at Lake Atitlán,' Aleta mused.

'Something to keep in the backs of our minds, anyway. Tomorrow we leave before dawn and head for Mauthausen, and we'll take the car. They'll be watching the trains.'

39

CIA HEADQUARTERS, LANGLEY, VIRGINIA

Ellen Rodriguez brushed her dark hair away from her tanned, freckled face and took the call on one of the operations room's secure lines. Brandon Gray, the CIA's young, ambitious chief of station in Berlin, sounded grim.

'The police in Frankfurt have just given a news conference. I'm sending it through now. Our asset on the Vienna train has been killed.'

'Tutankhamen . . . ?'

'Wiley will want to know.'

Thirty minutes later, Wiley and Larry Davis arrived together.

'Roll the video,' Wiley demanded.

Rodriguez nodded to the duty officer and the online edition of *Die Welt* appeared on screen, headlining the discovery of a body at Frankfurt Hauptbahnhof. The footage cut to the media conference conducted by Frankfurt's Erster Polizeihauptkommissar, Franz Reinhardt.

'In answer to your question, we can't be sure exactly where the murder took place.' Ellen Rodriguez stepped in again as translator.

'An estimate, Hauptkommissar?' The questions came from a young blonde reporter, who had elbowed her way to the front of the pack.

Reinhardt shook his head patiently. After nearly forty years in the Hessen State Kriminalpolizei, most of them as a detective, he was not about to be fazed by a pushy young journalist. 'The train originated in Vienna and departed at 10.40. It didn't arrive in Frankfurt until 17.36, nearly seven hours later. The murder could have been carried out virtually anywhere along that route.'

'What about the autopsy?' the young woman persisted. 'Surely the state of the body, rigor mortis, temperature . . . an examination will enable you to be more accurate?'

'A preliminary examination of the body has revealed that the victim was shot twice in the heart, at reasonably close range. I expect the results of the autopsy to be available some time later today, but I would caution you not to put too much emphasis on an autopsy. Determining the time of death is never an exact science,' Reinhardt said bluntly, looking directly at the journalist. 'In the first place, the temperature of death to which you refer, algor mortis, is only indicative. Under ideal conditions, a body will cool by one degree every hour; but that timespan can vary by up to six hours, which covers a lot of distance by train. Rigor mortis is just as problematic. That can vary from fifteen minutes to fifteen hours.' Some of the older journalists were smiling.

'Have you identified the body?'

'We have a passport, and we are trying to trace the deceased's family. Until we do, it would not be appropriate for me to comment further.'

'We've heard that the toilet cubicle was locked, Hauptkommissar. How do you account for that?' another journalist asked.

'Time will tell. For the moment, there is no apparent motive and no signs of a struggle, but we will be seeking to interview everyone who has travelled on this particular train, and we're asking anyone who has seen or heard anything suspicious to come forward immediately.'

Reinhardt retreated into his headquarters and the video was replaced by a live feed from the depths of the new and inelegant US\$130 million US Embassy abutting the side of Tiergarten Park at the prestigious 2 Pariser Platz Square. Security considerations during the building's construction had forced the German authorities to move an entire street. One of the major newspapers, *Süddeutsche Zeitung*, had dubbed it 'Fort Knox at the Brandenburg Gate'.

'Have we got anything more concrete than the party line from PC Plod?' Wiley demanded of the Berlin chief of station.

'The last contact we had with our asset was thirty minutes out of Würzburg. It appears that Tutankhamen took our man's cell phone, which might be his first big mistake. We've been tracking it and we know that Tutankhamen, and probably Nefertiti as well, terminated at Göttingen Hauptbahnhof. They're still in that vicinity and I've mobilised two assets to close on them.'

Ellen Rodriguez watched the exchange with interest. She had met Brandon Gray only once, during a conference when they'd had a heated argument over the place of women in the Agency. Along with many other Agency insiders, she had been surprised when Wiley had appointed Gray to one of the most senior posts in Europe. Brash, ambitious and every bit as arrogant as Wiley, the tall, wiry crew-cut Gray was often wrong, but never in doubt. She looked at the screen showing the progress of the blue crosshairs annotated with the cell phone and shook her head. It would be most unlike O'Connor to make such a basic error.

'That's assuming Tutankhamen's kept the cell phone on him,' she said.

'What do you mean?' Gray demanded, his anger bursting from the video screen.

'I mean that we recovered Sodano's cell phone on a barge, presumably dropped there by Tutankhamen to throw us off the scent. Why would he keep your asset's cell phone and allow you to track him?'

'To monitor messages, for starters!' Wiley exploded.

'Precisely, sir,' Gray responded. 'And perhaps Officer Rodriguez can explain how the cell phone might have got off the train at Göttingen of its own accord?'

Rodriguez remained silent, torn between her loyalty to the Agency and her respect for O'Connor.

'Sir, might it be time to bring the German and Austrian police into the loop? Without their full cooperation, it's proving hard to track passport movements,' Gray suggested.

'No,' Wiley barked, 'that will compromise our own operations. Track the passports through the back door.' He turned away from the screen and glared at Rodriguez. 'What've we got on Nefertiti?'

'We've just received her cell phone bills for the last twelve months,' Rodriguez replied evenly, 'so we're still sifting through them. In the last two weeks Nefertiti's cell phone traffic has been light – calls to her travel agent in Guatemala City, calls to the *Museo Nacional de Arqueologia y Etnologia* and the *Museo Popol Vuh*, also in Guatemala City. The only call that might be of interest, and it's the last one she made from her cell phone,' Rodriguez added pointedly, 'was three days ago from Vienna to the International Tracing Service in Bad Arolsen, a spa town in northern Germany. I doubt Tutankhamen and Nefertiti are in Göttingen – they're more likely headed for Bad Arolsen.'

Wiley turned back to the Berlin feed. 'Concentrate on Göttingen and give your assets there a green light, but get someone out to Bad Arolsen, just in case. Either way, we take them out!'

With an ease that came from nearly ten years driving twenty-tonne waste-collection vehicles, Bernhard Baecker guided the hydraulic forks into the slots on the industrial bin at the back of a large cinema centre. With the push of a button, the heavy bin was effortlessly hoisted into the air. The big Mercedes truck rocked on its suspension as the bin's contents tumbled noisily into the back, and its hydraulics whined as the compression rams came into play. Towards the front of the previously crushed payload, a Nokia cell phone, cushioned by a large amount of paper towel and tissue, continued to emit a signal. Baecker set the big bin back on its wheels, withdrew the hydraulic forks and put the truck into gear. 'That's the last one for the day, Kristian,' he said with a smile as he eased the big truck out of the complex and on to *Godehardstrasse* to the west of the medieval centre of Göttingen. 'I'm looking forward to a beer!'

'Just the one today, Bernhard,' Kristian Dieter, the younger man sitting beside him, replied. 'It's Sophie's fifth birthday tomorrow, and if I don't put the trampoline together tonight I'll be in big trouble!'

'You married guys. One day you'll wise up.' Baecker swung into the nearby busy *Industriestrasse* and picked up speed. '*Was in Gottes Namen!*' He slammed on the brakes and the deep klaxon of the truck's powerful air horns rent the air. The Audi overtaking them had inexplicably moved into the inside lane, slowed and then stopped, in an attempt to box them in. Two men in balaclavas, brandishing machine pistols leapt from the car and raced towards them.

'They've got guns, Bernhard!' Dieter yelled. Baecker selected reverse and began to back up, the two balaclava-clad men in hot pursuit.

'*Halten Sie der Lastwagen!*'

Baecker hit the brakes again, selected first gear and drove towards them. 'Get down!' he yelled at Dieter, but it was too late. One of the young thugs hired by the CIA to assassinate O'Connor and Aleta panicked. He unleashed a burst of fire which shattered the windscreen. Both men inside died instantly in a hail of bullets. Baecker slumped over the wheel and the twenty-tonne vehicle slewed off the road and mounted the footpath, ploughing into the front of a small café. The dozen or so patrons sitting at the outside tables, including two young mothers with their children in strollers, didn't stand a chance.

The two gunmen raced back to their car. The team leader floored the Audi and took off, leaving a trail of smoking rubber behind the squealing tyres. A blue-and-silver police car passing in the opposite direction negotiated a savage U-turn and took off in pursuit, siren blaring and blue roof-lights flashing. A gas bottle in the back of the café exploded and the fire quickly took hold. Thick black smoke belched from the shattered ruins. Survivors screamed. Some ran, their clothes in flames, others crawled out in agony as more sirens sounded in the distance.

40

GUATEMALA CITY

Low cloud hugged the highland volcanic ranges, drifting down into the valleys, as the pilot lined up the aircraft for the final approach into *Aeropuerto La Aurora*, Guatemala's international airport. Monsignor Jennings stared out the window from his business-class seat. Below, high-rise buildings competed for space with the slums of a teeming, vibrant city of over two million people, many of whom lived in abject poverty. Guatemala City was the country's third capital. The first, Ciudad Vieja, located just to the east, had been destroyed by floods and volcanic eruptions in 1541. The second, Antigua, also close by, had been destroyed by a violent earthquake 200 years later.

Jennings had intended to catch a 'chicken' bus to Panajachel on the northern shore of Lake Atitlán, but through the low cloud he caught sight of the city's Olympic stadium, with its distinctive blue seating that could hold 30 000 of the soccer-mad country's fans. Just to the north of the stadium was the city's Zone 1 and the red-light district. The old feeling stirred in his loins, and he resolved to spend the night in the city. The parish of San Pedro could wait another day. And in any case, it would give him a chance to talk to his contact at the *Museo Nacional de Arqueologia y Etnologia*. What had given cause for Weizman's excitement?

Clear of customs, Jennings waddled out of Guatemala's new terminal pulling his trolley bag behind him. He wore civilian clothes – jeans and a yellow sports shirt. The humidity and the heat were oppressive and already sweat was streaming down his florid face.

'*Zona Uno ¿cuánto?*' Jennings demanded of the driver of a battered yellow taxi outside the arrivals hall.

'*Cien quetzales*,' the dark, wizened Mayan driver replied.

'A hundred quetzales! Daylight robbery! *Setenta*. Seventy,' Jennings insisted, holding up seven fingers for emphasis. '*No mas!*'

The old taxi driver shrugged, and Jennings stepped inside. The city streets were choked with buses belching clouds of black diesel smoke, battered lorries with suspensions that had seen better days, brightly coloured chicken buses and the ubiquitous Toyota utes in various states of disrepair.

'Hotel Rio, Avenida 6a,' Jennings directed further.

Once they reached the hotel, Jennings paid the cab driver and hauled his luggage across the cracked tiles of the grimy reception foyer. The staff knew him well, and for a few quetzales would turn a blind eye to him bringing back a street boy or two.

'*Quiere chica señor? Muy limpio. Muy buen polvo.* You want girl, mister? Very clean. Very good fuck.' Monsignor Jennings waved the young tout away with an irritable flick of his wrist.

'*Maricon! Vete a la mierda!* Fuck off, you queer!' the young tout shouted.

Jennings ignored him and turned into a dimly lit lane behind the bus station in one of the sleaziest parts of Zona 1, and headed for his favourite pick-up joint, el Señor Chico Club. The entrance was unmarked. Jennings paid the ten quetzales cover charge to the security guard, tipping him another twenty. The moustachioed thickset security guard, his stomach bulging behind a grimy dark-blue shirt, smiled slyly and pocketed the money.

'*Bienvenidos de nuevo*, Señor Jennings. It's good to see you again. Reynaldo is not in yet, but he'll be here shortly.'

Reynaldo was only twelve, but he was like no other boy Jennings had ever known. A hot flush of anticipation flooded the dark depths of the monsignor's soul. Reynaldo, like the other rent-boys in el Señor Chico, operated from small dingy rooms upstairs. They were paid the equivalent of US$10 for thirty minutes, half of which went to the establishment; but for regulars like Señor Jennings, and for a price, Reynaldo would be allowed off the premises. Jennings pushed through the dirty curtain that shielded the club from the street and worked his way through sweating, steaming patrons gyrating to the Weather Girls' 'It's Raining Men'. The room reeked of the heavy, sweet, skunk-sage smell of pot, and strobe lights flickered through the smoke, momentarily illuminating the peeling blue paint on the flimsy walls. Young men danced with older men, mainly Europeans and Americans, their eyes glazed with a cocktail of ice, ecstasy and tequila. At the far side of the corrugated-iron bar, two young men were locked in a passionate embrace, each groping down the front of the other's jeans.

'*Ron Zacapa por favor . . . con cubitos de hielo.*'

'Certainly, Señor Jennings. One Zacapa on the rocks coming up.' The shirtless young barman flipped a heavy lowball tumbler into the air, caught it and scooped up some ice of questionable origin. He poured a shot of rum and slid the glass down the bar, his oiled torso gleaming in the reflected lights of the mirror ball.

'On the tab, señor?'

Jennings nodded and threw back the rum, immediately ordering another. Unlike Bacardi or any of the other better known rums, Ron Zacapa Centenario did not come from the Caribbean or Jamaica, nor was it made from molasses. One of the world's finest rums, it came from the first pressings of sugar-cane juice from Guatemalan farms. Distilled high in the mountains surrounding Quetzaltenango and aged in used American bourbon and whiskey barrels, the rich dark liqueur was made to be savoured, but Jennings needed a hit. He surveyed the room. At one end a worn wooden staircase led to the upstairs rooms that could be rented for 800 quetzales for four hours. The 'take out' price for Reynaldo would, he knew, be double that, but Jennings was prepared to pay. He felt a surge of anticipation as he spotted the young boy coming in through the back entrance.

'*Bienvenido a Ciudad de Guatemala, Señor Jennings.*'

'You're free tonight, Reynaldo?' Jennings' voice was thick. His eyes roved lustfully over the boy's slender form.

Reynaldo nodded, a glazed look on his handsome young face. It was a face devoid of humour; the joy of living once evident, extinguished. The authorities had tried hard to stamp out the child-sex trade, but as in any of the world's large cities it still flourished, if you knew where to look.

Once they were in the back of the taxi, Jennings' pudgy, sweaty hand wandered across Reynaldo's taut brown thigh.

The morning heat was already oppressive and Jennings gratefully entered the cooler surrounds of the pink low-set 1930s building that housed the *Museo Nacional de Arqueologia y Etnologia*. Jennings waddled past the softly lit glass cases, his dirty runners squeaking on the highly polished tile floor. The first cases held rare blades, knives and spearpoints the ancients had carved from obsidian, the hard black glass formed when volcanic lava cooled without crystallisation, enabling it to be ground to molecular thinness, many times sharper than a modern surgical scalpel. Priceless milky-green jade masks, eyes inlaid with mother of pearl and obsidian, stared lifelessly from the next cabinet, secured amongst red-and-blue statues and pottery that had been recovered from the royal tombs in the pyramids of Tikal and Palenque, but Jennings didn't spare them a glance. He was intent on finding his contact. At that moment a guard signalled Jennings towards a corner of the exhibition hall devoid of exhibits, a corner that both men knew was blind to the CCTV cameras. Carlos was stocky, with jet-black hair and a square brown face. His dark eyes shifted nervously around the room.

'Doctor Weizman. You said she was here two months ago?' Jennings inquired, wiping the sweat from his pink forehead.

'*Sí*. She had permission to visit the storerooms. She was quite excited, señor.'

'Do you know why?'

'I think it was one of the stelae, a smaller one that has always been stored in one of the back rooms.'

'I need to see it.'

Carlos shrugged apologetically. 'That would be difficult, Señor . . . without permission.'

Jennings thrust a dirty hundred-quetzale note into the guard's hand.

Carlos smiled. 'Follow me, señor, but stay close to the wall.'

Not long after, Jennings examined the small limestone stela with excitement. 'This is from Tikal. How long has the museum had this?'

'I think it dates from the Nazi expedition to Tikal in the 1930s. The Nazis are not popular here, señor, so it has never been on display.'

'And the museum records?'

Carlos shrugged again. 'Copying records is strictly against the rules, señor.'

'I need the records quickly, Carlos, understand? *Prontamente! ¿Entienden?*' Jennings demanded irritably as he pressed another dirty note into Carlos' hand.

Monsignor Jennings reached Lake Atitlán in the late afternoon and by the time he reached the northern town of Panajachel, the last ferry had departed for the southern shore and San Pedro.

Jennings was tired and irritable and was in no mood to pay the hundred quetzales the old boatman was asking.

'Fuel is very expensive, señor. You have to pay for my return trip.'

'*Cuarenta quetzales*,' Jennings insisted, gesturing rudely with four fingers. The old man shrugged, took the key out of the ignition of his small fibreglass runabout and walked towards the shore, leaving Jennings fuming beside the boat.

'*Sesenta quetzales*. Sixty. That's my final offer,' Jennings shouted.

The boatman shrugged and kept walking. Jennings looked around but the lake shore was deserted, empty boats rocking gently against the other jetties. '*Ochenta!*' he yelled.

The boatman paused, turned and walked back along the shaky jetty. Eighty quetzales might only be a little more than US$10, but even after the cost of fuel, it would put food on the table for his grandchildren.

The boat rocked alarmingly as Jennings obeyed the boatman's instructions to move to the bow. The old but meticulously maintained forty-horsepower Evinrude started first time. The boatman cast off and the little launch gathered speed across the cold smooth waters. The sun was sinking behind the mountains above San Marcos, bathing the coffee plantations on the three soaring volcanoes of Atitlán, Tolimán and San Pedro with an orange glow, but Jennings was oblivious to the scenery. He sat just back from the bow, absorbed in the single page of acquisition notes from the *Museo Nacional*.

The stela had indeed been acquired as a result of the expedition Himmler had ordered to the jungles of Tikal in 1938, although the details of the transaction seemed shrouded in mystery. Of greater importance to Jennings was the appearance of the Greek letter Φ. It was the first time the Mayanist scholar had seen the letter inscribed on a stela. Was there a link between the Maya and the Greeks? And what did the numbers on the stela mean? Jennings understood well the ancients' use of bars and dots in a vigesimal or numeral system that was based on 20 rather than the decimal system based on 10, but the bars and dots on the small stela had been hard to make out.

Three hundred and twenty kilometres to the north-east, the last of the sun's rays struck the top of Temple III above the jungle canopy in Tikal. The rays almost lined up with Temple IV. The winter solstice was drawing closer.

41

CIA HEADQUARTERS, LANGLEY, VIRGINIA

Wiley took the call in his office.

'They're being held in the city watch-house.' The encrypted telephone connection to the US Embassy in Berlin was unusually clear, as was the message from the chief of station, Brandon Gray. 'The heat from the media is red-hot —'

'Not least because, like me, the media are mystified as to why two men in balaclavas would attack a fucking garbage truck!'

'Their instructions were to follow the cell phone and assassinate Tutankhamen and Nefertiti,' Gray said defensively. 'There's little doubt the cell phone was on board the truck, but there was no sign of either of the targets.'

'Has anyone tumbled to anything that might link us? What about the cell phone?'

'No, sir. The fire was intense, and the cell phone would have been destroyed. I'm worried about the assets, though. Germany abolished the death penalty in 1949, but the feeling here is overwhelmingly in favour of its reinstatement for cases like this. Either of them might talk.'

'That can't be allowed to happen! Terminate them both.'

'Even if we can find someone who's prepared to do it and able to get access,' Gray replied, hesitating, 'it'll be very expensive . . . '

'I don't give a fuck what it costs. Find someone on the inside!' Wiley slammed the receiver back onto its encryption cradle, got up from his desk and paced his office. The German Chancellor was already describing the crash as a massacre and she was demanding answers. He contemplated briefing the new director but immediately dismissed the notion. The old regime would have simply denied any involvement, but if the CIA connection surfaced on this new President's watch, Wiley knew he'd be finished. Four floors below, a heated argument between Larry Davis and Ellen Rodriguez was in full swing.

'Jesus Christ, Larry. I don't know what O'Connor or Weizman have done to get so far up the administration's nostril, but this is way out of control!' Rodriguez' green eyes were blazing. 'Ten people are dead, including two babies, because we've got a bunch of thugs out there. Amateurs firing at anything that moves!'

'If you're not up to this, Rodriguez . . . ' Wiley strode into the room. 'What've we got, apart from this clusterfuck in Göttingen?'

Davis mopped his bald pate. 'It appears the targets were not in Göttingen, but Bad Arolsen,' he said, glancing at Rodriguez. 'We got a look at the visitors' book and Nefertiti used her own name to sign in.'

'Why would she use her own name?'

Davis shrugged and Rodriguez stepped in. 'Probably because you have to book to search documents well in advance, and at the time Weizman made the phone call to the International Tracing Service, she wouldn't have been aware we had her in our crosshairs.'

'Was Tutankhamen with her?'

'She was accompanied by a man fitting his description,' Davis replied quickly.

'So where are they now?'

'Not sure, but we're sending more assets into Bad Arolsen,' said Davis.

'Which I think is a mistake.'

Wiley wheeled on Rodriguez. 'Why?'

'Firstly, Germany is not some third-world country where murders are part of everyday life,' Rodriguez replied evenly. 'Everyone from the Chancellor down is demanding answers to our latest effort in Göttingen and the police will be on high alert across the country. If we start pouring assets into a little village like Bad Arolsen, that's only going to draw the crabs. Secondly, the targets are highly unlikely to still be there.'

'And why is that?'

'I've worked with O'Connor before. He is, or was, one of our best agents. He hopes for the best and plans for the worst, so he'd expect us to be close on his heels. He won't stay exposed a moment longer than he has to.'

'So where do you suppose he might be now?'

'O'Connor already knows what we've got planned for Weizman, and knowing O'Connor, he'll be on to us – you,' she added, 'having exactly the same plans for him. Our contact in Bad Arolsen has reported that Weizman asked to see the documents for the Mauthausen concentration camp. They may be headed there, although just why O'Connor has sided with Weizman, I'm not sure. Perhaps it has something to do with that Mayan conference.'

'I'd stick to finding out where they are if I were you, Rodriguez,' Wiley responded, a menacing edge to his voice. He turned to his chief of staff. 'Get Vienna to stake out the border crossings to Austria, and I want observation on the trains and airports. Get hold of the rental car hirings in the area and get someone out to the Mauthausen concentration camp. I want these two on toast.'

42

MAUTHAUSEN

O'Connor parked the car outside Mauthausen's forbidding stone walls behind which, during the war, over 120 000 people had been murdered by the Nazis. With the exception of some of the cramped, squalid barracks, which had been torn down, the camp had remained as it was when Aleta's family was interned in 1938. The camp was maintained now as a memorial to the innocent souls who had been taken.

It was early, and a Sunday, so the car park was empty. The tourist buses would come later. O'Connor and Aleta walked towards the main gate in silence. Aleta's long dark hair trailed over her shoulders, moving gently in the light morning breeze.

Rusted iron bars protruded from the granite archway, the big eagle which they had once supported torn from its mount by prisoners when the camp was finally liberated by the US 11th Armored Division in May of 1945. The heavy wooden doors in the centre of the archway were closed. O'Connor and Aleta entered through a side arch beneath the observation towers and passed into the SS assembly compound, where the prisoners had been stripped naked and left for hours in the hot sun or freezing snow while their clothes were disinfected.

Aleta had researched the camp thoroughly before arriving in Austria, but even that had not prepared her for the grisly reality that confronted her when she entered the gas chambers. The chambers at Mauthausen could accommodate up to 120 prisoners and the Nazis had disguised them as shower rooms. Aleta choked back tears as she walked through the white tiled rooms, the shower heads and water pipes still in place. Each room had its entry through a heavy iron bulkhead door. The doors, now rusting, were made to be sealed and locked from the outside and were equipped with a centre peep-hole. The SS guards would observe the prisoners falling to the tiles and fighting for their lives, blood streaming from their ears and other orifices as deadly Cyclone-B hydrogen cyanide was vented into the room.

O'Connor and Aleta walked silently into the adjacent rooms, which contained the ovens used to incinerate the bodies the SS guards dragged from the 'shower rooms'.

'I need some air,' Aleta said finally, her face pale. They climbed the steps that led out of the gas chambers and walked past the barrack blocks and the brothel that had been set up for prisoners who collaborated with the Nazis. They passed through the massive granite 'prisoners' gate' and walked towards the quarry, where thousands of prisoners had died, whipped and worked to exhaustion digging out rocks with their bare hands.

The car park now hidden from view, neither O'Connor nor Aleta saw the Audi pull in and park at the far end. The CIA asset noted the blue strip with the white 'D' for Deutschland beneath the twelve gold stars of the European Union on the registration plate of the rental Volkswagen Passat. He transmitted the number to the chief of station in Berlin in a secure burst from his cell phone. Ten minutes later he received his instructions. 'Car hired in Kassel-Wilhelmshöhe by male fitting description of Tutankhamen. Nefertiti likely to be with him. Once confirmed, follow and terminate both targets at first opportunity.'

'Given what happened here,' Aleta said thoughtfully, 'it's surprising Israel doesn't show more compassion towards the Palestinians.'

'Some might argue the Israelis have the right to defend themselves against rocket attacks.'

'Yes. But the Israeli attacks in Gaza and Lebanon have been ruthlessly disproportionate: they've even bombed schools and UN posts.'

'That can hardly be compared to the Holocaust,' O'Connor suggested gently.

'Every life is precious. When you flatten places like Gaza, the most populated area on the planet – where one and a half million people are crowded into a tiny area that even the Vatican calls a concentration camp – you've made a decision to kill innocent civilians. If it were any other nation raining cluster bombs and white phosphorous on women and children, your people in Washington would be outraged. *White phosphorous!* A compound that clamps to the skin and keeps burning deep into the body. How do the Israelis justify that?'

O'Connor didn't reply, surprised by the ferocity of Aleta's views. Was it an Arab or a Jew, he wondered, who had said, 'A man without a country is a man without dignity. And our dignity is more important to us even than our life.' O'Connor was convinced the awful killing would continue on both sides until the Arab Islamists recognised Israel's unequivocal right to exist, and the Israelis withdrew from their illegal settlements and returned the land they had occupied since 1967 so a Palestinian state could become a reality.

They reached the 'staircase of death' and Aleta looked towards the cliff. 'There are 186 steps to the top,' she said. 'The prisoners were made to carry huge rocks up these stairs on their shoulders, as punishment.' Tears welled in her eyes. 'I think if my grandfather were alive today, he'd be urging the Israeli government and people to take a different course. I'm not blaming the Israeli people – they want peace just as much as the ordinary Palestinians – but the hardliners in the Israeli government will never rest until all Palestinian land is taken by force, and the Islamists will never rest until Israel is wiped off the map. It's madness, the same mindless madness that gave birth to von Heißen and Mauthausen.' She wiped her eyes and looked at O'Connor. 'It's time we went. There's less than three weeks to the winter solstice. If we're going to have any chance of finding the third figurine, let alone lining them up by 21 December, we'll need to move quickly.'

O'Connor nodded. It would be touch and go. Together, they walked in silence across the deserted quarry, a quarry where Jews and others had been murdered in their thousands. Their hands touched briefly, and Aleta made no effort to pull away.

'The big question now, I suppose, is how we get to Guatemala?' she asked as O'Connor pulled out of the car park.

'You've just won the job of navigator,' he said, handing the road map to Aleta. 'We'll head back along the Danube to Mauthausen town proper, then north on Route 123 to link up with the E55 into the Czech Republic.'

'Why the Czech Republic?'

'Wiley trusts no one, so he'll resist taking the German and Austrian police into his confidence, but he'll still have CIA assets watching the major border crossings. The Czech Republic won't be high on his agenda as he'll expect us to exit from either Vienna or one of the big German cities like Frankfurt.'

'So, Prague?'

O'Connor shook his head. 'The airports and train stations will be under heavy surveillance, and the CIA chief of station in Prague will have mobilised his own assets. But even the CIA doesn't have the resources to watch all the docks, and I have a contact in Hamburg. If we can bypass Prague and head back across the border through Dresden and on to Hamburg undetected, we've got a chance.' O'Connor glanced in the rear-view mirror. He'd mentally photographed the cars in the parking lot, and the black Audi that had been parked at the far end was now following at a discreet distance. 'We've got company again.'

The driver of the Audi waited until the road disappeared into a series of small hills before he closed the gap and lined up the Passat in the sights of his Brügger & Thomet MP9.

'Get down!' O'Connor yelled. The rear windscreen of the Passat shattered under a withering burst of sub-machine-gun fire. O'Connor swerved from side to side and another burst of fire crackled past the offside of the car into the pine forest. O'Connor floored the Passat, racing up the narrow twisting road, but the black Audi was gaining.

Whoever he was, he wasn't leaving any doubt about his intentions, O'Connor thought, drifting sideways into the next corner, only to be confronted by a massive B-double tanker coming the other way. The mountains reverberated to the blast from the truck's triple air horns as O'Connor spun the wheel, missing the tanker by centimetres.

'Hang on!' he yelled as he swerved past the rear end of the tanker and onto the other side of the road. O'Connor hit the brakes and the Audi shot past. He dropped the Passat into second and tramped the accelerator, the squealing tyres leaving a line of smoking rubber on the road. O'Connor waited until the valley to the north dropped away sharply before he closed in on the rear of the Audi. In a precision high-speed move, O'Connor veered to the right and tapped the rear fender of the Audi. The Audi spun, and O'Connor and Aleta ducked as the assassin let fly with another wild burst of gunfire. The Passat shot past and O'Connor glanced in the rear-view mirror in time to see the Audi hit a guide post. The car flipped and rolled down the steep embankment in a shower of sparks. O'Connor skidded the Passat to a halt and leapt out of the car. The Audi bounced off a rocky outcrop and dropped another twenty metres, exploding in a fiery ball beside the creek below.

Aleta's face was white. 'Who *are* these people?'

'When the CIA wants someone assassinated, they usually use one of their field officers, but if they want it done in a hurry, or if the target's a high enough priority, they employ what's known in the trade as an "asset", or, in our case, several assets.'

'And that guy is one of their *assets*?'

'Was. We've gained a little time, but not much,' O'Connor replied, thinking out loud. 'They've got our licence plates, but if I'm right, and Wiley hasn't asked the Austrian and German police for help yet, that might prove the difference.'

'And what are customs and immigration going to say at the border when we turn up in a car that's riddled with bullet holes, not to mention a back window that's been shot out?'

O'Connor smiled at her. 'You're learning. We'll graduate you as a spy yet!'

'No, thanks.'

'We'll need to pick up another car before we cross the Czech border.'

'Hire another one, you mean?'

'Only if we have to. Wiley seems to have the hire-car agencies tapped. We'll, ah, borrow one.'

Aleta shook her head.

O'Connor slowed on the outskirts of the Austrian town of Freistadt and turned west off the E55 towards the Bahnhof. The station was deserted but as he pulled into the car park, he counted six other cars.

'Keep a look out,' he said to Aleta, as he got out and walked over to an older model nondescript Toyota. He picked the door lock in an instant and tried a small flat-bladed screwdriver in the ignition. 'Sometimes it works, but not today,' he muttered as he snapped the plastic cover from the bottom of the steering column, exposing the ignition wiring: three pairs of wires running into the back of the ignition cylinder. O'Connor glanced at the *ACC OFF ON START* positions on the ignition switch and quickly went through a process of elimination. The green-and-yellow pair would probably provide the battery and accessories, he thought, and he punted on the red pair being power to the car and the brown pair providing the connection to the starter. Within thirty seconds he'd disconnected the green-and-yellow pair, as well as the red pair, bared the wires and twisted them together.

'*Und jetzt, das thema von . . .*'

O'Connor smiled to himself as the radio burst into action with the theme from the old war movie, *The Great Escape*. He quickly disconnected the brown wires and stripped them as well. The ends sparked as he touched them together and the engine fired.

'Follow me,' he said to Aleta, waiting until she'd got into the driver's seat of the Passat before heading out of the car park.

O'Connor pulled off the E55 and drove into a small forest to the north of Freistadt. There they transferred their luggage, containing the precious figurines, to the Toyota, and O'Connor hid the Passat amongst a thick clump of bushes.

'Just in case the owner reports his car stolen,' he said as he attached the Passat's registration plates to the Toyota.

'I'm curious . . .' Aleta said as they turned back on to the E55 and headed north towards the quiet Austrian–Czech border crossing.

'How I did that?' O'Connor grinned. 'Secret men's business.'

'No – although one day you can show me how – it's more that there were two BMWs and a late-model Mercedes in that car park. Why did you go for the old Toyota? Less likely to attract attention?'

'Yes, but there's a technical reason as well. Late-model cars have a radio-frequency identification chip in the ignition that needs a matching key, so you can't hot-wire them, and some keys have a precise resistance built into them that has to be matched with the resistance value in the car's memory. There are ways around it, but we won't need this one for long – we should be in Hamburg tomorrow.'

Inspector Erich Polzer of the Upper Austria Polizei and his wife alighted from the train and looked around the Freistadt Bahnhof car park.

'*Jemand hat gestohlen unser Auto!*' the Inspector exclaimed angrily, and reached for his cell phone.

43

SAN PEDRO, GUATEMALA

The last of the sun's rays painted the clouds seemingly streaming from the crater of San Pedro, the smallest of the three volcanoes towering sentinel over Lake Atitlán and the villages dotted around the foreshores. The boatman eased his *lancha* into the jetty at San Pedro, gently nudging the piles. The waters of the lake lapped the pier's old wooden steps and the boatman threw his hawser with unerring accuracy, securing the stern. Monsignor Jennings, handing the money to the boatman, climbed onto the gunwale and the boat tilted alarmingly. The boatman steadied it against the pier and shook his head as Jennings lost his footing and fell into the lake.

'*Imbécil!*' Jennings fumed, flailing back to the jetty and hauling himself onto the steps.

The old boatman shrugged and placed Jennings' suitcase on top of the jetty. With an expert flick, he unhitched the hawser from the jetty pile and backed into the inlet.

'*Adios, señor!*' The old boatman was still grinning as he headed into the dusk enveloping the smooth waters of the lake.

'*Tuc tuc, señor! Tuc tuc!*'

'*Aquí, señor, aquí!*'

A squabble had broken out between two young taxi drivers, neither of whom could have been older than twelve. One had illegally manoeuvred his *tuc tuc* under the rope at the end of the jetty, gaining the advantage over the other boy waiting at the rank. Jennings took the option that didn't involve walking, much to the anger of the boy who'd kept to the rules.

'*Que te jordan! Hijo de puta!* Fuck you, son of a bitch!'

Jennings' driver gave the other boy the bird, opened the throttle and powered the noisy little three-wheeler up the narrow road that led to the town square at the top of the hill.

'*Dónde a, señor?*'

'*La Iglesia,*' Jennings replied, pointing in the direction of the white-washed Catholic church that sat atop one of the foothills of Volcán San Pedro. Jennings, still dripping as he clung to the flimsy metal frame supporting the *tuc tuc*'s canvas, observed the young driver with interest. The boy's olive skin was flawless and Jennings began to mentally run his hand up the young man's inner thigh. The boy weaved artfully between tourists and locals browsing the small roadside stalls that offered everything from woven baskets to tacos, spices to *hambuergasas*. The local village women, wearing elegant *cortes*, walked the streets balancing large baskets of fruit and bread on their heads, seemingly without effort.

'*¿Como se llama usted?*' Jennings asked.

'*Me llamo Alonzo,*' the boy replied as he weaved across the crowded square at the top of the hill, bringing the *tuc tuc* to a halt opposite the path that led to the church.

'I'm the new priest here, Alonzo. Come and see me,' Jennings said, tipping the boy fifty quetzales. 'I'll make it worth your while.'

Jennings extended the carry handle on his bag and walked up the path to the steps of the large white-washed colonial building that dominated San Pedro. A stone statue of Saint Peter guarded the cobblestones, and rocks protected gardens filled with luscious palms, brilliant orange hibiscus, white nun orchids and pink confetti flowers. The massive cedar door creaked on its iron hinges.

A solitary nun kneeling in the front pew turned at the sound of Jennings' footfall echoing off the white stone walls, and went back to her prayers. Jennings walked up the centre aisle of the church and stopped at the nun's pew. Sensing his presence, Sister Juanita Gonzales opened her eyes and looked up to find an obese, red-faced man in a dripping safari suit staring down at her.

'Can I help you, señor?' she whispered.

'Monsignor Jennings.'

Sister Gonzales shot to her feet, banging her knee on the heavy wooden pew.

'Oh, Father. I'm so sorry, no one told us you were coming,' Sister Gonzales stammered, her round dark eyes full of concern. 'I'm Sister Gonzales,' she added. The beautiful young nun was slim and petite, her long dark hair hidden under the hood of her habit.

'I see,' Jennings replied irritably. 'Take me to my quarters.'

'Again, I'm most terribly sorry, Father,' said Sister Gonzales, hurriedly opening the blinds and windows of the tiny one-bedroom San Pedro presbytery, which commanded sweeping views over the lake. 'The presbytery's been vacant ever since Father Hernandez left, so it's terribly musty. We were planning to give it a thorough spring clean before your arrival.'

'The presbytery's been vacant all that time?'

'We've been without a permanent parish priest since Father Hernandez retired, although he lived here for many years until he left . . . ' Sister Gonzales' voice trailed off.

'And what was the reason for his leaving?' Jennings probed.

Sister Gonzales stared at the old wooden floorboards.

'I'm waiting!'

'No one really knows, Father. There are just rumours . . . '

'Yes?'

'Rumours of his past – that he might have been a Nazi. He left in a big hurry after the Israelis arrived,' Sister Gonzales added uncomfortably.

'You knew the Israelis were here?'

Sister Gonzales nodded. 'Someone in Panajachel warned Father Hernandez the Israelis were coming for him, and he left in a truck before they could get here.'

'A truck?'

'There is a back road that connects with the highway to the south. He took a big crate with him —'

'Containing?'

'No one knows, Father, but it was very heavy. It had to be loaded by forklift.'

Jennings grunted.

'Have you had dinner, Father? We're having black beans and tortillas tonight.' The young nun smiled enthusiastically.

'I'll eat out. That will be all.'

Jennings glanced around his new quarters, angry at the task he'd been given. San Pedro was a long way from the delights of the European capitals, and even those in Guatemala, he thought wistfully, remembering the previous night with Reynaldo. Perhaps some of the *tuc tuc* drivers held some promise. He unpacked his battered suitcase and placed his clothes in the oak wardrobe in the bedroom which was on a mezzanine floor, reached by a wooden staircase. The rest of the flat consisted of a downstairs sitting room with an old couch and a white wicker table and two wicker chairs. The kitchen had a small stove, connected to a gas bottle, and an old Kelvinator refrigerator. The bathroom was equally primitive. Several tiles were missing from the shower recess, which was screened by a yellowed shower curtain.

He walked back out into the sitting room, oblivious to the stunning vista of coffee plantations running down the sides of the volcanoes to a lake shore dotted with poinsettia trees, banana palms, Mexican honeysuckles, spiny yuccas and a host of other colourful palms and plants. Jennings opened a door under the stairs and switched on the light. The storeroom was dank and dusty; empty save for a pair of scuba tanks and a diving regulator. He lifted the tanks and underneath was an old diary. The Israelis had indeed forced von Heißen to get out in a rush, Jennings thought, as he retrieved the diary from the concrete floor.

44

HAMBURG

O'Connor parked the Toyota in a side street near the Hamburg Hauptbahnhof and hailed a cab to take them within walking distance of the Hansehof, a two-star hotel on *Simon-von-Utrecht Strasse*. He booked just one room, not wanting Aleta to be any more vulnerable than she already was.

'Bit of a comedown from the Imperial,' Aleta said with a grin, unable to resist having a dig.

'Yes, but this one's nondescript, and it has one big advantage at this stage of our journey.'

'And what might that be?' she asked as O'Connor inserted the key to their room.

'Twin beds.'

'You're incorrigible.'

'I've got one or two things to organise,' O'Connor said, stacking their suitcases on the luggage rack. 'Don't answer the door or the phone. I'll be back in an hour – two at the most.'

Aleta flicked on the television and settled in for the CNN news. A young journalist was standing amid the ruins of Salebata village on the southern side of the Pacific island of Samoa.

'Whole villages have been wiped off the map here, and the death toll will be high,' she announced. The camera panned across boats tossed like confetti into coconut palms, mud-covered stumps of concrete where houses had once stood, cars smashed onto their sides, and the roofs of those buildings still standing hanging drunkenly on debris that stretched along the shoreline. 'The quake, which struck at 3.48 p.m. eastern standard time, measured a massive 8.3 on the Richter scale, with an epicentre 100 kilometres south of Western Samoa. And in breaking news, another earthquake measuring 7.6 on the Richter scale has reportedly hit the Indonesian West Sumatra province, devastating the cities of Padang and Pariaman. The death toll is expected to be in the hundreds.'

The feed crossed to a seismologist at the Bureau of Meteorology in Sydney. 'Eighty per cent of the world's earthquakes occur around what is known as the Pacific Rim of Fire, a horseshoe-shaped series of trenches and tectonic plates that stretch for 40 000 kilometres.' The seismologist ran his pointer over a map that showed the fiery rim stretching from the coastline of South America up to Alaska, across to Siberia and down through Japan to New Zealand. 'It also contains over 450 volcanoes. In the case of Samoa the massive Pacific plate is now moving westwards at nearly a centimetre a year, thrusting under the Australian plate. Undersea earthquakes can trigger waves which move at speeds of up to 800 kilometres an hour. As they approach a shoreline, these killer waves can build to the height of a three-storey building, as happened in 2004 when a quarter of a million people lost their lives.'

For the next hour, Aleta watched the disasters unfold in Samoa and Indonesia, until the channel crossed to the Philippines, where a deadly typhoon was coming ashore near the north-eastern tip of Luzon. Depressed by the diet of destruction, Aleta started to flick through the cable channels. A preacher in a white suit from one of America's southern Baptist mega-churches suddenly appeared on the screen.

A pull-through announced 'The Jerry Buffett Hour – the hour that will *change* your life! – a weekly broadcast that goes to over 300 stations around the world'. The vision cut away to the 15 000-capacity auditorium of the Buffett Evangelical Centre. It was packed to the rafters, the congregation hanging on their preacher's every word. The cameraman had been well tutored in catching Jerry Buffett's best side, and he slowly zoomed in, capturing the tele-evangelist's tanned face, the square jaw and the intensity in his deep-blue eyes.

'As God's warnings, in the form of ever-increasing numbers of earthquakes and tsunamis, continue to exact their toll of death and destruction, the end time is closer than you think, my friends!' Buffett thundered. 'There are those who are sceptical of the coming Armageddon, but if the American people don't turn from their ways, if we don't turn back to the Lord, the prophet Isaiah is very clear!' Buffett grasped both sides of the massive lectern and began to read from the prophecies of Isaiah 24: ' "Behold . . . the earth shall reel to and fro like a drunkard, and it shall fall!" That, my friends, is clear warning of the coming geographical pole shift from one of the greatest prophets of the ages. Everything Isaiah has foretold has either come to pass or *will* come to pass. A geographic pole shift will be God's way of punishing a sinful world, just as he punished the ancient Israelites when they turned from the commandments and worshipped the golden calf. It's right here in Isaiah 13: "Therefore I will shake the heavens, and the earth shall remove out of her place." Those who focus on money, those who engage in sins of the flesh, those who have turned their backs on the Almighty God . . . His pole shift will swallow them in an instant!'

Buffett paused to let his words take effect, amidst gasps of fear and awe from the congregation. 'But those of you who truly fear the Lord – not Allah, or Yahweh or any other false god, but the one true God who revealed Himself as our Lord Jesus Christ – at the coming Armageddon, you will be swept up in the rapture and saved!' Buffett left the lectern and paced the huge stage, speaking more urgently. 'God's warning is not only in Isaiah, my friends; it's here in the Book of Revelation and it's in Luke 21, where the great physician and confidant of the Apostle Paul warns us very clearly of the coming catastrophe, foretelling of the sea roaring across the land.'

He strode back towards the lectern. 'There is a lot of nonsense being put about in the media,' he continued, more quietly again. 'Occasionally you will read about 2012 – about ancient savages and a missing codex – but there is only one codex we should take any notice of,' he said, his voice rising again as he held his Bible aloft, 'and that's the word of the *Lord*. Be ready, my friends! We know not the day or the hour, but all the signs are with us – tsunamis, earthquakes, wildfires and erupting volcanoes. Hurricane Katrina, God's punishment of a city renowned for sex and sinfulness, was just a mere taste of the real catastrophe that awaits us, for there are limits to the patience of even Almighty God!'

Aleta clicked off the television in disgust. She had long ago abandoned the idea of a wrathful God, who would extract retribution on his people, and she had never been able to accept the Christians' claim there was only one path. The key sounded in the lock and O'Connor entered with two big backpacks and a smaller plastic bag.

'We leave tomorrow night on a small container ship bound for Havana. From there we'll cross the Caribbean, go through the Panama Canal and head north for Puerto Quetzal on the Pacific coast of Guatemala.'

'Not quite your P&O cruise,' Aleta observed, her Spanish accent laced with humour.

'Not quite, no. The other problem is that there's only one cabin and we're going as husband and wife.'

'What?'

'The captain's a very strict Catholic, but don't worry – the bedding arrangements are bunks,' O'Connor replied with a grin. 'In the meantime,' he said, reaching into the plastic bag and hauling out a wad of quetzales, 'some local currency, and L'Oréal of Paris Super Blonde pre-lightener, as well as L'Oréal's Viking light ash blonde.'

'I presume they're for me.'

'Together with a pair of sharp scissors.'

Aleta made a face.

'Look, I know you're probably fond of your hair, and you've got good reason to be. It's gorgeous —'

'Spare me the flattery, Mr O'Connor.'

'But you've seen what these guys are like. For them, life's cheap. You're just a number and a pay cheque. These are old tricks, but if they buy just an hour or two, they might save your life.'

'I'm sorry. I don't mean to sound ungrateful, but your world takes a little getting used to. What time do we leave?'

'The ship sails on the tide tomorrow night, just before midnight. Here's your new passport,' O'Connor said, handing Aleta a cherry-coloured Ecuadorian passport embossed with the gold coat of arms incorporating a giant condor atop Mount Chimborazo. 'We've doctored your photograph to ash blonde,' he added with a grin.

'Ecuadorian?'

'They'll be looking for a Guatemalan. You speak Spanish, and so do the Ecuadorians.'

On the other side of the city, two police patrolmen cruised along *Greifswalder Strasse*, near Hamburg's main railway station, and stopped their silver-and-blue BMW patrol car alongside an old Toyota.

'The licence plates don't match,' the younger of the two policemen observed.

'*Nein*,' the other agreed, 'but the model and the dent in the left fender are identical. Feed the registration into the system and let's see what we get.'

Across the Atlantic, at the CIA's headquarters in Langley, it was not yet 6 a.m., but Howard Wiley had already arrived, frustrated and angry at the lack of progress.

He strode into the ops room. 'What've we got?' he demanded of his chief of staff.

'The Austrian police have found our asset's body in a burnt-out car in a creek bed. Our contact advised me a short while ago that a hire car fitting the description of the one Tutankhamen and Nefertiti were travelling in has been found in a forest near Freistadt,' Larry Davis replied, pointing to the small northern Austrian town on one of the electronic maps.

'What the hell are they doing up there?'

'We're still checking,' Davis replied.

'They'll probably use the Czech Republic to try and throw us off the scent,' Ellen Rodriguez offered. She had deep black shadows under her eyes. With the exception of Davis, who had only just beaten his boss into the room, Operation Maya had been working through the night.

'And what do you base that on, *Officer* Rodriguez?' Wiley sneered.

'Call it a hunch if you like, but we've been watching the big airports and train stations and O'Connor would expect that. We're going to need more than inside contacts for these two. If we're going to have any hope of tracking which border crossings they're using, we need to bring the Austrian, German and Czech police and customs agencies into the loop.'

'And the next thing we'll be up to our armpits in alligators, trying to explain to Congress and the White House why we blew up a garbage truck in a foreign country!' Wiley turned back to his chief of staff. 'What information do we have on their destination?'

Davis looked uncomfortable and raised his eyebrows at Rodriguez.

'My guess is they'll try for Guatemala, probably Tikal, as soon as they can, since that's where the Maya Codex is rumoured to be,' she said. As per your instructions, I've alerted the Guatemala station. They've got the airports and major border checkpoints covered and they're working on possible locations for the codex.'

'Trains?' Wiley demanded.

Rodriguez took a deep breath. 'Guatemalan railways were shut down in 2007.'

Wiley glared at her. 'Be that as it may, I want these two found and eliminated before they cause any more problems for us in Germany or the Czech Republic or wherever the fuck they are at the moment. In the meantime, I want every border crossing into Guatemala covered, and that includes Mexico, Belize, Honduras and El Salvador, as well as the ports. And I want that codex!' Wiley motioned Davis into the little room known as the 'cone of silence' to one side of the operations room.

'Rodriguez is becoming a pain in the ass, and she's far too cosy with the White House for my liking. There's a briefing on HAARP in Alaska the day after tomorrow. Fuck her off up there as the CIA representative until I can arrange to get her out of here – permanently.'

45

GAKONA, ALASKA

The fresh snow drifts outside HAARP's operations room sparkled under the cold early-December sun. The Director of Gakona, Dr Nathaniel B. Hershey, was very solidly built. In his younger days, the nuclear physicist had played quarterback for the Washington Redskins, and he still worked out every day, but not today. Today he was providing a personal briefing on the capabilities of HAARP to the vice chiefs of the navy, army and air force, as well as the assistant commandant of the Marines, the CIA and a brace of high-powered civilians from the Pentagon.

'Here at HAARP, we're at the cutting edge of science,' Dr Hershey began. 'Within a few short years we've got to the stage where we can generate 3.6 million watts on the ground, and because we have very large phased-array antennae that cover nearly fifteen hectares, we can direct that energy into a narrow beam wherever we want to aim it, blasting the ionosphere with over three gigawatts, or three billion watts, of electromagnetic power.'

Ellen Rodriguez' eyes widened. Rodriguez was not only fluent in Spanish and German; as a teenager, she had graduated *summa cum laude* from a little-known college in the Bronx and won a scholarship to Columbia University, where she'd majored in environmental physics. She had done as much research on HAARP as she could in the short time before she left Langley, and she had already reached the conclusion that messing with the earth's delicate balance was madness.

Dr Hershey flashed up a display of the ionosphere, the upper part of the atmosphere that stretched from eighty to 1000 kilometres above the earth and consisted of electrons and charged particles or ions. 'As most of you are aware, the ionosphere plays an important part in communications, acting as a mirror for radio waves, enabling us to communicate over long distances. What is not so well understood is the effect that it might have on intercontinental ballistic missiles fired from Russia, China, or, in the future, from rogue states like North Korea or Iran.'

'Can it be used to deflect them?' asked the nuggetty little four-star commandant from the Marine Corps.

'That's one of the things we're aiming to find out, General,' Dr Hershey replied, flashing up another PowerPoint slide. 'By aiming three billion watts at a single point in the ionosphere, we believe we can actually lift it by up to eighty kilometres at a particular point, and it's quite possible that could be used to deflect any incoming missiles off course.'

'If you blast the ionosphere with three billion watts, Dr Hershey, and hold a piece of it eighty kilometres out to space, all that energy has to go somewhere, and that somewhere will be into the particles that make up the ionosphere itself, am I right?' Rodriguez was up the back of the small briefing room, but her voice held an authority that turned the heads of those far more senior in the front row.

'I'm not sure where you're going with this,' Hershey countered, his blue-grey eyes suddenly steely. He had answered questions like this on open days, but he hadn't expected one in the middle of a top-secret briefing.

'If I'm right, three billion watts of energy will throw huge amounts of heat into the ionosphere, way past the normal balance. Isn't there a chance that all of that energy might discharge back? Much the same way as a lightning bolt discharges energy, only in this case, hundreds of times more powerful?'

Dr Hershey smiled through pursed lips. 'I would draw the analogy of putting your finger in a bucket of water; you take your finger out, and the hole is repaired immediately.' Hershey glared at Tyler Jackson, the CIA's most senior scientist at HAARP, silently asking how someone like Officer Rodriguez had been allowed into the briefing.

'I couldn't have put it better myself, Dr Hershey,' the Marine Corps general drawled. 'Now, if the handbag brigade up the back doesn't mind, I'd like to hear the rest of what you've got to say.'

Hershey smirked. 'Thank you, General. As part of this program, we intend to conduct three major experiments. The first, which I've briefly outlined, will involve a ten-minute burst of extremely high energy aimed at a point above the northern Pacific. Prior to the beam firing, the air force will launch a long-range missile from Vandenberg Air Force Base in California, which we will then deflect off course, towards the Arctic Ocean.'

The Vice Chief of Staff of the United States Air Force nodded enthusiastically. 'In the past, as part of the National Missile Defense program, we've launched interceptor missiles from Kwajalein Atoll in the Marshall Islands, but they haven't been one hundred per cent effective. This will add another string to our bow.'

Rodriguez shook her head, convinced that no one in the room had any idea what they were playing with.

'The second experiment will involve the generation of extremely low-frequency electromagnetic waves, or ELF,' Hershey continued, pointing to the screen showing layers of the earth's atmosphere. 'At altitudes of between a hundred and 150 kilometres above the earth, we have what are known as electrojets. Essentially these are rivers of electrons or electricity running through the ionosphere above the earth. We intend to blast beams of extremely high energy into them, which will change the nature of the electrojets and generate beams of ELF that can be used to communicate with our submarines over very long distances.' It was the Vice Chief of the Navy's turn to nod his approval.

'ELF waves can also be used to effectively X-ray the earth, and this, we hope, will assist us to find tunnels in countries like Iran, which is burying its nuclear plants so deep even our satellite-based sensors are having difficulty picking them up.' Hershey paused to let HAARP's potential sink in. Rodriguez seized her chance to get the people in the room to think beyond the parade ground.

'Seismic tomography has long been in use, Dr Hershey, to search for oil and gas deposits, for example,' she began, 'and for the benefit of those in this room who may not be familiar with the technique, crude oil and natural gas will return sounds at different frequencies that enable geologists to identify the substance and its location. But those techniques employ energy in the range of thirty to forty watts, which is more than sufficient to get through solid rock. We're talking here about pounding the earth's surface with three *billion* watts. Do we have any idea what might happen to the earth's delicate balance if you unleash that sort of energy?'

Dr Hershey took a deep breath and raised his eyes to the ceiling. 'That's why we do experiments, Dr Rodriguez – to find out,' he replied icily. 'And if you think the Russians, the Indians and the Chinese haven't built research stations similar to this one, think again.' He grabbed the remote and thumbed through a number of slides, stopping at a satellite image of an aerial array in the province of Nizhny Novgorod in central Russia. 'Taken from one of our KeyHole satellites just last month,' Hershey explained. 'We've got resolution down to half a metre, and you can clearly see the streets and buildings in the small town of Vasilsursk on the River Volga, close to which is the Russian ionospheric heating facility, Sura . . . here.' Hershey glared at Rodriguez and aimed his laser pointer at the screen showing a crossed dipole array of 144 antennae in a 300-metre square grid. 'That station was set up in 1981, well before this facility, and has an effective radiated power of 190 million watts.'

'Well, that's all right, then,' Rodriguez muttered under her breath.

'The Chinese aren't sitting on the sidelines, either,' Hershey continued, flicking the remote. 'This image was taken only last week, above the Xinjiang Uighur Autonomous region, which is China's most western and largest province, and strategically one of the most important.' Hershey again focused his laser pointer. 'It's bigger than Western Europe and borders Tibet to the south, Mongolia to the east,

Russia to the north, and India, Pakistan, Kazakhstan, Kyrgyzstan, Tajikistan, and Afghanistan to the west. And this next image clearly shows the antennae array of the Xinjiang ionospheric laboratory, located at 40° 24′ North and 93° 38′ East.'

'We know the Russians are working on controlling the weather, but how much do we know about Chinese capability?' the Vice Chief of Naval Operations asked.

'Not as much as we'd like, sir, but I'm assured the CIA is working on that problem as we speak.'

'Whoever controls the weather controls the world, Dr Hershey,' the admiral observed. 'The Russians have already made some progress using explosive devices to bend the jet stream above Siberia, which will reduce the severity of their winter, and I've also seen reports that they're working on controlling hurricanes and cyclones.'

'Absolutely right, Admiral, which brings me to an outline of our third major experiment,' Dr Hershey responded, glancing at Rodriguez. 'The research is not yet complete, but based on our findings to date, we've every reason to believe that hurricanes, tornados, volcanoes and earthquakes can all be controlled and initiated at will. It's a form of weather warfare we intend to perfect before the Russians and the Chinese beat us to it.'

Neither Jackson nor Rodriguez was surprised when they were excluded from the informal discussions over lunch, and the two dined together in the canteen.

'Your concerns are absolutely valid,' Jackson said as they shared a barely passable coffee at the end of their meal. 'We're able to generate ELF with the power to identify deep underground tunnels, and blast them with heat waves, but there's a problem with accuracy.'

'Can that be overcome?'

'In theory. Using the ionosphere as a lens to reflect the waves back to a target is too imprecise, so they're planning to use a Minuteman missile which can be manoeuvred into a known position. The outer casing will be specifically configured to act as the reflecting lens.'

Rodriguez handed Jackson a card. 'That cell's clean . . . the system won't pick it up. If things get worse, call me. I used to work at the White House, and my former boss, Andrew Reed, is now the President's Chief of Staff.'

46

HAMBURG

O'Connor directed the taxi driver past the railway sidings to the end of *Buchheisterstrasse*. He retrieved the backpacks containing the precious figurines from the trunk of the taxi, paid the driver, scanned the length of *Buchheisterstrasse*, and then the dockside itself. Satisfied, he nodded to Aleta. 'Let's go.'

Dark clouds scudded across the midnight sky, and behind them a three-quarter moon was intermittently reflected off the inky waters of the Elbe, 120 kilometres upstream from the river mouth on the North Atlantic. Together, they walked unhurriedly along the concrete dock, past warehouses and containers and the massive forklifts used to manoeuvre them to the loading cranes. The rusted shape of the MV *Galapagos*, a 15 000-tonne container ship, loomed at the far end of the dock, smoke wisping from her blackened funnel as the engineers worked up the required head of steam for departure.

'Are customs and immigration going to be waiting for us?' Aleta asked nervously.

'With a bit of luck, they won't be too bothered with a small cargo vessel, particularly at this time of night. Although the captain will probably ask to see your passport, and depending on how busy he is with the final loading arrangements, he might see us in his cabin. Just be your charming self – but not too charming; we don't want to excite the crew on the first night,' O'Connor added with a mischievous grin.

'If we were anywhere else I'd kick you in the shins!' Aleta said, smiling to herself. The prospect of sailing across the Atlantic with this dashing Irishman was as exciting as it was nerve-racking, but her smile quickly faded as she caught sight of two men in uniform descending the ship's gangplank.

'Keep walking. Just act normally,' O'Connor said softly, weighing up his options as the two men approached.

'Who the fuck does she think she is?' Howard Wiley fumed at his chief of staff, shaking with rage at the 'please explain' he'd received from the CIA's director. Rodriguez' questions at the HAARP briefing had raised eyebrows in more than one corridor of power.

'I don't think she understands the potential of the HAARP experiments,' Larry Davis agreed, sweating more than usual as he absorbed the full force of Wiley's tirade.

'Rodriguez wouldn't know if a goddamned San Francisco trolley car was up her ass until the people got off . . . and in her case you'd have to ring the fucking bell. I want her head on a plate the minute she steps back into this building. She's fired!'

'And if she goes to the media?'

'We'll have her behind bars. She's signed up to the Intelligence Authorization Act like every other motherfucker around here, and if she so much as thinks about opening that big mouth of hers, I'll have her in the slammer faster than she can blink.'

'With respect, Deputy Director – and I'm not defending Rodriguez here – the Authorization Act didn't protect Valerie Plame, and if Rodriguez sues —'

'Let her! She won't win, and we'll clean out the bitch's bank balance in the process.'

'She wouldn't win, sir,' Davis persisted, 'but the peaceniks would be all over us like a rash. So far, they haven't been able to stir up much media interest in HAARP, but this would give them air time, and the director will be more pissed than he is already.'

'So what are you suggesting?'

'The chief of station in Guatemala City's just resigned. Why don't you send Rodriguez down there in his place?'

'As chief of station? Are you out of your mind, Davis?'

'Think about it, sir. Guatemala's an armpit and we were short-staffed down there even before this codex thing came on the radar, let alone now the chief of station's resigned. Rodriguez will be working like a dog from the day she arrives. You can claim it's a promotion into the field; it gets you off the hook with the equal opportunity wankers and gets her out of our hair. And if it all turns to custard, you can remove her, and she'll probably resign.'

'It's a pity we don't have anyone at the North Pole,' Wiley

grumbled. 'She could freeze her tits off up there. All right, make it happen,' he said finally. 'In the meantime, what's the word on Tutankhamen and that other bitch?'

'We're still checking. We've traced them to Hamburg, but they may have left by train.'

'I want them found – and fast!'

'*Guten Abend.*' O'Connor flashed a smile at the two officers approaching along the dock.

'*Abend,*' one of them replied.

'Who were they?' Aleta asked, breathing a little easier after the two men had passed.

O'Connor shrugged. 'Don't know, but Merchant Marine, not customs or police. Watch your step,' he said as they reached the gangplank.

'You're cutting it fine,' the ship's steward observed haughtily as they reached the deck. 'We sail in twenty minutes.'

'Sorry about that,' O'Connor apologised.

'The captain's on the bridge,' the steward sniffed. 'I'll show you to your cabin and then he'll want to see your passports. Follow me,' and he minced his way down the port companionway.

'Opening bat for the other side,' O'Connor whispered.

'Stop it!' Aleta whispered back, suppressing a fit of the giggles.

Aleta and O'Connor stood at the rail of the port wing of the bridge.
Aleta watched the two tugs herding their charge away from the dock
towards the middle of the Elbe. Powerful lights lit the for'ard decks
of the MV *Galapagos* as the crew worked to get the heavy mooring
hawsers aboard. O'Connor scanned the docks up to *Buchheisterstrasse*,
searching for any signs of anyone on their trail.

'The captain didn't seem too interested in the paperwork,' Aleta
observed as the MV *Galapagos* moved slowly out into midstream.

'One of the reasons I timed our arrival to just before sailing: he's
got a lot of things on his plate right now, and he won't relax until he's
clear of the English Channel and out into the Atlantic.'

'Slow ahead,' the captain ordered. Below decks, a single gleaming
steel shaft, driven by the massive Hitachi-Man marine diesel engine
began to turn.

Howard Wiley looked into the biometric security scanner outside
the door of the Operation Maya ops room. In an instant the powerful
system computed the algorithms and analysed the pattern on Wiley's
iris. No two irises were the same; even identical twins had different
irises. The security Wiley had installed on Operation Maya was far
tighter than fingerprint recognition. The light glowed green and he
stepped into the room, just as a message alert from the Berlin station
pinged on Larry Davis's computer screen:

Information just to hand indicates Tutankhamen and Nefertiti departed Hamburg by sea. MV *Galapagos*, a 15 000-tonne

container ship, left Buchheisterstrasse docks nine hours ago,
bound for Havana and then Puerto Quetzal on Pacific coast
of Guatemala.

'Fuck! Can we get someone on board?'

Davis shook his head. 'She'll be clear of the mouth of the Elbe and
into the English Channel by now.'

'Tell Rodriguez that when she gets to Guatemala City, her first
task is to organise for one of the crew to fall ill in Havana and arrange
a swap. Tutankhamen and Nefertiti can simply disappear over the
side, and the sharks will do the rest.'

'The ship's steward is not such a bad guy once you get to know him.
He even keeps a half-decent cellar,' O'Connor said, extracting the
cork from a bottle of Alsace riesling. They had been at sea over a
week, and O'Connor had made it his business to speak to every
member of the crew. He now felt reasonably confident they'd got
out of Hamburg without a tag . . . for the moment. Initially the MV
Galapagos had made good progress. They were now well out into the
mid-North Atlantic, to the west of the Azores group, but rising seas
had forced the captain to slow to ten knots. Dinner over, O'Connor
and Aleta had repaired to their cabin just below the bridge, with its
view over the for'ard decks through the big square portholes.

'Cheers.' O'Connor raised his glass. Aleta raised hers, and
gripped the table as the *Galapagos* rolled to starboard and buried
herself into a massive wave. White water exploded over the bow

and foamed over the for'ard containers before streaming back through the scuppers.

'They lose about 10 000 containers a year in seas like this,' O'Connor observed idly, savouring the delicate citrus flavours of the riesling. 'One washed up on a beach in Somalia last year full of thousands of bags of potato chips – made the kids' day.'

Aleta smiled and turned to stare at the dark mountainous seas ahead. The wind moaned in the rigging of the ship's cranes and tore at the foaming crests beyond. She looked back at O'Connor. 'You know, if someone had told me that one day I'd be sitting in a cabin with an Irishman, guarding two priceless figurines and sipping riesling – which is very nice by the way – while on the run from a bunch of hitmen, I would have thought they'd lost their marbles.'

'This is life and we're living it, but unfortunately your life's not going to be the same for a while, at least not until we find the codex.' O'Connor paused, weighing up how much hurt his next question might cause. 'What happened in San Marcos? If that's not too painful a question.' O'Connor was still puzzled as to why some of the most powerful men in Washington wanted Aleta dead.

Aleta sighed. 'No, it's not too painful, although I still want those responsible brought to justice.' She gripped the table again as the *Galapagos* ploughed into the base of another massive wave. The whole ship shuddered, her bow disappearing from view in another explosion of white foam. 'I was only eight at the time. My father was a lay preacher in the little Catholic church at San Marcos.'

'Yet he started out life as Jewish?'

Aleta nodded. 'Papa was Jewish through and through, but as I mentioned to you at Mauthausen, Archbishop Angelo Roncalli, who later became Pope John XXIII, helped my father escape the Nazis. Roncalli used to sit up until three in the morning forging Catholic baptism certificates for Jewish children.' Aleta's eyes were moist. 'Papa said that Roncalli was everything a priest should be. My aunt Rebekkah drowned during their escape, but Papa never forgot Roncalli's kindness. My grandparents were both Jewish, and they had great faith, but I think Papa practised his own faith as a Catholic out of respect for Roncalli. Papa was occasionally asked to preach at the bigger Catholic church in San Pedros, fifteen minutes by boat from San Marcos.' Aleta took O'Connor back to 1982 and the north-west shores of the beautiful lake.

Ariel Weizman gripped the rails of the pulpit of the cavernous white-washed church that stood over San Pedro and the lake. His dark curly hair had long turned grey and his face was gently lined with the wisdom and heartache of the years. Some of the villagers shifted nervously in the big wooden pews, their dark eyes fearful and alert.

'As we celebrate mass here in San Pedro today, we remember in our prayers Archbishop Óscar Romero,' Ariel began. 'It's two years to the day since Archbishop Romero was brutally gunned down while celebrating the Holy Mass, just across the border in El Salvador. Archbishop Romero's "crime" was to demand an end to the torture, rape and murder of his people. The leader of San Salvador's death squads, Major Roberto D'Aubuisson, has never been brought to justice. "Blowtorch Bob" was a nickname D'Aubuisson earned from his favourite form of torture, and he was also known for throwing babies into the air and shooting them for target practice. Yet D'Aubuisson is an honoured guest whenever he visits Washington.' Ariel glanced at his family sitting in the front pew. The twin boys were restless, but little Aleta was looking at him, her big brown eyes as inquisitive as ever, her dark shiny hair tied back in a ponytail. Misha, Ariel's wife of fifteen years, scolded the twins softly, a tender smile on her face.

'In Central and South America, the United States is supporting brutal regimes that are systematically murdering the local populations. The Sixth Commandment is very clear,' he continued, 'and in Exodus, and in Deuteronomy, God has spoken, yet in Chile, the United States has supported the overthrow of the democratically elected Salvador Allende, and replaced him with Augusto Pinochet, a murderous thug. With the support of the CIA, Pinochet's men are torturing and murdering tens of thousands of Chileans opposed to his brutal regime. The United States of America is fond of preaching democracy, but only if it gets the results it wants.' Ariel paused. The *campesinos*, the simple folk of San Pedro who eked out a subsistence living amongst the coffee plantations and maize farms, were nervous; but Ariel knew that unless someone spoke out on their behalf, the killing would continue.

On the other side of the town square Howard Wiley was standing next to a dilapidated store – *Cristo viene!* Christ is coming! painted in red on the wooden walls. Wiley scanned the courtyard of the San Pedro church. Appointed as the CIA's chief of station at the US Embassy in Guatemala City two years previously, at thirty-one he was one of the Agency's youngest field commanders. Wiley turned to Major Ramales, the Guatemalan Army officer commanding the death squads assigned to put down the growing insurrection around Lake Atitlán.

'Everything is ready, Comandante?'

Ramales fingered his trimmed black moustache. '*Sí*. You only have to give the word.'

Wiley adjusted his earpiece. Ariel Weizman's homily was coming through loud and clear.

'Here in Guatemala, President Reagan is supporting General Montt, another ruthless thug trained by the Americans at their School of the Americas at Fort Benning in Georgia. This is not the first time the United States has put a government of its choosing in power in Guatemala,' Ariel reminded his congregation. 'Many of you will recall that the Eisenhower administration and the CIA toppled the democratically elected President Arbenz and replaced him with another of their puppets, Colonel Armas. I appeal today to General Montt: send your soldiers back to their barracks, where they will no longer be able to rape and murder our women and children —'

Ariel's sermon was interrupted by soldiers in camouflage uniforms shouldering open the heavy doors of the church, crashing them back against the white-washed stone masonry. More soldiers stormed into the church and immediately opened up with machine guns and automatic rifles in a deafening burst of fire. Bullets ricocheted off the stone walls and shattered the ornate glass windows. The old stone church was rent by the screams of the congregation, many dying where they sat. Ariel clutched his chest, the bloodstain on his shirt spreading as he slumped forward onto the pulpit railing. Aleta screamed as her mother's lifeless form toppled into the aisle. Blood spurted below Misha's neck from a ruptured aorta. The twins, who had been standing on the pew seat, were cut down together as the soldiers repeatedly raked the villagers with bursts of fire. Tears running down her cheeks, Aleta crawled between the pews and out through a side door of the church.

Some time later, numb with shock and horror, Aleta peered through the bushes in the church garden as the soldiers threw the last of the bodies onto the big trucks drawn up outside the church. A young boy moaned and stirred amongst the corpses and a soldier jumped up onto the truck. In a series of brutal swipes with a razor-sharp machete, he hacked off the boy's head. In the distance, on the foothills of Volcán San Pedro, more soldiers were unloading their grisly cargo, throwing the bodies of the villagers into a deep pit dug the previous day.

Aleta could not have known that while most of the *campesinos* were dead, some, including one of her brothers, were still alive. Explosions rocked the volcanic hillside. Whenever there was movement in the pit, a soldier would yell '*Granada!*' and hurl a hand grenade at the bodies. Tears continued to stream down Aleta's cheeks as she watched the truck drive away, leaving just the officers in the town square, laughing and joking with a short white man wearing a fawn safari suit. He had a pale, freckly face and spiky red hair. Eventually the white man and an officer got into a staff car and drove down towards the little dock at the bottom of the hill.

The container vessel shouldered her way through another massive wave, the crest curling angrily over her bow. 'I am terribly, terribly sorry,' O'Connor said simply. 'The CIA has made some unconscionable mistakes over the years, and the campaigns in the Americas were amongst the worst. But thank you for telling me. It couldn't have been easy.'

'Time is a great healer, Curtis . . . but you never forget.'

'Would you know the man with the red hair if you saw him again?'

'Oh, yes. Even though it was years ago, that's one face that's indelibly seared on my memory. Why do you ask?'

'Howard Wiley, the man who's trying to kill us, is now in charge of all the CIA's spy rings and overseas operations. In 1982 he was chief of station in Guatemala City – and his most striking physical attribute, apart from his lack of height, is his spiky red hair.'

Aleta's eyes widened. 'Short?'

'Around five-foot four. Quite vertically challenged, is our DDO. I think this explains why he wants you out of the way.'

'And it explains something else. Papa was asked to preach that day because Father Hernandez was supposedly going to be away in Guatemala City. But how could Wiley know I was there?'

'The CIA have a file on anyone, *anyone* they think might pose a threat, either to their operations overseas, or to America itself. When you wrote that article in *The Mayan Archaeologist* linking the School of the Americas to the training of death squads in Central America, it would have rung alarm bells for Wiley. He can't be certain you were at the church on that day, but he knows you were born in San Marcos and that Ariel was your father. People like Wiley don't leave anything to luck. If he suspects there is the slightest chance you can link him to the killings, he won't hesitate.'

'So he'll get me in the end . . .' Aleta shuddered.

'Not while I'm around.'

Trust this man with your life. Aleta sipped her riesling, pondering the shaman's words. 'What I don't understand is if Wiley is now running the CIA's spy ring, why have you stayed so long?'

O'Connor didn't reply immediately. It had been a long time since he'd been alone with an intelligent, beautiful woman, and even longer since anyone had been able to penetrate his outer shell. 'I've always been grateful for getting a new start in America,' he said finally. 'When I joined the CIA, I just wanted to do my bit for my adopted country, a country I was proud of – or used to be, until the last administration came along.'

Aleta listened, trying to fathom O'Connor. To her, he was still an enigma. He was confident but unassuming. Hard as nails, yet possessed of a roguish sense of humour and a soft Irish brogue. She felt her attraction for this man growing. 'I don't even know where you were born, other than, I presume, Ireland,' she said, her voice gentler now. 'You now know a little more about me, but I still know very little about you.'

O'Connor refilled the wine glasses. 'I've never tried to disguise my accent. I was born in a place called Ballingarry. It's a small village in County Tipperary, near the border of Kilkenny in the south. My father used to work in the coalmines, but he died when I was ten.'

'I'm sorry. I know how hard that must have been.'

'Thank you, but don't be. I was the last of five kids by a wide margin – my father referred to me as "the accident". I used to hide before the drunken bastard came home because if he found me, he'd beat me up.'

'Did things get better after he died?' she asked, shocked.

'Not much. We moved to a tenement house in Sheriff Street in Dublin, near the docks on the Liffey, which was a pretty tough neighbourhood. My mother worked as a cleaner at night, and got her kicks screwing her way through the day. Eventually one of her men friends paid for me to go to a Catholic boarding school in Dublin run by the Christian Brothers.'

Aleta noticed his face cloud as he took her back to the slums of inner-city Dublin in the late 1970s.

'So, O'Connor. I'm told you're in need of a bit of discipline. What have you got to say to that, eh?' The head brother of Saint Joseph's, Brother Michael, was obese, his round, pudgy face the same colour as the salmon walls of his sparsely furnished office. His sandy-coloured hair was thinning at the temples; his eyes an icy grey.

Curtis winced as Brother Michael lashed him across the face with a heavy leather strap.

'I asked you a question, you little Dublin shite! Answer, boy!' Brother Michael said more slowly and menacingly, 'or bejaysus I'll beat you within an inch of your life.'

'I'm here because my mother's boyfriend paid for me to come here,' Curtis responded defiantly. He fought back the tears as the strap again sliced into his cheek.

'You sodding little gobshite!' Brother Michael lashed Curtis again and shoved him headfirst into the wall. A silver crucifix of Jesus rattled against the plaster above Curtis's head. 'Get out of my sight!'

Brother Michael propelled Curtis out of his office into the corridor, where he crashed into one of the bigger boys.

'What da fook? I'm gonna bleedin' nut the fookin' head of you, ya bleedin' bollocks ya!'

'Tell your mother to get married,' Curtis responded, ducking deftly out of the way of the bigger boy's swinging right arm.

Later that night, as the newest boy in the dormitory, Curtis had his first experience with Brother Brendan, the house master.

'Lights out, you scum!' The tall, sinister Brother Brendan walked silently down the middle aisle that separated the rows of bunks. He stopped at the bottom of Curtis's bed. Curtis pretended to be asleep, watching through barely open eyelids. Brother Brendan silently approached the head of the bed, breathing heavily, beads of sweat appearing on his pallid face. He slid his hand under the sheets and onto Curtis's thigh. In an instant Curtis clamped the brother's skinny wrist with his left hand and wrenched Brother Brendan's thumb back sharply with his right.

'*Aaggghhhh!*' Brother Brendan's high-pitched yell reverberated off the darkened dormitory walls.

'Touch me again, you fucking pervert, and I'll break your fucking arm!'

Brother Brendan fled without a word.

Curtis waited nearly an hour. When he was sure everyone was asleep, he quietly retrieved his clothes from the locker beside his bed, dressed and crept out of the dormitory.

Staying in the shadows of the three-metre-high brick wall that surrounded Saint Joseph's, Curtis made his way to a large oak tree where he paused and checked the dimly lit buildings behind him.

Satisfied that none of the brothers were about, he flung the battered leather satchel containing the few things he owned over the wall and scaled the tree. Curtis glanced up and down but the laneway was deserted. He quietly grasped the top of the wall, slid down until he hung at full stretch and dropped to the ground. The traffic on nearby Thomas Road was light, but Curtis eventually hitched a ride to the docks area on a truck carrying a load of Guinness.

It was after midnight when he reached the tenement house in Sheriff Street, but the light was still on in his mother's bedroom. Curtis pushed open the old wooden front door and climbed the stairs; but he stopped at the top of the landing. The door to his mother's room was ajar and she was naked on the bed. A man Curtis had never seen before was astride her.

'Give it to me! Give me that fat cock!'

Curtis crept into his old room and closed the door, numb to a world over which he had no control.

'At least I had some very good years with my family,' Aleta said softly. The *Galapagos* rolled and shuddered yet again, spume flying from the crests of the huge waves as the gale howled over the foam-covered containers. 'What happened? Did you go back to school?'

'I left the next morning. My aunt Shaylee lived on the other side of the city and she and her husband took me in, something for which I'll always be grateful. Without them, I'd probably be driving a crane down at the docks.'

'University?'

O'Connor nodded. 'I won a scholarship to Trinity College and did my doctorate at the School of Biochemistry and Immunology. Worked for "big pharma" for a while in the States, but didn't like their ethics, so I joined the CIA . . . and here we are,' he said with a grin. '*Prost.*'

'*Prost.*' Aleta raised her glass to the man she was beginning to understand, although she knew she'd only scratched the surface. They clinked glasses, and O'Connor got up from the table and stood at the window, watching another wave explode onto the decks, tumbling over the containers before exhausting itself in the scuppers. The *Galapagos* shook herself free, crested the wave and charged towards the next.

Aleta joined him at the big square porthole. For a long while they stood close, watching the storm, finishing their wine.

O'Connor put his arm around Aleta's slim waist, half expecting her to take his hand away, but she nestled into him, resting her head and her now short blonde hair on his shoulder. Her perfume was a sensual mix of jasmine and caesalpinia; foxglove and vanilla; citron and cedar. It might be aptly named, he thought wryly, having spied the elegant red bottle earlier in the day: Trouble by Boucheron. A flash of forked lightning hit the sea barely two nautical miles from the ship; 120 000 amps travelling at 60 000 metres every second turned the strike point on the ocean into a boiling inferno. The deck and containers were bathed in a powerful and eerie blue light, and O'Connor momentarily reflected on the power of the transmitter at Gakona. The thunder crackled above them and shook the *Galapagos*' superstructure. He turned towards Aleta. Their lips met, softly at first, and then more urgently. They held each other tightly, moving with the roll of the ship. O'Connor ran his hand slowly down the small of Aleta's back and she responded, moulding herself against him.

47

GUATEMALA CITY

From her office inside the secure area of the American Embassy building in the tree-lined Avenida Reforma of Guatemala City's Zone 10, Ellen Rodriguez scanned the latest satellite information on the position of the *Galapagos*. She fed the data into the computer and reset the calculation for the *Galapagos'* arrival. At its present speed and course, the *Galapagos* would reach Havana in three days at 1135 local time.

Rodriguez looked at her watch. It was after 10 p.m. and still there was no word on getting an asset on board the container ship. For the moment there was little she could do but wait for her counterpart in the US quasi-embassy in Havana, the quaintly named 'United States Interests Section', to get in contact. She prepared to head home. 'Home' was the Howard Johnson Inn across the road, and was likely to remain so for some time. In the week since she'd arrived, she'd been in the office before dawn, and rarely left before ten, sometimes midnight. Finding a place of her own would have to wait, she thought ruefully. Rodriguez was preparing to shut down her encrypted links when an alert appeared on her screen.

TOP SECRET

NOFORN

OPERATION MAYA

CHIEF OF STATION EYES ONLY

Asset identified. Briefed re. Tutankhamen and Nefertiti. *Galapagos* scheduled to berth Haiphong Terminal, Maritima. Estimated duration of stay, no more than twenty-four hours but expect crew to take shore leave. Arrangements in hand to -manufacture requirement for crew replacement. Will advise soonest.

COS. Havana.

Rodriguez shut down her computer, torn again between her duty to the Firm and her feelings about the plan to eliminate Curtis O'Connor. In her experience Officer O'Connor was one of the finest agents ever to walk out of Langley's doors. Even if they got an asset on board the *Galapagos*, he would have to be good. Very good. Ellen Rodriguez prepared to leave. On the other side of the Atlantic in Rome, it was now very early in the morning.

Cardinal Felici acknowledged the salute of the Swiss Guard and entered the Vatican's secret archives, adjacent to the Vatican library.

If the guard found it strange that the second-most senior cardinal in the Vatican was up and about at 5.30 in the morning, his face was inscrutable. The archives contained more than eighty kilometres of shelving, but Cardinal Felici was only interested in reacquainting himself with one document. He made his way into the vault beneath the *Cortile della Pigna*, the massive Roman bronze pinecone in the courtyard of the Belvedere above.

Felici extracted the document from the crimson cover embossed with the gold coat of arms of the Vatican State. Sister Lúcia, just a child at the time, had handwritten her account of the third warning on a small single sheet of paper. Felici reflected on the public version of the third warning of Fátima released by Pope John Paul II. That, he knew, had been a mistake and had only fuelled the controversy. Too many people had seen the original warning, including Bishop Venancio, the auxiliary bishop of Fátima; and too many people knew this warning had been recorded on a single sheet of paper. Felici had been in Guatemala at the time, and had not been able to prevent the clumsy 26 June release, which the Vatican had committed to *four* sheets of paper, passing off the young Lúcia's vision of a city in ruins as unremarkable. Had the real identity of the city in ruins been made public, the shock would have reverberated around the world. Felici adjusted his glasses and focused on Sister Lúcia's original account.

> I write in obedience to you, my God, who commands me to do so through his Excellency the Bishop of Leira and through your most Holy Mother and mine.
>
> After the two parts which I have already

explained, at the left of Our Lady and a little above, we saw Archangel Raguel, the Archangel of Justice with a flaming sword in one hand and a pair of scales in the other. Seated on the scales were two younger angels, one a boy, one a girl, but the scales were out of balance, tipped in favour of the male. Archangel Raguel's sword hilt was gold, embossed with the Greek letter phi.

As we watched, huge pyramids rose above the horizon. Warriors from the great civilisations of the past streamed from within them. The Maya, the Inca, the Egyptians, the Hopi Indians, the Cherokees, all of them formed up *en masse* behind Our Lady. Prominent amongst them were the Maya. The Mayan king was flanked by a Mayan prince and princess, each wearing a jade talisman in the shape of the Greek letter phi. Above them sat the prophets: Abraham, Moses, Elijah, Jeremiah, Ezekiel, Daniel, and the last great prophet, Muhammad. Below them sat the seers: Cassandra, Saint Malachy, Hildegard of Bingen, Savonarola, Nostradamus and Edgar Cayce. Saint Malachy was the first to step forward.

Malachy, a bishop who was born in Armagh in Northern Ireland in 1094, had accurately predicted the reformation more than 300 years before it occurred. More astonishingly still, Malachy had arrived in Rome in 1140, accompanied by a number of monks. He had fallen into a trance on the Janiculum Hill above the old city, where he started talking in Latin. His scribe faithfully took down all his utterances; it was nearly dawn by the time Malachy had finished. When he woke, Malachy confirmed to his companions that God had given him a vision of the identity of every Pope until the end of time. The list was extraordinarily accurate, and Felici shivered involuntarily as he thought of the prediction for John XXIII: 'Saint Malachy was holding a long scroll in front of him, and he continued to read in Latin: *Pastor et Nauta.*'

Shepherd and sailor. In 1958 the American Cardinal Francis Spellman had hired a boat and sailed up and down the Tiber with a cargo of sheep, in the hope that he might fulfil Malachy's prediction for the conclave, but to no avail. Although it had indeed been a shepherd and a sailor whom God had chosen. The keys of Peter had been handed to John XXIII. Angelo Roncalli had previously been the patriarch of the maritime city of Venice.

The accuracy of Malachy's predictions weighed heavily on Felici's ambitions. Malachy had designated the second-last Pope before the end of time as *de Gloria Olivae*. Felici knew that 'from the glory of the olive' was a reference to the olive branch being a symbol of the order of Saint Benedict; Benedict XVI was the name Joseph Ratzinger had chosen. Aged seventy-eight at the time of his election, Benedict XVI was one of the oldest in the history of the papacy. Malachy had insisted that the last Pope would be known as 'Peter the Roman', bringing to an end the rock upon which Peter had built the original church, as well as the end of the world itself. Felici took

a deep breath and went back to the final part of the real secret of
Fátima, to Sister Lúcia's record of the Virgin Mary's appearance.

The Archangel Raguel spoke in a voice of
great authority. 'Penance! This is the last
of your warnings!' Then came a series of
visions. Immense, uncontrollable wildfires
raged across great swathes of Spain and
Italy. In Australia exhausted men and women
battled impossible odds to try to save their
homes but to no avail. In the United States
California was ablaze, as were the Balkans
and Africa. Hurricanes of enormous power
pounded the coastlines of the continents.
Earthquakes rent the ground from beneath
San Francisco, New York, Tokyo and London.
The earth trembled as her massive tectonic
plates ground together.

An intense white light emanated from Our
Lady but it seemed strangely blocked above
the Basilica of Saint Peter. Great bolts
of blue lightning crackled from the tip of
Raguel's sword, reducing Saint Peter's and
the rest of Vatican City to smoking rubble. Hundreds of children swarmed over the
walls, chasing the priests from where they
were hiding. The Pope appeared amongst the
rubble, his white robes stained with blood,

until he too was cut down by Raguel's sword.

Beyond the walls of the Vatican, the Tiber had been reduced to stinking mud. Suddenly there was a vision of three enormous interlocking toothed wheels, each larger than the other, and each tooth was designated with a Mayan hieroglyph. The two largest wheels slowly turned until the teeth meshed in an enormous flash of energy, giving a date of 21 December 2012. Our Lady, the Archangel Raguel, all the prophets and seers and the old civilisations faded back towards the company of heaven, leaving planet earth wobbling in its orbit, the changing positions of the poles and the equator devastating the entire world.

Cardinal Felici replaced Sister Lúcia's letter in its crimson folder and sealed it in the vault, where he was determined it would remain.

48

HAVANA

The *Galapagos* was due to sail in three hours and all but one of the crew had returned from shore leave. O'Connor surveyed the Havana docks from his position beneath the port wing of the bridge. The traffic on *Primer Anillo del Puerto*, the main road connecting the ports on the south side of the harbour, was heavy. Containers were piled up on the concrete docks serviced by railroad and trucking companies. Beyond them, huge forklifts charged to and from three giant warehouses. The *Galapagos* was taking on cargo, and O'Connor watched as the crane operator eased a big thirty-tonne container of machinery into position.

Fifteen minutes later the last crew member, one O'Connor had not seen before, reached the bottom of the gangplank. O'Connor wandered over to the rail where the ship's steward was standing, dragging on a cigarette.

'New crew member, Alfredo?'

Alfredo shrugged and smiled. '*Sí*. One of the crew – too much fucking, too much to drink. This one's Sicilian. He's probably no better, and I've got to share a cabin with him.' Alfredo stubbed his cigarette out on the rail and disappeared through the nearest bulkhead, leaving O'Connor to watch the new arrival negotiate the gangplank.

The Sicilian was thickset and muscled, with black hair and a thick black moustache, his face pockmarked and scarred. O'Connor was immediately on high alert.

'We've got company again,' he told Aleta as he closed the cabin door behind him.

'Who? Where?'

'It may be coincidence, but I don't think so. One of the crew supposedly had too much to drink and they've had to replace him. It's plausible, but it's also a classic move in CIA asset substitution.' O'Connor opened his bag and took out the small compact CIA toolkit he carried, as well as a heavy door-hasp. 'High-quality hair dye is not the only thing they sell in Hamburg.'

'What do you need that for?'

'Our new friend, if he's one of Wiley's buddies, will pick the lock on this cabin in an instant, but this one will be tougher to crack,' he said, marking the spots for the heavy-duty bolts. Ten minutes later he shouldered the cabin door from the companionway outside, but it held fast.

O'Connor waited until just before sailing time. He instructed Aleta to remain in the cabin and made his way to the port bridge-wing. The last container was being loaded and two tugs were standing by, one for'ard of the bow and one aft of the stern. The captain was on the starboard bridge wing, barking orders to the deck crew through the tannoy system. The Sicilian had been assigned duty on the for'ard hawser. O'Connor made his way off the bridge, down a series of steep narrow companionways, reaching the crew quarters in less than two minutes. The door to Alfredo's cabin was unlocked, but the Sicilian had secured his gear in one of two lockers screwed to a bulkhead in the cramped quarters. The brass padlock was child's play for O'Connor. He chose a diamond-shaped lock pick and a small tension wrench and had it open in an instant.

The Glock pistol, complete with silencer, was in a small worn leather pouch at the bottom of the Sicilian's kit bag. O'Connor sat on one of the bunks, quickly extracted the magazine, checked the chamber was empty, pulled the slide back, released the lock lever and removed the slide from the Glock. The countless hours of arms training at Camp Peary in Virginia kicked in and seconds later O'Connor had taken out the recoil mechanism and the barrel and put them to one side. He took a small punch from his bag, placed it between the firing pin and the firing pin sleeve and pressed down to take the pressure from the spring, allowing the slide backing plate to be prised free.

Suddenly the deck vibrated as deep in the bowels of the ship the massive drive shaft began to turn. Above decks, the crew had stowed the mooring hawsers and the Sicilian was making his way aft along the companionway that housed a maze of pipes beneath the containers. O'Connor removed the firing pin from the slide mechanism and pocketed it. He quickly replaced the slide backing plate, reassembled the barrel and recoil mechanism, replaced the slide on the pistol, rammed the magazine full of nine-millimetre rounds back into the butt and returned the gun to where he'd found it.

'What's the situation?' Howard Wiley demanded over the secure video that linked Langley with the US Embassy in Avenida Reforma.

'The asset has confirmed he's on board, but the satellite images are showing the *Galapagos* has only just left Havana harbour. I'll let you know as soon as we have confirmation of success,' Rodriguez replied evenly.

'How long before the ship reaches Guatemala?'

'Six to seven days, depending on the weather.'

'*What?*'

'It's 2000 nautical miles from Havana to Puerto Quetzal.'

'They're not on a tramp steamer, Rodriguez, those things do twenty knots.'

Rodriguez sighed inwardly. 'Their route will take them west out of Havana and into the Yucatán Channel between Cuba and Mexico, where a gale warning is still current, which will prevent them doing more than eight or nine knots. From there they'll head south to the Panama Canal, and that's over eighty kilometres long. Depending on traffic, it will take about ten hours to navigate.'

'Ten hours for eighty kilometres gives them a speed of less than four fucking knots.'

Rodriguez told herself to remain calm. 'From the Caribbean side, there are three sets of locks at Gatun which will raise them eighty-five feet up to Lake Gatun itself, and at the far end they have to negotiate another set of locks at Pedro Miguel and another two at Miraflores, which will lower them into the Pacific. It's not a racetrack, sir. And in any case I fail to see what the speed of the ship has to do with the mission.'

'That's why you're in bumblefuck-nowheresville and I'm in Langley, Rodriguez. Has it occurred to you that the mission on board the *Galapagos* may not succeed?'

'Based on O'Connor's performance to date, that's entirely possible . . . sir.'

'So what arrangements have you made for that eventuality?'

'With respect, sir, we've only just managed to get an asset on board the *Galapagos*.'

'What've we got in Puerto Quetzal?' Wiley demanded of his chief of staff. Larry Davis shook his head. 'Get someone there – now!' Wiley glared back into the video camera.

'The speed of the ship determines how much time we have to get another asset in position, Rodriguez.'

'Might that not be better organised from here, sir – in country?'

'No!' With that, the video screen went blank.

Rodriguez leaned back in her chair. '*Mierda!*' she swore, shaking her head.

'These people don't give up, do they?' Aleta observed when O'Connor returned to the cabin.

'Nope, but then, neither do we.'

Nine hours later, the *Galapagos* rounded Cape San Antonio,

the westernmost tip of Cuba, and headed south into the Caribbean towards Panama. The gale warning was still in force, and the winds tore foaming white spume from the backs of angry, rolling waves, although the ship's roll had abated. To the west the sun had set over the Mexican coast, and the bars and nightclubs were in full swing in Cancun and Playa del Carmen's Fifth Avenue, the centre of the Mayan Riviera.

O'Connor wondered when the Sicilian might strike and he put himself in the hitman's place. He would probably make his move some time after midnight, when the minimum number of crew would be awake and on duty. O'Connor resolved to turn the confrontation on its head, to provide the Sicilian an opportunity to strike, but on O'Connor's terms. He looked at his watch. It had just gone 10 p.m. He turned to Aleta, who was sitting at the table beneath the porthole, working on her grandfather's notes and the angles of deflection of the sun's rays that a third figurine might produce. 'I may be gone for some time,' he said, 'but don't worry – unlike the British explorer, I will return.'

'Where are you going?' Aleta asked.

'Secret men's business . . . a little something that has to be attended to. This is 101 stuff, but on no account open the door, even if a key turns the lock, okay? It may not be me.'

Aleta nodded fearfully. 'Be careful.'

She watched the bow of the ship dipping and rising more gracefully now, with the occasional large wave exploding over the for'ard containers. The white caps were intermittently caught by the moon, illuminated through gaps in the clouds scudding across from the west. Silently Aleta wrestled with her thoughts, and the irony of finding herself caring for a man who had been sent to Vienna to kill her.

O'Connor took up a position near a stanchion at the stern of the ship, leaning against the rail but looking back towards the superstructure. The Sicilian would want a clear shot and to dispose of his target quickly. That would mean a close-quarters kill. Twenty minutes later, the asset walked through the aft bulkhead and onto the stern deck beneath the containers.

'You're up late. Can't sleep?' The Sicilian spoke Spanish with a thick Italian accent. He approached slowly, his right hand in his trouser pocket. His dark eyes were focused and cold.

'*Potrei dire lo stesso per voi*. I could say the same for you.' O'Connor's use of the Sicilian's native Italian had the desired effect, momentarily unnerving the Sicilian. He drew the Glock from his pocket and pointed it at O'Connor, the long silencer barely a foot from O'Connor's chest.

'*Forse questo vi aiuterà, bastardo*. Perhaps this will help you.' The Sicilian pulled the trigger but the mechanism went forward with a dull *clunk*. The assassin frantically reached to recock the slide but O'Connor's reaction was lightning fast. In a movement perfected by the Israeli Defense Forces, he pivoted ninety degrees on his left leg, and with a sliding step, he rammed his right knee into the Sicilian's groin. The assassin grunted in pain and made another attempt to load the Glock, his head lowered. O'Connor slammed his elbow behind the Sicilian's ear, sidestepped, straightened his right leg, swept it behind the Sicilian's knee and slammed the assassin's head onto the steel deck. The Glock clattered against the aft bulkhead.

Dazed, the Sicilian got to his knees. O'Connor straddled his neck and with one hand under his chin and the other clamped to his hair, rolled his target sideways onto the deck. Ankles crossed, O'Connor held the Sicilian's head in a vice-like grip while he choked him with his legs. The big man flailed helplessly, but gradually his protests grew weaker. O'Connor continued to crush his neck until he was sure the Sicilian was dead. He checked his pockets for identification, but they were empty. O'Connor took him in a fireman's lift, pushed up and heaved him over the rail. Dispassionately he watched his would-be-killer's body plunge into the *Galapagos'* moonlit boiling wake, ten metres below.

O'Connor retrieved the Glock and stood at the stern rail, staring at the diminishing silvery turmoil of the wake until his heart rate dropped back to its normal sixty beats a minute. He hadn't seen his assassin surface, and if a Caribbean reef shark didn't get him, then the tigers or great whites certainly would. Satisfied that he and Aleta were safe again, at least until they got to Puerto Quetzal, he headed back to the cabin, wondering if she was still awake. It would be good to feel the softness of her skin against his.

The sun was setting across the Pacific when a week later O'Connor scanned the docks of the Guatemalan port of Puerto Quetzal. The ship had docked three hours earlier, but he had returned to the cabin after talking the captain into letting them stay on board for another night.

'You're in no hurry to get off?' Aleta asked.

O'Connor shook his head and handed her his binoculars. 'See the taxi parked at the end of the wharf?' He pointed past the stacks of containers and warehouses to a yellow taxi parked beside the port administration buildings. 'He's already cruised up and down the wharf three times.'

'Looking for us?'

'The last knucklehead will have been ordered to report on the success of his mission. When Langley didn't hear from him, they'll have put in a back-up plan. That's him at the end of the docks.'

'A taxi driver?'

'Probably. They did pretty well to get someone on board the *Gala-pagos*, but getting an asset into a place like Puerto Quetzal at short notice wouldn't be easy. This guy's a rank amateur, but I don't want to start a shoot-out at the O. K. Corral. He'll have already reported that we haven't disembarked, which will have them in a quandary. They'll be wondering if we're still on board or if their man was successful but somehow came to grief in the process. For the moment they'll be confused, and it's a waiting game.'

'A chicken bus leaves about 5 a.m. from Puerta de Hierro, about half a mile east of here.'

O'Connor raised an eyebrow.

'Trust me; I've been here before, or at least not far from here, on a dig.'

'Excellent. We'll sneak off early tomorrow morning, and with a bit of luck, James Bond up there will be fast asleep in his cab.'

O'Connor scanned the taxi cab with his night-vision sight and grinned. 'I can almost hear him snoring. Time to go.'

He followed Aleta down the gangplank and together they crossed the dimly lit concrete dock to the safety of the closest warehouse. O'Connor checked the taxi again and then led the way between two warehouse buildings, and on past some oil storage-tanks. Even at four in the morning, the road tankers were lined up to refuel, so O'Connor and Aleta kept to the shadows, making their way along the dirt easement beside the oil pipes. Ten minutes later, they reached a back-road entrance and walked for another kilometre on a dirt road that ran past a housing estate.

'Seems like quite a wealthy area,' O'Connor observed, with a nod of his head towards the houses with pools, which had been built on the series of canals, most with their own jetty.

'Puerta de Hierro's eclectic and deceptive,' Aleta replied, pulling the wheel of her bag out of a pothole in the dirt road. 'Houses are a lot cheaper in Guatemala, and the big shipping companies subsidise their employees. This is all part of the María Linda River, and a little further down the coast is Iztapa, which means 'river of salt'; there are lots of saltpans. But many of the Guatemalans on the other side of Highway 9 are dirt poor,' she said, nodding towards the main road. To the east the sky was just beginning to lighten behind the jungle-clad mountains of the highlands.

The bus terminal was small by Guatemalan standards, and just four vehicles were loading – old retired US school buses reincarnated as part of the Guatemalan transport system.

O'Connor scanned the bus terminal while Aleta approached the *ayudante*, the 'driver's helper' on the nearest bus. 'Escuintla?' Aleta asked, looking for the bus that would take them to the next big town.

'No. That one over there,' the *ayudante* said with a big smile, pointing to a brightly coloured bus with 'Linda' painted in vivid turquoise on the top of the windscreen, and on the back and sides. The rest of the bus was painted in bright reds and yellows, and the chrome on the old International reflected the lights of the bus terminal. Painted yellow flames issued from the below the big square hood.

The next *ayudante* offered to put their bags on the roof of the bus with the rest of the menagerie: baskets, tyres, chairs, tables, brightly coloured canvas bags, empty paint cans and assorted parcels of varying sizes wrapped in bright-blue plastic.

Aleta shook her head and slipped him a five-quetzale note, the equivalent of about sixty cents. The *ayudante* smiled and helped Aleta onto the bus with her bag. Not that she needed to have tipped him to ensure they could take their bags on. She had to ease her way down the aisle of the already crowded bus past two pigs, a large sack of carrots, three sacks of potatoes and a caged rooster. O'Connor stacked the backpacks containing the precious figurines in the luggage rack above them, and they took an empty bench seat in front of a woman in *traje*, the traditional dress of her village: a colourful handwoven *huipil* blouse, and the long *corte* skirt secured with a woven belt – the whole a kaleidoscope of tangerines, purples, aquamarines, scarlets and mustard yellows.

Twenty minutes later, the chicken bus pulled out of *Puerta de Hierro*, leaving a cloud of black smoke in its wake.

49

VANDENBERG AIR FORCE BASE, SANTA BARBARA, CALIFORNIA

A gentle swell broke over a darkened Point Sal on the Californian coast, to the north of Santa Barbara. Two hours behind Guatemala City, the Point Sal beach was deserted. The security guards had cleared and secured the area just before dusk. Further south, a huge eighteen-metre-high LGM-30 Minuteman nuclear missile stood ready in test-launch silo Lima Foxtrot-26 at the northern end of Vandenberg Air Force Base. The heavy concrete slab on top of the silo was still closed; the gleaming missile beneath it weighing thirty tonnes. The missile's range of 13 000 kilometres was more than enough to hit any target in Russia, China, Korea or the Middle East; and on the few occasions that a target might be out of reach, the US Navy's Ohio-class nuclear-powered submarines were on continuous deployment, equipped with Trident nuclear missiles, which could be launched from beneath the surface of the ocean. America had the world well covered, and although this morning's launch would not include a nuclear warhead, the experiment being directed out of Gakona would serve to boost America's position as the dominant world power. A short distance away, in a heavily guarded hangar, technicians were already working on another Minuteman missile, the casing of which would act as a lens to deflect the high-powered ELF beam into Iran.

Air Force Lieutenant Colonel Dan Williams checked the digital clock in the control centre. He knew this was no normal test, and the tall lanky commander of the 576th Flight Test Squadron could feel the tension in the room. The 5.15 a.m. test flight was shrouded in secrecy, not least because the missile track would take it over populated areas of the United States and Canada, across Alaska and out to the north of Siberia. Williams glanced at the tracking screen above the array of consoles and computer screens that monitored every aspect of the launch. All going well, a powerful burst of electromagnetic radiation from the base in Gakona would deflect the missile back into the Arctic Ocean, to the north of the Beaufort Sea. Williams turned to Captain Chavez, the young electronics whiz who'd been assigned as the missile-test launch director.

'Pass to Gakona: ready for launch.'

Chavez acknowledged the command and Williams reached for the secure handset that would connect him to *Looking Glass*, the modified 707 Boeing E6-Mercury command and control aircraft cruising at 29 000 feet above the launch silo. Tonight, in addition to its crew of twenty-two, *Looking Glass* was carrying a two-star admiral as the Airborne Emergency Action Officer, or AEAO. Should an attack on the United States knock out nuclear ground-control stations in the Pentagon, Offutt Air Force Base in Nebraska, and Site 'R' on Raven

Rock Mountain in Pennsylvania, the AEAO on the 'doomsday plane' would be in position to assume the role of mission control.

'*Looking Glass*, this is launch director, over.'

'Launch director, this is *Looking Glass*; loud and clear, over.' The airborne launch colonel and captain were strapped into their seats at the command console, a suite of computer screens and control dials located behind the cockpit. It was just one of the many consoles in an E6-B cabin jammed with avionics that enabled the aircraft crew to monitor communications from super-high frequencies down to the very low frequencies critical for maintaining contact with nuclear-armed submarines. Each officer was entrusted with a separate key, both of which were required to execute a nuclear strike.

'*Looking Glass*, activate launch command on my mark: five, four, three two, one, *mark*.' The launch colonel and captain nodded to one another and turned their keys. A high-speed burst transmission activated the control computers on the ground.

'Launch director, this is *Looking Glass*; transmission complete, over.'

Four ballistic gas actuators fired and the 110-tonne reinforced-concrete silo cover slid forward on its rails, revealing the gleaming missile below.

'Roger, *Looking Glass*; we have ignition, out.' The first of the three solid-stage motors erupted in a roar of flame and smoke, and the thirty-tonne missile rose majestically from its underground silo and up into the early-morning sky.

Four thousand kilometres further north, Curtis O'Connor's old colleague, Tyler Jackson, was monitoring the control screens in the Gakona command centre, watching events unfold with a growing sense of foreboding.

'One point five miles in altitude, one nautical mile down range, travelling at 900 miles per hour . . . all systems green.' Captain Chavez's voice sounded excited as he watched the live footage. The huge Thiokol TU-122 first-stage motor generated 200 000 pounds of thrust as it powered the missile towards the ionosphere above, leaving a long fiery exhaust trail.

'Mach one . . . we're now supersonic . . . first-stage engine operating normally . . . first stage jettisoned . . . second-stage engine ignition . . . fifty nautical miles altitude . . . all systems green.'

Heavy flakes of snow were falling outside the Gakona control centre, and the big diesels that powered the thirty transmitter shelters were at full capacity. Each shelter contained twelve transmitters, each in turn generating 10 000 watts of radio-frequency power. Every one of the 360 transmitters had been switched to the high-frequency dipole antennae, all of which were at the maximum end of the ten megahertz range. Tyler Jackson watched as Gakona's mission controller vectored a staggering three billion watts of electromagnetic energy into the ionosphere and into the path of the massive missile, now travelling at over 16 000 kilometres per hour. Sixty nautical miles above Gakona, the sensitive ionospheric layer heated to 40 000 degrees Celsius, creating a boiling plasma plume of electrons. The powerful transmitter lifted thirty square kilometres of the earth's protective shield into the path of the missile.

'All stations, this is launch director. We've lost communications with the missile at this time . . . missile not responding . . . missile is now sixty degrees off course . . . computed bearing one two zero degrees.'

Tyler Jackson stifled a gasp. The one-tonne nose cone was headed for North Korea.

50

GUATEMALA CITY

The cell phone rang out inside the taxi on the wharf at Puerto Quetzal. Rodriguez pursed her lips, exasperated at Wiley's insistence on organising the asset in Puerto Quetzal from Washington. She had been dialling the secure cell phone since 4 a.m. without success, and there was no word on either O'Connor or Weizman. Langley was an hour ahead of Guatemala City and Rodriguez knew it wouldn't be long before Wiley would be on the secure line demanding answers. She dialled the number again. This time a sleepy voice answered.

'*¿Sí?*'

'*¿Qué está pasando?* What's happening? Is there anything to report?'

'*¿Cómo?*'

Rodriguez took a deep breath. 'Tutankhamen. Nefertiti?'

'Ah. *Sí* . . . They not come,' the taxi driver replied in halting English.

Five minutes later, Rodriguez put down the phone, convinced that *Fawlty Towers'* Manuel and Langley's asset had a lot in common.

At CIA's headquarters, Howard Wiley scanned the latest intelligence report from Cardinal Felici at the Vatican:

OPERATION MAYA

DDO EYES ONLY

Contact in San Pedro confirms Hernandez made a hasty departure from the presbytery where he lived. Point of interest is a quantity of scuba gear left behind. Will advise.

Felici

Scuba gear. Wiley pondered whether Lake Atitlán might be the repository for something of great interest. His thoughts were interrupted by a knock on the door.

'Come.'

'I thought you ought to know, sir. The media are carrying a story on this morning's Minuteman test . . . CNC are about to cross live,' Larry Davis announced.

'What the fuck? That's a top-secret firing!' Wiley reached for the remote.

'I've spoken briefly with Gakona. It seems there's been a malfunction. Input into the computer may have been out by a decimal point, which they think has caused the missile to impact the wrong side of the ionospheric shield, sending it south-west instead of north-east – here it is now.'

A 'breaking news' pull-through was scrolling across the bottom of CNC's coverage of the Australian Open golf tournament: MYSTERY OBJECT PLUNGES INTO SEA OF JAPAN, 300 METRES FROM CRUISE SHIP. RUSSIA ACCUSES THE UNITED STATES OF TARGETING NORTH KOREA.

'This is Lee-Ann Ramirez; we interrupt this coverage of the Australian Open with breaking news. We cross to our Pentagon reporter, Sheldon Murkowski. Sheldon, I know it's early in the morning in Washington, but is there any response yet from either the Pentagon or the White House to the accusations by the Kremlin that the US has fired a missile towards Korea?'

'Lee-Ann, the Pentagon has not yet released a statement, but the mystery cone-shaped object, reportedly the size of a small car, was seen by dozens of tourists on board a Japanese cruise liner as it plunged into the ocean off the island of Hokkaido just before 6.30 p.m. local time.'

'These are very serious allegations, Sheldon. Do we know what the Kremlin is basing them on?'

'The Russian Defence Minister, Vladimir Andropov, was quite determined in his remarks. A Russian satellite-tracking station near Vladivostok followed the missile from the west coast of the United States at around 5.15 a.m., Californian time. Minister Andropov claims it was initially tracked across Alaska, but then it inexplicably altered course two minutes into the launch. We expect that either the Pentagon or the White House will hold a media conference shortly, Lee-Ann.'

'That was Sheldon Murkowski, reporting from the Pentagon. And in other breaking news, a violent storm has blacked out communications over most of Japan and in parts of Korea and southern China. Authorities claim the storm arrived without warning and is the most violent in recorded history.' The broadcast cut to live footage of Tokyo. The evening sky over the Japanese capital was a strange orange-purple. There were very few clouds, yet the city was being struck repeatedly with huge lightning strikes.

In scenes reminiscent of the September 11 strike on the World Trade Centre in New York, a jagged, forked silver-indigo flash exploded onto the Midtown tower, Tokyo's tallest building, demolishing the Ritz-Carlton hotel and the rest of the top twenty storeys, which tumbled into the crowded CBD below. Almost immediately after, another immensely powerful flash struck the 750-year-old Great Buddha of Kamakura, splitting the eighty-four-tonne statue down the middle. Nearby, Yuigahama Beach was being peppered with strikes at temperatures approaching 30000 degrees Celsius, which instantly melted the silica, fusing the sand into fulgurites – hollow glass tubes that penetrated metres into the beach. More powerful bolts struck the ancient heart of the city of Tokyo and more still had thundered into the area around Shinjuku, reducing to a pile of rubble the world's busiest train station, used by four million commuters every day.

'Already there is speculation that the events off Hokkaido and the violent storms above Tokyo may somehow be connected. We'll bring you updates on this unfolding drama as they come to hand. This is Lee-Ann Ramirez, returning you to Australia.'

Wiley got up and walked over to the large map of the world

mounted on the far wall of his office. 'The impact area's around the Mariana Trench?'

'A little to the north,' Davis confirmed.

'Fuck 'em. Just deny it. They won't find anything out there, and the media will lose interest.'

'Well, that will be up to the Pentagon, and perhaps the White House, sir.'

'Neither of whom would know shit from clay. Get on to their press secretaries and tell them it's only a suggestion, but remind them who's making it. In the meantime I want a team of divers up at Lake Atitlán,' Wiley said, handing Davis a hard copy of Felici's report. 'Hernandez was a qualified high-altitude diver, and I've got a hunch he didn't buy all that gear to go fishing. Any word on Tutankhamen or Nefertiti?'

Davis shook his head. 'The asset's got the ship in sight, but no one's disembarked.'

'For fuck's sake! Get Rodriguez on the secure video. I want some answers.'

51

GUATEMALAN HIGHLANDS

O'Connor surveyed the busy bus terminal at Escuintla, a rural city of 70 000 people on the border of the Guatemalan highlands and the Pacific Plain. He followed Aleta aboard a chicken bus even more brightly coloured and crowded than the one from Puerta de Hierro. A half-hour later, the bus clawed its way up the narrow winding road that led into the mountains towards Panajachel. O'Connor shook his head as the driver pulled out to overtake another bus belching black smoke, the roof festooned with pots, pans, bicycles, and wicker baskets. Together they approached a blind corner and still the driver persisted, drawing level with the other bus. Suddenly a mini-van appeared around the corner. The bus driver leant on the air horns and the mini-van swerved into the foliage overhanging the road, missing the side of the bus by centimetres. A group of young boys on the bench seat at the back of the bus cheered.

'Do you have to apply for a licence in this country, or does it come on the back of the cereal packets?'

Aleta smiled. 'You get used to it. There are T-shirts in Panajachel with 'I Survived' on the front and a photo of a chicken bus on the back. I'll get you one.'

'We've got to get there first,' O'Connor replied, leaning towards Aleta as a man with a piglet under one arm made his way past them to the front of the bus.

It was midafternoon by the time they arrived at the Panajachel terminal. Aleta and O'Connor shouldered their backpacks and made their way down the cobblestoned main street. Bright-red *tuc tucs* buzzed up and down, looking for fares. Woven mats and rugs juxtaposed with brightly coloured dresses and pants hung from poles beneath the corrugated-iron awnings above the stores. Power cables and phone lines were festooned around poles in spaghetti-like bundles strung above the street. Wonderful aromas of spices and freshly ground coffee beans filled the air. O'Connor maintained a constant watch on the crowd as they walked down *Avenida Santander* towards the shore of Lake Atitlán, past vendors sitting underneath their yellow and red umbrellas, with their offerings of mangoes and candied nuts. Aleta smiled at a little boy with big brown eyes. The boy hung on to his mother's skirt and shyly returned the smile as his mother hoisted a huge basket of bananas onto her head.

They reached a paved-stone path that led down to the jetties, and as they rounded a large tree Lake Atitlán came into view. Across the lake to the south stood Volcán Tolimán with Volcán Atitlán behind it, each soaring over 10 000 feet. Clouds streamed off both peaks, giving the impression they might erupt at any moment. Further to the west, the third of Lake Atitlán's volcanoes, Volcán San Pedro, towered over the little town that had given the powerful mountain its name.

'*¿Cuánto a San Marcos?*' O'Connor asked the old boatman.

'*Ochenta quetzales* ... for you. For the beautiful lady, *sesenta quetzales.*'

O'Connor grinned. '*¿Cómo se llama usted?*'

'Fidel,' the old mariner replied.

'Okay, Fidel, let's go.' O'Connor stowed the backpacks containing the priceless cargo under the cabin awning and steadied the gunwale for Aleta. The boatman went astern, spun the ten-seater runabout on a quetzale and headed out between two rickety wooden piles.

The high-pitched hum of the Evinrude, and the occasional *thwack thwack* of the bow hitting the water interrupted the silent splendour of the great lake.

'Penny, or I should say quetzale, for your thoughts? Does this bring back painful memories?' O'Connor asked gently.

'I try to concentrate on the good times. It will be enough if we can find the third figurine and get to Tikal before the winter solstice. My father would have done the same.'

'Which gives us less than three days ... '

Forty minutes later, they rounded the last little promontory and the boatman eased the throttle.

'That's José on the jetty!' Aleta said, pointing excitedly.

'The shaman? How did he know we were coming?' O'Connor was instantly alert.

'Maybe it's just coincidence?'

Arana waved and Fidel threw him the mooring rope.

'*Muchas gracias.*' O'Connor thanked the old mariner and slipped him 200 quetzales. Fidel fumbled in his pocket for change.

O'Connor shook his head. '*No, para usted*. For you.'

'*Gracias, gracias!*'

'*Mi placer.*'

'*Bienvenido a San Marcos!*' José kissed Aleta on both cheeks. 'And you must be Curtis. Welcome.' José adopted a Western gesture and shook O'Connor firmly by the hand. He turned to Fidel, and told him to wait.

'Come, your rooms are waiting for you.'

'Separate . . . what a pity,' O'Connor said softly. Aleta dug him in the ribs.

Not very far across the lake in the larger town of San Pedro, two ex-navy SEALs, skilled in high-altitude diving and now employed by the CIA as mercenaries, checked into the Mikaso Hotel on the shores of Lake Atitlán.

Arana's wife, Sayra, set dinner outside in the garden. The house was perched on a rise, a short distance from the lake's shore. Sayra had prepared a *topado*: a rich stew of lake crabs and fish, coriander, tomatoes, coconut milk and plantains, a cousin of the banana. After dinner, Sayra retired, leaving Arana alone with O'Connor and Aleta.

'It's now the eighteenth of December, José. The solstice is less than three days away.'

Arana smiled enigmatically. 'You have come to the right place, Aleta. As I said to you in Vienna, this is a sacred mission of profound importance. But I must remind you again that the figurine and the codex are fiercely protected, the former by Mother Nature herself, the latter by the ingenuity of my forefathers. More than one fortune seeker has paid the ultimate price. The ancients ensured that the codex would only be found by someone possessing the inner spiritual balance to understand it correctly. That person may be you, Aleta, but we will only know that if you are ultimately successful.' Arana turned to O'Connor. 'The Vatican now has a man in San Pedro, the Mayanist scholar, Monsignor Jennings. He's been appointed to the Catholic church there, and he's taken over the presbytery that used to be occupied by Father Hernandez.'

'Aleta and I were speculating that Father Hernandez might actually be Karl von Heißen, the German SS officer who escaped through the ratlines set up by the Vatican and the CIA at the end of World War Two.'

'And you would be correct. Von Heißen was aided by il Signor Felici, a gentleman to His Holiness Pope Pius XII, and father of Cardinal Salvatore Felici. Unfortunately for Cardinal Felici, von Heißen kept very detailed diaries.'

'*Aha*. It's all falling into place,' O'Connor thought out loud. 'If Cardinal Felici's past, in this case his father's involvement with Nazi criminals, ever surfaced, Felici's career and his chances of becoming the next pontiff would be finished.'

'Although that's not the only reason the Vatican is very worried about this part of the world. The Maya Codex threatens the uniqueness of the message of Christ,' Aleta said.

'Upon which the Vatican depends for its very existence. I should have a look at Monsignor Jennings' living arrangements. Is there any way I can get across to San Pedro at this time of night?' O'Connor asked.

'Fidel is waiting for you at the jetty. Monsignor Jennings usually drinks at the Buddha Bar. It's on the shore of San Pedro not far from the main tourist area.'

'Please take care,' Aleta said.

'Already he means something to you,' Arana observed with a gentle smile after O'Connor had left.

'More than I thought, even if it is like living on the run with Indiana Jones. You're the one who said I should trust him with my life.'

'And now you're going to have to trust me. Do you recall me telling you about the need to replenish your inner spirit?'

Aleta nodded.

'Tonight, we're going to cleanse that inner spirit, which will also relieve your depression. I want you to lie over here,' Arana said, indicating a garden bench covered with big soft cushions. 'Have you ever been hypnotised?'

'No. Is it safe?'

'I did say you will have to trust me. The mind has different states, Aleta. When we're awake, we're in what is known as the beta state, the state in which we're alert: we're thinking and our brainwaves are pulsing at somewhere between fifteen and thirty cycles per second. At eight to fifteen cycles per second we fall into the more relaxed alpha state, usually when we're drifting in and out of sleep, or even absorbed in a movie.' He paused, allowing Aleta to make herself comfortable.

'You're becoming more relaxed,' Arana said softly, passing his hand above Aleta's eyes. 'Close your eyes and we will move towards the theta state, when your brainwaves slow . . . slow . . . slower . . . to just four or five cycles per second. The state we reach when entering a deep sleep; a state that you will enter softly and quietly. At the end of this,' the shaman continued even more softly, 'I will count to three, and you will gently awake.'

Aleta could feel herself drifting, partly because she was deeply tired, and partly because she was back in her home village under the care of a man in whom she had complete trust. The pillows were soft and comfortable and she drifted further. Her eyelids were heavy, and she had neither the strength nor the energy to open them.

'You are walking into a deep tunnel now. You are descending stone steps that lead deeper and deeper into this tunnel. Deeper . . . and deeper . . . and deeper. The steps keep going down . . . and down . . . and down. You've reached a dimly lit stone corridor. It smells dank and musty down here.' Arana waved a wild orchid in front of Aleta's face but she wrinkled her nose distastefully. It was a test that his patient had entered a deep trance. Aleta was now open to the power of suggestion. To cleanse her spirit Arana would have to take her back in time. It was a technique the ancients had been using for centuries, a technique that modern psychiatry and hypnotherapy had only recently explained, coining the phrase 'past-life regression' therapy. Though each individual was different, the shaman knew every human being had lived through past lives; it was just that the memories were inaccessible in the present life. Arana also knew well that hypnosis could remove those barriers.

'As you walk along this tunnel, you will see doors to your left and right, Aleta,' he continued, still speaking in soft, even tones. 'I want you to choose a door and open it.'

'There is a brightly coloured door on my left . . . I'm opening it now.'

Aleta began to sway to the rhythm of the drums.

'Where are you?'

'I'm in Tikal. My name is Princess Akhushtal.' Aleta had gone back to 790 AD, to the great city-state of Tikal, one of several very powerful cities in the jungles of the Yucatán Peninsula. Calakmul and Naranjo, controlled by a warrior queen, Lady Six Sky, lay further to the north. The peace between the cities was fragile.

'What do you see?'

'Tikal is very busy today,' Princess Akhushtal said excitedly. 'It's the winter solstice tomorrow, and at dawn the High Priest will be conducting a ceremony with the jade statues to determine the resting place for the Maya Codex. But the High Priest is very worried.'

From the viewing platform where she was sitting with her father, King Yax Ain II, Princess Akhushtal surveyed the great ball court below. The muscled warriors wore thick rolls of padding to protect their ribs from a massive black leather ball over a metre in diameter as they jostled for position. The rules of the ball game prevented them kicking the ball or touching it with their hands; instead they used their heavily padded forearms and occasionally their foreheads. Headdresses of horns and quetzal and macaw feathers identified the different sides.

Princess Akhushtal's gaze shifted from the ball court to the towering salmon-coloured pyramids at either end of the main plaza — the Temple of the Great Jaguar and the Temple of the Mask. The soaring monuments had been built fifty years before and contained the tombs of royal members of the Great Jaguar clan: King Hasaw Chan K'awil and his queen, Lady Twelve Macaw. Further to the east of the plaza, the Tikal markets were bustling with traders. The stores were shaded with sackcloth awnings. Racks of exquisitely woven cloth were suspended beneath. Rugs, pottery and baskets of spices, nuts and fruits spilled on to the main thoroughfares. The women, dressed in multicoloured blouses, balanced their purchases in wicker baskets on their heads. Noblemen in feathered headdresses reclined on wicker lounges that were carried aloft amongst the crowds by their servants. Beyond the marketplace, Akhushtal could see the sentries on top of Temple IV and Temple V, the 'skyscraper pyramids', the tallest structures in the Meso-American world. Below them, the gates on the causeways that connected the great city with the jungle were heavily guarded by the King's warriors.

'The drums are beating louder now and the game is coming to an end. My father is getting to his feet and the ball players have all turned and bowed in our direction.'

Aleta shifted restlessly on her pillows but Arana remained silent and waited.

'My father is meeting with the High Priest now. The High Priest is warning of a great catastrophe for the Maya if we don't change course.'

'You must find a way to make peace with Calakmul and Naranjo,' the High Priest informed the King in grave tones. The respected Mayan elder was tall and dressed in a white sackcloth robe and hood, his brown weathered face etched with lines of wisdom. He maintained a commanding presence, even in the company of King

Yax Ain II. 'If these wars continue, not only will there be more casualties on both sides, but the entire Mayan civilisation will come under threat. The wars are destroying the environment on which your people depend for their very existence.'

'The people of Calakmul and Naranjo are very stubborn,' the King complained. 'I have a duty to maintain our way of life. We are the pre-eminent city, and they must conform to our customs and traditions. If necessary, we will force them to adopt our way of living.' The muscled, well-built warrior King was seated on a low stool, resplendent in a headdress of red, blue and green feathers from the prized quetzal bird, his protective leather battle-dress fastened at the belt by a huge jade emblem.

'The dominant society and culture must take the lead, but that does not mean we should not accept other cultures,' the High Priest persisted. 'It's not a weakness to sit down and reach agreement. It's a strength.'

'It will be perceived as a weakness, especially by the council of advisors,' the King grumbled.

'We are coming to the end of the tenth *baktun*. It will be a time of great upheaval and loss,' the High Priest warned, reminding King Yax Ain II that the current *baktun*, a cycle of 394 years, was coming to its conclusion. 'The destruction we experienced at the end of the last *baktun* will repeat itself.'

The King looked thoughtful.

'The signs will keep repeating until we take notice of the warnings – or sow the seeds of our own destruction, and eventually the destruction of the entire planet.'

'The entire planet?'

'The destruction at the end of this *baktun* will be widespread, particularly amongst your own people, but the destruction of the entire planet is not scheduled to occur until the end of the thirteenth *baktun*: in the year 2012.'

'And what happens in 2012?' the King asked, a sceptical edge to his voice.

'The thirteenth *baktun* and December 2012 will signify the end of the grand cycle: the end of the Age of the Fifth Sun. For the people of 2012, they will ignore the damage they do to the environment. They won't be able to reach agreement. And their wars will be based on competing religions. The adherents of those religions will each claim that only they possess the one true path, but unless they learn to accept that there are many paths and many cultures, the clash between religions will destroy them all.'

'The year 2012 is many *baktuns* away,' the King responded dismissively.

'Nevertheless, we have a duty to warn future civilisations of the difficulties we face, and what may await them.'

'And how do we do that?'

'The warnings have been transcribed into a codex. At the ceremony of the solstice tomorrow, the Keepers of the Temples, the jade figurines, will be placed on top of Pyramids I, IV and V. At sunrise, the sun's rays will be captured by the crystals and deflected. The final diffraction will signify the resting place for the Maya Codex, which will remain hidden until long after you and I have gone. One who is amongst us now will return to unlock the secret, but if they are to be successful, they will need to find the sequence of numbers that is at the base of the universe itself. That sequence contains a common number from which a subtraction of one will give its reciprocal, and to which the addition of one will give its square.'

Aleta shifted on her pillows again, frowning as she wrestled with the mathematical predictions of the High Priest, but then relaxing, as if the equation were solved.

'What is happening now?' Arana prompted.

'The sky is streaked with pinks and soft purples . . . the dawn is approaching. The howler monkeys are swinging through the trees above us. I'm accompanying my father towards the Great Plaza, where his subjects are already gathered in their thousands. Together, we are ascending the steps of the Temple of the Great Jaguar. The High Priest is waiting for us at the summit. Up . . . up . . . up we are climbing. The drums are beating, louder now, and fires of incense are burning at the base of the temple, where the warriors are drawn up in their legions. We are reaching the top . . . the High Priest is bowing . . . my father is taking his seat on his throne, and now I am able to be seated as well. The priests are hovering around the jade figurines. They have positioned one on the roof comb above us and another to the west on top of Temple IV, and yet a third has been positioned to the south on top of Temple V. The High Priest has lifted a golden conch shell to his lips. It has a keyhole in the middle, and the sound is reverberating through the jungle.'

The shaman watched his patient carefully, aware of what was coming. Aleta was moving from side to side on her pillows, moving to the rising crescendo of the drums.

'The sky is getting lighter above the jungle, which spreads like a dark-green canopy out to the east. The High Priest is looking towards the point where the sky is the brightest, where the sun will rise on the shortest day of the year – now! The first rays of the sun have struck the crystal in the jade figurine on top of Temple I.' A narrow, searing beam of deep-green laser-like light energised the crystal on the top of Temple I, only to be immediately deflected on a precise angle to strike the crystal on the jade figurine on top of Temple IV to the west, from where it energised the crystal on top of Temple V. Aleta turned her head suddenly. 'The light beam! It's been deflected towards . . . wait . . . I can't see it . . . oh, no!'

The screams were coming from the direction of the city gates at the bottom of the causeway that led up to the markets. One after another, the thatched-roofed huts on either side were going up in flames. Thousands of bloodthirsty warriors from the rival city of Calakmul fought with the guards at the gates, beheading them and ripping their still-beating hearts out of their chests. Now they were streaming on towards the plaza. Fierce battles broke out as Tikal's warriors raced to meet them to defend their King.

The High Priest was strangely calm; for him the surprise dawn attack had been inevitable. He shook his head sadly. The city-states, he knew, would continue fighting until they destroyed themselves and, ultimately, the Mayan civilisation. He quietly signalled to the priests who were preparing to entomb the Maya Codex. Through the chaos and smoke of the raging battle, the laser-like beam held steady on the mechanism that controlled a secret entrance to a complex across from Temple V. The priests held the precious codex aloft to indicate they had seen their High Priest's signal, and one of them descended a shaft and entered the passageway to the chamber. The sun climbed higher and the beam faded from view. The High Priest signalled to the priests on each temple that the jade figurines were to be sealed in the secret chambers that had been prepared on top of each pyramid.

'No! No! The Calakmul warriors have reached the base of our pyramid. My father's warriors are being overwhelmed . . . speared . . . beheaded. They are fighting hard but the other side is gaining. Oh, no! They're swarming up the steps towards *us* . . . No! No!'

O'Connor found the Buddha Bar not far from the shores of the lake, and he mentally filed his escape routes. A Tibetan flag flew over the main entrance. Statues and images of the Buddha added an Asian ambience to the ochre Spanish-style building, which contained a huge wooden Buddha that had been used on the set of *Apocalypse Now*. O'Connor scanned the crowd in the dimly lit ground-floor bar. It was full, but O'Connor quickly determined they were mainly backpackers playing pool and smoking weed, a pastime that was *de rigueur* in San Pedro. He checked to see if he was being followed, and climbed the stairs to the second-floor restaurant.

The big casual horseshoe booths were crowded with tourists and locals, save for one at the far end. O'Connor recognised Jennings immediately. He was sitting next to a boy whom O'Connor judged to be not more than fifteen. Jennings was sipping a whisky and the boy a Coke, prompting O'Connor to wonder what might be in the boy's glass.

O'Connor took the next flight of stairs to survey the rooftop bar, which had a 360-degree view of the darkened lake. It, too, was crowded with backpackers. The sweet, pungent smell of weed hung heavily around the balcony where the two ex-navy SEALs were standing with their backs to O'Connor. One of them had a neatly trimmed beard, but the short military-style haircuts were a dead giveaway. O'Connor retreated downstairs, where Jennings was returning from the bar with another whisky and another 'Coke' for the boy. A shiver ran down O'Connor's spine as Jennings placed his hand on the boy's thigh. O'Connor had to fight a powerful urge to blow his cover and free the boy from the fat priest's grasp. Instead, he headed back out towards the main street, and threaded his way through the late-night shoppers and the *tuc tucs* buzzing across the cobblestones, past the brightly coloured buildings, one of which was painted with a huge sign, declaring Jesus as Lord of San Pedro La Laguna.

O'Connor reached the top of the steep road, hardly having raised his heartbeat. He paused beside a shop, long enough to scan the occupants of the dimly lit square and analyse the layout of the big white-washed church standing opposite at the summit of the hill. The presbytery would be the little building to one side, he concluded. He headed around the perimeter of the square and approached through the cover of the palm trees and church gardens.

The lock was elementary and O'Connor closed the oak door quietly behind him. He flicked on his pocket torch and began a systematic search of Jennings' small apartment. The kitchen table, which appeared to double as a desk, revealed nothing of interest. Nor did the kitchenette or the small bathroom, but when he searched the cupboard under the stairs, he found the scuba gear, just as Jennings had. O'Connor climbed the narrow stairs to the mezzanine bedroom above. In the bottom of the wardrobe O'Connor found a small trunk. He picked the lock and inside he found a stack of

NAMBLA Bulletins, the official magazine of the North American Man/Boy Love Association. On the topmost magazine Jennings had scrawled 'very cute' across the photo of the boy on the cover.

O'Connor relocked the trunk and turned his attention to the man-hole cover in the ceiling. He dragged across the only chair in the room, hoisted himself into the ceiling and played the torchlight over the piles of rat droppings scattered amongst the old beams. The light picked out three small dusty trunks at the far end of the confined roof space, and O'Connor eased himself along the central joist. The dust was an indicator that the trunks almost certainly did not to belong to Jennings. Again, he picked the locks and opened the first trunk. Diaries. Dozens of them. O'Connor thumbed through the upper-most one and found the last entry had been made twelve months before von Heißen had fled. Was there one diary missing? O'Connor wondered as he opened the second, and then the third trunk, which contained the diaries covering von Heißen's time at Mauthausen. They were in chronological order, and, curious, O'Connor located the diary for 1938. Five minutes later he let out a soft whistle as he found von Heißen's meticulous entry for Heinrich Himmler's visit to Mauthausen.

Reichsführer Himmler sehr zufrieden mit Geburtstag . . . Reichsführer Himmler very pleased with celebrations for the Führer's birthday. Forty-eight Jewish scum executed – one for each year of the Führer's glorious life.

Himmler personally congratulated me on the smooth functioning of Konzentrationslager Mauthausen, giving strong intimation that promotion to Standartenführer is being considered!

Herr Doktor Richtoff's preparation for high-altitude medical experiments well in hand.

Himmler agreed to execution of Weizman scum. Weizman dealt with on the stairs. His bitch and brats will be Herr Doktor Richtoff's first 'patients'.

If Mossad had been hard on von Heißen's heels, how could they have missed these? There was only one explanation that made any sense to O'Connor. Mossad were *so* close, they would have kept pursuing him. O'Connor kept the diary with the incriminating evidence of the shootings and dropped back into Jennings' bedroom, where he searched the bedside table. In the drawer he found the last of von Heißen's diaries, and nestled inside the front cover, he discovered the original *huun* map containing the backbearings from the volcanoes – the same one confiscated from Ariel Weizman more than seventy years ago.

Paydirt! But as O'Connor began to thumb through the pages, he heard the sound of a key turning in the front door.

Aleta was sweating profusely; twitching nervously on the pillows. The shaman knew it was time to bring her out.

'You're coming out of this room now, Aleta,' he intoned gently. 'You're moving back towards the door through which you entered . . . moving back to the stone passageway . . . closing the door behind you. You're calmer now . . . calmer.' Aleta stopped twitching and almost immediately her breathing began to slow.

'One . . . two . . . three,' José intoned softly.

'Was I dreaming?' Aleta asked.

José smiled and shook his head. 'It's quite a common reaction; but no, you weren't dreaming. That was just one of your past lives, although undoubtedly one of the more significant, and there are several reasons you've relived it just now.' Arana paused, allowing Aleta to readjust to her surroundings. A cool breeze was coming in off the lake and the night was clear. Without the glow of city lights, the stars seemed far brighter and more numerous – just as they had to the Maya, centuries before.

'Did you learn anything?' Arana continued.

'The laser beams ... the three statues were placed on top of Pyramid I, Pyramid IV and Pyramid V ... but I didn't see where the final deflection fell.'

'Now that you know which pyramids are in the matrix, it will be enough for you to discover the final figurine; and provided you can position all three by the winter solstice, you will still have a chance to recover the codex.'

'With only three days left, that's looking increasingly unlikely,' Aleta said.

'How are you feeling?'

'It's as if a great load has been lifted.'

The Mayan elder smiled. 'Then the cleansing has been a success.'

'I'm not sure what the golden conch shell with the keyhole outline in the middle meant, though.' Aleta mused.

'The significance of that, like the significance of balance, will become apparent very soon,' José replied enigmatically.

Monsignor Jennings quickly checked behind him before ushering the young boy inside.

'Have a seat, Eduardo. Make yourself comfortable,' Jennings said, indicating the sofa against the staircase. He headed for the tiny kitchenette and poured himself a generous Chivas Regal, and a double shot of Johnny Walker Red Label and Coke for Eduardo. Jennings brought the Coke back and sat down beside Eduardo, recalling the wonderful words of Oscar Wilde: *The great affection of an elder for a younger man . . . that is as pure as it is perfect . . . so much misunderstood that it may be described as the 'Love that dare not speak its name'. It is beautiful, it is fine, it is the noblest form of affection. There is nothing unnatural about it. It is intellectual, and it repeatedly exists between an elder and a younger man, when the elder man has intellect, and the younger man has all the joy, hope and glamour of life before him. That it should be so, the world does not understand. The world mocks at it and sometimes puts one in the pillory for it.* Jennings knew the words by heart. He sat and admired Eduardo's slim, taut brown form and placed his hand on Eduardo's thigh.

'*Cien quetzales,*' Eduardo intoned woodenly.

'*Más tarde.* Later,' Jennings said, placing Eduardo's hand on his own growing erection.

Eduardo withdrew his hand. '*Cien quetzales . . . o no contrato.*' Eduardo might have been only fourteen, but he was already street smart.

'*¿Cuánto para toda la noche.* How much for all night?' Jennings asked throatily, feeling for his wallet.

'*Quinientos quetzales.*' This amount would feed Eduardo's brothers and sisters for a fortnight.

'*Cien quetzales.* The rest later,' Jennings said, handing over a grimy cherry-coloured note. Rivulets of sweat ran down his pudgy cheeks and he shifted lengthways on the couch. Breathing heavily, Jennings unzipped his own fly and ran his hand up the inside of Eduardo's thigh, fondling the boy into an erection before pulling Eduardo's head down onto his own enlarged member.

O'Connor quietly photographed the pair from the mezzanine bedroom above. He wondered if, even when faced with the photographs, the Catholic Church would act, but he promised himself the fat priest would rot in gaol one way or another. For now, time was running out. Confident that Jennings was totally absorbed, O'Connor crept down the stairs.

'Suck me, boy . . . suck me,' Jennings wheezed. 'Oh yes. That is *so* good.'

O'Connor controlled his anger and quietly slipped out the front door. He headed back down towards the docks, where Fidel was waiting, two of von Heißen's diaries and the map safely in his hand.

'Santa Cruz. *La tienda de buceo, por favor, Fidel.*' The dive shop would be closed, but O'Connor was sure money would overcome that inconvenience.

'*Sí,*' Fidel nodded with a smile and eased the little launch away from the wooden jetty.

A short distance away one of the ex-navy SEALs was standing on the balcony of the Mikaso, scanning the shores of the lake. Hank Sanders trained his high-resolution night-vision binoculars on the little boat as it gathered speed, and he watched it head for the village of Santa Cruz on the northern side of the lake.

'Hey, Mitch, come and have a look at this. See the guy sitting in

the back of the boat? Looks like our man?' he said, handing over
the binoculars.

'Hard to say,' Mitch Crawford said, 'but if it is, I wonder where
he's headed at this time of night.'

Twenty minutes later, they had their answer. Sanders and Crawford watched the launch pull into Santa Cruz's jetty, the nearby dive
shop clearly visible.

Crawford kept his night-vision binoculars trained on Fidel's small
lancha as the boatman eased it into the jetty at San Marcos. He
watched as Fidel and O'Connor carried the diving gear up to where
Aleta was still in deep conversation with José.

'Looks as if the boatman's staying the night as well. It's dive on,
I reckon.'

'Probably not tonight,' Crawford replied, sharpening his diving
knife, 'otherwise they would have left the gear on the jetty. My guess
is early tomorrow morning. Either way, it doesn't matter. The gear
and the boat's ready.' The burly tattooed ex-Marine diver spat over
the balcony. 'They won't know what's hit 'em.'

O'Connor sat on the end of Aleta's garden lounge. 'Your grandfather's original *huun* bark map,' he announced quietly. 'I found it in
a diary at Jennings' presbytery, along with some scuba-diving gear,
so I'm assuming that von Heißen left it behind.'

'He must have left in one hell of a hurry,' said Aleta.

'Mossad tends to have that effect on some people.'

'Do you think they got him?'

O'Connor shook his head. 'Adolf Eichmann worked for Mercedes Benz in Buenos Aires for years, but when the Israeli team of Mossad and Shabak agents finally captured him in 1960, it made world headlines. Von Heißen is now the most wanted Nazi known to be still alive – we would have heard if they'd been successful. There are three trunks of diaries still in the roof of Jennings' presbytery, but we'll go back for those.' O'Connor opened the *huun* bark map. 'Look at this.'

'The backbearings!' Aleta whispered.

'Exactly, and they intersect just off that point.' O'Connor indicated a small rocky promontory jutting out into the lake about a kilometre away. 'Someone, I presume your grandfather, has embossed the bottom of the map with the Greek letter phi, and there's a mark under the dot point, see? A short line.'

'Von Heißen may already have the figurine . . . assuming it was in the lake in the first place.'

'The scuba gear suggests he investigated the lake, although whether he was aware of the third figurine is a moot point. But there's only one way to find out.'

They both looked at Arana. 'If it's meant to be, it will be,' he said calmly. 'When will you dive?'

O'Connor looked at his watch. 'It's nearly 11 p.m. now, and we've had a very long day. From a safety point of view, we'll be more alert after a few hours' sleep, not to mention a little more acclimatised to the altitude.'

52

LAKE ATITLÁN, GUATEMALA

Fidel was waiting as O'Connor and Aleta, already in their wetsuits, walked down the dirt path to the jetty. The lake was like glass, the faint pink of dawn caressing the lake's three sentinel volcanoes.

Across the lake, Sanders put down his night-vision binoculars and went inside to wake his partner. It was time to move.

O'Connor and Aleta made a slow and deliberate final check of the gear: cylinders, both stages of the regulators, tank-pressure gauges, depth gauges, compasses, BCDs – the buoyancy compensation devices – safety reels, weights, wrist dive computers, torches and dive lights. O'Connor checked the fastenings on the dive knife above Aleta's booties and made a final check of his own.

Fidel eased the *lancha* away from the jetty and under O'Connor's instruction, motored out to a point about fifty metres off the small promontory that jutted out into the lake. O'Connor took bearings on each of the three volcanoes and mentally calculated the backbearings.

'Another ten metres, Fidel,' he directed, pointing north-west. It took nearly ten minutes of manoeuvring and adjustment until O'Connor felt they were over the spot indicated on the map.

'Keep the volcanoes on these two lines,' O'Connor said, indicating directions to two prominent buildings on the far shores of the lake. He turned to Aleta. 'Ready?'

Aleta nodded.

They sat on the gunwale and adjusted the straps on their big yellow fins. Aleta returned O'Connor's 'O', her thumb and forefinger together, the rest of her fingers pointed upwards: the diver's universal 'I'm okay/are you okay?' O'Connor put his regulator in his mouth, kept one hand over his mask, clamped the trailing hoses to his chest with the other, and rolled backwards into the lake. Out of habit, Aleta checked that the lake was clear behind her then followed O'Connor into the cold dark water. They both surfaced, and O'Connor gave the thumbs down signal to descend. Aleta raised her BCD hose, pressed the deflation button and followed O'Connor into the depths. Three metres below the surface, O'Connor stopped for a 'bubble check'. He looked for any signs of leaks on Aleta's gear and Aleta returned the favour.

O'Connor probed the depths with his powerful torch beam, looking for signs of the promontory. Lake Atitlán was close to 5000 feet above sea level and more than 300 metres deep. He had ensured the necessary altitude and freshwater adjustments were programed into both their wrist dive computers, but a high-altitude dive meant the atmospheric pressure was lower than at sea level: there would be a greater reduction in pressure when they surfaced. The distance to the nearest decompression chamber didn't bear thinking about.

The water was very clear and O'Connor continued to search with his torch as they descended. The promontory had dropped away sharply, forming an underwater cliff-face, but at a gauge reading of fifteen metres, O'Connor was relieved to see that it had levelled out into a plateau. He and Aleta touched bottom and a large black crab scuttled away, leaving puffs of grey volcanic dust in its wake. O'Connor unhooked a long white nylon rope from his weight belt and, holding one end, gave the rest of it to Aleta to anchor on the floor of the lake. She gave him the 'O', and he swam out until Aleta held it fast at the five-metre mark. O'Connor began to swim in a circle in the classic 'rope search'. The beams of their torches pierced the darkness, producing an eerie underwater kaleidoscope, and illuminating a grey stony bottom. Clear patches gave way to underwater plants and gossamer-like seaweed. Occasionally a large bass would be caught in the light.

The first 360-degree traverse revealed nothing of interest, and O'Connor tugged on the rope for Aleta to let it out another five metres. He swam another circle, and another. On the lake side, the promontory dropped away further, and on the next pass O'Connor's gauge was showing twenty metres; but he kept swimming, slowly searching the bottom with his powerful torch. As he came back towards the promontory, the bottom began to slope up again to eighteen metres, and then sixteen metres, when suddenly he saw it. The entrance to the underwater cave was a small but unmistakeable 'squeeze'. O'Connor inspected the broken plants at the entrance. It was hard to tell just how long ago, but the entrance had definitely been disturbed.

At the jetty at San Pedro, the CIA mercenaries were checking their gear.

O'Connor gave three short tugs on the rope, signalling Aleta to join him. He pointed to the entrance, recoiled the rope and hooked it to his belt. Once they had negotiated the squeeze, it opened into a wide cavernous passageway. Aleta looked around her in amazement. The grey stony bottom had given way to stalagmites, some of which had joined stalactites to form underwater columns. It was as if they had entered an underwater city. A little further on, a volcanic shelf appeared, and O'Connor gave the thumbs up to surface. At the six-metre mark, he called a halt and they waited for a three-minute safety stop before rising to the top.

'Can you believe this?' Aleta exclaimed. Her voice echoed in the huge underwater chamber. O'Connor looked around. Over millions of years, well before the chamber had flooded, fresh water had cascaded and dripped from the cavities above. The water held vast quantities of dissolved limestone and volcanic dust, and the calcite had gradually precipitated into brilliantly coloured geological formations in deep reds, purples, blues, ochres and yellows. Above them, glow-worms had attached themselves to the roof. Hundreds of sticky beaded strands, which the glow-worms manufactured from their mouth glands, formed a shimmering but deadly curtain for any insect attracted by the light show. Once an insect became enmeshed in the deathtrap, the glow-worm simply pulled in the long silvery-blue line and ate its prey alive.

O'Connor hauled himself onto the limestone shelf and helped Aleta out of the water. They divested themselves of their tanks and fins and began to explore. The shelf stretched for a hundred metres before sloping down again into the crystal-clear waters of the cave.

'I wonder how far this goes?'

O'Connor shrugged. 'Some of these caves go a long way; there's one across the border in Mexico that's over 150 kilometres long.'

'Gives a lot of scope for hiding things. Does the line on the map make any sense?'

O'Connor steadied his wrist compass and searched the walls with his torch. Suddenly he stopped.

'Look! Up there!' he exclaimed, flashing his torch two metres above Aleta's head. 'Without the map, you'd never know it, but there's another ledge.' He gained a foothold on the limestone wall and levered himself up to the smaller ledge, at the end of which was an entrance to a much smaller cave. O'Connor eased his way through the narrow opening to discover another colony of glow-worms, their lethal curtain glimmering at the far end of the cave. He played his torch over the rough limestone floor. On one side of the cave four metal ingots, each indented with the eagle and swastika of the Third Reich, glinted in the light beam.

Aleta squeezed into the cave beside him and gasped.

'Some of von Heißen's ill-gotten gains,' O'Connor said grimly, knowing the probable origin would have been the gold fillings of thousands of Jews.

'Why would he have left them here? Maybe there wasn't enough time to get them out.'

'That'd be my guess, along with there not being enough space in his truck for the trunks in the ceiling. As for the gold, each of these ingots weighs around 400 ounces, which on today's market is worth over US$400 000. We're looking at about one and half million dollars worth here, so God knows how much he's got away with.' O'Connor shone his torch around the rest of the cave. 'No sign of the figurine.'

'Do you think he might have found it down here?'

'I suspect not. Von Heißen was a meticulous diary keeper. The last entry in the final diary was dated the day before he left, and there's no mention of it.' O'Connor ran his torch back and forth over the limestone, but after ten minutes' searching there was still no clue as to where the figurine might be hidden. Finally he aimed his torch beam at the far corner, towards the 'curtain of death'.

'There, on the floor, just in front of the glow-worms!' Aleta tugged at O'Connor's wetsuit. 'There's a faint outline of a nautilus conch shell! Do you remember my grandfather's notes?'

'The Fibonacci sequence . . . look for Φ.'

'Yes!' she exclaimed, realising that the outline in the limestone was not only sacred to many civilisations and religions, but that the spiral of the shell grew in accordance with the Fibonacci sequence.

The High Priest's words resonated with the icon on the cave floor. *One who is amongst us now will return to unlock the secret, but if they are to be successful, they will need to find the sequence of numbers that is at the base of the universe itself. That sequence contains a common number from which a subtraction of one will give its reciprocal, and to which the addition of one will give its square.* Phi and the Fibonacci sequence represented the golden mean, which was at the base of the universe. Aleta knew well that if you divided any number in the sequence by its predecessor, the result was always 1.618. If you subtracted one, you got 0.618, which was the reciprocal, or 1/1.618; and if you added one, then the resultant 2.618 was the square of 1.618.

'We haven't got time to go in to it now,' she said, kneeling and using her knife to carefully scrape away the limestone that had accumulated over the sacred icon, 'but while you were crawling around Jennings' ceiling, José subjected me to some regression therapy. For the Maya, the conch shell opened a portal to their ancestors.' Her pulse began to race as O'Connor joined her, and their scraping revealed a rectangle that formed a border around the shell.

Outside the cave, Crawford and Sanders had reached the grey stony bed of the lake. Fidel's boat drifted aimlessly above them. Crawford spotted the rope first and signalled. He pointed to his eyes and then to the rope. Both divers followed the rope towards the cave's underwater entrance.

53

GAKONA, ALASKA

The wind was still howling up the Copper River Valley, buffeting the control station at Gakona, but for Dr Tyler Jackson, alarm bells were ringing over what was about to unfold, and he didn't notice. Howard Wiley had arrived on a flying visit for a briefing. The satellite image on the screen was marked *TOP SECRET*, pinpointing the location of the Islamic Revolutionary Guard base at Fordo near Qom, one of Iran's holiest cities and a major seat of Islamic academic endeavour.

'As you're aware,' Gakona's director, Dr Nathaniel B. Hershey, began, 'for some time we've suspected the Iranians have been constructing a nuclear facility deep within the mountains near Qom. The infra-red satellite imagery has not been able to penetrate the solid rocks, nor is it likely that our conventional weapons will be able to inflict any significant damage.' Hershey flashed up a diagram that showed the intended path of the extremely high-energy but low-frequency radio waves HAARP was capable of generating.

'The second experiment in the Operation Aether series will beam three billion watts of energy directly into the suspected Iranian complex. If all goes well, anything inside the mountain will be destroyed. H-hour for the transmission burst will be in three days from now, at 0300 hours, our time. That's 1530 hours Iranian local time, when the maximum number of workers will be on duty.' Hershey went on to explain the details of the impact of the high-energy heat burst. He paused at the end of his briefing to allow questions. Jackson seized his chance, determined to sound one last warning.

'There is, of course, a risk with this experiment,' he began. A look of thunder appeared on Hershey's square rugged face. 'Deep-earth tomography has never been tried on this scale before, and the results are therefore unknown. It's not inconceivable that this massive burst of energy may upset the earth's rotational spin. The earthquake off Sumatra that caused the devastating tsunamis in 2004 measured 9 on the Richter scale, and we have incontrovertible evidence that it increased the earth's wobble, moving the poles by several centimetres. Three billion watts of energy may have an even more devastating effect than a natural earthquake.'

'That is pure conjecture, Dr Jackson,' Hershey responded icily.

Wiley turned in his seat and glared at the senior CIA scientist. 'Isn't that why we do experiments, Dr Jackson? To see if they work?'

'We should learn from history, sir. In 1954, as you know, we detonated the first hydrogen bomb on the Bikini Atoll. The experiment Castle Bravo was expected to yield four megatons. Castle Bravo yielded nearly four times that, devastating the population, vaporising the test island, and leaving a mile-wide crater on the lagoon floor. The radioactive fallout reached as far as Australia, India and Japan. We're in a similar situation with Operation Aether: we don't *know* what might happen here. Worse still, we're moving towards a once-in-26 000-year planetary alignment, which culminates in December 2012, when the Maya predicted the earth would be exposed to the power of a massive black hole at the centre of the Milky Way galaxy. We should at least postpone the launch of the missile and the ELF beam until after 2012, when the earth will most likely be in a more stable orbit.'

'Mystical nonsense from a bunch of savages. And it may have escaped your attention, Dr Jackson, but by 2012, the Iranians will have the bomb.' Wiley made a mental note to organise an early retirement for his aging scientist, and he stood to address the thirty or so other defense and civilian employees.

'There's been a lot of crap put about in the media recently,' he began. 'A lot of rubbish about targeting North Korea. So, I've launched an investigation. Let there be no doubt in anyone's mind: when I discover who's been leaking information to the media about our classified missile launches, they'll wish they were dead. All of you are signatories to the Intelligence Authorization Act, and the fastest way to lose your balls or your tits is to breach it. This facility is for peaceful purposes, and that remains the official line. We don't discuss intelligence or classified operations, period!'

As soon as he could leave the briefing room, Jackson went straight to his office. This experiment held the same uncertainties as Castle Bravo, but on a potentially far more devastating scale. Somehow he would have to find a way to focus international attention on the madness that was Aether.

54

LAKE ATITLÁN, GUATEMALA

Aleta's pulse was racing as O'Connor's knife uncovered the last of the rectangle bordering the shell icon. A rectangle that, like the nautilus shell it enclosed, was in a precise ratio of 1:1.618 or Φ.

'The nautilus shell – biological engineering at its best,' he observed, replacing his knife in the sheath above his bootie. 'As it moves to a new chamber, it fills the old one with a gas and then seals it with mother of pearl. Very ingenious.'

'A logarithmic spiral, so that each chamber is proportional to the last,' Aleta agreed, fighting to contain her excitement.

O'Connor dug out the last of the sascab, the same Mayan mortar made from crushed and burnt limestone that Aleta's grandfather had encountered in Tikal, but no amount of levering would prise the block free. Aleta inserted her knife into the faint outline of a keyhole in the centre spiral of the shell. She gasped as a subterranean mechanism was activated and the heavy block of limestone slid slowly into the cave floor, and then sideways into a specially constructed recess, the whole device hinged on large bronze bearings.

'How did you know to do that?'

'It's a long story, but look!' Aleta grabbed O'Connor by the arm. The limestone block had slid back to reveal the third figurine nestling at the bottom of the cavity, the crystal and the black and gold-rimmed obsidian glistening in the light of the glow-worms.

O'Connor moved to extract the figurine but Aleta grabbed him. 'No! Wait!' She broke off a piece of nearby creamy-orange stalactite and lowered it into one end of the cavity, touching the crystal at the top of the figurine.

O'Connor winced as a razor-sharp, spring-loaded blade sliced the stalactite in two and returned to its recess in one side of the cavity. Aleta broke off another long piece and touched the other end of the figurine. The vicious spring-loaded blade from the opposite side was lightning fast. O'Connor took a deep breath and exhaled, feeling his wrist. The blade would have sliced his hand off in an instant. 'How did you . . . ?'

'How did I know? The ancient Maya put great store in the energy of the jaguar, but that energy is feminine. José warned me that the ancients knew our world would eventually be dominated by the male, and that the codex and this figurine would be fiercely protected by a principle of balance.'

'So the figurine is on some sort of mechanical bed, and if you tilt it, you lose your arm,' O'Connor said, thinking out loud. 'Do you suppose that ring in the centre of the figurine might be the balance point?' He pointed to a small jade circle protruding from one of the lower branches of the Tree of Life carving.

'A very good chance. If you look closely, there are two indents on the edges of the cavity that mark the centre.'

O'Connor fashioned another two probes out of long, slender stalagmites and, holding them like a pair of tweezers, he lowered the end of the rope from his belt. The leading tip of one of the stalagmites hit the ring slightly off centre and both blades flashed from their recesses, slicing the stalagmites in two. It took three attempts before he managed to thread the rope through the ring. He handed Aleta one end.

'Those two grooves: we can slot the rope into them and use them as guides.'

Aleta nodded and she and O'Connor carefully walked backwards on either side of the cavity, slowly raising the priceless figurine to the top of the recess. They swung it to one side, the glow-worm lights reflected in the crystal even more eerily than before.

'The lost feminine,' Aleta exclaimed. At the base of the jade Tree of Life, the ancients had carved a powerful female jaguar with two cubs, one male, the other female.

O'Connor checked his watch. Less than seventy-two hours to the solstice. He reached for the two nylon specimen bags he carried on his dive belt, and they loaded the figurine into one and the gold into the other. Together, they manoeuvred the precious cargo down to the main ledge below.

From behind a large stalagmite in the dark recesses of the cave, the two ex-navy SEALs watched as O'Connor and Aleta checked their gear and prepared to leave.

'I'll take the gold,' O'Connor said. Aleta raised her eyebrows in mock admonition.

'Only because it's the heaviest, smart ass.'

'At least it'll be lighter in the water. Thank God for good old Archimedes.'

O'Connor set off with the gold, tracking the rope that led back to the underwater entrance. Aleta followed with the precious figurine, reeling in the rope as she swam, but they had only travelled about thirty metres when O'Connor sensed the vibrations behind him. He turned in time to see Aleta being attacked. Her assailant had ripped off her mask and slashed her breathing hose. A second attacker was powering towards him, knife drawn.

He dropped the gold, which fell to the floor of the cave, landing in a puff of silt. In an instant, he recalled the training he'd done at the Naval Amphibious Base on the Silver Strand isthmus near San Diego. The Chief Petty Officer instructor had been one of the hardest men O'Connor had ever encountered, and his words rang clearly in O'Connor's head: 'If you're attacked underwater, *let your opponent come to you*. Then get behind them – go over them or under them, but get behind them – and turn them upside down.'

O'Connor drew his own knife and waited for his assailant. At the last moment he dived underneath him, twisted, ripped off his attacker's face mask from behind and cut his air hose. The ex-navy SEAL was strong, but O'Connor turned him upside down in a choke hold and glanced behind. Aleta, with no face mask and no way of breathing, was sinking to the bottom of the cave. Her attacker had retrieved the figurine and was powering towards O'Connor, who plunged his own knife into the femoral artery of his still-struggling adversary. A cloud of blood exploded around them. O'Connor pushed him away and waited for the second asset to press his attack.

He glanced over to where Aleta was struggling; her equipment snagged on a big stalagmite, air bubbles exploding from her fractured regulator, but there was nothing he could do.

The second diver hesitated, then swam rapidly for the entrance of the cave, still clutching the figurine. O'Connor dived towards Aleta, freed her from the stalagmite and together they shot to the surface. Aleta gasped for breath and coughed up water and O'Connor hauled her up onto the limestone shelf.

'I'll be okay,' she coughed. 'The figurine!'

'I'll be back!' O'Connor inserted his mouthpiece and stepped back into the water. The body of the first assailant was lying on the bottom of the cave and O'Connor swam strongly towards the narrow entrance. The second CIA asset had cleared the squeeze and O'Connor surfaced in time to see him climbing over the stern of his boat. Fidel's boat was drifting but Fidel was nowhere to be seen.

Acting on an impulse, O'Connor dived back to the bottom of the lake and retrieved the nylon rope from its anchor point. O'Connor resurfaced, and the rope, freed of its anchoring point, floated on top of the lake. O'Connor quickly laid it out to form a mesh on the surface and positioned himself in the middle. The second diver started the outboard and gunned it to full throttle, aiming his boat straight at him. O'Connor waited until the last moment and then dived. The propeller sliced the first lengths of the rope, but the next length fouled it and the shear pin snapped. The propeller came loose, spinning to the bottom of the lake in a shower of foaming bubbles. Free of the propeller, the Evinrude outboard screamed in protest.

O'Connor followed the slowing boat above him, holding his breath, knowing his adversary would be looking for the tell-tale signs of exhalation bubbles on the surface. He came up underneath the bow and drew his knife. He cautiously swam to one side and as he'd expected, the second diver was scanning the waters behind the boat. O'Connor eased his way down the side of the boat, supporting himself on the gunwale, but his attacker suddenly turned. With unerring accuracy born of hours of practice, O'Connor let fly with his knife. It flashed through the air, piercing the startled diver's neck.

'*Aaggghhhh!*' His opponent grasped his neck and tumbled backwards over the stern. O'Connor dived and swam through the clouding bloody water, gripping his opponent in a final choke hold. The diver's struggles gradually weakened until they ceased altogether and O'Connor let go, watching the lifeless body sink to the floor of the lake. He clambered over the stern of the boat and retrieved the nylon bag containing the figurine. Fidel's boat was drifting some 200 metres to the north. O'Connor sat on the gunwale, clasped the figurine to his chest and rolled back into the water in a backwards somersault.

When O'Connor surfaced, Aleta was still sitting on the ledge, trying to cut and refit her slashed breathing hose.

'Are you okay?'

Aleta nodded. 'Are they still out there?'

'They're both dead, but I think they got to Fidel.'

'Bastards! These people don't fucking give up, do they?'

'No, and it's not over yet. But if we can get to Tikal before the solstice, we might still have a chance.' He placed the figurine on the ledge and dived back to the floor of the cave to retrieve Aleta's face mask and the bag containing the ingots. 'Your regulator's stuffed,' he said when he returned to the ledge, 'so we'll buddy breathe.'

'Thank you, Curtis. You saved my life, again.'

He grinned. 'All part of the service.' Together, they stepped back into the now-clear, emerald waters of the cave. With the figurine and the gold safely back in their grasp, they swam slowly towards the entrance, sharing O'Connor's regulator every three breaths. Outside the cave and about fifteen metres above them, the hulls of the two *lanchas* were clearly visible. O'Connor gave Aleta the thumbs up towards the one that still had a propeller.

Fidel was lying unconscious on the bottom of the boat, his shirt stained with blood. O'Connor grabbed a towel to stem the flow. 'San Pedro will have the best medical facilities – or Panajachel?'

'There's a doctor at San Marcos,' Aleta replied, gunning the motor.

José Arana was waiting for them at the little jetty and together he and O'Connor carried Fidel to the doctor's house, where Arana remained to wait for news.

When José returned, Aleta was sitting with O'Connor in the garden, explaining what she'd learned during her regression therapy.

'The doctor said he'll be okay,' Arana said, 'but if you hadn't got to him when you did, Fidel would no longer be with us.' He picked up the carved jade figurine, admiring the ancient craftsmanship. 'You've done well,' he said.

'Did you know that one of us might have lost an arm?' Aleta asked, an edge to her voice.

'I warned you that both the last figurine and the codex itself would be fiercely protected,' Arana replied simply, 'but more importantly you have less than three days until the solstice.'

'We have a little task to complete in San Pedro before we leave,' O'Connor said. 'Von Heißen's diaries contain compelling evidence of the atrocities the Nazis committed at Mauthausen . . . and they also contain evidence of the CIA's involvement in the Guatemalan death squads. Jennings obviously doesn't know they're there, but we need to recover them to a safe place.'

'How are we going to distract Jennings?' Aleta asked. 'Mass will be finished in half an hour.'

'How do you feel about confession?'

'What?'

'I saw a notice on the porch of the church. Jennings conducts confessions after Mass, and if you hold him up in the confessional, I'll have time to get the trunks out of the ceiling and down to the launch.'

'And what if he recognises me?'

'He won't. Not if your face is covered by a niqab.'

'A Muslim full-face veil? He can't give confession to a Muslim!'

'Pretend you're going through a crisis of faith, and that you're going to convert. That should give me long enough!'

'I'll be there for a week. Besides, I'll stand out like a sore thumb.'

'Not really,' Arana said. 'There are quite a few Muslims in the Lake Atitlán community, and we all coexist without any problems. Besides, every picture you have ever seen of the Virgin Mary depicts her in a veil. That's just a Christian version of the hijab.'

55

SAN PEDRO, GUATEMALA

Aleta waited on the main steps outside the church until the last of the congregation had shaken their priest by the hand, while O'Connor took up a position in the gardens. Even at a distance, Jennings' surprise and irritation at Aleta's request for him to hear a Muslim renounce her faith in a Catholic confessional was clearly audible, and O'Connor watched as the two disappeared back inside the church. Confident that Aleta would tie Jennings up in knots, he headed for the presbytery.

Monsignor Jennings slammed the door of the little wooden confessional shut and switched on the red light above the door. Aleta closed the curtain on her side, knelt on the tattered cushion and waited until Jennings slid open the worn cedar partition. Through the holes, Aleta could make out Jennings' shadowy figure. He was breathing heavily. It had been many years since Aleta had been in a confessional, but she remembered the tortuous procedure of a teenager's imagined sins as if it were yesterday. She remembered, too, the lives the hypocrite on the other side of the screen had destroyed.

'My friends tell me that unless I renounce Islam and become a Catholic I will burn in hell,' Aleta whispered.

'And your friends are correct. You must renounce your current beliefs and embrace the one true faith.'

'But we both worship the one God?'

Jennings snorted. 'God has revealed much more of Himself to Catholics than to any other faith. He is God the Father, God the Son and God the Holy Spirit. Those who do not take Jesus as their Saviour, or who do, but embrace other denominations of Christianity, are gravely deluded . . .'

Aleta listened, willing the minutes by as Jennings launched into full stride, delivering a verbal broadside against other faiths. 'Unless you accept the Catholic faith in all of its beauty and majesty, you are doomed, my girl.'

Aleta glanced at her watch. O'Connor had estimated he'd need fifteen minutes to recover the trunks from the ceiling and get them back to the jetty. She needed to keep Jennings going for a while longer.

'I have another problem, Father.'

'And what's that?' Jennings asked irritably.

'I masturbate . . . a lot. Is that a sin, Father?' Aleta could feel the fat priest's piggy little stare boring through the holes in the partition, and she fought to quell a fit of the giggles.

'It is a very serious sin! Matthew makes it very clear that when your right hand causes you to sin, it should be cut off. The Catholic God is a very jealous God, and if you abuse your body for an act of self-gratification, that is sexual idolatry, a mortal sin for which you will surely burn in hell. If you don't turn away from this false faith, and if you don't reject sex for pure pleasure, I can't help you.'

'Thank you, Father. Can I ask how you manage to do without sex?'

'How dare you? How *dare* you? You will leave this church now!'

Aleta slipped out of the confessional, leaving Jennings fuming on the other side of the partition.

Security around the Vandenberg Air Force Base was tighter than usual. A heavy swell was coming in across a dark Pacific Ocean, and a searchlight probed the white caps as additional guards patrolled the Point Sal beach. The specially modified thirty-tonne LGM-30 Minuteman missile was in the last stages of being readied in test-launch silo Lima Foxtrot-26. A short distance away, the technicians were carrying out a series of final checks on the equipment on board *Looking Glass*. The crew of the E6-Mercury command and control aircraft were already strapped in their seats. They would vector the missile into a precise position for the massive ELF attack on the Iranian tunnel systems, an attack that would penetrate as far as the earth's core. Nearly 4000 kilometres to the north, the command and control centre at Gakona was at full strength, where the scientists and technicians were testing HAARP's elaborate circuitry. Tyler Jackson shifted nervously in his swivel chair, weighing up his options. The countdown to H-hour had begun.

'The *hide* of that hypocritical bastard,' Aleta swore, as they powered back across the lake towards San Marcos, the three trunks of diaries weighing down the stern.

'Did he say it was okay to masturbate with your *left* hand?'

She gave O'Connor a playful cuff over the ear. 'Do you think we'll make it?' she asked, suddenly more serious.

'It'll be touch and go. The solstice dawn's the day after tomorrow and Tikal's over 300 kilometres away. When Wiley discovers what's happened to 'Lloyd Bridges' and 'Buster Crabb' out there, he'll be incandescent. But José's organised a four-wheel drive so we can take the back road out of here – just in case Wiley's lined up any more guerrillas to block our path.'

Howard Wiley's anger rose as Ellen Rodriguez brought him up to date via the secure video link from the US Embassy in Guatemala City. Wiley's face was once again the colour of his hair, and he clenched and unclenched his right fist.

'The body was found floating on Lake Atitlán, not far from the shore near San Marcos. The authorities have not identified it, but it's almost certainly one of ours . . . found in a full diving suit with a knife wound to the throat.'

'How can you be sure it's one of ours?' Wiley rasped.

'My contact tells me the body has a US Navy SEAL emblem tattooed on his left arm.'

'Shit! And the other one?'

'Missing . . . presumed dead.'

'That's one hell of an assumption, Rodriguez!'

'They were after O'Connor,' Rodriguez replied calmly, 'and he was seen in San Pedro *after* the first body was found.'

'So where is he now?'

'My guess is that both he and Weizman are headed for Tikal.'

'We briefed five more assets yesterday. Are they there yet?'

'As yet, they've not reported in.'

'For fuck's sake, Rodriguez! What sort of a nickel-and-dime show are you running down there?'

Rodriguez kept her counsel.

'Get your ass up to Tikal and take charge of this bullshit. I want roadblocks, round-the-clock surveillance, and I want Tutankhamen and Nefertiti dead as soon as they show their faces . . . and I want that codex!' With that, the screen went blank.

Rodriguez shook her head in frustration. Whatever the Wileys of this world thought of Guatemala, it was a sovereign country, and roadblocks might be a bit tricky.

O'Connor kept to the speed limit, not wanting to attract any unwarranted attention, and as the hours slipped by, the stunted lowland bushes of Petén gradually gave way to the deep rainforests of Tikal. The site of the ancient Mayan city was now a national park, and O'Connor slowed to a stop at the gates.

The park attendant waited until the old four-wheel drive was out of sight before he called the number he'd been given. He had no idea who the man and woman in the battered Toyota were, nor did he much care. They matched the description he'd been given, and the American woman had paid him handsomely.

'So what's the plan? Or are you just making it up as we go along?' Aleta asked.

'Pretty much,' O'Connor replied with his disarming grin. The four-wheel drive bounced alarmingly out of a large pothole. 'There's a pretty reasonable lodge where we could stay the night, only a few hundred metres from the pyramids.'

'Won't they be looking there?'

'They will, which is why we'll avoid it . . . A pity really.'

'So where does that leave us? If you can get that mind of yours above your navel.' Aleta was smiling.

'Before we left San Marcos, José told me he'd be in contact with one of the elders in a village across the river. José's taken a more direct route, so he's probably there already. It's the same village your grand-father visited. According to José, there's a track about a kilometre ahead that branches off the main road.'

The track, not much used except by the villagers, was barely wide enough for the Toyota to pass. O'Connor drove slowly through the overhanging undergrowth. Vines and ferns grew abundantly between the huge mahogany and ceiba trees. Forty minutes later they came to the river, and the same bridge Levi had crossed seventy years before.

'Aren't you going to hide the vehicle?' Aleta asked, as she hoisted her backpack with one of the figurines.

'No point,' O'Connor replied, shouldering his own backpack, which contained the other two. 'Langley will have a twenty-four-hour satellite footprint over this place, and they'll already have this vehicle fingered. But once we get over the bridge, it will be hard for them to track us under the canopy. They'll need people on the ground, although they'll be working on that too.' O'Connor negotiated the rickety rope bridge and Aleta followed, treading warily on the worn cedar logs that swayed above the swift-flowing river nearly ten metres below. Safely on the other side, O'Connor led the way, pushing through the foliage along the narrow track that wound towards the old Mayan village. Suddenly he stopped, and Aleta almost cannoned into him. He moved off the track, motioning Aleta to follow. 'We've got company again,' he mouthed, putting his finger to his lips and pointing up the track.

Aleta peered through the thick jungle, but she could see nothing. 'More assets?' she whispered.

'I'm not sure. It could be men from the village . . . I caught a movement about 150 metres away.'

Aleta jumped as the jungle parted beside her and José Arana stepped into view.

'You are right to be cautious. Your enemies are not far from here; they arrived in Tikal last night.'

'You startled me, José!' Aleta remonstrated, her heart still racing.

'You didn't waste any time, O'Connor said, acknowledging Arana's mastery of the jungle.

Arana smiled disarmingly. 'There is very little time to waste. Follow me, and we'll join the welcoming party.'

In the seventy intervening years since Levi Weizman had been in the village, little had changed. There had been a small increase in the population, but smoke from the same cooking fires drifted towards the river. The women still soaked maize kernels in lime, grinding them into *masa* dough, and the griddles were warming, ready for the tortillas. The dinner menu hadn't changed much either: a savoury aroma of chicken simmering in jalapeno chillies, diced peppers, oregano and limes wafted into the jungle. The younger women, the grand-daughters of those Levi had observed, had taken over the task of working the backstrap looms and they were weaving the *huipils* and *traje* in the same bright colours and designs that identified the village.

The elders, the descendants of those who had once ruled Tikal, were dressed in their traditional red and yellow cotton shirts, *pantalons* and straw hats. O'Connor and Aleta were solemnly introduced. No one knew better than the elders the magnitude of what might be about to take place.

56

TIKAL, GUATEMALA

Ellen Rodriguez arrived in Tikal in a nondescript embassy four-wheel drive bearing local plates. She scanned the car park of the Jungle Lodge for any sign of the Toyota reported by the guard at the park gates, but no vehicle fitted that description. After checking into her room, she took a mango juice in the lobby and waited until the desk was manned by just one of the staff, an older dark-skinned man with a thin black moustache.

'Would it be possible to see the guest list?'

'I'm sorry, senora, but it's against company policy.'

Rodriguez slipped him a 200-quetzale note.

'But I will see what I can do,' he said, his face expressionless as he pocketed the money. A short while later, he returned with a sealed envelope.

Back in the privacy of her room, Rodriguez worked her way down the list. She knew O'Connor too well to expect him to book in under his own name, but she was looking for two people, a man and a woman, who might have checked in some time after the report from the gate guard. Rodriguez came to the end of the list and sighed with frustration. No one had checked in as a couple, or two singles in the timeframe. So where were O'Connor and Weizman, she wondered. She looked at her watch. It was time to meet with the latest thugs Wiley had organised from Washington. Rodriguez smiled grimly to herself. The chase for O'Connor had left a trail littered with bodies, and she was beginning to hope that her old colleague might prevail again, but with five assets deployed, she knew the odds were now stacked even more heavily against him. Tomorrow was the winter solstice, and soon O'Connor would have to come out into the open.

Wiley's assets were supposed to rendezvous with Rodriguez near the base of Pyramid I, pretending to be part of a night tour of the ruins, but as she approached the Great Plaza, Howard Wiley detached himself from the main tourist group. Rodriguez stifled a gasp. No matter how important an operation was to Washington, it was unprecedented for the Deputy Director of Operations to appear in the field. If someone in Tikal recognised Wiley from a Senate hearing in Washington, the whole operation would be compromised.

'I'm taking personal command, Rodriguez. This operation's been a balls-up from the word go. You can brief me in your room.'

'But, sir . . . the assets . . . '

'They're under my direct command. This time I want no mistakes.'

'Would you like something to drink, sir?' Rodriguez asked as she closed the door to her bungalow. Her tone was icy.

'A scotch.'

Rodriguez handed him a miniature Johnny Walker Red Label from the room service bar.

'So what do you have?' Wiley demanded.

'O'Connor and Weizman entered the park about two hours ago, but since then they've not been sighted. I've checked the records of the hotel, but no one has arrived in the timeframe. For the moment, they've disappeared, but they can't be far away.'

'Langley has a satellite image of a vehicle on what looks to be a disused track,' Wiley said. 'We've also got real-time footage of two people crossing a bridge, but after that they were lost to the jungle canopy.' He pulled a map of the ruins of Tikal and the surrounding area out of his soft leather attaché case and laid it on the coffee table. 'My guess is that they're headed for this village here.'

'And the assets?'

'Three of them have been deployed in the ruins, with instructions to shoot on sight.'

'You don't think that might attract attention?'

'I don't give a fuck, Rodriguez. There are enough shoot-outs between Mexican drug lords in this part of the world to rival John Wayne on steroids. The other two assets are on their way to the village. If the two people crossing the bridge were Tutankhamen and Nefertiti, we'll get them there. Either way, they're cactus.'

'So what about the codex? Wouldn't it be better to keep them under observation until they lead us to it?'

'That's the problem with you, Rodriguez – you leave too much to chance. It probably hasn't occurred to you, but whatever information our friends picked up around Lake Atitlán, they'll have on them. I'm just as capable of deciphering that as they are. Now, do you have anything else?'

'You and Langley seem to have it pretty well covered, *sir.* '

'Good.' Wiley drained his scotch and folded the map. 'I'm in Bungalow Eleven. If anything breaks out at that tin-pot organisation you run in Guatemala City, I'm to be informed immediately.'

More than one door closed as Wiley left. The other was the silent sound of a door closing on a career to which Rodriguez had devoted her entire working life. With only hours to go to the winter solstice, and the second experiment in Operation Aether, she set her cell phone alarm for 3 a.m.

57

TIKAL, GUATEMALA

The two assets moved silently along the jungle track towards the village where Arana and the elders, along with O'Connor and Aleta, were deep in conversation around the central fire. All listened carefully as Aleta outlined Levi Weizman's notes on the confluence of the sun's winter solstice rays with the crystals embedded in the gold-rimmed obsidian at the top of each figurine.

'The second map was given to my grandfather by your predecessors,' she said, laying the ancient *huun* bark document out on the ground. 'It's a precise triangle that corresponds to the angles between Pyramids I, IV and V.'

Arana nodded quietly in approval.

'My grandfather found the male figurine, the one with the male jaguar at its base, in Pyramid I, so I'm surmising that at the solstice tomorrow, the male figurine should be positioned on top of the Pyramid I roof comb. Each figurine has a hole in the base in the shape of the Greek letter Φ, and they're each in a different position on the base, so it's possible that may assist with the positioning.'

Again, Arana nodded in agreement.

'If my theory is correct,' Aleta continued, 'the female figurine with the jaguar and her cubs needs to be positioned on top of Temple IV, where it came from originally. The final neutral figurine needs to be positioned on top of Temple V, where my grandfather discovered it, and where it can capture the deflected rays from both the male and female figurines.'

'You have done well, Aleta, but what then?' Arana prompted.

'It's hypothesis, but I'm hoping my grandfather was right when he theorised that the final beam deflection will indicate the location of the codex.'

'The problem is, José,' O'Connor interjected, 'we'll need help to safeguard the figurines once they've been positioned —'

A blood-curdling scream, followed closely by another, pierced the jungle foliage.

'Two of your enemies have been foolish enough to approach the village on the main track,' said Arana. 'If they were skilled in moving through the jungle at night, they might have been more difficult to detect, but there are more than twenty warriors protecting the village.' He turned towards the village elders and consulted with them in the ancient language of the Maya. The village chief occasionally glanced at Aleta with a questioning look. Was this the one who had been sent to unlock the secrets of the Maya Codex?

'The elders are in agreement,' Arana said finally. You have both done remarkably well to get this far, and perhaps the time is upon us; but we can't help you position the figurines. Our forefathers were very clear that the codex would be found only by the one who was destined to do so. Our warriors can guard the figurines once you have placed them; but once again I must warn you, the codex itself is fiercely protected.' Arana looked gravely at Aleta. 'Even more so than the figurine you discovered in Lake Atitlán, although the principle of balance remains the same.'

It was well past midnight by the time the warriors from the cordon around the village had silently assembled, their war paint gleaming in the flickering firelight.

'It's time we moved,' Arana said to Aleta and O'Connor. 'Sunrise is at 6.49 a.m., which is a little over three hours from now.' He nodded to the warriors and four of them immediately set off along the old jungle track that led back towards the bridge and the ancient Mayan ruins.

'Aren't we going with them?' Aleta asked.

'That's the scout party,' O'Connor said. 'If any of Wiley's guerrillas are lying in wait, they'll give us early warning.'

Aleta shivered. 'Probably with their lives,' she replied bitterly.

'They'll do that willingly,' Arana told her. 'Sacrifice for the greater good is part of Mayan culture.'

A spine-tingling roar carried through the mists of the jungle. One of Tikal's few remaining jaguars was on the prowl.

'It's an omen,' Arana observed, nodding to another warrior carrying a long fiery torch. They moved off in single file, ten warriors leading the way with their torches, followed by O'Connor and Aleta with the figurines. Arana and the elders completed the main body, followed by another ten warriors protecting the rear of the column.

Thirty minutes later they reached the scout party, which had propped on the outskirts of the ruins. Arana gave orders for the torches to be extinguished, and once again the scout party moved forward, more cautiously now. When they reached the edge of the Great Plaza, the lead scout suddenly stopped and the rest of the party melted off the track. O'Connor and Arana moved forward to join them, and the lead scout pointed towards the comb on top of Pyramid I. The temple was bathed in eerie moonlight and O'Connor picked it immediately. He pulled his night sight from its pouch and adjusted the focus. A man was sitting against one side of the comb, cradling an automatic rifle.

'Another one of Wiley's thugs,' O'Connor muttered, turning to Arana. 'I'll take him from the rear side of the pyramid,' he said, screwing a red filter onto the end of his torch. 'When you see my signal, tell the scouts I want them to create a diversion.'

O'Connor skirted the main plaza and the side of Pyramid I that was furthest from the gunman. He quietly began to climb the weathered limestone steps, keeping his eyes on the decorative limestone comb at the top. O'Connor froze as the gunman rose to his feet. He was young, and his movements were jumpy. Never a good sign. The young gunman waved his rifle towards Pyramid IV, as if seeking reassurance, before sitting back down again, his back to the comb.

Clearly there was another thug on Pyramid IV. O'Connor resumed his stealthy climb towards the top, planning to garrotte his quarry from behind. That tactic would avoid a noisy gun battle, although the nearest police station was fifty kilometres away in

Flores. O'Connor paused, took his torch from his pocket and flashed it three times towards the warriors hidden in the jungle below, the red filter ensuring the light could only be seen from a direct line. The warriors pulled on long creeper vines and the jungle began to shake. The gunman leapt to his feet, nervously traversing the base of the pyramid with his rifle. O'Connor quietly covered the last few metres. At the last moment, the young gunman turned but it was too late. In one swift movement O'Connor whipped the garrotte around his quarry's neck. The rifle clattered onto the top limestone step as the hired mercenary flailed helplessly. He was strong, and he dragged O'Connor past the edge of the comb before he collapsed. O'Connor held the choke until he was certain the gunman was dead.

Ellen Rodriguez groped for the cell phone, thinking it was the alarm, only to find Tyler Jackson on the line.

'Ellen, you need to listen carefully. We don't have much time.'

'What's happened?'

'We're about to launch a missile from Vandenberg which will be vectored into a position above Iran. It will act as a lens, focusing a tomography beam to destroy the nuclear facilities at Fordo.'

'I'm with you, Tyler, but I'm not sure I can do much to stop that.'

'You used to work at the White House – what about the Chief of Staff, Andrew Reed?'

'Yes, but we're going to need some powerful arguments to stop this. The Iranians are getting close to having the bomb, and the President will have given this attack the green light.'

'No doubt snowed by the Israeli Lobby and the hawks at the Pentagon, but he won't have all the facts. No one has any idea what might happen as our solar system moves towards the centre of the galaxy. There's a supermassive black hole at the centre of the Milky Way, and we're about to punch three billion watts of energy into the core of the planet when it's in its most unstable orbit in 26 000 years. Are you on email?'

'Yes, but I'll have to fire up the laptop.'

'By the time you've done that, the email will be there.' Jackson attached an image of the earth's structure and a map to the email and pressed the 'send' button.

'Hang on . . . it's just coming through now.'

'If you open the first attachment, you should be able to see an image of the earth's layers?'

'Yes – the core, the mantle and the outer crust.'

'Good. You'll see from the diagram that the core has a diameter of 7000 kilometres, which consists of solid iron surrounded by molten metals. You will also see that the middle layer, or mantle, is 2800 kilometres thick and is made up of hot silicates . . . around 3000 degrees Celsius, but it's the earth's crust I'm worried about most.'

'I'm not sure I follow.'

'The crust runs from the top of Everest at a height of around eight kilometres down to the Mariana Trench in the deepest part of the ocean off Japan, eleven kilometres under the surface; but overall, the crust is only seventy kilometres thick. In some areas under the oceans it's only five kilometres thick, and it's flexible. We don't notice it, but the earth spins at over 1600 kilometres an hour. If you're a child playing on a merry-go-round in the park, the centrifugal force will spin you to the outside, and even throw you off, if it's going fast enough. But in the case of the planet, that same force means the crust bulges significantly at the equator.'

'I'm still not sure how this is an argument to stop the rocket firing?'

'It's the bulge at the equator that determines the position of the oceans. If a powerful enough force changes the earth's axis, making it spin at a different slant, the position of the oceans will *change*. That's what makes this Aether experiment so dangerous. If a top is spinning on a table and you give it a shove, it'll wobble and crash . . . but the earth isn't constrained by a table or anything else: if something like three billion watts of energy stirs up the molten outer core, the Chandler wobble will increase. There'll be a series of earthquakes even more powerful than Haiti or Chile, after which the earth will stabilise – still spinning at the same speed, but on a different slant or axis.'

Rodriguez shivered at the enormity of what Tyler Jackson was saying. 'And we will have changed the position of the equator.'

'The position of the poles will change as well,' Jackson argued. 'With a *magnetic* pole shift, the north and south poles just flip, and that's bad enough – that destroys navigation systems, kills migratory birds and a whole host of other things. But with a *geographic* pole shift, the bulging of the equator would change both the position and the depth of the oceans. London, Washington, New York, Tokyo, Sydney – they'll all be under water. In the US sixty per cent of the population live on, or near the coast. In Japan and Australia it's eighty per cent. It doesn't matter where you go, most people live on or near the coast. If you open the second attachment, it contains a map that shows how the world will look after a geographic pole shift.'

Rodriguez stared in disbelief. Vast tracts of the United States, Europe, China, Japan, India, Russia and South America had disappeared from view, while new land masses around Cuba and Florida and between Australia and Papua New Guinea had suddenly appeared.

'Has this ever happened before?' she asked.

'People dismiss cities like Atlantis as science fiction, but it's not that Atlantis sank . . . As you can see from the map, when a geographic pole shift occurs, the position of the oceans change and whole continents disappear. They are covered in water while new land masses appear.'

'Is there any evidence?'

'Not in the history books, because we've only been recording our history for about 6000 years, but the evidence is there – and it's right under our noses. The work we're doing on ice cores from the Arctic and the Antarctic is going to surprise a lot of scientists. Drilling on the bottom of the Ross Sea clearly indicates that 6000 years ago, the Antarctic was ice-free, and deep ice cores are revealing fossilised forests.'

'So the poles haven't always been where they are today?'

'No. And we're now finding increasing evidence of lost cities on the bottom of the ocean: further signs of a past geographic pole shift. At the bottom of the map you will see side-scan sonar images of what look like ancient roads and pyramids. A team of highly respected marine archaeologists has found evidence of what might turn out to be a Mayan city off the coast of Cuba. And as recently as two years ago marble and stone formations were found in shallow waters off the Bimini islands in the Bahamas.'

'How long have we got?'

'A few hours – no more.'

'I'll do what I can, Tyler. If I can swing it, are you prepared to brief the President by video link?'

'Absolutely.'

Rodriguez hung up and put a call through to Andrew Reed's private cell phone.

'Jesus Christ, Ellen. Are you guys smoking something illegal down there?' Reed, none too happy at being woken in the small hours of the morning, or at the discussion being carried out over an open line, was less than sympathetic; but the conversation was interrupted by the sound of gunfire coming from the ancient city.

The bullets missed O'Connor by centimetres, ricocheting off the comb masonry. O'Connor grabbed the gunman's rifle and took cover. The limestone masonry disintegrated further as the second mercenary switched to automatic and sprayed the top of the pyramid. O'Connor descended a dozen or so large steps and then worked his way round the other side of the pyramid to where he could get a clear view. Pyramid IV was bathed in moonlight and he detected a small movement behind the right-hand side of the comb. He adjusted the butt of the rifle into his shoulder, lined up the crosshairs on the telescopic sight and waited. Suddenly his target leapt out from behind the comb and opened fire on O'Connor. The bullets whined over O'Connor's head but he ignored them, calmly adjusting the sight. He took the first pressure on the trigger and then squeezed off a single shot. The gunman arched back, still firing bullets into the early-morning sky, a small bloody hole in the centre of his forehead. O'Connor watched as he tumbled down more than a hundred steps and into the jungle below.

O'Connor signalled with his torch and Aleta, backpack on her shoulders and accompanied by four warriors, appeared from the fringe of the jungle and began the ascent. To the east, across the top of the dark jungle canopy that stretched as far as O'Connor could see, the velvet night was beginning to soften. He looked at his watch. The dawn of the winter solstice was barely thirty minutes away. Howard Wiley, awakened by the gunfire, was quietly heading for the ruins.

'We don't have much time,' Aleta said, breathing hard as she reached the top of Pyramid I.

O'Connor levered himself onto the top of the comb and switched on his filtered torch. The limestone was old and weathered, but at the very centre of the comb the faint etching was unmistakeable.

'Phi!' Aleta whispered excitedly, pointing to the Φ that had been carved in the limestone.

'And it's surrounded by a groove, which will hold the base of the figurine,' O'Connor said, feeling the slight indentation in the stone. Aleta scrambled off the comb and retrieved the male figurine from her backpack. She handed it up to O'Connor and climbed back to the top. With the aid of his torch, O'Connor lined up the Φ on the base of the figurine with the Φ on the top of the comb and slotted the figurine into position. The crystal glinted in the early-morning light.

O'Connor scanned the eastern horizon. The sky was getting lighter still. He turned to signal the warriors to guard the figurine, but four of them had already taken up their positions, one on each corner of the pyramid summit. O'Connor grabbed Aleta's empty backpack and together they descended the steep steps to the jungle below. O'Connor took the female figurine and put it into Aleta's backpack, leaving the neutral in his own. He shouldered the pack and he and Aleta, accompanied by four more warriors, made their way down the jungle track which led to Pyramid IV. They raced up the big limestone steps. Breathing hard, O'Connor scrambled to the top of the comb. It was fainter than the one on Pyramid I, but both the Φ and the groove were unmistakeable. Aleta handed up the ancient female figurine, and O'Connor aligned the two Φs and positioned it into the groove.

'What are you like with a rifle?' he asked, retrieving the second gunman's weapon.

'I used to belong to a pistol club, but I can do rifle.'

Leaving four warriors to guard Pyramid IV, O'Connor and Aleta doubled down the hundred or so steps to where Arana and the rest of the warriors were waiting.

'We've got less than ten minutes and Pyramid V's 500 metres away,' O'Connor said, shouldering the final neutral figurine.

'The elders and I will remain in the Great Plaza,' Arana announced. 'May the gods of the Maya be with you.'

O'Connor and Aleta set off down the jungle track behind the remaining warriors, their Mayan war paint shining in the misty half-light. A troop of howler monkeys swung noisily through the branches of the strangler figs above, their squat black faces staring down as their predecessors had for centuries. But the group had only gone 300 metres when a burst of machine-pistol fire shattered the mists of the jungle. Two warriors died instantly, and O'Connor winced as a bullet struck his rifle from his grasp.

Instinctively Aleta took cover amongst the buttresses of a strangler fig and dropped to one knee. The fiery red flashes from the gunman's machine pistol as he raked the track with bullets gave away his position near the base of Pyramid V. Aleta calmly adjusted the crosshairs and squeezed off three rounds.

'*Aaggghhhh!!*' The firing stopped and the gunman tumbled onto the track barely fifty metres away.

'You're not just a pretty face, are you?' O'Connor said admiringly, as he retrieved his rifle and emerged back on the track.

'You're bleeding! Are you okay?'

'It's a flesh wound.' O'Connor signalled the remaining warriors to move on.

They reached Pyramid V and O'Connor and Aleta bounded up the steps.

'Two minutes,' O'Connor announced, and he scrambled to the top of the comb. 'It's here!' The Φ and the groove were just visible. Aleta handed up the neutral figurine ,and O'Connor slotted the artefact into the limestone. 'Lie flat, just in case,' he said. Together they looked towards the east. The jungle canopy spread like a verdant green carpet as far as the eye could see. Here and there, the distinctive top of a giant ceiba tree soared above its chicle, balsa and buttressed fig neighbours. Howler monkeys swung amongst the vines below, their harsh calls mingling with the squawks of the macaws, the chirps of the hummingbirds and the *kyowh-kyowh* of the orange-breasted falcon. The horizon glowed in a mixture of orange and yellow; the point of the coming winter-solstice sun glowing more fiercely than the rest.

'Twenty seconds,' O'Connor whispered. 'Ten . . .'

Aleta's heart began to race. It was as if she were sitting on the launch pad at Cape Canaveral.

'Now!' Rays of light that had travelled at 300 000 kilometres a second, from a sun that was 150 million kilometres away, pierced the mists above the jungle. O'Connor focused his binoculars on the crystal on top of Pyramid I. The male figurine had already energised, and at a precise angle of 287 degrees a powerful laser-like beam of bright-green light deflected towards the top of Pyramid IV, energising the crystal on the female figurine, sending another searing beam of green light to power up the crystal beside them. It crackled and sizzled like a lightning conductor, deflecting yet again. Aleta and O'Connor followed the beam to a point in the ruins just 300 metres away.

'The Pyramid of the Lost World!' O'Connor exclaimed, focusing his binoculars. 'Take a bearing,' he said, handing Aleta his compass. Aleta ducked under the beam and aligned the compass sight from behind the sizzling, crackling crystal.

'Two hundred and sixty-nine degrees!'

'It's hitting one of the limestone steps of the pyramid a metre or so above the ground.' As O'Connor mentally marked the spot, the sun rose higher above the jungle and the power in the crystals and the laser beams began to fade. A police siren could be heard faintly in the distance. Close by in his hiding place in the ancient Central Acropolis, Howard Wiley focused his own binoculars and watched Tutankhamen and Nefertiti scramble down Pyramid V towards the warriors waiting at the base of the steps.

Rifles in hand, O'Connor and Aleta moved down the jungle track leading to Mundo Perdido, the Pyramid of the Lost World. Early archaeologists were struck by the great pyramid soaring above jungle teeming with dangerous and exotic wildlife, the sight evoking a comparison with Conan Doyle's primitive world of the same name. Cautiously, O'Connor and Aleta approached the lower steps of the pyramid. O'Connor signalled for the warriors to post sentries and keep watch. The police siren was getting louder.

'There's a burn mark on the limestone, see? Above the first step.' Aleta pointed to a spot still glowing softly on the weathered stone.

'A hidden chamber?' O'Connor wondered aloud.

'The ancients were superb engineers. There may be a mechanism embedded in the step.' Aleta took an archaeologist's chisel and hammer from her knapsack. She chiselled around the still softly glowing green spot and suddenly she hit metal. 'It's a lever!' she exclaimed, as she deftly removed the surrounding masonry. O'Connor extended his hand towards the bronze lever, which was in the shape of a jaguar.

'No!' Aleta commanded, grabbing his wrist. Arana's words rang in her ears: *The codex itself is fiercely protected . . . even more so than the figurine that you discovered in Lake Atitlán.* 'We need your rope.'

Aleta fastened one end around the neck of the jaguar lever and they retreated to the ten-metre extent of the cord. Aleta pulled at the lever, but it didn't budge and O'Connor swung on to the cord with her. Together they dug their boots into the soil and the lever slowly moved towards them. Suddenly the side of the temple shook, and four massive steps disappeared, revealing a shaft at the base of the pyramid, immediately below where Aleta and O'Connor had been. Ancient dust drifted up from the tonnes of rubble that had fallen six metres to the bottom. O'Connor anchored the rope to a nearby tree and dropped it into the shaft. Using his boots as a brake, he slowly lowered himself down the rope towards the fallen steps. Once he reached the bottom, Aleta followed.

'Look! More steps and a tunnel leading further into the pyramid!' Aleta exclaimed, pointing past the rubble. O'Connor threw a large limestone rock down the stone steps, wary that another yawning chasm might open in front of them. The sound of the falling rock echoed down a passageway that had been sealed for over 1200 years. Aleta followed him down the steps and into the tunnel. Protected from the weather, the limestone walls were painted a bright salmon pink, and the ceiling was high, coming together in a typical Mayan pointed arch.

'The original colour of all the pyramids,' Aleta observed. 'Red cinnabar, the colour of the east . . . the colour of life.'

'And the hieroglyphics?' Every few paces, the ancients had embedded a jade tablet into the walls.

'I can't decipher them all immediately, but this one is very clear,' Aleta replied, a shiver running down her spine. ' "Death will come swiftly to he who, without authority, disturbs the resting place of the codex." Curtis! It's here!'

Above them, the Flores police car roared up the jungle track to the Mendez Causeway and screeched to a halt just short of the Great Plaza, the siren dying. Howard Wiley emerged from his hiding place in the Central Acropolis. He skirted the Great Plaza and moved down the track towards the Pyramid of the Lost World. Ellen Rodriguez followed Wiley at a distance, taking up a position amongst the three small pyramids to the east of the Lost World Pyramid; each aligned with the equinoxes, and the summer and winter solstices. Wiley approached the exposed shaft on the Lost World Pyramid and Rodriguez watched as he scanned the surrounding area. Wiley checked his pistol and climbed down the rope into the shaft.

O'Connor used his powerful torch to probe the red-cinnabar walls of the stone passage and its high arched ceilings. The gradient grew steeper as he and Aleta descended deeper and deeper into Mundo Perdido. Nearly sixty metres further on they were confronted with steps leading down to what appeared to be a stone wall with a huge jade calendar-wheel embedded in the centre. Beside it a smaller jade wheel with an even smaller inner wheel meshed with the larger one like gears in a gear box. At either side of the top of the steps, two polished wooden poles were fixed to the walls, each topped with an ancient oil lamp. O'Connor took one of the poles off the wall and began to probe the steps. Aleta removed the other one and did likewise, wary that the steps might open and swallow them both, but the steps held firm.

'It's the *Haab*, the Mayan long-count calendar, and the sacred *Tzolk'in*, the short-count calendar,' Aleta observed excitedly when they reached the wall. She ran her hand over the exquisitely carved wheels, each embedded with hieroglyphs and the Mayan numbering system of dots and dashes denoting the days and dates. 'The long-count is based on the cycles of the earth and the smaller short-count is based on the cycles of the Pleiades star cluster in the Taurus constellation,' she explained. 'Together, they not only give the day and date in any one year, but the precise date in three other cycles: a 52-year cycle, the longer sun cycle of 5125 years, and the great cycle of 25 625 years. We're now in the end times. The fifth great cycle of the sun will end on 21 December 2012 – a rare meshing of the calendar gears.'

O'Connor probed the stone masonry with his torch beam. 'Trouble is, we seem to be at a dead end.'

Aleta shone her own torch on the hieroglyphs on the wheels. She grabbed O'Connor's elbow. 'I don't think so. The calendars are meshed on 4 *Ahau*, 8 *Cumku* – today's date! There's a mechanism behind these wheels that's been keeping perfect time for over 1200 years. Are you thinking what I'm thinking?'

O'Connor nodded. 'Perhaps there is a setting that might open the wall?'

'Exactly. The Mayan system of cyclical meshing calendars could predict dates four, forty or 40 000 years in advance, so I'm wondering if the setting we're looking for is 21 December 2012?' Aleta pocketed her torch and placed her hands either side of the *Haab* wheel. She applied pressure and the great wheel began to rotate of its own accord – slowly at first, then moving more quickly. Aleta stepped back as the jade hieroglyphs and dots and dashes meshed in perfect synchronicity, the days, weeks and months speeding by. The wheels began to slow until the *Ik* and *Kank'in* teeth on the great *Haab* and the sacred

Tzolk'in, together with the dots and dashes on the inner wheel, meshed in a flash of energy. Aleta gasped. '21 December 2012!' A mechanism deep within the pyramid began to rumble and the stone wall with the embedded sacred calendars slid slowly into a stone recess.

'Duck!' O'Connor picked up the vicious swinging ball in his torch beam and he tackled Aleta to the ground. From high in the ceiling of the tomb, a huge bronze ball embedded with razor-sharp spikes whistled over the prostrate forms of Aleta and O'Connor and smashed into the stone steps beyond. Aleta's face was white as she got shakily to her feet. 'Thank you. Once again, you saved my life,' she said in a whisper.

'One good turn deserves another,' O'Connor replied, but he knew it had been close. Together they played their torches into the gloom of the vast rectangular cavern beyond. Aleta put her hand to her mouth at the sight of the inestimable riches. The cavern was filled with hundreds of priceless jade artefacts. Lidded tripod vessels, engraved with images of the rain god, the sun god and cormorants and turtles, lined the walls. In the centre of the cavern stood a large raised stone tomb, covered by a massive red-cinnabar capstone engraved with the *Haab* and *Tzolk'in* calendars. The tomb was surrounded by necklace beads, anklets and bracelets made from different shades and hues of jade.

O'Connor and Aleta approached cautiously and Aleta stifled another gasp.

'What's wrong?' In the reflected torchlight, O'Connor could see the colour had drained from Aleta's face.

'The body inside that tomb is that of Princess Akhushtal,' Aleta replied, focusing her torch beam on a set of hieroglyphics engraved below an exquisite jade mortuary mask at the top of the capstone.

'She was the daughter of King Yax Ain II, and the calendars on top of the tomb are set at Friday 21 December 2012.'

'Vandenberg control, *Looking Glass*, ready.'

'*Looking Glass*, you are cleared for immediate departure on Runway 30; contact departures when airborne.'

'*Looking Glass*, thank you and good day.'

Air Force Colonel Bill Glassic lined up the Boeing 707 E6-Mercury command and control aircraft on the centre line, applied the brakes and advanced the throttles to sixty per cent, allowing the engines to spool up. Satisfied, he released the brakes and slowly pushed all four throttles forward.

'EPR set, eighty knots,' the first officer called. 'Vee-one.' Glassic removed his right hand from the throttle levers and concentrated on the runway ahead. *Looking Glass* had passed the point where the flight could be aborted.

'Rotate . . . Vee-two . . .'

Glassic eased the 707's nosewheel off the runway and waited until a positive climb was indicated on the pressure altimeter. The landing gear retracted with a thump and *Looking Glass* began the climb to the missile-launch control altitude of 29 000 feet.

O'Connor ran his torch along the walls of the tomb. More jade tablets were embedded in the stone, each engraved with hieroglyphs.

A series of colourful murals in brilliant reds, emerald greens, turquoise blues and iridescent yellows depicted the presentation of jaguar skins to past Mayan kings. Lamp poles were fastened to the walls at regular intervals. They had been made from *tinto*, a logwood from the swamps, a wood that was highly durable and resistant to deterioration. O'Connor removed one and felt the wick at the top. It was perfectly preserved and he retrieved a box of matches from his backpack and lit it. The wick burned feebly at first, but as the oil was drawn from the ceramic container, the lamp shed an eerie, flickering light amongst the priceless artefacts. O'Connor used the lamp to light four more of the closest poles.

'Curtis! Look!' Aleta shone her torch at the centre of the far wall. The recess was painted in brilliant reds, blues and greens. The firelight was reflected in a pedestal made of polished black obsidian. On top stood a magnificent half-metre-high urn made from a mosaic of rich, smoky jade. The lid handles were exquisitely carved into the forms of two jaguars: one male, the other female. O'Connor started to move slowly towards it, but he was stopped in his tracks.

'Put your hands above your heads. Both of you!' Wiley snarled. The DDO stepped out of the gloom of the passageway, the gunmetal of his pistol glinting in the flickering tomb light. Wiley kept his pistol pointed towards Aleta and O'Connor while he collected the two rifles from where they lay on the floor, and he slid them back towards the passageway. 'Your pistol, O'Connor. Slide it over. One false move and the bitch gets it in the head.'

O'Connor slid his pistol across the stone floor and Wiley kicked it towards the rifles. 'So, what do you suppose that urn might contain, *hmm?*' Wiley asked, waving his pistol at Aleta. She didn't answer.

In the confined space of the tomb Wiley's pistol shot was deafening. Aleta jumped as the bullet passed between her legs and ricocheted off the stone floor. 'I asked you a question, bitch!'

She hadn't seen him in over thirty years, but the face of the man behind the murders of her father and mother, her two brothers, and thousands of Guatemalan descendants of the great Maya was seared indelibly on her brain.

'It would appear that the honour of uncovering one of the greatest archaeological finds since the tomb of Tutankhamen has fallen to you, Mr Wiley,' she replied, struggling to keep her voice even.

Wiley could picture the headlines. 'Stand back!' he ordered, waving his pistol and motioning O'Connor and Aleta back towards the side wall. Wiley kept his pistol aimed in their direction and moved sideways towards the recess. When he reached the urn, he lifted it from where it had rested for over a thousand years.

'*Aaggghhhh!*' The pressure plate beneath the urn activated another mechanism and six spears, each tipped with the deadly poison of the fer-de-lance, fired from hidden slots in the recess walls. Two of the spears pierced Wiley's thighs and his pistol clattered onto the ancient stones. The urn settled back onto the pressure plate just as Ellen Rodriguez, pistol drawn, appeared from the passageway.

'Rodriguez – keep them covered,' Wiley ordered, reaching to remove the two spears; but the barbs were deep. The poison took effect immediately and he slumped to the floor.

'Not this time, Mr Wiley.' Rodriguez calmly picked up Wiley's pistol and pocketed it.

'You double-crossing bitch. You'll burn in San Quentin for this.'

'On the contrary, Mr Wiley. When the administration finds out what you've been up to, it's you who will find yourself on the inside.'

'You stupid cow,' Wiley responded, gasping for breath, 'this operation has been approved at the highest levels.'

'Something I'm sure the Senate Committee on Intelligence will find very interesting.' Rodriguez turned to Aleta. 'Do you think it's safe to recover the urn?'

'It's stood here for centuries, to be discovered by one who will be able to warn the world of its contents.' José appeared from the passage, his wizened face a coppery bronze in the flickering light of the oil lamps. He was accompanied by four warriors and he nodded to one carrying a small ceramic jar containing the antidote to the poison, indicating he should administer it to the now-unconscious Wiley.

'It is safe,' José said to Aleta.

Aleta gingerly lifted the priceless urn and removed it from the pedestal, setting it down beside the tomb of Princess Akhushtal. Her heart racing, she tried to lift the lid, but it was sealed with pitch.

The four ballistic gas actuators fired simultaneously, and the exhausts trails of vapour streamed into the pre-dawn air. The massive reinforced-concrete cover on launch silo Lima Foxtrot-26 slid silently to one side, revealing the eighteen-metre modified Minuteman 3 missile. In the Vandenberg control centre Air Force Lieutenant Colonel Dan Williams ran his eye over the myriad consoles and screens that would track the mission to Iran. All systems were showing green.

O'Connor proffered a knife and Aleta ran the blade beneath the rim of the jade. She gently prised the lid open and stepped back as foul air that had been trapped within the urn for hundreds of years escaped. At the bottom of the urn was a large leather-covered package. Aleta's hands trembled as she unwrapped the outer covering.

'The Maya Codex!' she whispered in awe, cradling the priceless artefact. A tear ran down her cheek as she remembered her grandfather. Had it not been for the Nazis, he might have revealed its contents to the world. She placed the codex on the floor of the tomb and carefully opened it, page by *huun* page.

Rodriguez' cell phone buzzed quietly in the background, and she moved back up the passage to get a better signal.

'Any word from the White House?' Jackson asked. 'They're scheduled to launch in less than an hour.'

'I tried, Tyler, but Reed's not buying it. They're more concerned about stopping the Iranians than the Chandler wobble – which I doubt they understand.'

Tyler Jackson shook his head as he hung up the phone. It was absolute madness, but like the Castle Bravo experiment, no one was listening.

Rodriguez returned to the tomb to find Aleta, O'Connor and José huddled over the codex.

'Can you decipher it?' José asked. He had left even the task of deciphering the warning to the one whom the ancients had intended to issue it.

Aleta nodded. 'It will take time to unravel it in detail, but the warning is clearly there. Although . . .' Aleta paused, a puzzled tone to her voice, 'it appears to be in two parts. There's a short path that finishes before December 2012, and a longer path, though both of them lead to the destruction of the human race.'

'What's the short path?' O'Connor asked.

'It deals with the earth and its axis,' Aleta said, reading the hieroglyphs by torchlight. 'My God!' she gasped. 'There's a tilting, and a geographic pole shift, followed by an annihilation of cities near the coast. And there's a shooting star . . . no, wait . . . it's coming *from* the earth, not *to* it – it's some kind of rocket.'

It was Rodriguez' turn to gasp in amazement. She grabbed O'Connor by the arm and explained the calls she'd had from Tyler Jackson.

'Tyler's one of the best scientists I've ever worked with, Ellen, and if he's concerned, the White House should be too.'

'The Chandler wobble?'

'The Chandler wobble's very real, and we saw the effect of the Chile earthquake. That involved a shard of the earth's crust sliding under the South American plate, which redistributed a whole chunk of the earth's mass. Three billion watts of radiated power might push the planet past the point of balance. But the President can't assess that risk if he's not been briefed on it.'

Rodriguez speed-dialled Andrew Reed's number.

'For Christ's sake, Ellen, we had this fucking conversation at three o'clock this morning. The answer's no – what part of that don't you understand?'

'Then we'll announce what you're doing to the media.'

'And you'll not only be fired, you'll finish up behind bars.'

'You guys have got no idea what the CIA is up to down here, so shut the fuck up and listen.' Rodriguez briefed her old boss, taking a risk over the open line. When she'd finished, there was silence on the other end. 'Did you get that, Andrew?'

'There's a cabinet meeting shortly, but I'll delay it. Is this Jackson available?'

'Waiting for someone to call him in Gakona.'

59

TIKAL, GUATEMALA

It was the world's greatest archaeological announcement since the discovery of the tomb of Tutankhamen. The hotel conference room, even though it seated over a hundred people, was way too small. The media conference had, perforce, been moved to the Great Plaza of Tikal, flanked by the massive Pyramid I and II: the Temple of the Great Jaguar and the Temple of the Mask.

José performed an ancient Mayan blessing and introduced Aleta as one of the finest archaeologists of the age. She stepped confidently to the microphone, which had been positioned on the steps of the North Terrace on the northern side of the plaza. Cameras flashed incessantly and television cameramen and women vied for the best shots. The broadcast beamed live to over 150 countries. Aleta had wanted to begin by thanking O'Connor, but he'd firmly dissuaded her. The game in Washington wasn't over yet, he'd warned – not by a long shot. Just before Aleta took the microphone, Rodriguez handed her a note. It read: 'Test-firing of Minuteman cancelled'.

'The warnings are stark,' Aleta emphasised, after she'd given the assembled media a short introduction to the Maya and the codex. 'And the major warnings for our civilisation concern religion and the environment,' she said, avoiding any reference to the shorter warning on the rocket launch. 'The Maya built one of the greatest civilisations the world has ever seen; but the last recorded inscription on any stelae in Tikal is dated 13 August 869 AD, and by then the city was in deep trouble. By 950 AD, the entire Mayan civilisation had collapsed. The magnificent city-states, with their countless pyramids and temples, lay totally deserted. There has been much debate in academic circles as to the reasons, and until now the real cause has not been determined.'

Aleta's flawless command of English, with its delightful Spanish lilt, echoed authoritatively from the steps of the great pyramids. Three hundred kilometres away, Monsignor Jennings watched the proceedings on his black-and-white television. He threw the empty bottle of scotch clanging into the metal wastepaper basket. 'Fucking bitch,' he muttered, reaching for another bottle.

'It is now clear,' Aleta continued, 'that despite a series of warnings to the great Mayan kings – kings like Jaguar Claw, Zero Moon Bird, Hasaw and his wife, Lady Twelve Macaw, Yax Ain II – the city-states of Tikal, Calakmul and Naranjo, the latter controlled by the powerful warrior queen, Lady Six Sky, were engaged in vicious continual conflict. Conflict that ultimately destroyed both their environment and their ability to feed themselves, and ultimately, their civilisation. The Maya Codex makes plain that we will suffer the same fate unless we change course.' Aleta paused to let the warning hang above the ancient plaza. 'As a civilisation, we, like the Mayan city-states, are fearful of difference. We fight our wars in the name of religion, be it in Northern Ireland or in the Hindu Kush of Afghanistan, and we seem unable to tolerate, let alone accept, different cultures. Pakistan, for example, is close to being a failed state, and her nuclear weapons may fall into the hands of extremists. Those extremists would think nothing of engaging in suicide bombings on a nuclear scale, all in the name of their god, Allah.' The print-media journalists scribbled furiously.

'In the United States a powerful block of forty million evangelicals subscribes to the view that Christ cannot return until all of the occupied Palestinian territories – Gaza, the West Bank – until every last square centimetre of the so-called Promised Land is returned to Israel.'

Ten thousand kilometres away, the Prefect of the Congregation for the Doctrine of the Faith, Cardinal Salvatore Felici, sat glued to the television in his opulent office in the *Palazzo della Sacra Inquisizione*.

'The Vatican has yet to release the real third warning of Fátima,' Aleta charged, 'but a single page of notes, handwritten by Sister Lúcia, has been hidden away in the Vatican's secret archives. When the Virgin Mary appeared to Lúcia in 1917, she issued a similar warning to that contained in the Maya Codex. The Virgin's warning was preceded by Saint Malachy's claim of a vision from God given to him on the Janiculum Hill above Rome in 1140, a vision that has proved to be an extraordinarily accurate forecast of who was to take the Keys of Peter, and there is every indication that the last papacy will end in December 2012.' Some of the media reached for their phones. 'Nor are the ideas of Christ unique,' Aleta declared. 'The codex makes plain that the message of how we should do the right thing by our neighbour is common to a great many religions – Christianity, Judaism, Buddhism, Islam – and if you were brought up as a child in Baghdad, it is not Christ's resurrection you would be taught to believe in, but rather the resurrection of the great Prophet Muhammad on his night journey from Mecca to Jerusalem and back again. No one can claim they have the only path. There are many paths to the Omega, as the codex makes clear, because religion is an accident of birth. If we do not learn to get along and respect our different cultures, religion will be one of the forces that destroys us.'

Cardinal Felici snapped a pencil.

'But the most strident warning in the codex concerns our treatment of the environment, because it was this, in the end, that destroyed the mighty Mayan civilisation and forced them to abandon their cities. The conference in Copenhagen, like every environmental conference before it, was an abject failure, yet the evidence of dramatic changes in weather patterns is there for everyone to see. The Maya Codex is clear: if we don't change course, the sceptics who advocate protection of jobs will find there are no jobs left to protect. Finally,' Aleta said, 'the Maya Codex is quite clear about the coming confluence of our solar system with a supermassive black hole at the centre of the Milky Way.' There was a look of expectation on the face of every journalist in the plaza. 'NASA has confirmed the ancient astronomers were right, down to the last second. Added to that, the scientific evidence is clear that the earth's magnetic field is now at its lowest strength in recorded history, and the poles are moving across the wastes of the Arctic and Antarctic at over thirty kilometres a year. Sunspot power is rising dramatically, and will peak in 2012, but I would caution against extreme action.'

Arana nodded knowingly from where he was standing beside O'Connor near the base of Pyramid I.

'Governments should instead put in place plans for a possible pole shift, and issues such as the effect on communications should be addressed; that is only prudent. Governments should also ensure that our knowledge banks are stored in the ether, that hardware backups are secured on higher ground, and that plans for evacuation from coastal areas are developed and rehearsed. But again, I would warn against any alarmist action, because my dear friends amongst the Mayan elders have a different view.' Aleta turned to acknowledge José and the other elders and warriors.

'The elders are aware that 21 December 2012 will open a spiritual portal – a portal of great energy and hope, but it will only be accessible to individuals who are prepared to reassess their priorities, those committed to a more peaceful, calmer existence. The portal will also be accessible to powerful countries, but only those countries which realign their foreign policies towards a fairer and more balanced view of the world, and encourage their citizens towards not tolerance, but *acceptance* of different cultures. If that happens, there is great hope. If not, the codex is very clear. We will suffer the same fate as the powerful Maya.'

The Mayan warriors stood guard outside O'Connor and Aleta's chalet. Inside, José was taking his leave.

'We can't thank you enough, José,' Aleta said, her eyes moist as she kissed the shaman on both cheeks.

'It is enough that you have recovered the codex,' he replied, shaking O'Connor's hand. 'Although I fear the world will debate this for a short time, just as they have climate change, and the media will move on. When that happens, remember the Inca,' he said enigmatically. And with that, he was gone.

'Are we in the clear?' Aleta asked.

O'Connor shook his head. 'Washington will deny any knowledge of CIA involvement here, and of the experiments in Gakona. That's standard procedure. Deny and deny and keep denying in the hope the media will lose interest, until incontrovertible evidence surfaces that demands a retraction. There are powerful forces in Washington who still want my guts for garters, and as long as Wiley's still alive and kicking, he won't rest until he's silenced me.'

'And me. So what do we do now?'

'I've got some old friends in Mossad. They're getting close to von Heißen's trail in Peru, which coincidentally, is the home of the Inca. There's a cargo ship leaving Puerto Quetzal in two days' time, and the captain's an atheist.'

'Single bunks?'

'Double bed.'

'Count me in.'

AUTHOR'S NOTE AND ACKNOWLEDGEMENTS

On a sultry day in February 2008, I flew back from the highland jungles of Guatemala, and into Guatemala City. Because of cultural celebrations, it had been hard to find accommodation in the city centre. Instead, I finished up in a delightful hotel, the Vista Real: an oasis of fountains and gardens in the hills above the city opposite the Agua and Fuego volcanoes. The next morning, the hotel's equally delightful staff were gracious in their accommodation of my less-than-perfect Spanish. They assured me, '*Sí, señor. Será bien.*' All would be well. Someone would come for me. A short while later, a black vehicle pulled up in the driveway and a man came into the foyer.

'*¿ Señor d'Hagé? Jerónimo Lancerio. Mucho gusto.*'

Typical of the wonderful hospitality of the Guatemalans, the Minister for Culture himself had come up into the hills, on a very busy day in the cultural calendar, to pick me up. At Ministro Lancerio's headquarters I was given a series of briefings on Mayan culture and his department's plans for the future, which are impressive. I am deeply grateful to the Minister and his staff for their time, including Señor Tzunam B'alam. My thanks to Señor Jorge Chaclan and Charlie Hogg and his staff at Brahma Kumaris, who organised the meetings.

I am also grateful to the Nobel Laureate, Rigoberta Menchú, who provided her assistant, Aura Leticia Cuxe Pirir to facilitate translation. In 1992, Rigoberta received the Nobel Peace Prize 'in recognition of her work for social justice and ethno-cultural reconciliation based on respect for the rights of indigenous peoples'. Like the fictional Ariel Weizman, Rigoberta lost her mother and father and several members of her family at the hands of a brutal

Guatemalan military. The dark hand of the CIA has never been far from these killings, and the US School of the Americas at Fort Benning, Georgia, was at the forefront of training murderous thugs, prompting the then US President Clinton in March 1999 to express regret for the US role in Guatemala's thirty-six-year civil war, saying that Washington 'was wrong' to have supported Guatemalan security forces who tortured, kidnapped and murdered thousands of rural Mayans.

Much has been written about the coming events of 2012. The rare galactic planetary alignment is factual. Whether or not that translates into a pole shift remains to be seen, although the earth's changing magnetic field and an increase in sunspot activity may be portents. There is an alignment, too, between many of the ancient cultures. The Incas (the subject of the next book in this trilogy), the Aztecs, Hopis, Pueblo Native Americans, Cherokees (whose calendar also ends in 2012), Zulus, Maoris and the ancient Egyptians (the subject of the last book in this trilogy) all have traditions and prophecies for 2012, ranging from the apocalyptic to an increase in consciousness for those souls advanced enough to make the adjustment. Most forecast an increase in spirituality, at the expense of the dogma of religion, which would be no bad thing. The Mayan elders have not had much to say – yet, eschewing the more sensational coverage regarding 2012 such as that depicted in the recent movie, *2012*. Notwithstanding, most agree that unprecedented change is upon us, and the increase in volcanic eruptions, earthquakes, floods, wildfires and tsunamis may well be warnings that we continue to ignore. In November 1992, some of our finest minds – 1700 scientists, including *over a hundred Nobel laureates* – warned that: 'Human beings and the natural world are on a collision course. Human activities inflict harsh and often irreversible damage on the environment and on critical resources. If not checked, many of our current practices put at serious risk the future that we wish for human society and the plant and animal kingdoms, and may so alter the living world that it will be unable to sustain life in the manner that we know.' We took little notice in 1992, just as nearly twenty years later, we have failed dismally to take any action at Copenhagen. As Aleta Weizman puts it, 'The sceptics who advocate protection of jobs in front of protection of the environment will soon find there are no jobs to protect.'

The activities and characters at Gakona are fictional, but the HAARP (High Frequency Active Auroral Research Program) facility is very real, and worried scientists and environmentalists have questioned the real purpose of the facility. If it is a harmless exploration of the upper atmosphere, why is it run by US Defense? The military has long been experimenting with how the weather might be controlled. Is there a link between HAARP and the current increase in earthquakes? Scientists have also pondered the dangers the current HAARP experiments may pose, much as the experiments associated with the atomic bomb produced unmitigated catastrophes. The Castle Bravo experiment referred to in this novel was the codename for the testing of a US thermonuclear hydrogen bomb at Bikini Atoll in 1954. Without going into detail, scientists made an horrendous error when they assumed the lithium-7 isotope, which made up sixty per cent of the lithium content of the Castle Bravo bomb, would be inert. Far from inert, the lithium-7 isotope was highly fissionable, and the bomb yielded fifteen megatons – way in excess of the expected five megatons. Radioactivity was increased a thousandfold and monitoring equipment was vaporised by the blast. The crews of naval ships monitoring the tests and thousands of islanders were affected, with resultant widespread cancer. Traces of the fallout reached as far as Australia, Japan, India and parts of Europe. Like the characters, the Gakona experiments in this novel are fictional, but . . .

There are many people involved in the production of a novel, and the superb team at Penguin has been at the forefront. The delightfully forthright, yet diplomatic Bob Sessions; my publisher, Ben Ball; the unsung heroes in design, including Elissa Webb; Sally Bateman and her great PR team; and Peg McColl who, at my request, continues to woo Italian publishers (the bottle of Moët still stands, Peg). Thank you to the consultant designer, Dave Altheim, for another wonderful cover, and to Bridget Maidment and Arwen Summers for their perceptive editing. Last, but certainly not least amongst the men and women of Camberwell Road, is my editor, Belinda Byrne, whose contribution has been invaluable.

Monsignor Jennings is fictional, but sadly, there has been no shortage of Catholic 'role models' on which to base his character. That said, there are myriad Catholic priests around the world who deserve our utmost respect and affection. Nor is paedophilia confined to the Catholic Church. Priests of other denominations as well as teachers in some of our most prestigious schools have molested children and ruined countless young lives. But it is the Vatican's and the wider Catholic Church's consistent, repeated and criminal cover-up of this activity 'for the good of the Catholic Church' that puts paedophilia so deservedly in the spotlight. If the evidence that has recently (and not so recently) come to light is substantiated, the Catholic Church stands guilty of abusing human rights – the very rights it claims to uphold.

It is not widely known, but starting with Saint Peter, for the first thousand years of the Catholic Church, Catholic priests were able to marry. The charismatic Christ had absolutely nothing to say on the issue, and indeed, he enjoyed a special relationship with women. Celibacy for Catholic priests wasn't introduced until 1022, when Pope Benedict VIII banned marriages and also found it necessary to ban mistresses. A major (although not the only) factor was inheritance. The Vatican was worried that on a married priest's death, his assets would go to his family, and not the Church. A later order by Pope Innocent II forced married priests to divorce their wives, many of whom finished up destitute. Few of us (less than one per cent) are wired to be celibate, and contrary to the claims of some prominent pro-Catholic journalists, research indicates *as few as two per cent* of the clergy achieve pure celibacy. Pope Benedict XVI now has the opportunity to reverse the decision of his predecessor. That is not to say the abolition of celibacy will solve the paedophilia problem in the Catholic Church, but it would at least provide priests with a healthy, wholesome outlet for natural sex drives (both heterosexual and homosexual). The fictional Cardinal Felici protected Monsignor Jennings' criminal activities, for the good of the Catholic Church. Now there is a real-life stench emanating from a sewer in Rome, coming not from the Tiber, but from within the walls of the Vatican itself.

In writing this novel, many others outside Penguin have also provided advice, encouragement and occasional solace. To Robyn, who has seen me when the going has been at its roughest, and to Antoinette and friends, my heartfelt thanks. My agent, Clare Forster (Curtis Brown), has given unstintingly of her time, reading the manuscript and, as always, providing insightful advice; I am very lucky to have her on my team. To Kate, Nic and Patrick at the Stockmarket Café in Leura, and patrons like Stephen Measday, Guy and Jayne, Rod and Bronwyn, and the other locals who frequent the long wooden table to solve the problems of the world. To Mary Rodwell, the director and founder of ACERN, the Australian Close Encounter Resource Network, for her counsel on understanding the phenomenon of past lives. To Tom, Wendy, Jodie, Tom, Kathie, Imogen, Tegan, Judy and the rest of the staff at Megalong Books. To Caroline Ladewig, who read some of the early drafts, and provided the sort of wonderful feedback you'd expect from one who lectures in English, a very big thank you. I'm also indebted to other scholars, such as Dr José Argüelles, Dr Carl Johan Calleman, Professor Michael D. Coe, Maurice Cotterell, Barbara Hand Clow, Adrian Gilbert, John Major Jenkins, Geoff Stray, and many others. To include them all would be to footnote a novel.

Historians may note my adjustment of some of the chronology and timing of real events, particularly in Nazi Germany. That has been done to suit the plotlines, and again, any errors are mine alone.

Finally, to my two boys, David and Mark (to whom whose partner and spouse this novel is dedicated), the former a senior fireman, the latter a detective, who continue to scratch their heads as to what their father might be up to.

SOMMAIRE

MAFIA, MAFIAS

Marcelle Padovani

DÉCOUVERTES GALLIMARD
CULTURE ET SOCIÉTÉ

« Il faut se persuader, dit l'historien Enzo Ciconte, que l'histoire des mafias n'est pas un problème de pauvreté et de sous-développement mais de richesse ; que la mafia n'est pas seulement une histoire de criminels mais l'histoire de l'État ; que les mafias ne sont pas un souci du seul Mezzogiorno mais de l'Italie, de l'Europe, voire du monde ; et enfin que les mafias, qu'on le veuille ou non, ont des valeurs. » Munis de ce viatique en guise d'avertissement à ne pas tomber dans des analyses faciles, entrons donc au royaume de la mafia. Des mafias.

CHAPITRE 1

UNE MAFIA, DES MAFIAS

Des Corléonais qui se déguisent en *mafiosi* pour le carnaval… Cette photo, signée Franco Zecchin (page de gauche), raconte comment les Siciliens ont assez d'humour pour exhiber les accessoires typiques de Cosa Nostra : la *coppola* (« casquette ») et le fusil à canon scié. Ceux de la Calabre (ci-contre) glorifient les vendettas.

La 'Ndrangheta calabraise

Protégée par son image d'organisation criminelle archaïque et tranquille, vaguement médiévale dans ses méthodes, une mafia occupe aujourd'hui le devant de la scène italienne : la 'Ndrangheta de Calabre. Elle a supplanté sa consœur sicilienne Cosa Nostra aux niveaux national et international. Sa discrétion, son choix du profil bas, sa réticence à occuper la scène médiatique, joints justement à son prétendu archaïsme, lui ont permis de grandir dans l'ombre. De s'organiser et de prospérer. À l'abri des réflecteurs. En évitant autant que possible les assassinats spectaculaires « à la corléonaise », et les coups d'éclat. En ayant l'air, en somme, de ne pas payer de mine. Et pourtant… il s'agit d'une mafia extrêmement dangereuse, classée en 2008 par l'administration américaine au nombre des cinq sociétés du crime les plus redoutables dans le monde, qui gère 80 % du trafic de cocaïne.

Sa force ? Son organisation en *locali* (des groupes d'une cinquantaine d'affiliés), solidement implantés dans les zones de trafic les plus sensibles ; et sa

San Luca, cette petite ville anodine au cœur de l'Aspromonte calabrais – 4 100 habitants –, est en fait le sanctuaire de la 'Ndrangheta. D'ici partaient les ravisseurs de riches héritiers de l'Italie du Nord, et ici ils revenaient pour les cacher dans des grottes inaccessibles. En attendant que soit versée la rançon qui les libérerait. C'est ici encore que les femmes mafieuses jouaient les vivandières. C'est ici enfin que la police a découvert en 2007 un réseau de tunnels souterrains, avec chambres confortables, cuisines et frigos bien remplis, où se cachaient les *latitanti*, les « fugitifs ». Un deuxième San Luca, à 20 mètres sous terre.

réputation de fiabilité totale (car elle paye cash ses achats de drogue ou d'armes, et elle n'est pas affaiblie ou délégitimée par le phénomène des « repentis »). Sa force incontournable sur le marché de l'illégalité lui vient donc du caractère rigoureusement familial de son organisation : lorsqu'un *'ndranghetista* est coffré, il est impensable qu'il ouvre la bouche, si ce n'est pour décliner son identité, parce qu'il trahirait non seulement ses alliés et complices, mais ses proches parents, ses frères, fils ou neveux. Sa famille de sang.

La présence internationale de la 'Ndrangheta a sauté aux yeux lors du massacre de Duisbourg (15 août 2007), à cause du nombre de morts (six), de leur âge (souvent des adolescents) et du fait que les *mafiosi* aient pu agir sans aucun problème dans la très tranquille Allemagne, à plus de 2 000 kilomètres de la capitale de la 'Ndrangheta, que l'on situe à San Luca, dans la Calabre profonde. On a réalisé alors que ces Calabrais criminels avaient sérieusement investi à l'étranger (en particulier en Allemagne, avec plus de trois cents pizzerias, et en Belgique, avec un quartier entier de Bruxelles). Et on s'est souvenu que dès 1998, la 'Ndrangheta avait été impliquée dans un trafic de combustible nucléaire destiné au Zaïre, puis en 1999 dans un trafic d'armes et d'explosifs en faveur de l'IRA irlandaise, et en 2004 en faveur de l'ETA basque. Que, si elle transporte et produit de la cocaïne, c'est grâce à ses rapports privilégiés avec les AUC (Autodefensas Unidas de Colombia), le bras armé du narcotrafic colombien, et les FARC. Qu'elle est devenue en tout état de cause

Le restaurant Da Bruno, géré par des *mafiosi* calabrais à Duisbourg, est devenu célèbre le 15 août 2007, lors d'une vendetta sanglante de la 'Ndrangheta. Provoquant la stupeur des habitants qui laissent un *Warum !* (« Pourquoi ? ») sur le lieu du crime (ci-dessus), tandis que la presse allemande consacre ses unes à l'événement (ci-contre). C'est la première fois que le crime organisé calabrais venait déranger le monde ordonné germanique. Mais les enquêteurs italiens se plaignent amèrement que les autorités locales, qui n'ont pas entrepris de dessiner une carte des investissements *mafiosi* en Allemagne, aient sous-estimé la gravité de ce crime.

extrêmement savante dans l'art du recyclage. Et qu'elle a choisi d'investir dans la pierre.

Une conversation entre deux 'ndranghetistes (transcrite à partir d'une écoute téléphonique) à l'automne 1989 est révélatrice de la vocation transnationale de l'organisation. X appelle Y : « Le mur de Berlin est tombé... Vas-y... Achète tout. » « Tout quoi ? », interroge Y.

CORRIERE DELLA SERA

Il padrino, latitante da 43 anni, si nascondeva in un casolare a Corleone. La folla

Catturato il capo della mafia:

« Tout ce qui peut être acheté à l'Est... Immeubles... Hôtels... Restaurants... », réplique X.

La 'Ndrangheta est ainsi devenue la spécialiste numéro un de l'investissement immobilier. En Italie aussi. Et aussi dans la Ville éternelle. « Une grande partie des activités de service (hôtels, restaurants, etc.) est sous son contrôle à Rome », signale Vincenzo Macrì, magistrat à la Direction nationale antimafia.

Les bruits selon lesquels le restaurant La Rampa, aux pieds des escaliers de la Piazza di Spagna, et le Café de Paris, sur la Via Veneto, étaient entre ses mains, ont semé la panique dans la

Deux policiers de Palerme exposent devant les caméras les photos de leur dernière prise en 2007 (ci-dessous) : Salvatore Lo Piccolo (accompagné de son fils Sandro), qui était devenu le « parrain » de Cosa Nostra. Les deux ont été surpris lors d'un « sommet » *mafioso* à Giardinello (Palerme).

Ces visages en série illustrent l'efficacité des forces de répression. Toute la « Coupole » de Cosa Nostra est désormais sous les verrous. De gauche à droite : Bernardo Provenzano, le parrain « bucolique » qui, en fuite depuis 1963, se cachait dans une ferme de Corleone en mangeant de la chicorée sauvage et de la *ricotta* ; Giovanni Brusca,

bastardo. Grasso: protezioni politiche, indagheremo

, sono Provenzano»

capitale à la fin 2008. Quoi qu'il en soit, ces bruits confirment que la 'Ndrangheta a réussi son examen de passage du stade de mafia rurale, spécialiste en enlèvements crapuleux, à celui de holding national et international particulièrement habile au plan managérial et financier. Sur le chiffre d'affaires italien de l'illégalité, qui représenterait d'après l'institut Eurispes 9,5 % du PIB, la mafia calabraise s'adjuge 3,4 %. Or ce chiffre d'affaires frôle les 40 milliards d'euros (c'est une estimation).

La Cosa Nostra sicilienne

L'avancée foudroyante de la 'Ndrangheta sur le marché du crime s'accompagne du déclin – probablement provisoire – de sa consœur sicilienne Cosa Nostra. Car cette vénérable mafia traverse une très mauvaise passe : tous ses boss sont en taule, de Salvatore (dit Totò) Riina à Bernardo Provenzano, en passant par Leoluca Bagarella, Giovanni Brusca, Salvatore Lo Piccolo, etc. Seul manque à l'appel en ce début 2009 Matteo Messina Denaro, boss de Trapani, dont on dit qu'il devrait être le prochain parrain de l'organisation, mais il est traqué par les fins limiers du commissaire Giuseppe Linarès, qui aura tôt ou tard sa peau.

l'homme qui a appuyé sur la télécommande pour faire sauter le juge Falcone en 1992, et qui a été coffré quatre ans après; Leoluca Bagarella, killer impitoyable – 100 homicides ! –, qui était le bras droit de Totò Riina (ci-dessus), lequel sourit derrière les barreaux de sa cage lors de son premier procès à Palerme. Car même dans les situations les plus difficiles, le boss doit toujours montrer son autocontrôle.

Autre signe de crise profonde : la « Coupole », le gouvernement de Cosa Nostra, ne s'est plus réunie depuis 1993. Et l'opinion publique de son côté affiche plus volontiers son rejet avec des commerçants qui ne paient plus le *pizzo*, le « pourcentage », à Palerme et ailleurs, et le mouvement Addio pizzo qui l'accompagne. Avec aussi l'organisation patronale Confindustria qui a lancé une campagne moralisatrice contre cette pratique diffuse dans toute l'île : seront expulsés des rangs du patronat tous ceux dont il sera prouvé qu'ils continuent à verser leur obole à la mafia. Du jamais vu sous les cieux de Cosa Nostra.

   L'impression de déclin et d'isolement est confirmée par la chute libre de l'organisation mafieuse dans le trafic international de drogue, et par les tentatives, plutôt gauches, d'y remédier. Comme celle qui a conduit en 2007 en taule Salvatore Lo Piccolo, boss palermitain, au moment où il essayait de rebâtir l'Old Bridge, le « vieux pont », entre mafia sicilienne et mafia américaine, pour renouer ensemble le fil perdu du bon vieux

Le visage transfiguré « à la Andy Warhol » (ci-dessous) de Matteo Messina Denaro, le dernier parrain...

À Palerme, les *ragazzi* (« jeunes gens ») d'Addio pizzo (« Adieu le pourcentage ») célèbrent à leur façon la capture des Lo Piccolo, le 5 novembre 2007 (ci-contre). Leur mouvement est né en 2004 pour stopper les extorsions, le racket et les « pourcentages », que, d'après les magistrats, 80 % des commerçants de la capitale sicilienne versent à Cosa Nostra. Leur slogan : « Un peuple qui verse le

trafic de stupéfiants. L'état d'âme du *mafioso* s'en ressent. Et Matteo Messina Denaro peut ainsi envoyer en 2004 un *pizzino* (« petit mot ») désespéré à son boss de l'époque, Bernardo Provenzano : « Vous me demandez un plaisir à Marsala... mais je ne peux vous aider, parce qu'ici les coups de bâton pleuvent, et je crois qu'à la fin "ils" arrêteront même les chaises quand "ils" auront fini d'arrêter les personnes... » Cette mafia à genoux, les « os brisés », comme dit à son tour le « repenti » Antonino Giuffrè dans ses confessions à la police, semble sur le point de disparaître. « Certains de nos amis, ajoute Giuffrè, ont pensé "rendons les armes et n'en parlons plus", l'organisation doit être dissoute »...

Mais il ne faudrait pas trop s'apitoyer sur le blues de l'homme d'honneur. Oui, Cosa Nostra est en crise, mais Cosa Nostra n'est pas finie. On peut être sûr qu'elle restera à l'avenir loin de la *coppola* (la typique casquette mafieuse), des figuiers de Barbarie et de la *lupara*, le fusil à canon scié. Loin donc des accessoires et du folklore qui firent, d'une certaine façon, sa gloire. Et plus tard sa disgrâce.

pizzo est un peuple sans dignité. » Et un autre : « Contre le *pizzo*, change tes consommations. » Il s'agit donc pour eux d'inciter les Siciliens à une consommation critique, en les invitant à s'approvisionner dans les magasins *free pizzo*, qui affichent l'autocollant ci-dessus.

Mais il est plus que prématuré de fêter son enterrement, ne fût-ce que parce que Cosa Nostra a mis sur pied un modèle parfait, extrêmement cartésien, d'organisation criminelle. Valable sous tous les cieux.

La Camorra napolitaine

Des quatre mafias actuellement existantes dans la Péninsule, une autre profite de l'effacement provisoire de Cosa Nostra : la Camorra napolitaine. Cette nouvelle mafia – pas si nouvelle par bien des aspects – traverse une phase de protagonisme aigu, sanguinaire et impitoyable, que l'écrivain Roberto Saviano a fait connaître dans le monde avec son *Gomorra*. Réussissant à focaliser l'attention sur les petits groupes de boss-managers, agents recruteurs d'ados prêts à tout, qui valorisent la structuration horizontale de leur organisation et sont devenus des experts en terreur sur leur territoire. Conséquences de cette focalisation médiatique : les forces de l'ordre ont concentré, avec un certain succès,

Les ordures (ci-dessus, une plage de Naples envahie de déchets) sont l'un des principaux business de la Camorra : Roberto Saviano l'a révélé dans *Gomorra* (ci-dessous, couverture de la première édition italienne).

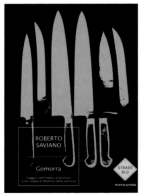

leur attention sur le groupe émergent des Casalesi, les camorristes de Casal di Principe, qui ont d'ailleurs juré l'élimination physique de Saviano : imitateurs de la Cosa Nostra du temps des Corléonais, ils jouent au massacre tout en s'insérant dans toutes les sources de profit, dont le stockage et le transport des ordures. Cette double face leur permet de pratiquer l'intimidation violente d'un côté et, de l'autre, la poursuite de rapports juteux avec le monde politique local, parfois même dans les rangs de la gauche, car il est devenu difficile, dans les hautes sphères du pouvoir, de distinguer entre un manager-killer et un manager-comme il faut. C'est l'aspect le plus déconcertant et le plus dur à combattre de cette Camorra assassine, qui flirte en complet veston avec le décisionnisme des administrateurs locaux.

Mais cette organisation n'est plus la représentante des intérêts de la plèbe napolitaine, ce qu'elle sut être au début de son existence. Elle est devenue « Le Système », c'est-à-dire quelque chose d'impitoyable, de rationnel et d'organisé, qui a réussi à provoquer plus de 3 600 morts en vingt-six ans, comme dit

Ces poids lourds qui descendent vers Siculiana (en haut) illustrent les ambitions de la Camorra : elle ne se contente plus d'empoisonner Naples (ci-dessus, couverture de *L'Espresso* du 11 septembre 2008), mais rêve d'étendre son influence jusqu'aux terres siciliennes.

Saviano. Une sorte de criminalité du IIIᵉ millénaire, qui se marie harmonieusement avec la branche gagnante de la nouvelle économie. Quiconque déboule à Secondigliano, à dix minutes du centre de Naples, pourrait croire qu'il va rencontrer la misère absolue. Or il se trouve au cœur du marché, justement, de la nouvelle économie. Le port reçoit chaque jour des dizaines de conteneurs remplis de montres, vêtements, jeux vidéo, qui iront se répandre dans toute l'Europe, mais sur lesquels

Tout le Mezzogiorno (en couleurs) est contaminé par les mafias. Seule la Basilicate (en beige) semble échapper à la contagion. La plus connue et la plus organisée est Cosa Nostra. La plus récente et la plus internationale, la 'Ndrangheta, tient

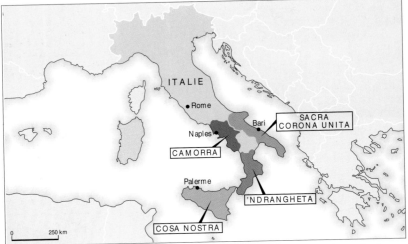

il est rare que les droits de douane aient été payés (1 600 000 tonnes de marchandises y débarquent chaque année rien que de la Chine).

C'est donc au port que commence l'aventure économique du « Système ». De moins en moins provinciale, cette criminalité particulièrement violente est infiltrée également dans les travaux publics, les investissements immobiliers, les extorsions, la drogue et les jeux de hasard. Ses boss ont pour modèle « les brokers américains, pas Al Capone », comme dit le journaliste napolitain Franco Mancusi. Ou bien les héros des films de Tarantino. L'un d'eux, Walter Schiavone, a voulu qu'on lui construise une villa fastueuse,

la Calabre; et la plus « cinématographique » et désordonnée, la Camorra, la Campanie – la Sacra Corona Unita des Pouilles étant plus marginale. Toutes ont en commun d'exploiter systématiquement les sources de profit : pizzo, usure, trafic d'armes, de stupéfiants et d'êtres humains. Sans oublier les fraudes à la Communauté européenne, les appels d'offres et les sous-traitances.

"Ormai tutta l'Italia è invasa dalla mafia"

sur l'exemple de celle du gangster cubain de Miami, Tony Montana, dans le film *Scarface*. Un délire architectonique avec des escaliers majestueux, typiquement hollywoodiens. Le style de consommation des gens du « Système » se doit lui aussi d'être somptueux.

C'est sans doute la force et la limite de la Camorra, cette organisation sans hiérarchie et sans « Coupole », polycentrique et multiforme – 236 groupes recensés ! –, extrêmement moderne. Elle qui était née sous la protection espagnole au XVIIᵉ siècle (le mot *camorra* pourrait venir de *gamurri*, la veste courte des bandits espagnols, ou encore de *morra*, qui signifie « regroupement de malfaiteurs »). Ces agrégations fluides, réfractaires à toute organisation centralisée – les tentatives de centralisation avec la NCO (Nuova Camorra Organizzata), puis avec la NF (Nuova Famiglia) et enfin avec la NMC (Nuova Mafia Campana) ont toutes échoué –, passeront donc à l'histoire avec leur chiffre d'affaires malgré tout consistant : 12,5 milliards d'euros (estimation de l'institut Eurispes).

La Sacra Corona Unita des Pouilles

La quatrième mafia qui a sévi dans la Péninsule en ce début de millénaire s'appelle la Sacra Corona Unita. Née dans les Pouilles, elle s'était spécialisée dans le trafic d'êtres humains, dans les années 1990, au moment du débarquement en Italie de masses d'Albanais qui fuyaient leur patrie parce qu'ils avaient faim. La Sacra Corona traverse aujourd'hui une phase de repli, due surtout aux accords de coopération sur l'immigration signés entre l'Italie et l'Albanie.

Il ne faut pas croire que l'emprise mafieuse n'existe qu'au sud de Rome. Déjà en 1990 (ci-contre, l'interview du juge Falcone à *La Repubblica*), les responsables de l'Antimafia dénonçaient la diffusion généralisée du phénomène criminel dans l'ensemble de la Péninsule. Milan, par exemple, est considérée comme la deuxième capitale de la 'Ndrangheta après San Luca. Rome pullule d'investissements 'ndranghetistes, comme Rimini, Bologne, Florence ou encore Tranto (en bas, titre le *La Republica*). Avec cette conséquence paradoxale qu'un jour le *made in Italy* risque de se confondre avec le *made by mafia*.

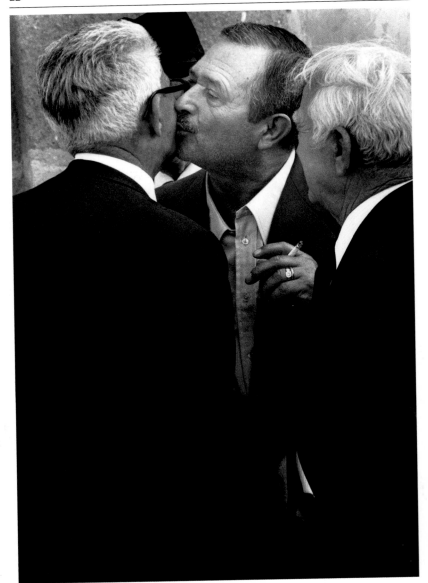

Les modalités d'action des différentes mafias répondent à des caractéristiques analogues : le recours habituel à la violence comme méthode de gouvernement ; la pratique de l'*omertà* comme règle d'étanchéité de l'« organisation » ; l'offre de protection aux populations en échange de leur silence, avec son corollaire du « contrôle du territoire » ; l'utilisation de codes et rituels comparables pour l'affiliation ; la capacité à s'insérer dans les affaires légales grâce aux liens privilégiés entretenus avec le pouvoir ; la pratique d'un certain langage.

CHAPITRE 2

LE MODÈLE MAFIA

Les photographes (page de gauche, un cliché de Franco Zecchin) ont contribué à l'étude de la « phénoménologie » de la mafia : en croquant les contacts corps à corps, les baisers entre hommes, si typiques de la mafiosité. À droite, une carte postale de 1901 des trois larrons : le brigand calabrais, le camorriste et le *mafioso*.

Naissance de la mafia en Sicile au temps des Bourbons

Au début du XIXᵉ siècle, lorsque prend fin le système féodal que les Normands avaient instauré au XIᵉ siècle et qui permettait à la noblesse sicilienne de défendre ses privilèges et de rendre la justice sur ses terres comme si la royauté n'avait jamais existé, les « barons », désarçonnés par leur perte de légitimité, embauchent une force clandestine violente, les futurs *mafiosi*, pour surveiller leurs propriétés, les *feudi*. Et les tenir à l'abri du banditisme et des ambitions des paysans (qui ont « faim de terre »). C'est dire combien cette abolition de la féodalité a laissé désarmée et sans autorité la noblesse rurale, habituée depuis des siècles à se comporter à sa guise sur ses *latifondi* et à y régner comme seule et unique détentrice de l'autorité, même si théoriquement c'était le vice-roi qui gouvernait depuis Palerme.

Les Branciforte étaient de vrais seigneurs à Mazzarino, province de Caltanisetta, et leur noblesse remonte au roi Frédéric II. Leur forteresse (au sommet de cette miniature, ci-dessous) est encore visible aujourd'hui, ainsi que le château de Mazzarino, du XIVᵉ siècle.

Les hommes en armes que les barons embauchent et qui sont donc des salariés du *feudo*, défendront la propriété avec une grande efficacité, jusqu'à en devenir progressivement les maîtres véritables : ainsi est née la mafia. Avec déjà un rôle ambigu : la défense des droits légitimes des propriétaires à profiter de leurs biens, mêlée à la volonté de s'accaparer, y compris par l'intimidation et la violence, ces mêmes biens.

Les origines de la Camorra et de la 'Ndrangheta

Un phénomène équivalent se retrouve en Campanie et en Calabre où Camorra et 'Ndrangheta s'affirment à la même époque pour leur capacité à rendre la justice dans la situation très mouvementée du

Mais les nobles ont cessé d'être le pivot de la société sicilienne, avec leurs richesses inouïes et la puissance de leurs dynasties. On en retrouve des traces dans le roman *I Vicerè* (*Les Vice-Rois*), publié en 1894 par Federico de Roberto, et dans des films comme *Le Guépard*, touné par Visconti en 1963. Le bras armé de la noblesse a toujours été le *campiere* (page de droite, en bas).

PER MIRACOLO IL CARABINIERE LANZA SALVA IL CONTE MAGRI 24 MAGGIO 1867

Mezzogiorno pendant les décennies qui précèdent l'unité italienne. Il faut se souvenir que le brigandage est né en Calabre après l'unité (1861). Financé par les Bourbons, il a assumé très vite les caractéristiques d'une lutte des classes paysannes avec des formes anarchisantes. C'est sur les cendres du brigandage que naîtront les 'ndrine – cellules de base de la 'Ndrangheta – pour protéger, comme en Sicile, les privilèges des propriétaires terriens. Ces 'ndrine prendront de plus en plus d'importance dans les latifondi, poussant le capomafia, « chef de mafia », à jouer un rôle de juge de paix, qui intervient pour défendre l'honneur des femmes, avec tout ce qu'il faut de mariages réparateurs en cas de besoin, et pour régler tous les litiges de propriété ou de voisinage. S'enracine ainsi dans les couches populaires l'idée que les mafias sont nées pour secourir les faibles contre toutes les injustices. Et le phénomène mafieux deviendra progressivement un élément structurel de l'histoire de la Péninsule. Parce qu'il n'est évidemment pas seulement un phénomène criminel, mais offre une structure valable d'ascension sociale et d'accumulation de la richesse. Une structure qui joue le rôle de l'État, suppléant sa carence, dans les régions méridionales.

Dans l'imagerie populaire, l'ex-voto (à gauche) est un mélange de superstition et de rationalisme. Ici, un brigand, qui avait braqué son pistolet sur un couple, est arrêté par un carabinier, le 24 mai 1867... mais celui qui sauve miraculeusement le couple est en fait saint Sébastien, l'État n'étant que son instrument... On retrouve donc même dans ces peintures naïves la fameuse méfiance sicilienne envers les institutions. Les ex-voto sont en tout cas des remerciements vibrants qui tapissent encore de nombreuses églises.

La mafia, un pouvoir légitime ?

Le mot *mafia*, qui signifie « beauté », « perfection »,
« excellence » – d'après le sociologue sicilien
Giuseppe Pitrè, on dit à Palerme d'une fille qu'elle
est *mafiusa, mafiusedda*, pour signifier qu'elle est
belle, ou même d'un balai qu'il est *mafioso* pour
signifier qu'il est fonctionnel –, le mot, donc, a dès le
départ une connotation positive. Viendront ensuite
les explications de type économique et moral pour
justifier l'extraordinaire tolérance des populations
méridionales à l'égard de leurs organisations
criminelles. Ici, on ne peut que s'attarder
sur le rapport mafia-État, qui est la clé
de lecture la plus convaincante de la
prolifération, de la durée et de la force

Les *campieri* ont
continué jusqu'aux
années 1950 à tourner
autour des *latifondi*
pour les protéger
contre toute intrusion
(ci-dessous, en Sicile).

des mafias italiennes. Et sur le fait que des régions entières font plus confiance au gouvernement criminel qu'aux institutions légales. Au point que « l'histoire de la mafia a pu se confondre avec celle de l'État », comme le soutient Ciconte.

L'écrivain Andrea Camilleri raconte que son grand-père, qui possédait au début du siècle dernier deux mines de soufre dans la province d'Agrigente, confiait chaque semaine la paye des mineurs en argent liquide à un homme à cheval, qui traversait tranquillement, sans problème, des passages montagneux exposés et dangereux. Un inconnu, ou plutôt plusieurs inconnus accompagnaient discrètement son voyage, signalant par un sifflement que la voie était libre. Pas de police. Pas de carabiniers. Pas de gardes du corps. « Les siffleurs, dit Camilleri, étaient des *mafiosi* rémunérés par mon grand-père pour protéger ce parcours hebdomadaire. Des *mafiosi* qui garantissaient la régularité de leur paye aux travailleurs. C'était déjà un système qui remplaçait l'État. »

Parmi les créateurs se consacrant à la figuration populaire de la mafia, une mention spéciale revient à Mimmo Cuticchio, marionnettiste et peintre de rideaux de scène tel ce *Beati Paoli*, réalisé en 1987 (ci-dessus). Les Beati, qui ont encore un siège derrière l'église de Santa Maria del Gesù à Palerme, seraient nés au XIIe siècle pour s'opposer à la justice officielle des rois et des seigneurs. Leur lieu d'élection : les souterrains de la capitale sicilienne, où ils prononçaient des sentences sans appel, immédiatement exécutoires. Le livre *I Beati Paoli*, de Luigi Natoli (1909), réédité en 1971 avec une préface d'Umberto Eco, aide à comprendre pourquoi les Beati peuvent être considérés comme les ancêtres de la mafia.

*Briganti di Barile
(colà condannati alle)
prigioni.*

Le phénomène des brigands (ci-contre, la « bande à Barile ») est étroitement lié à la crise économique dans le Mezzogiorno. Certains groupes anticléricaux et antiroyalistes subventionnaient au XIXᵉ siècle ces bandes et les lançaient contre l'armée régulière. Elles furent durement réprimées, jusqu'à ce que la Commission parlementaire d'enquête de 1863 mette en évidence les causes sociales du brigandage. En Sicile, les brigands se retrouvèrent vite aux côtés de la mafia contre l'État-ennemi (en bas, les cadavres des chefs de bande Leone et Rinaldi, « recomposés » après leur exécution).

Banda Barile

Capibanda siciliani

e NALDI

Antonino Leone
da Ventimiglia (Termini Imerese)

Placido Rinaldi
da S. Mauro Castelverde

Des dizaines d'exemples, même plus récents, tendent à accréditer le rôle « étatique » de Cosa Nostra. Le journaliste Francesco La Licata raconte comment une de ses tantes, en graves difficultés économiques dans les années 1970, va mettre ses bijoux au mont-de-piété de Palerme. Elle doit les retirer un an après. Or elle se présente au mont un an plus tard avec une demi-heure de retard par rapport à l'échéance. Le fonctionnaire la renvoie : « Trop tard ! » La femme rentre chez elle en sanglots et va pleurer chez sa voisine, qui lui dit : « Ne t'inquiète pas, on va chez Don Carlo. » Don Carlo est un homme débonnaire qui trône en débardeur du côté de la Vucciria. Il écoute. Il dit : « Revenez demain. » Et le lendemain il lui donne ses bijoux, en réclamant seulement la somme qu'elle aurait légalement dû verser la veille pour rentrer en leur possession. Qui osera dire que Don Carlo n'a pas agi comme un État intelligent, face à un État légal, insensible et aveugle ?

Le raisonnement est identique du côté de la Camorra et de la 'Ndrangheta, qui fait dire à l'anthropologue napolitain Marino Niola qu'il est tout à fait compréhensible que les populations se rangent « du côté du plus fort » : « Si la légalité offrait des avantages, les Napolitains, et les Calabrais, seraient de son côté. Or la légalité ne parvient pas à convaincre qu'elle est plus avantageuse : l'ordre public est garanti plus par les camorristes que par les forces de police ; les offres de travail et d'ascension sociale viennent plus de la société du crime que des bureaux d'embauche ; les jeunes enfin trouvent dans les organisations criminelles un employeur et

Les habitants des *bassi* (« bas quartiers ») du centre historique de Palerme (ci-dessous, photo signée Ferdinando Scianna) étaient dans les années 1960 aussi prolifiques que misérables. Mais la dureté de la vie et le spectacle répété de la mort ont continué bien après de faire partie du quotidien dans la capitale sicilienne.

un modèle culturel en harmonie avec la société de consommation. Car le boss est riche et a du succès même auprès des femmes. »

Si les « gens du Nord » peuvent diagnostiquer une faiblesse dans le rapport connivent des « gens du Sud » avec les mafias, il faudrait leur expliquer qu'en l'absence de l'État le Méridional ne se sent protégé que s'il fait partie d'un clan, d'une association, d'une secte, d'une loge ou d'une mafia ; que l'État, les rares fois où il se manifeste dans le Mezzogiorno, se présente généralement comme un ennemi de la population locale ; et enfin que la mort n'a pas au Sud la même valeur qu'ailleurs. On y flirte avec la mort, la mort violente, plus naturellement que dans le reste de la Péninsule. Un jeune aspirant camorriste racontait à Roberto Saviano : « Tous ceux que je connais sont morts ou ont fini en taule. Je veux devenir un boss. Je veux avoir des supermarchés, des usines, des femmes. Et puis je veux mourir. Mais comme un homme vrai, quelqu'un qui commande vraiment. Je veux mourir assassiné. »

Si l'enfance peut jouer à mimer la guerre mafieuse (ci-dessous, à Catane, en 1982, photo de Franco Zecchin), elle est vite rattrapée par les terrifiants drames de la réalité : par exemple, par les homicides, « exquis » ou non, qui peuplent la vie de tous les jours. « Celui qui naît dans une famille mafieuse, ou plus simplement dans un contexte où la prédominance de la mafia est forte, subit dès l'enfance l'influence des modèles criminels. Ces enfants vivent une violence formatrice. » C'est Don Luigi Ciotti, fondateur de l'association Libera, qui parle.

Cosa Nostra, le modèle d'organisation criminelle

Le *sentire mafioso* – cette façon d'être en harmonie avec les valeurs du monde mafieux – a débouché sur la formulation d'un véritable modèle d'organisation criminelle, signé Cosa Nostra. Car Cosa Nostra est structurée de manière cartésienne et rationnelle. Chaque famille mafieuse (composée du « chef de famille », du « sous-chef », du « conseiller », du *capo decina* – « chef de dizaine » –, et des « soldats » ou « hommes d'honneur ») forme un *mandamento*, qui a un siège de droit à la « Commission interprovinciale », ou « Coupole », de Cosa Nostra. Le chef de famille et le conseiller sont élus démocratiquement. La Commission provinciale est composée de tous les *capi mandamento*, qui en élisent le chef, le sous-chef et le « secrétaire » (celui qui s'occupe des rendez-vous de la Commission). Son rôle est de permettre un équilibre entre les affaires des différentes familles, d'éviter que l'une ne déborde sur les intérêts des autres. On y délibère

Les contacts entre hommes, visages rapprochés, corps contre corps, sont considérés comme typiques de la mafiosité (ci-dessous, la procession des Mystères à Trapani en 1984, photo de Franco Zecchin). Giuseppe Pitrè, fin observateur des mœurs siciliennes de la fin du XIXᵉ siècle, y ajoutait un code de communication particulier, fait de silences et de gestes. Pour dire « non », une légère contraction de l'angle gauche de la bouche suffit. Pour dire « rien », il faut passer l'ongle du pouce sur les dents supérieures. Pour dire « faire l'amour », il suffit de se lécher la pulpe du majeur…

Palerme
- Descendants Lo Piccolo
- Capizzi
- Lo Presti

Messine
- Clans de Mistretta et Barcellona

Catane
- Familles Santapaola et Ercolano

Trapani
- Matteo Messina Denaro

Syracuse
- Nardo
- Bottaro

Raguse
- Le Stidde

0   50 km

Le territoire sicilien est tapissé de familles mafieuses, avec une forte prépondérance dans les provinces de Palerme, Catane et Trapani. On estime à 5 000 le nombre total des hommes d'honneur. « Une petite armée », disait Giovanni Falcone, soulignant qu'ils sont aussi appelés « soldats ». Tout le pouvoir dans l'« organisation » prend sa source dans le « chef de famille », appelé aussi « représentant ». C'est lui qui choisit les soldats et leurs *capi-decina* qui les encadrent par groupe de dix. Au-dessus, le *capo-mandamento*, ou chef de circonscription, qui a un rôle de coordination provinciale. Encore au-dessus : le parrain avec sa Commission interprovinciale ou « Coupole », sorte de gouvernement de l'île.

des grands choix et on y décide des homicides « exquis », comme celui du juge Giovanni Falcone.

Cette structure, extrêmement fonctionnelle et assez démocratique, a été officialisée en 1984 par les confessions du « repenti » Tommaso Buscetta au juge Falcone. On a compris alors qu'à côté de l'État légal il y avait cette Coupole, ce gouvernement occulte, infiniment plus efficace pour le contrôle du territoire – pas de vols ni de hold-up qui troublent la sérénité des populations, les seuls crimes autorisés étant ceux programmés par Cosa Nostra –, plus rapide et expéditif pour rendre la justice – ses sentences sont sans appel –, et plus équilibré, au fond, sur le thème de la solidarité (avec, par exemple, le chèque mensuel versé aux familles des hommes d'honneur en prison). On a alors réalisé que la mafia, ce n'était pas seulement le trafic de drogue et les règlements de compte, le racket et le pompage des ressources publiques, mais aussi un tissu socio-économique et un monde de « valeurs » qui offrent des garanties et des opportunités aux populations.

Il suffit pour s'en rendre compte de lire les *pizzini* qu'échangeaient dans les années 2000 les « parrains », même pour résoudre de petits problèmes quotidiens. Untel demande à son boss de référence, au nom d'un pâtissier ami qui cherche

Commission ou «Coupole»

Représentants

Chefs de famille

Hommes d'honneur ou «soldats»

de la bonne *ricotta* pour ses *cassate*, l'adresse d'un berger de confiance. Un autre cherche à ravitailler son supermarché avec une marque de détergents de bonne qualité. Ces *pizzini* sont une mine d'informations révélatrices du réseau parallèle constitué par la mafia. On y traite également de problèmes sentimentaux, de coups de pouce, de requêtes d'un bon hôpital ou d'une bonne faculté pour y faire étudier les enfants. On y prodigue les conseils affectueux, comme cet homme d'honneur qui écrit au fils du boss Salvatore Lo Piccolo, en 2006 : « Pense à bien couvrir mon parrain, maintenant qu'il fait froid, le soir quand il s'endort devant la télé. »

l'importo' era, un mil
andati via e non har
può vedere se si pos

De précieux *pizzini* – ces petits mots pliés et repliés pour échanger entre *capi* et faire converger sur le « boss des boss » toute information utile – ont été retrouvés chez

La correspondance par *pizzini* portés au boss par une personne de confiance est une garantie supplémentaire d'étanchéité. Surtout depuis la répression féroce qui a menacé l'existence même de Cosa Nostra. Pas de téléphones. Pas de portables qui peuvent être mis sous écoute. Seulement des petits mots archaïques qui voyagent dans les poches d'un ou deux fidèles, et reviennent à la case départ avec la réponse du parrain. Matteo Messina Denaro, boss de Trapani, entretenait ainsi avec Provenzano une intense correspondance. Il explique dans un *pizzino* daté de mai 2004 : « La personne qui vous portera mes lettres est un parent, je l'appellerai dorénavant 121. »

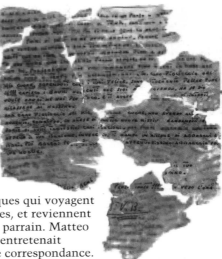

Salvatore Lo Piccolo ou encore Provenzano, qui les gardait dans une valise dans sa ferme de Corleone (ci-dessus). Pour rendre encore plus imperméable Cosa Nostra, les *pizzini* étaient chiffrés : à chaque nombre correspondait un homme d'honneur (page de droite).

Autres modèles

Les autres sociétés criminelles péninsulaires ne sont pas arrivées à ce point de perfection organisationnelle. La structure de la 'Ndrangheta, par exemple, est à l'opposé de celle de Cosa Nostra : non homogène, non pyramidale, non dirigée par un chef incontesté, chaque *'ndrina* ayant

```
do e seicento milioni. Sono
dato niente. Se   per favore
o recuperare queste cose.
```

Près de San Luca, en Calabre, à 865 mètres d'altitude, se tient chaque 2 septembre, la fête de la Madonna dei Polsi : fête religieuse très courue depuis le XVIIᵉ siècle,

son activité sur son territoire et l'organisant à sa guise. La hiérarchie veut cependant que le *mammasantissima* joue un rôle de boss, avec son « comptable », son « maître de journée », son *puntarolo* (« celui qui a été piqué » et ses « camorristes ». À la base de chaque *'ndrina*, il y a les *picciotti*, « jeunes d'honneur », qui obéissent aux ordres. L'ensemble des *'ndrine* s'appelle aussi *onorata società*, sorte de confédération souple qui n'aura jamais la rigidité de la Coupole de Cosa Nostra. Chaque année au mois de septembre, les *'ndrine* se réunissent pour la fête de la Madonna dei Polsi.

A 5.	B 4.	C 3.	D 2.	E 1.	F 6.	G 7.	H 8
I 9.	L 10.	M 15.	N 14.	O 13.	P 12		
Q 11.	R 16.	S 17.	T 18.	U 19.	V 20		
Z 21					84		

fête mafieuse aussi, car elle est généralement suivie d'une rencontre au sommet des *'ndrine*, pour y discuter business. La police y est très présente aussi.

C'est donc le caractère territorial de l'organisation qui domine en Calabre, territorial et familial, avec ses *locali* d'une cinquantaine d'adhérents, qui restent l'unité fondamentale d'agrégation. Dans un *locale*, on peut trouver plusieurs familles de sang autour d'une famille dominante, dont les liens sont généralement renforcés par des pratiques endogamiques.

La 'Ndrangheta a des codes écrits, par exemple le jurement (ci-dessous) du nouveau « frère », qui s'engage à rester fidèle et à n'adhérer à aucune autre organisation.

Les mariages n'étant qu'un moyen de sceller des alliances, résoudre des conflits et éviter des vendettas. Le modèle organisationnel de la 'Ndrangheta reproduit donc celui des sociétés patriarcales, où la famille demeure la cellule primaire.

GIURAMENTO - DEL - NUOVO - FRATELLO -
D. GIURO - SOPRA - QUESTA - ARMA - E- DI-
FRONTE - A: QUESTI - FRATELLI - DI-NON-
PARTECIPARE - A - NESSUNA - SOCIETA - E-
A - NESSUNA - ORGANIZZAZIONE - TRANNE
AL - SACRO - VANGELO - GIURO - DI - ESSERE -
FEDELE - DIVIDENDO - SORTE - E - VITA -
CON - I - MIEI - SACRI - FRATELLI.

Son expansion horizontale a montré ses limites lors des « guerres » et des *faide* (« conflits ») entre familles, qui ont abouti au massacre de Duisbourg.

Autre grande différence avec Cosa Nostra : la 'Ndrangheta fait usage depuis toujours – et pas seulement dans des *pizzini* – de codes écrits. Le premier remonte à 1888, contient 17 articles et déjà une formule de jurement entre « frères de sang ». Les guerres ou conflits internes ont été longs, exténuants, et on ne sait pas encore si la *pax mafiosa* qui a suivi le massacre de Duisbourg sera durable, ni si la tentative de confédérer sérieusement les intérêts divergents des *'ndrine* a obtenu de vrais résultats.

Entrer dans la « carrière »...

Les analogies de toute façon restent grandes pour ce qui regarde le bagage « culturel » et organisationnel des *mafiosi*. Et d'abord sur le comment on entre dans la mafia. Contrairement à la légende, il n'est pas facile de devenir un homme d'honneur, ni à Palerme ni à Reggio de Calabre (à Naples, le problème est un peu différent). L'impétrant doit avoir fait ses preuves, montré son sang-froid et son habileté à manier les armes, et sa capacité

à exécuter les ordres sans rechigner ni discuter. Avoir commis un homicide sur commande est une bonne carte de visite. Le jour du baptême, en général dans une salle discrète, si possible à la campagne, les hommes de la « Famille » mafieuse sont réunis. Le candidat est introduit, on lui perce le doigt (pouce ou index), on lui met une image pieuse dans la main à laquelle on donne le feu. Le candidat passe l'image en flammes d'une main dans l'autre jusqu'à ce qu'elle se réduise en cendres, en murmurant : « Que mes chairs brûlent comme cette image si je ne respecte pas mon serment. » Il s'est implicitement engagé à « défendre les faibles et les opprimés », à « aider les autres », à « venger dans le sang les offenses reçues » et à « garder le silence le plus absolu, sous peine de mort, sur tout ce qui concerne l'"organisation" ».

Lorsque Matteo Garrone tourne *Gomorra* en 2007, d'après le roman de Roberto Saviano, personne n'aurait imaginé qu'il rencontrerait un tel succès. C'est son côté documentaire qui frappera le public, et le fait que la plupart des acteurs sont des adolescents de Naples. Celui qu'on voit au premier plan (ci-dessous) a d'ailleurs eu depuis des soucis avec la justice. Un autre est tombé dans un guet-apens camorriste. Il n'avait pas 17 ans.

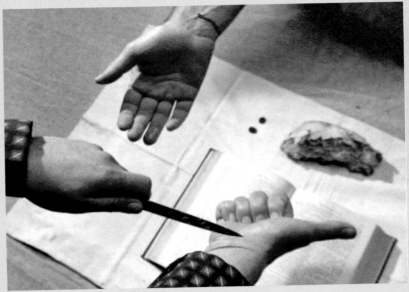

Dans la Camorra, comme le raconte Roberto Saviano, entre 12 et 17 ans, une simple accolade ou une main serrée suffisent pour devenir membre de l'organisation. Pour les plus âgés, il y a un peu plus de pathos. Raffaele Cutolo, lorsqu'il fonde la Nuova Camorra Organizzata (NCO), déclare, en bénissant le lieu de réunion de la NCO : « Je baptise cet endroit comme le baptisèrent nos trois vieux ancêtres Osso, Mastrosso et Carcagnosso. » L'entrée dans l'« O » est alors vécue comme un moment crucial dans la vie d'un individu, une espèce de baptême. On utilise lors de la cérémonie d'initiation, comme dans Cosa Nostra, le doigt piqué par la pointe d'un couteau et l'image sacrée (ici, la Madone de Pompei) qui brûle en passant d'une main dans l'autre. Mais il s'agit d'un rituel introduit dans les années récentes, sur simple imitation de Cosa Nostra. À la fin du baptême, l'accolade avec les « frères » qui sont déjà membres de l'organisation. L'initiation – ici, en prison, dans le film *Il camorrista*, de Giuseppe Tornatore (1986) –, se fait normalement en présence de toute la famille mafieuse ou, au moins, de cinq de ses membres.

... à Cosa Nostra...

Tel est en tout cas le tout premier
récit « de l'intérieur » fait par
un affilié à Cosa Nostra, lorsqu'il
devient en 1973 le « repenti »
numéro un de l'histoire de la
mafia. Il s'appelle Leonardo Vitale
et peu de gens à l'époque
donneront crédit à ses
affirmations. Après le serment,
le nouvel adhérent, toujours
d'après Vitale, est présenté
au chef de famille, et on lui donne
quelques informations sur
Cosa Nostra, et un grand nombre
de règles de comportement à
respecter : « Tu ne voleras point ;
tu ne poursuivras point de tes
assiduités la femme d'un ami ;
tu ne demanderas jamais aucune

explication sur ce qui t'est ordonné ; tu ne
chercheras jamais à savoir ce qui appartient aux
autres familles ; tu n'oublieras jamais que tu es
un homme d'honneur devant la police et les
magistrats. »

   Mais attention : ces règles sont valables
uniquement à l'intérieur du monde de Cosa Nostra :
rien n'empêche le *mafioso* de voler à l'extérieur (sur
les aides de l'État, sur les profits des commerçants,
etc.), ni d'avoir des histoires avec des filles lorsqu'il
est en déplacement. Le tout est que ne soit pas mise
en jeu la fonctionnalité de l'État-Cosa Nostra.
Et que les apparences soient sauvées. Un des
derniers boss siciliens arrêtés, Salvatore Lo Piccolo,
confirme en 2007 que le bagage de base du *mafioso*
n'a pas changé. On a trouvé dans ses poches au
moment de son arrestation des images de saints,
des coupures de journaux, un procès-verbal
d'interrogatoire, et la liste, écrite à la main,
des droits et devoirs du *capomafia*, en parfaite
continuité avec la liste établie par Vitale, laquelle
s'organise en huit points :

Le procès est devenu
un événement crucial
dans la vie du *mafioso*,
mais, même en prison,
il continue à
communiquer par
gestes. Page de droite,
un inculpé du procès
Spatola (Palerme, 1983)
menace le photographe
Franco Zecchin avec des
mouvements des doigts
et de la bouche. Pour
Leonardo Vitale (ci-
dessus), la menace se
transformera en
assassinat. Car Vitale
est le premier « repenti »
de Cosa Nostra, celui
qui, dès 1973, donne
aux magistrats la clé de
lecture des rites de Cosa
Nostra. Jugé par l'État
pour ses homicides, il
sera ensuite éliminé par
la mafia. C'était avant
que soit votée la loi sur
les « repentis », en 1991.

1 – On ne peut se présenter tout seul à un autre « ami », la présence d'une tierce personne est nécessaire ;

2 – On ne regarde pas les femmes des amis ;

3 – On ne fréquente pas les « sbires » (les flics) ;

4 – On ne fréquente pas les tavernes et les cercles ;

5 – On respecte sa femme ;

6 – On doit être disponible à tout instant pour la Commission, même si l'on a une épouse qui est sur le point d'accoucher ;

7 – On doit toujours dire la vérité ;

8 – On ne peut en aucun cas entrer dans Cosa Nostra si on a des problèmes de « cornes » en famille ou si l'on a un parent dans les forces de l'ordre…

… à la 'Ndrangheta et à la Sacra Corona Unita

Dans la 'Ndrangheta, le rituel d'affiliation est analogue, avec quelques particularités locales. Le candidat se pique le doigt ou le bras avec une aiguille ou un couteau pointu, faisant tomber quelques gouttes de sang sur l'image de l'archange saint Michel, qui est ensuite enflammée.

Avant que n'entre en vigueur la loi sur l'association de malfaiteurs de type mafieux (1982) et avant que le « maxi procès » (1987) ne condamne de façon définitive dix-neuf *mafiosi* à la perpétuité, le procès était une espèce de promenade pour les inculpés, de laquelle ils sortaient avec une « insuffisance de preuves » qui ne faisait qu'accroître leur prestige dans l'organisation et dans la société. D'où l'air parfaitement décontracté, quelquefois même arrogant, des inculpés, qui savaient qu'ils ne risquaient pas grand-chose.

« Comme le feu brûle cette image, vous brûlerez vous aussi si vous commettez une infamie », dit le maître de cérémonie. Mais le rituel peut varier selon le grade auquel on se trouve : si l'on est *picciotto*, au plus bas degré de l'affiliation, on se contentera souvent d'un serment verbal ; si l'on est « camorriste », le jurement se fera avec l'image de l'Archange et les cendres sur la plaie ; si l'on est *sgarrista*, il s'agira d'une croix tracée au couteau sur la phalange du pouce ; si l'on est *santista*, *vangelista* ou *trequartista*, l'incision en forme de croix se fera sur l'épaule.

Dans la Sacra Corona Unita, la dernière des mafias, suffisamment organisée pour mériter le titre de « quatrième mafia », les rituels sont comparables à ceux de la 'Ndrangheta. Très fragmentée, incisive et dangereuse malgré sa date de naissance récente (1981), la Sacra Corona Unita, constituée de trois sociétés – la mineure, la majeure et la secrète –, a ses rites de passage d'une société à l'autre. Aux *picciotti* et *camorristi* de la société mineure, qui ont surtout des tâches de surveillance, quarante jours suffisent, avant l'affiliation, pour démontrer leur bravoure. Leur jurement : « Je jure sur la pointe de ce poignard taché de sang d'être fidèle à ce corps de société ; de partager jusqu'à la dernière goutte de sang avec un pied dans la tombe et l'autre enchaîné pour donner une forte embrassade à la prison. »

Le fétichisme du *mafioso* est tel qu'il peut conserver dans sa poche – tel Tommaso Ventura, l'une des six victimes de la tuerie de Duisbourg à l'été 2007 – l'image sainte qu'il a brûlée dans sa main le jour de son initiation (ci-dessus). Cette image sainte marque l'adhérent pour la vie. Quand il s'agit de la 'Ndrangheta, l'impétrant aura d'abord été présenté à l'*onorata società* par un affilié plus ancien. Il devra jurer fidélité à l'organisation. Dans la Camorra (à gauche), une espèce de justicier rappelle que Camorra rime avec *fedeltà* (« fidélité »).

Quand le *picciotto*
ou le camorriste arrivent
dans la société majeure,
ils deviennent *sgarrista*
ou *santista*. Sgarrista,
s'il a commis
au moins trois
homicides,
santista quand
il atteint
le sommet de sa carrière criminelle. Le rite prévoit
alors qu'une capsule de cyanure lui soit donnée,
avec une carabine calibre 12 ou un fusil à canon
scié. La capsule invite l'affilié à se donner la mort
plutôt que d'ouvrir la bouche en cas d'arrestation.

Parlant de ces rites archaïques d'affiliation, qui
se sont perpétués même après sa mort en 1992,
le juge Giovanni Falcone soutenait : « On peut
sourire à l'idée qu'un criminel, au visage dur
comme la pierre, ayant déjà commis pas mal de
méfaits, mette une image pieuse dans sa main, jure
solennellement de défendre les faibles, et de ne pas
regarder la femme des autres. On peut en sourire
comme d'un cérémonial archaïque ou d'une
supercherie. Il s'agit pourtant d'une affaire très
sérieuse, et qui engage un individu pour la vie.
L'entrée dans la mafia ressemble à une entrée en
religion : on ne cesse jamais d'être prêtre. Mafieux
non plus. » « On entre dans cosa nostra par le sang,
avec un index piqué par une aiguille ou un couteau,
et on n'en sort que par le sang », ajoutait Giovanni
Falcone. Ces vérités sont valable pour toutes les
organisations criminelles italiennes.

La *lupara*,
traditionnel fusil
à canon scié, typique
du monde paysan puis
des homicides mafieux,
et qui laissait des trous
béants dans le corps des
victimes, est passée de
mode. Cosa Nostra lui
préfère les calibres 38
et autres 357 Magnum,
chargés de projectiles
à expansion. Mais
il y a encore mieux :
l'étranglement de
la victime, car c'est du
travail « propre », sans
écoulement de sang ni
coups de feu. Il suffit,
après, de dissoudre
le corps dans l'acide.
La Camorra, elle, n'en
est pas encore arrivée
là et continue de
collectionner les engins
de mort (ci-dessus, les
armes saisies en 2009
à Torre Annunziata,
près de Naples).

On a longtemps cru que les filles, épouses et mères de Cosa Nostra, enveloppées dans leurs châles noirs, aveuglées par l'*omertà*, clouées à leur foyer, ne prenaient pas part à la saga criminelle des hommes. Et qu'elles ne savaient rien. Or, la « femme d'honneur » existe. Elle est l'autre moitié de la mafia.

CHAPITRE 3

FEMMES D'HONNEUR

Y a-t-il quelque chose en commun entre la moderne Rosetta Cutolo (page de gauche) – une vraie boss accusée de neuf homicides et qui géra la Nuova Camorra jusqu'en 1990 – et cette terre cuite caricaturale destinée aux touristes, qui vante la *mafiusa*, la femme du *mafioso* ? Oui : une aptitude au commandement, les mères restant dans tout le Mezzogiorno le centre de toutes les valeurs et de toute autorité. En 1995, une année record, les femmes inculpées pour association mafieuse furent au nombre de quatre-vingt-neuf.

Mafieuses?

Qui l'eût cru? Même en 1985, alors que le délit d'«association mafieuse» – le fameux «416 bis» – est en vigueur depuis trois ans déjà, et qu'il permet de poursuivre un prévenu, ou une prévenue, pour simple participation à une organisation criminelle, même sans avoir personnellement commis aucun délit, des magistrats de Palerme refusent de condamner une femme. Elle s'appelle Francesca Citardi, épouse du boss Giovanni Bontate et fille de parrains notoires. Elle a été convoquée devant les juges parce qu'elle est sociétaire majoritaire de l'entreprise Calliope, créée par son mari pour recycler de l'argent sale en Sicile, et qu'on la soupçonne d'être complice de ses activités illégales. Mais les juges – des hommes – émettent cette curieuse sentence: on ne peut évaluer, disent-ils, les responsabilités de chaque personne qu'en fonction du «rôle précis qu'elle joue dans l'organisation mafieuse». Surtout, lorsque «de par son tempérament, ou de son insuffisante émancipation par rapport au pouvoir masculin traditionnel, cette personne est culturellement portée à n'avoir aucune fonction active dans les affaires du couple, mais plutôt à subir, en acceptant des choix faits par d'autres». On croit rêver: parce qu'elle est femme, Francesca Citardi n'a pas assez d'autonomie pour être une criminelle. Le quotidien palermitain *L'Ora* pourra titrer justement, au lendemain de cette sentence historique: «Mafieuse? Non, femme seulement»...

Michelina de Cesare, belle et courageuse brigande (ci-dessous), fit la guerre aux armées piémontaises qui avaient envahi le royaume des Deux-Siciles en 1861. Arrêtée et torturée, elle meurt en 1868 à l'âge de 27 ans, pour avoir refusé de rompre l'*omertà*. Son corps martyrisé, exposé aux populations pour les terrifier, ne servit qu'à faire de la propagande en faveur des brigandes, véritables pasionarias habiles à manier les armes et jouissant d'une grande liberté de mœurs.

Le scénario est identique en 1988 pour Benedetta Palazzolo, femme du parrain Bernardo Provenzano.

À l'époque, elle s'occupe activement des propriétés de son homme, qui est en fuite. Et elle a à son nom des biens mobiliers et immobiliers. Qu'importe! Les magistrats de Palerme décident qu'au fond, elle se contente de profiter de sa situation d'épouse, un « statut qui en soi n'est susceptible ni de criminalisation ni de sanction ». Benedetta Palazzolo, d'après eux, ne s'est jamais interrogée sur la provenance des centaines de millions de lires qui pleuvaient sur son foyer et dont elle était la gestionnaire.

Un dernier exemple, celui de Vincenzina Marchese, épouse du parrain Leoluca Bagarella : on découvre à son domicile en 1990, au cours d'une perquisition, un certain nombre de revolvers. On l'accuse d'abord de détention d'armes, mais elle est très vite lavée de tout soupçon. La raison ? Ces revolvers, écrivent les juges, elle ne sait même pas s'en servir. Pourquoi ? Parce qu'elle est une femme !

C'est ainsi que la magistrature sicilienne, imprégnée jusqu'à la moelle de culture machiste, a farci ses sentences de stéréotypes aberrants, reproduisant en son sein les valeurs mafieuses sur le rôle de la femme, et mettant ces dernières à l'abri de la loi. Le raisonnement est simple : les femmes ne sont pas membres de Cosa Nostra ; elles ne comptent pour rien dans l'organisation ; elles ne sauraient être responsables de quoi que ce soit.

Fille de boss, épouse d'un killer patenté (100 homicides!) et sœur d'un « repenti », Vincenzina Marchese (ci-dessous) n'a pas résisté à ces contradictions. Mariée le 29 avril 1991 avec Leoluca Bagarella (ci-contre), elle s'est ôté la vie trois ans après, à 40 ans à peine. Elle souffrait d'une profonde

crise d'identité : elle avait accepté d'épouser un *viddanu*, un paysan de Corleone, elle qui venait d'une espèce de noblesse mafieuse palermitaine. Mais le coup fatal fut l'annonce de la collaboration avec la justice de son frère, Giuseppe Marchese, qui avait fait partie du commando ayant assassiné le juge Falcone. Elle avait l'impression d'être elle aussi devenue une « infâme ».

Le 15 novembre 1983, un boss de Palerme, Benedetto Grado, est descendu par un commando *mafioso*. Le photographe Franco Zecchin a tout le temps de faire son cliché avant que n'arrivent les forces de l'ordre, souvent informées des crimes après les journalistes. C'étaient les terribles années 1981-1983, qui firent plus de mille morts dans les rangs de Cosa Nostra : pour la première fois dans l'histoire de la mafia, la primauté des « familles » palermitaines était mise en discussion par les Corléonais. Celles qui acceptaient de passer un accord avec les *viddani*, les paysans de Corleone, avaient la vie sauve. Les autres devaient s'enfuir à l'étranger (aux États-Unis principalement) pour échapper à la mitraille mafieuse. Ou mourir, comme les Grado, une vieille famille d'hommes d'honneur palermitains, spécialisée dans le trafic de drogue et le recyclage de l'argent sale, et l'une des représentantes de l'aile « modérée » de la mafia sicilienne, hostile à la guerre ouverte avec l'État. Les femmes de Grado ont ici la raideur et l'autocontrôle de vraies boss mafieuses : pas de scènes de douleur de type « méridional » ; une grande retenue due au rang que leur famille occupe dans la société du crime.

Discrète, mais puissante

La magistrate Teresa Principato (ci-contre) est devenue la spécialiste des femmes de la mafia, auxquelles elle a consacré un livre, *Les Vestales du sacré et de l'honneur* (1997). C'est une Palermitaine authentique qui, grâce à sa connaissance de la mentalité mafieuse, a pu conduire l'interrogatoire de célèbres *mafiose*, telles Grazia Ribisi et Giusy Vitale.

❝La femme a un rôle fondamental dans la famille. Elle doit transmettre les valeurs, éduquer les enfants selon le modèle paternel. J'ai connu une femme qui avait conservé pendant des années la veste trempée de sang de son mari assassiné. Puis elle l'a donnée à son fils, le jour où l'assassin est sorti de prison. Une façon de lui ordonner la *vendetta*, de lui faire comprendre qu'il était de son devoir de tuer le tueur de son père.❞
—— Teresa Principato

« Il y a une équivoque de fond dans ces sentences, dit aujourd'hui la magistrate Teresa Principato : des juges hommes se sont employés à confirmer les préjugés des *mafiosi*. C'est un fait que les statuts non écrits de Cosa Nostra refusent l'adhésion des femmes, des flics et des gays. Parce qu'ils ne sont pas fiables. Les femmes de par leur nature. Les flics de par leur métier. Et les gays parce qu'ils peuvent être l'objet de chantages. » Ce sera la même Teresa Principato, forte de ses soupçons sur ce qu'elle appelle le « *protagonismo* criminel féminin », qui mettra pour la première fois en 1998 des puces électroniques et des caméras dans le parloir de la prison de l'Ucciardone à Palerme, où le parrain de Partinico, Vito Vitale, reçoit régulièrement sa sœur Giusy. On découvrira ainsi que Vito passe subrepticement à Giusy des papiers sur lesquels sont inscrits des noms. Et Giusy commente, donne ou refuse son consentement. Les enquêteurs ont donc surpris pour la première fois une femme dans l'exercice de ses fonctions de mafieuse. Les noms qu'elle écarte, c'est

parce que, dit-elle, ils ne sont pas en mesure d'assurer la régence de la circonscription mafieuse en l'absence de Vito. Puis elle avance des conseils sur la conduite à tenir vis-à-vis de Bernardo Provenzano, etc. La preuve est faite qu'une femme peut commander dans la mafia.

En une décennie d'ailleurs, le nombre de femmes poursuivies pour le délit d'« association mafieuse » sera passé de 0 en 1989 à 77 en 1998, avec une pointe de 89 en 1995. Parmi ces femmes rattrapées par la justice, on compte des noms devenus célèbres, tel celui de Grazia Ribisi, de Palma di Montechiaro (province d'Agrigente), qui avait littéralement pris le pouvoir après l'assassinat de ses deux frères. Grâce aux écoutes téléphoniques réalisées à son domicile, les enquêteurs comprennent qu'elle connaît à la perfection

Giusy Vitale (ci-dessous) est la sœur de Vito (page de gauche, en bas) : lorsque son frère est arrêté en 1998, elle devient le boss de Partinico. Sa fière allure de commandante en chef a fait frémir les mafiologues. On avait enfin sous la main un exemplaire de *mafiosa* dans l'exercice de ses fonctions.

l'organigramme de Cosa Nostra et qu'elle est capable de programmer une série consistante d'assassinats. On n'oubliera pas non plus Maria Catena Cammarata, de la famille de Riesi, qui remplaçait son frère Pino et jouissait d'une véritable délégation de pouvoir pour des tâches engageantes, et pas seulement pour organiser une assistance décente à ses frères en fuite. La dernière en date de ces boss en jupons est Concetta Scalisi, arrêtée à Catane en 2001, en compagnie de ses gardes du corps (des femmes, elles aussi). La féminisation de la plus machiste des organisations criminelles est donc un phénomène généralisé. Faut-il se réjouir de cette nouvelle égalité hommes-femmes ?

Et pourtant ce boss en jupons était quasi analphabète : ses frères lui avaient interdit d'aller à l'école. Arrêtée à son tour, elle s'enferme dans un silence méprisant pendant quatre ans et demi. Puis elle rencontre au parloir son fils de 12 ans qui lui demande ce qu'est la mafia. Incapable de le lui expliquer, elle décide de collaborer avec la justice.

Adhérentes à plein titre

Le processus d'émancipation est comparable dans la 'Ndrangheta calabraise. C'est dans les années 1970 que les femmes se mettent à révéler une forte propension à la prise de responsabilités. Car ce sont elles qui approvisionnent les séquestrés que leurs hommes gardent enchaînés dans des grottes de l'Aspromonte, en attendant que les familles paient la rançon demandée. Elles savent parfaitement ce qu'elles font, ces femmes, lorsqu'elles prennent le chemin de la montagne avec du pain, de l'eau et du fromage. Une statistique : à San Luca – la capitale de la 'Ndrangheta, 4 600 habitants, où l'on a compté cinquante séquestrations de personnes et où chaque famille a eu un parent en prison –, les femmes vivandières étaient à l'époque les

Premier séquestré célèbre de la 'Ndrangheta, Paul Getty Jr. (ci-dessous) fut enlevé à Rome dans la nuit du 7 juillet 1973 et libéré le 13 décembre suivant contre un milliard sept cent millions de lires.

Scomparso a Roma il nipote di Paul Getty
Giunge una telefonata: «Preparate i soldi»

principales protagonistes du crime. La technique des séquestrations avait débuté en 1973 avec l'enlèvement de Paul Getty Jr., le petit-fils du milliardaire américain : il laissera dans l'aventure un morceau d'oreille que ses geôliers ont coupée pour convaincre la famille que l'affaire était sérieuse. Eh bien, ce sont les femmes de San Luca qui sont allées « soigner » le jeune Getty lors de sa mutilation.

Mais jusqu'ici aucune d'entre elles n'avait dû rendre compte devant la justice de son activité criminelle de soutien logistique à l'organisation. Dans son rapport pour l'an 2000, la DIA (Direzione Investigativa Antimafia) surprendra tout le monde en révélant que, sur les 7 358 affiliés à la 'Ndrangheta dans la province de Reggio de Calabre, 255 sont des femmes. Adhérentes à plein titre. Ce phénomène nouveau confirme que la mafia au féminin commence à émerger même dans les statistiques et que les femmes ne se contentent plus d'une fonction « alimentaire » de couverture, mais qu'elles jouent un rôle décisif, notamment dans les vendettas. Parce qu'elles sont les gardiennes de

Comme elles se ressemblent ces femmes qui, en 1972 à Seminara (page de gauche), enterrent avec des gestes de tragédie grecque une victime de la mafia calabraise, et celles qui, le 24 août 2007, participent à San Luca aux funérailles de trois des six victimes de la tuerie de Duisbourg (ci-dessus). En réalité un monde les sépare : celui de la richesse, venue des enlèvements, puis du trafic de drogue et d'armes, et du recyclage. Les femmes de San Luca sont aujourd'hui assez malignes pour promouvoir un cessez-le-feu entre familles mafieuses, éviter la surexposition médiatique et judiciaire liée à Duisbourg.

la mémoire. Parce que ce sont elles qui transmettent la culture et les valeurs mafieuses à leurs enfants. Parce qu'elles se sont émancipées, voyageant de par le monde comme des hommes. Deux

La légendaire Pupetta Maresca se marie voile en tête en 1955 avec l'amour de sa vie, Pasquale Simonetti (ci-contre). Lorsqu'elle est arrêtée en 1982 (en bas), elle a pris l'allure d'une femme dynamique et moderne.

d'entre elles, la femme et la sœur du boss Nirta en fuite en Hollande, ont été arrêtées en novembre 2008 à Amsterdam, où elles étaient venues passer le week-end avec le fugitif. Car l'argent des séquestrations de personnes a été sagement réinvesti dans l'immobilier (Allemagne de l'Est) et dans la drogue (Hollande).

Les femmes sont, de plus, devenues un élément décisif du système d'alliances des 'ndrine calabraises : rien de tel qu'un bon mariage pour sceller l'accord entre deux familles mafieuses. L'endogamie est un pivot essentiel de l'organisation.

Pupetta, Rosetta, « Erminia »...

Dans la Camorra napolitaine, le phénomène de libération féminine par le crime est curieusement plus ancien que dans les mafias sicilienne et calabraise. Un cas célèbre, celui de Pupetta Maresca, membre de la Nuova Famiglia, remonte aux années 1950. Pupetta était connue pour sa beauté tapageuse. Elle s'amourache un jour d'un *guapo*, un « délinquant », dit « Pasquale 'e Nola ». Mais il est assassiné en 1955 par un rival. Que fait Pupetta ? Enceinte jusqu'aux dents, elle se rend à Naples et tue l'assassin, Antonio Esposito, sous les yeux de tous. Autre cas : celui de Rosetta Cutolo, sœur du boss Raffaele, leader de la Nuova Camorra Organizzata. Rosetta apprend à gérer les affaires lorsque son frère est arrêté, recevant dans sa luxueuse maison d'Ottaviano les différents groupes criminels de la Famille, et organisant la fuite de son frère de l'hôpital de la prison d'Avellino.

On peut citer enfin le cas d'« Erminia », dite « Céleste » à cause de ses yeux bleus. Ce boss du quartier Forcella à Naples a été dénichée par les carabiniers à la fin 2001, après dix mois de traque dans les *vicoli* (« ruelles ») de la ville. Elle se cachait tout bêtement à son domicile, derrière un panneau coulissant qui tapissait le mur de sa chambre à coucher. Elle n'a pas bronché lorsqu'on lui a passé les menottes. Elle a seulement imploré « Laissez-moi faire mon brushing » et appelé sa coiffeuse à domicile. Puis elle a enfilé un fourreau couleur léopard et pris son sac Vuitton : « Je suis à vous. » Destination : la prison. « Lady Camorra » – c'était un autre de ses surnoms – gérait depuis deux ans les affaires du clan Giuliano, après l'arrestation de ses cinq frères, Luigi, Carmine, Raffaele, Guglielmo et Salvatore. « Cette femme est un leader », confiera aux journalistes le commandant des carabiniers qui organisa sa traque. « Elle a des qualités réservées d'habitude aux hommes : le charisme et les capacités organisationnelles. »

Mafia et cinéma ont toujours fait bon ménage, avec les *Parrain* et *Good Fellows* américains, mais aussi avec les films italiens, en particulier *La Sfida* (*Le Défi*), de Francesco Rosi, qui porte à l'écran la vie de Pupetta Maresca et de son camorriste de mari (affiche, page de gauche). Le boss Bernardo Provenzano gardait une cassette du *Parrain* dans sa cache, tandis que Bernardo Brusca avait, lui, sur sa table de chevet un exemplaire en italien du livre de Giovanni Falcone, *Le Juge et les Hommes d'honneur*. Les *mafiosi* ne dédaignent pas non plus le spectacle et le sport. Ici, le joueur de foot Maradona, prêté par l'Argentine au club de Naples, s'exhibe avec « Erminia » Giuliano, membre éminent du clan camorriste du même nom.

N'oublions pas enfin Teresa Granato, dite « La dame noire », boss et femme de boss, qui après avoir géré à Naples une petite armée de dealers, a été exécutée à 44 ans en 2000, en pleine rue, par deux tueurs en scooter appartenant à un groupe rival. Abattue de plusieurs balles, comme un homme.

Ninetta Bagarella ou l'étrange destin d'une « grande dame » de Cosa Nostra (page de droite) : elle assiste ici à la première audience du procès qui verra son mari condamné à la

RAID A SOMMA VESUVIANA

La vittima
44 anni, era legata al clan Orefice e riforniva di eroina e cocaina i mercanti di morte della zona

La ipotesi
Maria Teresa Granato gestiva una banda di pusher. Non è escluso che sia stata punita per uno sgarro

Il luogo dell'agguato a Somma Vesuviana. La trafficante di droga, colpita in piazza poco dopo mezzogiorno di ieri

Trafficante di droga trucidata

... et le double jeu d'Agata

Nous sommes en 1997 à Gravina près de Catane (Sicile). Agata Finocchiaro, 40 ans, ancien membre du clan mafieux du Mapassoto qui a abandonné sa terre natale pour ouvrir un pressing à Turin, décide brusquement de revenir sur ses pas. La raison ? Cosa Nostra, après avoir assassiné son frère, vient de descendre son neveu âgé de 17 ans. Trop c'est trop. Agata liquide sa teinturerie et redescend sur Catane. Pour se venger. Elle se remet dans le cercle *mafioso*, cherche des informations, se glisse dans le lit du boss soupçonné d'être l'assassin. Avec courage, car il s'agit d'un petit monstre appelé Marcello Gambuzza. Après six mois de ces liaisons dangereuses, Agata a assez de preuves de la culpabilité de son amant. Elle va le dénoncer aux carabiniers. « Bravo », ont dû penser les enquêteurs de l'Antimafia. Mais, ô surprise, après s'être vengée, Agata reprend goût au pouvoir. Très appréciée pour son aplomb, voilà que les membres de sa famille d'origine lui

perpétuité. Institutrice de son état, elle s'était amourachée de Salvatore Riina, dit U curtu (« le petit »), qu'elle suivra dans la gloire et la déchéance, partageant avec lui la clandestinité durant plus de vingt ans. Mère de quatre enfants qu'elle a fait étudier à domicile, elle est revenue à Corleone le lendemain de l'arrestation de Riina, le 15 janvier 1993. Maria Teresa Granato n'a pas eu le temps, elle, de devenir une « lady » *mafiosa*. *Pusher* à Naples, elle a été descendue de cinq balles en plein visage le 23 octobre 2000. Elle avait 44 ans (ci-dessus).

L'affection, la famille, les sentiments sont fondamentaux dans le monde mafieux. En bas, Alessandro Lo Piccolo, fils de Salvatore, envoie une bise à son papa lors de leur arrestation. Ce beau gosse de 32 ans était entouré d'une nuée de dames très affectueuses, qui lui expédiaient des *pizzini* d'amour – « Tu me manques », « Vivre sans toi est angoissant », « J'en ai marre de mendier de l'amour », « L'amour, c'est ce que j'éprouve pour toi » –, retrouvés dans la cache des Lo Piccolo, à côté de montres de valeur, de blousons signés, achetés dans les meilleures boutiques de Palerme.

ra la folla

offrent d'en prendre la tête. Elle accepte. Malchance : de maudites écoutes téléphoniques brisent sa carrière fulgurante, car elles mettent en évidence son double jeu. Agata est arrêtée en février 2000.

Les nouveaux piliers du crime

Il faut donc se rendre à l'évidence : maintenant que l'Antimafia se fait de plus en plus efficace, et que les *mafiosi* finissent plus facilement en prison, une nouvelle génération prend tout doucement la relève, et elle se décline au féminin.

Et les femmes des boss démontrent qu'elles peuvent devenir plus mafieuses que les mafieux. Lorsque le phénomène des « repentis » a pris pied à Palerme, rendant précaire l'existence des organisations criminelles, ce sont elles, les femmes, qui se sont précipitées pour défendre l'organisation contre les *canarini*, les « collabos », les « vendus ».

Le juge Giovanni Falcone racontait volontiers cet épisode qui regarde le premier aspirant palermitain au « repentir » dans la famille des Corléonais, un certain Vincenzo Buffa. Le bruit de sa collaboration s'était répandu dans la ville. Alors, à l'ouverture du procès, avant même que Buffa ait pu dire un mot, sa femme et sa sœur se mettent à hurler dans le public : « C'est un fou… un malade… cet homme est mort… nous sommes en deuil. » Résultat : impressionné par le chœur de ses femmes, Buffa s'empresse de se rétracter. Même scénario avec Giuseppa Favaloro, dont le mari était devenu un collaborateur de la justice. Lorsque son procès s'ouvre, elle s'exclame : « Ce n'est pas un repenti… c'est un infâme… dès que j'ai appris sa collaboration, j'ai ouvert les

armoires, j'ai décroché ses vêtements et je les ai brûlés. À mes trois enfants j'ai dit : "Mes petits, vous n'avez plus de père." » Admirable Giuseppa. Fantastique tragédienne.

Mais on n'a rien inventé sous le soleil des mafias. Les femmes méridionales, protagonistes depuis toujours du traditionalisme social, vestales du « familisme amoral » raconté dans les années 1960 par Edward Banfield, ne font que perpétuer

L'histoire de Cosa Nostra est aussi celle des femmes qui ont su résister à la mafia. Palerme, 30 janvier 1962 (ci-contre) : Serafina Battaglia est la première femme de la mafia à briser la loi du silence en dénonçant à la police les assassins de son fils. Palerme, 10 février 1986 (page de gauche) : Michela Buscemi a traîné devant la justice les assassins de son frère, coupable d'avoir vendu des cigarettes de contrebande sans l'accord de son boss. Parmi ces héroïnes de

la tradition : garantir la cohésion de la famille mafieuse et sa pérennité. Chaîne de transmission des valeurs mafieuses (honneur, vendetta, *omertà*), garantes de la réputation de leurs hommes, véritables Antigone, capables d'interpeller leurs époux ou fils d'un méprisant « *Ma tu omo sei ?* » (« Mais toi, tu serais un homme ? ») lorsqu'ils hésitent à venger dans le sang l'honneur bafoué de la famille, les femmes sont devenues le principal pilier du crime. Et alors que beaucoup d'hommes ont maintenant perdu confiance dans le modèle mafia, au point de briser le tabou séculaire du silence et de devenir des « repentis » (plus de sept cents aujourd'hui !), les femmes, elles, lui vouent une fidélité sans bornes. « Les femmes, elles ne jugent pas. Elles acceptent ou elles refusent. Et lorsqu'elles acceptent, elles le font pour de bon », écrivait, philosophe, un mafieux anonyme dans son livre *Homme d'honneur* (Mondadori, 1992).

l'Antimafia, c'est Rita Atria (ci-dessus) qui mérite le plus l'attention : bien qu'appartenant à une famille mafieuse de Partanna, lorsque son père et son frère sont tués, elle s'adresse au juge Paolo Borsellino, qui devient son point de référence. Mais quand celui-ci est assassiné, le 19 juillet 1992, Rita, 17 ans, se suicide : « La mafia elle est en nous... Borsellino tu es mort pour ce en quoi tu croyais. Moi sans toi, je suis morte. »

« Considérer Cosa Nostra comme un anti-État est une erreur grossière. Cosa Nostra, très souvent, a été l'État. Et elle a de toute façon toujours eu tendance à avoir des hommes, des institutions qui pouvaient la faire participer au système de pouvoir. »

Piero Grasso,
procureur national antimafia,
La Mafia invisible, 2001

CHAPITRE 4

LES CONNIVENCES

Lorsque, le 12 mars 1992, Salvatore Lima, député démo-chrétien et plénipotentiaire de Giulio Andreotti (ci-contre) est assassiné (page de gauche), on comprend que l'ère de l'attaque frontale contre l'État a commencé. Que Cosa Nostra n'a plus confiance dans ses référents habituels. Et qu'elle tient à le faire savoir. À sa manière : sanglante.

De la collusion...

Impossible de ne pas s'étonner du long silence – un silence assourdissant – des hiérarchies catholiques face à la mafia. Impossible de ne pas noter également que, dans toutes les organisations mafieuses, les rites d'affiliation prévoient la présence de la Madone, ou des saints, sous la forme d'images pieuses : elles apportent une sorte de caution divine au crime organisé. Les 'ndranghetistes calabrais vénèrent particulièrement la Madonna dei Polsi, au sanctuaire de laquelle ils se rendent régulièrement le premier dimanche de septembre, au cœur de l'Aspromonte. La Madonna dei Polsi est d'ailleurs considérée comme la « Mamma » de la 'Ndrangheta.

Le 12 juillet 1954, les pleureuses officielles de Cosa Nostra célèbrent à Villalba la mort de Don Calogero Vizzini (ci-dessus). Les *capimafia* jouissent alors d'un grand prestige dans la population sicilienne, de par leur rôle de « juges de paix », puis d'« antifascistes » qui, à partir de mai 1943, ont collaboré avec les forces alliées. En 1944, Don Calogero parcourait l'île à bord d'un char américain, désignant les maires acquis au gouvernement provisoire.

Dans Cosa Nostra, on utilise aussi la Madone, ou l'archange saint Michel ou sainte Rosalie ou d'autres saints, comme symbole de la fidélité de l'impétrant à l'organisation. Mais Cosa Nostra a bénéficié d'autres appuis moins surnaturels de la part de l'Église. Personne n'oubliera l'ineffable cardinal Ernesto Ruffini, prélat de Sicile dans les années 1960, qui affirmait depuis sa chaire de la cathédrale de Palerme que « la mafia n'existe pas ».

C'est l'époque où les hiérarchies avaient choisi de vivre plutôt avec la mafia qu'avec le « communisme » et d'utiliser l'organisation criminelle pour mieux combattre le danger d'une imminente colonisation de l'Occident par les Soviétiques… Cosa Nostra devait ainsi éviter la « barbarie ». Mais même bien plus tard, il s'est trouvé un autre évêque, dans les années 1990, monseigneur Angelo Rizzo, prélat de Raguse, pour oser soutenir : « Je veux rappeler le danger que représente l'athéisme communiste par rapport à l'athéisme mafieux, et les morts par avortement qui sont plus nombreux que les morts de mafia »… Aux temps du cardinal Ruffini en tout cas, le Parti communiste italien (PCI) facilitait les choses puisqu'il était en première ligne dans la bataille contre la mafia, et contre l'« obscurantisme religieux ».

En 1954, à la mort du parrain de Villalba, Don Calogero Vizzini, le PCI avait violemment protesté contre la pose d'une plaque commémorative sur la façade de l'église qui disait : « Ce fut un *galantuomo*, un gentilhomme », à l'initiative du

Connu comme le « curé de la mafia », Don Mario Frittitta a été arrêté en novembre 1997 (ci-dessus) et condamné à deux ans et quatre mois de réclusion pour « association mafieuse ». Il dit pour sa défense qu'il avait voulu assurer la rédemption, en l'induisant au repentir, du boss Pietro Aglieri. Celui-ci, féru de religion, avait construit un autel dans sa cache de fugitif, et Don Frittitta ne manquait jamais d'y célébrer la messe. Il semble même que ce curé audacieux ait célébré des mariages clandestins entre *mafiosi*. Les carabiniers d'Aversa (ci-contre), de leur côté, mettent sous séquestre, en septembre 2008 les biens du clan Setola à Casal di Principe (près de Naples) : les statues de Madone et de saints ne manquent pas, bien sûr, mais ce ne sont que des détails dans ces villas de rêve dont les garages sont peuplés de voitures de luxe.

curé du lieu. On pouvait donc à l'époque être mafieux et catholique. Mieux : mafieux et vénéré par les représentants de l'Église.

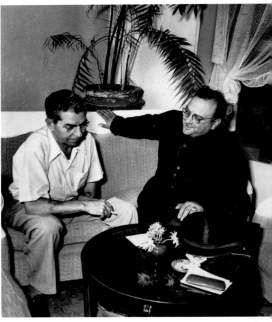

Les « repentis » de Cosa Nostra le confirment aujourd'hui : ils n'ont jamais pensé que leur foi pouvait entrer en conflit avec leurs agissements criminels ; ils ont toujours respecté les sacrements, baptisé leurs enfants et célébré leur mariage à l'église ; ils ne se sentent pas en contradiction avec les règles de l'Évangile. C'est donc devenu indéniable : la mafia n'est pas née hors de l'Église ou contre elle, même si les valeurs mafieuses sont la négation des valeurs chrétiennes. « L'Église a nourri la mafia dans son sein », va jusqu'à soutenir en 1993 la revue des prêtres contestataires de Palerme, *Segno*.

Mais ce sont les raisons économiques qui expliquent probablement le mieux l'aveuglement systématique de l'Église : les mafieux ont toujours été les grands aumôniers des paroisses en difficulté. Pour refaire un toit ou un clocher, pour venir en aide aux besogneux. Cette manne criminelle – mais l'argent a-t-il une odeur dans les paroisses siciliennes ? – justifiait aux yeux des curés de base les baptêmes clandestins célébrés lorsqu'un boss en fuite ne pouvait se montrer à visage découvert ; les communions faites dans l'ombre ; les correspondances entre prêtres et mafieux (on citera celle que le boss Pietro Aglieri entretint même après son arrestation avec

Les mafieux ne sont pas plus observants que la moyenne de la population, mais ils ont besoin plus que d'autres des valeurs catholiques pour assurer la cohésion de leur « famille », naturelle ou criminelle, et éviter toute forme de désordre (y compris de type sexuel) qui introduirait un élément d'instabilité dans son fonctionnement et constituerait un danger. Page de droite, le *mafioso* Salvatore Contorno, dit la « primevère de Santa Maria del Gesù », faisant baptiser un de ses enfants dans une église de Palerme.

le prêtre de sa paroisse à Palerme, et le fait que le même Aglieri s'était fait construire un autel privé dans son appartement où ce prêtre venait célébrer la messe).

Qu'il y ait eu des sacerdoces rattrapés par la justice ne surprendra pas outre mesure, tel celui de l'archevêque de Monreale, monseigneur Cassisa, qui recevait régulièrement la femme du parrain Totò Riina, avant et après qu'il eut été arrêté, et qui fut soupçonné par les juges d'avoir reçu des « enveloppes » sur les appels d'offres pour la restauration du dôme de sa cathédrale.

... à l'anathème

Puis arrive le tournant des années 1980, lorsque la mafia commence ses « crimes exquis » contre les représentants des institutions. C'est alors – en 1981 exactement – que le pape Jean-Paul II envoie une directive – la première du genre – aux évêques de l'île, leur demandant un « engagement précis de lutte contre les maux de la Sicile et surtout contre la mafia ».

« La mafia n'est pas un péché. Si tu dois te confesser, choisis un prêtre intelligent, capable de comprendre ces choses et qui ne te fasse pas perdre trop de temps » : c'est un certain Guttadauro, médecin de l'hôpital de Palerme, qui prononce ces mots, ne sachant pas qu'il est sur écoute. Des mots qui serviront à l'arrêter comme membre de Cosa Nostra, et sont révélateurs du cynisme avec lequel les hommes d'honneur prennent contact avec la religion. Pour s'en servir. « La religion n'est pas la foi », disent des théologiens. Elle est seulement un ensemble de rites, de textes et de symboles auxquels le mafieux peut adhérer.

C'est l'époque où le cardinal de Palerme, monseigneur Salvatore Pappalardo, à la suite de l'assassinat du général Carlo Alberto Dalla Chiesa, préfet de Palerme, fait appel, le 3 septembre 1982, à la « conscience antimafieuse » de l'Église, dénonçant les « frères assassins, ouvriers du mal » et réclamant une législation efficace contre la mafia. Il sera suivi par un modeste curé du quartier de la Vucciria, padre Angelo la Rosa, qui monte sur les étals du marché, au milieu des thons éventrés et des poulpes frémissants, et improvise un violent discours

Symbolique cliché (ci-dessous) : le général Carlo Alberto Dalla Chiesa, envoyé en mai 1982 en Sicile en tant que préfet ; le cardinal de Palerme Salvatore Pappalardo, qui incarne dans la ville le pouvoir de l'Église, et ses contradictions ; le maire Nello Martellucci, un démo-chrétien local dont personne ne peut

antimafia après un homicide particulièrement odieux. Et c'est encore le pape, en visite à Agrigente, qui donnera sa touche finale au tournant antimafieux de la hiérarchie : « Pour l'amour de Dieu, *mafiosi*, convertissez-vous. Un jour viendra le jugement de Dieu et vous devrez rendre compte de vos mauvaises actions. » Suivi de la conférence épiscopale sicilienne qui menace d'excommunication tous ceux qui « sont responsables d'homicides volontaires ». Cette fois, le message est clair. Mais il aura fallu quelques attentats spectaculaires pour que l'Église affirme enfin qu'il n'est pas possible d'être chrétien et *mafioso*.

garantir qu'il est exempt de contacts *mafiosi*, et qui témoigne, lui, des ambiguïtés de la politique. Ces trois pouvoirs sont les trois piliers du « système Sicile ». Le général sera fauché par la mitraille mafieuse le 3 septembre 1982. Le cardinal prononcera aussitôt une magnifique homélie dans la cathédrale de Palerme. Le maire, lui, poursuivra sa carrière de politicien local.

L'engagement des petits prêtres

On aura alors des témoignages parfois poignants de l'engagement antimafia des prêtres, surtout dans la base. Des « prêtres en tranchée » comme ils ont été baptisés : padre Antonio Garau, padre Paolo Turturro, padre Ennio Pintacuda, padre Giacomo Ribaudo, qui sont devenus des héros en entrant dans la ligne de mire de Cosa Nostra. À la saison des « petits juges » courageux succédait la saison des « petits prêtres ». Le plus symbolique d'entre eux : padre Pino Puglisi. Il prouvera par sa vie d'abord, puis par sa mort en 1993, qu'on ne peut vivre chrétiennement dans un quartier contrôlé par la mafia. Qu'on ne peut y ouvrir ni un centre social ni un centre culturel, ni même un terrain de foot. Parce qu'on dispute à la mafia son hégémonie sur les consciences. Padre Puglisi commença à être une menace pour l'ordre mafieux non par ses exhortations du haut de sa chaire, mais par ses actions : lorsqu'il emmena les gosses du quartier en balade au bord de la mer dans un autobus en location, ou dans un cinéma de Palerme, trouvant donc des occupations qui distrayaient les enfants de leur destin de futurs *mafiosi*. Padre Puglisi a été assassiné d'une balle dans la nuque le soir de son anniversaire : parce qu'il donnait une réponse alternative concrète à la criminalité. Et devenait gênant pour les sources de profit de Cosa Nostra. « En tuant un prêtre c'est Dieu que vous frappez », tonnera Jean-Paul II.

Don Pino Puglisi incarne le visage propre et antimafieux de l'Église (à gauche). Assassiné d'une balle dans la nuque le 15 septembre 1993, le jour de ses 56 ans, parce qu'il dérangeait l'ordre mafieux dans le quartier Brancaccio, avec son Centre Padre Nostro et ses équipées avec les gosses, il sera proposé comme « béat » en 1999 par le cardinal de Palerme. Avec l'accord du pape Jean-Paul II qui, avec sa visite à Palerme en 1982 (ci-dessous, photo Franco Zecchin), a imprimé un tournant dans le rapport Église-mafia.

Mafia et politique

« Il popolo siciliano ha sete
di libertà e fame di terra.. »

VOTIAMO

« Les chefs de la mafia sont sous la
protection des sénateurs, députés et
autres personnages influents qui
les prennent sous leur tutelle et les
défendent, pour être ensuite à leur tour
protégés et défendus par eux, rapporte en 1898 le
préfet de police de Palerme Ermanno Sangiorgio.
Un phénomène que je m'abstiendrai de qualifier mais
que j'ai le devoir de signaler à mes supérieurs. »

Depuis qu'elles existent, les mafias ont toujours
cherché un rapport fructueux avec le pouvoir.
Passant tranquillement de la féodalité au royaume
des Deux-Siciles, puis aux différentes étapes de
la monarchie constitutionnelle, puis du fascisme à
l'antifascisme, et du séparatisme au libéralisme,
avant de rencontrer celui qui reste le parti de
leur cœur, la Démocratie chrétienne. Quel bonheur
pour elles, au moins jusqu'aux années 1980-1985,
lorsqu'un véritable système politico-gangstérisque
règne sur le Sud, et surtout sur la Sicile, avec des
députés démo-chrétiens fiers de porter sur les fonts
baptismaux les enfants des *mafiosi* et des ministres
joyeux d'être les témoins de noces d'un *capomafia*
de quartier !

N'oublions pas les voitures officielles de la Région
Sicile qui suivirent le fourgon mortuaire du boss
des boss Don Calogero Vizzini le 11 juillet 1954 à
Villalba, avec cette couronne « Les amis de
Palerme »… N'oublions pas surtout – et c'est moins

L'expédition des Mille,
célèbre épisode du
Risorgimento, a lieu
en 1860, lorsque des
volontaires, commandés
par Garibaldi,
débarquent en Sicile
et la conquièrent au
royaume des Savoie.
Ce fut un pas décisif
pour l'unité italienne.
De nombreux paysans,
qui avaient faim de
terre, s'étaient révoltés
avant même l'arrivée
de Garibaldi, réclamant
une réforme agraire.
Ils furent écrasés par
les soldats des Bourbons,
hostiles à toute réforme
et à toute unification,
et qui n'hésitèrent pas
à faire fusiller femmes
et enfants (en haut, à
gauche, ex-voto). Le
17 mars 1861, Victor-
Emmanuel II de Savoie
sera cependant proclamé
premier roi d'Italie.

folklorique – le pacte politique passé entre Cosa Nostra et la Démocratie chrétienne à la fin de la guerre. Nous sommes le 1er mai 1947 – une date historique – à Portella della Ginestra, un lieu-dit à une heure de Palerme. Les paysans qui ont « faim de terre » et ont souvent procédé à des occupations de *latifondi* se retrouvent avec les ouvriers des chantiers navals et des PME locales pour fêter le 1er Mai des travailleurs. Ils seront accueillis sur le plateau de Portella par la mitraille mafieuse du bandit Salvatore Giuliano, embauché expressément par les notables démo-chrétiens pour isoler les « communistes » sur fond de guerre froide naissante.

Dans les années de l'après-guerre, le PCI prend fait et cause pour les paysans qui revendiquent lors des élections de 1948 une redistribution des terres (affiche, page de gauche).

Mais dès le 1er mai 1947, les tentatives de réforme agraire avaient subi un brutal coup d'arrêt avec la fusillade de Portella della Ginestra (ci-contre, rideau de scène, peint dans les années 1950) organisée par le bandit Salvatore Giuliano (ci-dessus) aux ordres de la mafia et de la Démocratie chrétienne locale, lesquelles voulaient éviter tout bouleversement social et toute modification du régime de propriété. Malgré cet épouvantable massacre aux conséquences funestes – 11 morts et 56 blessés –, Giuliano restera une espèce de héros populaire.

Salvatore Giuliano
est assassiné à
Castelvetrano
(province de Trapani)
le 5 juillet 1950 lors
d'un guet-apens
(ci-contre, le corps du
bandit au milieu de ses
concitoyens atterrés).
Il avait eu le temps,
dans sa brève vie
– 28 ans ! –, d'avoir
des accointances avec
la mafia et d'être
séparatiste. Militant
du Movimento
indipendentista
siciliano (MIS), il avait
même écrit au
président Truman en
janvier 1947 pour lui
demander d'appuyer
le détachement de la
Sicile de l'Italie et
son rattachement
aux États-Unis. Et
il souhaitait l'« appui
moral » américain
pour « éliminer les
communistes de l'île ».
Ses multiples
allégeances alliées à
sa pratique de brigand
en firent vite un
personnage gênant,
qui ne pouvait qu'être
éliminé. Il inspirera
un beau film à
Francesco Rosi
(*Salvatore Giuliano*,
1962), un exemple de
cinéma politique.
Car Rosi procédait à
un véritable travail
d'enquête avant de
se lancer dans ses
tournages, contribuant
ainsi à illustrer, sinon
à résoudre, quelques-
uns des mystères de
l'après-guerre italien.

Le résultat ? Un coup de frein sec aux luttes paysannes, un halte-là à la progression du PCI, et un bilan tragique de 11 morts. Le prix à payer pour libérer la Sicile du « danger bolchevique »...

Les porteurs de voix de la Démocratie chrétienne

La collaboration mafia-Démocratie chrétienne s'insinuera de manière physiologique dans le déroulement de la vie quotidienne des administrations. Avec les mafieux porteurs de voix pour les élections locales mais aussi nationales, et

Principal parti au banc des accusés : la Démocratie chrétienne (ci-dessous, en campagne électorale en 1955). Elle s'adaptera vite à la guerre froide à partir de 1947, devenant le fer de lance de l'anticommunisme. Et s'alliant pour ce faire même avec la mafia.

GIUSEPPE IMPASTATO
RIVOLUZIONARIO E MILITANTE COMUNISTA
ASSASSINATO DALLA MAFIA DEMOCRISTIANA
N. 5-1-1948   M. 9-5-1978

Ci-contre, la plaque commémorative de l'assassinat, en 1978, de Giuseppe Impastato, militant d'extrême gauche, devant laquelle posent sa mère et son frère. La Démocratie chrétienne s'allie aussi avec les « pouvoirs forts », tels les grands argentiers Nino et Ignazio Salvo (ci-dessous et en bas), puissants répondants économiques de la Démocratie chrétienne et membres influents de Cosa Nostra. Les Salvo étaient affiliés à la « famille » de Salemi. Ignazio fut condamné pour association mafieuse, puis assassiné par les Corléonais en 1992.

les politiciens prêts à écouter les raisons de la mafia. Car la mafia a besoin de la politique. Pour faire voter des lois qui facilitent ses chances de profit (avec le relâchement du contrôle des changes par exemple, ou du contrôle des exportations de capitaux, ou de la régulation des marchés). Pour obtenir des permis de construire faciles, des adjudications pas trop regardantes, des licences d'exploitation favorables ou des transmissions de propriété pas trop limpides. Alors oui, la mafia apporte des voix et organise le consensus, dans le plus pur style clientélaire, mais ce n'est jamais pour rien. Le « système Sicile » recevra sa bénédiction au niveau national avec les différents secrétariats de la Démocratie chrétienne qui feront semblant de ne pas voir la pollution mafieuse toujours au nom de la nécessaire lutte contre le « communisme ».

Le maximum de la collusion mafia-Démocratie chrétienne a été symbolisé, probablement à tort, par l'affaire Andreotti. Giulio Andreotti, grand catholique et grand boss démo-chrétien, onze fois ministre et sept fois président

L'homme symbole de cette Démocratie chrétienne qui, au nom de la guerre au bolchevisme, flirta avec le crime organisé : Giulio Andreotti, 90 ans en 2009 (ci-contre, lors du procès Pecorelli en 1998). Pivot de la vie politique italienne durant cinquante ans, il sera jugé par le tribunal de Palerme pour « association mafieuse ». Absous en 1999, il sera en 2003 à la fois absous et condamné, puisque la sentence parle d'une « authentique, stable et amicale disponibilité de l'inculpé envers les *mafiosi* jusqu'en 1980 ». Mais s'agissant de faits anciens, la prescription est de rigueur. Le cinéma ne pouvait pas ne pas s'emparer du personnage : le film *Il Divo*, de Paolo Sorrentino, illustre, entre autres, le baiser supposé (en haut) entre Andreotti (à droite) et Totò Riina, le parrain de Cosa Nostra (à gauche). Les deux plus grands adversaires d'Andreotti, et les deux plus grands combattants antimafia, Giovanni Falcone et Paolo Borsellino, seront assassinés en 1992, le premier le 23 mai, le second le 19 juillet.

du Conseil, est accusé dans les années 1990 d'être le grand manitou de Cosa Nostra, le politicien qui tire les ficelles de la mafia. Un « repenti » racontera même que l'accord scélérat entre la Démocratie chrétienne et les *mafiosi* a été scellé d'un baiser entre Andreotti et Totò Riina, le chef des Corléonais. Mais l'enquête et le procès qui s'ensuivent aboutissent à l'absolution, au moins à partir de 1980 (pour les faits antérieurs, il y avait prescription), du patron de la Démocratie chrétienne. Il était d'ailleurs difficile qu'il en fût autrement, les responsabilités étant dans ce cas plus d'ordre politique et moral que d'ordre pénal. Le grand coupable fut donc déclaré innocent.

C'est en fait dans les années 1983-1985 que l'entente Démocratie chrétienne-mafia s'était brisée, avec la victoire des Corléonais de Totò Riina sur les « modérés » de Palerme. Totò Riina inaugure alors les saisons des attentats anti-institutionnels avec l'assassinat du juge Rocco Chinnici (1983). Il ne la

complétera qu'en 1992 – une année terrible – en faisant sauter le député démo-chrétien Salvatore Lima, les juges Falcone et Borsellino, et le grand argentier sicilien Ignazio Salvo. Totò Riina avait décidé cette année-là de prendre de front l'État pour le contraindre à une espèce de négociation : il voulait dicter ses conditions sur le problème des détenus *mafiosi* en régime dur, sur celui des séquestrations de biens, et sur la révision des procès. Il sera arrêté le 15 janvier 1993. Mais par la suite, dans la mesure où l'État, et le gouvernement, cessaient d'être un monopole démo-chrétien, la mafia sicilienne et les mafias en général ont réorienté leurs indications de vote en faveur des nouveaux arrivants dans les sphères du pouvoir : les berlusconiens de Forza Italia et les centristes de Pierferdinando Casini, en somme, les héritiers de feue la Démocratie chrétienne. Car il reste difficile pour la mafia de se ranger du côté des rebelles, des révolutionnaires ou tout simplement des progressistes.

Certains pensent que Cosa Nostra n'a pas été seule à vouloir l'élimination des juges Falcone et Borsellino (ci-dessous, en une de quotidiens italiens).

la Repubblica

Una tonnellata di tritolo: 5 morti e 7 feriti. Mea culpa dei partiti a Roma

Falcone assassinato

Strage di mafia, è morta anche la moglie

Shock a Montecitorio: oggi il Presidente

Non c'è più tempo

Edizione speciale domani Repubblica sarà in edicola

COLPITO DALLA MAFIA IL CANDIDATO ALLA SUPERPROCURA, L'UOMO CHE INDAGAVA SUI KILLER DI FALCONE

Massacro, ucciso Borsellino

Autobomba a Palermo: assassinati il giudice e cinque agenti della scorta tra cui una donna

Scalfaro: guai a noi se non saremo uniti, forti, credibili. Mancino e Parisi contestati dai poliziotti

Les cousins d'Amérique

Les *connections* entre la Sicile et les États-Unis, ou plutôt entre Palerme et Manhattan, commencent dès le XIXᵉ siècle, dans les années 1860 exactement. Au départ, il s'agissait d'organiser l'importation des oranges, des citrons, de l'huile d'olive et des fromages siciliens. La drogue ne fera son apparition que plus tard, dans les années 1920, cachée justement dans les caisses d'agrumes ou les barils d'huile d'olive. Le mot « mafia » se manifeste aussitôt dans la presse américaine pour évoquer les activités, criminelles ou non, des Siciliens ou des Italiens. Ce qui provoque la réaction du journal des immigrés, *Il Progresso italo-americano*, qui lance la dénomination de « Mano Nera » pour éviter que l'on parle de « mafia sicilo-américaine ». Une façon élégante de tenter de sauver la face aux Siciliens. « Un véritable pont va relier les faubourgs de Palerme et les *slums* de New York, mais aussi de La Nouvelle-Orléans », écrit l'historien Salvatore Lupo. Des deux côtés de l'Atlantique, on ne peut que noter dès lors la communauté de mœurs et de philosophies criminelles qui unit les mafias. Des deux côtés, on offrira aussi la fameuse « protection » du *pizzo*, l'impôt versé à l'État-mafia pour pouvoir « être tranquille ». Des deux côtés, le vrai *mafioso* ne sera en tout cas jamais perçu comme un criminel de droit commun. Le lien entre les deux organisations criminelles deviendra donc structurel.

La prohibition sera d'une grande utilité aux mafias, parce qu'elle provoquera une atténuation sensible de la frontière entre légalité et illégalité. Pour bon nombre de citoyens, il semblera légitime de consommer de l'alcool de contrebande : c'est l'époque où les *bootleggers* deviennent d'ailleurs des opérateurs normaux du marché, et où le fameux Al Capone peut soutenir que tout ce qu'il fait, c'est de « répondre à la demande du public ». La prohibition aidera donc les *mafiosi* à sortir des *slums*. Un rapport du FBI, daté de 1938, signale déjà, comme le relève Salvatore Lupo, que la mafia américaine est « organisée en familles, avec un président élu,

Dans *Là où fleurit le citronnier*, Antonino Buttita raconte, et illustre, le « pont » instauré dès la fin du XIXᵉ siècle entre Cosa Nostra et ses antennes américaines. En effet, les agrumes siciliens commencent à être exportés dans le monde entier, et surtout aux États-Unis. Si les affiches publicitaires (ci-dessus, celle des Cicero Brothers) sont de véritables œuvres d'art, dans les caisses de citrons, il y avait aussi de la drogue. Ce fut le début d'un juteux trafic de stupéfiants. À l'ombre des citronniers.

Deux *mafiosi* siculo-américains célèbres. En bas, Lucky Luciano, beau gosse, dit-on, mais surtout richissime criminel qui domina la mafia américaine. Revenu en Italie en 1946, il y organisera un colossal trafic de drogue. Francesco Rosi lui dédia un film en 1973.

Ci-dessus, Al Capone, un gangster légendaire qui domina la Chicago des années 1930. Et qui a été incarné au cinéma par Rod Steiger, Ben Gazzarra et Robert De Niro.

ou un "représentant" », et que « ces familles siègent à la Commission ou "Grand Council" », laquelle a un rôle de « chambre de compensation des conflits ».

Lucky Luciano, mafieux ou héros ?

Lorsque survient la guerre et que les autorités américaines cherchent à communiquer non officiellement (le gouvernement italien était fasciste) avec la Péninsule, il leur semble normal de s'adresser aux *mafiosi* italiens, à travers leurs coreligionnaires américains, reconnaissant automatiquement aux premiers un statut de force militaire : puisqu'ils étaient en état de contrôler leur territoire ! Car les *mafiosi* haïssaient le fascisme, non pas tant par amour de la démocratie que par rejet viscéral de la répression féroce que le préfet Cesare Mori, au nom de Mussolini, avait entreprise dans le sud de l'Italie.

Le boss Calogero Vizzini pour la Sicile et Lucky Luciano pour les États-Unis sont donc les protagonistes du débarquement allié dans l'île. L'historien Michele Pantaleone raconte que les avions américains qui survolaient la campagne autour de Palerme lançaient des tracts et des mouchoirs sur lesquels était gravée la lettre « L » pour signifier aux populations que le débarquement avait le consentement de Lucky Luciano et donc de Cosa Nostra. La mafia italo-américaine donnera ainsi les noms des premiers maires antifascistes en remplacement des *podestà* mussoliniens. Lucky Luciano sera libéré des prisons américaines en janvier 1946, avec vingt ans d'avance sur l'échéance normale : tel fut le prix de sa collaboration. Lors de son expulsion des États-Unis, une cérémonie publique, avec les dockers de New York alignés en rangs d'oignons, lui rendit les honneurs. Lucky s'installera d'abord à Rome, puis à Naples. Jouissant d'une popularité extrême, il lui arrivera de signer des autographes à des marins américains de la base de l'Otan.

Natif de Lercara Freddi (Sicile) en 1897, Luciano est considéré comme le père du crime organisé moderne. Après avoir trafiqué dans l'alcool, la drogue et la prostitution, mais aussi dans le recyclage des déchets, le bâtiment et les transports, il était devenu un grand boss. Arrêté et condamné à 50 ans de prison, il dirige la Cosa Nostra américaine de derrière les barreaux… Jusqu'au moment où, après avoir préparer avec lui le débarquement allié (ci-dessus, les habitants de Pollina regardent passer les chars américains le 8 mai 1943), le gouvernement des États-Unis met Luciano en liberté en échange de ses informations.

Mais Lucky continue ses trafics. En 1948, il rencontre Charles Gambino à Palerme. Le boss italien exilé et le boss américain émergent passent un accord pour le trafic de drogue : le premier fournira la matière première (l'héroïne) et le second la distribuera à New York. Il ne faudra pas attendre longtemps – 1954 – pour que la Commission Kefauver ne stimagtise cet accord, allant jusqu'à écrire que « l'Italie est le centre mondial de l'héroïne et Luciano en est le patron ».

Lucky Luciano devient vite un héros (ci-dessus, il pose sur une plage de Capri), s'installe à Naples puis à Palerme, où il réorganise la Cosa Nostra sicilienne. Il meurt à Naples, en 1962. Habile à ne pas laisser de traces et à cultiver les protections

Drogue et Pizza Connection

L'année 1957 sera décisive pour les rapports italo-américains. Du 12 au 16 octobre, un sommet mafieux historique se tiendra à l'hôtel des Palmes à Palerme, avec Joe Bonanno et Giuseppe Genco Russo, pour peaufiner les tenants et les aboutissants du trafic international de drogue, et pour jeter les bases d'un « gouvernement » de Cosa Nostra : la Coupole est née ces jours-là dans la capitale sicilienne. Le sommet des Palmes ressemblait en tout état de cause à un traité de paix et d'amitié entre deux peuples… Il sera suivi du sommet d'Appalachin (État de New York), interrompu, lui, par une irruption de la police.

et les connivences, Luciano a été récemment cité par *Time Magazine* comme l'un des vingt hommes les plus influents du XXe siècle.

Mais il faudra attendre vingt ans pour que les magistratures américaine et italienne agissent de concert contre les deux mafias. Avec les grands procès de 1985-1987, à New York, sous la dénomination de « Pizza Connection » (enquête menée par le procureur Rudolph Giuliani), et avec le « maxi procès » de 1986-1987 à Palerme (mené par le juge Giovanni Falcone). Un coup dur pour les deux mafias. Elles ne s'en

La guerre contre Cosa Nostra a été menée avec persévérance par toutes les administrations américaines, jusqu'à la quasi-extinction de cette organisation. Rudolph Giuliani (page de gauche),

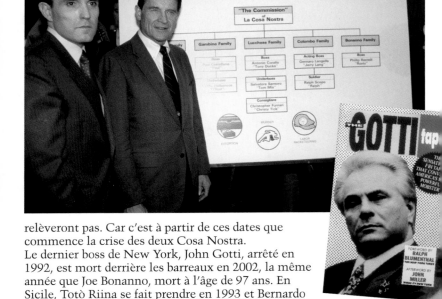

relèveront pas. Car c'est à partir de ces dates que commence la crise des deux Cosa Nostra.
Le dernier boss de New York, John Gotti, arrêté en 1992, est mort derrière les barreaux en 2002, la même année que Joe Bonanno, mort à l'âge de 97 ans. En Sicile, Totò Riina se fait prendre en 1993 et Bernardo Provenzano en 2006.

Une dernière tentative de travail commun entre les deux mafias sera tentée avec les exilés de la « guerre des mafias » sicilienne, qui s'étaient réfugiés aux États-Unis pour échapper à la folie meurtrière des Corléonais après leur victoire sur les Palermitains en 1981. Il s'agissait de reconstituer l'Old Bridge, sous l'égide de Salvatore Lo Piccolo. Mais celui-ci sera arrêté en plein boulot en 2007.

procureur de Manhattan, se distingue dans les années 1980 par sa bataille contre les familles Castellano, Gambino et Gotti. John Gotti (ci-dessus) mourra en prison en 2002 à l'âge de 61 ans. Ce sera le dernier des parrains.

CORRIERE DELLA SERA

Blitz di polizia e Fbi a Palermo e New York. Presi i boss del nuovo patto criminale

Italia-Usa, colpo ai padrini

Nel mirino le famiglie Gambino e Inzerillo: 90 arresti

La storia

Le due mafie

Il New Jersey e quel cadavere nell'auto

di GIOVANNI BIANCONI

PALERMO — «C'è una bomba nella macchina parcheggiata davanti all'hotel Hilton di Mont Laurel», disse la voce anonima che aveva telefonato all'ufficio di polizia del New Jersey.

Son idée était de reproduire les vieux schémas du commerce d'agrumes du XIXe siècle. Pour créer les conditions d'une réinsertion dans le juteux trafic de stupéfiants, Lo Piccolo voulait lancer une « Pasta Connection ». Nous sommes en 2003. Niccolò Notaro, 300 000 euros en poche, part de Palerme pour New York. Il est licencié en droit et parle bien l'anglais : un vrai nouveau *mafioso*. Avec cet argent, prélevé dans les caisses de la « famille » de Villabate, il est chargé par Lo Piccolo d'implanter un nouveau business lié à la distribution des pâtes aux États-Unis. Il crée la Haskell International Trading, signe un accord avec Nestlé-Italie pour obtenir l'exclusivité de la distribution sur le territoire américain. L'accord est signé le 16 mai 2003. La campagne de promotion est mise sur pied, Nick Notaro a bien travaillé, les voyages recommencent entre la capitale sicilienne et l'américaine. Mais quelque chose va s'enrayer à peine trois ans après. L'Old Bridge est démantelé par la police italienne. Lo Piccolo est arrêté avec son fils. La tentative des Siciliens de se réinsérer à plein titre dans le trafic de stupéfiants a donc échoué. Pour combien de temps ?

En février 2008, une maxi opération antimafia (ci-dessus) conduite par les polices américaine et italienne aboutit à 90 arrestations (60 à New York et 30 à Palerme). L'Old Bridge entre la Sicile et les États-Unis va-t-il s'effondrer ? Ces hommes prospéraient dans le secteur alimentaire et le bâtiment en montant de complexes opérations financières. Mais leur vrai but était de renouer ensemble le fil du trafic de drogue. Ce sont les *pizzini* des *mafiosi* siciliens qui ont trahi leurs amis d'outre-Atlantique. Interprétés par la police sicilienne, ils ont conduit tout droit aux Inzerillo et Gambino des États-Unis.

La mafia est la première entreprise italienne avec 90 milliards d'euros de chiffre d'affaires, soit 7 % du PIB, dit le rapport SOS Impresa de la Confesercenti (Confédération des commerçants) en 2007. Pour l'institut Eurispes, le chiffre d'affaires total des mafias atteindrait 130 milliards d'euros en 2008, dont 59 issus du trafic de drogue, 9 du racket, 12,6 de l'usure, et 16 de l'écomafia. La différence de chiffres tient au fait qu'il ne s'agit que d'évaluations, la mafia n'étant ni cotée en Bourse ni soumise au contrôle d'un quelconque comptable.

CHAPITRE 5

L'ÉCONOMIE DE LA MAFIA

C'est sur les traces du bon vieux trafic de cigarettes (ci-contre, dans les *vicoli* de Naples) que commence le trafic de drogue dans les années 1960 (page gauche, de la cocaïne en provenance de Panamá). Depuis, les trajets se sont perfectionnés. L'héroïne moyen-orientale peut très bien arriver en Italie du Sénégal via la Hollande, et la cocaïne colombienne, de la Belgique via l'Espagne.

Avec l'ouverture du chantier du
pont sur le détroit de Messine
(fin 2009-début 2010), deux
mafias se frottent sûrement les
mains. Celle qui règne du côté
de Ganzirri (Sicile), à savoir
Cosa Nostra, et, à
3,3 kilomètres de distance
– la longueur exacte du pont –,
celle qui règne du côté de
Cannitelli (Calabre), autrement
dit la 'Ndrangheta. « Le pont ? Lorsqu'il sera fini,
dans dix ans, il aura servi surtout à unir les deux
mafias », diagnostiquent, amers, les écolos de Reggio
de Calabre, hostiles à cette construction
mégalomane, à l'utilité économique discutable,
mais à l'impact sur l'environnement désastreux.
Le pont chevauchera l'un des plus beaux paysages
du monde, ce détroit historique qui sépare la
Calabre de la Sicile, et donc le continent de l'île,
parsemé d'écueils (Charybde et Scylla !) et
qu'Homère célébra avec passion.

Le pont des soupirs…
le pont des merveilles…
le pont des horreurs…
On en parle depuis un
demi-siècle de ce pont
sur le détroit de
Messine (ci-dessus, la
contestation des Verts
italiens qui dénoncent
le « pont entre l'État
et la mafia »), mais
le gouvernement
Berlusconi semble,
cette fois, décidé à passer
à l'acte (ci-dessous,
la maquette du pont).

Au royaume des travaux publics, la mafia est reine des sous-traitances

Les travaux publics sont une des principales sources de profit des mafias italiennes. Sans cesse renouvelable : le bâtiment et les infrastructures donnent et donneront toujours du travail. Or les mafias ont appris de longue date à s'insérer dans les financements publics. Bien sûr, il ne s'agit pas pour elles de créer des sociétés *ad hoc*, ce serait trop criant, et c'est interdit par la loi sur la transparence dans les travaux publics. Mais se manifester sur le terrain au moment des sous-traitances, c'est permis. La mafia est devenue la reine des sous-traitances. Avec ses tracteurs, ses excavateurs, ses bennes, ses camions. Avec sa main-d'œuvre locale qu'elle contrôle

La folie des chantiers du Mezzogiorno (ci-dessous, construction du village touristique de Castellaneta Marina dans les Pouilles) détruit progressivement des paysages séculaires. De Campomarino à Nova Siri (côte allant de la Basilicate aux Pouilles), une série de mégaconstructions

sévèrement – pas de grèves avec le personnel garanti par Cosa Nostra ou la 'Ndrangheta ! Et avec son absence totale de préjugés.

Un exemple, toujours lié à la construction du pont et des deux énormes pylônes qui le supporteront : pour déblayer les détritus, non seulement Cosa Nostra et la 'Ndrangheta seront à l'œuvre avec leurs excavatrices, mais elles transporteront aussi le terreau, les pierres, les rochers et les troncs d'arbres. Où ? Si ce n'est dans le détroit même, probablement à quelques kilomètres de distance des piliers. Car la beauté du paysage, le bien-être des populations ou la sauvegarde des espèces en danger ne sont pas le principal souci des mafias. Et comme il s'agira de centaines de milliers de tonnes, les écolos redoutent qu'à la longue elles ne fassent remonter le niveau de la mer et ne détruisent au passage l'équilibre écologique de cette partie vitale de la Méditerranée, où circulent en masse les thons et les espadons.

hôtelières ont poussé entre 2000 et 2007, sur 150 kilomètres. Sur tous ces travaux, les mafias locales ont leur mot à dire et leur pourcentage à prendre. Malgré le vote de lois qui interdisent aux entreprises en odeur de mafia de participer aux appels d'offres – elles doivent produire un « certificat antimafia » pour y être autorisées –, les *mafiosi* du bâtiment réussissent généralement à s'insérer grâce aux sous-traitances multiples (par exemple le transport des matériaux), plus difficilement contrôlables.

Bien avant que la Camorra n'occupe le devant de la scène et que *Gomorra* ne crève l'écran, le cinéaste Francesco Rosi avait signé en 1963 un beau film d'engagement politique, *Le mani sulla città* (*Main basse sur la ville*), avec Rod Steiger dans le rôle principal. Sa dénonciation impitoyable de la corruption et de la spéculation immobilière à Naples – même si la ville n'est jamais nommée – met en scène un ineffable constructeur immobilier, Eduardo Nottola, qui est aussi conseiller communal. Un conflit d'intérêts qui deviendra banal au fil des ans en Italie… Et que les amnisties successives ne feront qu'accentuer. Eduardo Nottola non seulement survivra au scandale (des morts sur un de ses chantiers et un enfant qui perd ses jambes), mais il deviendra assesseur au bâtiment. Avec la bénédiction de la Démocratie chrétienne et de l'évêque de Naples.

La logique a été identique en 1977 pour la construction du Vᵉ centre sidérurgique de Gioia Tauro (Calabre) et du port, qui est devenu depuis le principal terminal pour les conteneurs qui transitent d'Asie ou d'Amérique du Nord vers l'Europe : avec ses 3 millions d'unités qui jettent l'ancre chaque année, Gioia Tauro a remplacé Malte pour le *transhipment*. Les sous-traitances avaient alors été soigneusement divisées entre les différentes familles de la plaine de Gioia Tauro sous l'égide des Piromalli, chefs de file des *mafiosi* locaux. Elles s'étaient également occupées de l'embauche de la main-d'œuvre. Le phénomène s'était déjà produit pour la construction de l'autoroute du Soleil et de l'université de Cosenza. Ces investissements publics avaient alors aidé et accompagné la croissance des mafias – c'étaient les années 1970-1980.

« Le risque Mezzogiorno »

Ce fut une décennie féconde pour la mutation génétique du crime organisé, qui légalisa alors son rapport avec les politiciens locaux, les grands investisseurs nationaux et la bourgeoisie du lieu. C'est l'époque où le groupe Ferruzzi de Raul Gardini (chimie) et le groupe Fininvest de Silvio Berlusconi, pourtant tous deux originaires de l'Italie du Nord, versent des pourcentages juteux aux mafias pour garantir la protection de leurs outils de travail (les émetteurs de la Fininvest pour Berlusconi). Son bras droit Marcello Dell'Utri a d'ailleurs subi une condamnation définitive pour cet épisode

IL PAR
CHE A
L'affare subappa

Les aides à fonds perdus (donc sans intérêts et sans remboursement du capital) dont la Cassa per il Mezzogiorno (en haut, annonce de l'un de ses financements) fut responsable ont largement contribué à alimenter la mentalité « assistée » des gens du Sud. En remplissant les poches du crime organisé. « Plutôt qu'une cure, ces fonds sont une maladie », soutiennent les économistes les plus sérieux.

délictueux. Les entreprises s'étaient donc persuadées à l'époque que le problème « mafia » était seulement un problème de coût supplémentaire qu'on aurait pu appeler « le risque Mezzogiorno ». Évalué à environ 3 % du coût total de la facture, il pouvait ressembler à un énième impôt local qu'il valait mieux se résigner à honorer. Le juge Giovanni Falcone, tellement effrayé de la diffusion de ces pratiques et de l'exploitation mafieuse de l'argent de la collectivité, avait même proposé de bloquer tous les financements à fonds perdus destinés au Sud. Comme mesure de précaution.

C'est le procureur national antimafia Piero Grasso qui a lancé l'alarme dès la mi-avril 2009 (ci-contre, article de *La Repubblica*, 14 avril) : l'après-séisme à L'Aquila risque de faire l'affaire des mafias : « Nous pouvons affirmer que la corruption est un phénomène très diffus dans les Abruzzes, et que l'administration publique y est particulièrement corruptible. Ce sont deux données qui facilitent automatiquement les infiltrations mafieuses. » La Camorra, la 'Ndrangheta et même Cosa Nostra ont d'ailleurs déjà laissé des traces de leur passage dans cette zone montagneuse à cheval entre le centre et le Sud. On a ainsi relevé en 2009 que 1 600 000 euros provenant du trésor du *mafioso* sicilien Ciancimino avaient atterri dans les caisses de trois sociétés abruzzaises. Les appels d'offres que la reconstruction implique ainsi que la gestion des ordures et détritus ne peuvent qu'être au centre des intérêts des mafias. Ce qui a conduit le parquet national antimafia à dépêcher quatre de ses experts pour contrôler de près le pedigree des seize entreprises du bâtiment candidates à la reconstruction.

O DEL CEMENTO
DIA L'ABRUZZO

bra dei clan: perché il dopo terremoto fa paura

Le pompage des ressources publiques (et privées) est donc la principale spécialité de la mafia. Les tremblements de terre aussi ont prouvé leur « utilité », particulièrement celui de 1980 en Campanie, qui permit à la Camorra napolitaine de réaliser un véritable saut qualitatif. Ses entreprises se présentèrent, ponctuelles, au moment de la reconstruction, avec leurs camions, qui garantissaient le déblaiement des ruines, et leurs ouvriers, qui assurèrent l'installation des premiers préfabriqués.

« Si le tremblement de terre n'avait pas existé, il aurait fallu l'inventer », dit l'historien Enzo Ciconte. Une chose est sûre : là où il y a développement, richesse et investissement, il y a mafia. Au Sud en tout cas.

Mettersi a posto

Un phénomène analogue se produit pour le *pizzo*, le « pourcentage », cette rente ordinaire de l'organisation mafieuse. Le *pizzo* a une double fonction : assurer un revenu minimum garanti pour le paiement des dépenses courantes, par exemple les chèques mensuels aux détenus et à leurs familles, sans oublier les veuves et les orphelins ; et garantir un contrôle capillaire du territoire, qui représente la vraie force des mafias, leur police locale, le signe de leur profond enracinement. Le mécanisme du *pizzo* est simple, même s'il est à double sens : le *mafioso* vient offrir au commerçant – du marchand ambulant au restaurateur en passant par le boucher, le coiffeur, l'agence bancaire ou le garage – la protection de l'organisation en échange d'un versement mensuel – parfois annuel –, l'équivalent d'une prime d'assurance, pour être garanti contre tout vol, hold-up, effraction ou incendie. Le chiffre est donc variable selon leurs activités économiques et

« Se mettre en règle » : c'est le conseil amical que les proches des mafias conseillent à quiconque ouvre une nouvelle activité productive. « Se mettre en règle » signifie verser le *pizzo* (ci-dessous, les comptes rendus pointilleux des sommes payées à la « famille » de Salvatore Lo Piccolo) ou bien risquer l'attentat (page de droite, le célèbre restaurant de Portici [Naples] Ciro a Mare, qui offre un excellent poisson et qui a sauté en janvier 2009 pour n'avoir pas su *mettersi a posto*).

selon leur caractère plus ou moins florissant.
Il est conseillé aux négoces qui ouvrent pour la
première fois de *mettersi a posto*, « se mettre en
règle ».

Telle est la formule magique, le conseil
impérieux, l'ordre en définitive, qui
marque le premier contact du *mafioso*
avec le commerçant. Les modalités
d'approche sont souvent grossières.
L'invitation peut être verbale, ou sous
la forme d'un billet glissé sous le rideau
de fer avec le chiffre de la rançon exigée
et l'opportunité de se mettre « en
rapport avec les amis ». Les missives
sont souvent écrites par des
analphabètes, mais leur contenu est
sans équivoque : ou l'on paie ou l'on
sera victime d'un attentat. Ainsi, en
2006, ce boucher de Messine qui trouve
sous sa porte ce billet : « Cher
commerçant, je te fais savoir que d'ici à
la fin du mois il faut 30 000 euros si tu
ne veux pas que ta boucherie saute. »
Ou ce négoce de luxe de Palerme :

Libero Grassi : un
héros de l'Antimafia,
le premier chef
d'entreprise sicilien qui
ait payé de sa vie son
refus du *pizzo*.

« Ciao, très cher ami, d'ici 15 jours il faut
50 000 euros, sinon ton magasin brûlera. Si tu as
des amis consulte-les. » Ou encore cette parfumerie,
toujours à Palerme : « Très cher ami, prépare
25 000 euros, on viendra te trouver. Si tu as des
amis, parles-en avec eux. Salutations distinguées et
à bientôt. » Les « amis », ce sont des voisins, des
commerçants qui vivent dans le même quartier, qui
expliqueront au « nouveau venu » qu'il vit dans la
zone de contrôle de tel ou tel chef *mafioso*. Et qu'il
vaut mieux « se mettre en règle ». Faire semblant,
en quelque sorte, qu'il s'agit d'un nouvel impôt
d'État – l'État mafieux – qui protège mieux qu'une
compagnie d'assurances. D'ailleurs à Palerme,
les sociétés d'assurances ne sont guère présentes…

Mais le problème du *pizzo* est assez complexe,
il a des dimensions « culturelles » enracinées.
Sinon, comment expliquer qu'un boutiquier
palermitain victime du *pizzo* – les écoutes
téléphoniques le prouvent – suggère à son maître
chanteur de sortir du magasin pour empocher son
enveloppe car la police a installé des caméras qui
contrôlent les locaux à l'intérieur ?

De Naples (à gauche) à Palerme (ci-contre) en passant par Reggio de Calabre (en bas), il se confirme en ce début de IIIᵉ millénaire que le *pizzo* reste la rente préférée des mafias. Alors, ceux qui repoussent le chantage, lorsqu'ils n'y laissent pas la vie, sont souvent contraints de fermer boutique ou de changer de métier. On comprend dans ces conditions que dans certains quartiers des grandes villes du Sud, plus de la moitié des commerçants préfèrent verser leur obole. Mais au *pizzo* s'est ajoutée l'usure. Car pour faire face à la crise économique, nombre de commerçants sont tentés d'avoir recours au crédit parallèle, même si les taux d'intérêt varient de 120 à 240 %.

Trafics en tous genres

À ce pompage systématique et parfois consensuel des ressources, publiques et privées, les mafias ajoutent des sources de profit plus risquées mais plus juteuses : les différents trafics de cigarettes, de drogue, d'armes et parfois d'êtres humains (ce fut le cas pour la Sacra Corona Unita des Pouilles). Pour ce qui est de la drogue, l'Italie a commencé dans les années 1960 à jouer un rôle de pays de transit : le produit (le pavot), parti de Turquie ou du Liban, une fois passé en France chez les « Marseillais » qui l'avaient transformé en héroïne, arrivait en Sicile où les familles mafieuses se chargeaient de le revendre aux Américains. Les Siciliens n'étaient donc au départ que des associés des « Marseillais », mais ils savaient mieux que quiconque utiliser les bons vieux réseaux du trafic de cigarettes. Puis ils se mirent à raffiner eux-mêmes, sous l'égide d'un chimiste formé à l'école de Marseille, Francesco Marino Mannoia, arrêté plus tard par les soins du juge Falcone, qui le persuada de se « repentir ». Et il raconta la véritable histoire du raffinage d'héroïne.

Des kilos de cocaïne cachés dans des caisses de calmars surgelés : c'est l'opération anti-drogue de janvier 2009 dans le port de Naples (ci-dessous).

La 'Ndrangheta, elle aussi, a suivi un chemin analogue dans les années 1970, toujours à la remorque des réseaux du trafic de cigarettes : les contrebandiers calabrais furent les premiers « courriers de la drogue » avec les familles Macrì et Piromalli. Ils avaient investi dans les stupéfiants

Son enlèvement a duré plus de deux ans (1988-1990) : Cesare Casella a raconté dans un livre sa longue prison aux mains de la 'Ndrangheta (page de

l'argent des rançons de plus de deux cents enlèvements réalisés par leurs soins dans la Péninsule. Ce fut leur pécule de départ. Aujourd'hui, les 'Ndranghetistes assurent 80 % du trafic international de stupéfiants. Et empochent des millions d'euros. Ils y ont ajouté le trafic d'armes, parfois de substances nucléaires et de bijoux. Dans la Camorra napolitaine, l'entrée dans la drogue s'est faite sous l'égide de Cosa Nostra, avec des boss napolitains qui avaient la double affiliation, celle camorriste et celle de la mafia sicilienne. Ainsi pour les parrains Salvatore et Michele Zaza. Avec le déclin, provisoire mais évident, de Cosa Nostra sur le marché international des stupéfiants, ce sont donc ses alliés qui en assurent le trafic actuel. Mais les élèves ont maintenant dépassé leurs maîtres.

droite, en haut).
Sa rançon a servi à financer l'entrée de cette organisation dans le trafic de stupéfiants (ci-dessus, saisie d'un chargement en 2007 à Milan).

« Les lois ne servent à rien si elles ne sont pas accompagnées d'une solide volonté politique : celle-ci ne se formera que lorsque le pays tout entier sera conscient de la nécessité de combattre le crime organisé. Alors se poseront les vrais problèmes, qui ne sont pas d'ordre législatif, mais professionnel. Le cadre et les structures existent. Il faut les faire marcher avec des hommes professionnellement compétents. Souvent, lorsque j'évoque ce problème, je vois s'arrondir les yeux de mes interlocuteurs comme si je disais quelque chose d'indécent. »

Giovanni Falcone, *Le Juge et les Hommes d'honneur*, 1991

CHAPITRE 6

L'ANTIMAFIA

Deux magistrats antimafia (à gauche) qui étaient comme frères et qui ont été assassinés à deux mois de distance, en 1992, lorsque Cosa Nostra lança sa grande offensive contre l'État : Giovanni Falcone et Paolo Borsellino étaient tous deux palermitains et connaissaient sur le bout des doigts la mafia et la mentalité mafieuse. La Pieuvre (ci-contre) ne leur a pas pardonné.

« U maxi » !

Le mot « Antimafia » est sûrement un néologisme. Il
n'empêche que la lutte contre la mafia est aussi une
réalité bien tangible. À partir du « maxi procès » (dit
« U maxi » par les *mafiosi*) de Palerme en 1986-1987
en tout cas. Instruit par le juge Giovanni Falcone, il
comptera 474 inculpés, 8 607 pages d'accusations et
800 000 pages de procès-verbaux d'interrogatoire,
25 « repentis » et une salle d'audience spectaculaire
construite à deux pas de la prison de l'Ucciardone,
pour éviter les déplacements des détenus (considérés
comme dangereux). Son issue donne encore
des frissons dans le monde du crime organisé :
19 perpétuités et 2 665 années de prison

Le 10 février 1986 à
Palerme, le « maxi
procès » contre la mafia
s'ouvre dans la salle-
bunker du tribunal
(ci-dessus, annonce d'*Il
Corriere della sera*), avec
une salle d'audience
construite pour
l'occasion, à l'épreuve de
tout type d'attentat, et
sévèrement contrôlée
(ci-contre). Les inculpés
sont au nombre de 474,
du jamais vu en Italie.
C'est en tout cas
la première réaction
d'envergure de l'État
contre Cosa Nostra.

seront infligés au Gotha de Cosa Nostra. Pour la première fois, tous les chefs mafieux, les membres de la Coupole, de Michele Greco à Totò Riina, sont au banc des accusés et subissent donc de lourdes condamnations. Pour la première fois, les magistrats appliquent la loi La Torre, qui a introduit dans

Le « maxi procès » sanctionne 120 homicides et des décennies de trafic de drogue et d'extorsions. Sur les 474 inculpés, 119 – en fuite – furent condamnés par

Il maxiprocesso a Cosa Nostra: ieri sera il verdetto

Condanne a vita (sono 19) a tutti i componenti la «cupola» Liggio non è stato giudicato. Pene complessive per 2.265 anni

Ergastolo ai boss

le code pénal le délit d'« association mafieuse ». Pour la première fois, un procès mafieux ne s'achève pas par des « absolutions au bénéfice du doute ». Les preuves, elles, sont là; elles ont été minutieusement accumulées par le « Pool antimafia » de Palerme, et de nombreux témoins sont présents pour les confirmer à l'audience. Le « maxi procès » sera la première réponse massive mais démocratique d'un État secoué par une série d'« attentats anti-institutionnels ». Qui passe à l'attaque mais en restant dans le cadre de la légalité.

contumace. Et il ne fut pas tenu compte des comportements aberrants de certains prévenus qui s'étaient cousu la bouche pour signifier leur refus de parler, tandis que d'autres avaient quotidiennement menacé de se couper la gorge.

Fascisme et mafia

Le « maxi procès » fut le contraire de la répression
indiscriminée, autoritaire et souvent illégale, que
le fascisme instaura entre 1924 et 1929. Non
seulement en Sicile mais dans tout le Mezzogiorno.
Où les garanties constitutionnelles furent
suspendues. Où les tortures dans les prisons
devinrent monnaie courante, ainsi que les procès
sommaires, les violences injustifiées et les
déportations. Pour l'historien Francesco Renda
(*Mafia. Quattro studi*, 1970), c'est « toute une classe
enchaînée qui s'est trouvée inculpée aux côtés des
mafiosi – les paysans, les pauvres gens de la
campagne, privés de leurs droits civiques et
politiques les plus
élémentaires – victime de la
plus épouvantable terreur et
de la haine la plus aveugle ».
Des milliers d'innocents
tombèrent sous le coup de
la furie dévastatrice du
général Cesare Mori,
nommé en 1924 préfet de
Sicile par Benito Mussolini.
Le parti fasciste, qui se
voulait le seul médiateur
possible dans les sociétés
méridionales, ne pouvait en
effet accepter de partager
avec quelque organisation
que ce soit, légale ou
illégale, le système
clientélaire, la distribution
des faveurs, le contrôle
des bureaux d'embauche.
En somme ce qui constitue
les instruments de base
du monde *mafioso*. Mais
jamais le fascisme ne s'en
prendra à la « haute mafia »,
l'*alta mafia* des banques,
des salons, de l'industrie,

Le célèbre général
Cesare Mori (ici, en
mai 1928 à Binova,
sur une photo inédite)
racontera en 1932
sa guerre contre les
mafias, dans *La Mafia
à couteaux tirés*.
Envoyé par Mussolini
pour mater les « terres
infidèles », il fut
surnommé le « préfet
de fer » : ce sera le titre
du film de Pasquale
Squittieri (1977) avec
Giuliano Gemma et
Claudia Cardinale. Son
héritage reste très
discuté.

S.E. Mori parla al popolo

31. *Ai piedi di Gangi liberata dai banditi le popolazioni delle Madonie in masse imponenti si raccolgono intorno al Prefetto Mori inneggiando alla liberazione.*

des hobereaux de la campagne. Alors, si l'homme d'honneur a eu à se plaindre de Mussolini et de Mori, allant jusqu'à se ranger parfois aux côtés des antifascistes, les hautes sphères de Cosa Nostra n'ont eu, elles, qu'à s'en réjouir.

Ce sont les mêmes hautes sphères qui se hâteront à la Libération de prendre langue avec les partis conservateurs et les hiérarchies catholiques. Leur but : sauver l'ordre en place. La propriété. Le système social existant. Ce qui voulait dire barrer la route aux *braccianti* (« journaliers ») et autres salariés agricoles qui voulaient profiter de la fin de la guerre pour changer la société. En s'alliant même aux communistes.

CESARE MORI

CON LA MAFIA
AI FERRI CORTI

CON 16 ILLUSTRAZIONI
FUORI TESTO

A. MONDADORI · EDITORE

Autoritaire, inflexible, peu orthodoxe dans ses méthodes, Mori (ici, face à la foule à Gangi) traîna devant les cours de justice des brigands, des *mafiosi*, mais aussi des innocents. Beaucoup pensent qu'il a été utilisé par le fascisme pour éliminer la mafia « basse » tout en sauvegardant la « haute ». Mori a eu conscience des limites de son action : « Le coup mortel contre la mafia nous le porterons lorsqu'il nous sera consenti de faire des ratissages pas seulement dans les figuiers de Barbarie mais aussi dans les antichambres des préfectures, des bureaux de police, des palais des patrons et même de quelques ministères. »

Un nouvel instrument de lutte : le « délit d'association mafieuse »

Entre ces deux réponses extrêmes – la répression fasciste et le « maxi procès » – l'histoire de l'Antimafia suit son train-train : moins éclatant sans doute, mais très instructif. Elle commence avec l'offensive parlementaire contre le crime datée de juillet 1963 lorsque, après l'assassinat de sept carabiniers à Ciaculli près de Palerme, la première Commission d'enquête sur la mafia est instaurée. Elle contribuera de façon notable à la connaissance du phénomène et à l'implication des classes dirigeantes péninsulaires dans

1. Dopo l'articolo 416 del cod
«Art. 416-bis. - Associaz

l'aventure de l'Antimafia. L'année décisive cependant est l'année 1982, lorsque le secrétaire régional du PCI, Pio La Torre, et le général Carlo Alberto Dalla Chiesa sont assassinés à Palerme. Ce général-préfet avait été envoyé en « terre infidèle » pour donner un signal de la volonté de l'État de répondre à Cosa Nostra après une série d'attentats spectaculaires. D'y répondre même en termes de législation nouvelle.

Un véritable arsenal antimafia sera ainsi élaboré, que le Parlement européen donnera en exemple aux autres membres de l'Union dix ans après. Leur conseiller de prendre pour modèle ne fût-ce que le seul « délit d'association mafieuse » dans leur trousseau de lois contre le crime organisé.

Le fameux article 416 bis du code pénal (ci-dessus) est voté le 19 septembre 1982 après l'assassinat du général Carlo Alberto Dalla Chiesa et de sa femme (en haut), le 3 septembre de la même année. Il introduit le délit d'association mafieuse, punissable de 3 à 5 ans de réclusion, même sans délit. Il prédispose également la confiscation des biens des *mafiosi* arrêtés.

Ce délit, instauré par la « loi La Torre », permet de condamner un inculpé pour un crime auquel il n'a pas pris part (et c'est important dans le Sud, parce que les témoins font généralement défaut dans les procès de mafia), mais pour le simple fait qu'il est membre de l'organisation criminelle qui l'a programmé. Pour apporter les preuves du délit associatif, il est très utile de pouvoir établir par exemple que des méthodes telles que l'intimidation, la menace ou la violence ont été utilisées par le prévenu.

En 1982, le mot fin est donc mis aux procès farces qui se concluaient par l'absolution des inculpés faute de témoins visuels, et dont l'issue, heureuse pour le *mafioso*, ne faisait

penale è aggiunto il seguente:
e di tipo mafioso.

qu'accroître son prestige dans la population. Le boss Luciano Leggio avait ainsi accumulé neuf procès et neuf absolutions pour « insuffisance de preuves » avant que le délit d'association mafieuse ne fût introduit. Ce nouveau délit a d'ailleurs été inséré directement dans le code pénal : c'est le fameux article 416 bis. Redoutable et redouté par les criminels.

Menaces sur les biens mafieux

Autre grande innovation de la loi La Torre : l'introduction de mesures de confiscation des biens *mafiosi*. Ce n'est plus seulement la personne du mafieux qui est frappée, mais aussi son patrimoine,

Luciano Leggio, dit Liggio, originaire de Corleone, a le profil type du *mafioso* arrogant (ici, lors d'un procès). Sanguinaire et sans pitié, il commença sa carrière de criminel en 1945, à l'âge de 20 ans, en assassinant un *campiere* dont il prit la place. Il devait ensuite éliminer le syndicaliste Placido Rizzotto, puis le *capomafia* Michele Navarra, qu'il remplaça comme chef des Corléonais. Condamné au « maxi procès » de 1986-1987, il finit ses jours en prison en 1993.

ses propriétés, ses actions, etc. Les biens confisqués ne sont pas remis en vente avec le système des enchères publiques (ils pourraient être rachetés par des prête-noms), mais cédés à des associations, des communautés, des groupes, des coopératives de citoyens. L'association Libera, créée en 1995 par Don Luigi Ciotti pour diffuser la « culture de la légalité », et qui regroupe 1 500 communautés, groupes, unités de base antimafia, s'est spécialisée dans la gestion des biens mis sous séquestre. Un exemple : l'immense propriété du boss Inzerillo à Palerme où une centaine de *ragazzi* de Don Ciotti produisent depuis plus de dix ans une excellente huile d'olive « libérée de la mafia ». Des dizaines de coopératives Libera terra ont également été créées, dans les Pouilles, la Calabre, la Campanie. Et même une coopérative dans le bâtiment qui a pris la place de la Calcestruzzi de Trapani (Sicile), bannie pour activités mafieuses. Ces initiatives subissent parfois des intimidations criminelles, mais le soutien de l'opinion, et la mobilisation, même médiatique, que garantit Don Ciotti, ont empêché jusqu'ici toute marche arrière.

Grâce au « 416 bis », les séquestrations de biens se sont multipliées (ci-dessus, des Ferrari mises sous séquestre à Caserte, dans le garage de l'avocat Mario Natale, tenu pour un prête-nom du clan camorriste des Casalesi). Les terres confisquées sont le plus souvent confiées à l'association Libera (budget 2008 : trois millions d'euros), qui produit et vend des denrées « libres » et gère les biens « libérés ». Ses fameuses « caravanes de la légalité » parcourent l'Italie en tous sens : à l'été 2009, Libera a même inauguré une caravane de cinéma qui stationne dans les terres libérées en projetant des films dédiés au crime organisé.

farina di
CECI
da agricoltura biologica

LIBERA
TERRA
• Corleone

dalle terre liberate dalla mafia
le cooperative aderiscono a LIBERA associazioni. Nomi. Numeri contro le mafie

Les « repentis »

Il faut ensuite faire un saut jusqu'en 1991
pour qu'enfin soit votée une loi qui favorise la
collaboration des mafieux avec la magistrature :
en instaurant d'importantes réductions de
peine aux « repentis » (tel est le terme hâtif
qui a alors été adopté même s'il ne correspond
généralement pas à un parcours moral
ou religieux) qui vident leur sac avec les
représentants de l'État. Lequel offre en échange une
protection inspirée par le système des « Marshall »
américains : un chèque mensuel et un changement
d'identité ainsi que le transfert de leur famille proche
dans une localité protégée, et en tout cas, hors de la
Sicile, des Pouilles ou de la Campanie. On compte
actuellement 785 « repentis » de la mafia, ce qui veut
dire 2 703 personnes à protéger en incluant les
familles. Le plus célèbre d'entre eux, Tommaso
Buscetta, arrêté au Brésil en 1984, et interrogé par
le juge Giovanni Falcone, décida avec lui de passer
à table. Avec un grand sérieux et une vision globale
du crime organisé (c'était aussi un gros trafiquant

Antonio Castro est
un des fondateurs de
Libera terra, qui veut
être exemplaire même
dans la qualité des
produits – bio – qu'elle
cultive (ci-dessus,
farine de pois chiches,
mise en vente en 2008).
Ses coopératives
les plus célèbres sont
la Pio La Torre et
la Placido Rizzotto,
du nom de deux
victimes illustres
de Cosa Nostra.

de drogue, raison pour laquelle il fut surnommé « le boss des deux mondes »), il raconta pendant des mois la véritable histoire de Cosa Nostra.

Sur cet épisode majeur de la lutte contre les mafias, le juge Falcone, qui s'était farouchement battu pour l'adoption de la loi en faveur des « repentis », écrira : « Quand […] l'État a montré une (provisoire) disponibilité

à combattre, le côté cérémonieux du *mafioso* à l'égard du magistrat s'est atténué, et les traits de caractère de chacun se sont montrés au grand jour : certains se sont mis à hurler, d'autres sont devenus insolents jusqu'à la menace, d'autres carrément fous, d'autres ont refusé de répondre, en priant d'ailleurs le juge de "ne pas leur en vouloir", d'autres enfin ont collaboré, comme cela se produit dans n'importe quel pays civilisé » (*Le Juge et les Hommes d'honneur*, 1991). On peut ajouter à l'arsenal antimafia le fameux article 41 bis du code carcéral qui condamne à l'isolement total le *mafioso*. Par exemple la vitre blindée qui sépare le condamné de ses visiteurs, même s'il s'agit de sa famille rapprochée.

Tommaso Buscetta est le « repenti » par excellence, celui qui, disait Falcone, « nous a ouvert les portes sur Cosa Nostra ». C'est en juillet 1984, après avoir été arrêté par la police brésilienne, que « le boss des deux mondes » est interrogé à Brasília par Falcone. Il décide de collaborer avec la justice italienne. Transféré dans la Péninsule (ci-dessus), il remplira des centaines de pages de confessions, n'hésitant pas à confirmer devant les tribunaux (ci-contre, en 1986, à Palerme), malgré les *lazzi* des *mafiosi* en cage, ses accusations contre Cosa Nostra. En échange, il obtiendra vite la liberté, sera pris en charge par les Marshall américains, changera de nom et mourra de sa belle mort en 2000, à New York. Entre-temps, Cosa Nostra aura assassiné une vingtaine de ses parents en Sicile.

C'est avec le juge Falcone (ci-contre, au palais de justice de Palerme) que commence la saison des « repentis ». Il arrive même que des candidats à l'abandon de Cosa Nostra, tel Gaspare Mutolo (en bas, lors de sa première arrestation en 1976), fassent savoir à Falcone leur désir de collaborer avec l'État. À l'automne 1991, Mutolo, autorisé à parler avec le magistrat le plus estimé par Cosa Nostra, explique alors le rôle des démo-chrétiens Salvatore Lima, Giulio Andreotti et des services secrets de Bruno Contrada. Bien qu'auteur de trente homicides, sera vite remis en liberté. Il vit aujourd'hui sous un faux nom dans une grande ville, s'est converti à la restauration et à la peinture. Mutolo, né en 1940, est souvent cité comme l'exemple type du « repenti heureux », celui qui a réussi sa conversion à la vie civile.

De nombreuses modifications, hélas, ont par la suite été introduites. Car on tend, dans les rangs de la politique, avec le temps qui passe, à vouloir atténuer le caractère drastique des mesures adoptées. Malgré leur extraordinaire efficacité. Et c'est alors que recommence le parcours à obstacles des « solitaires de l'Antimafia », tel le procureur national Piero Grasso – l'instauration d'un parquet centralisé et de services de la répression unifiés avait été décidée en 1991, toujours sous l'impulsion du juge Falcone – qui l'a raconté dans un livre (*La Mafia invisible*, 2001). Par-delà les sous-évaluations aveugles du danger mafieux de la part de l'exécutif, par-delà sa tendance à répondre au coup par coup, de façon émotive, aux événements délictueux siciliens, calabrais ou napolitains, Piero Grasso dénonce par exemple la loi de 2001 qui corrige celle de 1991 en rendant plus laborieuse la collaboration des « repentis ». Qui ne pourront dorénavant obtenir les premiers bénéfices de leurs confessions qu'après avoir exécuté au moins un quart de leur peine, ou dix ans en cas de perpétuité. Cette même loi élimine les déclarations au coup par coup, obligeant le candidat au « repentir » à dire tout ce qu'il sait dans un laps de temps maximum de six mois. Ce qui est peu lorsqu'un inculpé doit être interrogé par plusieurs parquets.

Le métier de magistrat antimafia est toujours dangereux mais, en Sicile, il peut coûter la vie. Ceux qui l'ont choisi aux temps héroïques (1980-1990) devaient bien sûr se battre contre la mafia, mais aussi contre l'État, le Conseil supérieur de la magistrature, qui ne comprenait pas grand-chose à la dangerosité des organisations criminelles. Ni à l'importance de la spécialisation des juges et de la centralisation des enquêtes. Lorsque Rocco Chinnici inventa le « Pool antimafia » de Palerme, avec Falcone (page de gauche, en haut, tout à gauche), Borsellino (ci-contre, en haut) et Ayala (en bas, à gauche, avec Falcone), ce fut une révolution : les informations sur la mafia étaient enfin centralisées. C'est ainsi que naquit le « maxi procès ». Nombre de magistrats restent aujourd'hui compétents, mais le travail d'équipe est fini. Dans la bataille contre la 'Ndrangheta, Nicola Gratteri (ci-contre) doit se sentir bien seul. Et il doit parfois se trouver davantage épaulé par la police que par ses pairs.

Vers une mafia ordinaire ?

Mais Piero Grasso dénonce aussi un autre coup de frein à la lutte antimafia, qui vient de l'évolution des organisations criminelles elles-mêmes. En choisissant une stratégie d'immersion dans la société, après la folie des attentats anti-institutionnels à répétition, elles ont fini par convaincre les représentants de l'État qu'ils ont gagné la bataille. Que la mafia ne tue plus, et donc qu'elle n'est plus dangereuse. Or quand la mafia ne tue pas – même l'écrivain sicilien Leonardo Sciascia le disait –, c'est qu'elle engrange des bénéfices, qu'elle est occupée à s'infiltrer dans toutes les sources possibles de profit, et qu'elle développe son visage légal. Aussi dangereux que son visage sanguinaire. Pour Cosa Nostra, pense Grasso, l'éclipse actuelle, le choix de devenir une « mafia invisible », lui fait faire un parcours analogue à celui de la mafia américaine. Laquelle a su depuis près de dix ans tirer un trait sur le monde du crime. Les vieilles familles sont devenues des multinationales, des entreprises propres, qui ont de moins en moins recours aux canaux illicites de profit. La « mafia invisible » est d'ailleurs d'une grande commodité pour les partis politiques qui sont habitués à traiter avec elle pour en recevoir

Un cliché symbolique de 2006 : à gauche, Giovanni De Gennaro, dit le « super flic », avec lequel Falcone conduisit ses enquêtes les plus fructueuses, et qui pilota avec lui le « repentir » de Tommaso Buscetta ; au centre, le ministre de l'Intérieur Giuseppe Pisanu, efficace responsable de la guerre contre le crime organisé ; à droite, Piero Grasso, devenu procureur national antimafia. Ils représentent les trois piliers de la bataille : policier, politique et judiciaire. La création en 1991 d'une Direzione Investigativa Antimafia qui fait collaborer toutes les forces de police sous une seule direction en est l'illustration. Tout comme celle de la Direction nationale antimafia (ou Parquet), née la même année.

quelque bénéfice électoral. Aux États-Unis, mais plus encore en Italie.

Que manque-t-il donc à ce pays pour battre définitivement le crime organisé ? C'est la question que se posait à haute voix Giovanni Falcone, symbole et héros de l'Antimafia, avant d'être assassiné le 23 mai 1992 à Palerme. Les lois sont là, disait-il, l'appareil répressif marche bien (la police italienne est en effet l'une des plus efficaces d'Europe contre le crime organisé), les prisons sont pleines de *mafiosi*… Pourquoi n'est-il pas encore possible de déraciner le mal ? Et il revenait sans cesse à cette maudite mobilisation fluctuante, épisodique, inconstante de la classe politique, qui s'est trop habituée à naviguer d'un état d'urgence à l'autre en oubliant le danger *mafioso* dans les périodes de calme plat… Un diagnostic qui coïncide avec celui de Piero Grasso. Le problème, disait alors Falcone, ce ne sont plus les lois, mais la volonté de les appliquer durablement. Quand la mafia tue. Et même quand elle ne tue pas.

Mai 1992 : le juge Falcone, sa femme et son escorte viennent de sauter sur l'autoroute Punta Raisi-Palerme (en bas). La société italienne semble complètement déboussolée. Et la presse témoigne de son désarroi lorsqu'elle interroge : « Comment gagner cette guerre ». On devine une myriade d'incertitudes sur les probabilités de la remporter.

TÉMOIGNAGES
ET DOCUMENTS

La mafia, déjà, au XIXᵉ siècle

Les observateurs n'ont pas attendu le XXIᵉ siècle pour découvrir la mafia. Des voyageurs français ou anglais, mais aussi une petite armée d'autochtones tels le « sbire » Alongi, l'écrivain Linares ou le sociologue Pitrè avaient exprimé – avec des décennies d'avance ! – des concepts très modernes sur l'extraordinaire voisinage culturel entre la mafia et la mentalité mafieuse.

Le rapport Mafia-État

Vu par l'écrivain britannique Patrick Brydone en 1770.

De qui était composé ce corps de garde ? Je te le donne en mille : des plus audacieux et consommés forbans qui aient jamais existé. Dans un autre pays ils auraient déjà subi le supplice de la roue, ou les chaînes ; ici au contraire ils sont publiquement protégés et universellement craints et respectés. [...] Ils ont une conception très romantique et très haute de ce qu'ils appellent leur point d'honneur. En eux, il y a un absurde mélange de vice perpétré de vertu, si je peux utiliser ce terme, qui gouverne leurs actions.

Patrick Brydone, *Viaggio in Sicilia e a Malta* [1770], Ed Longanesi, 1968

La Calabre

Vue par un officier français, Duret de Tavel, envoyé sur ces terres infidèles par Murat en 1810.

Les Calabrais sont de stature moyenne, bien proportionnés et musclés. Ils ont une peau sombre, des traits marqués, des yeux vifs et brûlants. Comme les Espagnols, avec lesquels ils ont beaucoup de choses en commun, ils portent en toutes saisons de grands manteaux noirs qui leur donnent un aspect sombre et lugubre. La forme de leurs chapeaux, très hauts et coniques, est bizarre et malheureuse. À cause des haines qui opposent les familles, ils sortent toujours armés de fusils, de poignards, et d'une ceinture en forme de giberne qui contient des cartouches. [...] À la tombée de la nuit, ils se barricadent à la maison et seuls des motifs urgents peuvent les contraindre à sortir. Le brigand, et celui qui cultive la terre se ressemblent tellement qu'on ne sait pas bien comment les distinguer : ils ont les mêmes coutumes, ils portent les mêmes vêtements et le même armement. [...] Les Calabrais, même ceux qui de par leur condition devraient être ennemis du désordre, manifestent un inexplicable sentiment d'indulgence envers les brigands : ce sont des pauvres diables, disent-ils avec compassion.

Séjour d'un officier français en Calabre, ou Lettres propres à faire connatre l'état ancien et moderne de la Calabre... Éditions Béchet aîné, 1820

Les « Beati Paoli »

Vus par Vincenzo Linarès, écrivain palermitain en 1840.

Ils se réunissaient pour exercer leurs fonctions despotiques et secrètes sous le nom de « Beati Paoli ». Gens du peuple, artisans, marins, hommes de loi, formaient ce corps terrible qui s'attribuait le droit de juger les actions des hommes, de réexaminer les sentences, de réparer les torts infligés par le pouvoir et les tribunaux constitués. Leurs attentions ne s'adressaient pas aux hautes sphères politiques. [...] Les Beati Paoli se rencontraient en grand secret sur le coup de minuit. Ils faisaient leurs procès en hâte... Leurs jugements étaient brefs, leurs votes libres, leurs peines rapides et fèroces... Le magistrat corrompu, le noble arrogant, l'employé malhonnête étaient soumis à un examen severe... Telle était la justice des Beati Paoli.

Vincenzo Linarès, *Racconti popolari*, Editions Lorenzo Dato, 1840

Les Siciliens

Vus par le policier G. Alongi en 1886.

La note dominante du caractère sicilien est un sentiment exagéré de soi-même, un égoïsme sans fin, un orgueil et une plénitude individuelle... En toute bonne foi le Sicilien se considère comme le plus habile, le plus intelligent, le plus éduqué, le plus riche, le plus vertueux, le plus digne homme du monde [...] Au besoin d'être homme, il sacrifie tout autre sentiment [...] Les femmes ont des vestiges de cannibalisme car elles embrassent et sucent leurs enfants sur le visage, dans le cou, les bras nus et d'autres parties du corps, jusqu'à les faire pleurer de façon convulsive, et en leur disant : « Comme tu es doux, je te mange, je te ronge tout entier »... Moi-même, accouru auprès d'un mort, j'ai trouvé sa femme et son fils qui embrassaient ses blessures sanguinolentes, faisaient semblant de les sucer et, le museau couvert de sang, criaient : « Je veux boire de la même manière le sang de son assassin, je meurs de soif. »

Giovanni Alongi [1886] in *La Maffia*, Sellerio, 1977

La mafia

La mafia n'est ni une secte ni une association, elle n'a pas plus de règlements que de statuts.

Un *mafioso* n'est pas un voleur, pas un malandrin ; et si – le mot connaissant un récent succès – un voleur ou un malandrin a été qualifié de *mafioso*, c'est par un public peu cultivé qui n'a pas pris le temps de réfléchir au sens du mot, et n'a pas prêté attention au fait qu'aux yeux d'un voleur ou un malandrin, un *mafioso* est simplement un homme courageux, expérimenté, et qui n'a rien à cacher. Et dans ce sens être mafieux est une qualité nécessaire, indispensable. La mafia est la conscience de son propre être, une conception excessive de la force individuelle comme « unique et seul arbitre de chaque différend, de tout conflit d'intérêt ou d'idée » ; un concept qui rend intolérable la supériorité, ou pire encore, le pouvoir d'autrui. Le *mafioso* veut être respecté et respecte la plupart du temps. S'il est offensé, il ne fait pas appel à la Justice, il ne s'en remet pas à la Loi ; ce serait faire preuve de faiblesse, enfreindre l'*omertà*, loi qui considère celui qui en appelle au magistrat pour obtenir réparation comme un ignoble traître.

Le *mafioso* sait obtenir raison tout seul, et lorsqu'il n'en a pas la force (ou qu'il se méfie), il le fait au moyen d'autres individus qui partagent ses idées et sa façon de penser. Même sans les connaître il s'en remet à eux ; un seul mouvement des yeux ou des lèvres, un mot suffit pour se faire comprendre et pour être assuré qu'il obtiendra réparation de l'offense ou, du moins, qu'elle sera vengée.

Mais celui qui n'a pas la force ou la capacité de se faire justice lui-même, et doit recourir à un ou plusieurs hommes dont il estime la force et le courage (il suffit d'une arme) – ce qui se dit *farisi la cosca*, faire appel au clan – est un lâche, ou comme on dit un *carugnuni*, une charogne : car quel genre d'homme n'a ni force ni courage ?

Giuseppe Pitrè, *Usi, costumi credenze e pregiu dizi del popolo siciliano*, Palerme, 1889, traduction Olivia Gili

La question méridionale

Leopoldo Franchetti et Sydney Sonnino étaient deux jeunes universitaires qui dédièrent à la « question méridionale » un livre extraordinaire, publié en 1877 après un long séjour en Sicile, et que l'éditeur Donzelli a republié en 2000. Franchetti s'intéressa aux « Conditions politiques et administratives » de l'île tandis que Sonnino consacrait son enquête aux « Paysans ».

Le voyageur qui débarque à Palerme, s'il y reste quelques jours, s'il ouvre un quelconque journal, s'il prête l'oreille aux conversations, s'il pose lui-même quelques questions, sent tout changer autour de lui. Les couleurs, l'aspect de chaque chose. Il entend dire que dans tel endroit quelqu'un a été tué d'un coup de fusil parti de derrière un mur, tiré par le gardien du jardin, parce que le propriétaire l'avait pris à son service à la place d'un autre qui avait été suggéré par une de ces personnes qui se chargent de distribuer le travail dans les propriétés des autres, et de choisir ceux à qui donner les terres en location. Un peu plus loin, un propriétaire qui voulait louer ses jardins à sa façon a senti passer une balle un centimètre au-dessus de sa tête, en guise d'avertissement bénévole, et ensuite il s'est soumis. Ailleurs, un jeune qui avait eu l'abnégation suffisante pour se dédier à la fondation et à la gestion de crèches dans les environs de Palerme, a pris un coup de fusil. Ce n'était pas par vendetta, ou par rancœur ; mais parce que certaines personnes, qui dominent la plèbe dans les environs, redoutaient qu'en se dédiant aux classes pauvres, cet homme puisse acquérir une certaine influence qu'elles auraient voulu garder en exclusivité pour elles-mêmes. Les violences, les homicides, prennent des formes étranges. On raconte qu'un ex-frère, qui dans un patelin voisin de Palerme avait pris la tête des abus de pouvoir et des crimes, allait ensuite apporter le réconfort de la religion à certains de ceux qu'il avait fait blesser. Après avoir entendu un certain nombre de ces anecdotes, tout le parfum des fleurs d'oranger et de citronnier laisse la place à une odeur de cadavre. Les auteurs de ces délits ont ils subi quelque procès, ont ils été condamnés ? Pratiquement aucun, et si par hasard l'un d'eux a été arrêté sur un soupçon, il s'est retrouvé en liberté pour absence de preuves, et parce qu'on n'a pas trouvé de témoins à sa charge.

Quelle est la raison de la puissance inouïe qu'ont ces personnes ? Où se cache la force qui leur assure

TÉMOIGNAGES ET DOCUMENTS 117

l'impunité ? Lorsqu'on demande si elles se sont constituées en associations, si elles ont des statuts, et des peines pour punir les traîtres : tous répondent qu'ils l'ignorent, et beaucoup qu'ils ne le croient pas. Le pays n'est pas dominé par quelque secte secrète de malfaiteurs. Il n'y a rien de mystérieux dans les délits commis. Parmi leurs auteurs, on trouve il est vrai des repris de justice, qui essaient d'échapper à de nouvelles poursuites. Mais la justice est la seule à ne pas savoir où ils se trouvent. Par ailleurs il est de notoriété publique qu'Untel ou Tel autre, un bourgeois, un propriétaire, un métayer, éventuellement conseiller communal, a constitué et accru son patrimoine en se mêlant des affaires des autres, en leur imposant sa volonté, et en faisant tuer ceux qui ne s'y soumettaient pas. Que tel autre, qui se promène tranquillement dans les rues, a plus d'un homicide sur la conscience. La violence s'exerce ouvertement, tranquillement, régulièrement ; elle fait partie de l'ordre normal des choses. Elle n'a besoin d'aucun effort, d'aucun ordre, d'aucune organisation. Entre celui qui donne l'ordre de commettre un délit, et celui qui l'exécute, souvent il ne semble pas y avoir de rapports continus, réglés par des normes fixes. Ce sont des personnes qui ayant besoin de commettre une violence, et trouvant sous leur main, pour ainsi dire dans la rue, les instruments adaptés à leurs fins, en font usage. [...]

Un tel type de société n'est pas nouveau dans l'histoire. Mais la Sicile en a développé complètement tous les symptômes. D'un côté on note une fidélité, une énergie dans l'amitié et dans les rapports d'inférieur à supérieur, qui n'a ni limites, ni scrupules, ni remords. Les individus se regroupent autour d'un ou plusieurs puissants, quelle que soit la raison de leur puissance : la richesse,

l'énergie, l'astuce ou autre chose. Les intérêts deviennent peu à peu communs. Les plus puissants utilisent leur force et leur influence au service des autres, les moins puissants mettent à disposition les moyens dont ils disposent. Chaque personne qui a besoin d'aide pour quelque raison que ce soit, pour faire respecter ses droits ou pour commettre une violence, est un nouveau client. Les responsables de chaque clientèle, n'ayant pas la moindre idée de ce que peut être l'intérêt collectif, cherchent à enrôler en faveur de cette même clientèle toutes les forces disponibles, sans aucune distinction. Ces responsables cherchent donc l'alliance des malfaiteurs comme celle des représentants du pouvoir judiciaire ou politique. Et pour sceller chacune de ces alliances, ils emploient les moyens qu'il faut. Ils aident le malfaiteur à fuir la justice, en organisant son évasion s'il est en prison, son absolution (et on imagine avec quels moyens) s'il subit un procès et ne peut s'évader.

Le malfaiteur devient ainsi un client. Il se mettra au service des personnes qui l'ont sauvé. Et qui pour se procurer l'alliance des autorités judiciaires et politiques emploient la corruption, la tromperie, l'intimidation. Et si ces moyens ne marchent pas, les responsables de clientèle s'arrangent pour faire croire ou bien qu'ils ont réussi, ou bien qu'ils ont trouvé dans les sphères supérieures du gouvernement les instruments pour punir le fonctionnaire récalcitrant.

Leopoldo Franchetti,
*Condizioni politiche
e amministrative della Sicilia*,
réédition Donzelli,
2000

Camorra, camorras

Pasquale Villari (1827-1917) est un intellectuel méridionaliste qui publie justement ses Lettres méridionales *en 1878. On ne peut qu'être frappé de la justesse de son analyse. Villari dit en d'autres termes ce que Roberto Saviano dénoncera 128 ans plus tard, dans* Gomorra.

De l'organisation...

Je commencerai par la Camorra, en notant que la loi sur la sécurité publique suppose que le camorriste ne fasse pas autre chose que s'enrichir indûment sur les biens d'autrui. Alors qu'il menace et procède à des intimidations, et pas seulement pour s'enrichir ; qu'il impose des taxes ; s'empare de ce qui appartient aux autres sans rien payer ; fait commettre des délits ; en commet lui-même, en obligeant d'autres à en prendre la responsabilité ; protège les coupables contre la justice ; exerce son métier, si l'on peut dire, sur tout : dans les rues, dans les maisons, dans les foyers des théâtres, sur les lieux de travail, sur les crimes commis, sur le jeu. L'organisation la plus parfaite de la Camorra, on la trouve dans les prisons où règne le camorriste. Et en l'y envoyant on croit le punir, alors qu'on lui donne les moyens de mieux poursuivre son œuvre. Mais ce que la loi ne semble pas soupçonner, et que beaucoup ignorent, c'est que la Camorra ne règne pas uniquement dans les rangs inférieurs de la société ; il y a aussi des camorristes en gants blancs et en habit noir, dont les noms et les délits sont connus de tous. La forme que la Camorra prend dans les différents lieux et chez les personnes où elle s'exerce, est extrêmement variée.

Il n'y a pas longtemps, j'ai écrit à un maire adjoint de Naples, amoureux de son pays, vieux libéral, et patriote sûr : « Dis-moi quelque chose de la Camorra. Est-ce qu'elle avance ou qu'elle recule ? Est-elle en voie d'être extirpée ? »

Il m'a fait une réponse que je ne reporte pas tout entière parce qu'elle pourrait sembler exagérée à beaucoup. Je copie seulement la conclusion de sa lettre : « De nombreuses ordonnances municipales ne peuvent atteindre leur objectif que si ce dernier coïncide avec les intérêts de la Camorra. Naples commence à être propre depuis que la Camorra avec ses sous-traitances en tire profit. Et moi, en tant que maire adjoint de... [ndt : les pointillés sont dans le texte original], j'ai pu contraindre 1 157 propriétaires à restaurer et repeindre en blanc leurs maisons et leurs villas, qui sont entourées de murs, seulement parce que, sans que je le sache, la Camorra locale a dirigé l'opération, en accord avec un huissier de la mairie. »

Cet état de choses fait peur, devient de plus en plus terrifiant à partir du moment où on s'en approche et on en constate l'extension.

Pour que la Camorra devienne forte, il faut qu'un certain nombre de citoyens, ou une classe entière, se plie aux menaces d'un petit nombre, ou d'un grand nombre, pourvu qu'ils soient organisés. Dès que ces conditions se réalisent dans des proportions assez importantes, on comprend alors de quelle façon la maladie réussit à s'étendre, et à prendre des apparences différentes en fonction des différentes couches sociales qu'elle atteint. Le mal est aussi contagieux que le bien, et l'oppression, surtout celle exercée par la Camorra, corrompt l'opprimé et l'oppresseur, et aussi celui qui reste spectateur et ne réagit pas de toutes ses forces. [...]

La ville de Naples est celle dans laquelle la plèbe se trouve non pas dans la plus grande misère, parce que ce n'est pas la pire des situations ; mais dans le plus grand abandon, le plus grand découragement, le plus terrible abrutissement. Tout était permis contre elle sous les Bourbon. Le *galantuomo*, le gentilhomme, pouvait sans crainte, même en plein jour et dans la rue, faire usage de son bâton, parce que la police penchait toujours de son côté. Les aumônes données par les privés ; ou par les couvents qui distribuaient la soupe ; ou par les Œuvres pieuses ; ou par le gouvernement qui donnait du pain – tout cela alimentait la misère et la rendait permanente. La Camorra naissait alors naturellement parmi ces hommes ; elle était comme leur gouvernement naturel, et pour cela se voyait soutenue et encouragée par les Bourbon, comme un moyen de faire régner l'ordre. C'est comme cela que le camorriste faisait régner la terreur, par la menace. C'est comme cela qu'il

enrôlait des gamins de 14 ou 16 ans, pour leur apprendre à voler par exemple un mouchoir, qui restait en sa possession, en lui donnant en échange, comme une espèce de faveur, quelques sous. C'est comme cela qu'il pouvait faire ce qu'il voulait des hommes et des femmes. Et comme il accomplissait ses propres vendettas mais aussi celles des autres, il ne suscitait pas seulement la terreur, mais aussi l'admiration et l'affection chez ceux-là même qu'il opprimait. Une fois la maladie déclarée, elle se répandait à vue d'œil. Et dès que ce spectacle ne suscitait plus le dégoût, que l'oppression et la violence ne semblaient plus être des délits, beaucoup d'autres les mirent en pratique, qui appartenaient à d'autres couches sociales, lesquelles, en d'autres temps, auraient trouvé dans leur conscience un obstacle invincible."

Pasquale Villari,
Lettere meridionali ed altri scritti sulla questione sociale in Italia,
1878, rééd. Loescher, 1972

... au Système

Le Système avait alimenté le marché international de l'habillement, royaume de l'élégance italienne. Chaque recoin de la planète pouvait être atteint par les entreprises, les hommes et les produits du Système. Système : un mot qu'ici tout le monde connaît mais qui, pour les autres, reste encore à déchiffrer, une référence inaccessible à ceux qui ignorent quelles sont les dynamiques du pouvoir de l'économie criminelle. Le mot camorra n'existe pas, c'est un mot de flics, utilisé par les magistrats, les journalistes et les scénaristes. Un mot qui fait sourire les affiliés, une indication vague, un terme bon pour les universitaires et appartenant à l'histoire. Celui que les membres d'un clan

utilisent pour se désigner est Système :
« J'appartiens au Système de
Secondigliano. » Un terme éloquent, qui
évoque un mécanisme plutôt qu'une
structure. Car l'organisation criminelle
repose directement sur l'économie, et la
dialectique commerciale est l'ossature
du clan.

Le Système de Secondigliano détenait
désormais tout le secteur du textile,
et la périphérie de Naples était le centre
de la production, le véritable poumon
industriel. Tout ce qu'il était impossible
d'exiger ailleurs, en raison de la rigidité
des contrats, des lois et des règles en
matière de copyright, on pouvait
l'obtenir au nord de Naples. Articulée
autour de la puissance économique des
clans, la périphérie permettait de brasser
des quantités considérables de capitaux,
inimaginables dans n'importe quelle
zone industrielle légale. Les clans
avaient créé des filières entières de
sous-traitance dans le textile et le travail
du cuir et des peaux, qui étaient en
mesure de produire des costumes, des
vestes, des chaussures et des chemises
identiques aux produits des grandes
maisons italiennes.

Ces entreprises bénéficiaient sur tout
le territoire d'une main-d'œuvre
extrêmement qualifiée qui s'était formée
durant des décennies dans la haute
couture, en créant les collections des
plus grands stylistes italiens et
européens. Les ouvriers qui avaient
travaillé au noir pour les grandes griffes
étaient recrutés par les clans, et non
seulement l'exécution était parfaite,
mais même les tissus étaient identiques,
achetés directement sur le marché
chinois ou envoyés par les marques aux
ateliers clandestins qui prenaient part
aux enchères. Les vêtements contrefaits
des clans de Secondigliano n'avaient
donc rien à voir avec les mauvaises

copies habituelles, vaguement
ressemblantes, qu'on essaie de faire
passer pour des originaux ; c'était une
sorte de vrai-faux. Il ne manquait que
la dernière étape, l'accord de la maison
mère, sa marque, mais les clans se
passaient de cet accord et ne
demandaient rien à personne. Du reste,
partout dans le monde le client était
intéressé par la qualité et par le modèle.
La marque y était la qualité aussi, il n'y
avait donc aucune différence. Les clans
de Secondigliano avaient créé un réseau
commercial présent sur tous les
continents et capable d'acquérir des
chaînes de boutiques et de dominer ainsi
le marché de l'habillement sur le plan
international. Leur organisation
économique s'intéressait également au
marché des magasins d'usine, les outlets.
Les produits de qualité à peine
inférieure étaient destinés à un autre
marché, celui des vendeurs de rue
africains et des étals des marchés. Rien
de ce qui était produit ne se perdait.
De l'atelier à la boutique, du
commerçant au distributeur, des
centaines d'entreprises et de travailleurs
prenaient part au processus, des milliers
d'ouvriers et de patrons qui brûlaient de
jouer un rôle dans la grande affaire
montée par les clans de Secondigliano.

Tout était coordonné et géré par le
Directoire. J'entendais sans arrêt ce
terme. Dans chaque discussion au café
du coin à propos d'une affaire, ou
chaque fois que quelqu'un protestait
contre le manque de travail : « C'est une
décision du Directoire. » « Le Directoire
devrait se bouger et viser encore plus
haut. » On aurait dit des extraits de
conversations datant de l'époque
napoléonienne. C'est le nom que les
magistrats de la DDA de Naples avaient
donné à une structure économique,
financière et opérationnelle composée

d'entrepreneurs et de parrains représentant diverses familles de la camorra dans la zone nord de Naples. Une structure aux visées purement économiques. Comme l'organe collégial de la Révolution française, le Directoire incarne le pouvoir réel de l'organisation, bien plus que son bras armé et ses escadrons de tueurs.

[...]

Les grandes griffes de la mode italienne ont commencé à protester contre la contrefaçon, un marché aux mains des clans de Secondigliano, seulement après que l'Antimafia eut dévoilé tout son fonctionnement. Avant cela, jamais elles n'avaient envisagé la moindre campagne publicitaire, jamais elles n'avaient porté plainte, jamais elles n'avaient informé la presse des mécanismes de production parallèle dont elles étaient victimes. Difficile de comprendre pourquoi les marques n'ont jamais pris position contre les clans. Les explications sont multiples. S'en prendre à la contrefaçon signifiait renoncer définitivement à la main-d'œuvre peu coûteuse dont elles se servaient en Campanie et dans les Pouilles. Les clans auraient fermé les voies d'accès au bassin des usines textiles de la périphérie napolitaine et entravé toute relation avec celles d'Europe de l'Est et d'Extrême-Orient. Porter plainte aurait fait perdre des milliers de débouchés commerciaux, puisque les clans géraient directement de très nombreux points de vente. La distribution, les représentants et les transports dépendent dans bien des zones des familles criminelles, et les coûts de distribution se seraient immédiatement envolés. Du reste, les clans ne faisaient rien qui pût salir l'image des griffes, ils exploitaient simplement leur puissance publicitaire et symbolique. Ils produisaient des vêtements sans défauts, conformes aux modèles et à la qualité. Ils parvenaient à ne pas faire de concurrence symbolique aux marques, mais diffusaient plus largement des produits que les prix du marché rendaient inaccessibles au grand public. Ils favorisaient la diffusion de la marque. Si presque personne ne porte plus les vêtements des grands couturiers, si on ne les voit plus que sur le dos de mannequins anorexiques durant la saison des défilés, le marché s'éteint lentement et le prestige diminue lui aussi. En outre, les ateliers napolitains fabriquaient des robes et des pantalons contrefaits dans des tailles que les griffes ne produisent pas, pour des raisons d'image. Mais pour les clans seuls comptent les gains potentiels, pas l'image. Grâce à la contrefaçon de qualité et à l'argent du trafic de drogue, les familles de Secondigliano avaient pu acquérir des boutiques et des centres commerciaux, où les produits authentiques et les bonnes copies se mêlaient de plus en plus souvent, rendant toute distinction impossible. Le Système avait d'une certaine façon aidé la mode « officielle » à se développer, malgré la flambée des prix, exploitant au contraire la crise du marché. Il avait contribué à faire connaître la mode italienne dans le monde et gagné ainsi des sommes colossales.

Roberto Saviano,
*Gomorra. Dans l'empire
de la Camorra*,
traduit de l'italien
par Vincent Raynaud,
Gallimard, 2007

La mafia, de Sciascia à Falcone

Deux Siciliens. Le premier, né à Raclamuto, est un intellectuel et mourra à 68 ans, en 1989. Connu comme la « Cassandre sicilienne » en raison de son pessimisme sur la nature humaine et sur la possibilité de changer le cours de l'histoire. Le second, natif de Palerme, était, lui, optimiste sur l'issue de la bataille culturelle et répressive contre Cosa Nostra : Giovanni Falcone, tombé le 23 mai 1992, à 53 ans, sous la mitraille mafieuse. Cosa Nostra fut pour Sciascia un sujet de fascination littéraire, pour Falcone l'occasion de développer une nouvelle méthode de guerre contre le crime organisé.

La Sicile comme métaphore

Le plus célèbre et le plus célébré des écrivains siciliens, Leonardo Sciascia, raconte la Sicile comme métaphore, et les mystères qui entourent son produit le plus original : la mafia.

Je m'interroge souvent sur la puissance inaltérable de la Mafia. À l'observer et à la disséquer, j'ai appris à connaître désormais le sens de ses moindres manifestations. Et je sais que lorsque la Mafia traverse des périodes de crise interne où les règlements de compte viennent fleurir les pavés de Palerme, et où l'on commence à compter les morts des grandes familles mafieuses, eh bien, mon Dieu, les choses ne vont pas si mal puisque les mafieux s'entre-tuent. Je sais donc que lorsque la Mafia tire, c'est qu'elle a des problèmes. Mais quand elle ne tire pas, et qu'on la croit inexistante, écrasée, éliminée, moi je sais que pour elle la période est bonne, que les bénéfices, elle est en train de les engranger, et que son apparent silence dissimule ses profits.

L'État porte une grande responsabilité dans la fortune de la Mafia, on peut même dire que d'une certaine façon il l'a fait croître dans son sein. On a quelquefois accusé l'État pour les « erreurs » qu'il aurait commises dans sa lutte contre le phénomène mafioso ; s'il ne s'agissait que d'erreurs ! À dire vrai l'État n'a jamais vraiment lutté contre elle. À l'époque, oui, où l'État avait constitué une vraie Mafia, où il était même devenu totalement une Mafia – je veux dire sous le fascisme – alors il a tenté d'expulser la Mafia comme phénomène concurrentiel. Par la suite cette lutte a pris des aspects tantôt spectaculaires, tantôt dérisoires, avec des battues de carabiniers par exemple, comme si les boss se cachaient dans le maquis, mais jamais avec une volonté de déracinement réel. Il y a eu ainsi l'épisode de la Commission parlementaire d'enquête sur la Mafia, constituée sous la pression de l'opinion publique continentale et particulièrement du parti communiste. On a alors beaucoup parlé de la Mafia, peut-être même trop, car on a nourri l'espoir que des mesures de police et de justice allaient permettre de circonscrire le phénomène. Mais, chose étrange, rien de tel ne s'est produit, et la Mafia a au contraire eu l'intelligence de saisir l'occasion offerte par cette enquête pour opérer un renouvellement interne qui avait été rendu indispensable par la montée des nouvelles générations. Elle s'est libérée de ses personnages les plus folkloriques, les plus compromis, les plus « découverts », les plus usés, puis elle s'est présentée à l'opinion publique comme la victime de mesures parfaitement anticonstitutionnelles. Mais dans ses structures les plus vraies, dans son véritable tréfonds, dans son organisation la plus secrète, elle est restée elle-même et elle a continué ses affaires. L'idée de la Commission anti-Mafia était donc « polluée » dès le départ. Un signe ? Le fait par exemple que cette enquête ait été sollicitée à l'unanimité moins une voix par l'Assemblée régionale sicilienne : 89 députés ont donc été pour, alors qu'au moins 20 d'entre eux, de par leur lieu d'élection, et de par les personnes qui leur sont proches, étaient directement en collusion avec la Mafia ! La requête est suspecte. Passons ensuite à la composition de cette Commission : aucun expert des problèmes siciliens et de la Mafia n'en faisait partie, aucun expert si ce n'est le sénateur communiste Girolamo Li Causi, dont les interventions pendant les interrogatoires furent en effet les plus rigoureuses et les plus décidées. Les conséquences de la publication du rapport anti-Mafia ? Certaines franges de la basse force mafieuse ont été envoyées au *confino*, en relégation ; dans les trois mille pages qui le composent, on peut trouver une description minutieuse et intéressante du phénomène Mafia, un ensemble d'analyses qui seront ultérieurement utiles

à la connaissance et à la compréhension de cette spécialité sicilienne ; et on a l'occasion d'acquérir la certitude que le petit et moyen fonctionnaire, l'adjudant des carabiniers ou le commissaire de police, a fait plutôt correctement son devoir dans la bataille contre la Mafia. Les rapports de ces modestes représentants de la loi sur leurs juridictions sont presque toujours honnêtes et exacts, et si l'on avait suivi à temps leurs indications, il est vraisemblable qu'une campagne de propreté aurait pu être lancée et elle aurait pu contribuer au déracinement du phénomène. La machine de l'État en vérité s'est bloquée plus haut, au niveau des fonctionnaires des chefs-lieux de département et des ministères romains qui maintiennent des rapports étroits avec les politiques. On concevra que le bilan qu'on tire des actes de cette Commission ne soit guère optimiste. J'oubliais, pour éclairer tout de même un peu le tableau, de dire que ces trois mille pages et ces dix ans de travail de la Commission ont tout de même permis de mieux apprécier les rapports de la Mafia avec la démocratie chrétienne et au moins d'écarter provisoirement un personnage aussi compromis que Vito Ciancimino des responsabilités de maire de Palerme pour motif de collusion avec la Mafia. Je le répète : le seul « politique » de la Commission qui possédait les instruments nécessaires à une bonne dénonciation, c'était Li Causi, c'est dire combien il a dû se trouver isolé au milieu des autres enquêteurs !

Autres effets négatifs de la publication de ce rapport : il a été accompagné de deux rapports « de minorité », l'un rédigé par le parti communiste et l'autre, par les fascistes ; hélas, celui dont sont responsables les communistes est franchement moins intéressant pour moi, Sicilien, que celui du MSI. Car on peut y relever des noms, les noms de tel ou tel Intouchable. Voyez-vous, les fascistes étant seuls à se trouver dans l'opposition, ils étaient tellement hors du jeu qu'ils ne couraient aucun risque à procéder à de telles dénonciations. J'en tire une conclusion amère, et c'est que les partis de gauche ont eu tort de laisser l'exercice de l'opposition, et donc de la dénonciation, une fonction salutaire et capitale dans une démocratie, entre les mains des seuls fascistes. Une vraie révolution culturelle en Sicile ne sera pas possible tant qu'il n'y aura pas une bonne opposition.

Mais l'étude du phénomène mafieux ne conduit pas forcément qu'à des conclusions de type politique, il en est aussi de littéraires, et là, je reconnais volontiers qu'on peut diagnostiquer chez moi comme chez de nombreux Siciliens une ambiguïté à l'égard de la Mafia. Si sur le plan civil bien sûr nous la condamnons et nous souhaiterions qu'elle n'existe plus, que tous les mafieux, sympathiques et moins sympathiques, se retrouvent en prison s'ils le méritent, eh bien, sur le plan de la narration, de l'intérêt qu'un écrivain peut porter à ses personnages, et qu'il peut trouver à se les expliquer, la Mafia représente un phénomène passionnant. Cette vision tragique de l'existence, cette rigueur et cette sévérité dans le comportement, cette façon de savoir prendre des risques, jointe à cette volonté totalisante que l'on trouve chez les mafieux de tous les niveaux... Ils ont, au fond, ce que Montesquieu appelait la « vertu » pour les classes dirigeantes, ils sont même vertueux au sens simple du terme ; il est difficile de déceler chez eux le moindre scandale, ou le moindre adultère, ou le moindre drogué ou encore le plus petit sympathisant du gauchisme. Le mafieux hait le désordre et la non-observance des normes. Puritain, adepte des mœurs les plus austères, rigide dans son comportement

individuel et social, il ne doit pourtant pas faire sourire ; dans une société qui assiste impuissante à la dissolution des normes, le mafieux, lui, vit dans un système que Calvin souvent ne désavouerait pas.

J'ai connu un avocat spécialisé dans la défense des causes mafieuses. Un jour, un gros boss vient le trouver chez lui. L'avocat est en train de faire sa toilette, il reçoit malgré tout son visiteur, l'invitant à entrer dans la salle de bains. Le mafioso le regarde d'un air offensé, lui jette une serviette éponge en le priant de s'essuyer : « S'asciugasse », lui dit-il. Mais la pudeur n'est pas tout. Pour parfaire son souci des normes, le mafieux est capable de se comporter en fidèle observant religieux. Oui, il va à la messe ; non, il n'est pas particulièrement croyant ; mais les rites sociaux collectifs représentent pour lui un élément de satisfaction, une impression de normalité. Il hait toutes les formes de marginalité. Dans la religion, seule la confession lui répugne, pour des raisons aisément compréhensibles : d'abord, aller à confesse, ce n'est pas considéré comme un comportement d'homme ; ensuite, confesse ou pas confesse il est toujours dangereux de parler de ses propres affaires à un autre homme, fût-il prêtre assermenté. Il est ainsi devenu courant que le mafieux finisse par interdire à sa femme une fréquentation trop assidue du confessionnal. La curiosité des prêtres, m'a dit l'un d'eux, peut aller bien au-delà des affaires sexuelles... Mais le proverbe ne dit-il pas : « Monaci e parrini, senticci la missa e stoccacci li rini. » Moines et prêtres, écoute leur message, mais casse-leur les reins !

Leonardo Sciascia, *La Sicile comme métaphore*, Conversations en italien avec Marcelle Padovani, traduction et adaptation de Marcelle Padovani, Stock, 1979

Sur Cosa Nostra

L'interprétation des signes, des gestes, des messages, et des silences est l'une des principales activités de l'homme d'honneur. Et donc du magistrat. On connaît la proverbiale tendance des Siciliens à la discrétion, voire au mutisme : dans Cosa Nostra, elle est portée à son paroxysme. L'homme d'honneur ne doit parler que de ce qui le regarde directement ; et seulement si on lui a posé une question précise, et s'il est en mesure et en droit d'y répondre : tel est le principe qui régit les rapports internes à la mafia, et les relations de la mafia et de la société. Aux magistrats et aux forces de l'ordre de s'y conformer.

J'ai toujours été très prudent dans mon approche des mafiosi. En évitant les fausses complicités et les attitudes autoritaires ou arrogantes, en exprimant mon respect et en exigeant la réciproque. Inutile d'aller trouver un boss en prison si l'on n'a rien de précis à lui demander sur une enquête concernant la mafia, si l'on est mal informé, ou si l'on croit pouvoir se comporter avec lui comme avec un banal criminel de droit commun.

À la suite des déclarations de Calderone, un boss de Caltanisetta devait, en 1988, être interrogé par un de mes collègues. Lequel s'approche du mafioso et lui dit : « Vous êtes bien Untel ? Alors vous allez pouvoir me parler de Cosa Nostra ! » Ce mafioso, qui était en train de s'asseoir, se redresse et rétorque : « Cosa Nostra ? Cosa Nostra, cela veut dire une chose qui appartient à vous, une chose qui appartient à l'avocat ici présent, une chose qui m'appartient à moi. Eh bien, ma part à moi, je vous en fais cadeau. » Et il s'assied et s'installe dans un mutisme définitif.

Que voulez-vous, les membres de Cosa Nostra entendent être respectés. Et ils n'offrent leur respect qu'à ceux qui leur manifestent un minimum d'égards.

Un de mes collègues de Rome, pour sa part, va un jour de 1980 trouver le fameux Frank Coppola, qui vient d'être arrêté, et le provoque : « Signor Coppola, qu'est-ce que la mafia ? » Le vieux Coppola, qui en avait vu d'autres, réfléchit un moment et lui dit : « Monsieur le juge, il y a trois magistrats qui, actuellement, veulent devenir procureur de la République. L'un est très intelligent, le second très appuyé par les partis au gouvernement, et le troisième est un imbécile. Lequel sera choisi ? L'imbécile. C'est cela la mafia… »

Il y a, par exemple, quelque chose que de nombreuses personnes ne comprennent pas : quand un mafioso dit à quelqu'un « Signore », cela ne correspond pas du tout au « Mister » américain, au « Sir » britannique ni au « Monsieur » français. Cela veut dire simplement que l'interlocuteur n'a droit à aucun titre ; autrement, il serait appelé « Zu » (mon oncle) ou « Don » s'il s'agit d'un personnage important de l'organisation, ou « Dottore », etc. Au premier maxi-procès de Palerme en 1986, le repenti Salvatore Contorno, pour bien exprimer son mépris à l'endroit de Michele Greco, considéré comme le chef de la mafia, et pour signifier qu'à ses yeux il n'était personne, parlait en ces termes : « Il Signor Michele Greco »…

Quant à moi, il m'est arrivé d'aller en Allemagne fédérale interroger un chef mafieux qui, lorsqu'il me voit, m'apostrophe ainsi : « Signor Falcone »… Cette fois, c'est moi qui me fâche et qui me redresse d'un coup : « Non, vous, vous êtes le Signor Untel. Moi, je suis le juge Falcone. » Il a compris mon message et s'est excusé. Il savait très bien pourquoi je refusais ce « Signore » qui niait ma fonction et me réduisait à être un moins-que-rien. Notre travail de magistrat consiste donc à posséder aussi une sérieuse grille d'interprétation des signes : pour un Palermitain comme moi, cela fait partie de l'ordre normal des choses.

J'ai rencontré Buscetta pour la première fois en juillet 1984 à Brasilia. Il venait d'être arrêté, et j'avais dressé selon les règles une liste de questions qu'un magistrat brésilien posait à ma place au détenu. Dès mon entrée dans la salle d'interrogatoires, j'avais été surpris de voir Buscetta accompagné de sa femme, qu'il m'avait d'ailleurs présentée, et je me sentais sur le qui-vive. Buscetta répondait de façon évasive aux questions du Brésilien, et j'étais en train de me demander si je ne perdais pas mon temps, lorsque le Boss des Deux Mondes, comme disaient les journaux à l'époque, s'est adressé à moi : « Monsieur le juge, pour répondre à cette question, même la nuit n'y suffirait pas. » Je me tourne alors vers le magistrat italien qui m'accompagnait, et je lui dis : « Cet homme collaborera avec nous. » Sa phrase, en effet, était un signal incontestable de paix et d'ouverture.

Il faut savoir que tout est message, tout est extrêmement chargé de signification dans le monde de Cosa Nostra, qu'aucun détail n'y est jamais inutile. C'est d'ailleurs fascinant à observer, et cela exige une attention soutenue, sans failles. Tommaso Buscetta est, à cet égard, un modèle. Je crois que nous avons eu des rapports très codés.

Quand il est venu à Rome, en juillet 1984, je suis allé l'interroger accompagné du magistrat Vincenzo Pajno, procureur de la République de Palerme, un personnage beaucoup plus important que moi – c'était un signe que je voulais donner à Buscetta et il l'a apprécié. On s'est mis à parler de choses et d'autres, puis il m'a dit : « Je n'ai plus de cigarettes. » Je lui tends mon paquet : « Gardez-le, monsieur Buscetta, nous nous revoyons demain. » Le lendemain, il

a tenu à préciser : « J'ai accepté hier vos cigarettes, parce que le paquet était déjà entamé. Cela me semblait correct. Mais si vous m'en aviez offert une cartouche, ou même plusieurs paquets, je n'aurais pas été d'accord, parce que cela aurait signifié que vous vouliez m'humilier. »

On peut à bon droit diagnostiquer quelque chose de pathologique dans ces échanges de cérémonies, dans cet attachement aux détails. Mais quiconque vit quotidiennement avec le danger est obligé de donner une signification à la moindre vétille, et de l'interpréter par un constant travail de déchiffrage ; je dis bien quiconque, qu'il s'agisse du policier, du magistrat, ou du criminel.

Cela peut donner lieu à nombre d'anecdotes plutôt drôles. On sait dans quelle estime Cosa Nostra tient l'État italien, et combien elle préfère sa propre justice, rapide et directe, aux longs procès qui n'en finissent pas. Cosa Nostra ne rate jamais une occasion de dénigrer l'État ou de se moquer de son impuissance. Le commissaire Beppe Montana racontait qu'en avril 1982, alors qu'on parlait beaucoup, à Palerme et dans toute l'Italie, de l'arrivée imminente du général Carlo Alberto Dalla Chiesa dans la « capitale du crime », il se trouvait à Ciaculli et devait faire une descente dans un bar. Il y pénètre avec un détachement de policiers en tenue de combat, et il ne trouve qu'un vieux serveur. Lequel se lève, imperturbable, se dirige vers le mur et s'y aplatit les bras en l'air et les jambes écartées. Et pendant qu'on le fouille, il demande : « Que se passe-t-il ? Dalla Chiesa est déjà arrivé ? »

C'est dire quelle dérision les initiatives, même les plus sérieuses, suscitent chez les mafieux. Un policier m'a raconté que lorsque le haut-commissaire à la lutte contre la mafia, Domenico Sica, avait été nommé, avec pour principale tâche de coffrer les mafiosi en fuite (c'était en 1988), un boss de sa connaissance, en apprenant la nouvelle, s'est abîmé dans un profond silence, puis, de façon très allégorique, s'est mis à parler d'un de ses amis qui avait un chien, lequel était dévoré par les tiques. Personne ne savait comment libérer cette pauvre bête de ses tourments. Un voisin suggère un médicament d'une efficacité exceptionnelle, qu'il suffit de verser dans la bouche de la tique et elle meurt sur le champ. « Et comment on la prend, cette tique ? » demande le policier. – « Et le Haut-commissaire, comment il les attrape, les fugitifs ? » répond le boss.

Les blagues ne jouent pas seulement le rôle des aphorismes d'autrefois. Elles sont souvent, pour Cosa Nostra, un moyen de transmettre un message. Je parlais avec Buscetta d'un homicide. Lui était persuadé qu'il s'agissait d'un homicide mafieux, moi j'étais plutôt perplexe. Quand nous arrivons à la fin du procès-verbal, Buscetta me dit : « Je vais vous raconter une petite histoire. » J'ai tout de suite compris qu'il voulait me dire quelque chose de manière détournée. « Il y a un monsieur qui a une infection mal placée, sur les fesses ; il va chez le médecin et lui dit : "Docteur, j'étais en train de passer sous un fil de fer barbelé, je me suis fait cette écorchure, et elle s'est infectée." Le médecin l'examine et dit : "D'après ce que je vois, ce n'est pas une éraflure du type de celles que provoquent les fils de fer barbelés." L'autre répond : "Docteur, je vous confirme que je me suis fait mal comme ça, mais soignez-moi comme s'il s'agissait d'autre chose…" » Buscetta entendait me signaler de cette façon : « Vous ne croyez pas qu'il s'agit d'un crime mafieux, moi si. Faites votre enquête comme s'il s'agissait d'un crime mafieux. »

Giovanni Falcone et Marcelle Padovani,
Cosa Nostra, Éditions n° 1, 1991

Le troisième niveau ?

À la question « Existe-t-il un "troisième niveau" qui domine la mafia et lui donne des ordres ?, voici la réponse de Giovanni Falcone.

Le troisième niveau est une sottise solennelle. J'avais écrit en 1982, avec le juge Giuliano Turone, un rapport sur les techniques d'enquête en terre mafieuse. Et nous avions relevé d'abord que la mafia n'est pas une organisation qui fait des crimes malgré elle, mais que le crime est l'une de ses finalités. Ensuite, que si l'on veut essayer de comprendre la mafia, il faut séparer les délits qui sont une fin en soi, pour lesquels l'organisation s'est constituée, tels que la contrebande, ou les extorsions, des autres crimes, qui, bien qu'ils n'entrent pas directement dans le cadre de la constitution de l'organisation, en sont la conséquence éventuelle. L'homicide, par exemple, d'un affilié, parce qu'il a commis une faute interne. Et nous les avions appelés « délits de deuxième niveau ». Enfin nous avions évoqué les crimes qui ne sont ni structurels ni éventuels, mais qui, à un moment donné sont exécutés parce qu'ils servent à préserver l'organisation dans son ensemble, et nous les avions appelés « délits de troisième niveau ». Quand on élimine un préfet par exemple, ou un magistrat, ou un policier, qui menacent l'existence même de l'organisation. Or, les médias, et même certains magistrats, se sont mis à parler de ce « troisième niveau » comme du « niveau caché », celui où se nichent les vrais responsables. C'est-à-dire selon eux les hommes politiques… La voilà la sottise solennelle.

Conversation avec
Marcelle Padovani, 1991

Le monde des *mafiosi*

C'est comme un bréviaire pour entrer dans l'univers mafieux : avec sa manie du surnom (certains mafiosi *en ont 3 ou 4), son lexique, ses proverbes, et ses très humaines angoisses aussi. Témoin, cette extraordinaire lettre signée Matteo Messina Denaro, qui révèle non seulement une réflexion sincère sur le sens de l'existence, la foi, le rôle social de son auteur, mais aussi l'évolution de son univers mental.*

Les surnoms

Les surnoms sont très répandus dans les quatre mafias, pour des raisons d'étanchéité par rapport au monde extérieur, mais aussi comme clin d'œil, avec un côté « club » ou «famille ».

Ces surnoms donnés ou pris aux mafiosi font allusion :

- à leurs goûts : « Pizza » pour un fana de la napolitaine, « Champagne », « Damejane » pour un gros buveur;

- à des caractéristiques physiques : « Mozzarella » pour un mafieux très blanc de visage, « U cortu » (le petit), « O zuoppo » (le boiteux), « U sciancato » (le déhanché), «Viking » pour un grand blond ;

- à des manies : « Scarpapulita » (chaussure luisante), pour un obsédé de son apparence physique, « Mercédès » pour un fan de grosses voitures, « U pasticciere » (le pâtissier) pour un amateur de gâteaux, « Il Presidente » (le président), pour un mafioso lié à la politique, ou encore « Il senatore » (le sénateur)…

Mots clés du monde *mafioso*

- *Cadavere eccellente* : cadavre exquis (en général, un politicien assassiné par la mafia).
- *Fiancheggiatore* (le flanqueur) : il est lui aussi un instrument du crime, meme s'il n'en est pas toujours un acteur.Le *fiancheggiatore* aide, cache et surtout se tait. Il appartient à la «zone grise » qui sait mais ne dit mot, tout en n'étant pas membre effectif de l'organisation.
- *Feudo* : concept juridique qui englobe les propriétés d'origine féodale, et dont l'extension peut atteindre plusieurs milliers d'hectares.
- *Incaprettamento* : technique d'auto-étranglement et surtout de transport des cadavres, avec la victime qui a les pieds et les poings attachés dans le dos avec une corde, qui est passée également autour du cou. Comme un cabri (*capretto*).
- *Latifondio* : concept économique, qui peut reccouvrir le précédent, et qui désigne une grande propriété vouée à la culture extensive.
- *Latitante* : fugitif (celui qui essaie d'échapper à la justice).

- *Lupara* : fusil à canon scié, utilisé surtout dans la mafia rurale, et qui a un effet dévastateur sur le corps humain dans lequel il laisse des trous béants.
- *Lupara bianca* : *lupara* blanche, c'est-à-dire disparition pure et simple d'un corps que l'on ne retrouve jamais, mais dont on est sûr qu'il a été l'objet de l'attention des *mafiosi*.
- *Pentito* : le repenti, il s'agit d'un collaborateur de la justice, un phénomène qui s'est affirmé dans les années 1980-1990, et dont le plus célèbre est Tommaso Buscetta.
- *Pizzo* : la rente de la mafia, prélevée par Cosa Nostra comme un impôt auprès de quiconque exerce une activité productive.
- *Vendetta trasversale* (vengeance transversale) : elle frappe la famille du « repenti » lorsque ce dernier ne peut être personnellement atteint. Buscetta a perdu ainsi 20 parents, Contorno 30.

Proverbes mafieux

L'homme qui parle beaucoup ne gagne rien et s'enterre avec sa propre bouche.

Celui qui a une bouche a une épée (et peut donc tuer).

Celui qui est aveugle, sourd et muet vit cent ans en paix.

La loi est égale pour tous, mais celui qui a de l'argent s'en fout.

Avec l'argent et les bonnes amitiés on enc… la justice.

Le *mafioso* Matteo Messina Denaro, face à la mort

Matteo Messina Denaro (1962-) est un mafioso sicilien qui fut candidat à la succession de Bernardo Provenzano comme capo di tutti capi, à la tête de Cosa Nostra, mais il fut évincé par Salvatore Lo Piccolo, arrêté le 5 novembre 2007. Depuis, il est soupçonné d'avoir pris le contrôle de Cosa Nostra.

Quant à la mort, je crois avoir avec elle un rapport particulier. Elle a toujours tourné autour de moi et je sais la reconnaître. Jeune homme, je la défiais avec la légèreté de l'inconscience, aujourd'hui que je suis un homme mûr, je ne la défie plus, je la prends à coups de pied, parce que je ne la crains pas. Non pas tant par courage, mais parce que je n'aime pas la vie. Ceux qui se trouvent bien sur cette terre peuvent redouter la mort, et ceux qui ont quelque chose à perdre. Moi je ne vis pas bien ici-bas, et je n'ai rien à perdre, même pas l'affection. Quand la mort viendra, elle me trouvera vivant, la tête haute, et souriant, parce que ce moment sera l'un des rares moments heureux que j'aurai eus dans ma vie.

Il n'y a rien eu dans mon passé qui ait pu me prédisposer au surnaturel, ou au suprême, tout s'est passé indépendamment de ma volonté, et j'ai seulement subi les sensations que me dictait mon moi. Il y a eu une période où j'avais la foi, de façon très naturelle, puis tout à coup je me suis rendu compte que quelque chose en moi s'était cassé. J'avais perdu la foi. Je n'ai rien fait pour la retrouver, je me suis aperçu qu'au fond je vis très bien ainsi. Je me suis convaincu qu'après la vie il y a le rien, et je vis en suivant les lignes de mon destin, m'inquiétant seulement de garder entière ma dignité. Je suis un homme serein, en paix avec lui-même.

Lettre de Matteo Messina Denaro, datée du 22 mai 2005, trouvée dans la poche d'un homme d'honneur à qui il l'avait expédiée

La mafia dans la littérature

La mafia est entrée dans la littérature avec deux romanciers : Tomasi di Lampedusa et son Guépard *(1958), qui relate la fin de la noblesse et la montée en puissance des nouveaux bourgeois alliés à la mafia, et Leonardo Sciascia, qui raconte, lui, l'étonnement du policier rationaliste face au monde mafioso. Personne ne pourra soutenir que l'intelligentsia italienne a tardé à comprendre l'importance du problème des mafias. C'est l'État qui n'a pas suivi.*

Devant le tribunal des Beati Paoli

Premier tome de L'Histoire des Beati Napoli *(1909), de Luigi Natoli (1857-1941),* Le Bâtard de Palerme, *qui se déroule au XVIIIᵉ siècle à Palerme, met en scène le jeune noble Blasco de Castiglione, résolu à percer le mystère de sa naissance. Il y fait connaissance avec la secte des Beati Paoli, ancêtre de la Mafia.*

Le lendemain matin, en s'éveillant, Blasco vit sur la table de nuit une lettre ; il ne tarda pas à reconnaître qu'elle était du même type que celle qu'il avait reçue plusieurs mois auparavant.

– Oh, oh ! fit-il, il y a donc du neuf ?

La lettre était ainsi rédigée :

« Vous êtes un homme courageux mais vous avez eu le tort de vous opposer à une œuvre de justice. Attendez à minuit devant la porte du palais. Un passant vous dira : Vous avez l'hameçon ? Vous répondrez : Donnez-moi la torche, et vous suivrez l'homme. N'ayez aucune crainte et fiez-vous à nous. »

Pas de signature, mais le sceau de la main armée, qui frappe. Blasco sourit.

« Mais oui, parbleu ! d'une aventure à l'autre, voilà ce qui rend la vie un peu amusante. Curieux, ces Beati Paoli qui, au lieu de me tirer un coup de carabine ou de me poignarder, m'écrivent des petits billets, qui pourraient passer pour des mots d'amour ! »

[...] À minuit pile, il se plaça devant la grande porte, adossé à l'un des piliers qui l'encadraient. Il avait deux pistolets en poche et un poignard à la ceinture [...].

L'homme passa, le lorgna, lui donna le mot de passe. Blasco lui répondit comme convenu et lui emboîta le pas. Ils marchèrent un moment. Au coin de la rue de San Cosmo, l'homme s'arrêta, tira de sa poche un mouchoir de soie et lui dit :

– Que Votre Seigneurie me pardonne, mais il faut qu'elle se laisse mettre un bandeau et promette de ne pas l'enlever.

– Faites donc, je vous le promets.

Quand il fut ainsi aveuglé, l'homme le prit par la main et le guida. Blasco comprit que pour le désorienter on lui faisait faire des tours et des détours, et puis sous ses pas la rue fut en pente. Tout à coup, on le fit arrêter. Il entendit le bruit d'une clé et sentit sur son visage une bouffée d'air humide qui sentait le renfermé.

– Venez avec moi.

Derrière lui, la porte se referma. Ils passèrent encore un seuil, puis il eut l'impression de sortir dans un lieu découvert. En fait ils étaient entrés dans une petite cour sur laquelle un arbre étendait sa frondaison. La tête de Blasco frôla un rameau et il supposa qu'ils traversaient un petit jardin. Puis on redescendit et on le fit s'immobiliser une nouvelle fois. Une main le désarma rapidement de son épée, en accompagnant le geste d'une excuse.

– Que Votre Seigneurie me pardonne, mais il le faut.

Sous le bandeau, Blasco fronça le sourcil, dépité : mais il pensa qu'il se trouvait au siège de cette ténébreuse société et qu'enfin ce qui était pour les autres un mystère devenait pour lui une réalité. Outre que son courage confinait à la témérité, il avait confiance dans la lettre des Beati Paoli. Quand ils voulaient se débarrasser de quelqu'un, ils le supprimaient d'un coup de carabine, puisqu'ils tenaient à éviter de donner de la publicité à leurs punitions.

Blasco entendit un échange à voix basse au terme duquel la même voix lui dit :

– Entrez.

L'air lui parut plus chaud et il eut le sentiment d'être entouré de près par d'autres personnes. Une voix qui le fit tressaillir dit :

– Asseyez-vous, monsieur.

Deux mains le guidèrent doucement et il prit place sur un siège. La même voix ordonna :

– Enlevez-lui son bandeau.

Blasco fut contraint de refermer les yeux en passant de la plus profonde obscurité à la lumière vive de quatre torches qui étaient fixées à la muraille de la pièce où il se trouvait ; cela lui interdit d'examiner tout de suite les lieux. En rouvrant les yeux, il vit qu'il était dans une espèce de rotonde, à l'évidence une ancienne crypte taillée dans la roche, d'où partaient deux couloirs qui se perdaient dans les ténèbres. Le long de la muraille

étaient creusées des niches. Au milieu, sur une espèce d'autel de pierre étaient posés un crucifix, deux cierges et l'Évangile ouvert ; derrière l'autel, sur un haut siège austère, se tenait un homme masqué ; à ses côtés deux autres, masqués de même. Le long du mur, des hommes étaient assis, qui tous avaient le masque sur le visage. Blasco regarda à ses côtés, derrière lui. Quatre hommes le surveillaient, qui avaient eux aussi le visage dissimulé. Tous étaient vêtus d'une tunique noire, longue, semblable à une chasuble de pénitent, mais à leur ceinture brillait un long poignard.

Un silence grave et solennel régnait dans la salle : Blasco vit étinceler des yeux derrière les masques et sentit tous les regards sur lui. Saisi par un mélange de stupeur et de curiosité, il attendait. Le chef prit la parole :

– Blasco de Castiglione, vous vous trouvez devant le tribunal des Beati Paoli. Nous avons dû une première fois nous opposer aux initiatives de votre curiosité. À présent la voilà satisfaite. Mais nous, monsieur, nous avons le droit de vous demander pourquoi vous voulez vous opposer à notre œuvre.

Blasco ouvrit la bouche, mais le chef le prévint :

– Attendez ; ce n'est pas encore à vous de parler. Pour l'instant, vous devez écouter. Ce tribunal vous a donné plus d'une preuve de bienveillance, il vous a sauvé d'une tentative d'assassinat, il a puni un de vos ennemis en le couvrant de ridicule ; vous, sans le vouloir, et sans le savoir, avez empêché l'arrestation de deux de nos fidèles compagnons, mais vous avez aussi empêché ce tribunal d'accomplir un acte de justice…

– De lâcheté ! corrigea Blasco.

Un murmure menaçant parcourut la crypte ; sans se montrer offensé, le chef reprit gravement :

– De justice ! Vous ne savez pas ce

que vous dites.

– Je sais qu'une pauvre jeune fille sans défense était au pouvoir d'hommes armés qui l'emportaient, en la menaçant de mort ; et je sais qu'user de la force et de la violence contre les faibles est la pire des lâchetés…

– Œil pour œil, dent pour dent !... Ceci est écrit dans les livres saints ; et la sagesse populaire dit « l'arbre pèche et la branche est punie ». Une femme a été tuée et son enfant nouveau-né a été sauvé par miracle : il a grandi dans l'ombre, parce que son nom, sa richesse, son avenir avaient été usurpés. Il a vécu dans l'obscurité et ignore qui il est, parce que s'il tentait de reprendre son nom, s'il exigeait de reprendre son rang dans la société, l'homme qui a tué sa mère et qui a usurpé son nom et son état, lui ôterait la vie. Ce scélérat, découvert, a, l'un après l'autre, fait mourir les témoins de ses crimes : l'une est morte empoisonnée, d'autres pendus, un autre assassiné. La femme généreuse qui a recueilli l'enfant persécuté a été jetée dans les cachots du Saint Office. Le garçon, qui est aujourd'hui un jeune homme, gémit dans les souterrains du Château. Le bourreau a fouetté sur la place publique cette femme innocente, et flagellé jusqu'au sang le jeune homme.

Ainsi donc, pour empêcher que celui-ci meure dans un cul-de-basse-fosse, pour qu'il vive et puisse retrouver son nom, sa richesse, son rang, pour accomplir cette œuvre de justice et de piété, il n'y avait qu'un moyen : prendre en otage la fille de cet homme, l'obliger, par amour de son sang, à cesser une persécution féroce et à remettre ses victimes en liberté ! Blasco de Castiglione, vous avez empêché cet acte de justice, et vous êtes fait complice de ce scélérat !... Don Raimondo de la Motta vous a accusé d'être un des chefs de cette société, il vous a fait arrêter à Messine, a tenté de vous faire empoisonner et vous lui

prêtez votre bras, votre vaillance, pour qu'il poursuive son œuvre sanguinaire… Vous, un cœur loyal et généreux, vous avez muré l'antre obscur et mortifère dans lequel gémit Emanuele Albamonte, le vrai duc de la Motta ! Vous l'avez muré pour le compte d'un voleur, d'un assassin, la honte du genre humain. Blasco de Castiglione, vous êtes coupable et le tribunal va juger votre œuvre… […]

– Vous avez autre chose à me dire ? répéta-t-il. Laissez-moi donc vous répondre qu'il n'est pas juste de m'accuser de connivence avec le duc de la Motta. Je ne suis pas plus son complice que je ne fus le vôtre quand je me suis opposé à l'arrestation de Girolamo Ammirata. Vous pouvez faire ce que vous voulez de moi, mais ne touchez pas à l'intégrité de mes pensées et de ma conscience… Et maintenant dites-moi si vous m'avez invité pour entendre vos réprimandes paternelles…

– Blasco de Castiglione, dit sévèrement le chef, ne plaisantez pas. Ici personne ne rit.

– Je commencerai donc…

– Et vous finirez !

Blasco vit des mains plonger vers la poignée de leur coutelas et des yeux se tourner vers le chef, comme pour lui demander ce qu'il fallait faire. Mais celui-ci se contenta de poursuivre :

– Blasco de Castiglione, nous vous demandons de ne plus vous mettre sur notre route… […]

– Et si je m'y mettais ? Si je tentais, de toutes mes forces, de m'opposer à vos représailles ?

– Nous serions contraints d'employer la violence contre vous.

– Et alors, tuez-moi ; parce que je vous jure sur la mémoire de ma mère que pour poser la main sur Violante de la Motta, il vous faudra passer sur mon cadavre !

Le chef éclata de rire.

Sur un signe qu'il fit, d'un seul mouvement, vingt bras se détendirent, vingt lames menacèrent la poitrine de Blasco. Il pâlit légèrement, mais ne bougea pas, n'eut pas un geste de crainte. Le chef poursuivit :

– Je n'aurais qu'une parole à prononcer pour que vous tombiez ici, criblé de coups, et nul n'en saurait rien. Votre cadavre ne nous embarrasserait pas : si nous ne choisissons pas de l'enterrer ici, nous pourrions le faire retrouver sur quelque route de campagne, pour le plus grand plaisir de la justice qui vous recherche. Mais votre mort n'apporterait rien à notre cause ; nous ne voulons que votre neutralité absolue… Consentez-vous à nous la promettre ?

Au fond de son cœur, Blasco voyait toujours Violante ; il répondit :

– Je ne promets que ce que je puis tenir.

– Prenez garde, Blasco de Castiglione ; sans vous tuer, je peux aussi vous empêcher d'agir, en vous laissant ici, d'où vous ne sauriez sortir. Pourquoi voulez-vous me contraindre à pareille mesure ?…

– Faites. Je préfère rester ici, enfermé, que dehors, libre, mais réduit à l'impuissance par un serment.

– C'est votre dernier mot ?

– Oui…

– Pensez que, enfermé ici, vous ne pourrez plus jamais défendre ou protéger ceux qui vous tiennent à cœur…

Blasco ne répondit rien. Le chef reprit :

– Vous ne pourrez jamais nous accuser d'avoir été intolérants et violents. Frères, enfermez-le dans la « réflexion ».

Luigi Natoli, *Le Bâtard de Palerme, Histoire des Beati Paoli* (tome I), traduit de l'italien par Maruzza Loria et Serge Quadruppani, Éditions Métailié, 2000

Don Calogero, un « fléau de Dieu »

Le Guépard *(1958) de Giuseppe Tomasi di Lampedusa témoigne des derniers fastes d'une noblesse sicilienne contrainte à passer alliance avec les nouveaux riches, des rustres souvent liés à la mafia. Don Fabrizio, prince de Salina, assiste avec mélancolie à la fin d'une époque et donne en mariage à son neveu Tancrède la belle Angelica Sedàra, dont le père fait partie de la nouvelle classe des enrichis.*

« Après tout, Excellence, don Calogero Sedàra n'est pas pire que tant d'autres gens qui ont grimpé ces derniers mois. » L'éloge était modeste mais suffisant pour permettre à Don Fabrizio d'insister : « Parce que, voyez-vous, don Ciccio, moi, cela m'intéresse beaucoup de connaître la vérité sur don Calogero et sa famille. »

« La vérité, Excellence, c'est que don Calogero est très riche, et aussi très influent ; qu'il est avare (quand sa fille était au pensionnat lui et sa femme mangeaient un œuf au plat pour deux) mais que, s'il le faut, il sait dépenser ; et puisque chaque "tari" dépensé dans le monde finit toujours dans la poche de quelqu'un, ce qui est arrivé c'est que beaucoup de gens dépendent maintenant de lui ; et puis s'il est ami, il est ami, il faut le dire ; ses terres il les donne à quatre terrages et les paysans doivent se crever à le payer, mais il y a un mois il a prêté cinquante onces à Pasquale Tripi qui l'avait aidé dans la période du débarquement ; et sans intérêts, ce qui est le plus grand miracle que l'on ait vu depuis que sainte Rosalie a fait cesser la peste à Palerme. Et du reste, intelligent comme un diable : Votre Excellence aurait dû le voir le printemps dernier : il allait et venait sur tout le territoire comme une chauve-souris, en calèche, sur sa mule, à pied, par la pluie ou le beau temps ; et là où il était passé se formaient des sociétés secrètes, la voie se préparait pour ceux qui devaient venir. Un fléau de Dieu, Excellence, un fléau de Dieu ! Et nous ne voyons encore que les débuts de sa carrière ! dans quelques mois il va être député à Turin, et dans quelques années, quand les biens de l'Église seront mis en vente, en payant quatre sous, il prendra les fiefs de Marca et de Masciddàro, et il deviendra le plus gros propriétaire de la province. C'est ça don Calogero, Excellence, l'homme nouveau comme il doit être ; mais c'est dommage qu'il doive être ainsi. »

Don Fabrizio se souvint de la conversation qu'il avait eue quelques mois plus tôt avec le père Pirrone dans l'observatoire inondé de soleil ; ce qu'avait prédit le Jésuite se confirmait ; mais n'était-ce pas une bonne tactique que de s'insérer dans le nouveau mouvement et de le diriger, du moins en partie, en faveur de quelques individus de sa classe ? Le désagrément de la prochaine conversation avec don Calogero diminua. « Mais les autres de sa maison, don Ciccio, les autres, comment sont-ils vraiment ? »

« Excellence, la femme de don Calogero personne ne l'a vue depuis des années, sauf moi. Elle ne sort que pour aller à la messe, à la première messe, celle de cinq heures, quand il n'y a personne. À cette heure-là, il n'y a pas d'orgues ; mais une fois je me suis tiré de mon lit de très bonne heure exprès pour la voir. Donna Bastiana est entrée accompagnée de sa femme de chambre, et moi, gêné par le confessionnal derrière lequel je m'étais caché, je ne parvenais pas à voir grand-chose ; mais à la fin de l'office la chaleur fut trop forte pour la pauvre femme et elle écarta son voile noir. Parole d'honneur, Excellence, elle est belle comme le soleil ! et on ne peut pas donner tort à don Calogero si, cloporte comme il est, il veut la garder loin des autres. Pourtant, même des maisons les mieux

gardées les nouvelles finissent par filtrer ; les servantes parlent ; et il paraît que donna Bastiana est une espèce d'animal : elle ne sait pas lire, elle ne sait pas écrire, elle ne connaît pas l'heure, elle ne sait presque pas parler : une très belle jument, voluptueuse et fruste ; elle est même incapable d'aimer sa fille ; elle est bonne pour le lit et c'est tout. » Don Ciccio qui, pupille de reines et attaché aux princes, tenait beaucoup à la simplicité de ses manières qu'il estimait parfaites, souriait avec complaisance : il avait découvert la façon de prendre une petite revanche sur celui qui avait anéanti sa personnalité. « Du reste », continuait-il, « il ne pourrait pas en être autrement. Savez-vous, Excellence, savez-vous de qui donna Bastiana est la fille ? » Il se retourna, il se dressa sur la pointe des pieds et il indiqua du doigt un petit groupe de maisons éloignées qui semblaient glisser le long de l'escarpement sur une colline et y rester clouées à grand-peine par un misérable clocher : un bourg crucifié. « C'est la fille d'un de vos fermiers de Runci, il s'appelait Peppe Giunta et il était si sale et si farouche que tous l'appelaient "Peppe 'Mmerda". Excusez l'expression, Excellence. » […] « Deux ans après la fuite de don Calogero avec Bastiana on l'a retrouvé mort sur le chemin de Rampinzeri, avec douze "lupare" dans le dos. Toujours plein de chance ce don Calogero, car l'autre devenait importun et arrogant. »

Giuseppe Tomasi di Lampedusa, *Le Guépard*, traduit de l'italien par Jean-Paul Manganaro, nouvelle édition et postface de Gioacchino Lanza Tomasi, Éditions du Seuil, 2007

Le Jour de la chouette

En 1961, Leonardo Sciascia publie son premier roman policier. Comme il se doit, il y a bien un meurtre initial, celui d'un petit entrepreneur de travaux publics, et un policier, le capitaine de carabiniers Bellodi. Délaissant une piste « passionnelle » trop facile pour être fiable, Bellodi met peu à peu en lumière une piste moins évidente : celle de la mafia.

Le capitaine Bellodi lisait les informations sur la piste que, d'après ce journal sicilien, habituellement très prudent et peu porté à adresser la moindre critique aux « forces de l'ordre », il avait négligée. La piste passionnelle, naturellement. Laquelle, au mieux, pour un homme ignorant les données certaines obtenues par les enquêtes, aurait pu donner l'explication d'un des crimes, mais laissait les deux autres dans l'obscurité la plus complète. Sans doute le journaliste se trouvant à S. était-il allé se faire faire la barbe par don Ciccio, et le récit du roman de la femme de Nicolosi avec Passerello avait-il excité son imagination. « Cherchez la femme », disait, en résumé, le journaliste, en bon journaliste et en bon Sicilien. Au contraire, pensait le capitaine, le précepte qu'il aurait fallu inculquer à la police, en Sicile, était de ne pas chercher la femme, précisément parce qu'on finissait toujours par la trouver, et pour le plus grand préjudice de la justice.

En Sicile, pensait le capitaine Bellodi, le crime passionnel ne jaillit pas de la passion proprement dite, de la passion du cœur, mais d'une sorte de passion intellectuelle, d'une passion ou d'un souci de formalisme — comment dire ? — juridique. Dans le sens d'une abstraction, en vertu de laquelle les lois perdent graduellement leur consistance au point d'en arriver à une transparence formelle pour laquelle le mérite, c'est-à-dire le poids humain des actes, ne compte plus ; l'image de l'homme une

fois abolie, il n'existe plus que la loi se mirant dans la loi. Le personnage qui porte le nom de Ciampa, dans *Le Bonnet de fou* de Pirandello, ne parlait-il pas comme s'il avait eu dans la bouche toutes les Cours de cassation réunies, tant il analysait et reconstituait la forme sans jamais effleurer le mérite. Dès les premiers jours de son arrivée à C., Bellodi était tombé sur un Ciampa ; exactement le personnage de Pirandello, arrivé dans son bureau non pas en quête d'auteur — puisqu'il en avait déjà trouvé un, et un très grand — mais en quête de subtils procès-verbaux : aussi avait-il tenu à parler à un officier, le brigadier lui semblant incapable de suivre l'arabesque de sa logique.

Cela, pensait le capitaine, provient du fait que, dans la conscience du Sicilien, la famille est la seule institution réellement vivante : vivante plutôt comme un nœud dramatique fondé sur un contrat et sur le droit, qu'en tant qu'agrégat naturel et sentimental. C'est la famille qui est l'État du Sicilien. L'État, ce qui est l'État pour nous, est en dehors : c'est une entité de fait, réalisée par la force. Il impose les contributions, le service militaire, la guerre, le carabinier. Au sein de cette institution qu'est la famille, le Sicilien passe les frontières de sa solitude naturelle et tragique ; il se plie à la vie en commun en vertu de rapports contractuels sophistiqués. Ce serait trop lui demander que de vouloir lui faire franchir la frontière séparant la famille de l'État. Il peut s'enflammer à l'idée de l'État, aller jusqu'à en assumer le gouvernement : mais la forme précise et définitive de son droit et de son devoir, c'est la famille, qui permet un accès plus rapide à la solitude victorieuse.

Le capitaine Bellodi ruminait ces idées [...], lorsque le brigadier introduisit don Mariano Arena.

« Asseyez-vous », lui dit le capitaine, et don Mariano s'assit en le considérant fermement sous ses lourdes paupières. Un regard qui ne trahissait rien et s'éteignit dès qu'il remua la tête comme si ses pupilles, ayant basculé, étaient remontées dans sa tête et y étaient rentrées mécaniquement.

Le capitaine s'enquit auprès de lui : avait-il jamais été en rapport avec Calogero Dibella, dit Parrinieddu ?

Don Mariano lui demanda ce qu'il entendait par « rapport » : le simple fait de le connaître ? une amitié ? une communauté d'intérêts ?

– Choisissez vous-même, dit le capitaine.

– Il n'y a qu'une seule vérité, je n'ai pas à choisir : simple connaissance.

– Et quelle opinion aviez-vous de ce Dibella ?

– Il me faisait l'impression d'un homme sensé. Quelques petites erreurs de jeunesse ; mais, ensuite, il m'a eu l'air de marcher droit.

– Est-ce qu'il travaillait ?

– Vous savez cela mieux que moi.

– Je veux le savoir de vous.

– S'il s'agit de travailler avec une pioche, parce que c'était là le travail auquel son père l'avait destiné, Dibella travaillait autant que vous et moi… Peut-être était-ce un travail de tête ?

– Mais, d'après vous, quel travail de tête ?

– Je l'ignore, et je veux l'ignorer.

– Pourquoi ?

– Parce que cela ne m'intéresse pas. Dibella suivait son chemin, comme je suis le mien.

– Pourquoi parlez-vous de lui au passé ?

– Parce qu'on l'a tué… Je l'ai appris une heure avant que vous ne m'envoyiez les carabiniers.

– En fait, c'est Dibella qui vous les a envoyés, les carabiniers.

– Vous essayez de m'embrouiller les idées.

– Non. Je vais vous faire voir ce qu'a écrit Dibella quelques heures avant de mourir. »

Et le capitaine montra à don Mariano une photocopie de la lettre.

Don Mariano la prit et la regarda en l'éloignant de toute la longueur de son bras. Il expliqua qu'il ne voyait bien que de loin.

« Que vous en semble-t-il ? lui demanda le capitaine.

– Rien, lui répondit Arena en lui restituant la photocopie.

– Rien ?

– Absolument rien du tout.

– Cela ne vous fait pas l'effet d'une accusation ?

– Une accusation ? répéta don Mariano d'un air étonné. Moi, ça ne me semble rien du tout. Une feuille de papier avec mon nom dessus.

– Il y a un autre nom.

– Oui : Rosario Pizzuco.

– Vous le connaissez ?

– Je connais tout le pays.

– Mais Pizzuco en particulier ?

– Pas en particulier. Comme tout le monde.

– Vous n'êtes pas en relations d'affaires avec Pizzuco ?

– Permettez-moi une question. Quel genre d'affaires croyez-vous que je traite ?

– Nombreuses et très variées.

– Je ne fais pas d'affaires. Je vis de mes rentes.

Leonardo Sciascia,
Le Jour de la chouette, 1961,
in *Œuvres complètes. I. 1956-1971*,
édition établie, préfacée et annotée
par Mario Fusco, Fayard, 1999

BIBLIOGRAPHIE

– Giovanni Alongi, *La Mafia*, rééd. Sellerio, 1977.
– Pino Arlacchi, *La Mafia imprenditrice, L'éthique mafieuse et l'esprit du capitalisme*, Il Mulino / Contemporanea 2, 1983.
– Edward Banfield, *The Moral Basis of a Backward Society*, Gencoe, 1958.
– Clotilde Champeyrache, *Sociétés du crime. Un tour du monde des mafias*, CNRS éditions, 2007.
– Enzo Ciconte, *Storia criminale. La resistibile ascesa di mafia, 'ndrangheta e Camorra dall'ottocento ai giorni nostri*, Rubbettino, 2008.
– John Dickie, *Cosa Nostra. Histoire de la mafia sicilienne de 1860 à nos jours*, Buchet-Chastel, 2007.
– Danilo Dolci, *Conversazioni in Sicilia*, Einaudi, 1962.
– Giovanni Falcone (avec Marcelle Padovani), *Cosa Nostra, le juge et les hommes d'honneur*, Austral / Éditions nº 1, 1991.
– Eric Frattini, *Cosa Nostra : un siècle d'histoire*, Flammarion, 2003.
– Jean-François Gayraud, *Le Monde des mafias, géopolitique du crime organisé*, Odile Jacob, 2005.
– Piero Grasso (avec Saverio Lodato), *La Mafia invisible*, Mondadori, 2001.
– Piero Grasso (avec Francesco La Licata), *Pizzini, veleni e cicoria. La Mafia prima e dopo Provenzano*, Sperling & Kupfer, 2008.
– Nicola Gratteri, *Fratelli di sangue*, Pellegrini, 2006.
– Eric J. Habsbawm, *Primitive Rebels*, Einaudi, 1966.
– Francesco La Licata, *Storia di Giovanni Falcone*, Rizzoli, 1993.
– Claire Longrigg, *L'altra metà delle mafia*, Ponte alle Grazie, 1997.
– Salvatore Lupo, *Histoire de la mafia des origines à nos jours*, Flammarion, 2001.
– Salvatore Lupo, *Quando la mafia trovò l'America*, Einaudi, 2008.
– Marie-Anne Matard-Bonucci, *Histoire de la Mafia*, Éditions Complexe, 1994 ; Gallimard, Folio, 2009.
– Cesare Mori, *Con la mafia ai ferri corti*, Mondadori, 1932.
– Luigi Natoli, *I Beati Paoli*, Flaccovio, 1972.
– Antonio Nicaso et Lee Lamothe, *Les Liens du sang*, Les Éditions de l'Homme, 2001.
– Marcelle Padovani, *Les Dernières Années de la mafia*, Gallimard, Folio, 1987.
– Salvo Palazzolo, Michele Prestipino, *Il codice Provenzano*, Laterza, 2007.
– Giuseppe Pitré, *Usi, costumi credenze e pregiudizi del popolo siciliano*, Il Vespro, 1978.
– Teresa Principato, *Mafia, donne: le vestali del sacro e dell' onore*, Flaccovio, 1997.
– Francesco Rendà, *I Fasci siciliani*, Einaudi, 1977.
– William Reymond, *Mafia SA : les secrets du crime organisé*, Flammarion, 2001.
– Roberto Saviano, *Gomorra. Dans l'empire de la Camorra*, trad. de l'italien par Vincent Raynaud, Gallimard, Paris, 2007.
– Leonardo Sciascia, *Les Paroisses de Regalpetra*, Denoël, 1967.
– Leonardo Sciascia, *La Sicile comme métaphore*, conversation avec Marcelle Padovani, Stock, 1979.

15hg Arrestation de Giovanni Brusca à Palerme, 20 mai 1996.
15hd Arrestation de Leoluca Bagarella à Palerme, 24 juin 1995.
15b Le boss Totò Riina lors de son premier procès, à Palerme.
16 Graffiti sur les murs de Palerme, avril 2008.
17h Des membres d'Addio pizzo fêtent l'arrestation de Lo Piccolo à Palerme le 5 novembre 2007.
17b Sticker apposé sur un magasin de Palerme, octobre 2007.
18h Déchets sur une plage de Naples en décembre 2004.
18b *Gomorra*, de Roberto Saviano, Mondadori, 2006.
19h Camions de déchets près de Siculiana (Sicile) en janvier 2008.
19b Couverture de *L'Espresso*, septembre 2008.
20 Implantation dans la Péninsule des mafias, cartographie d'Édigraphie, Rouen.
21h et **21b** Titre, manchette et cartouche de *La Repubblica*, 19 septembre 1990.

CHAPITRE 2

22 Le baiser, Palerme 1978, photo Franco Zecchin.
23 Carte postale satirique italienne, 1901.
24 Plan de Mazzarino (Sicile) montrant les propriétés de la famille Branciforte. Palerme, Palazzo Branciforte Butera.

25h Ex-voto sicilien, « Par miracle, le carabinier Lanza sauve le comte Magri le 24 mai 1867 ». Coll. part.
25b Deux *gabellotti*, gravure, début XXᵉ siècle.
26h Emblème des Beati Paoli.
26-27 Groupe de *campieri* en Sicile, photo Nicola Scafidi.
27h *Beati Paoli* de Palerme, rideau de théâtre. Coll.part.
28 Bandits de la bande de Barile (Basilicate) capturés en 1860.
29h Brigands de la bande de Barile simulant une attaque, 1860.
29b Antonino Leone et Placido Rinaldi, chefs de bande siciliens, 1892.
30 Une famille dans le centre de Palerme, photo Ferdinando Scianna.
31 Catane, 1982, photo Franco Zecchin.
32 Procession des Mystères, Trapani, 1984, photo Franco Zecchin.
33h Carte des clans de Cosa Nostra, cartographie d'Édigraphie, Rouen.
33b Organisation de Cosa Nostra, dessin de Frédéric Bony.
34-35 Extrait d'un *pizzino* du boss Bernardo Provenzano.
34b *Pizzino* de Salvatore Lo Piccolo.
35m *Pizzino* codé de Bernardo Provenzano.
35b Procession au sanctuaire de la Madonna dei Polsi

à San Luca (Calabre), 2 septembre 2007.
36 Serment d'un nouvel affilié de la 'Ndrangheta.
37 Scène de *Gomorra*, film de Matteo Garrone, 2008.
38-39 Baptême d'un nouvel affilié de la Camorra en prison, photogrammes d'*Il Camorrista*, film de Giuseppe Tornatore, 1986.
40 Leonardo Vitale lors de son procès, Palerme, 1977, photo Franco Zecchin.
41 Un accusé au procès Spatola, Palerme, 1983, photo Franco Zecchin.
42h Image sainte brûlée trouvée dans la poche d'un *mafioso*, victime de la tuerie de Duisbourg.
42b Symbole de la Camorra.
43 Armes confisquées dans la zone contrôlée par le clan Gionta à Torre Annunziata (Naples), mars 2009.

CHAPITRE 3

44 Rosetta Cutolo, sœur de Raffaele Cutolo, 1980.
45 Statuette vendue aux touristes à Catane.
46 La brigande Michelina De Cesare en 1860.
47h Vincenzina Marchese lors de son mariage avec Leoluca Bagarella, avril 1991.
47b Vincenzina Marchese.
48-49 La femme et les filles de Benedetto Grado tué en 1983 à Palerme, photo Franco

Zecchin.
50h La magistrate Teresa Principato et son garde du corps, Palerme, avril 2001.
50b Arrestation de Vito Vitale, Palerme, avril 1998.
51 Giusy Vitale, juin 1998.
52h Funérailles d'une victime de la 'Ndrangheta à Seminara en 1972.
52m John Paul Getty Jr. lors de son enlèvement.
52b Manchette d'*Il Corriere della sera*, 14 juillet 1973.
53 Funérailles de trois victimes de Duisburg dans l'église Santa Maria della Pietà de San Luca, 24 août 2007.
54h Mariage de Pupetta Maresca et Pasquale Simonetti à Naples, 27 avril 1955.
54m Affiche de *La Sfida*, film de Francesco Rosi, 1958.
54b Pupetta Maresca en 1982.
55 « Erminia » Giuliano et Diego Maradona.
56 Article d'*Il Mattino*, 24 octobre 2000.
57h Antonietta Bagarella, la femme de Totò Riina, et ses enfants.
57m Lettre adressée à Alessandro Lo Piccolo en prison.
57bg *Idem.*
57bd Arrestation d'Alessandro Lo Piccolo à Palerme, 5 novembre 2007.
58b Michela Buscemi lors d'une commémoration, Partanna, 1992, photo Franco Zecchin.

Palerme, février 1986, photo Franco Zecchin.

99b Manchette d'*Il Mattino*, 17 décembre 1987.

100 « Son Excellence Mori parle au peuple », photo, Bivona, mai 1928.

101h La foule écoute le préfet Mori à Gangi, illustration *in* Cesare Mori, *Con la mafia ai ferri corti*, Mondadori, 1932.

101b Couverture de l'ouvrage de Cesare Mori, *Con la mafia ai ferri corti*, Mondadori, 1932.

102 Assassinat de Carlo Alberto Dalla Chiesa et de sa femme à Palerme le 3 septembre1982, photo Franco Zecchin.

102-103m Extrait de la loi La Torre du 13 septembre 1982 (article 416 bis du code pénal italien).

103 Luciano Liggio au tribunal de Palerme en 1986.

104 Ferrari saisies chez un prête-nom de la mafia, Caserte, septembre 2009.

105h Antonio Castro durant la moisson à San Giuseppe Jato sur une terre confisquée à la mafia, photo Franco Zecchin.

105m Farine de pois chiche produite sur une terre confisquée à la mafia.

106h Tommaso Buscetta à l'aéroport de Rome en septembre 1984.

106b Déposition de Tommaso Buscetta au « maxi procès » de

Palerme en 1986, photo Franco Zecchin.

107h Giovanni Falcone et son escorte au palais de justice de Palerme.

107b Le « repenti » Gaspare Mutolo lors de son arrestation en 1976

108h Le « pool antimafia » à Palerme en 1985.

108b Giuseppe Ayala et Giovanni Falcone à Palerme.

109hg Le juge Paolo Borsellino devant la préfecture de Palerme le 2 juin 1992.

109hd Logo de la DIA (Direzione Investigativa Antimafia).

109b Nicola Gratteri, procureur général de Reggio de Calabre.

110 Gianni De Gennaro, chef de la police, Giuseppe Pisanu, ministre de l'Intérieur, et Piero Grasso, procureur national antimafia, à Rome, 2006.

111h Couverture de *L'Espresso*, 2 août 1992.

111b Attentat contre Falcone à Capaci, 23 mai 1992.

112 Manifestation antimafia à Naples en mars 2009.

TÉMOIGNAGES ET DOCUMENTS

113 Caricature sur les connivences parue dans l'*Asino* lors du procès Notarbartolo en 1899.

INDEX

Luciano, Lucky 77-79.
Lupo, Salvatore 76.

M

Macrì,
– famille 95 ;
– Vincenzo 14.
Madonna dei Polsi 35,
35, 62.
*Mafia à couteaux tirés,
La* (C. Mori) *100*.
Mafia invisible, La
(P. Grasso) 61, 107.
Mafia. Quattro studi
(F. Renda) 100.
Main basse sur la ville
(F. Rosi) 87.
Malte 88.
Mancusi, Franco 20.
Manhattan 76.
Mannoia, Francesco
Marino 94.
Mapassoto 56.
Maradona, Diego *55*.
Marchese,
– Giuseppe *47* ;
– Vincenzina 47, *47*.
Maresca, Pupetta 54,
54, *55*.
Martellucci, Nello *66*.
« Maxi procès » *41*, 98-
99, 100, 102, *103*.
Mazzarino *24*.
Messina Denaro,
Matteo 15, *16*, 17, 34.
Messine 91 ;
– détroit de 84, *84*.
Mezzogiorno 11, *20*, *29*,
31, *45*, *85*, 88, 89, 100.
Miami 21.
Michel, saint 41, 62.
Milan *21*, *94*.
Mille, expédition des
68.
MIS (Movimento
indipendentista
siciliano) *71*.
Monreale 65.
Montana, Tony 21.
Mori, Cesare 77, 100-
102.
Mussolini, Benito 77,
100-*101*.
Mutolo, Gaspare
107.

Mystères, procession
des *32*.

N

Naples *18*, 20, 36, *37*,
43, 55, *55*, 56, 78, *83*,
87, *93*, *95*.
Natale, Mario *104*.
Natoli, Luigi 27.
Navarra, Michele *103*.
NCO (Nuova Camorra
Organizzata) 21, *39*,
45, 55.
'Ndrangheta 12-15, *20*,
21, 24, 25, 30, 34, 36,
36, 41-*42*, 52, 53, 84,
85, *89*, *94*, 95, *109*.
Nestlé-Italie 81.
New York 76, 78, 79,
80-*81*, *106*.
NF (Nuova Famiglia)
21, 54.
Niola, Marino 30.
Nirta, Giuseppe 54.
NMC (Nuova Mafia
Campana) 21.
Notaro, Niccolò 81.
Nouvelle Orléans 76.
Nova Siri *85*.

O

Ora, L' (quotidien) 46.
Otan 78.
Ottaviano 55.

P

Palazzolo, Benedetta 47.
Palerme *14-17*, 24, 26,
27, 30, *30*, *33*, 36, 46,
47, *49*, 50, *57*, 58, *59*,
62, 64-*66*, 68, 69, 74,
74, 76, 78, 79, 81, *81*,
91-*93*, 98-99, 102, 104,
106, *107*, *109*, 111.
Palma di Montechiaro
(Agrigente) 51.
Palmes, hôtel des
(Palerme) 79.
Panamá *83*.
Pantaleone, Michele 78.
Pappalardo,
monseigneur
Salvatore 66, *66*.
Parlement européen
102.

Parrain, Le
(F. F. Coppola) 55.
Partanna (Sicile) 59.
Partinico (Sicile) 50,
51.
PCI (Parti communiste
italien) 63, *69*, 102.
Pecorelli, procès *74*.
Piazza di Spagna
(Rome) 14.
Pintacuda, padre Ennio
67.
Piromalli, famille 88,
95.
Pisanu, Giuseppe *110*.
Pitrè, Giuseppe 26, *32*.
Pollina (Sicile) 78.
Portella della Ginestra
(Sicile) 69, *69*.
Pouilles *20*, 21, *85*, 94,
104, 105.
Principato, Teresa 50,
50.
*Progresso italo-
americano, Il*
(journal) 76.
Provenzano, Bernardo
15, *15*, 17, 34, *34*, 47,
51, *55*, 80.
Puglisi, padre Pino 67,
67.

R

Raguse 63.
Reggio de Calabre 36,
53, 84, *93*.
Renda, Francesco 100.
Repubblica, La
(quotidien) *21*, *89*.
Ribaudo, padre
Giacomo 67.
Ribisi, Grazia *50*, 51.
Riesi, Pino 51.
Riesi (Sicile) 51.
Riina, Salvatore (Totò)
15, *15*, *56*, 65, 74-75,
80, 99.
Rimini *21*.
Rinaldi, Placido *29*.
Risorgimento 68.
Rizzo, monseigneur
Angelo 63.
Rizzotto, Placido *103*.
Roberto, Federico de
24.

Rome 14, *21*, 78.
Rosa, padre Angelo la
66.
Rosalie, sainte 62.
Rosi, Francesco *55*, *71*,
77, *87*.
Ruffini, Ernesto 62, 63.

S

Sacra Corona Unita *20*,
21, 41, 42, 94.
Salemi (Sicile) *73*.
Salvatore Giuliano
(F. Rosi) *71*.
Salvo,
– Ignazio *73* ;
– Nino *73*.
Sangiorgio, Ermanno
68.
San Luca *12*, *21*, *35*, 52,
53, *53*.
Santa Maria del Gesù,
église (Palerme) 27.
Saviano, Roberto 18,
18, 19, 31, *37*, *39*.
Savoie, royaume de *68*.
Scalisi, Concetta 51.
Scarface (Q. Tarantino)
21.
Schiavone, Walter 20.
Scianna, Ferdinando
30.
Sciascia, Leonardo 110.
Secondigliano 20.
Segno (revue) 64.
Seminara 53.
Sénégal *83*.
Sfida, La [*Le Défi*]
(F. Rosi) 55.
Sicile 25, *25*, *29*, 65, *66*,
68, *68*, *71*, 72, 78, *78*,
80, *81*, 84, 94, 104, 105,
106, *109*.
Siciliana *19*.
Simonetti, Pasquale *54*.
Spatola, procès *40*.
Squittieri, Pasquale
100.
Steiger, Rod 77, *87*.
Système, Le (Camorra)
19, 20.

T

Tarantino, Quentin
20.

CRÉDITS PHOTOGRAPHIQUES

Akg-images / Dpa / Federico Gambarini 13h. Ansa / Archivio Red / Franco Lannino 51. Arlac Film / Reitalia / Titanus 38h, 38b, 39h, 39b. Coll. Barone Giovanni Giaconia 100. Maurizio Bizziccari, Rome 52h. Coll. Christophe L. 37, 86h, 86b, 87g, 87d. Cinecittà / Vides Cinematografica / Lux Films / Suevia Films 54m. Coll. part. 25b, 26h, 27h, 34-35, 35m, 36, 57m, 57bg, 90g. Controluce / Giorgio Sticchi 104. Corbis / Bettmann 54h, 78. Corbis / Bettmann / Underwood & Underwood 77m. Corbis / Robert Maass 80h. Corbis / Sygma / Rick Maiman 80b. Courrier International 97. Eyedea / Gamma 63h, 103. Eyedea / Gamma / Antonello Nusca 12. Archives Gallimard 20, 33h, 33b. Indigo Films / Lucky Red / Parco Films 74d, 75hg, 75hd. Leemage / AGF 16, 91b, 105m. Leemage / Costa 25h. Leemage / Fototeca Storica 14m, 21, 23, 28, 29h, 29b, 45, 46, 52b, 53, 56, 61, 68d, 69h, 75m, 75b, 81, 98m, 99b, 111h, 113. Leemage / Fotogramma Dos, 14h, 14b, 15hg, 15hd, 15b, 18h, 19b, 42b, 44, 47h, 47b, 52m, 54b, 55, 57h, 59m, 63b, 65, 74g, 79, 91h, 94h, 94b, 95, 107h, 107b, 108h, 108b, 109hd. Leemage / MP 64. Magnum / Bruno Barbey 83. Magnum / Ferdinando Scianna 30, 69b. Ministero della Giustizia 102-103m. Melo Minnella, Palerme 24. Mondadori 18b, 101h, 101b. A. Palma 144. Rea / Contrasto / Roberto Caccuri 84h, 85. Rea / Contrasto / Giuseppe Gerbasi 96h. Rea / Contrasto / Roberto Koch 1, 2-3. Rea / Contrasto / Angelo Palma 88. Rea / Contrasto / F. Pedone 17h. Rea / Contrasto / Shobha 9, 50h, 109b. Rea / Contrasto / A. Zambardino 43. Rea / Ropi 11, 13b, 34b, 35b, 42h, 93b. La Repubblica 89. Reuters / Ciro De Luca 112. Reuters / Tony Gentile 50b, 67h, 110. Reuters / A. Parrinello 19h. Reuters / Giuseppe Piazza 17b, 57bd. Pucci Scafidi Studio Fotografico, Palerme 26-27. Scala / De Agostini Picture Library 70-71. Enzo Sellerio, Palerme 72. Editions Sellerio, Palerme 2e plat, 68g, 77h. Sintesi / Tony Gentile 1er plat, 96b, 109hg, 111b. Sipa Press / AP 82, 106h. Sipa Press / Olycom 58-59, 60, 62, 92b. Sipa / Olympia 84b. Franco Zecchin 4, 5, 6-7, 10, 22, 31, 32, 40, 41, 48-49, 58b, 66, 67b, 73h, 73m, 73b, 93, 98b, 99h, 102, 105h, 106b.

REMERCIEMENTS

L'éditeur remercie Giorgio Longo, ainsi que la bibliothèque de l'Institut culturel italien, à Paris.

ÉDITION ET FABRICATION

DÉCOUVERTES GALLIMARD
COLLECTION CONÇUE PAR Pierre Marchand.
DIRECTION Elisabeth de Farcy. COORDINATION ÉDITORIALE Anne Lemaire.
GRAPHISME Alain Gouessant. COORDINATION ICONOGRAPHIQUE Isabelle de Latour.
SUIVI DE PRODUCTION Géraldine Blanc. SUIVI DE PARTENARIAT Madeleine Giai-Levra.
RESPONSABLE COMMUNICATION ET PRESSE Valérie Tolstoï. PRESSE David Ducreux.

MAFIA, MAFIAS
ÉDITION Caroline Larroche, assistée de Maria Cecilia Vignuzzi. ICONOGRAPHIE Anne Mensior.
MAQUETTE Valentina Leporé. LECTURE-CORRECTION Pierre Granet et Marie-Paule Rochelois.
PHOTOGRAVURE Station Graphique.

Marcelle Padovani, docteur en sciences politiques, est correspondante permanente du *Nouvel Observateur* en Italie. Elle est l'auteur de trois films-reportages sur la mafia et de sept ouvrages, dont *La Sicile comme métaphore*, avec Leonardo Sciascia (Stock, 1979), *Les Dernières Années de la mafia* (Folio Gallimard, 1987), *Sicile* (Collection Le point-Planète, 1991) et, avec Giovanni Falcone, *Cosa nostra, le juge et les hommes d'honneur* (Austral / Éditions n° 1, 1992).

Dépôt légal : octobre 2009
Numéro d'édition : 166017
ISBN : 978-2-07-039651-1
Imprimé en France par Pollina - n°L51587.